7 GOOD REASONS

NOT TO GROW UP

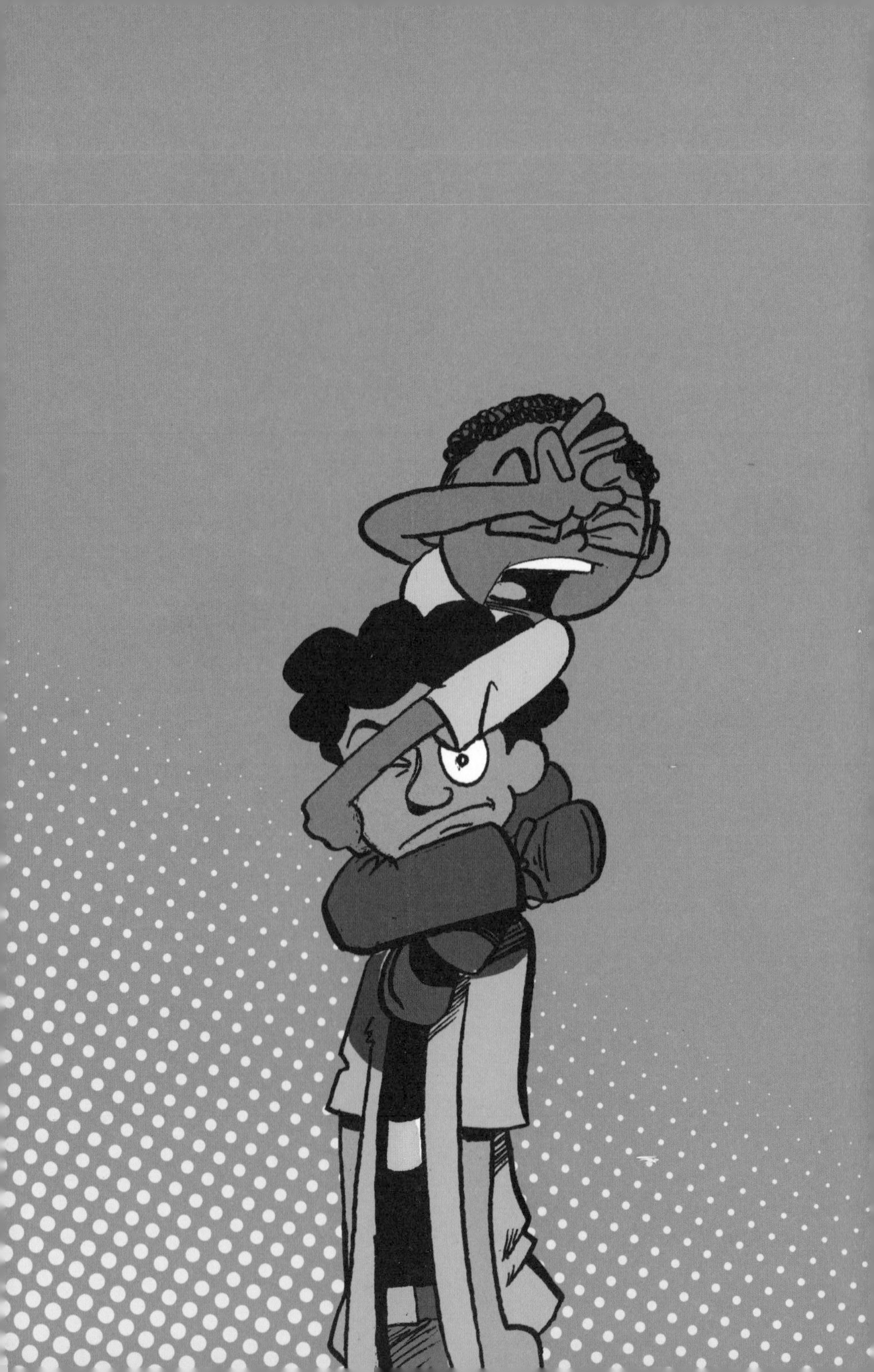

7 GOOD REASONS
NOT TO GROW UP

BY JIMMY GOWNLEY

graphix

An Imp

SCHOL

All rights reserved. Published by Graphix, an imprint of Scholastic Inc.,
Publishers since 1920. SCHOLASTIC, GRAPHIX, and associated logos
are trademarks and/or registered trademarks of Scholastic Inc.

The publisher does not have any control over and does not assume
any responsibility for author or third-party websites or their content.

This book is a work of fiction. Names, characters, places, and incidents are either the
product of the author's imagination or are used fictitiously, and any resemblance to
actual persons, living or dead, business establishments, events, or locales is entirely
coincidental.

Library of Congress Control Number: 2019950321

ISBN 978-0-545-85931-8 (hardcover)
ISBN 978-0-545-85932-5 (paperback)

10 9 8 7 6 5 4 3 2 1   20 21 22 23 24

Printed in China   62
First edition, November 2020

Book design by Steve Ponzo
Creative Director: Phil Falco
Publisher: David Saylor

To Rock Gownley (not his real name)
and to Pep, Harvey, Dave C., Beansoup,
and "Funky" (not real at all)

Special thanks to Studio Assistant, Anna Gownley

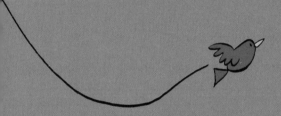

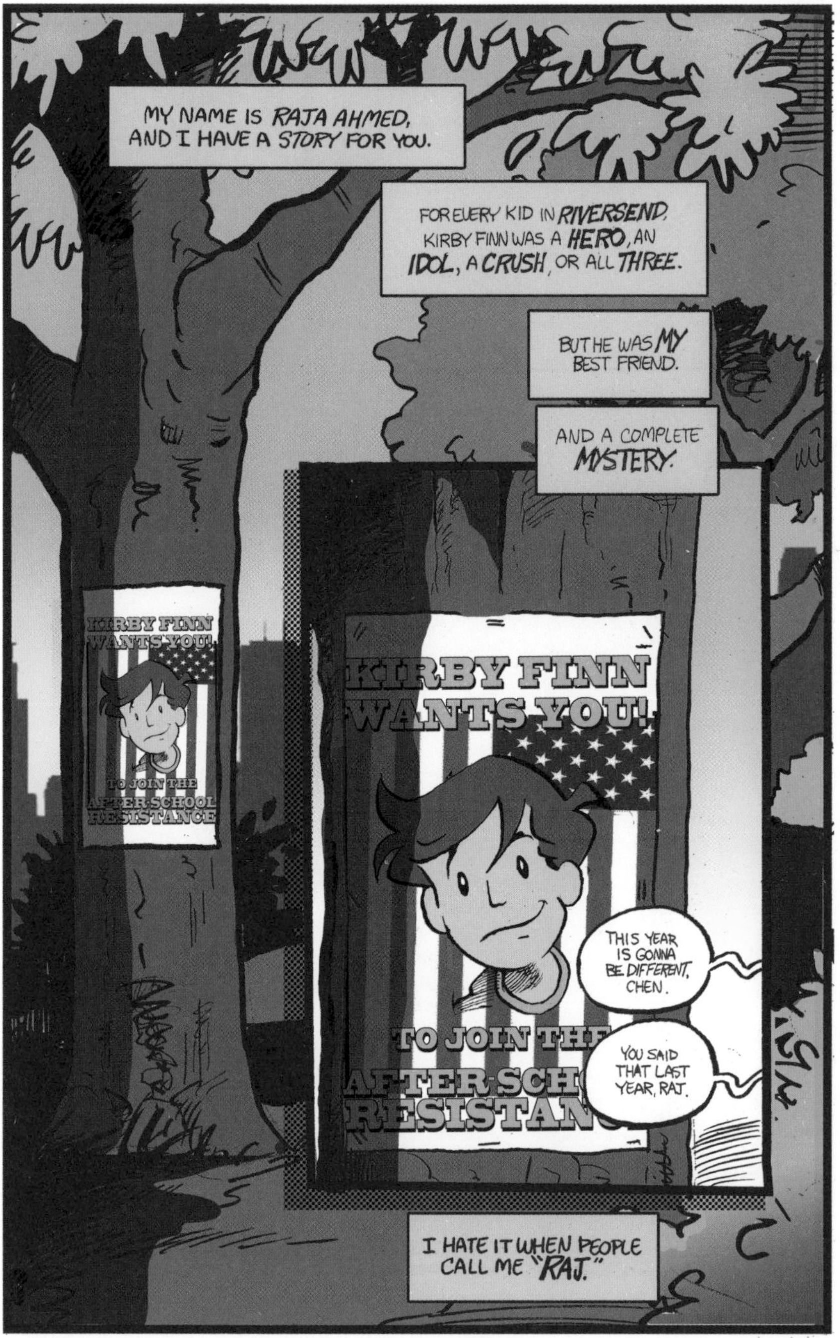
MY NAME IS RAJA AHMED, AND I HAVE A STORY FOR YOU.
FOR EVERY KID IN RIVERSEND, KIRBY FINN WAS A HERO, AN IDOL, A CRUSH, OR ALL THREE.
BUT HE WAS MY BEST FRIEND.
AND A COMPLETE MYSTERY.
KIRBY FINN WANTS YOU! TO JOIN THE AFTER-SCHOOL RESISTANCE
THIS YEAR IS GONNA BE DIFFERENT, CHEN.
YOU SAID THAT LAST YEAR, RAJ.
I HATE IT WHEN PEOPLE CALL ME "RAJ."

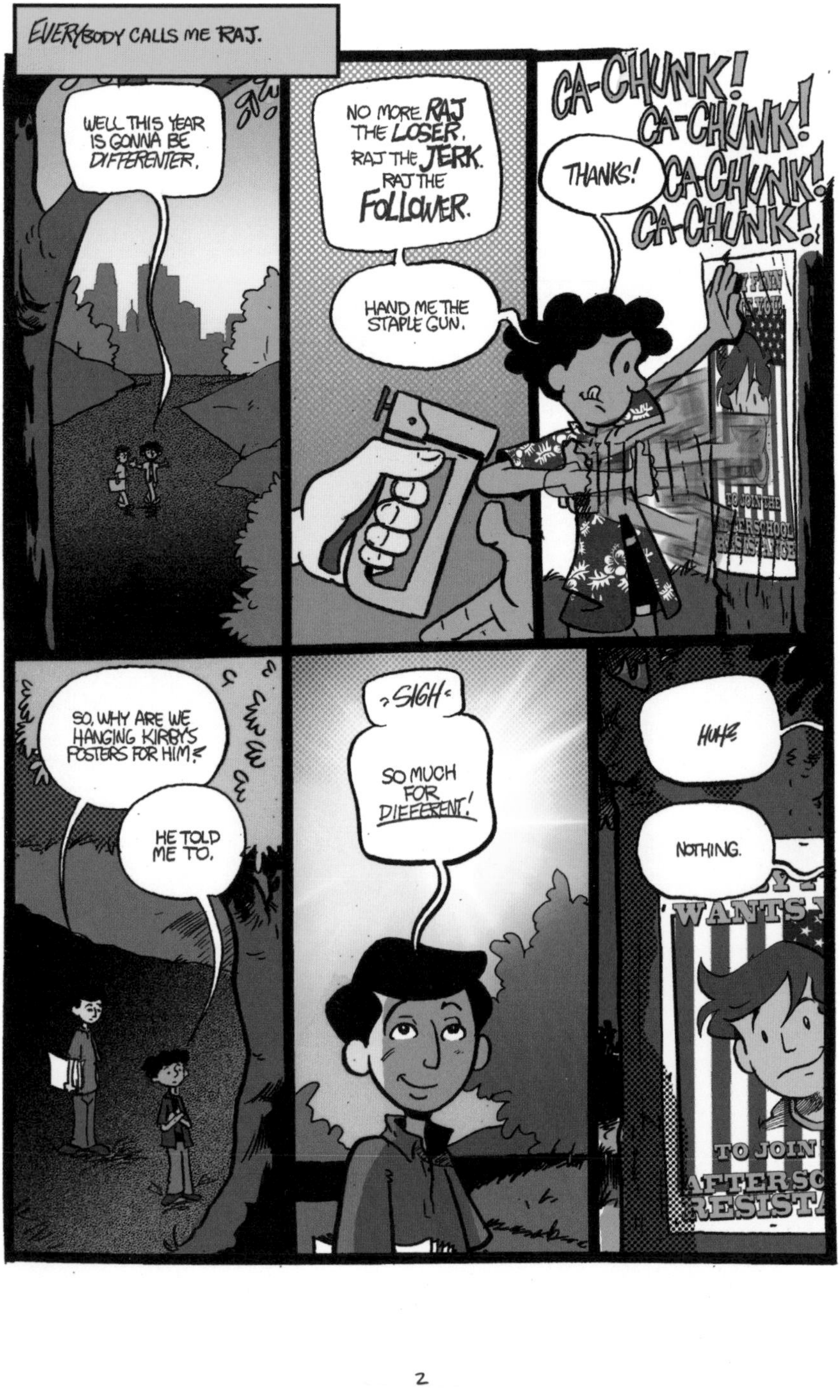
EVERYBODY CALLS ME RAJ.
WELL THIS YEAR IS GONNA BE DIFFERENTER.
NO MORE RAJ THE LOSER. RAJ THE JERK. RAJ THE FOLLOWER.
HAND ME THE STAPLE GUN.
CA-CHUNK! CA-CHUNK! CA-CHUNK! CA-CHUNK!
THANKS!
TO JOIN THE
AFTERSCHOOL RESISTANCE
SO, WHY ARE WE HANGING KIRBY'S POSTERS FOR HIM?
HE TOLD ME TO.
SIGH
SO MUCH FOR DIFFERENT!
HUH?
NOTHING.
WANTS
TO JOIN
AFTERSC
RESISTA

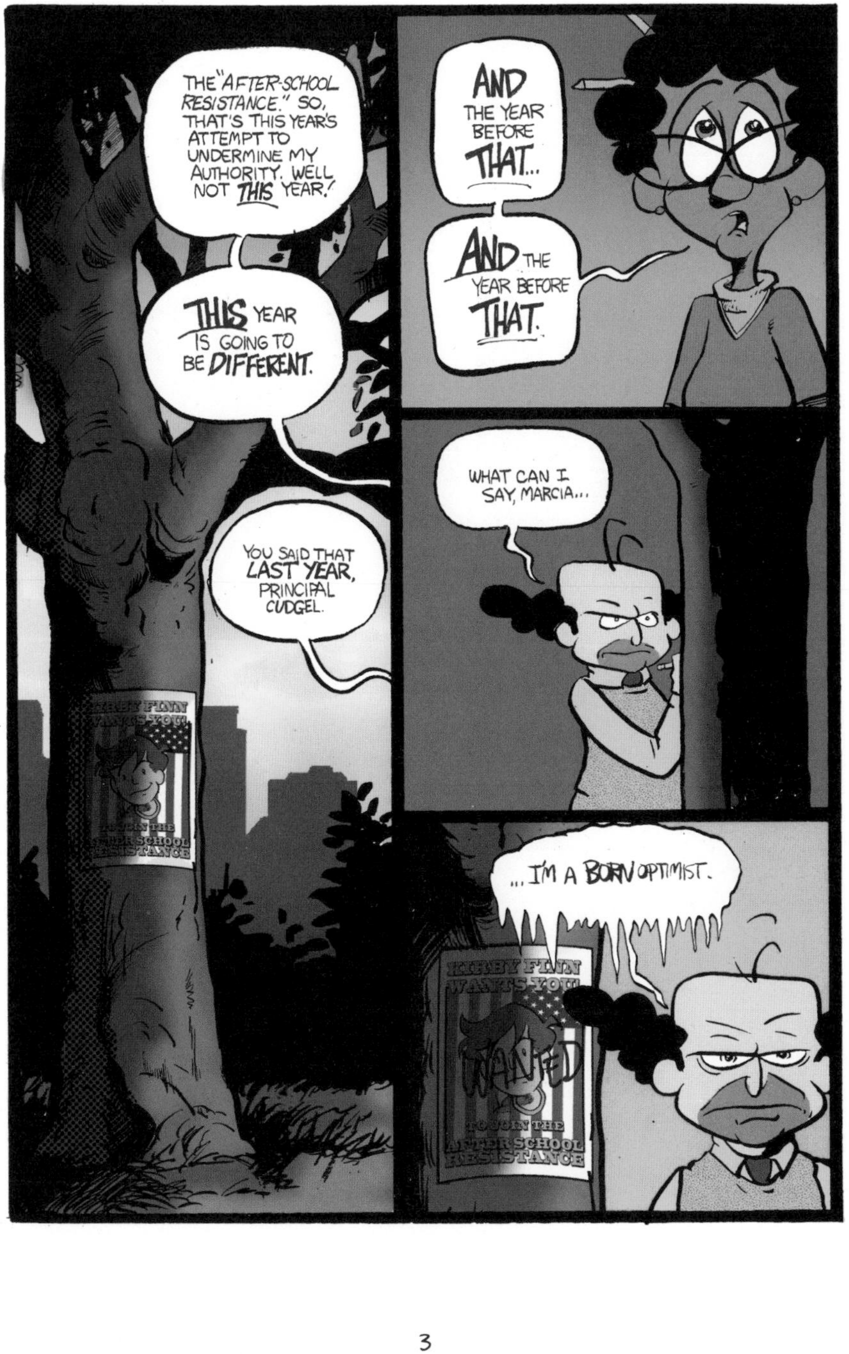
THE "AFTER-SCHOOL RESISTANCE." SO, THAT'S THIS YEAR'S ATTEMPT TO UNDERMINE MY AUTHORITY. WELL NOT THIS YEAR!
THIS YEAR IS GOING TO BE DIFFERENT.
YOU SAID THAT LAST YEAR, PRINCIPAL CUDGEL.
KIRBY FINN WANTS YOU! TO JOIN THE AFTER SCHOOL RESISTANCE
AND THE YEAR BEFORE THAT...
AND THE YEAR BEFORE THAT.
WHAT CAN I SAY, MARCIA...
...I'M A BORN OPTIMIST.
KIRBY FINN WANTS YOU! WANTED TO JOIN THE AFTER SCHOOL RESISTANCE

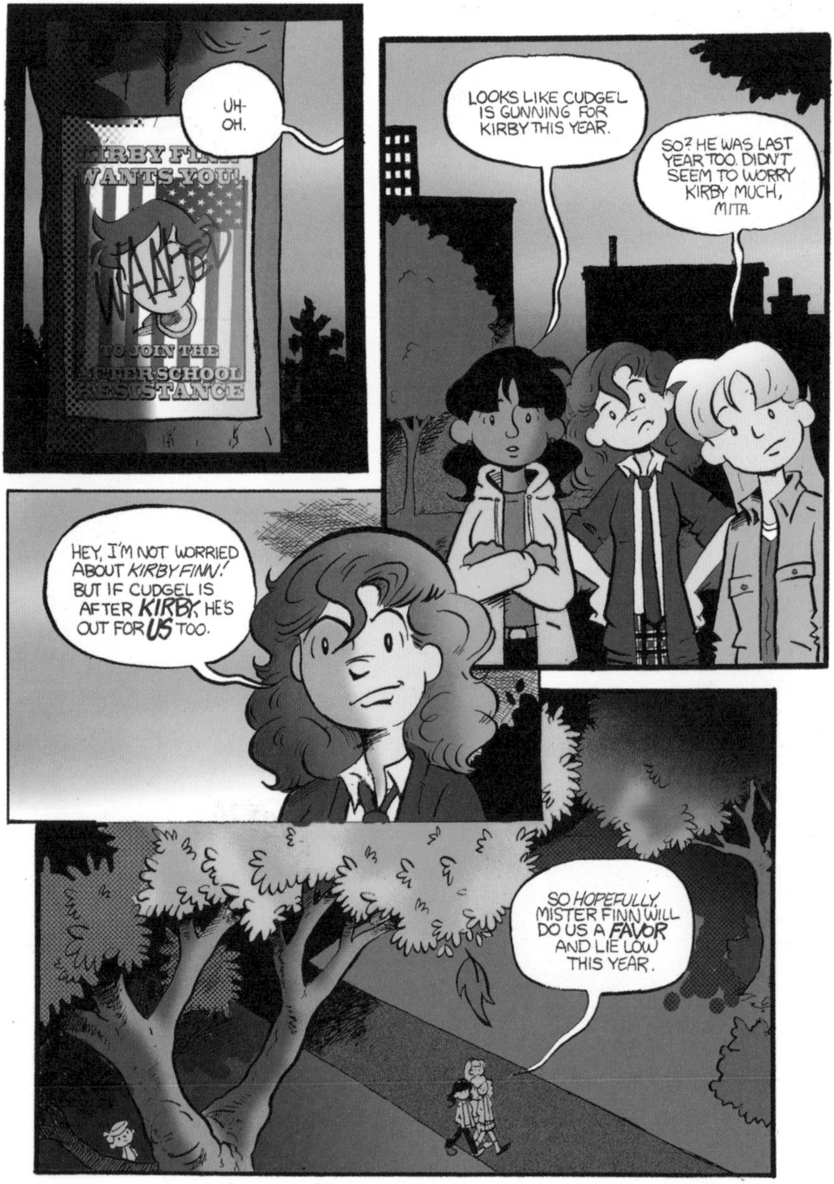
UH-OH.
KIRBY FINN WANTS YOU! TO JOIN THE AFTER-SCHOOL RESISTANCE
WANTED
LOOKS LIKE CUDGEL IS GUNNING FOR KIRBY THIS YEAR.
SO? HE WAS LAST YEAR TOO. DIDN'T SEEM TO WORRY KIRBY MUCH, MITA.
HEY, I'M NOT WORRIED ABOUT KIRBY FINN! BUT IF CUDGEL IS AFTER KIRBY, HE'S OUT FOR US TOO.
SO HOPEFULLY, MISTER FINN WILL DO US A FAVOR AND LIE LOW THIS YEAR.

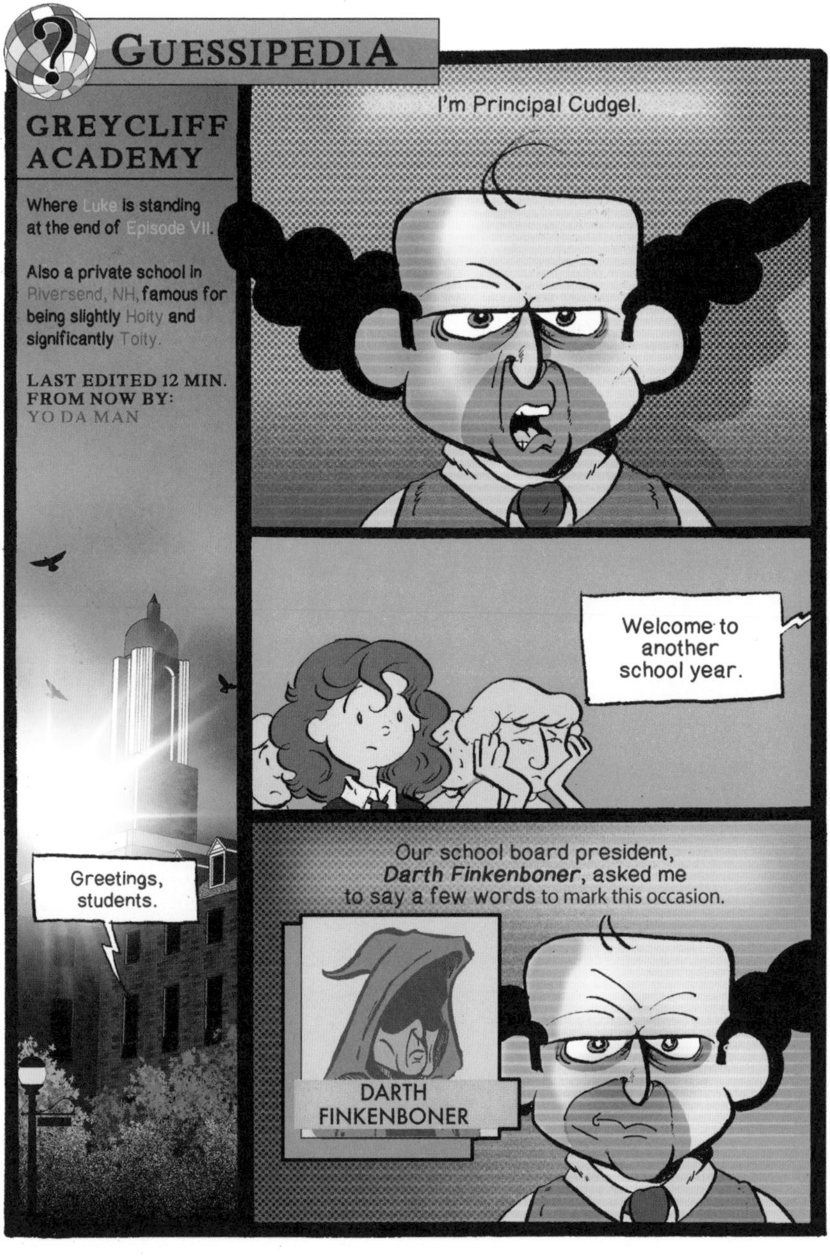
GUESSIPEDIA
GREYCLIFF ACADEMY
Where Luke is standing at the end of Episode VII.
Also a private school in Riversend, NH, famous for being slightly Hoity and significantly Toity.
LAST EDITED 12 MIN. FROM NOW BY: YO DA MAN
Greetings, students.
I'm Principal Cudgel.
Welcome to another school year.
Our school board president, *Darth Finkenboner*, asked me to say a few words to mark this occasion.
DARTH FINKENBONER

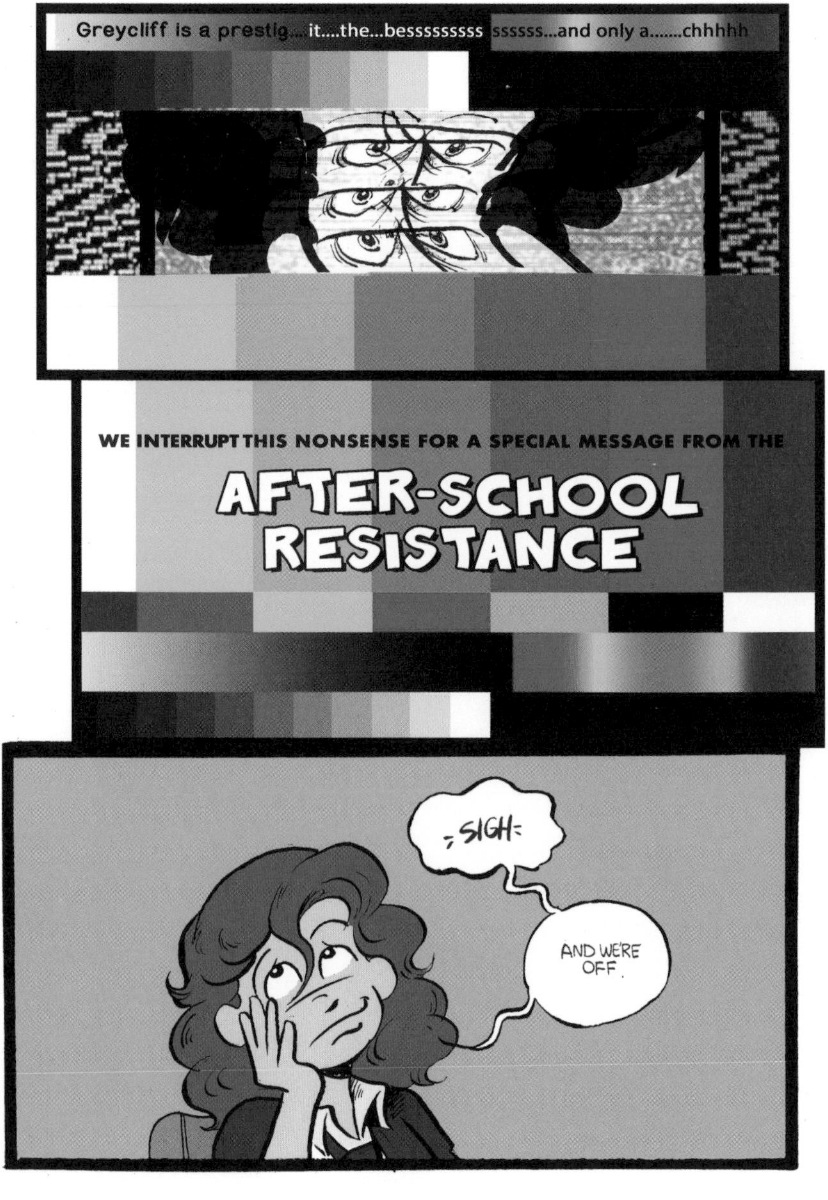
Greycliff is a prestig... it....the...bessssssssss ssssss...and only a.......chhhhh
WE INTERRUPT THIS NONSENSE FOR A SPECIAL MESSAGE FROM THE
AFTER-SCHOOL RESISTANCE
SIGH
AND WE'RE OFF.

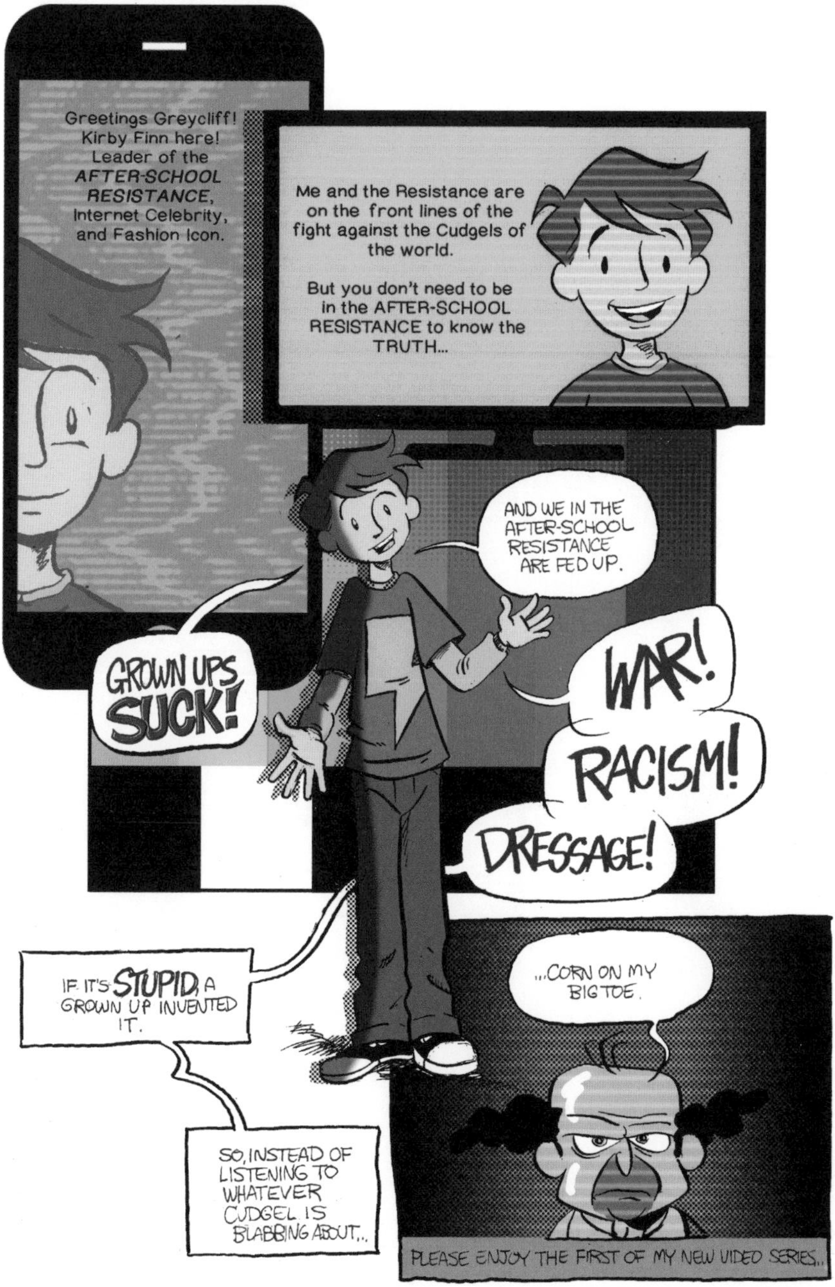
Greetings Greycliff! Kirby Finn here! Leader of the AFTER-SCHOOL RESISTANCE, Internet Celebrity, and Fashion Icon.
Me and the Resistance are on the front lines of the fight against the Cudgels of the world.
But you don't need to be in the AFTER-SCHOOL RESISTANCE to know the TRUTH...
GROWN UPS SUCK!
AND WE IN THE AFTER-SCHOOL RESISTANCE ARE FED UP.
WAR!
RACISM!
DRESSAGE!
IF IT'S STUPID, A GROWN UP INVENTED IT.
SO, INSTEAD OF LISTENING TO WHATEVER CUDGEL IS BLABBING ABOUT...
...CORN ON MY BIG TOE.
PLEASE ENJOY THE FIRST OF MY NEW VIDEO SERIES...

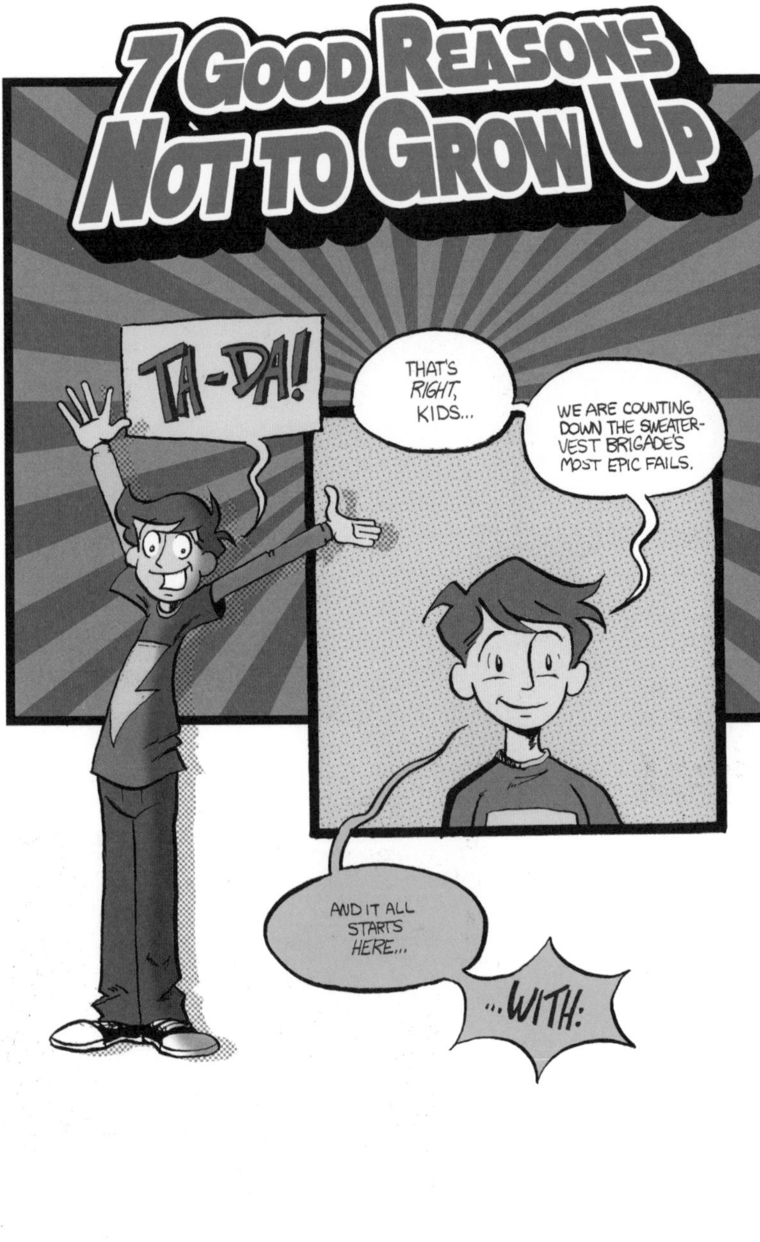
7 GOOD REASONS NOT TO GROW UP
TA-DA!
THAT'S RIGHT, KIDS...
WE ARE COUNTING DOWN THE SWEATER-VEST BRIGADE'S MOST EPIC FAILS.
AND IT ALL STARTS HERE...
...WITH:

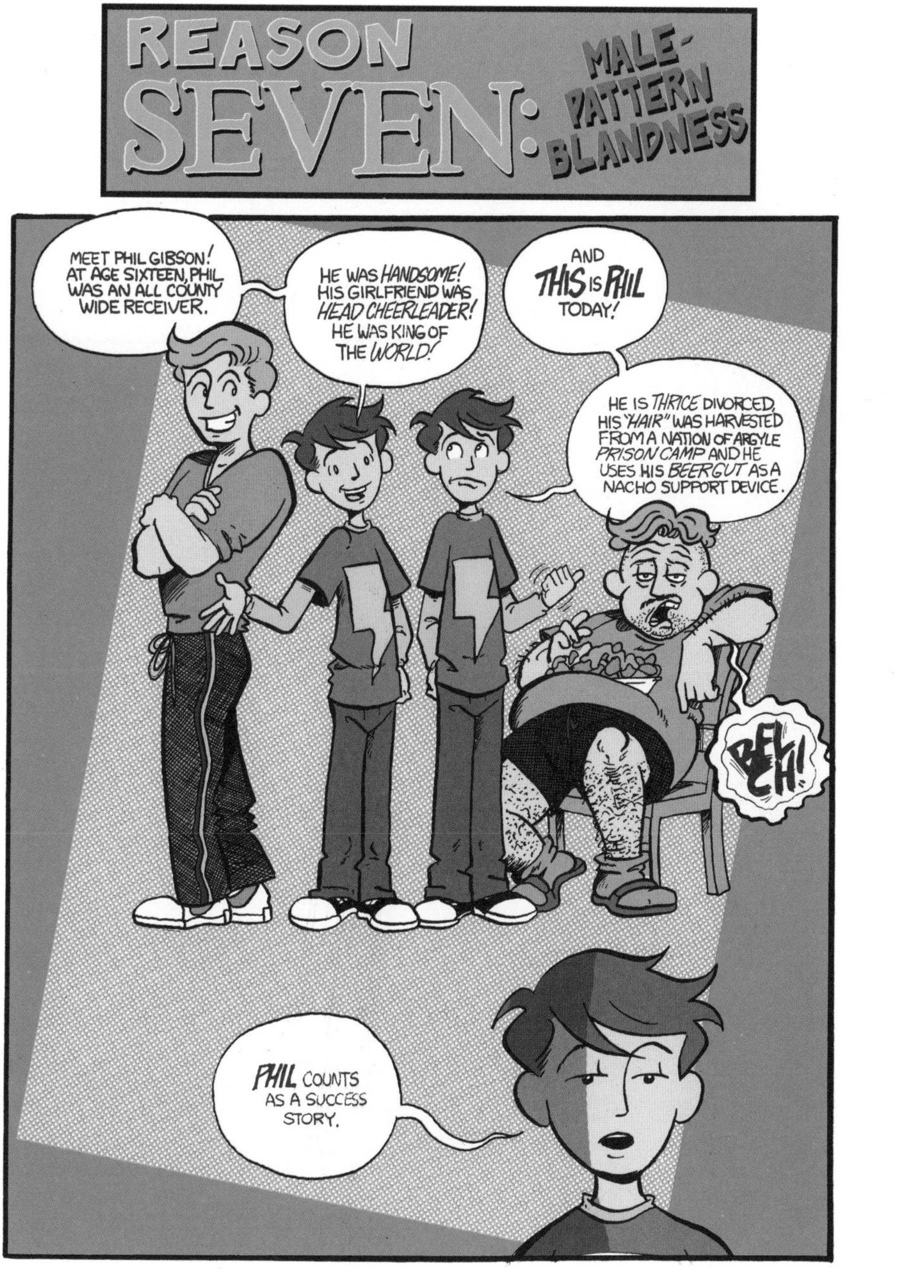
REASON SEVEN: MALE-PATTERN BLANDNESS
MEET PHIL GIBSON! AT AGE SIXTEEN, PHIL WAS AN ALL COUNTY WIDE RECEIVER.
HE WAS HANDSOME! HIS GIRLFRIEND WAS HEAD CHEERLEADER! HE WAS KING OF THE WORLD!
AND THIS IS PHIL TODAY!
HE IS THRICE DIVORCED, HIS "HAIR" WAS HARVESTED FROM A NATION OF ARGYLE PRISON CAMP AND HE USES HIS BEERGUT AS A NACHO SUPPORT DEVICE.
BELCH!
PHIL COUNTS AS A SUCCESS STORY.

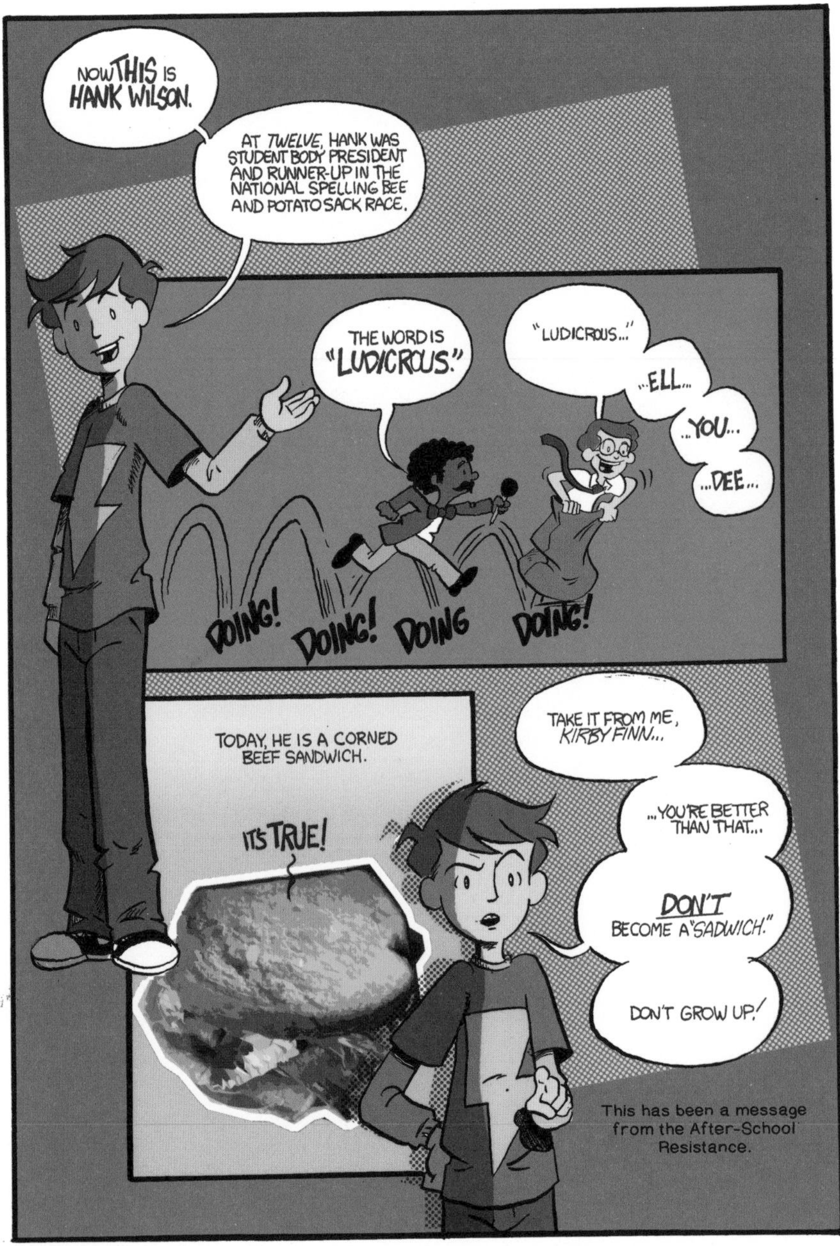
NOW THIS IS HANK WILSON.
AT TWELVE, HANK WAS STUDENT BODY PRESIDENT AND RUNNER-UP IN THE NATIONAL SPELLING BEE AND POTATO SACK RACE.
THE WORD IS "LUDICROUS."
"LUDICROUS..."
...ELL...
...YOU...
...DEE...
DOING!
DOING!
DOING
DOING!
TODAY, HE IS A CORNED BEEF SANDWICH.
IT'S TRUE!
TAKE IT FROM ME, KIRBY FINN...
...YOU'RE BETTER THAN THAT...
DON'T BECOME A "SADWICH."
DON'T GROW UP!
This has been a message from the After-School Resistance.

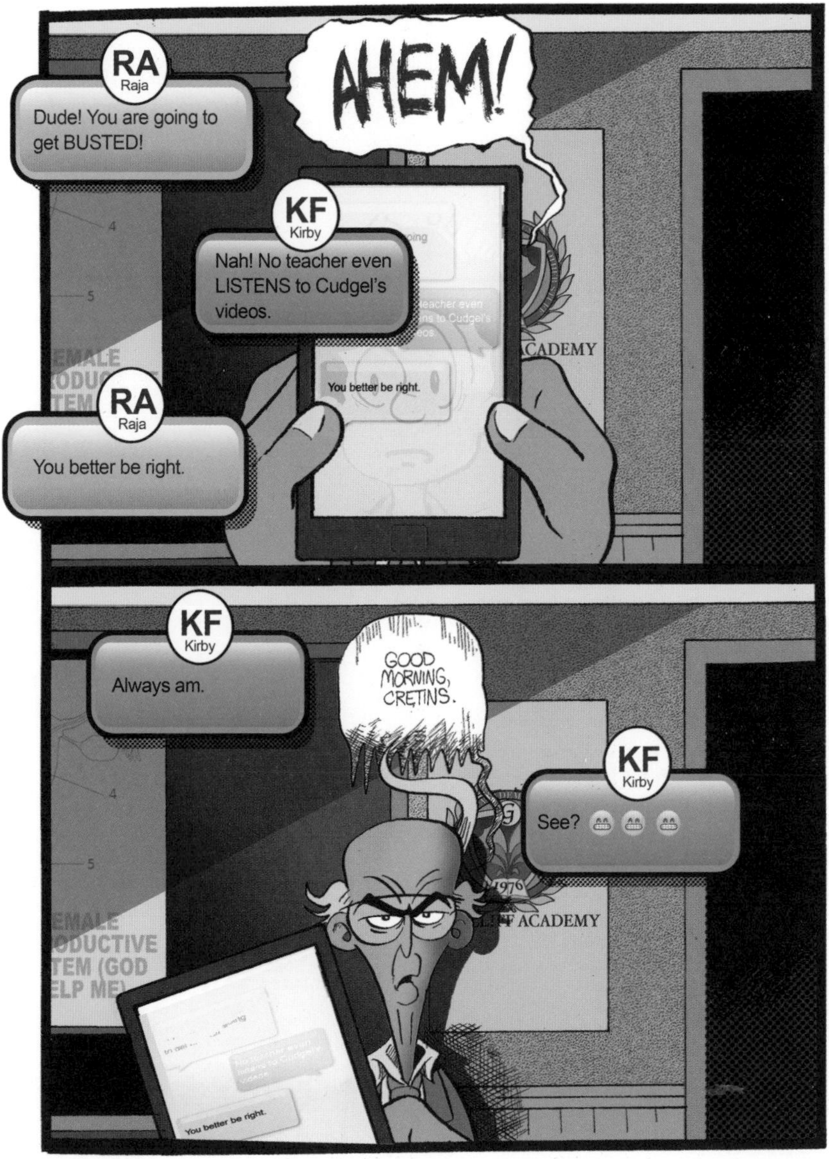
RA Raja
Dude! You are going to get BUSTED!
AHEM!
KF Kirby
Nah! No teacher even LISTENS to Cudgel's videos.
RA Raja
You better be right.
ACADEMY
KF Kirby
Always am.
GOOD MORNING, CRETINS.
KF Kirby
See?
You better be right.
ACADEMY

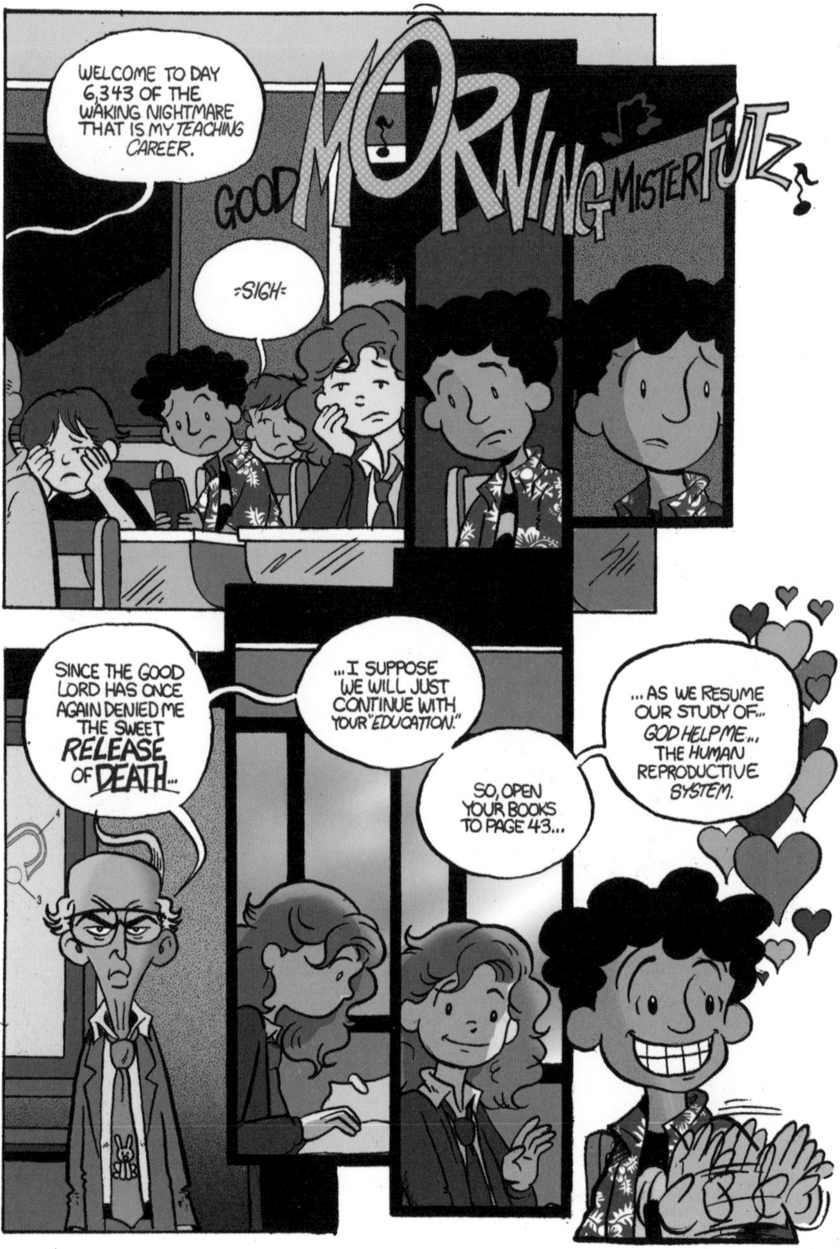
WELCOME TO DAY 6,343 OF THE WAKING NIGHTMARE THAT IS MY TEACHING CAREER.
GOOD MORNING MISTER FUTZ
=SIGH=
SINCE THE GOOD LORD HAS ONCE AGAIN DENIED ME THE SWEET RELEASE OF DEATH...
...I SUPPOSE WE WILL JUST CONTINUE WITH YOUR "EDUCATION."
SO, OPEN YOUR BOOKS TO PAGE 43...
...AS WE RESUME OUR STUDY OF... GOD HELP ME..., THE HUMAN REPRODUCTIVE SYSTEM.

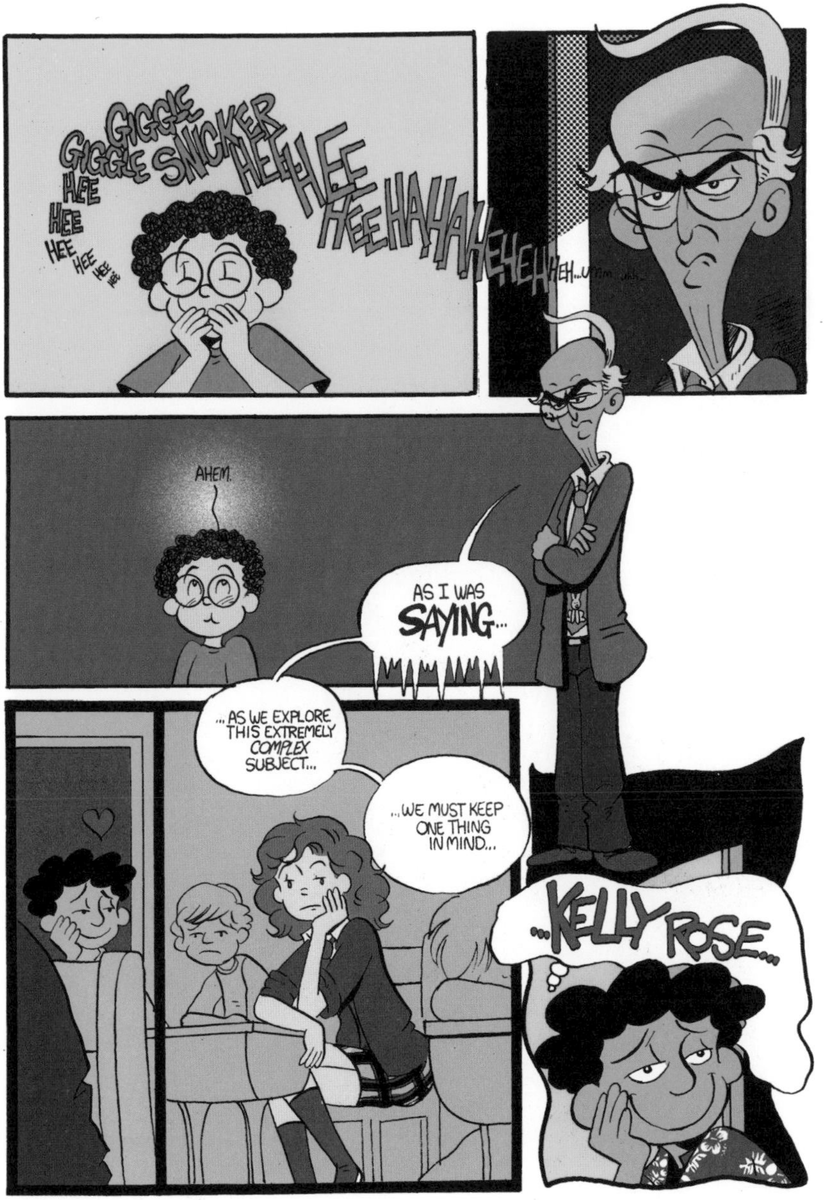
GIGGLE GIGGLE SNICKER HEE HEE HEE HEE HEE HEE HEE
HEE HEE HEE HA HA HA HEH HEH HEH HEH... umm... uhh...
AHEM.
AS I WAS SAYING...
...AS WE EXPLORE THIS EXTREMELY COMPLEX SUBJECT...
...WE MUST KEEP ONE THING IN MIND...
...KELLY ROSE...

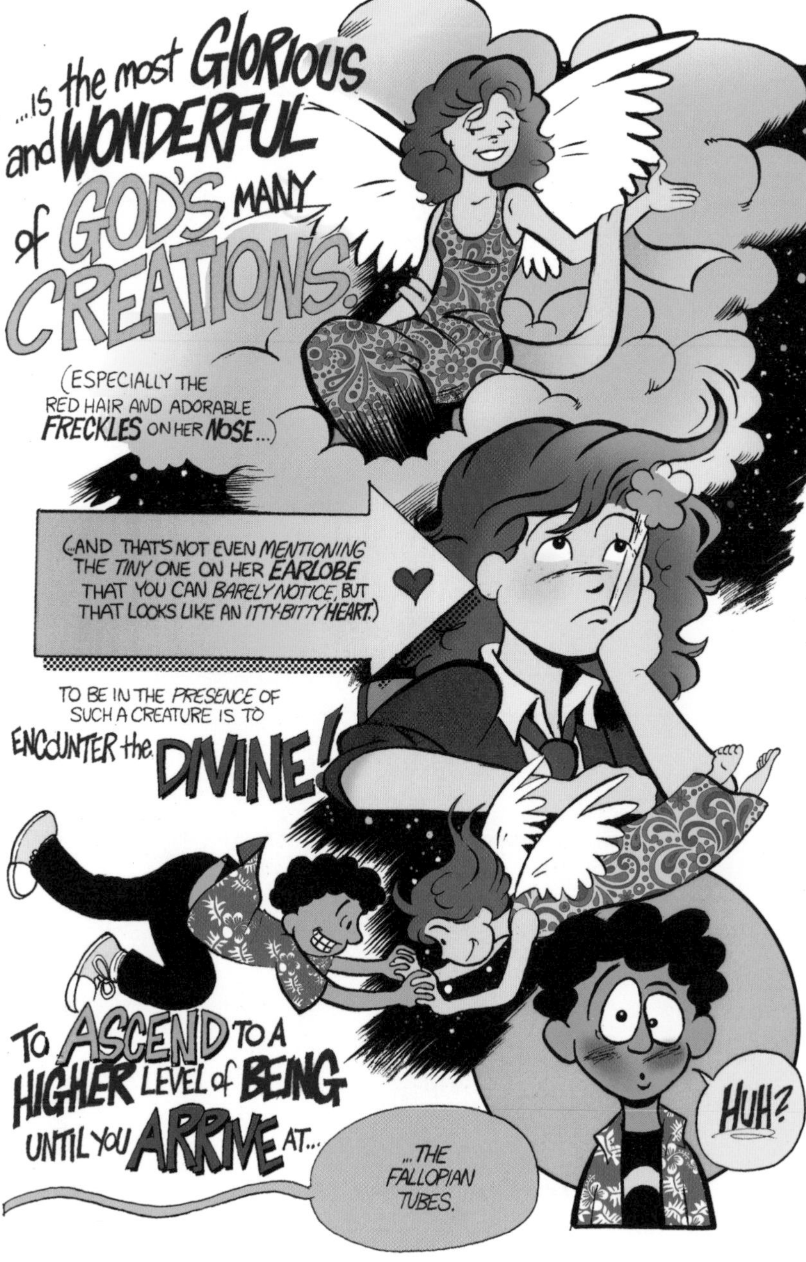
...IS the most GLORIOUS and WONDERFUL of GOD'S MANY CREATIONS.
(ESPECIALLY THE RED HAIR AND ADORABLE FRECKLES ON HER NOSE...)
(...AND THAT'S NOT EVEN MENTIONING THE TINY ONE ON HER EARLOBE THAT YOU CAN BARELY NOTICE, BUT THAT LOOKS LIKE AN ITTY-BITTY HEART.)
TO BE IN THE PRESENCE OF SUCH A CREATURE IS TO
ENCOUNTER the DIVINE!
TO ASCEND TO A HIGHER LEVEL of BEING UNTIL YOU ARRIVE AT...
...THE FALLOPIAN TUBES.
HUH?

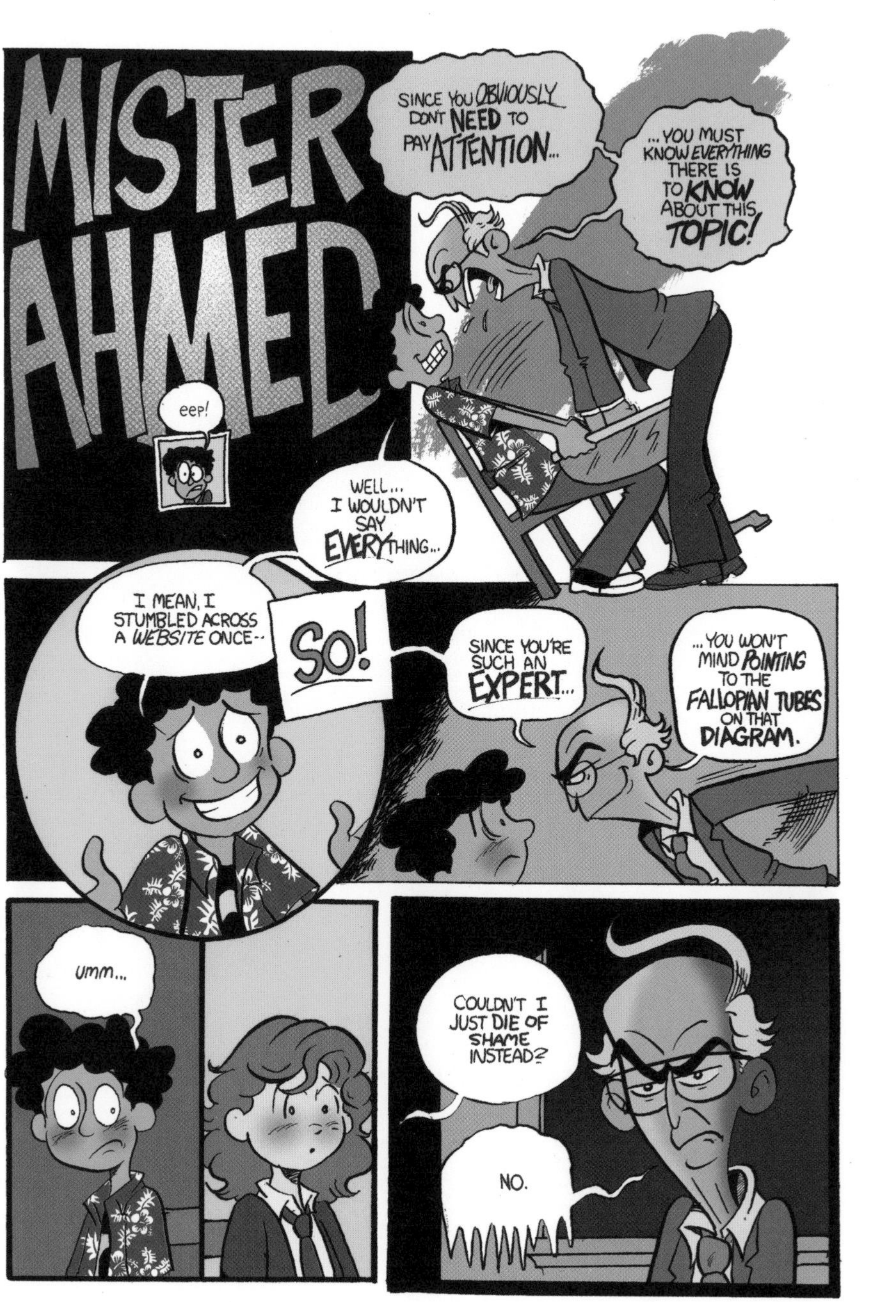
MISTER AHMED
SINCE YOU OBVIOUSLY DONT NEED TO PAY ATTENTION...
...YOU MUST KNOW EVERYTHING THERE IS TO KNOW ABOUT THIS TOPIC!
eep!
WELL... I WOULDN'T SAY EVERYTHING...
I MEAN, I STUMBLED ACROSS A WEBSITE ONCE--
SO!
SINCE YOU'RE SUCH AN EXPERT...
...YOU WON'T MIND POINTING TO THE FALLOPIAN TUBES ON THAT DIAGRAM.
umm...
COULDN'T I JUST DIE OF SHAME INSTEAD?
NO.

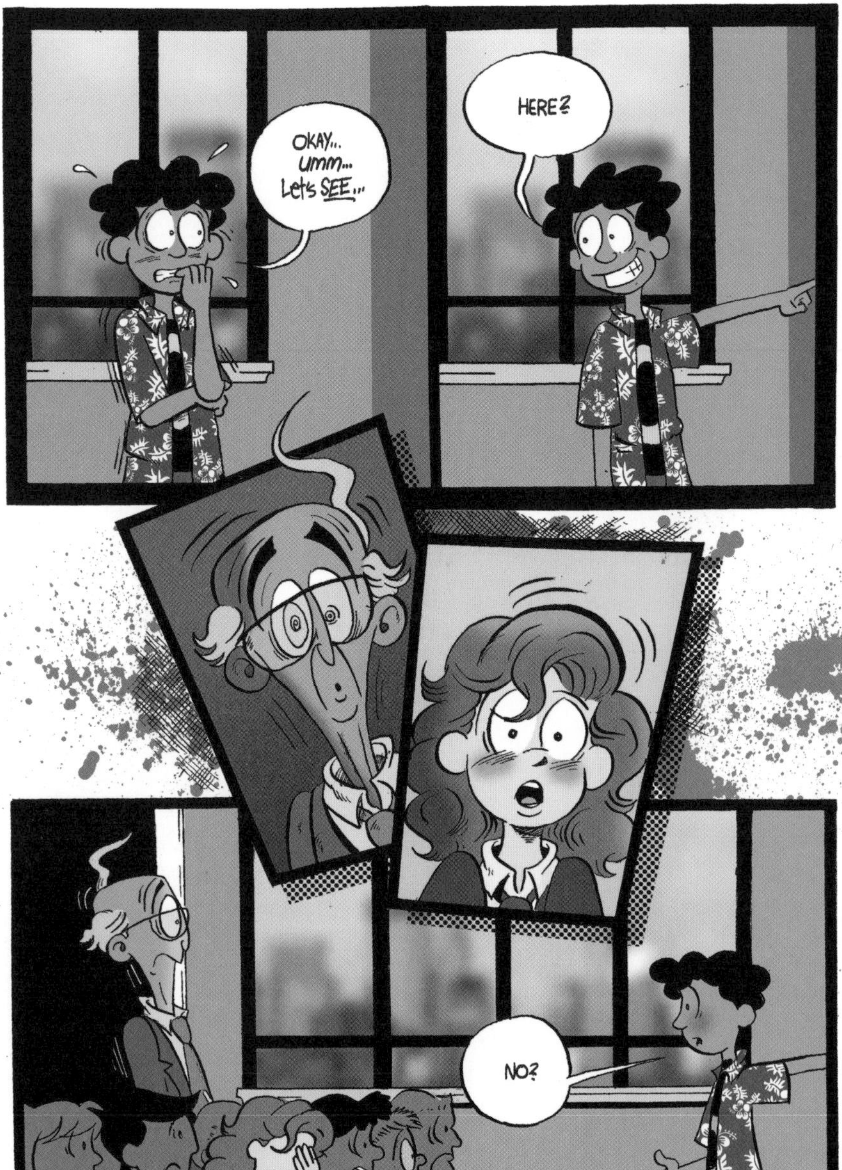

OKAY... UMM... Let's SEE...
HERE?
NO?

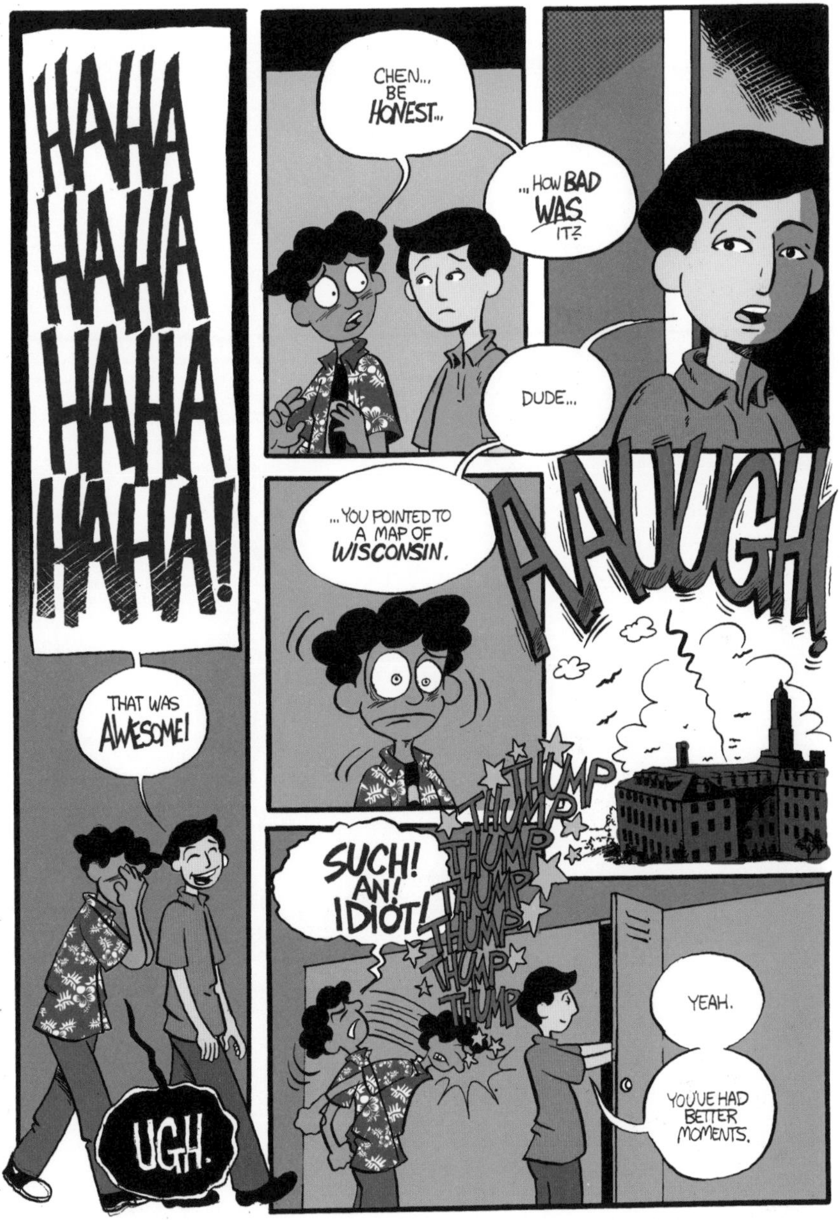
HAHA HAHA HAHA HAHA HAHA!
THAT WAS AWESOME!
UGH.
CHEN... BE HONEST...
...HOW BAD WAS IT?
DUDE...
...YOU POINTED TO A MAP OF WISCONSIN.
AAUGH!
THUMP THUMP THUMP THUMP THUMP THUMP THUMP THUMP
SUCH! AN! IDIOT!
YEAH.
YOU'VE HAD BETTER MOMENTS.

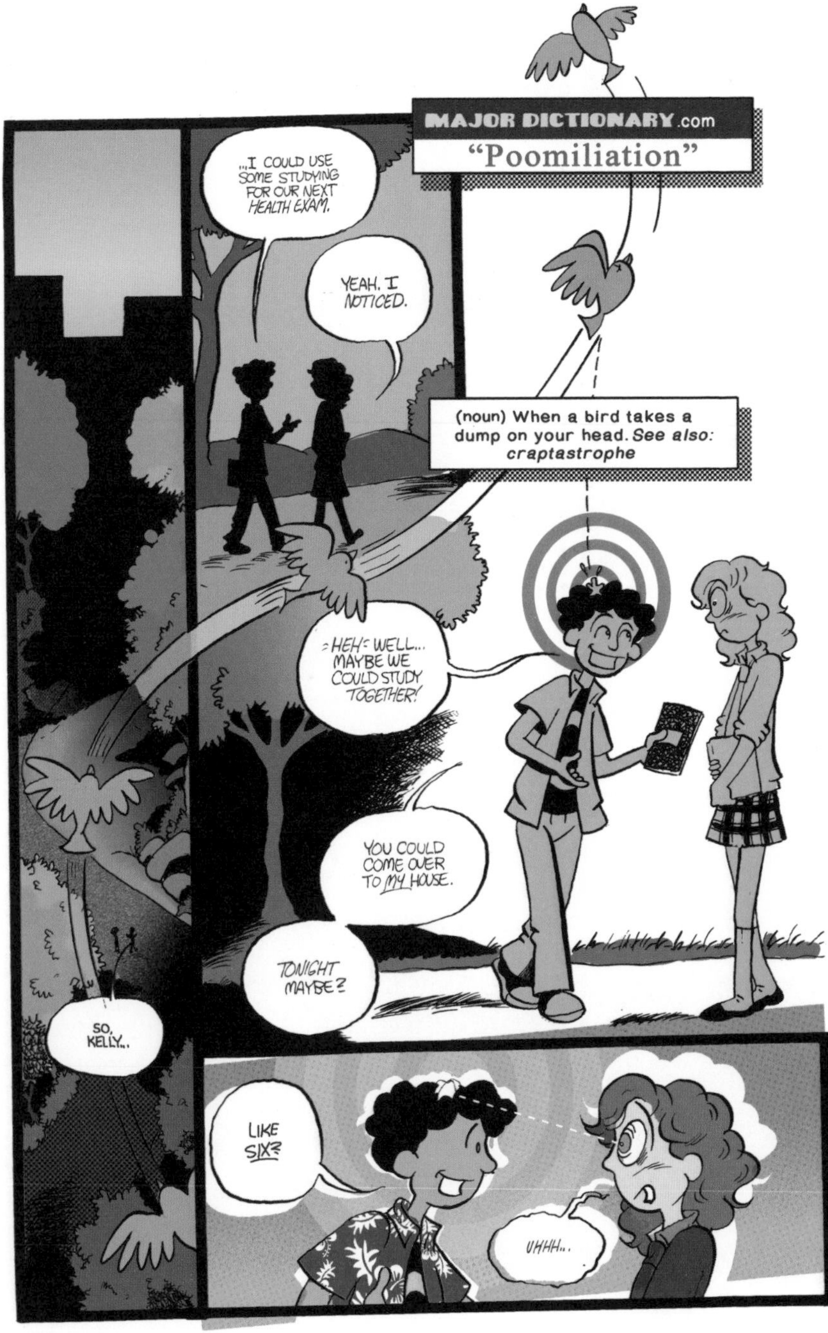
MAJOR DICTIONARY.com
"Poomiliation"
(noun) When a bird takes a dump on your head. See also: craptastrophe
SO, KELLY...
...I COULD USE SOME STUDYING FOR OUR NEXT HEALTH EXAM.
YEAH. I NOTICED.
=HEH= WELL... MAYBE WE COULD STUDY TOGETHER!
YOU COULD COME OVER TO MY HOUSE.
TONIGHT MAYBE?
LIKE SIX?
UHHH...

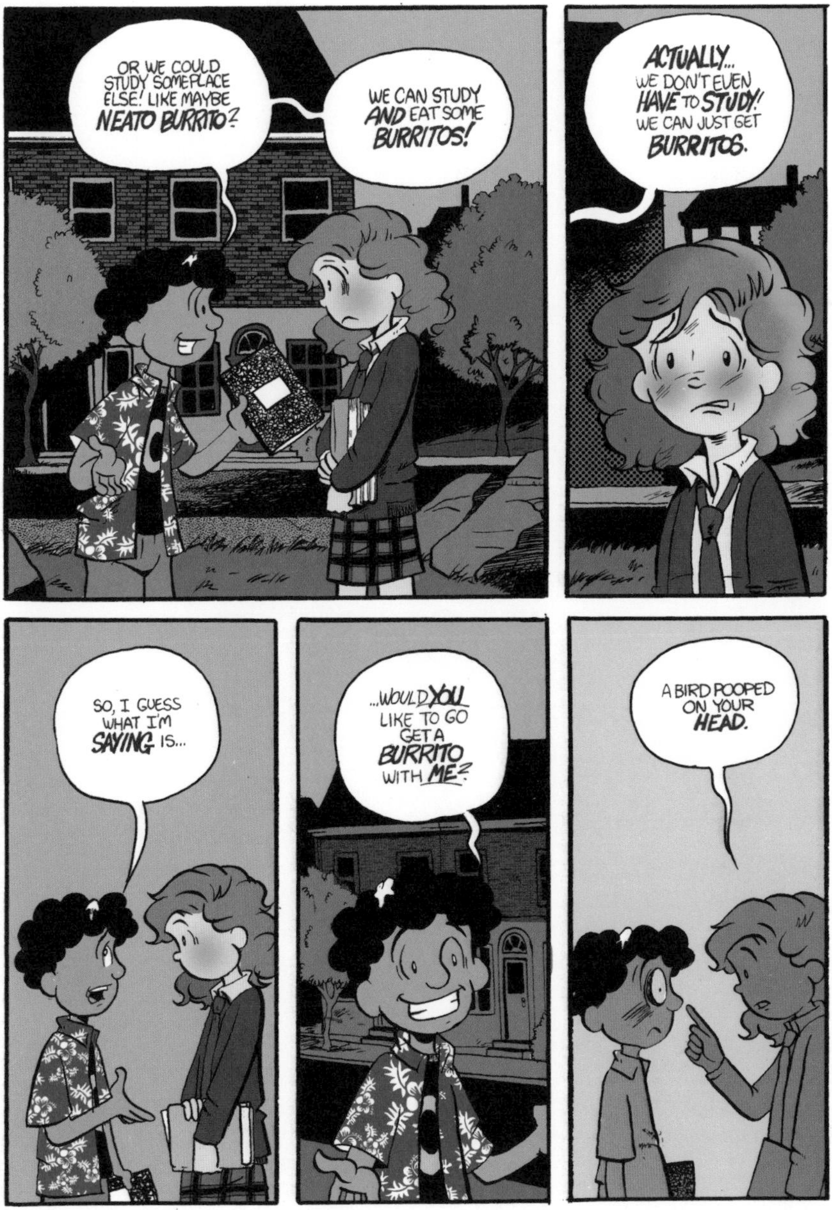
OR WE COULD STUDY SOMEPLACE ELSE! LIKE MAYBE NEATO BURRITO?
WE CAN STUDY AND EAT SOME BURRITOS!
ACTUALLY... WE DON'T EVEN HAVE TO STUDY! WE CAN JUST GET BURRITOS.
SO, I GUESS WHAT I'M SAYING IS...
...WOULD YOU LIKE TO GO GET A BURRITO WITH ME?
A BIRD POOPED ON YOUR HEAD.

I KNOW, RIGHT? ANYWAY, ACROSS TOWN...
...THIS WAS HAPPENING.
HMM... LET'S SEE...
IF I CROSS THE STATS FROM THE WEBSITE...
...AND INTERPOLATED THE ALGORITHM FROM THE OTHER THINGY...
DING!

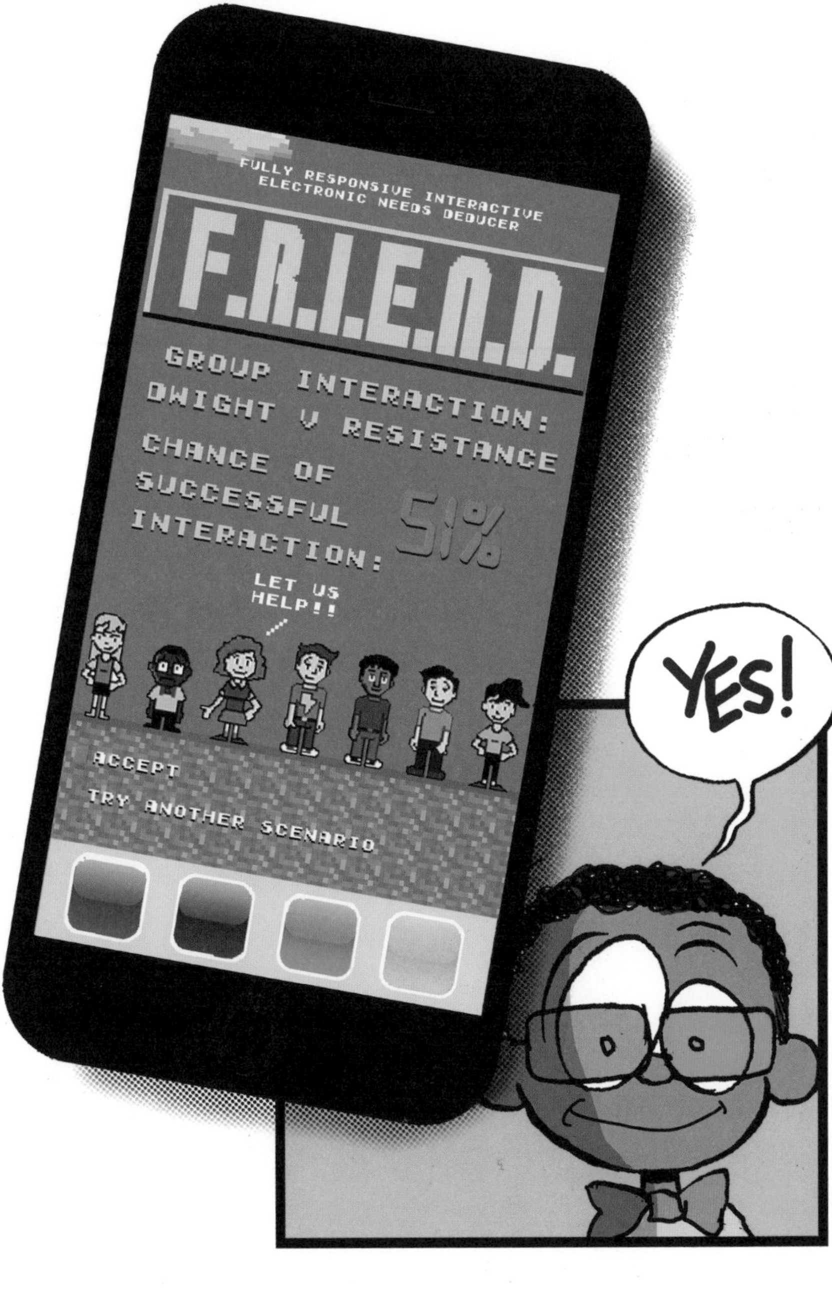
FULLY RESPONSIVE INTERACTIVE ELECTRONIC NEEDS DEDUCER
F.R.I.E.N.D.
GROUP INTERACTION: DWIGHT V RESISTANCE
CHANCE OF SUCCESSFUL INTERACTION: 51%
LET US HELP!!
ACCEPT
TRY ANOTHER SCENARIO
YES!

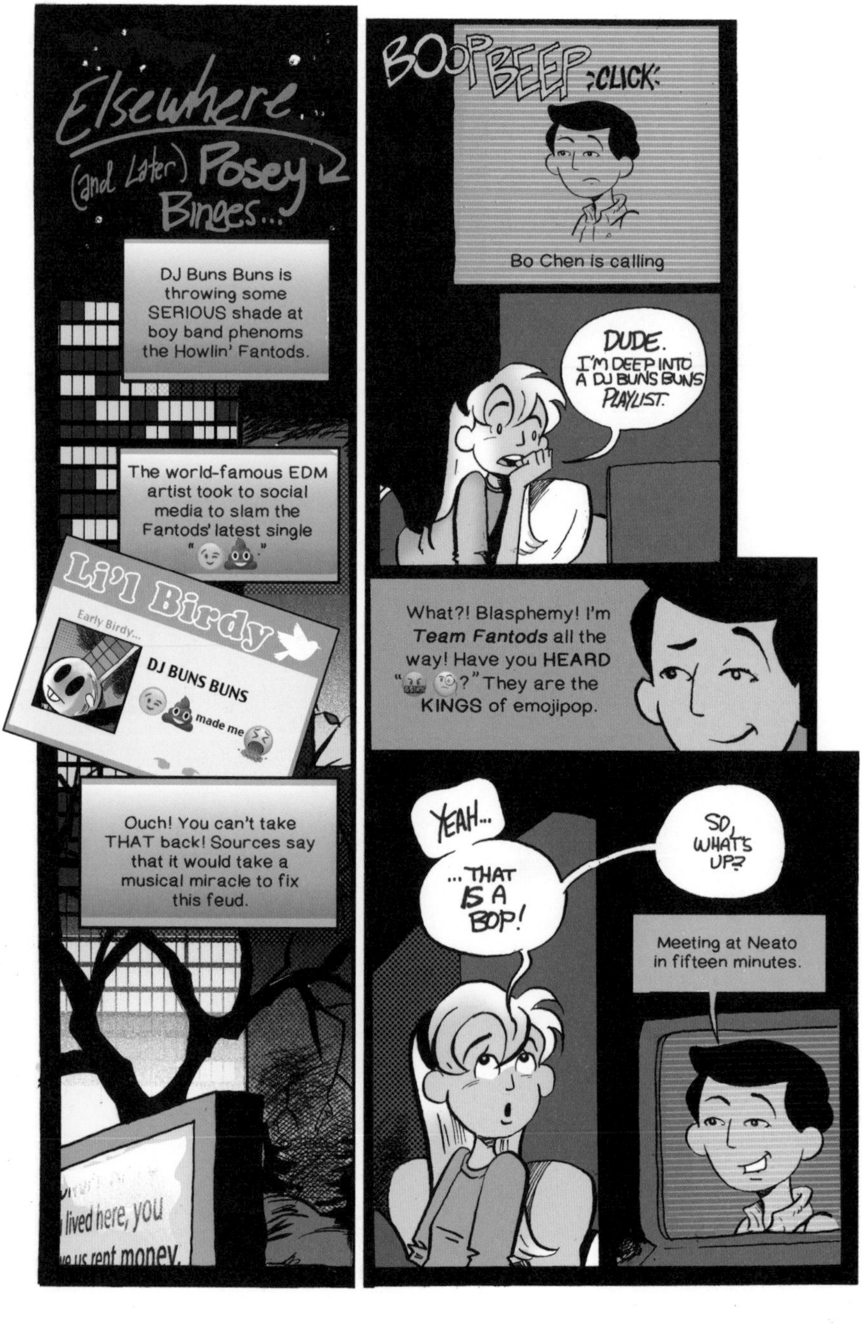
Elsewhere
(and Later) Posey Binges...
DJ Buns Buns is throwing some SERIOUS shade at boy band phenoms the Howlin' Fantods.
The world-famous EDM artist took to social media to slam the Fantods' latest single "😉💩."
Li'l Birdy
Early Birdy...
DJ BUNS BUNS
😉💩 made me 🤮
Ouch! You can't take THAT back! Sources say that it would take a musical miracle to fix this feud.
lived here, you
BOOP BEEP
CLICK
Bo Chen is calling
DUDE. I'M DEEP INTO A DJ BUNS BUNS PLAYLIST.
What?! Blasphemy! I'm *Team Fantods* all the way! Have you HEARD "🤬 🙄?" They are the KINGS of emojipop.
YEAH...
...THAT IS A BOP!
SO, WHAT'S UP?
Meeting at Neato in fifteen minutes.

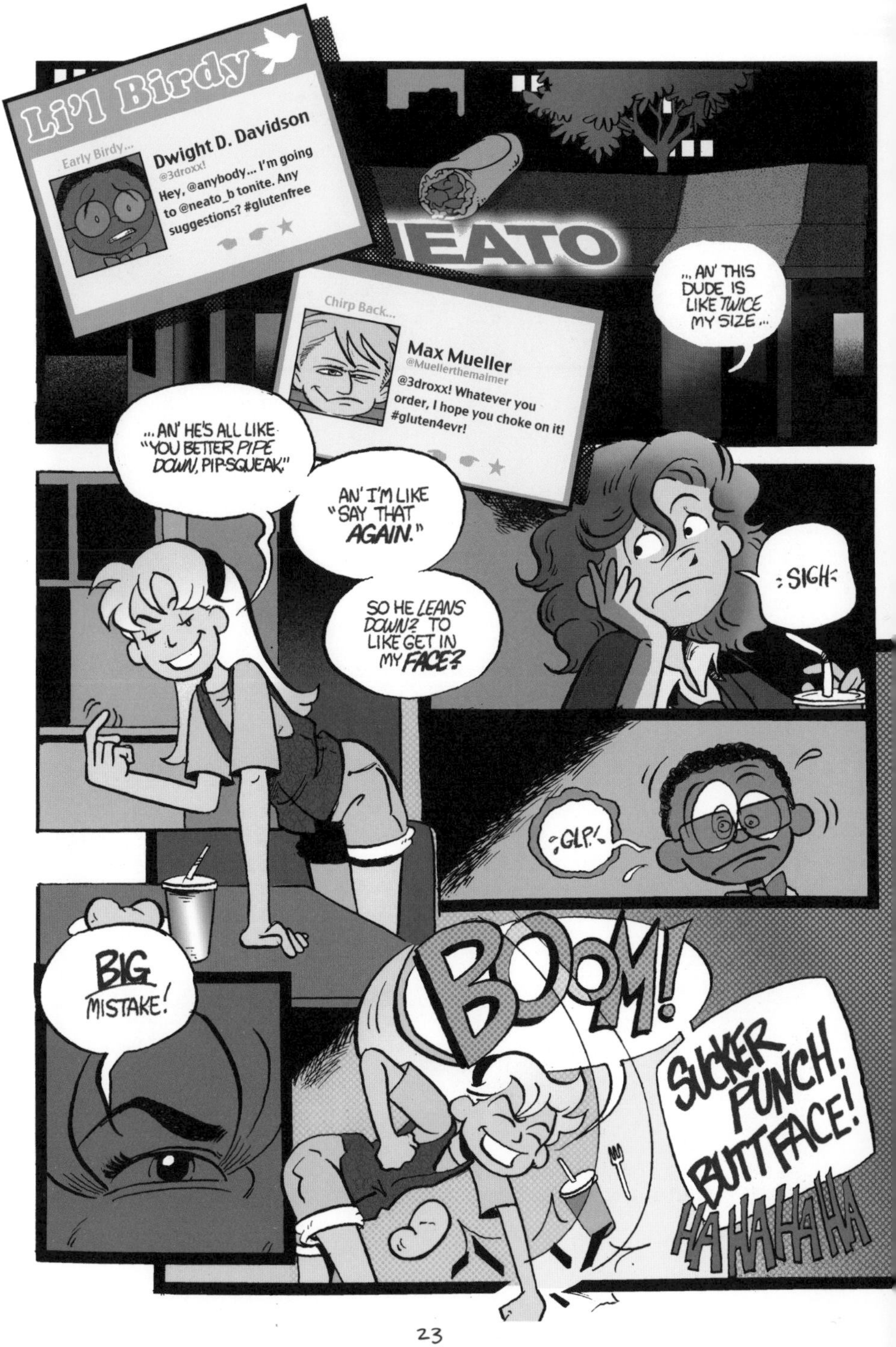

Li'l Birdy
Early Birdy...
Dwight D. Davidson
@3droxx!
Hey, @anybody... I'm going to @neato_b tonite. Any suggestions? #glutenfree
NEATO
Chirp Back...
Max Mueller
@Muellerthemaimer
@3droxx! Whatever you order, I hope you choke on it! #gluten4evr!
... AN' THIS DUDE IS LIKE TWICE MY SIZE...
... AN' HE'S ALL LIKE "YOU BETTER PIPE DOWN, PIP-SQUEAK."
AN' I'M LIKE "SAY THAT AGAIN."
SO HE LEANS DOWN? TO LIKE GET IN MY FACE?
SIGH
GLP!
BIG MISTAKE!
BOOM!
SUCKER PUNCH, BUTT FACE!
HA HA HA HA HA

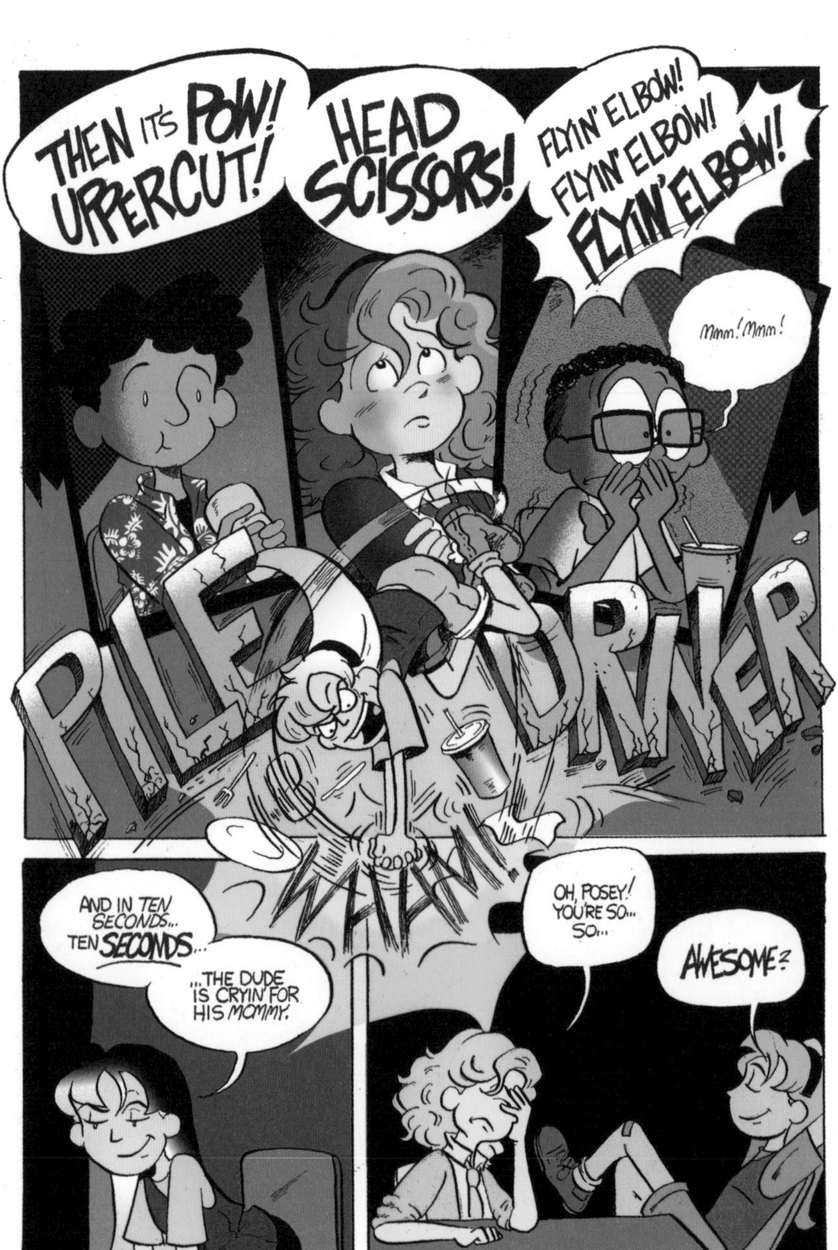

THEN IT'S POW! UPPERCUT!
HEAD SCISSORS!
FLYIN' ELBOW! FLYIN' ELBOW! FLYIN' ELBOW!
Mmm! Mmm!
PILE DRIVER
WHAM!
AND IN TEN SECONDS... TEN SECONDS...
...THE DUDE IS CRYIN' FOR HIS MOMMY.
OH, POSEY! YOU'RE SO... SO...
AWESOME?

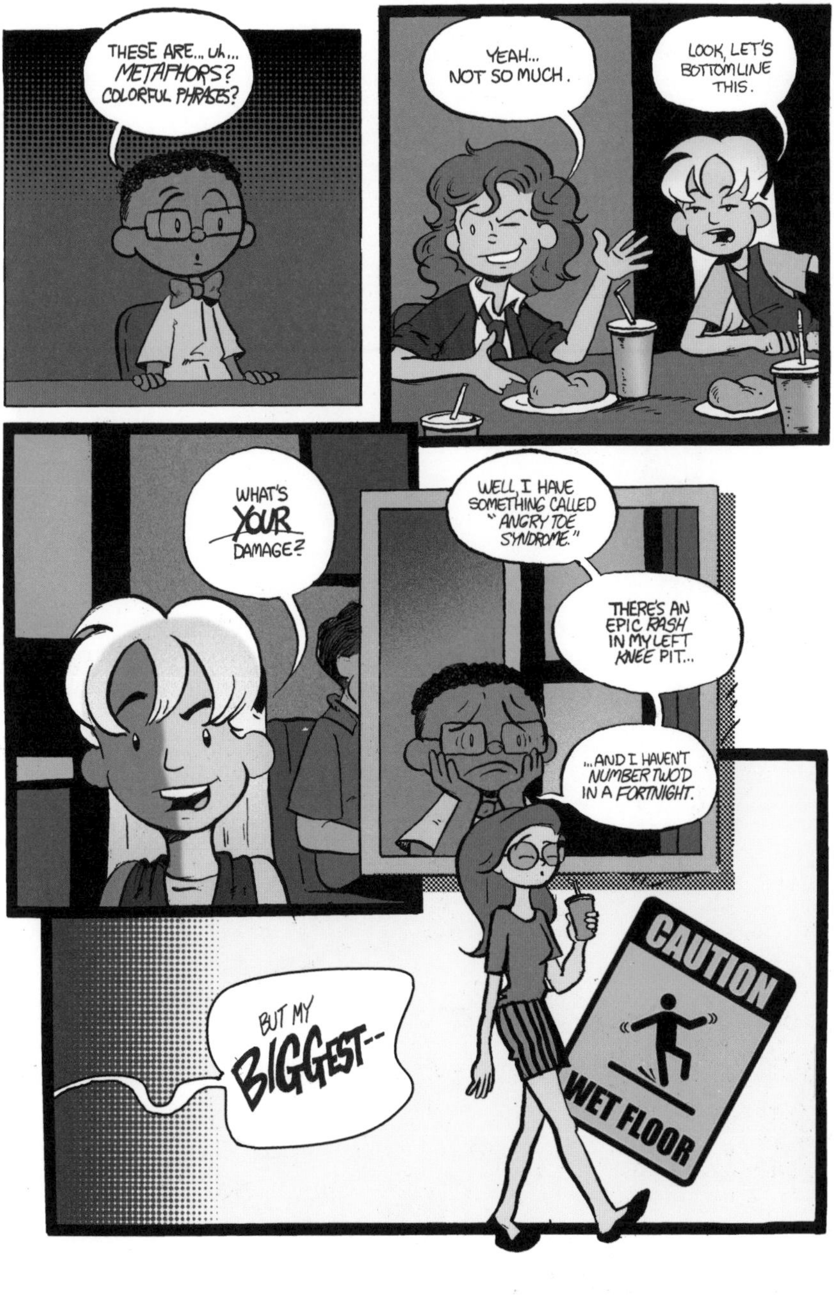
THESE ARE... uh... METAPHORS? COLORFUL PHRASES?
YEAH... NOT SO MUCH.
LOOK, LET'S BOTTOMLINE THIS.
WHAT'S YOUR DAMAGE?
WELL, I HAVE SOMETHING CALLED "ANGRY TOE SYNDROME."
THERE'S AN EPIC RASH IN MY LEFT KNEE PIT...
...AND I HAVEN'T NUMBER TWO'D IN A FORTNIGHT.
BUT MY BIGGEST--
CAUTION
WET FLOOR

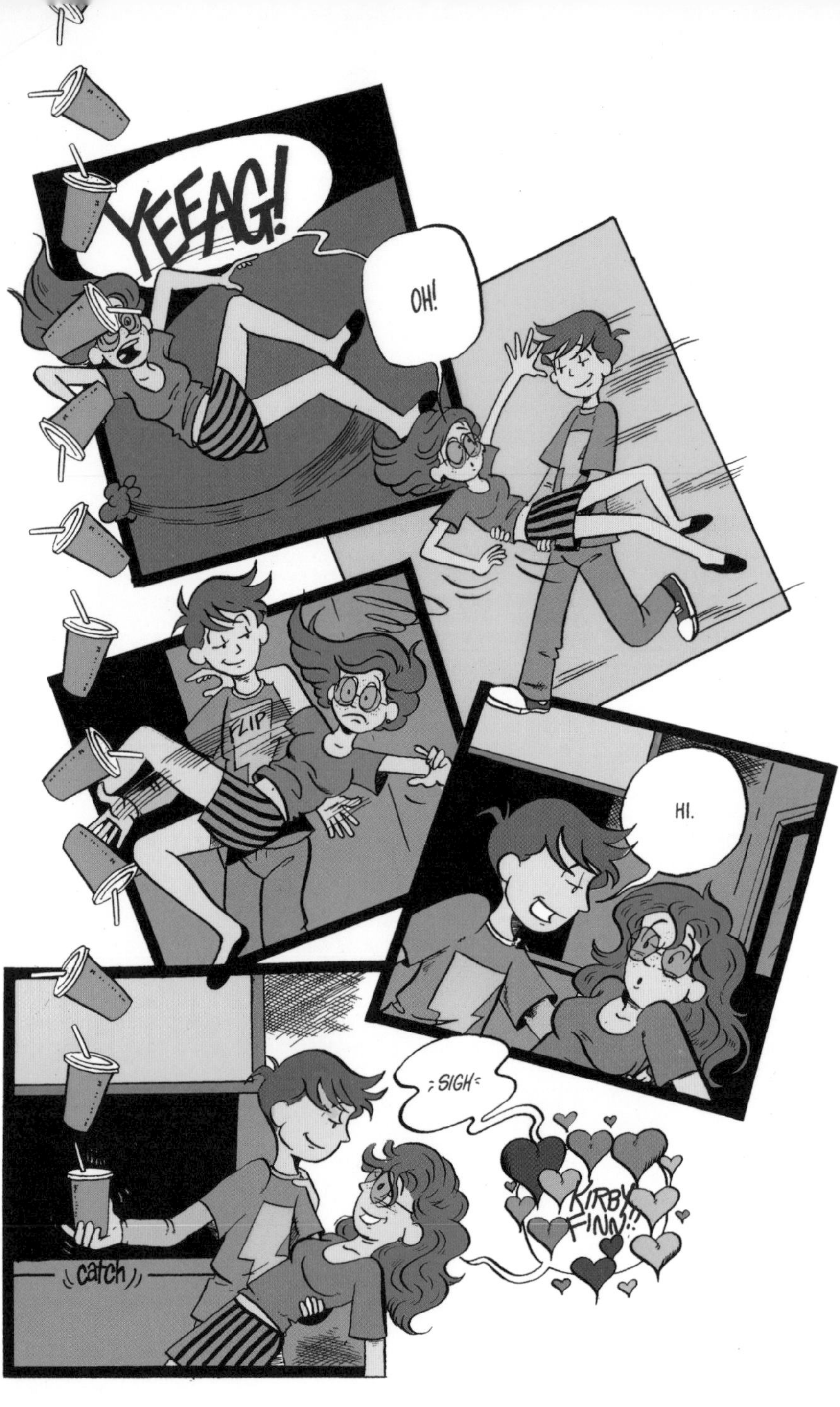
YEEAG!
OH!
FLIP
HI.
;SIGH;
catch
KIRBY!!
FINN!!

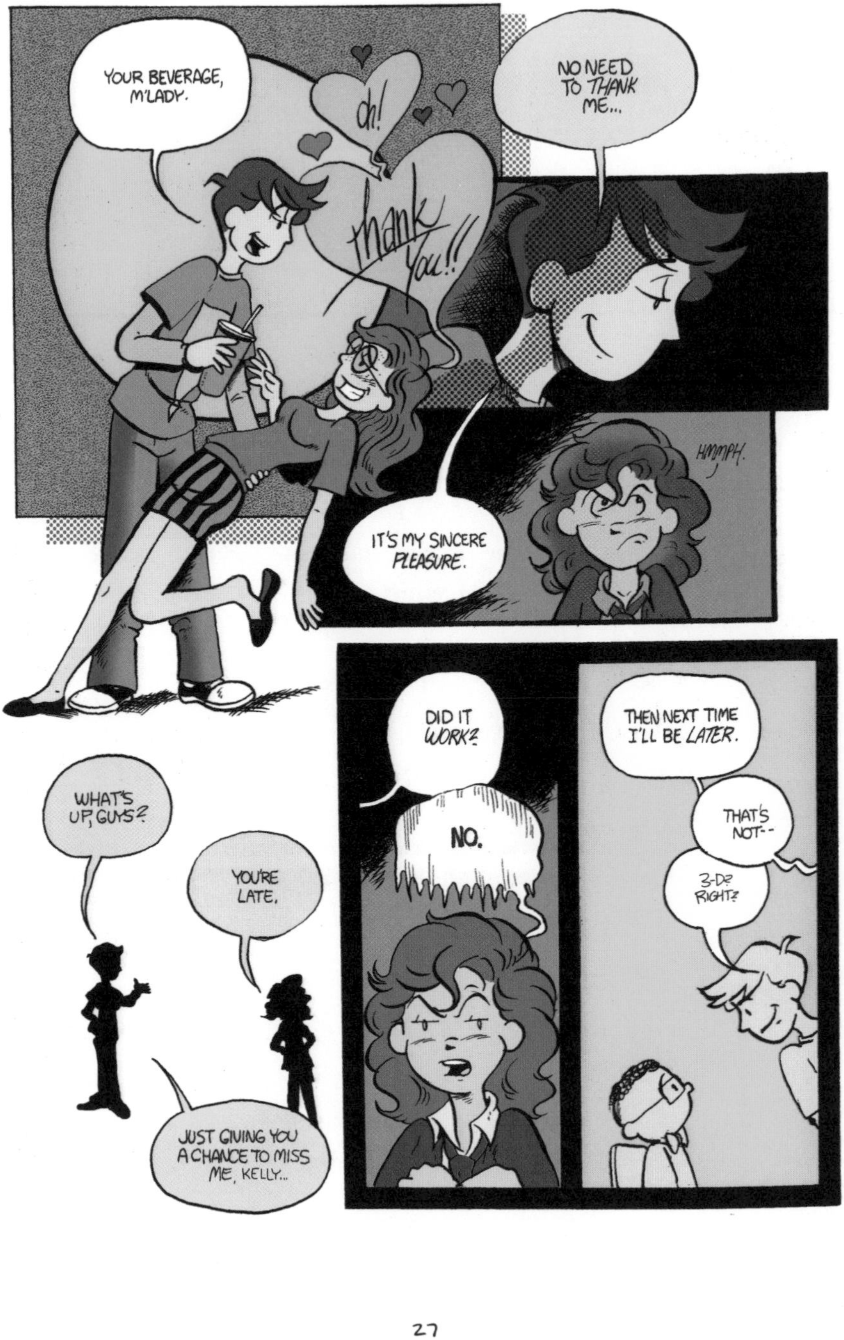
YOUR BEVERAGE, M'LADY.
oh!
thank You!!
NO NEED TO THANK ME...
IT'S MY SINCERE PLEASURE.
HMMPH.
WHAT'S UP, GUYS?
YOU'RE LATE.
JUST GIVING YOU A CHANCE TO MISS ME, KELLY...
DID IT WORK?
NO.
THEN NEXT TIME I'LL BE LATER.
THAT'S NOT--
3-D? RIGHT?

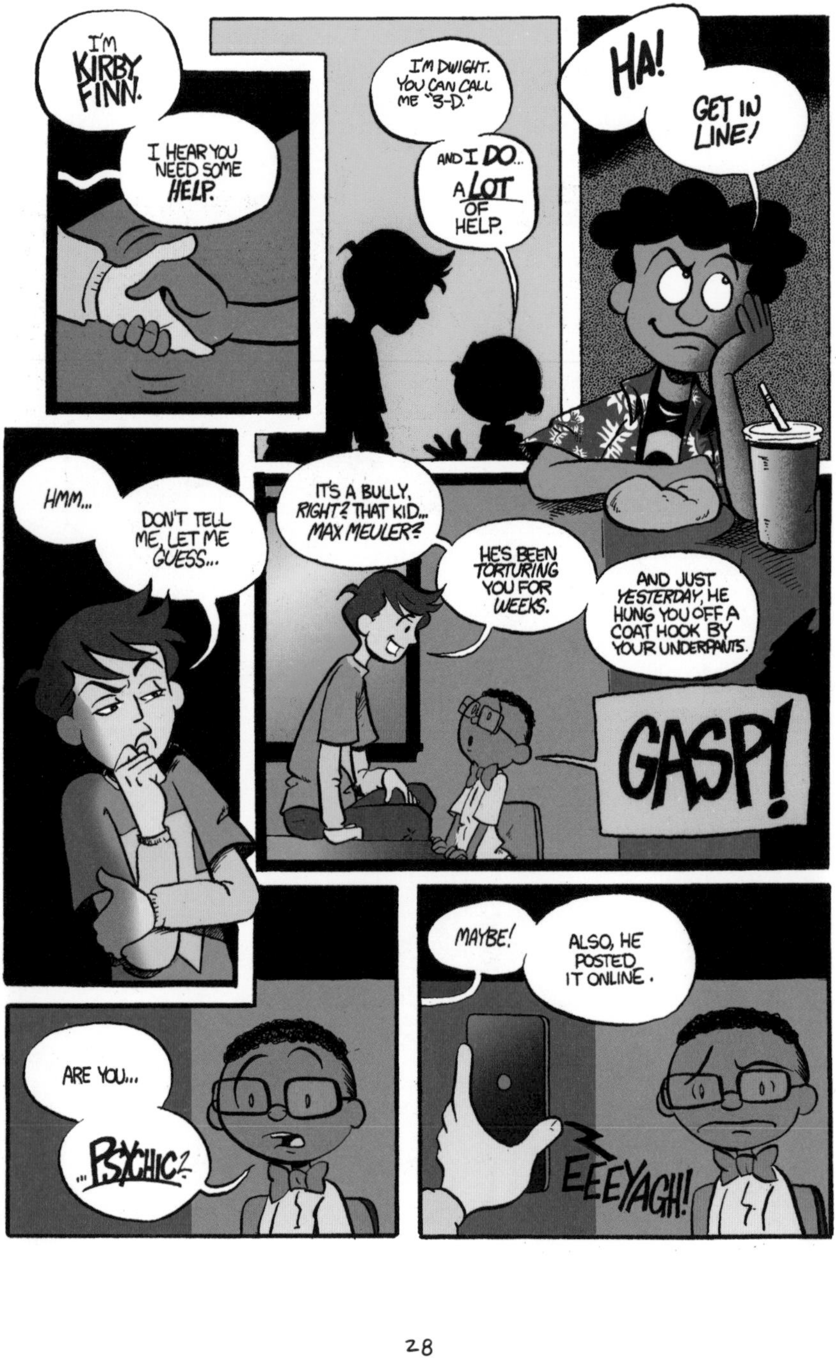
I'M KIRBY FINN.
I HEAR YOU NEED SOME HELP.
I'M DWIGHT. YOU CAN CALL ME "3-D."
AND I DO... A LOT OF HELP.
HA!
GET IN LINE!
HMM...
DON'T TELL ME, LET ME GUESS...
IT'S A BULLY, RIGHT? THAT KID... MAX MEULER?
HE'S BEEN TORTURING YOU FOR WEEKS.
AND JUST YESTERDAY, HE HUNG YOU OFF A COAT HOOK BY YOUR UNDERPANTS.
GASP!
ARE YOU...
...PSYCHIC?
MAYBE!
ALSO, HE POSTED IT ONLINE.
EEEYAGH!

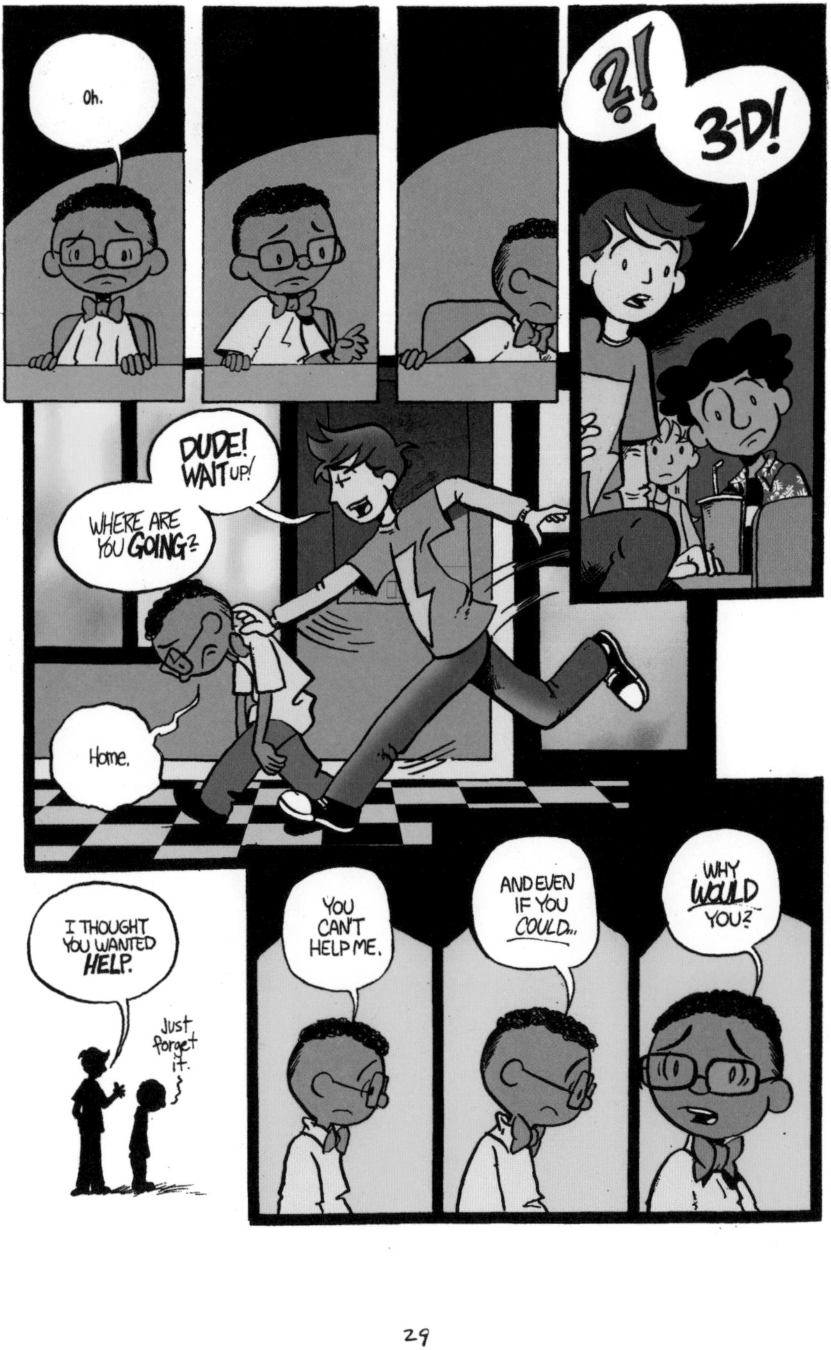
Oh.
?!
3-D!
DUDE! WAIT UP!
WHERE ARE YOU GOING?
Home.
I THOUGHT YOU WANTED HELP.
Just forget it.
YOU CAN'T HELP ME.
AND EVEN IF YOU COULD...
WHY WOULD YOU?

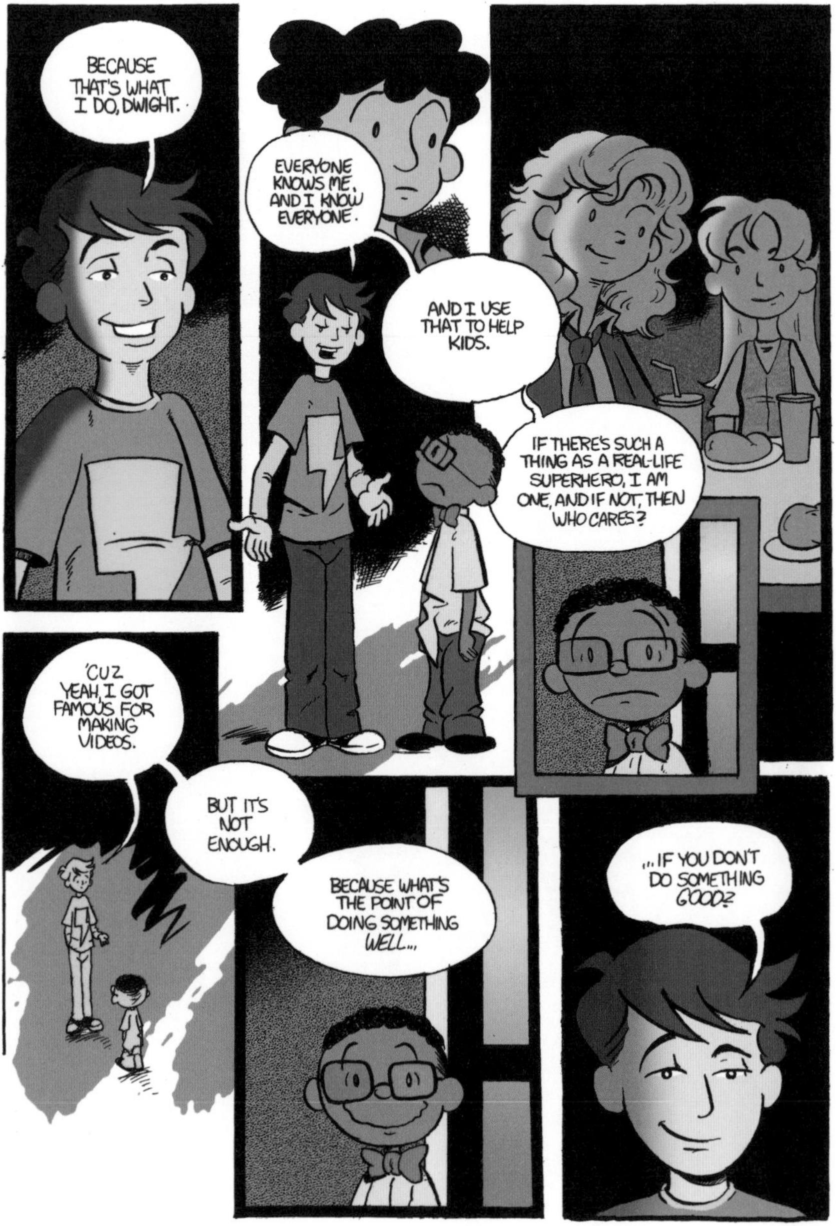
BECAUSE THAT'S WHAT I DO, DWIGHT.
EVERYONE KNOWS ME, AND I KNOW EVERYONE.
AND I USE THAT TO HELP KIDS.
IF THERE'S SUCH A THING AS A REAL-LIFE SUPERHERO, I AM ONE, AND IF NOT, THEN WHO CARES?
'CUZ YEAH, I GOT FAMOUS FOR MAKING VIDEOS.
BUT IT'S NOT ENOUGH.
BECAUSE WHAT'S THE POINT OF DOING SOMETHING *WELL*...
...IF YOU DON'T DO SOMETHING *GOOD*?

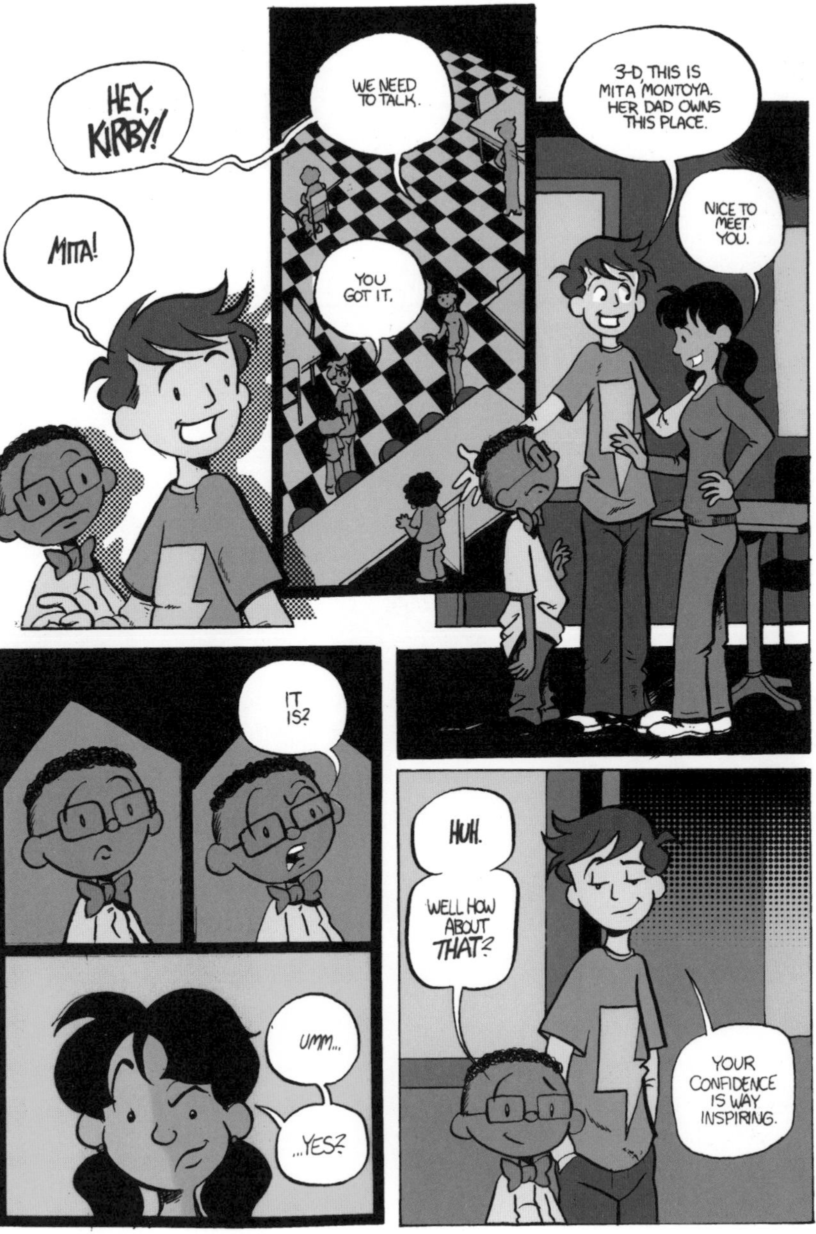
HEY, KIRBY!
WE NEED TO TALK.
MITA!
YOU GOT IT.
3-D, THIS IS MITA MONTOYA. HER DAD OWNS THIS PLACE.
NICE TO MEET YOU.
IT IS?
UMM...
...YES?
HUH.
WELL HOW ABOUT THAT?
YOUR CONFIDENCE IS WAY INSPIRING.

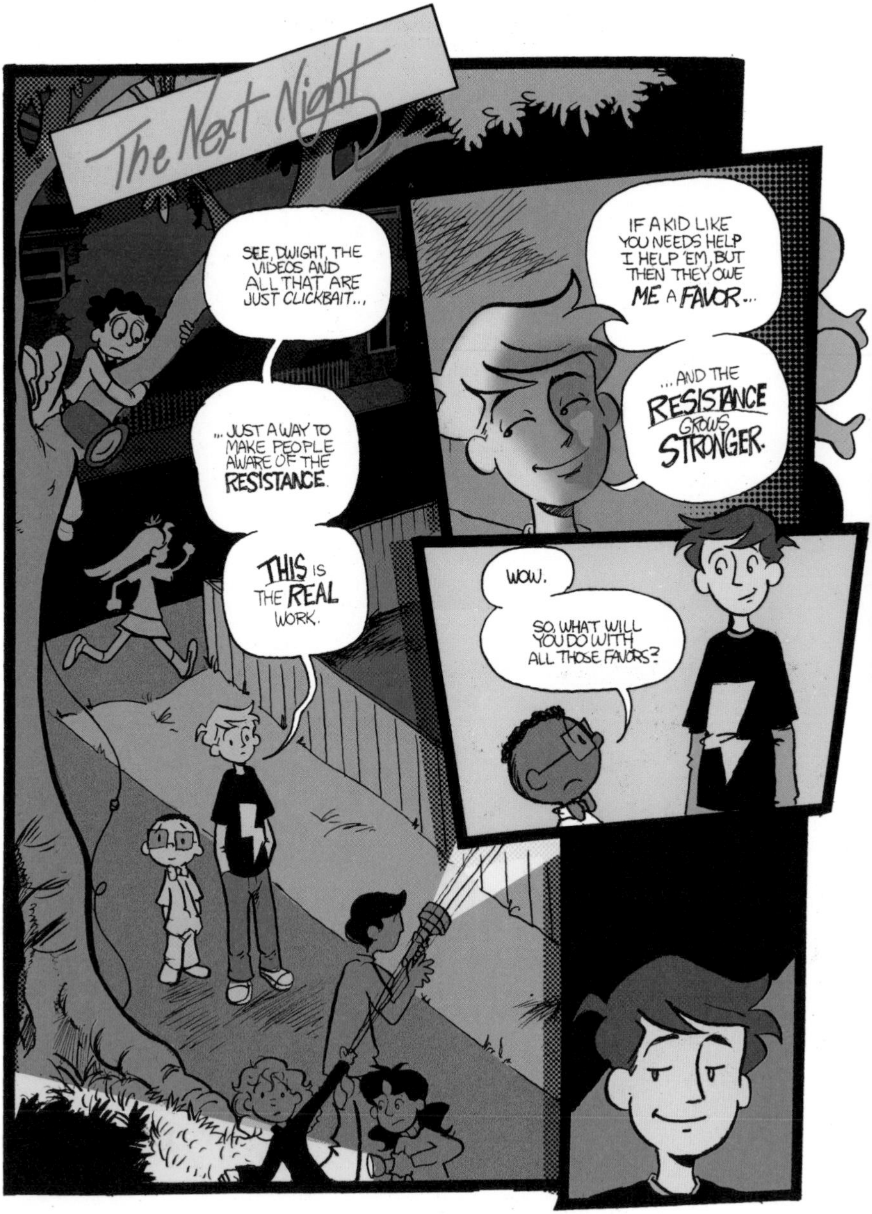
The Next Night
SEE, DWIGHT, THE VIDEOS AND ALL THAT ARE JUST CLICKBAIT...
...JUST A WAY TO MAKE PEOPLE AWARE OF THE RESISTANCE.
THIS IS THE REAL WORK.
IF A KID LIKE YOU NEEDS HELP I HELP 'EM, BUT THEN THEY OWE ME A FAVOR...
...AND THE RESISTANCE GROWS STRONGER.
WOW.
SO, WHAT WILL YOU DO WITH ALL THOSE FAVORS?

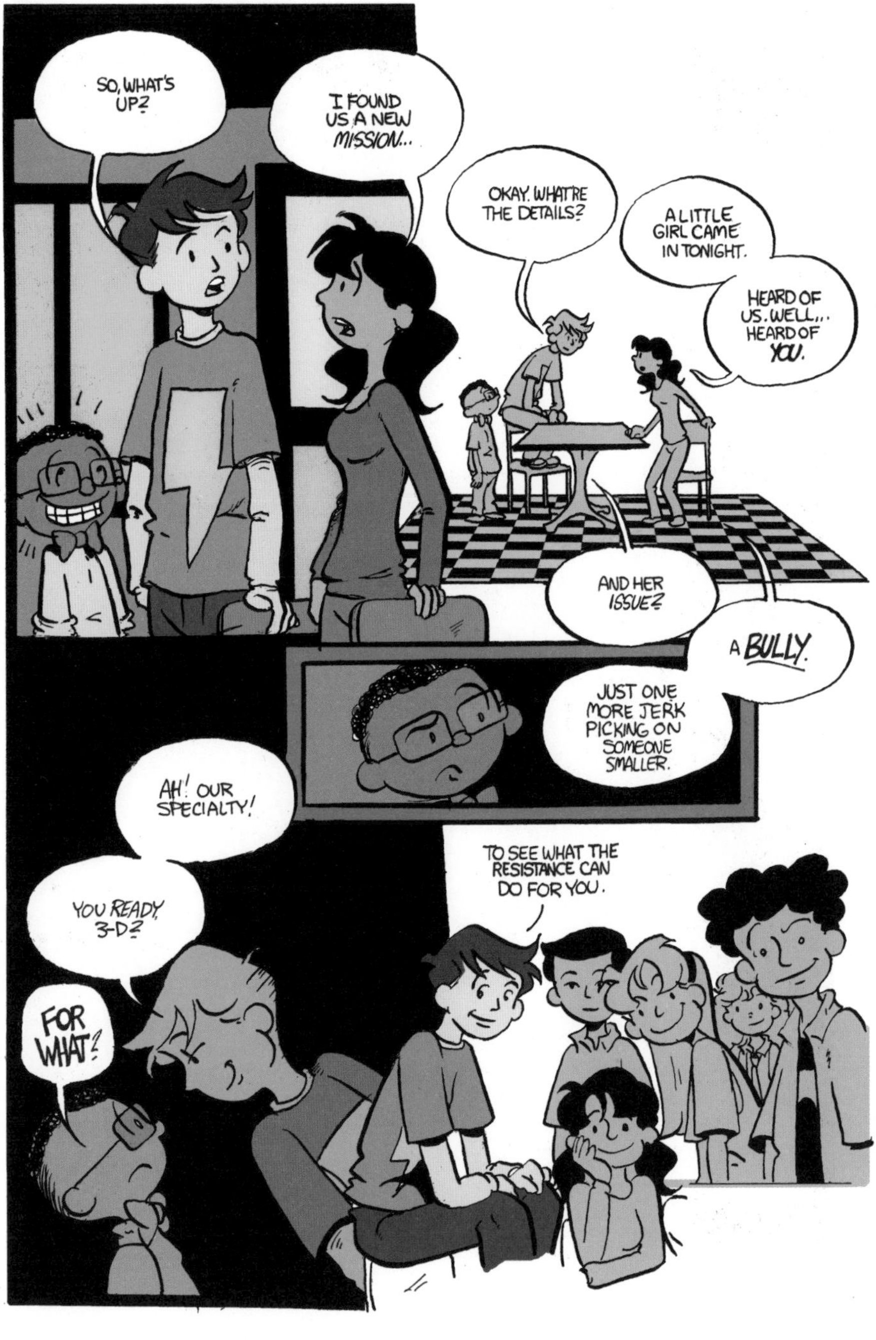
SO, WHAT'S UP?
I FOUND US A NEW MISSION...
OKAY. WHAT'RE THE DETAILS?
A LITTLE GIRL CAME IN TONIGHT.
HEARD OF US. WELL... HEARD OF YOU.
AND HER ISSUE?
A BULLY.
JUST ONE MORE JERK PICKING ON SOMEONE SMALLER.
AH! OUR SPECIALTY!
YOU READY, 3-D?
FOR WHAT?
TO SEE WHAT THE RESISTANCE CAN DO FOR YOU.

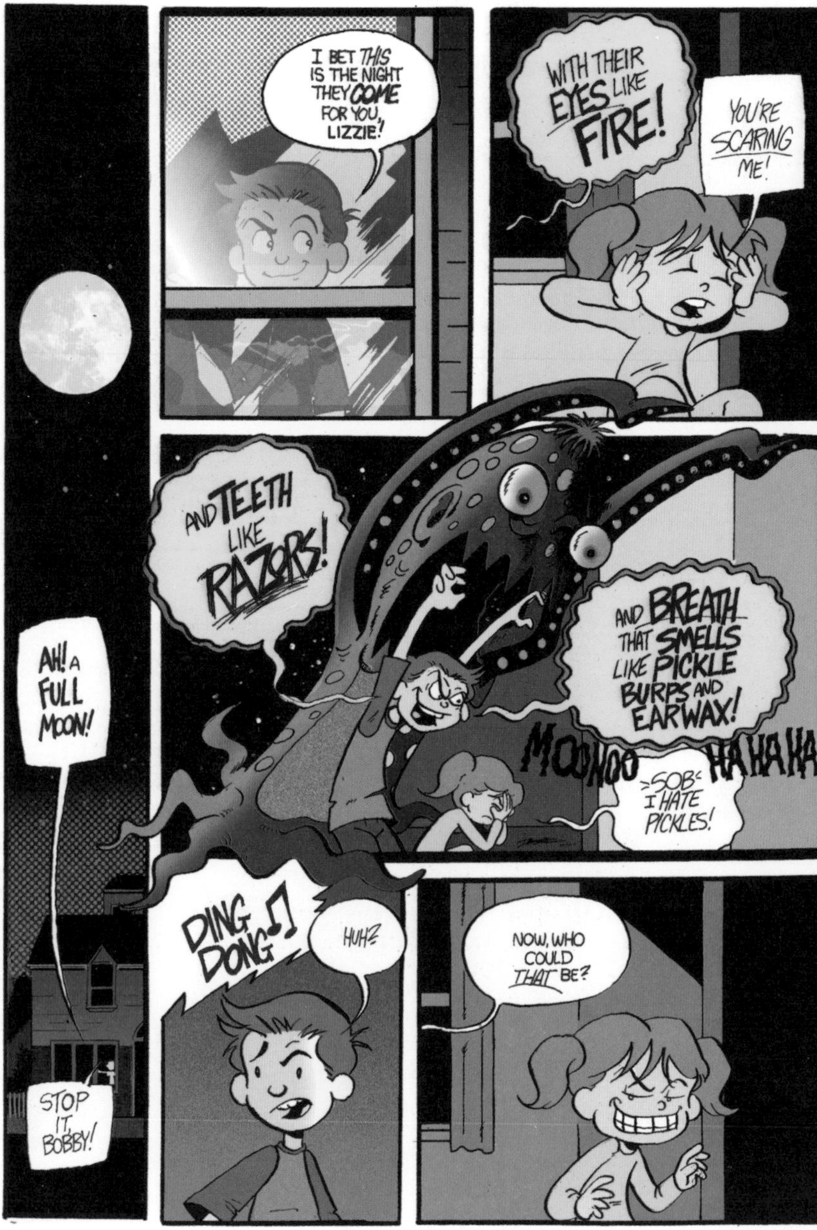
I BET THIS IS THE NIGHT THEY COME FOR YOU, LIZZIE!
WITH THEIR EYES LIKE FIRE!
YOU'RE SCARING ME!
AND TEETH LIKE RAZORS!
AND BREATH THAT SMELLS LIKE PICKLE BURPS AND EARWAX!
MOOHOO HAHAHA
SOB I HATE PICKLES!
AH! A FULL MOON!
STOP IT, BOBBY!
DING DONG
HUH?
NOW, WHO COULD THAT BE?

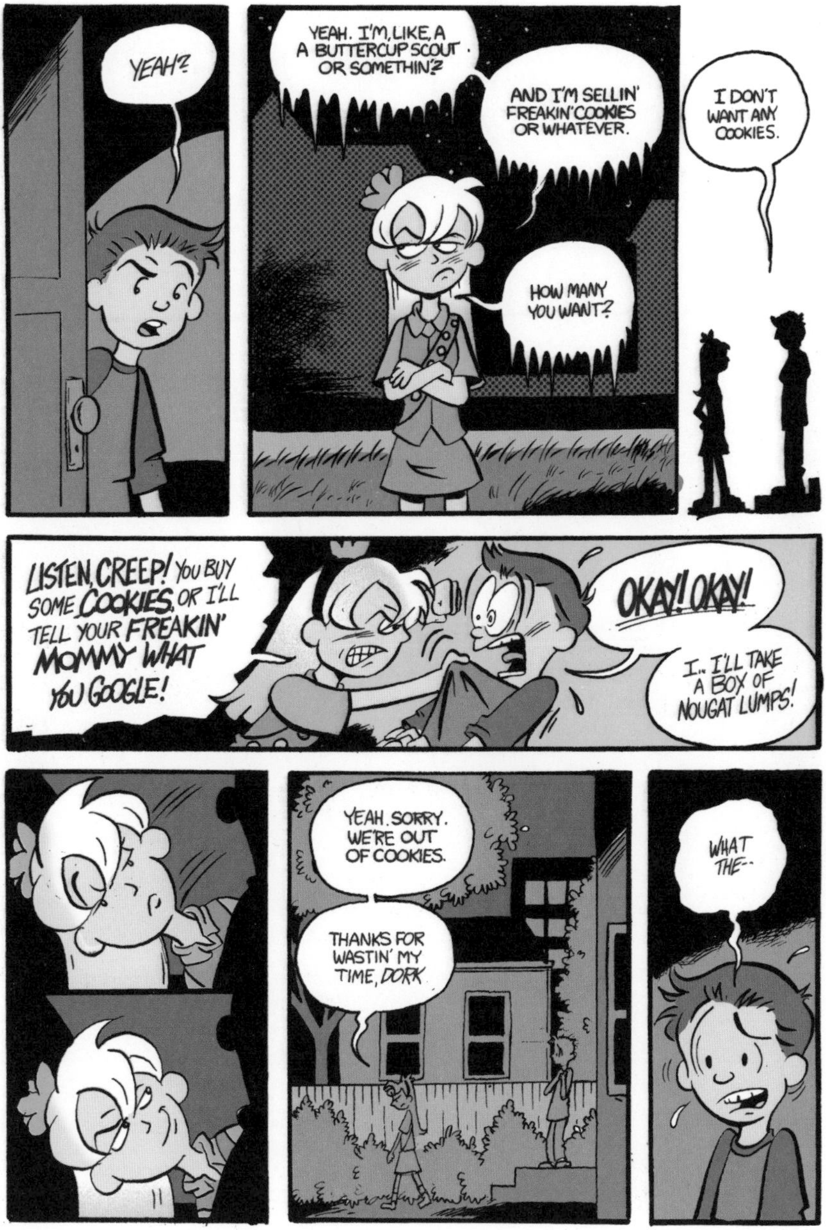
YEAH?
YEAH. I'M, LIKE, A A BUTTERCUP SCOUT OR SOMETHIN'?
AND I'M SELLIN' FREAKIN' COOKIES OR WHATEVER.
HOW MANY YOU WANT?
I DON'T WANT ANY COOKIES.
LISTEN, CREEP! YOU BUY SOME COOKIES, OR I'LL TELL YOUR FREAKIN' MOMMY WHAT YOU GOOGLE!
OKAY! OKAY!
I.. I'LL TAKE A BOX OF NOUGAT LUMPS!
YEAH. SORRY. WE'RE OUT OF COOKIES.
THANKS FOR WASTIN' MY TIME, DORK
WHAT THE--

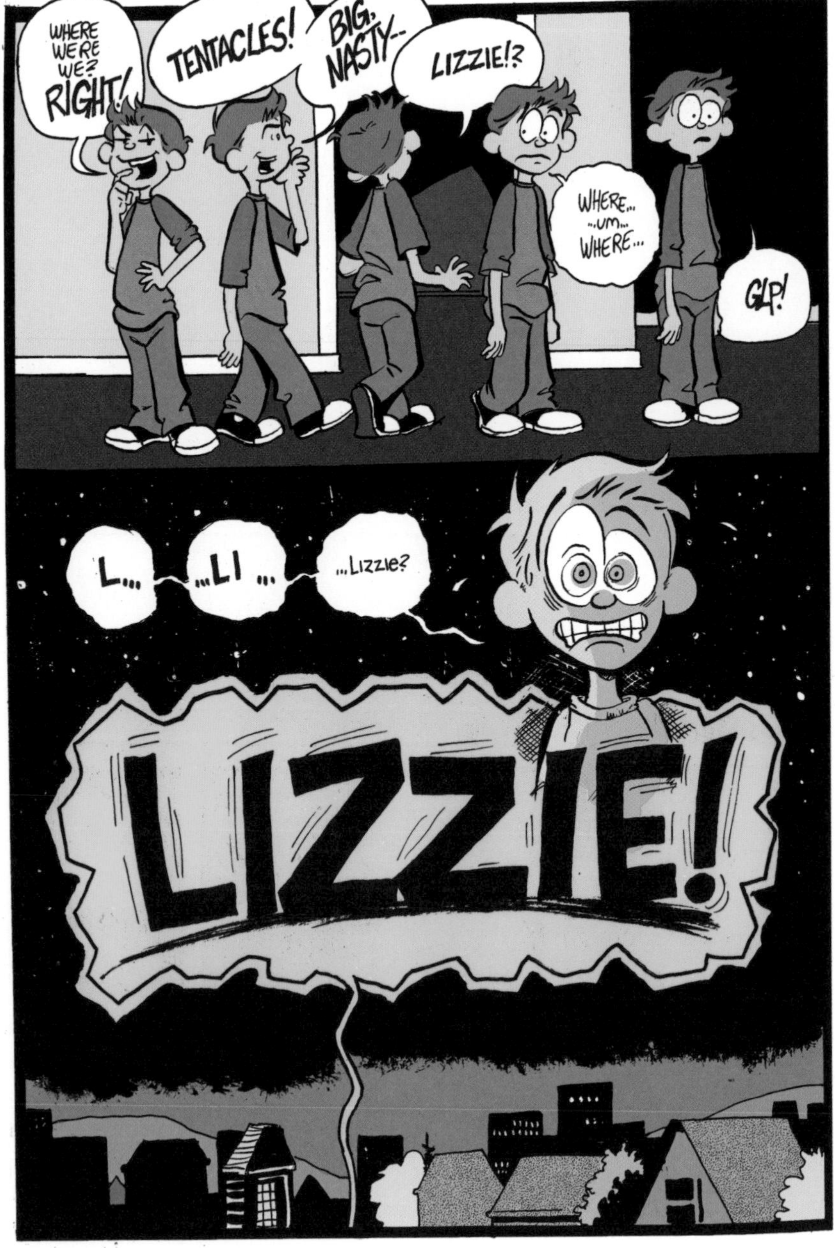
WHERE WE'RE WE? RIGHT!
TENTACLES!
BIG, NASTY--
LIZZIE!?
WHERE... ...UM... WHERE...
GLP!
L...
...LI ...
...Lizzie?
LIZZIE!

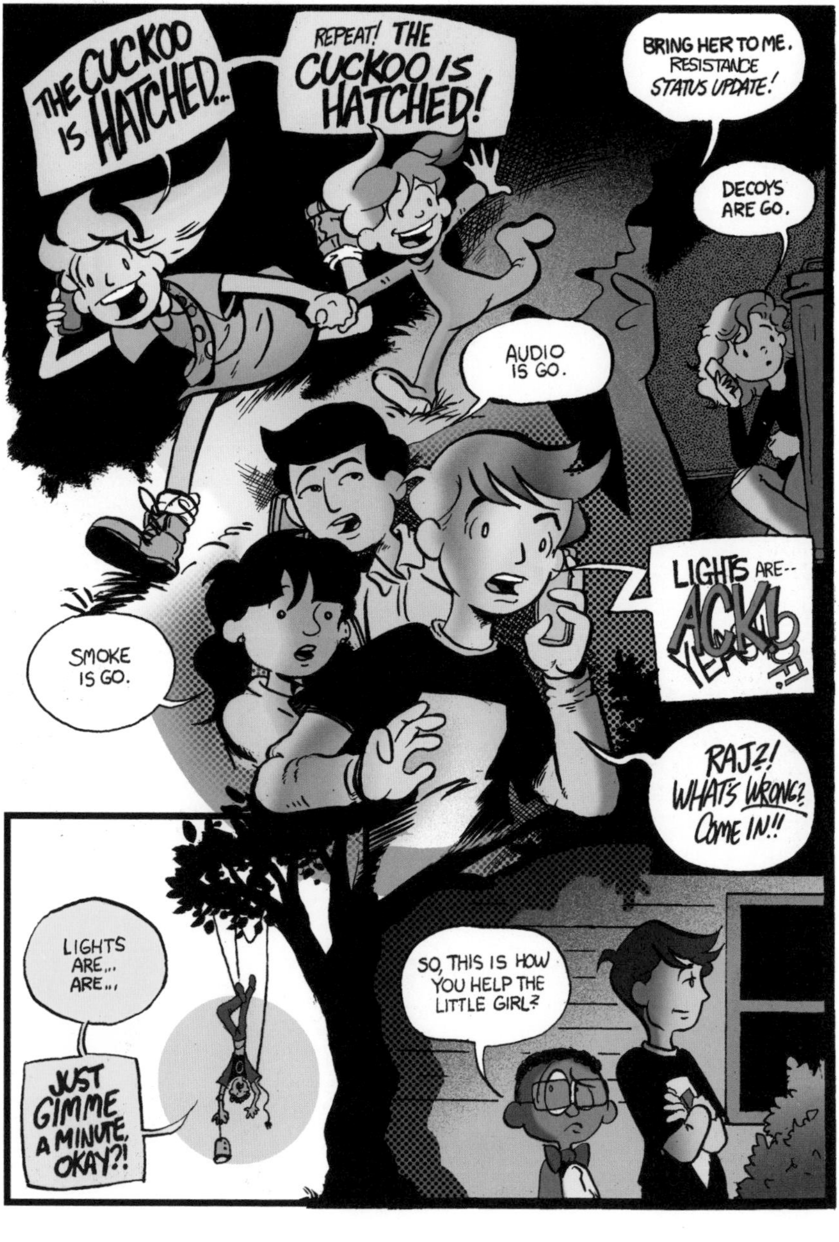
THE CUCKOO IS HATCHED...
REPEAT! THE CUCKOO IS HATCHED!
BRING HER TO ME. RESISTANCE STATUS UPDATE!
DECOYS ARE GO.
AUDIO IS GO.
SMOKE IS GO.
LIGHTS ARE-- ACK!
RAJ?! WHAT'S WRONG? COME IN!!
LIGHTS ARE... ARE...
JUST GIMME A MINUTE, OKAY?!
SO, THIS IS HOW YOU HELP THE LITTLE GIRL?

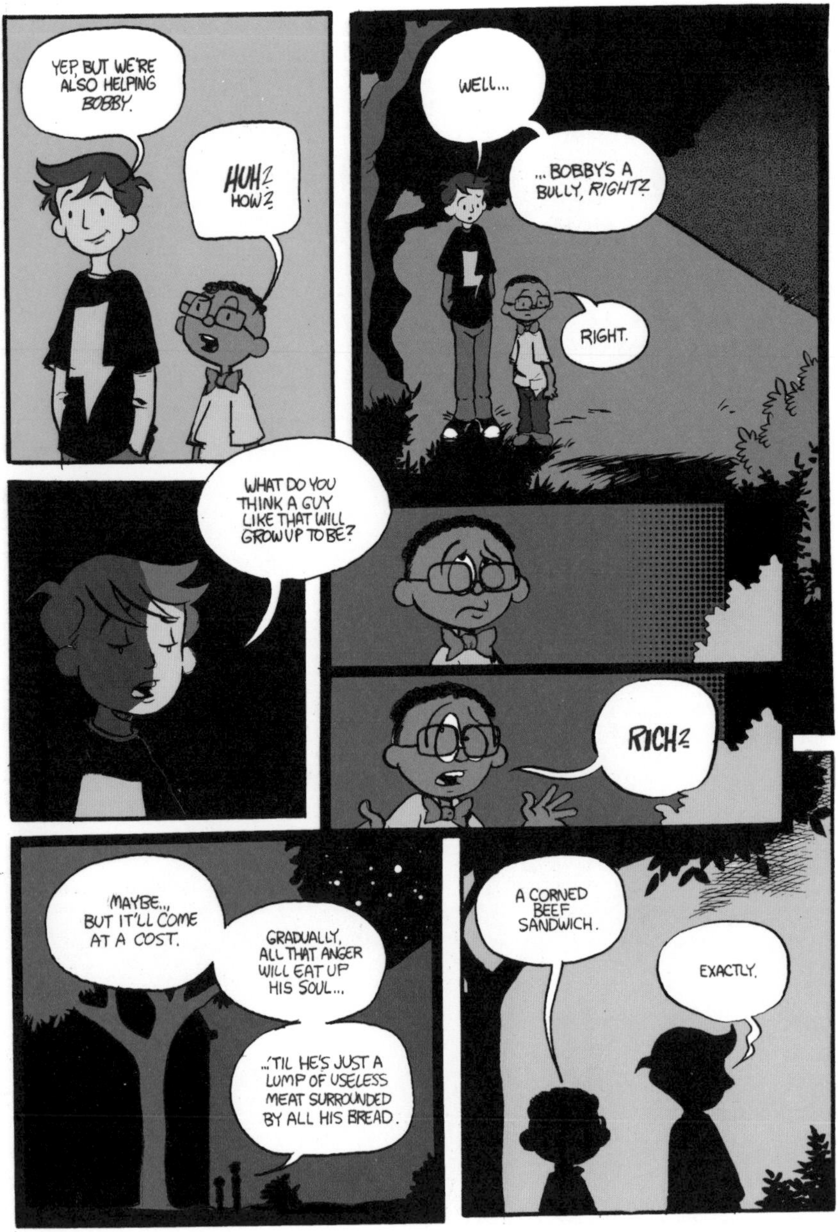
YEP, BUT WE'RE ALSO HELPING *BOBBY*.
HUH? HOW?
WELL...
...BOBBY'S A BULLY, *RIGHT*?
RIGHT.
WHAT DO YOU THINK A GUY LIKE THAT WILL GROW UP TO BE?
RICH?
MAYBE..., BUT IT'LL COME AT A COST.
GRADUALLY, ALL THAT ANGER WILL EAT UP HIS SOUL...
...'TIL HE'S JUST A LUMP OF USELESS MEAT SURROUNDED BY ALL HIS BREAD.
A CORNED BEEF SANDWICH.
EXACTLY.

"NOW, SHUT UP AND WATCH."

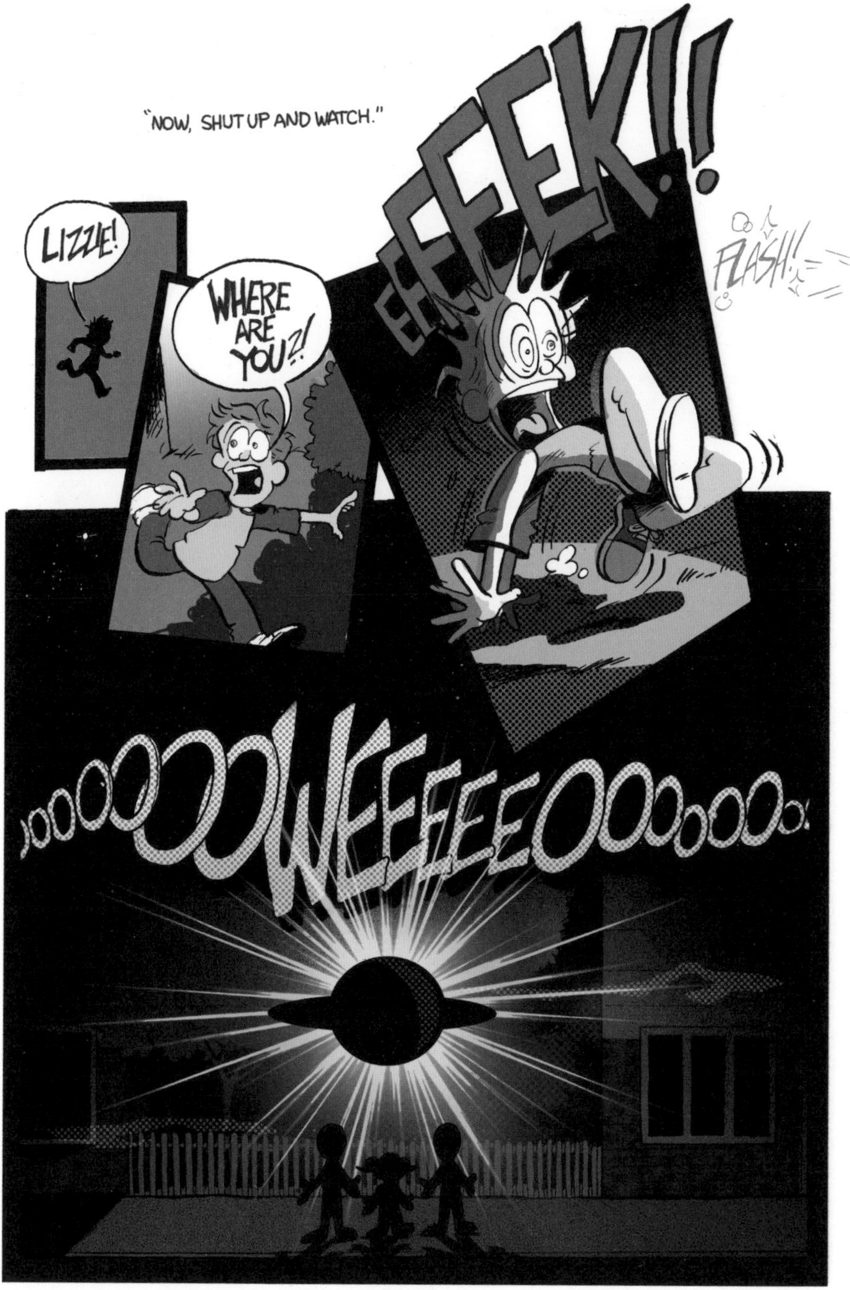
LIZZIE!
WHERE ARE YOU?!
EEEEEK!!!
FLASH!!
OOOOOOOOWEEEEEOOOOOOOO

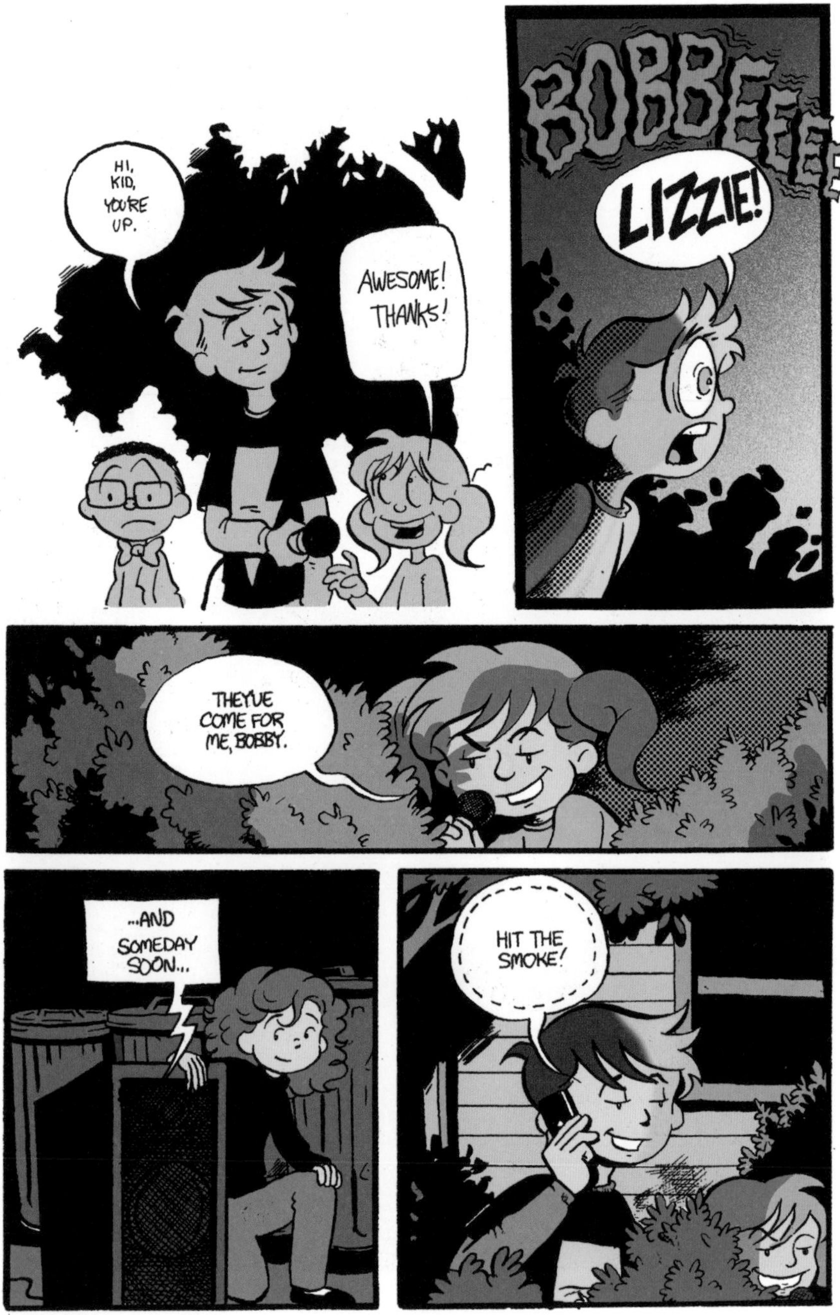

HI, KID, YOU'RE UP.
AWESOME! THANKS!
BOBBEEEE
LIZZIE!
THEY'VE COME FOR ME, BOBBY.
...AND SOMEDAY SOON...
HIT THE SMOKE!

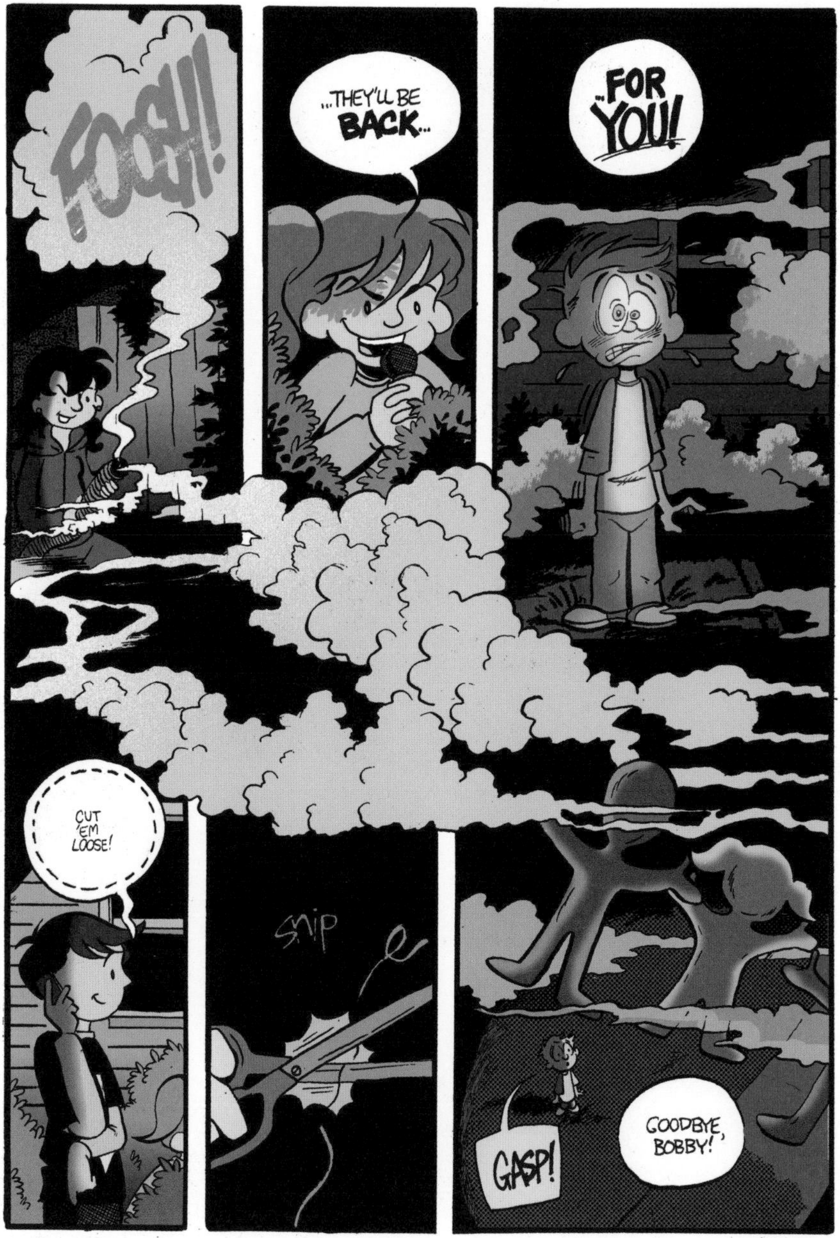
FOOSH!!
...THEY'LL BE BACK...
...FOR YOU!
CUT 'EM LOOSE!
SNIP
GASP!
GOODBYE, BOBBY!

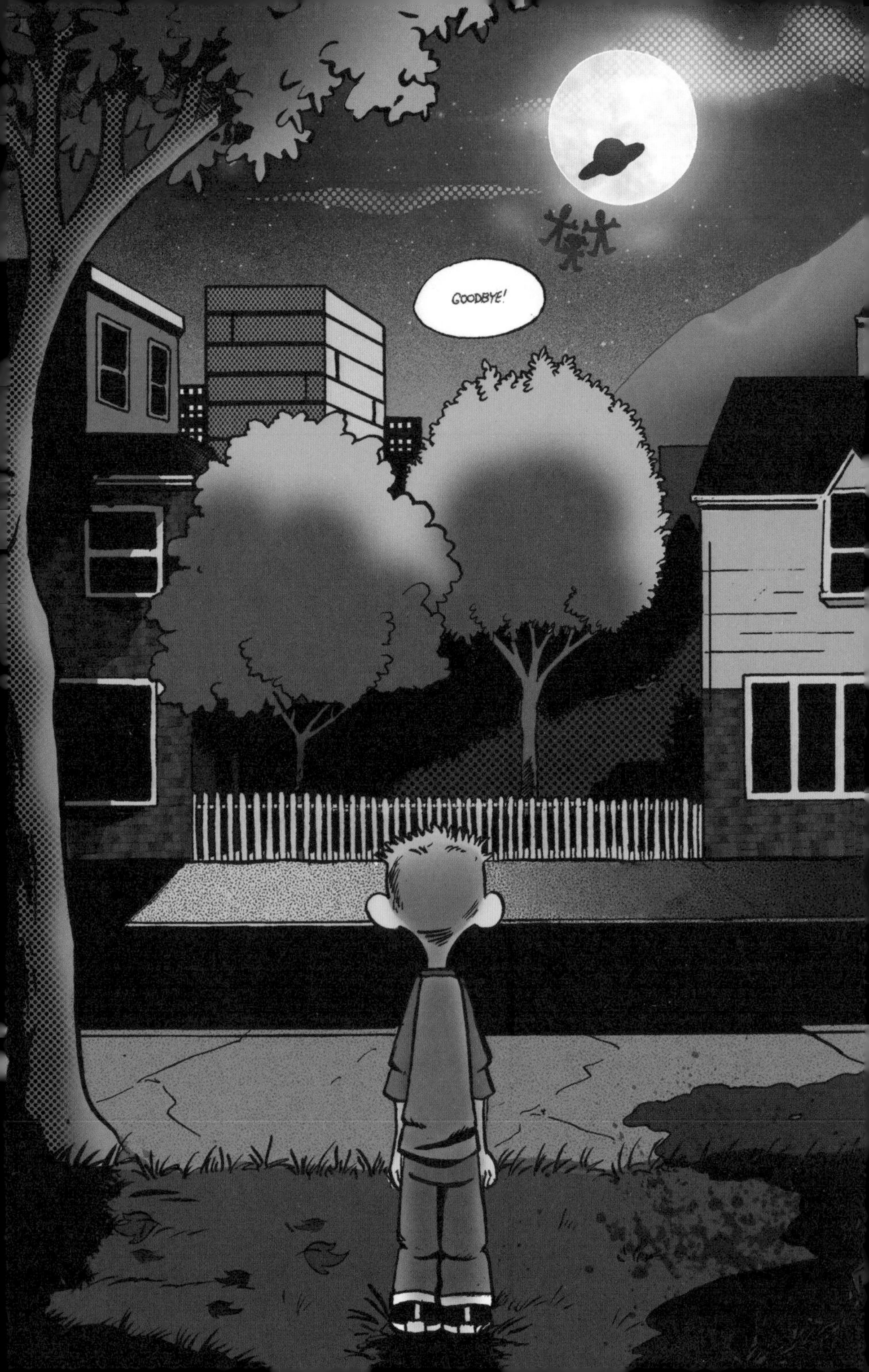
GOODBYE!

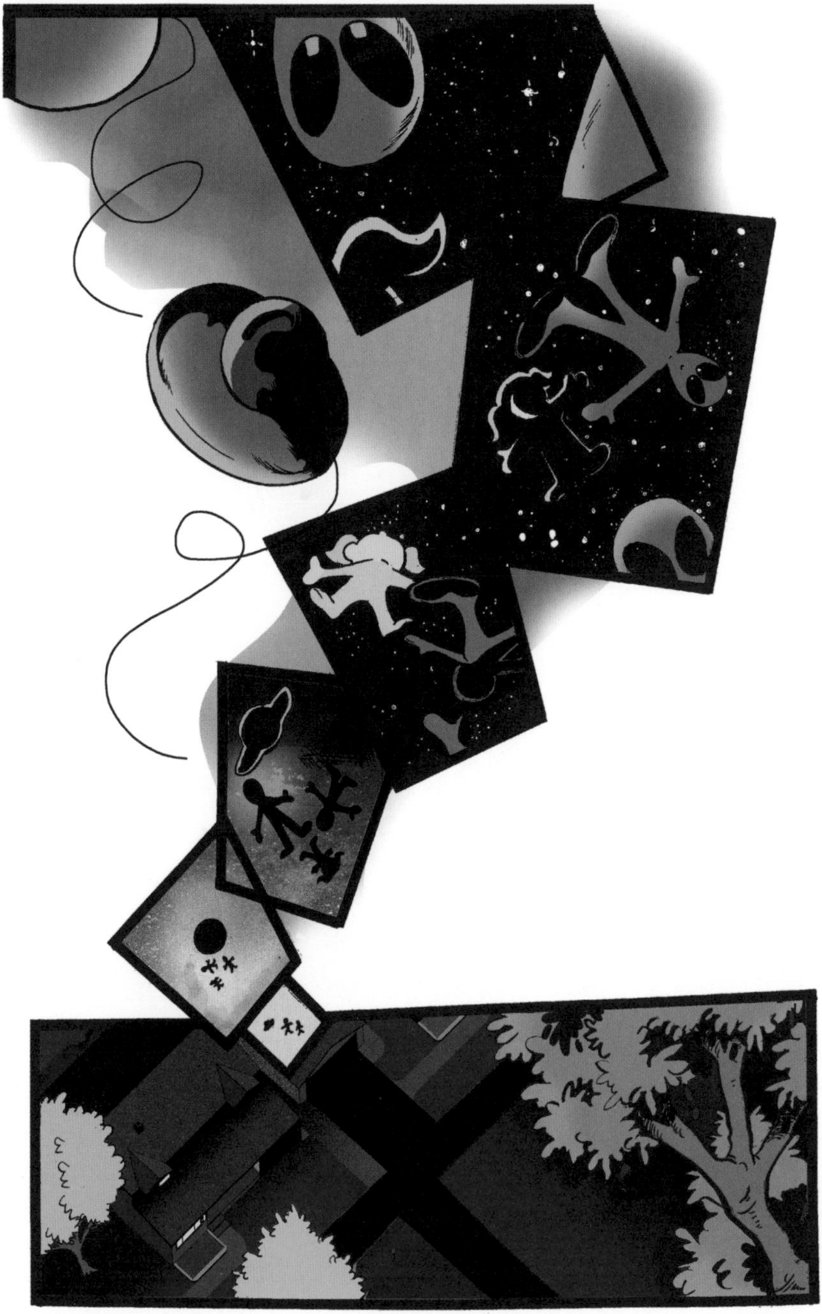

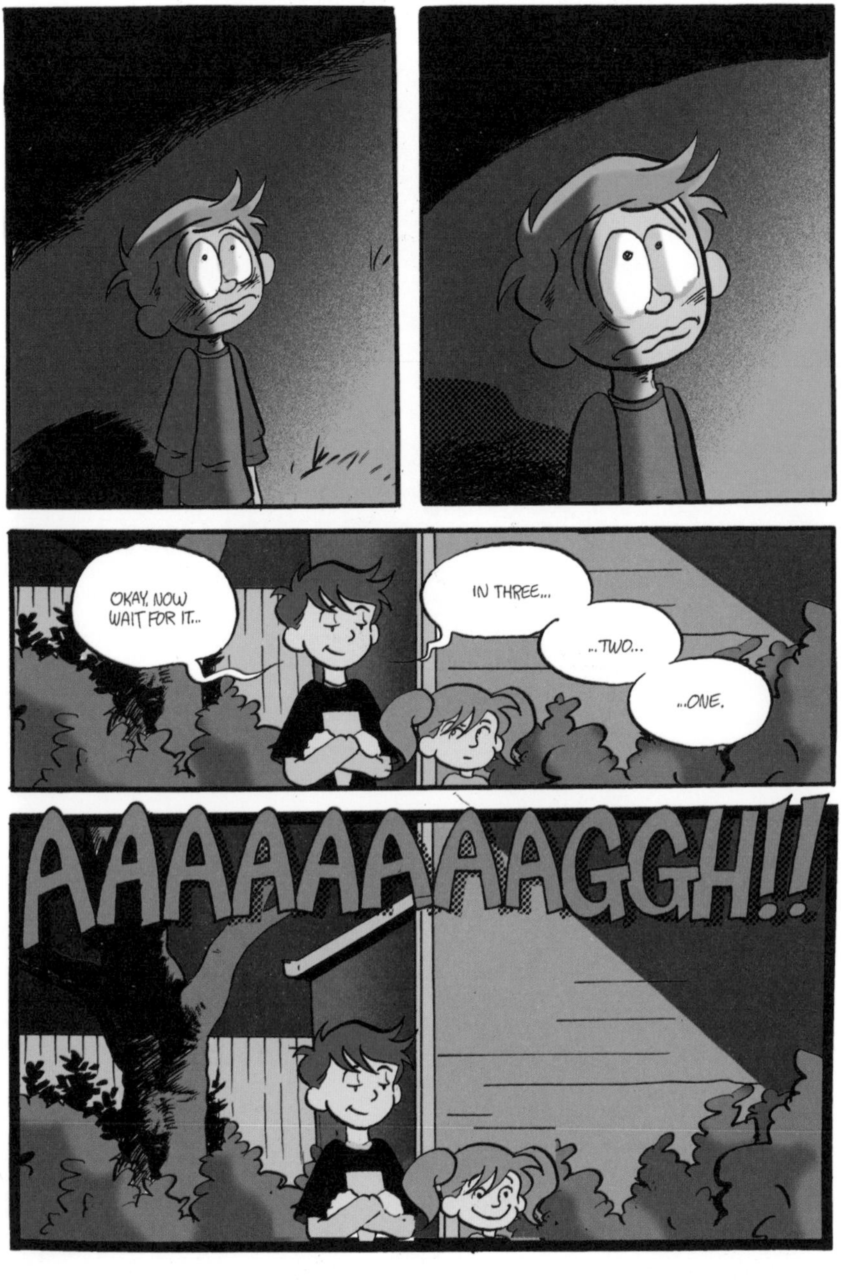
OKAY, NOW WAIT FOR IT...
IN THREE...
...TWO...
...ONE.
AAAAAAAAGGH!!

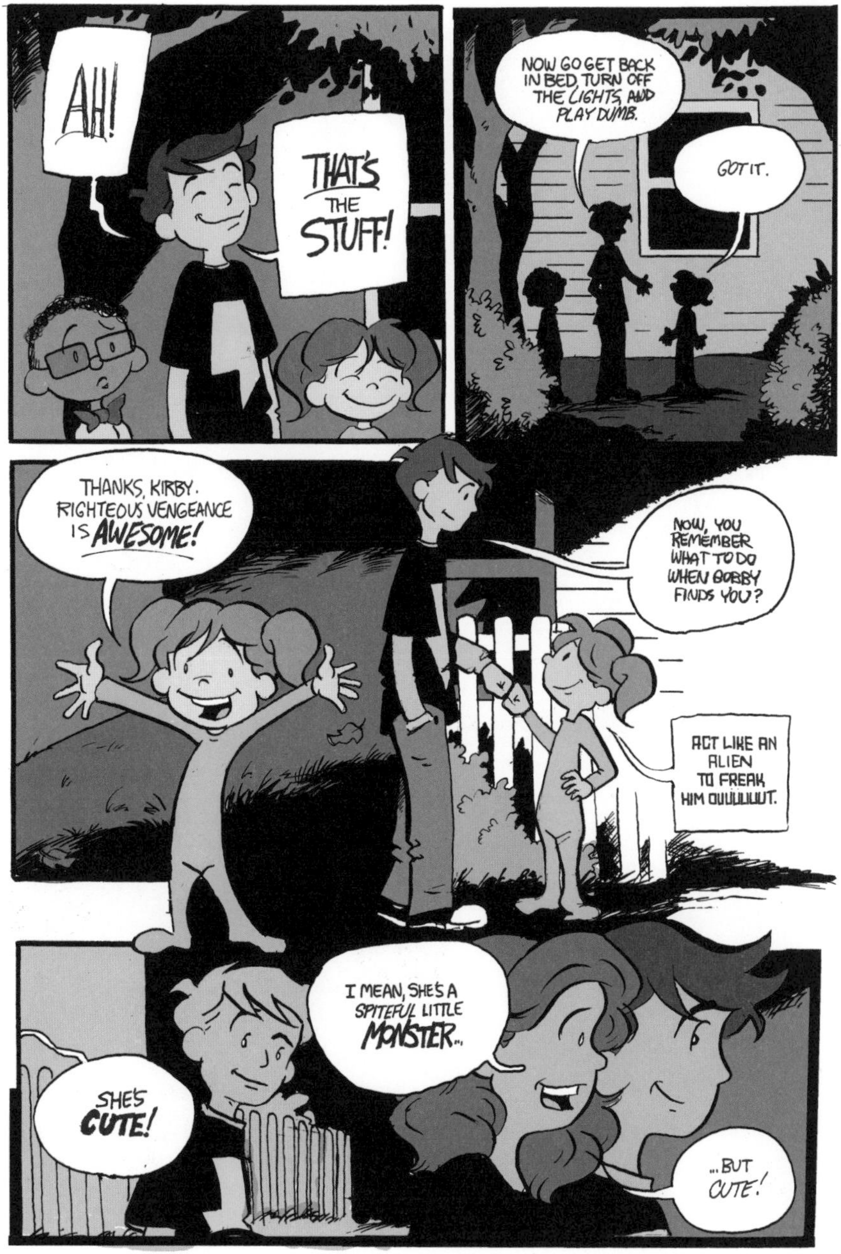
AH!
THAT'S THE STUFF!
NOW GO GET BACK IN BED, TURN OFF THE LIGHTS, AND PLAY DUMB.
GOT IT.
THANKS, KIRBY. RIGHTEOUS VENGEANCE IS AWESOME!
NOW, YOU REMEMBER WHAT TO DO WHEN BOBBY FINDS YOU?
ACT LIKE AN ALIEN TO FREAK HIM OUUUUUUT.
SHE'S CUTE!
I MEAN, SHE'S A SPITEFUL LITTLE MONSTER...
...BUT CUTE!

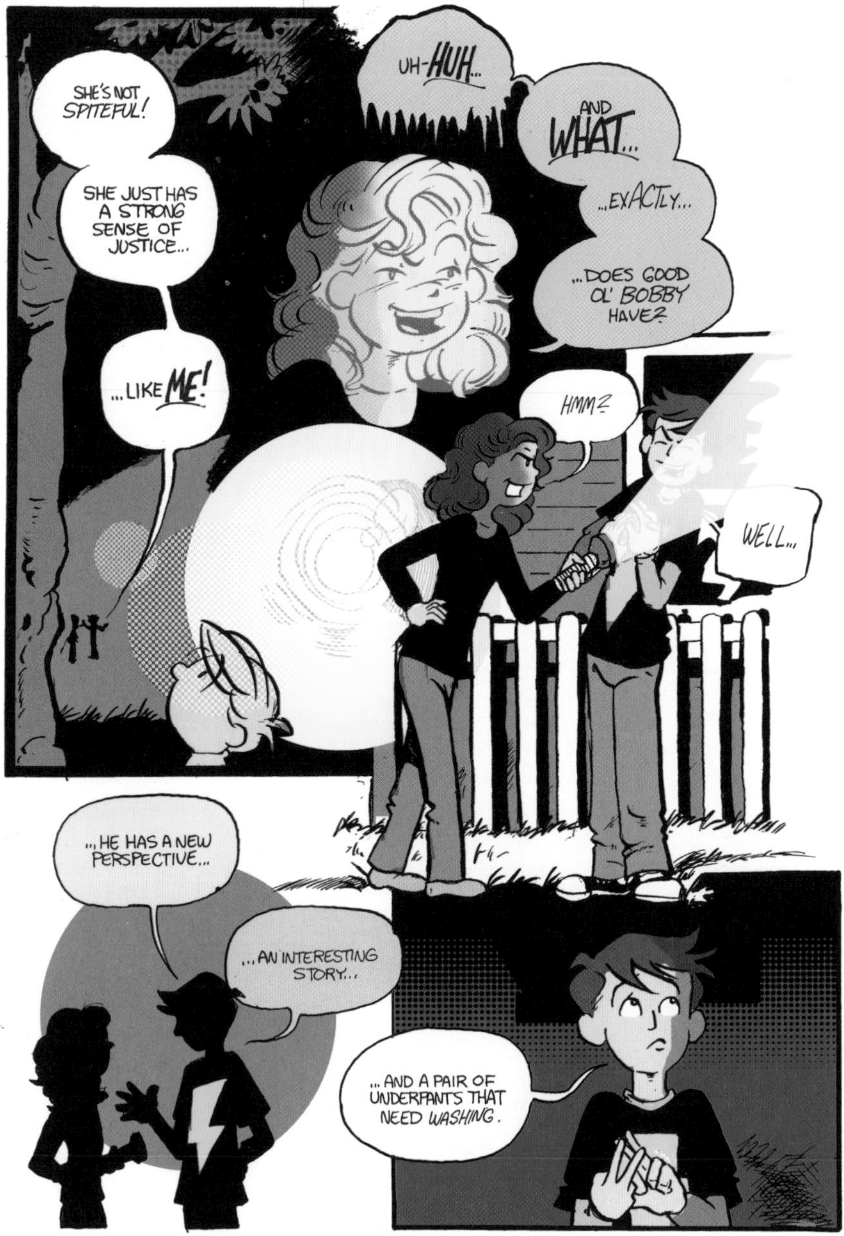
SHE'S NOT SPITEFUL!
SHE JUST HAS A STRONG SENSE OF JUSTICE...
...LIKE ME!
UH-HUH...
AND WHAT...
...EXACTLY...
...DOES GOOD OL' BOBBY HAVE?
HMM?
WELL...
...HE HAS A NEW PERSPECTIVE...
...AN INTERESTING STORY...
...AND A PAIR OF UNDERPANTS THAT NEED WASHING.

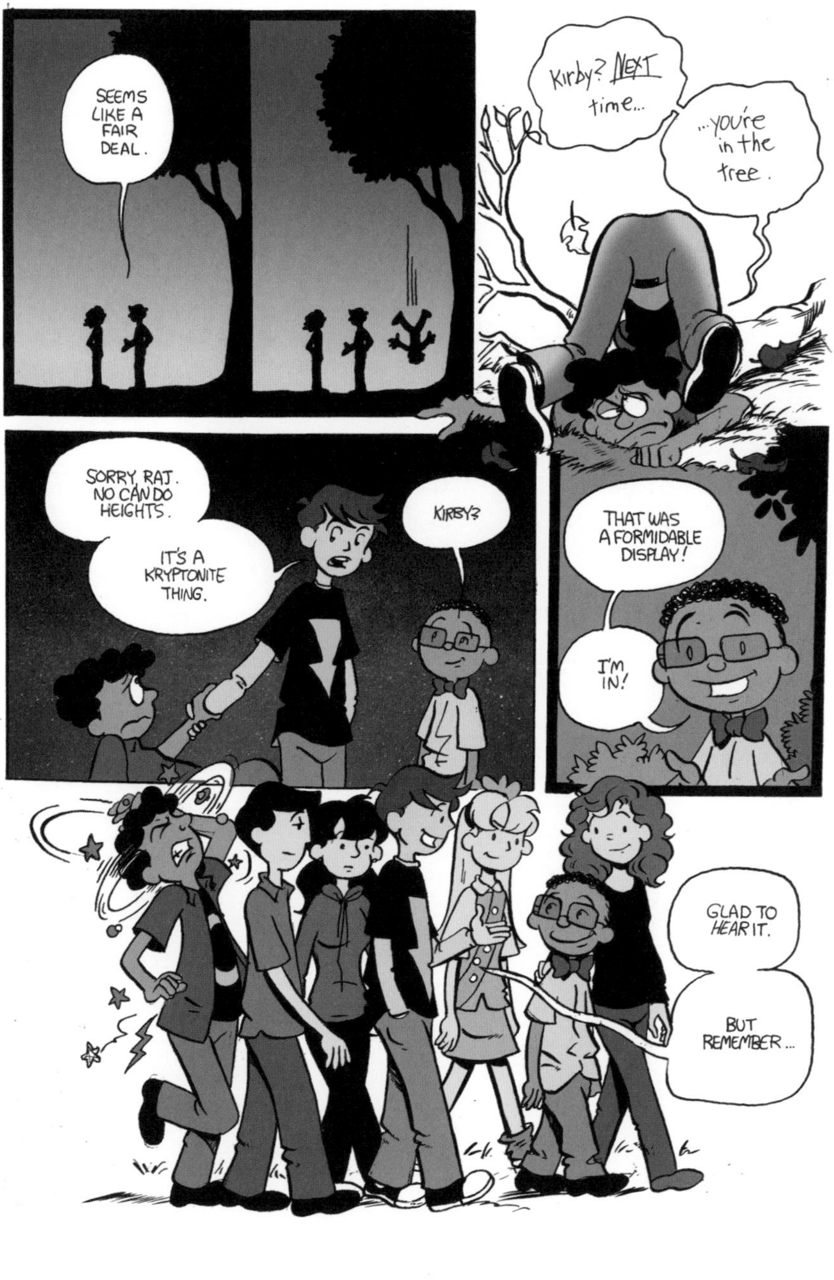
SEEMS LIKE A FAIR DEAL.
Kirby? NEXT time...
...you're in the tree.
SORRY, RAJ. NO CAN DO HEIGHTS.
IT'S A KRYPTONITE THING.
KIRBY?
THAT WAS A FORMIDABLE DISPLAY!
I'M IN!
GLAD TO HEAR IT.
BUT REMEMBER...

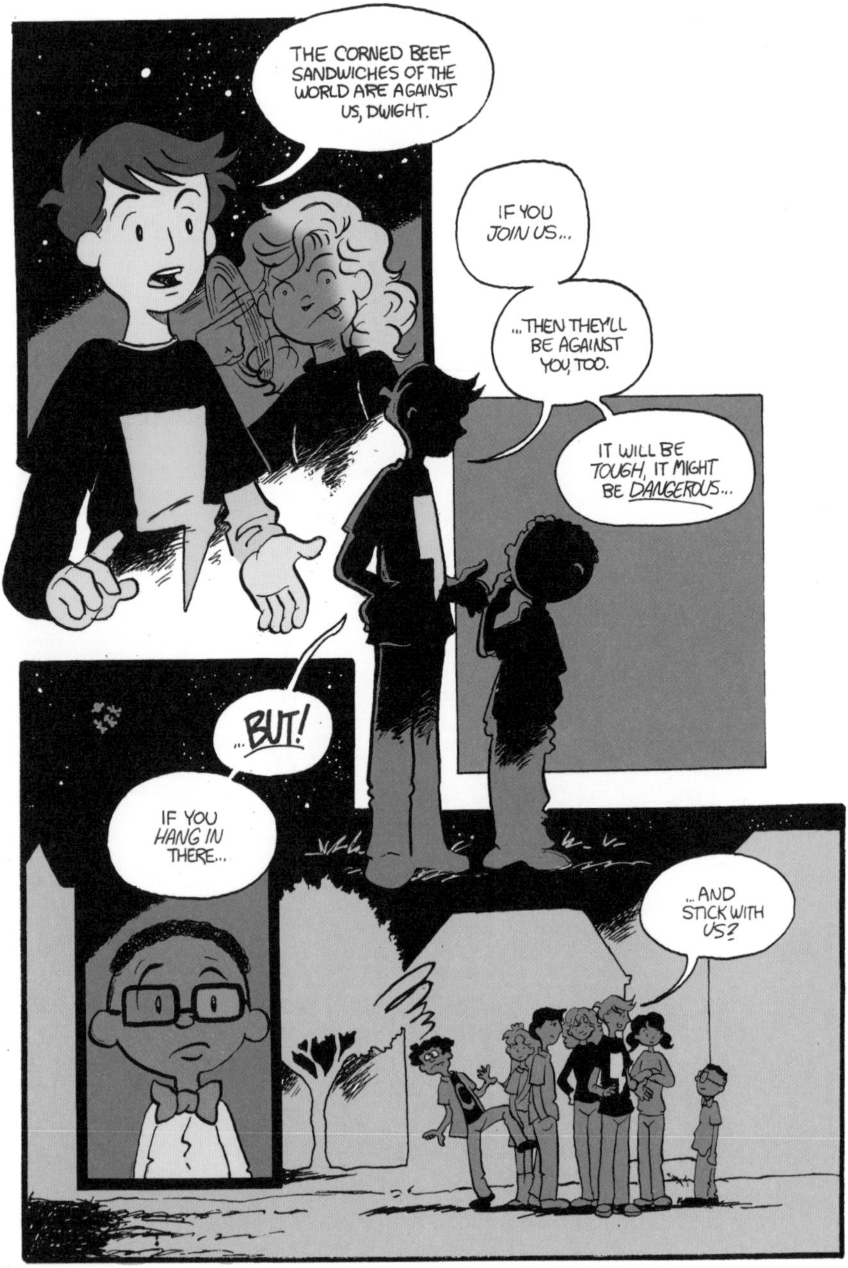
THE CORNED BEEF SANDWICHES OF THE WORLD ARE AGAINST US, DWIGHT.
IF YOU *JOIN US*...
...THEN THEY'LL BE AGAINST YOU, TOO.
IT WILL BE *TOUGH*, IT MIGHT BE *DANGEROUS*...
...*BUT!*
IF YOU *HANG IN* THERE...
...AND STICK WITH *US*?

THE SKY'S
THE LIMIT.

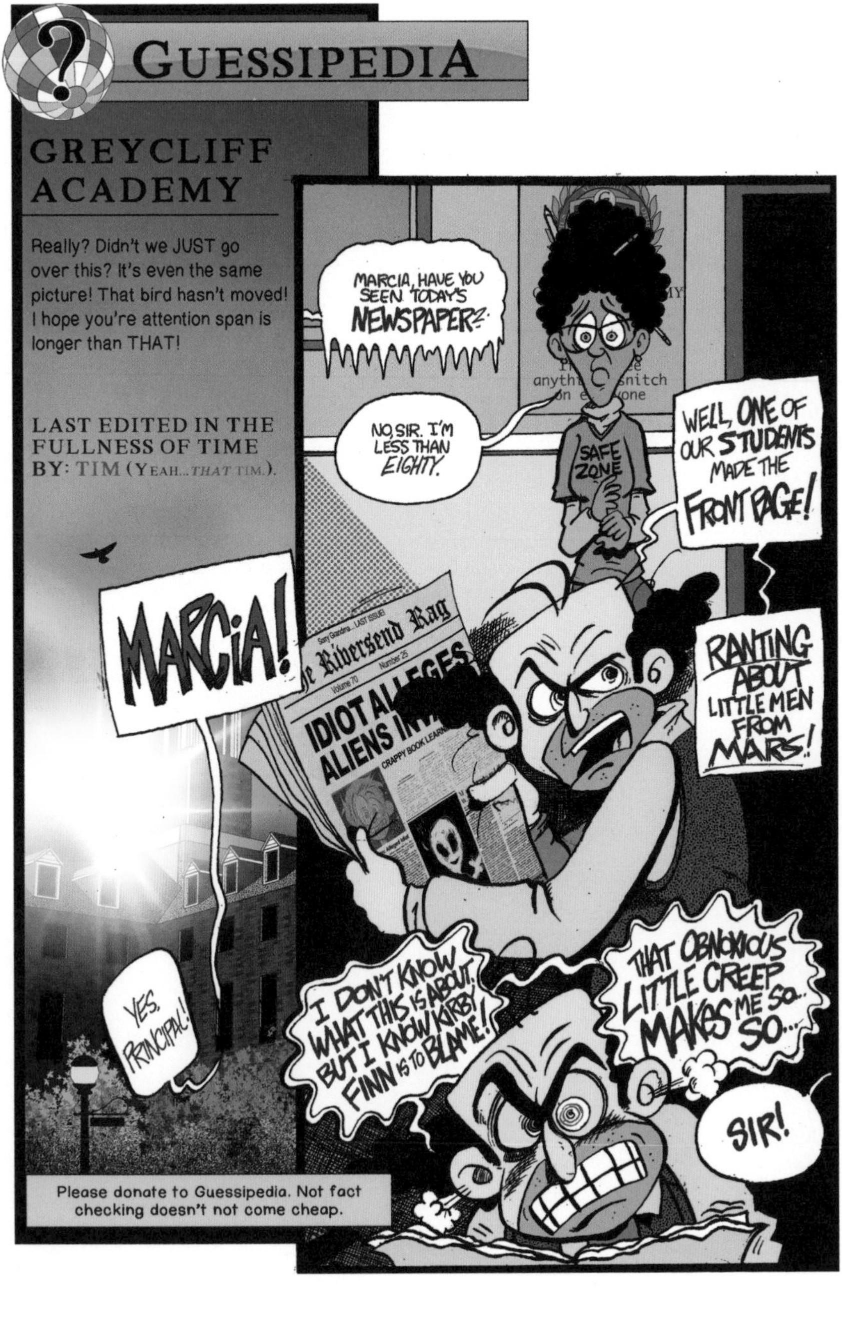
GUESSIPEDIA
GREYCLIFF ACADEMY
Really? Didn't we JUST go over this? It's even the same picture! That bird hasn't moved! I hope you're attention span is longer than THAT!
LAST EDITED IN THE FULLNESS OF TIME BY: TIM (YEAH...THAT TIM).
MARCIA!
YES, PRINCIPAL!
Please donate to Guessipedia. Not fact checking doesn't not come cheap.
MARCIA, HAVE YOU SEEN TODAY'S NEWSPAPER?
NO, SIR. I'M LESS THAN EIGHTY.
WELL, ONE OF OUR STUDENTS MADE THE FRONT PAGE!
RANTING ABOUT LITTLE MEN FROM MARS!
Sorry Grandma... LAST ISSUE!
Riversend Rag
Volume 70
Number 25
IDIOT ALLEGES
SAFE ZONE
I DON'T KNOW WHAT THIS IS ABOUT, BUT I KNOW KIRBY FINN IS TO BLAME!
THAT OBNOXIOUS LITTLE CREEP MAKES ME SO... SO...
SIR!

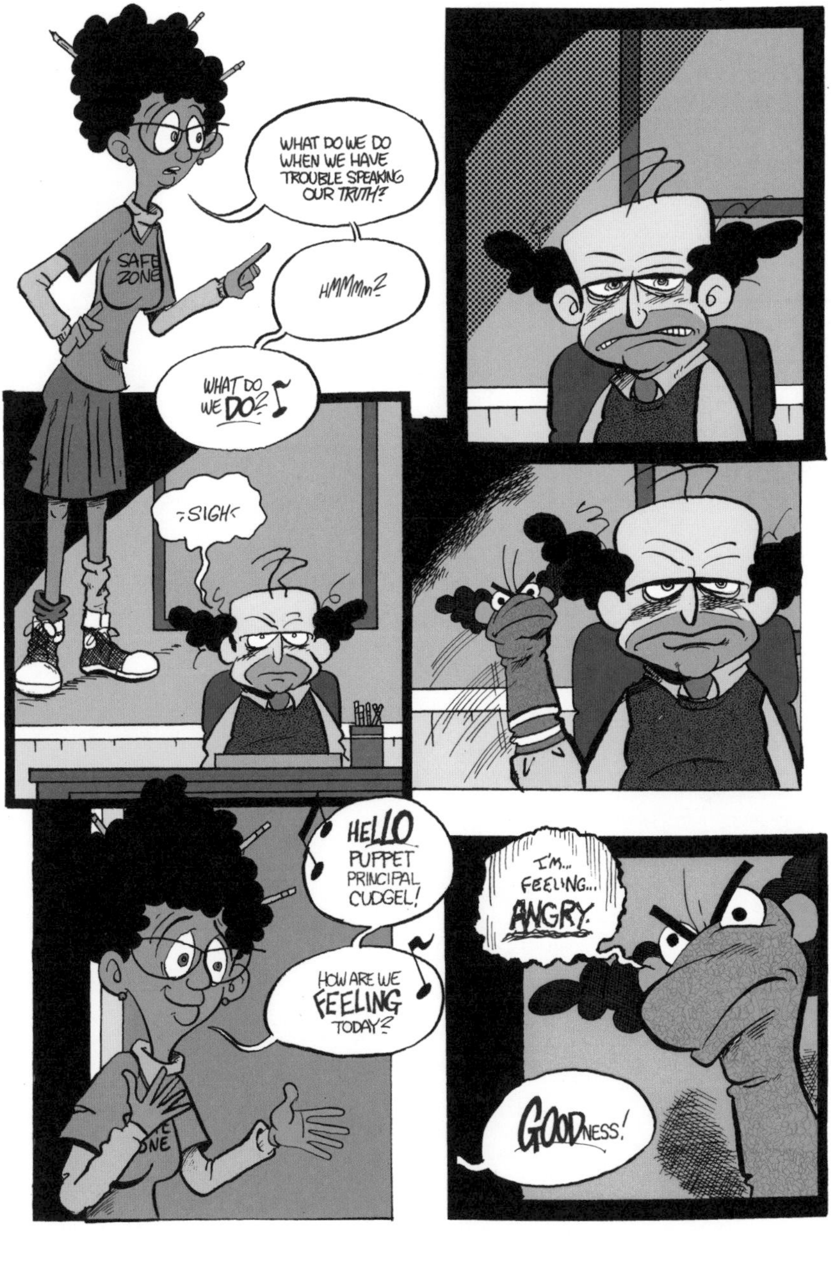

WHAT DO WE DO WHEN WE HAVE TROUBLE SPEAKING OUR TRUTH?
HMMMm?
WHAT DO WE DO?
SIGH
HELLO PUPPET PRINCIPAL CUDGEL!
HOW ARE WE FEELING TODAY?
I'M... FEELING... ANGRY.
GOODNESS!

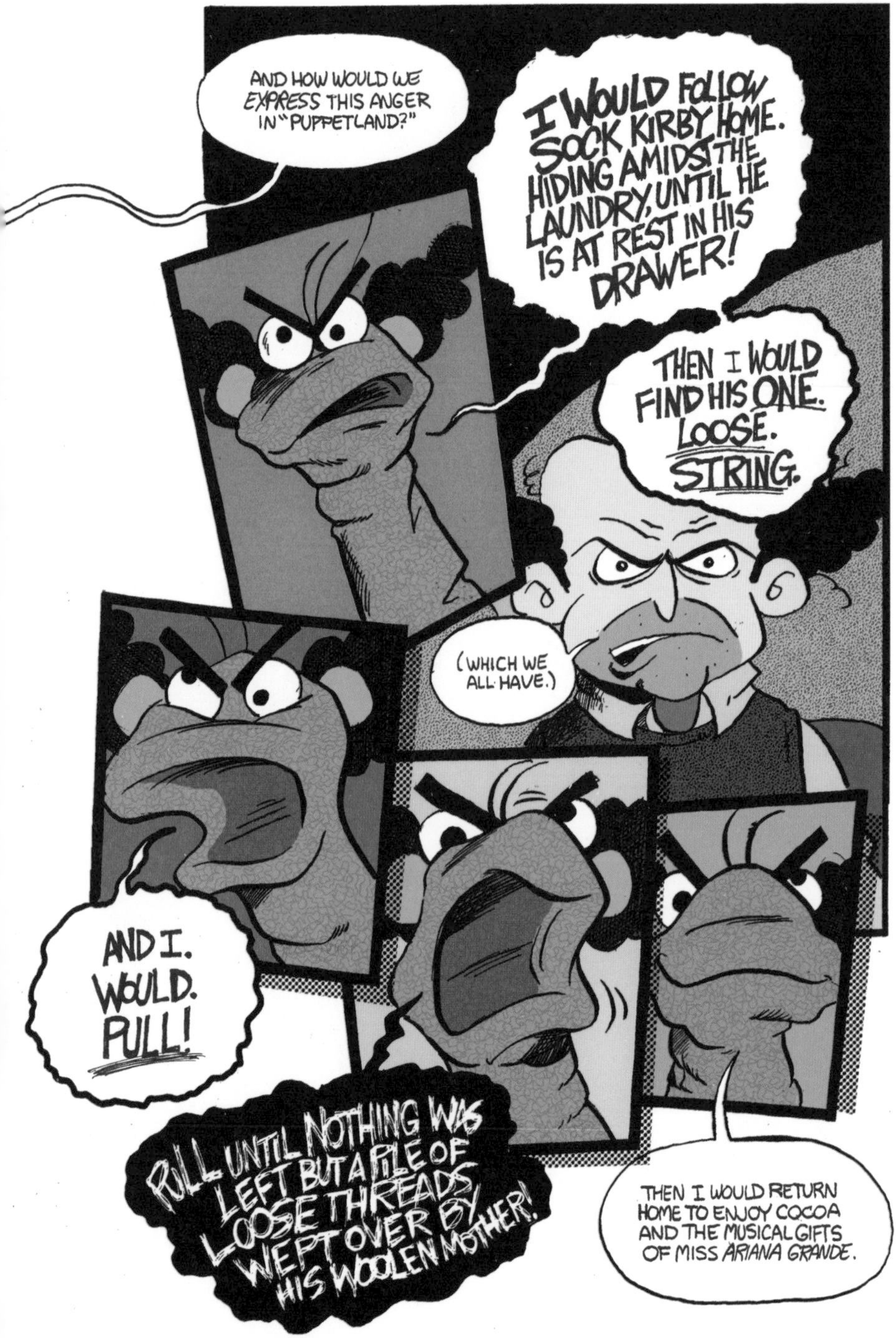
AND HOW WOULD WE EXPRESS THIS ANGER IN "PUPPETLAND?"
I WOULD FOLLOW SOCK KIRBY HOME. HIDING AMIDST THE LAUNDRY, UNTIL HE IS AT REST IN HIS DRAWER!
THEN I WOULD FIND HIS ONE. LOOSE. STRING.
(WHICH WE ALL HAVE.)
AND I. WOULD. PULL!
PULL UNTIL NOTHING WAS LEFT BUT A PILE OF LOOSE THREADS WEPT OVER BY HIS WOOLEN MOTHER!
THEN I WOULD RETURN HOME TO ENJOY COCOA AND THE MUSICAL GIFTS OF MISS ARIANA GRANDE.

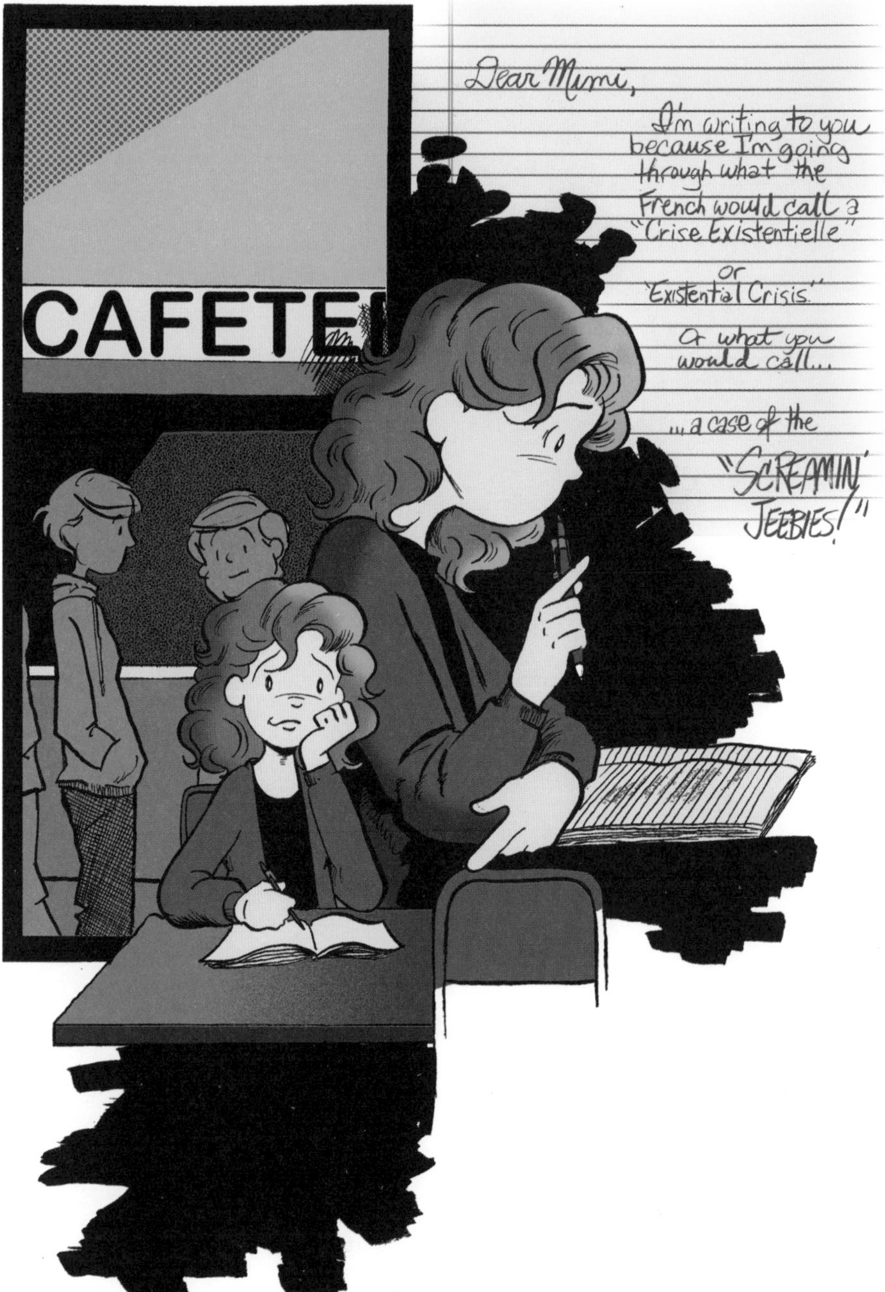
CAFETE
Dear Mimi,
I'm writing to you because I'm going through what the French would call a "Crise Existentielle"
or
"Existential Crisis."
Or what you would call...
...a case of the
"SCREAMIN' JEEBIES!"

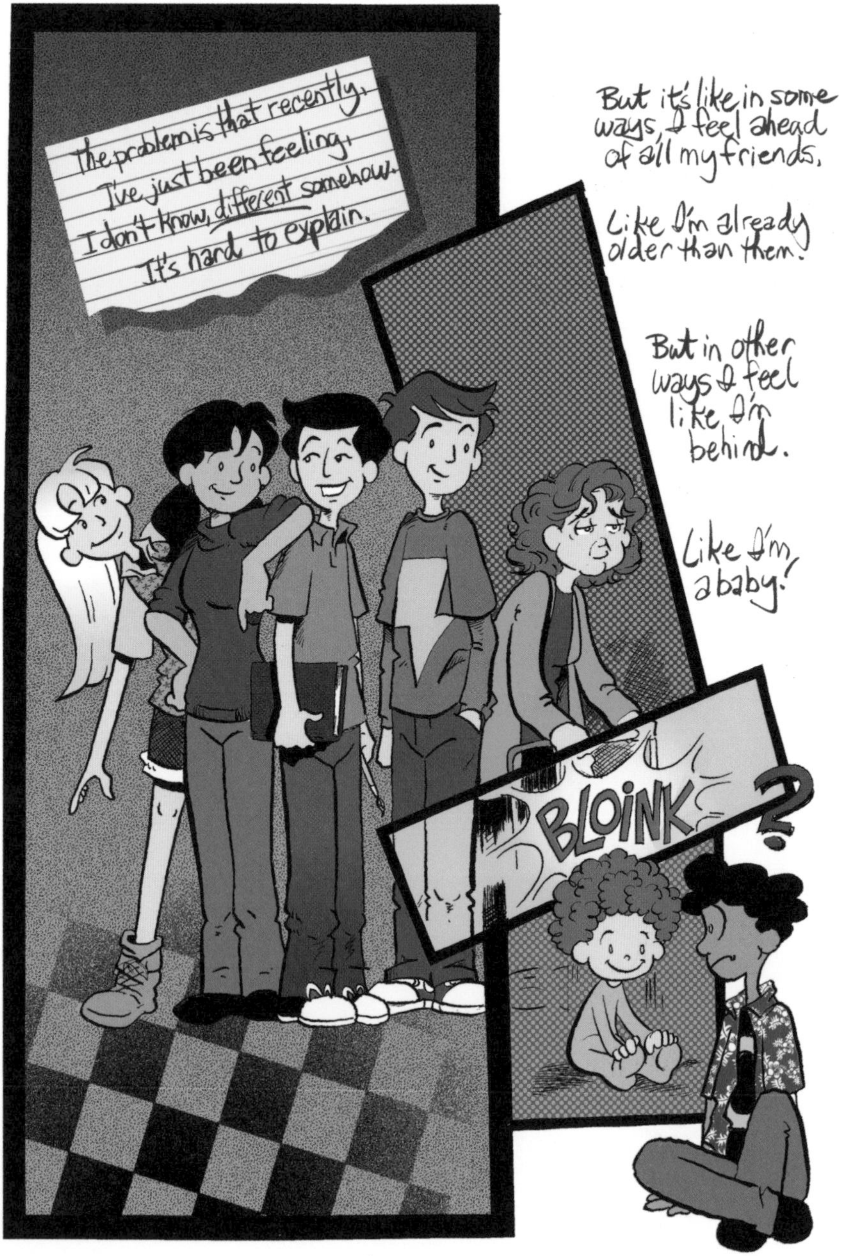
The problem is that recently, I've just been feeling, I don't know, different somehow. It's hard to explain.
But it's like in some ways, I feel ahead of all my friends.
Like I'm already older than them!
But in other ways I feel like I'm behind.
Like I'm a baby!
BLOINK
?

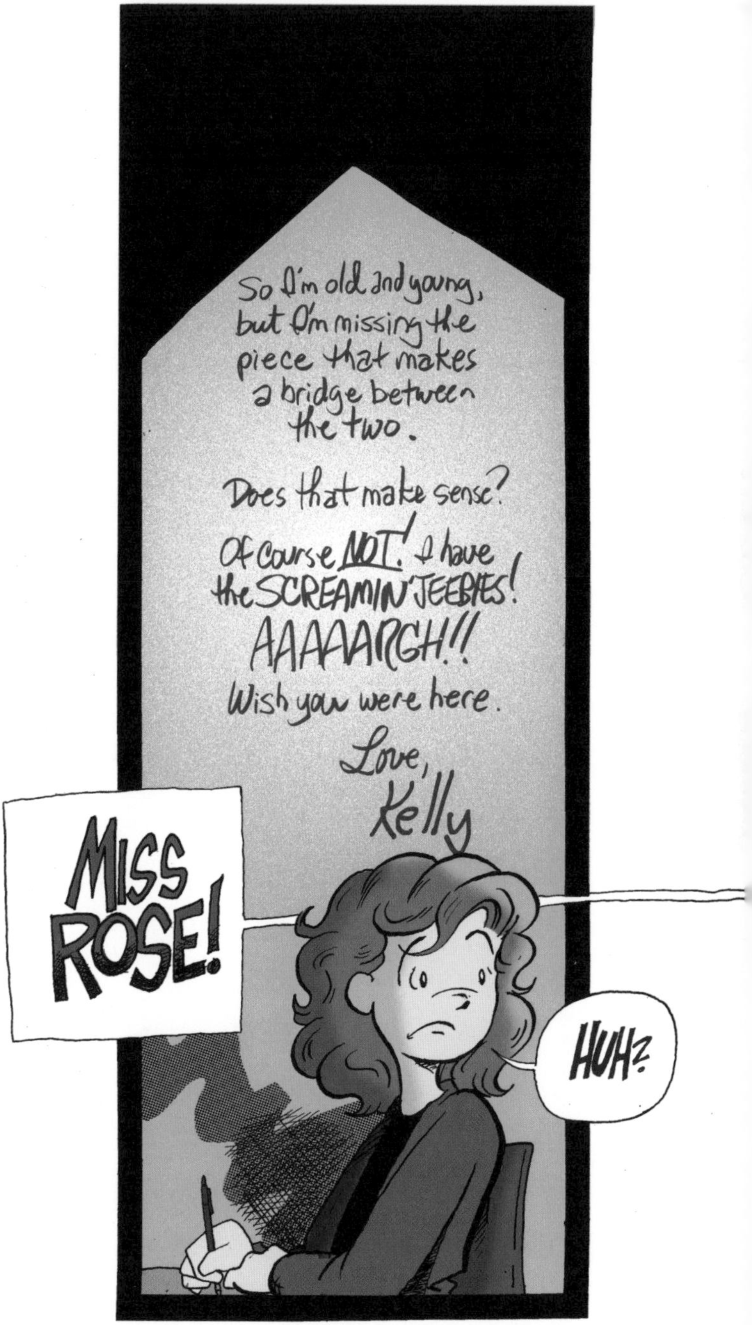

So I'm old and young, but I'm missing the piece that makes a bridge between the two.
Does that make sense?
Of course NOT! I have the SCREAMIN' JEEBIES!
AAAAARGH!!
Wish you were here.
Love,
Kelly
MISS ROSE!
HUH?

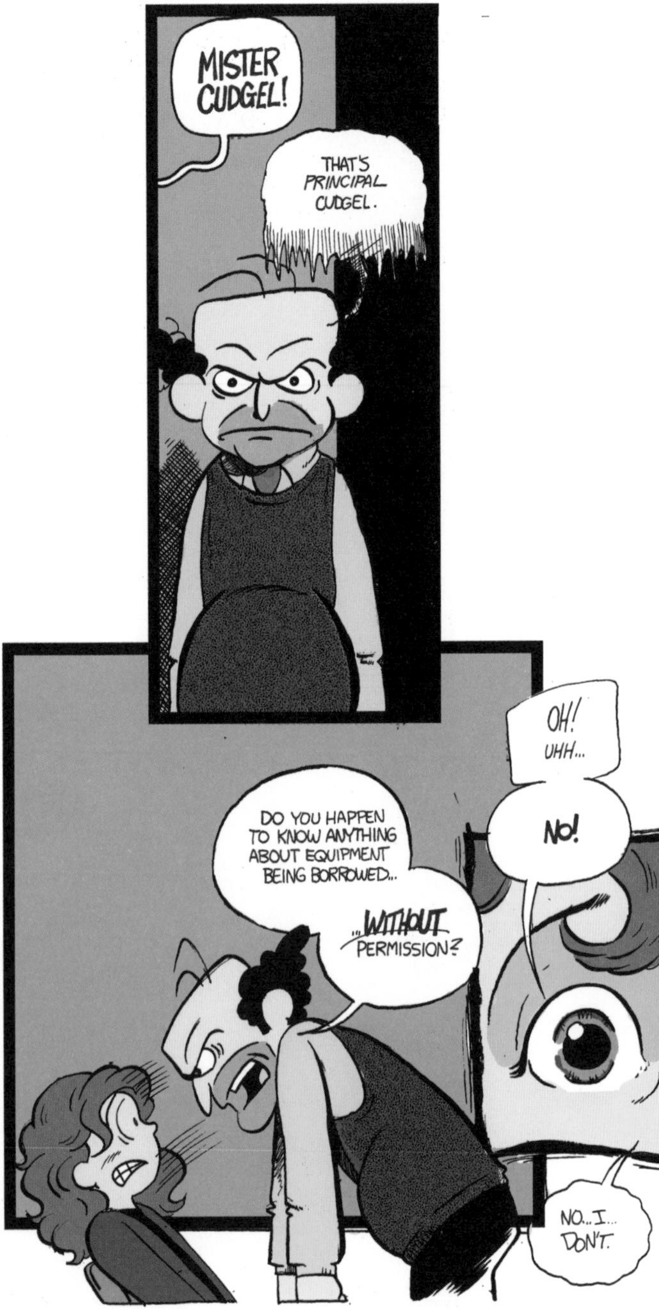
MISTER CUDGEL!
THAT'S PRINCIPAL CUDGEL.
OH! UHH...
NO!
DO YOU HAPPEN TO KNOW ANYTHING ABOUT EQUIPMENT BEING BORROWED...
...WITHOUT PERMISSION?
NO...I... DON'T.

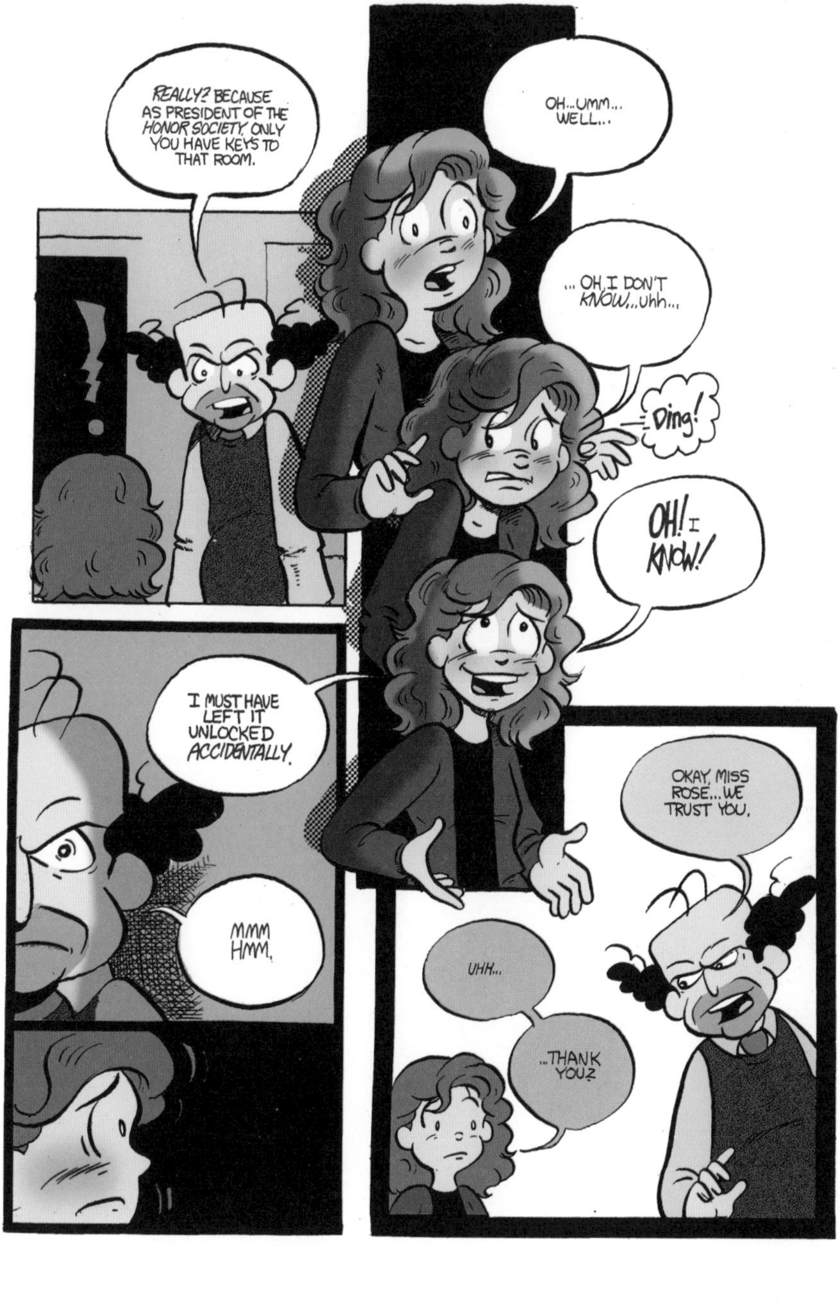
REALLY? BECAUSE AS PRESIDENT OF THE HONOR SOCIETY, ONLY YOU HAVE KEYS TO THAT ROOM.
OH...UMM... WELL...
...OH, I DON'T KNOW...uhh...
Ding!
OH! I KNOW!
I MUST HAVE LEFT IT UNLOCKED ACCIDENTALLY.
MMM HMM.
OKAY, MISS ROSE...WE TRUST YOU.
UHH...
...THANK YOU?

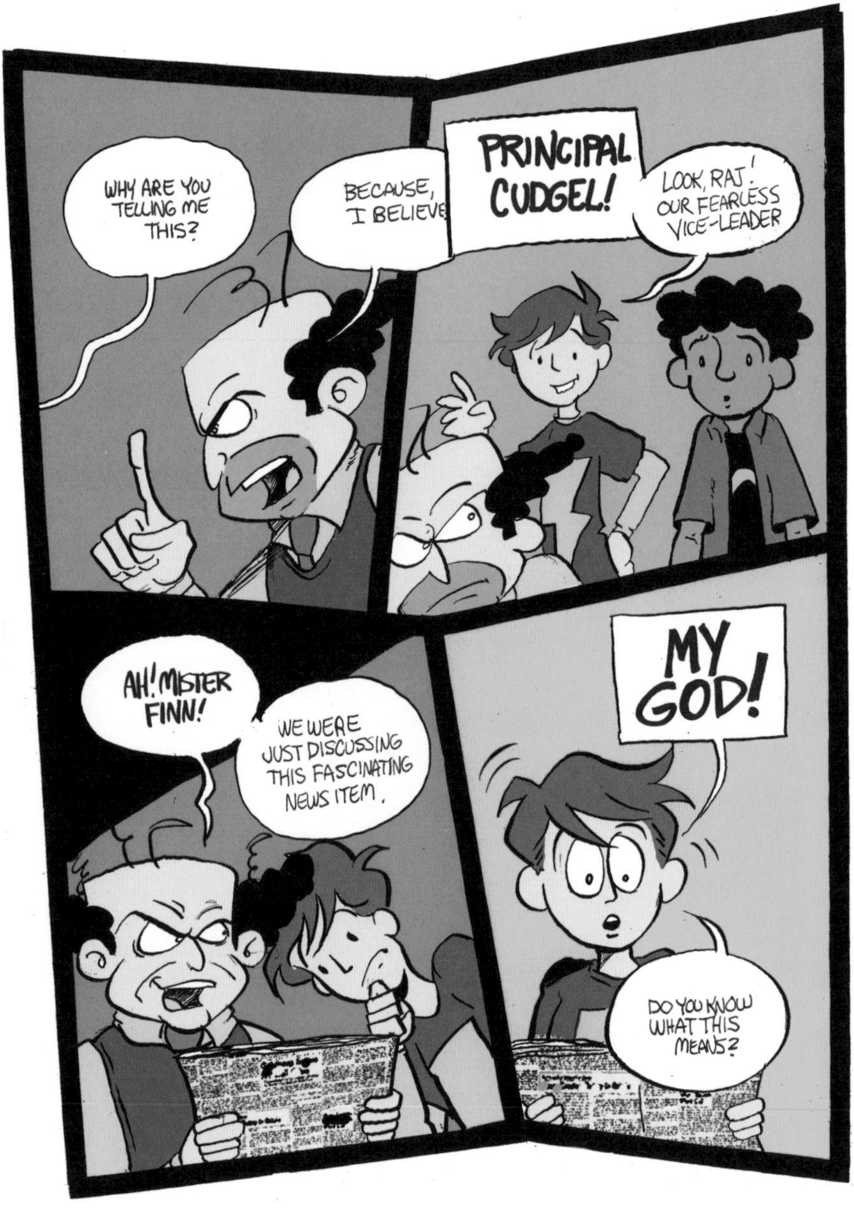

WHY ARE YOU TELLING ME THIS?
BECAUSE, I BELIEVE
PRINCIPAL CUDGEL!
LOOK, RAJ! OUR FEARLESS VICE-LEADER
AH! MISTER FINN!
WE WERE JUST DISCUSSING THIS FASCINATING NEWS ITEM.
MY GOD!
DO YOU KNOW WHAT THIS MEANS?

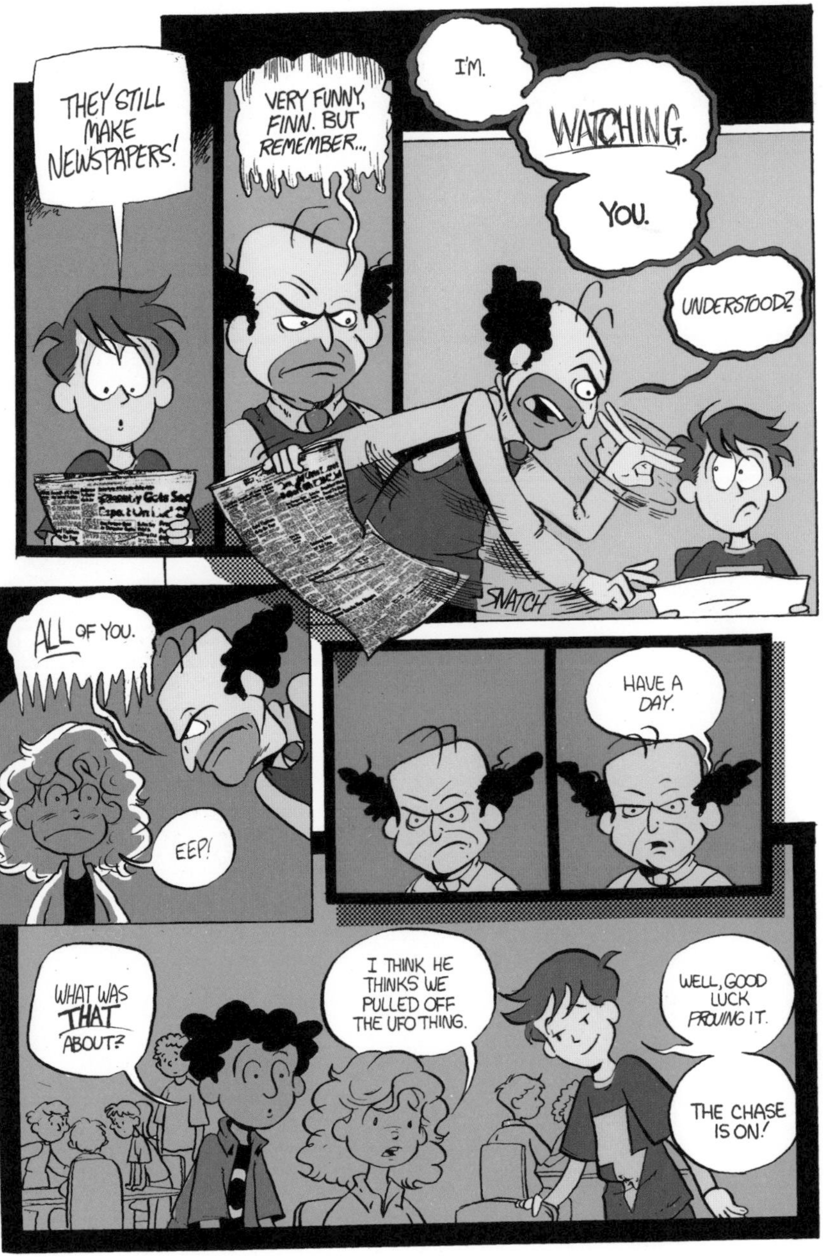
THEY STILL MAKE NEWSPAPERS!
VERY FUNNY, FINN. BUT REMEMBER...
I'M.
WATCHING.
YOU.
UNDERSTOOD?
SNATCH
ALL OF YOU.
EEP!
HAVE A DAY.
WHAT WAS THAT ABOUT?
I THINK HE THINKS WE PULLED OFF THE UFO THING.
WELL, GOOD LUCK PROVING IT.
THE CHASE IS ON!

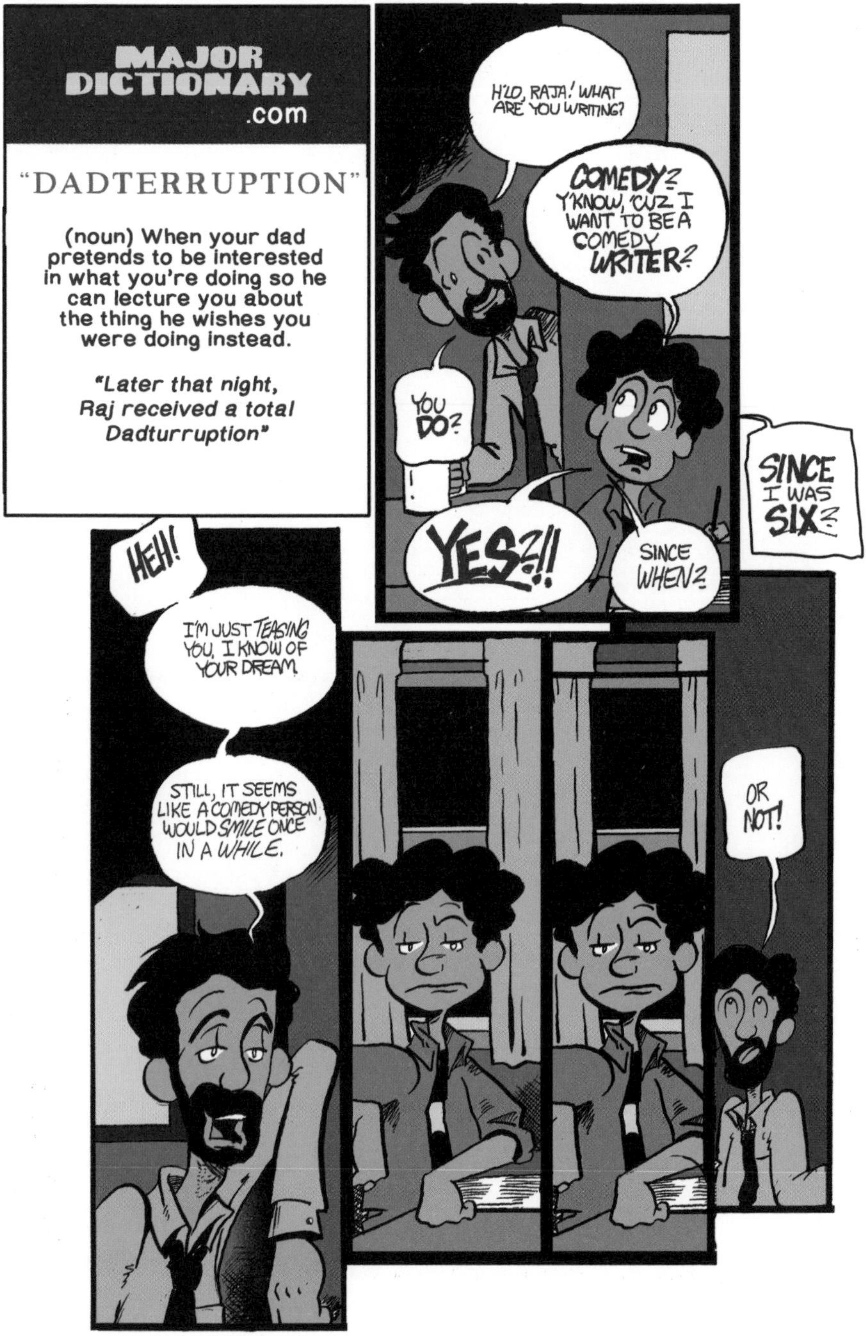
MAJOR DICTIONARY .com
"DADTERRUPTION"
(noun) When your dad pretends to be interested in what you're doing so he can lecture you about the thing he wishes you were doing instead.
"Later that night, Raj received a total Dadturruption"
H'LO, RAJA! WHAT ARE YOU WRITING?
COMEDY? Y'KNOW, 'CUZ I WANT TO BE A COMEDY WRITER?
YOU DO?
YES?!!
SINCE WHEN?
SINCE I WAS SIX?
HEH!
I'M JUST TEASING YOU. I KNOW OF YOUR DREAM.
STILL, IT SEEMS LIKE A COMEDY PERSON WOULD SMILE ONCE IN A WHILE.
OR NOT!

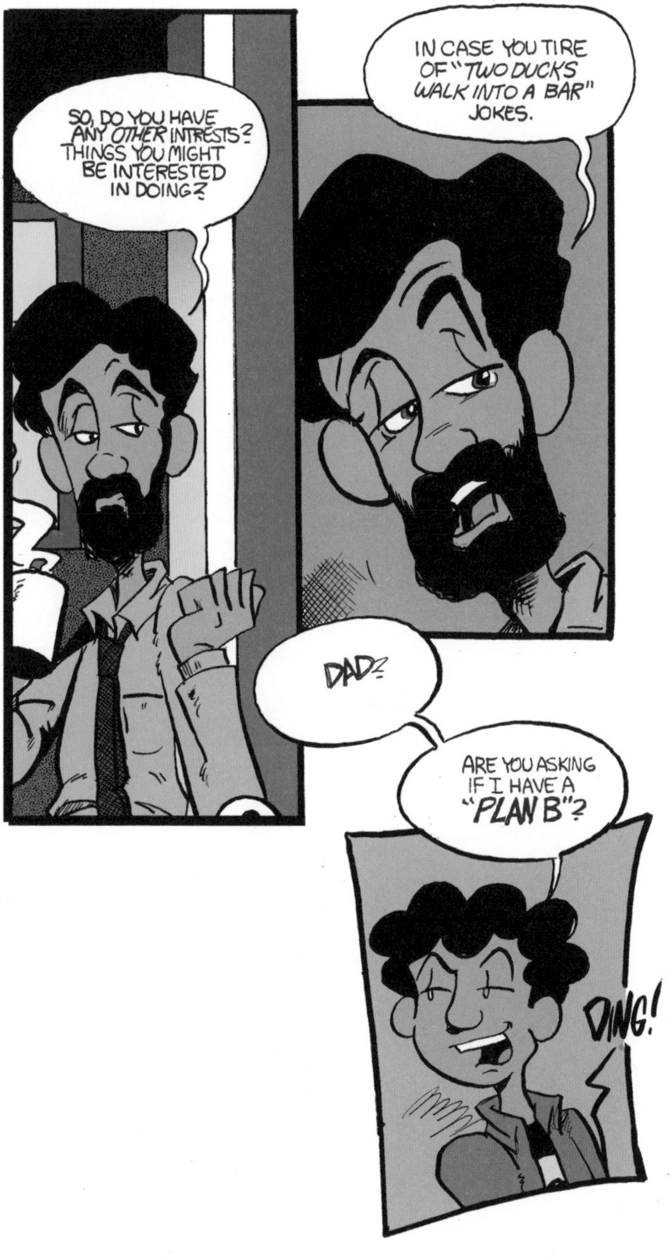
SO, DO YOU HAVE ANY OTHER INTRESTS? THINGS YOU MIGHT BE INTERESTED IN DOING?
IN CASE YOU TIRE OF "TWO DUCKS WALK INTO A BAR" JOKES.
DAD?
ARE YOU ASKING IF I HAVE A "PLAN B"?
DING!

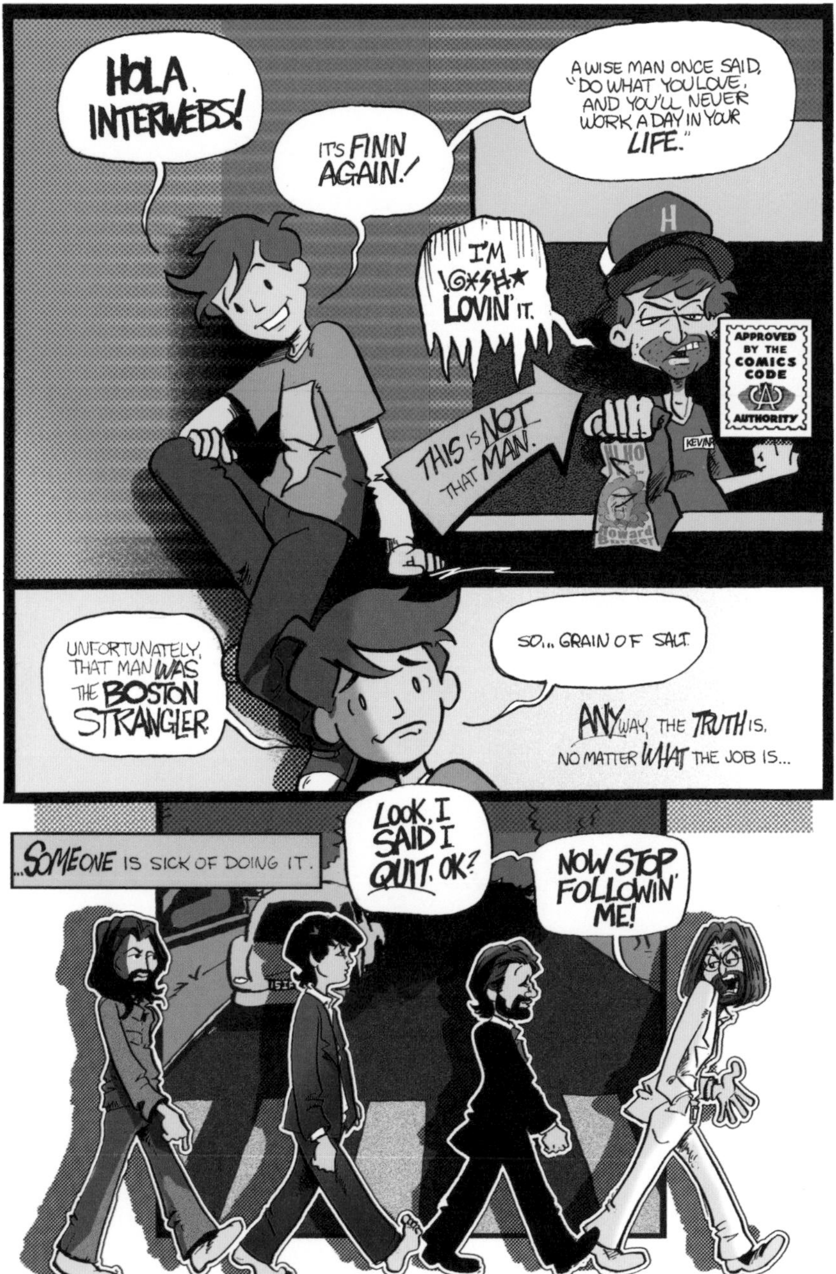
HOLA. INTERWEBS!
IT'S FINN AGAIN!
A WISE MAN ONCE SAID, "DO WHAT YOU LOVE, AND YOU'LL NEVER WORK A DAY IN YOUR LIFE."
I'M !@*$#★ LOVIN' IT.
THIS IS NOT THAT MAN.
APPROVED BY THE COMICS CODE AUTHORITY
UNFORTUNATELY, THAT MAN WAS THE BOSTON STRANGLER.
SO... GRAIN OF SALT.
ANYWAY, THE TRUTH IS, NO MATTER WHAT THE JOB IS...
...SOMEONE IS SICK OF DOING IT.
LOOK, I SAID I QUIT, OK?
NOW STOP FOLLOWIN' ME!

REASON SIX: THE BS OF PLANS B

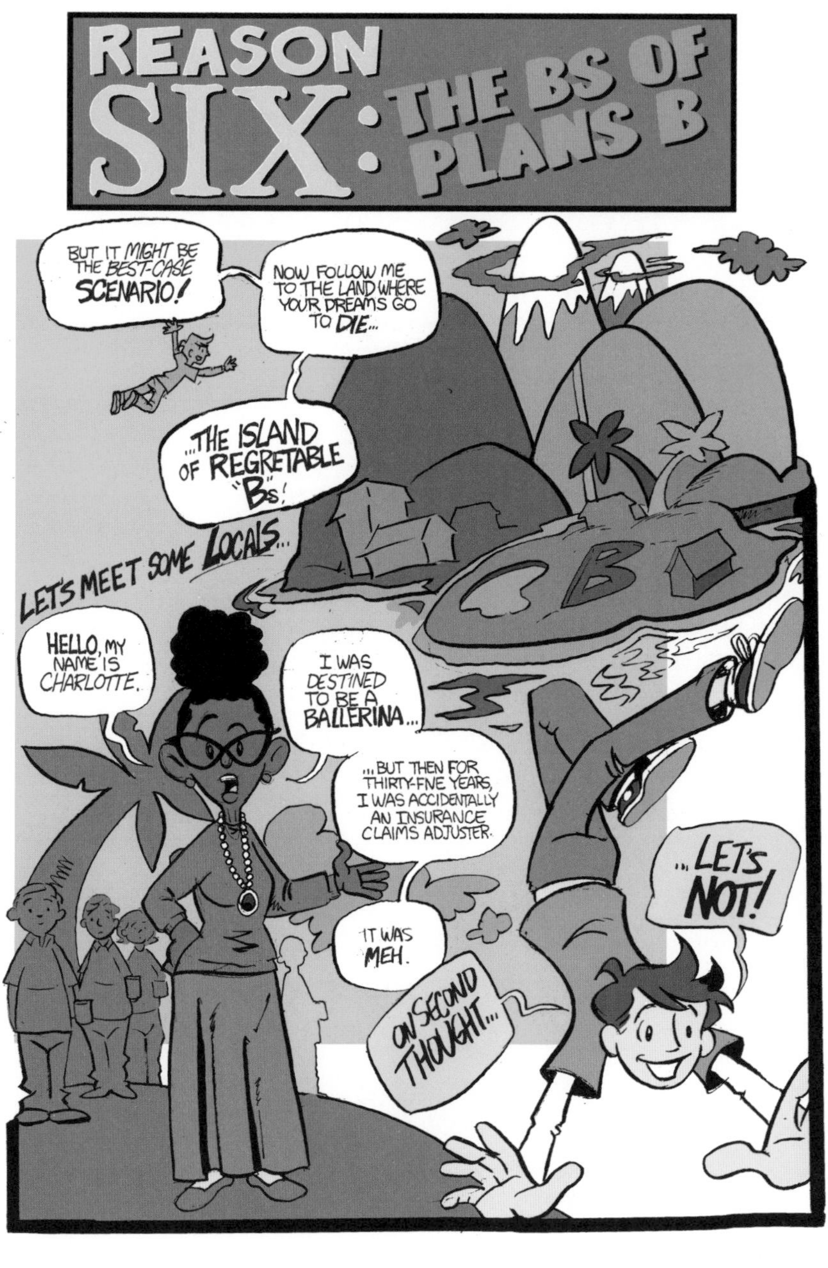
BUT IT MIGHT BE THE BEST-CASE SCENARIO!
NOW FOLLOW ME TO THE LAND WHERE YOUR DREAMS GO TO DIE...
...THE ISLAND OF REGRETABLE "B"s!
LET'S MEET SOME LOCALS...
HELLO, MY NAME IS CHARLOTTE.
I WAS DESTINED TO BE A BALLERINA...
...BUT THEN FOR THIRTY-FIVE YEARS, I WAS ACCIDENTALLY AN INSURANCE CLAIMS ADJUSTER.
IT WAS MEH.
ON SECOND THOUGHT...
...LET'S NOT!

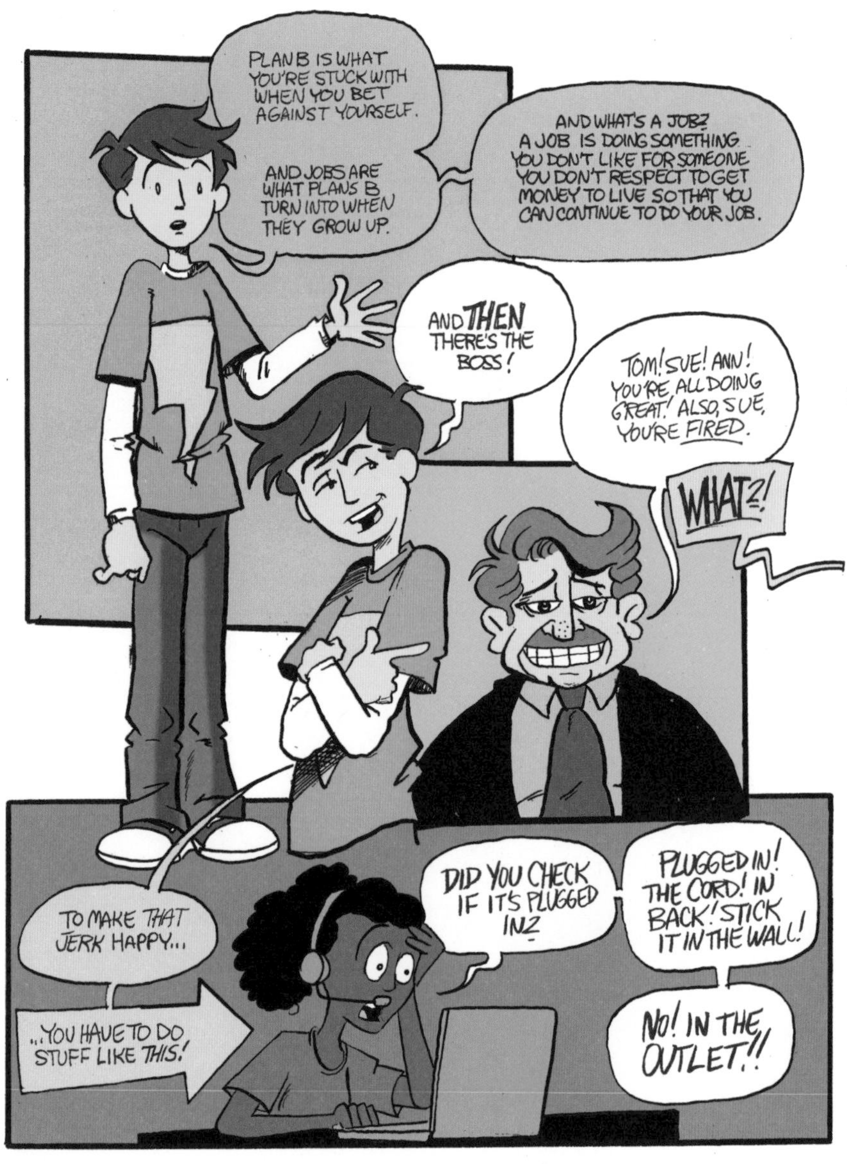
PLAN B IS WHAT YOU'RE STUCK WITH WHEN YOU BET AGAINST YOURSELF.
AND JOBS ARE WHAT PLANS B TURN INTO WHEN THEY GROW UP.
AND WHAT'S A JOB? A JOB IS DOING SOMETHING YOU DON'T LIKE FOR SOMEONE YOU DON'T RESPECT TO GET MONEY TO LIVE SO THAT YOU CAN CONTINUE TO DO YOUR JOB.
AND THEN THERE'S THE BOSS!
TOM! SUE! ANN! YOU'RE ALL DOING GREAT! ALSO, SUE, YOU'RE FIRED.
WHAT?!
TO MAKE THAT JERK HAPPY...
...YOU HAVE TO DO STUFF LIKE THIS!
DID YOU CHECK IF IT'S PLUGGED IN?
PLUGGED IN! THE CORD! IN BACK! STICK IT IN THE WALL!
NO! IN THE OUTLET!!

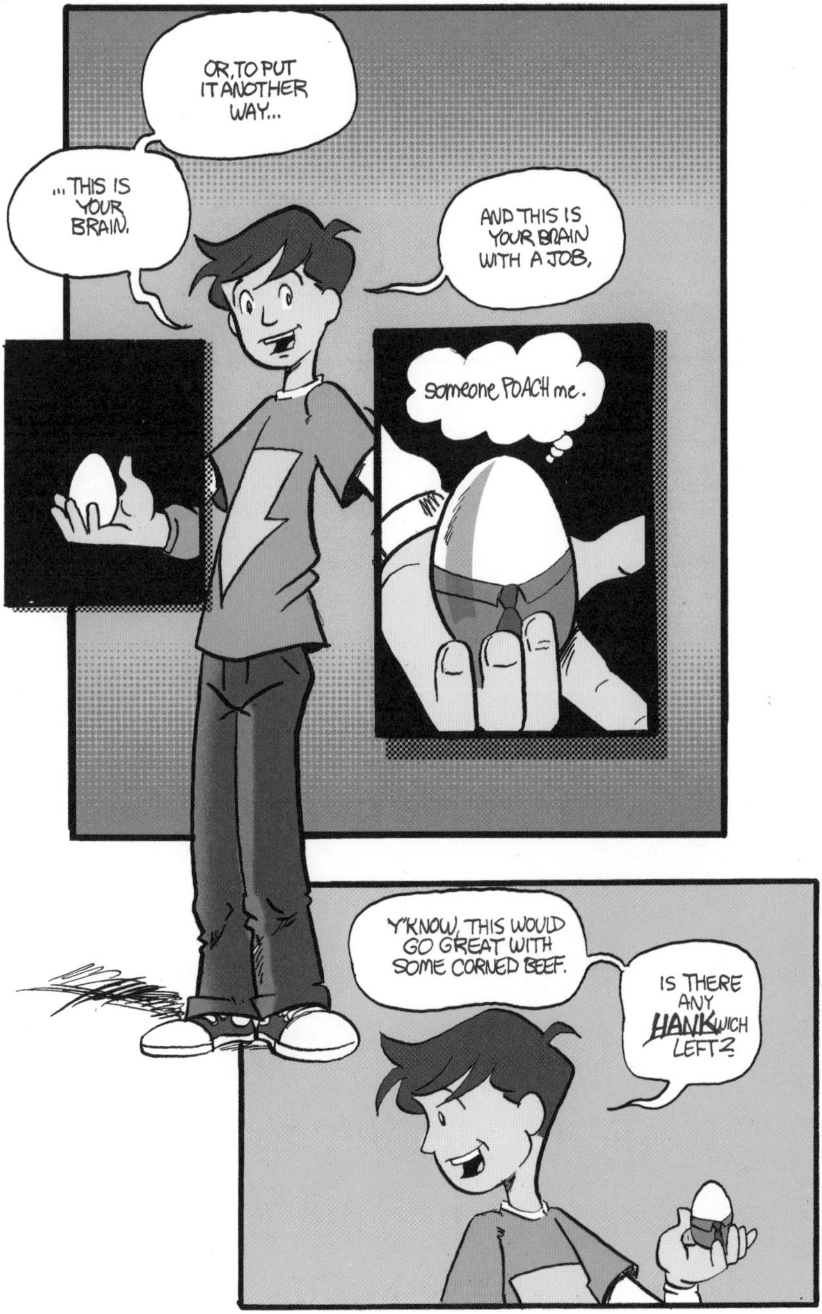
OR, TO PUT IT ANOTHER WAY...
...THIS IS YOUR BRAIN.
AND THIS IS YOUR BRAIN WITH A JOB.
someone POACH me.
Y'KNOW, THIS WOULD GO GREAT WITH SOME CORNED BEEF.
IS THERE ANY HANKWICH LEFT?

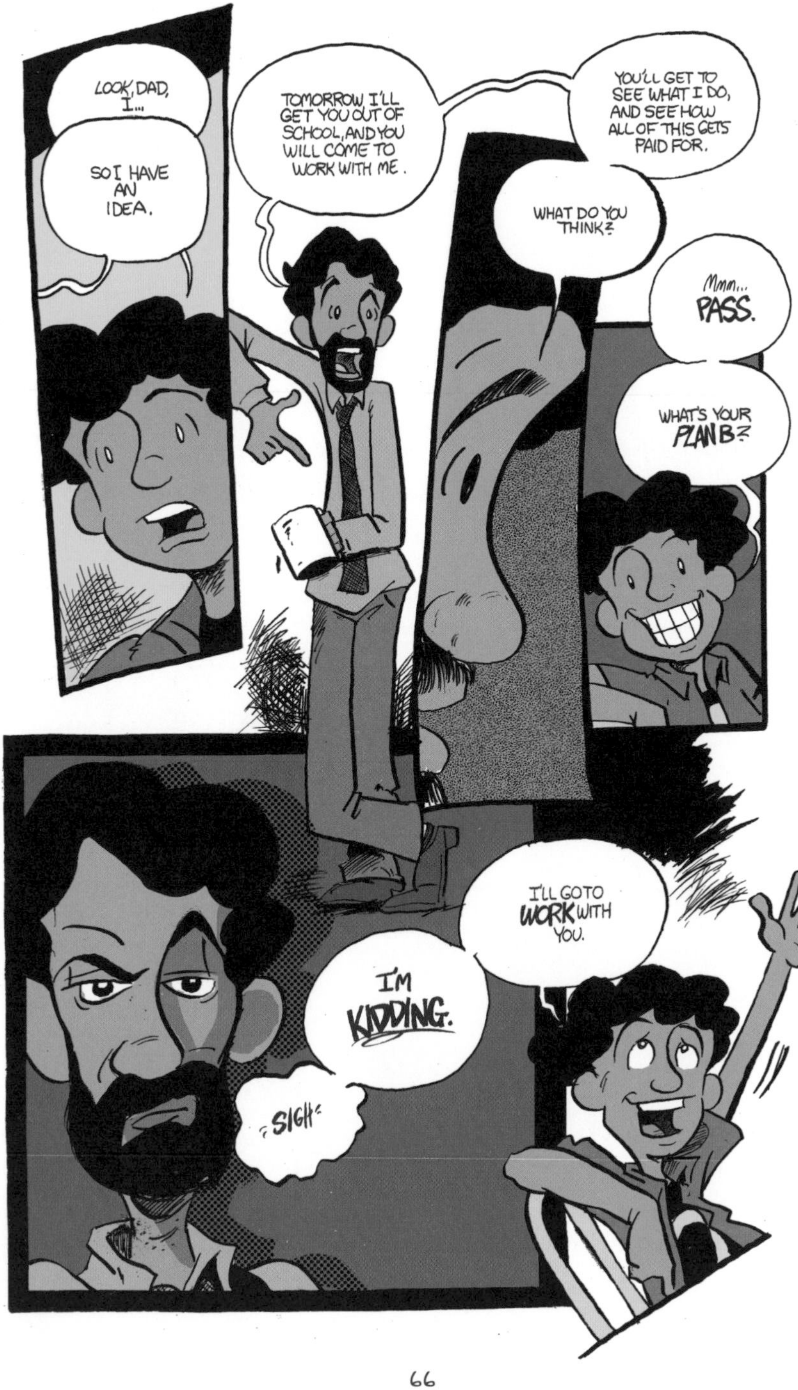
LOOK, DAD, I...
SO I HAVE AN IDEA.
TOMORROW I'LL GET YOU OUT OF SCHOOL, AND YOU WILL COME TO WORK WITH ME.
YOU'LL GET TO SEE WHAT I DO, AND SEE HOW ALL OF THIS GETS PAID FOR.
WHAT DO YOU THINK?
Mmm... PASS.
WHAT'S YOUR PLAN B?
I'M KIDDING.
SIGH
I'LL GO TO WORK WITH YOU.

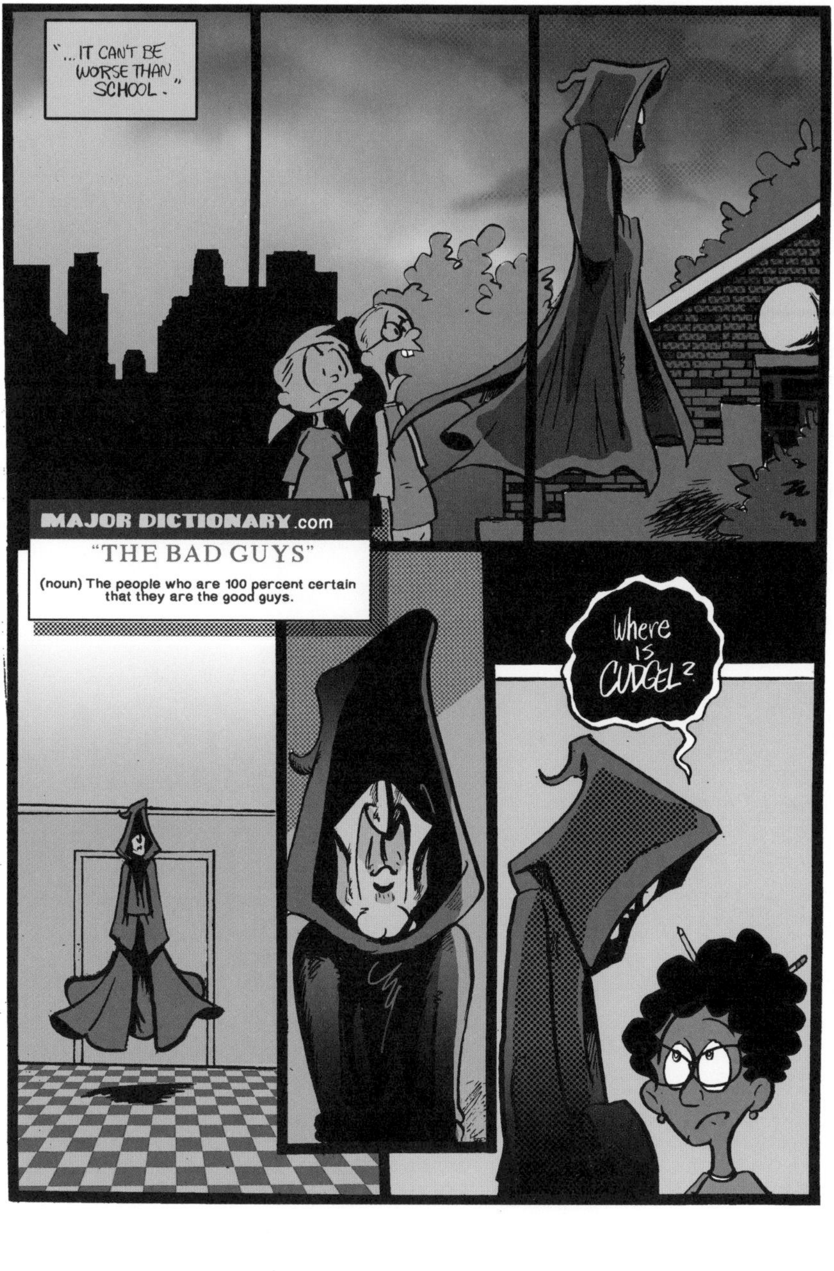
"...IT CAN'T BE WORSE THAN SCHOOL."
MAJOR DICTIONARY.com
"THE BAD GUYS"
(noun) The people who are 100 percent certain that they are the good guys.
Where is CUDGEL?

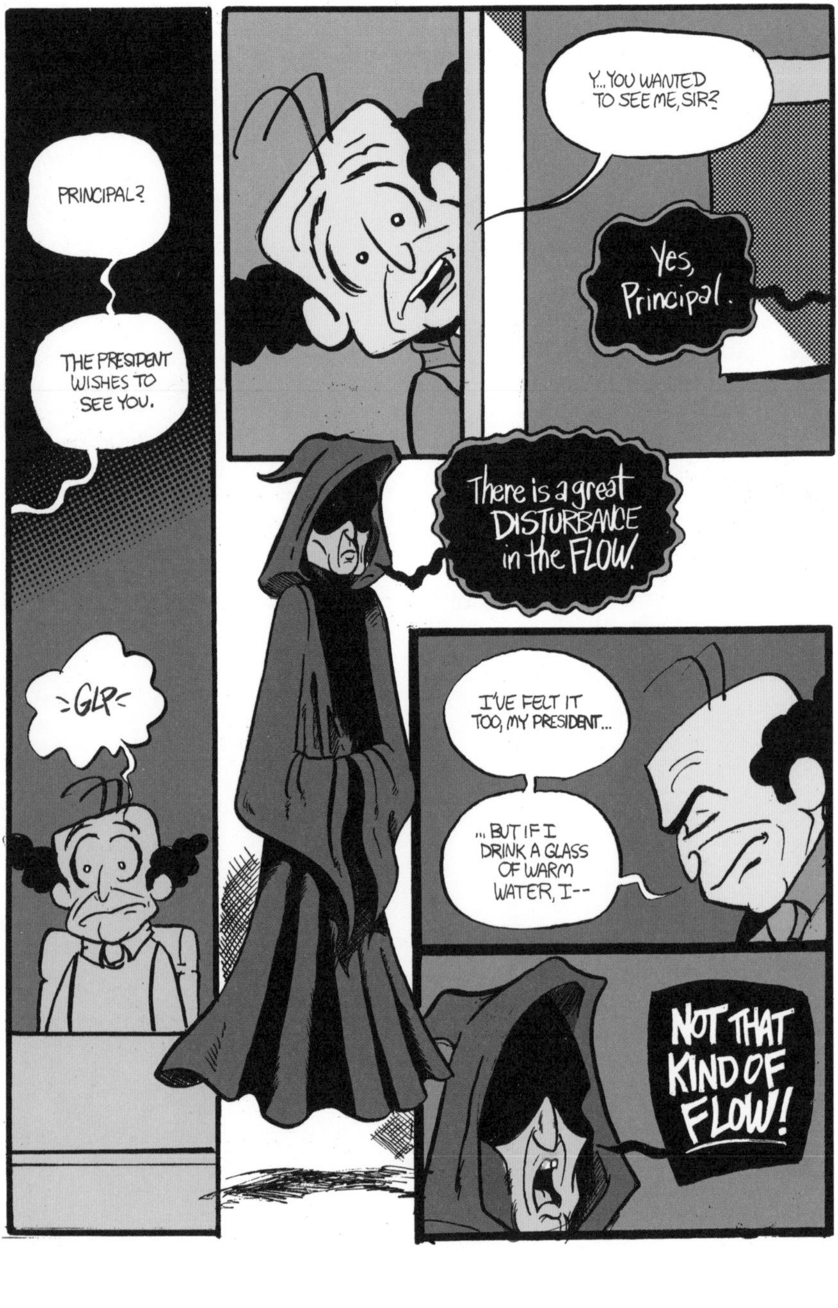
PRINCIPAL?
THE PRESIDENT WISHES TO SEE YOU.
Y...YOU WANTED TO SEE ME, SIR?
Yes, Principal.
There is a great DISTURBANCE in the FLOW.
GLP
I'VE FELT IT TOO, MY PRESIDENT...
...BUT IF I DRINK A GLASS OF WARM WATER, I--
NOT THAT KIND OF FLOW!

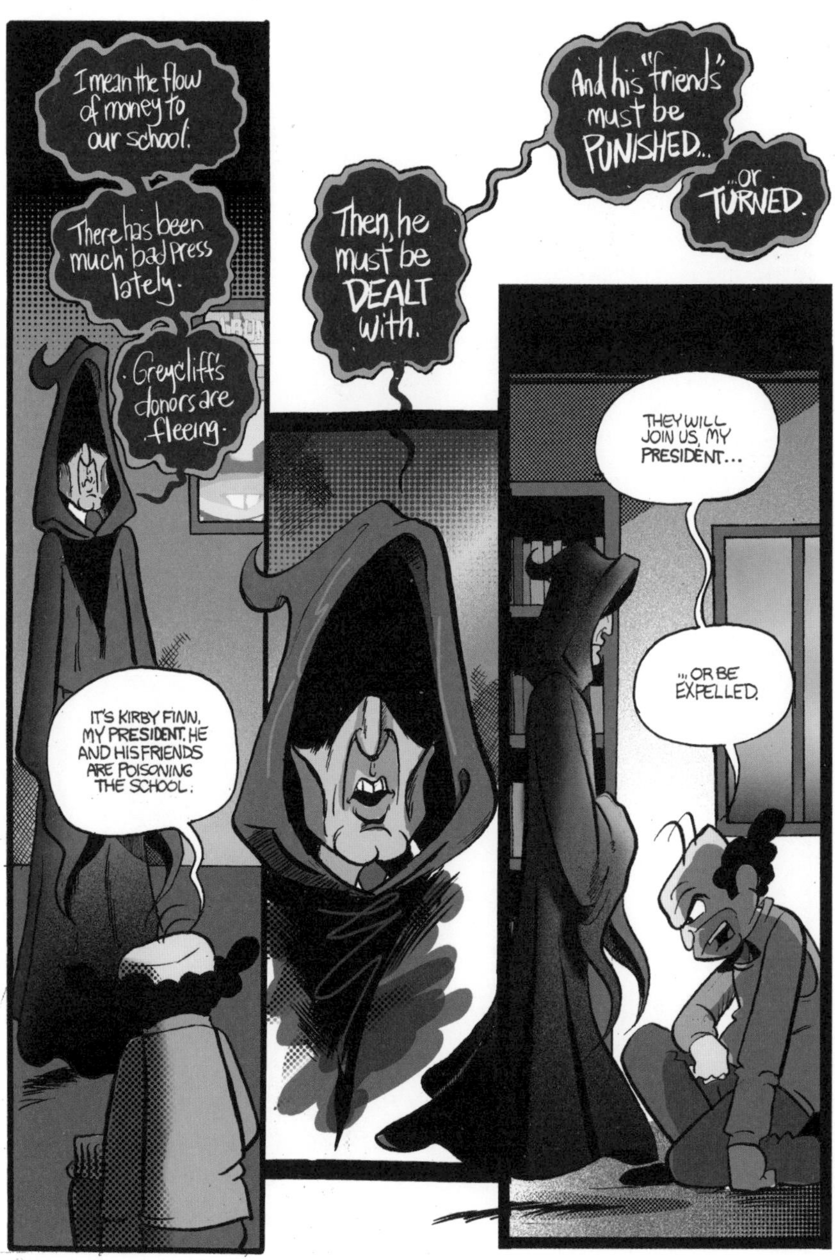
I mean the flow of money to our school.
There has been much bad press lately.
Greycliff's donors are fleeing.
IT'S KIRBY FINN, MY PRESIDENT. HE AND HIS FRIENDS ARE POISONING THE SCHOOL.
Then, he must be DEALT with.
And his "friends" must be PUNISHED...
...or TURNED.
THEY WILL JOIN US, MY PRESIDENT...
...OR BE EXPELLED.

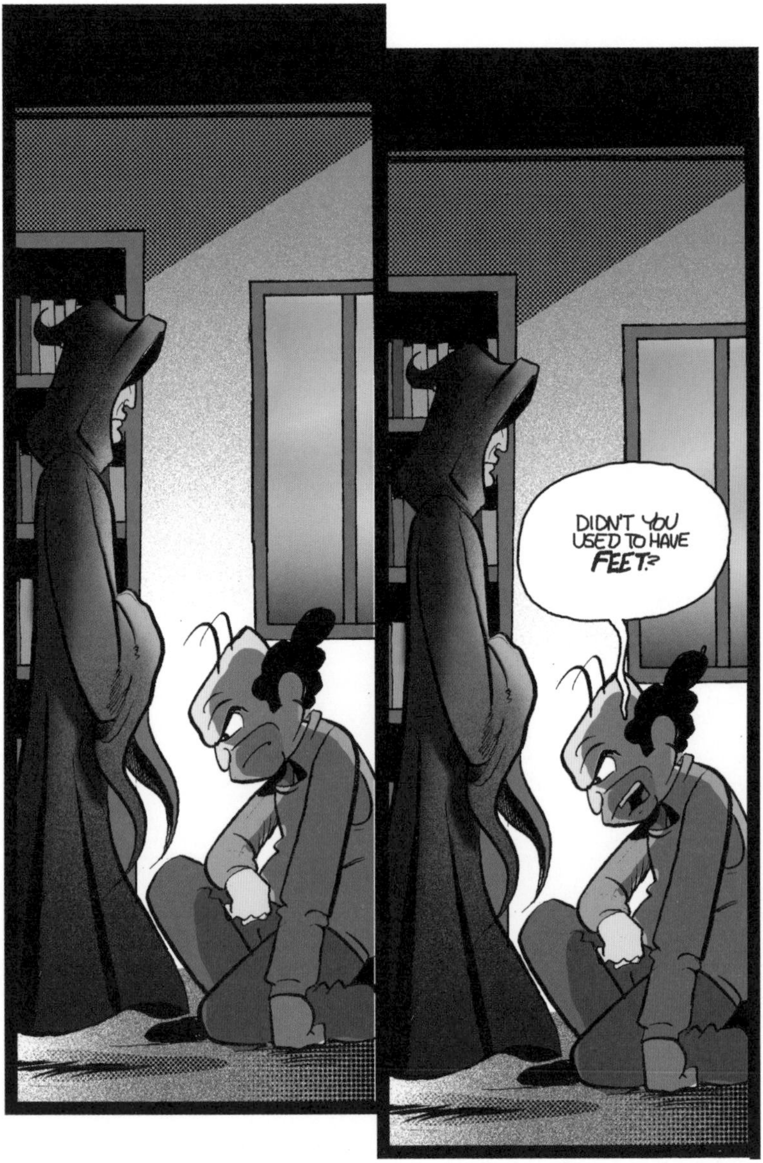
DIDN'T YOU USED TO HAVE FEET?

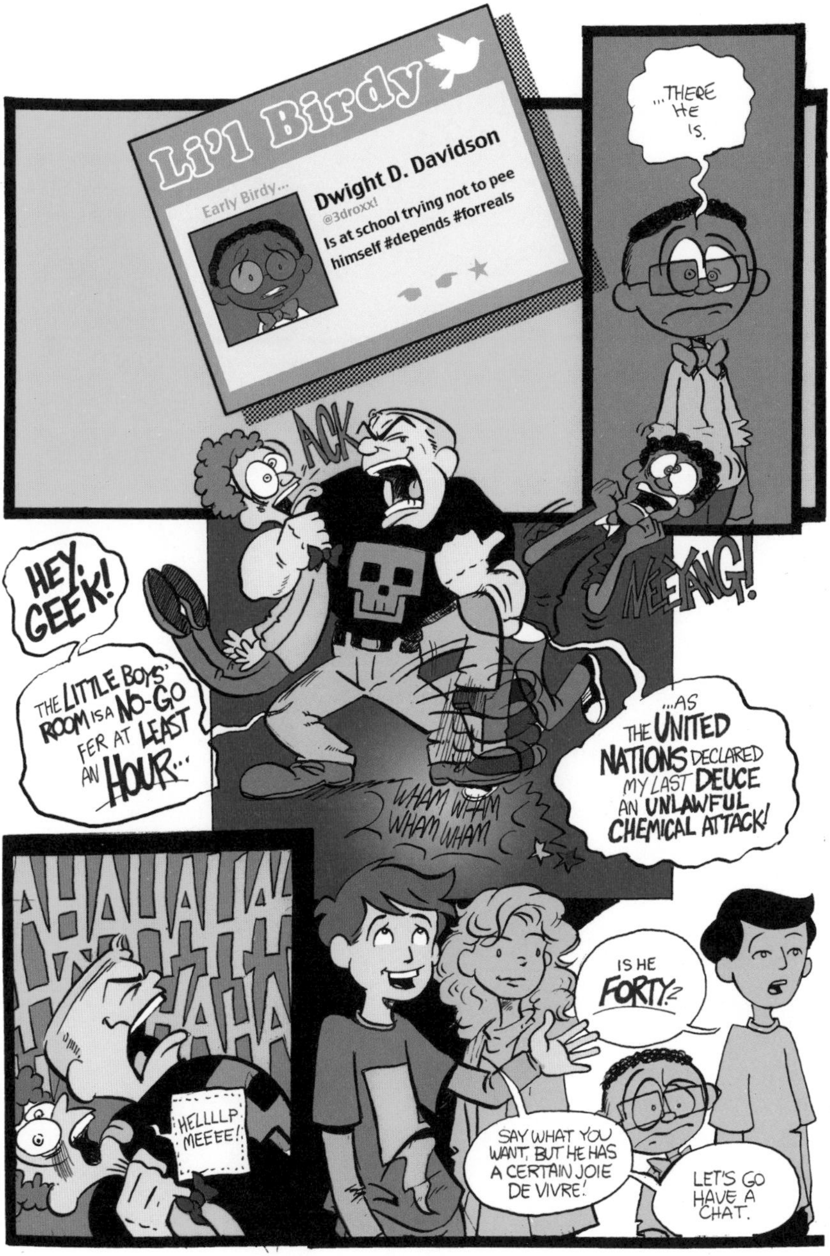
Li'l Birdy
Early Birdy...
Dwight D. Davidson
@3droxx!
Is at school trying not to pee himself #depends #forreals
...THERE HE IS.
ACK
HEY, GEEK!
MEEYANG!
THE LITTLE BOYS' ROOM IS A NO-GO FER AT LEAST AN HOUR...
...AS THE UNITED NATIONS DECLARED MY LAST DEUCE AN UNLAWFUL CHEMICAL ATTACK!
WHAM WHAM WHAM WHAM
AHAHAHAHAHAHAHA
HELLLLP MEEEE!
IS HE FORTY?
SAY WHAT YOU WANT, BUT HE HAS A CERTAIN JOIE DE VIVRE!
LET'S GO HAVE A CHAT.

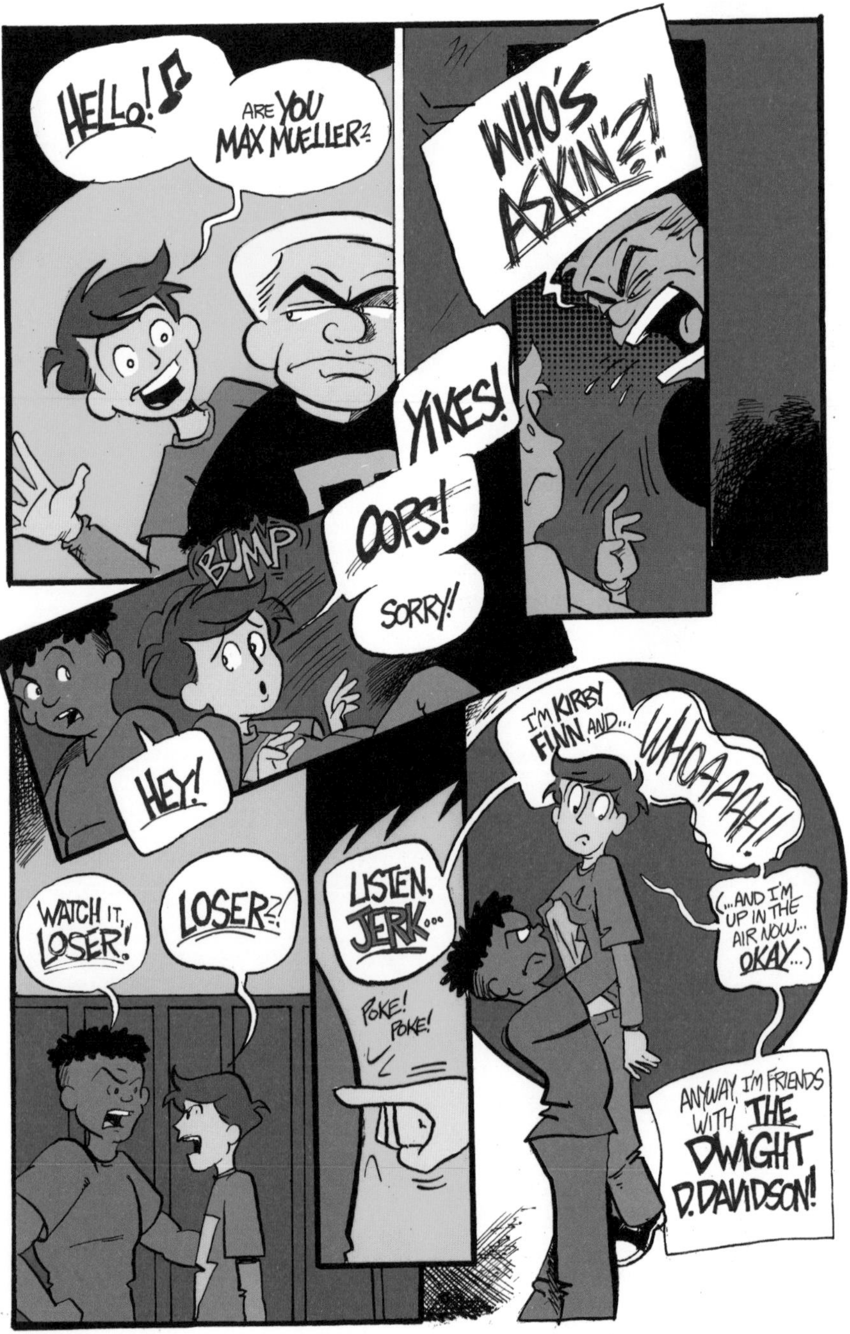

HELLO! ♫
ARE YOU MAX MUELLER?!
WHO'S ASKIN'?!"
YIKES!
OOPS!
BUMP
SORRY!
HEY!
WATCH IT, LOSER!
LOSER?!
LISTEN, JERK...
POKE! POKE!
I'M KIRBY FINN, AND...
WHOAAAH!
(...AND I'M UP IN THE AIR NOW... OKAY...)
ANYWAY, I'M FRIENDS WITH THE DWIGHT D. DAVIDSON!

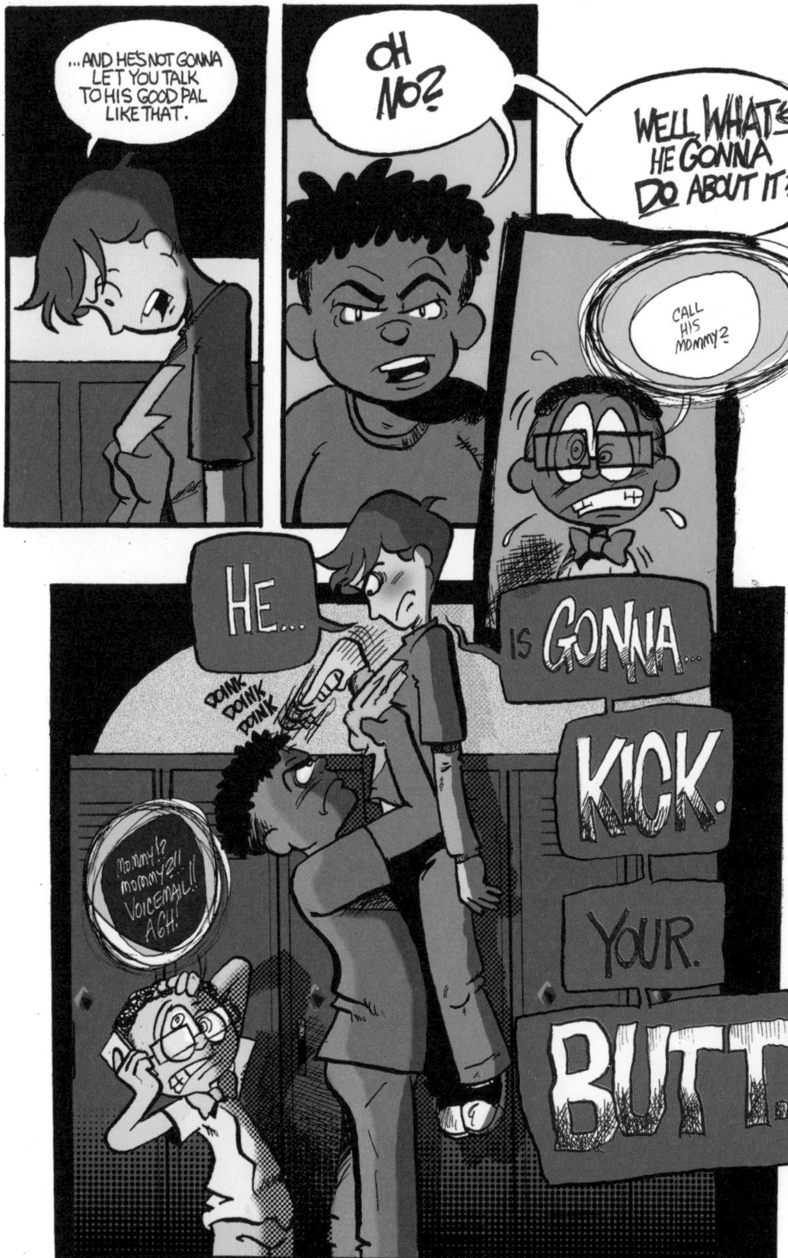
...AND HE'S NOT GONNA LET YOU TALK TO HIS GOOD PAL LIKE THAT.
OH NO?
WELL WHAT'S HE GONNA DO ABOUT IT?
CALL HIS MOMMY?
HE...
IS GONNA...
KICK.
YOUR.
BUTT.
DOINK DOINK DOINK
Mommy!? mommy?!! VOICEMAIL!! AGH!

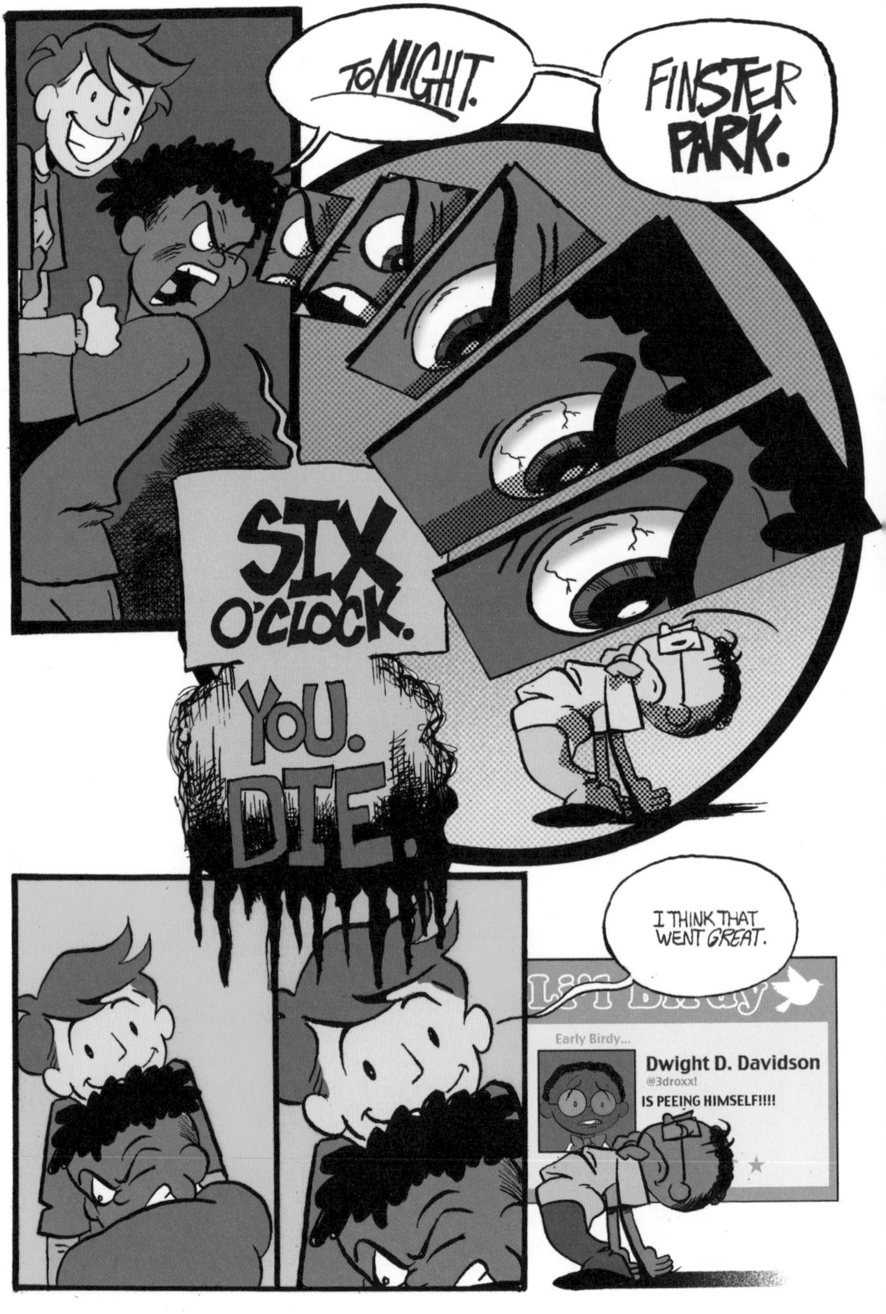
TONIGHT.
FINSTER PARK.
SIX O'CLOCK.
YOU. DIE.
I THINK THAT WENT GREAT.
Early Birdy...
Dwight D. Davidson
@3droxx!
IS PEEING HIMSELF!!!!

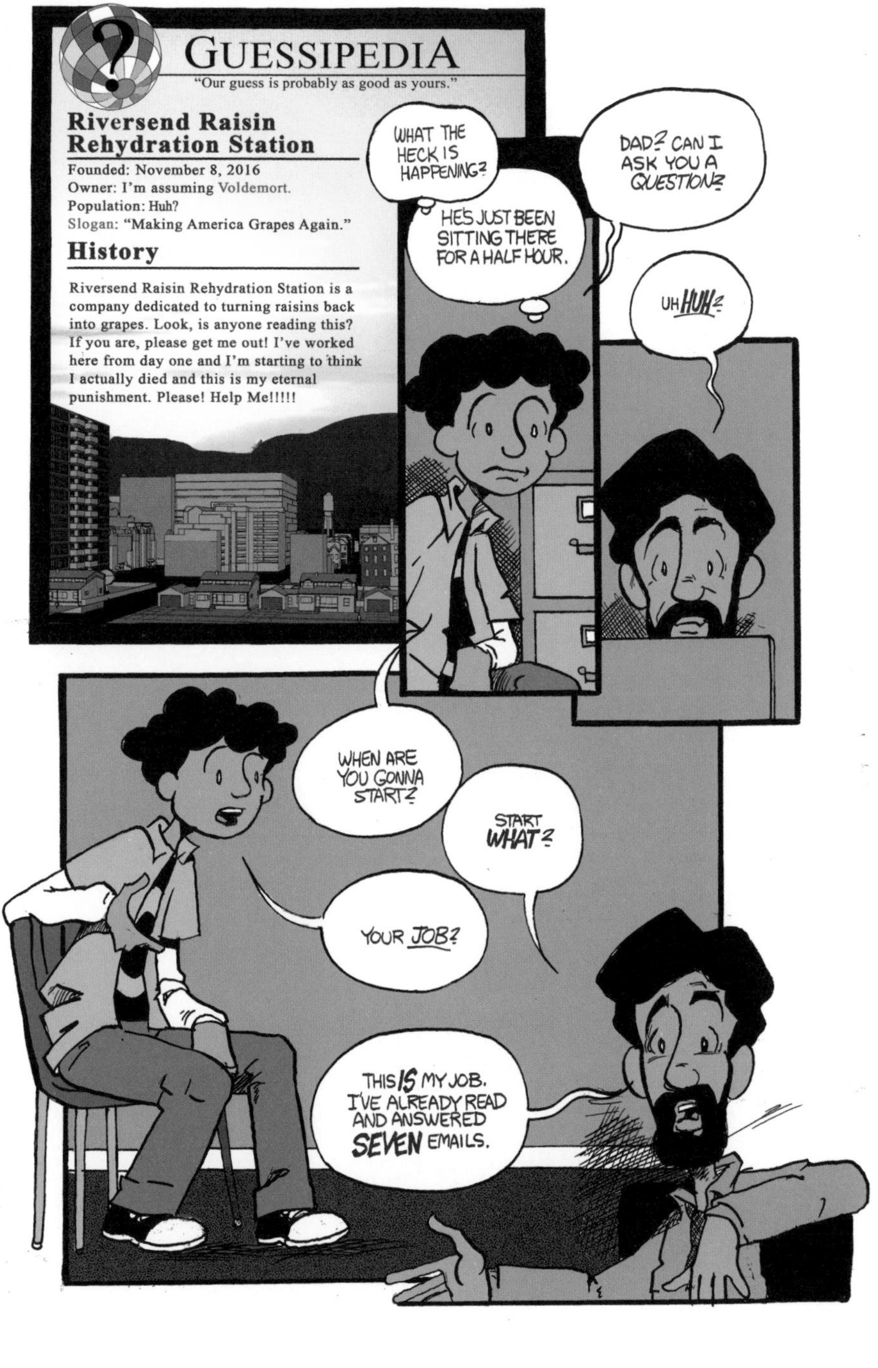
GUESSIPEDIA
"Our guess is probably as good as yours."
Riversend Raisin Rehydration Station
Founded: November 8, 2016
Owner: I'm assuming Voldemort.
Population: Huh?
Slogan: "Making America Grapes Again."
History
Riversend Raisin Rehydration Station is a company dedicated to turning raisins back into grapes. Look, is anyone reading this? If you are, please get me out! I've worked here from day one and I'm starting to think I actually died and this is my eternal punishment. Please! Help Me!!!!!
WHAT THE HECK IS HAPPENING?
HE'S JUST BEEN SITTING THERE FOR A HALF HOUR.
DAD? CAN I ASK YOU A QUESTION?
UH HUH?
WHEN ARE YOU GONNA START?
START WHAT?
YOUR JOB?
THIS IS MY JOB. I'VE ALREADY READ AND ANSWERED SEVEN EMAILS.

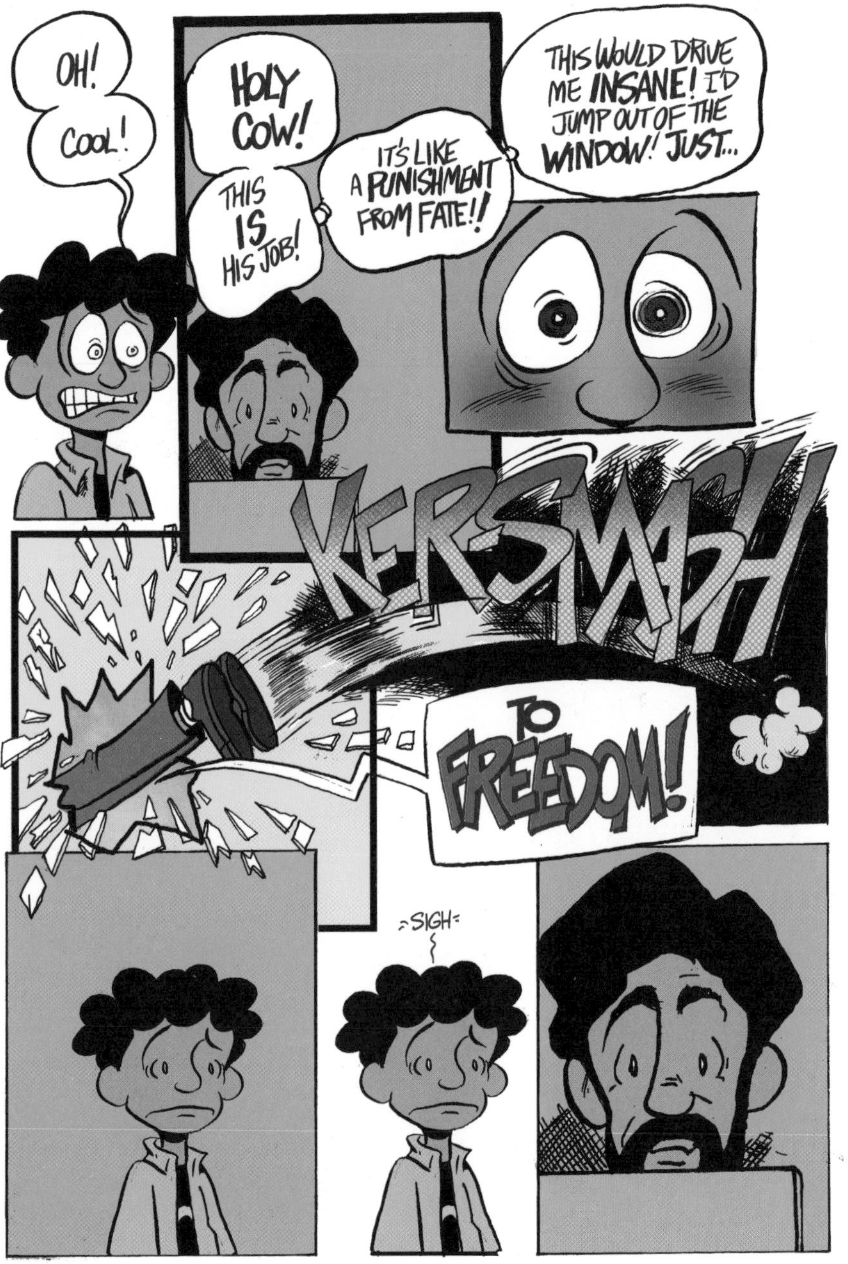
OH!
COOL!
HOLY COW!
THIS IS HIS JOB!
IT'S LIKE A PUNISHMENT FROM FATE!!
THIS WOULD DRIVE ME INSANE! I'D JUMP OUT OF THE WINDOW! JUST...
KERSMASH
TO FREEDOM!
SIGH

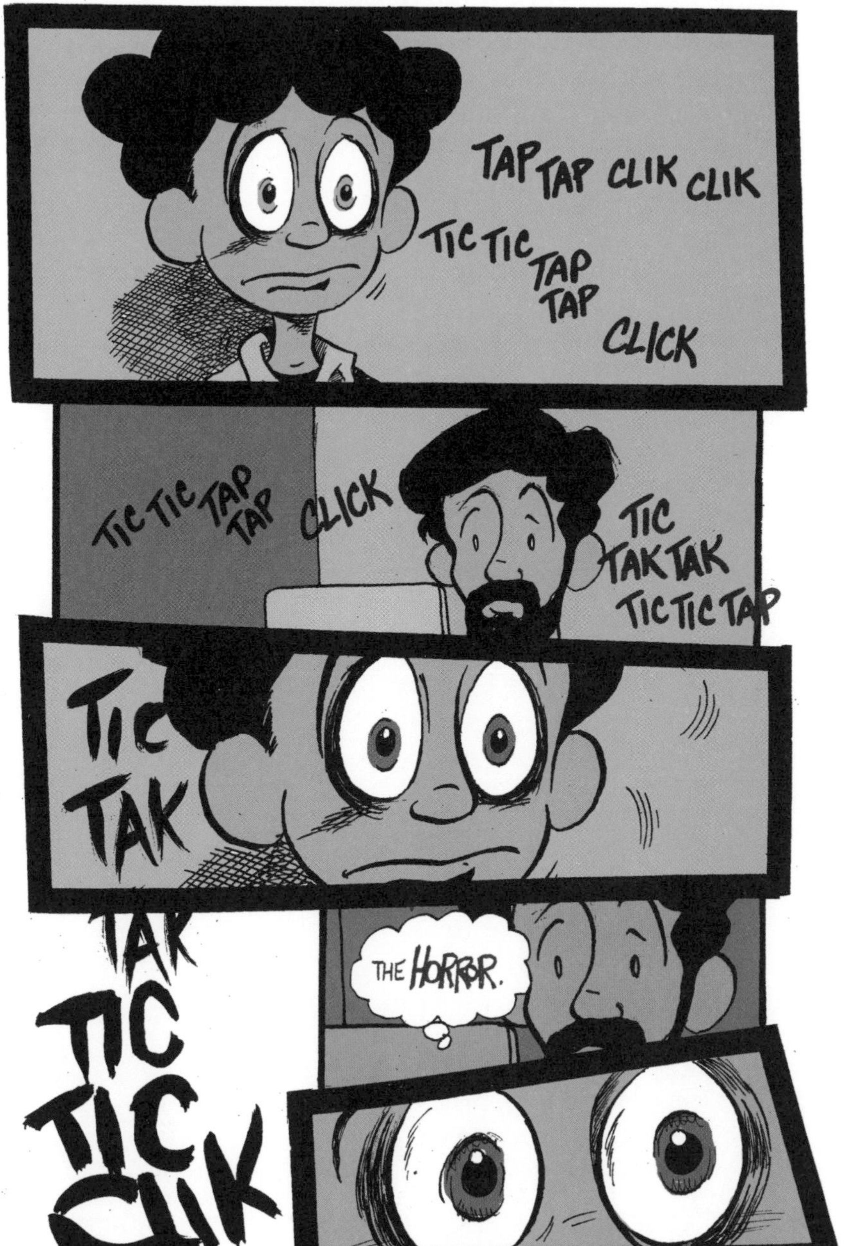
TAP TAP CLIK CLIK
TIC TIC TAP TAP
CLICK
TIC TIC TAP TAP
CLICK
TIC
TAK TAK
TIC TIC TAP
TIC
TAK
TIC
TIC
CLIK
THE HORROR.

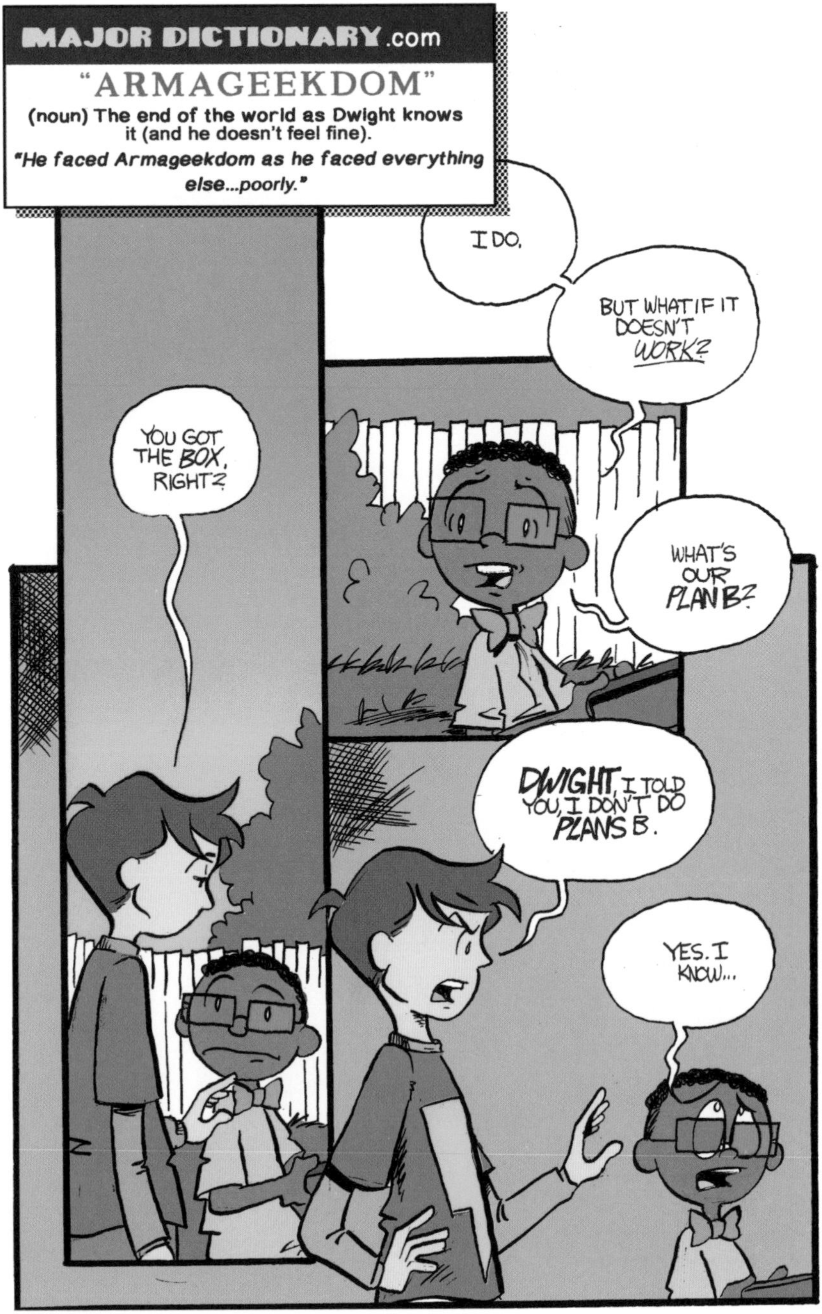
MAJOR DICTIONARY.com
"ARMAGEEKDOM"
(noun) The end of the world as Dwight knows it (and he doesn't feel fine).
"He faced Armageekdom as he faced everything else...poorly."
YOU GOT THE BOX, RIGHT?
I DO.
BUT WHAT IF IT DOESN'T WORK?
WHAT'S OUR PLAN B?
DWIGHT, I TOLD YOU, I DON'T DO PLANS B.
YES. I KNOW...

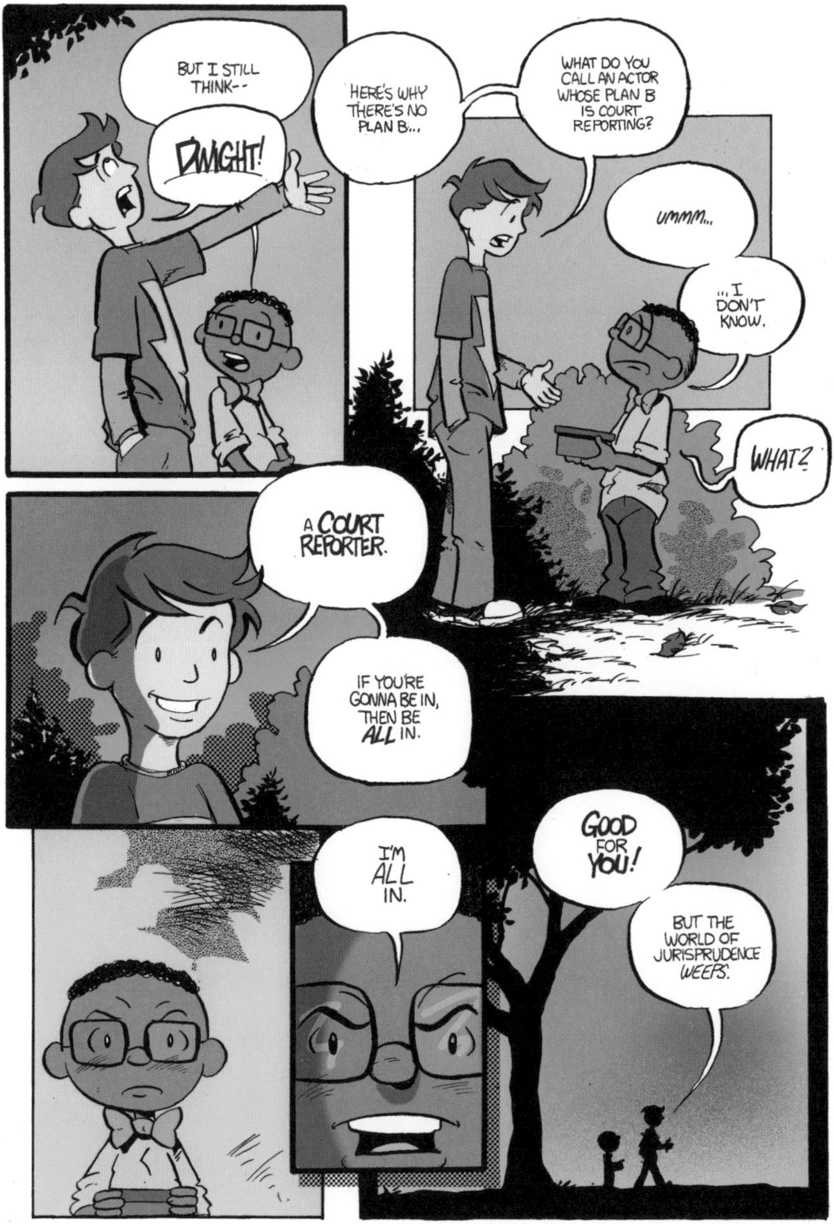
BUT I STILL THINK--
DWIGHT!
HERE'S WHY THERE'S NO PLAN B...
WHAT DO YOU CALL AN ACTOR WHOSE PLAN B IS COURT REPORTING?
UMMM...
...I DON'T KNOW.
WHAT?
A COURT REPORTER.
IF YOU'RE GONNA BE IN, THEN BE ALL IN.
I'M ALL IN.
GOOD FOR YOU!
BUT THE WORLD OF JURISPRUDENCE WEEPS.

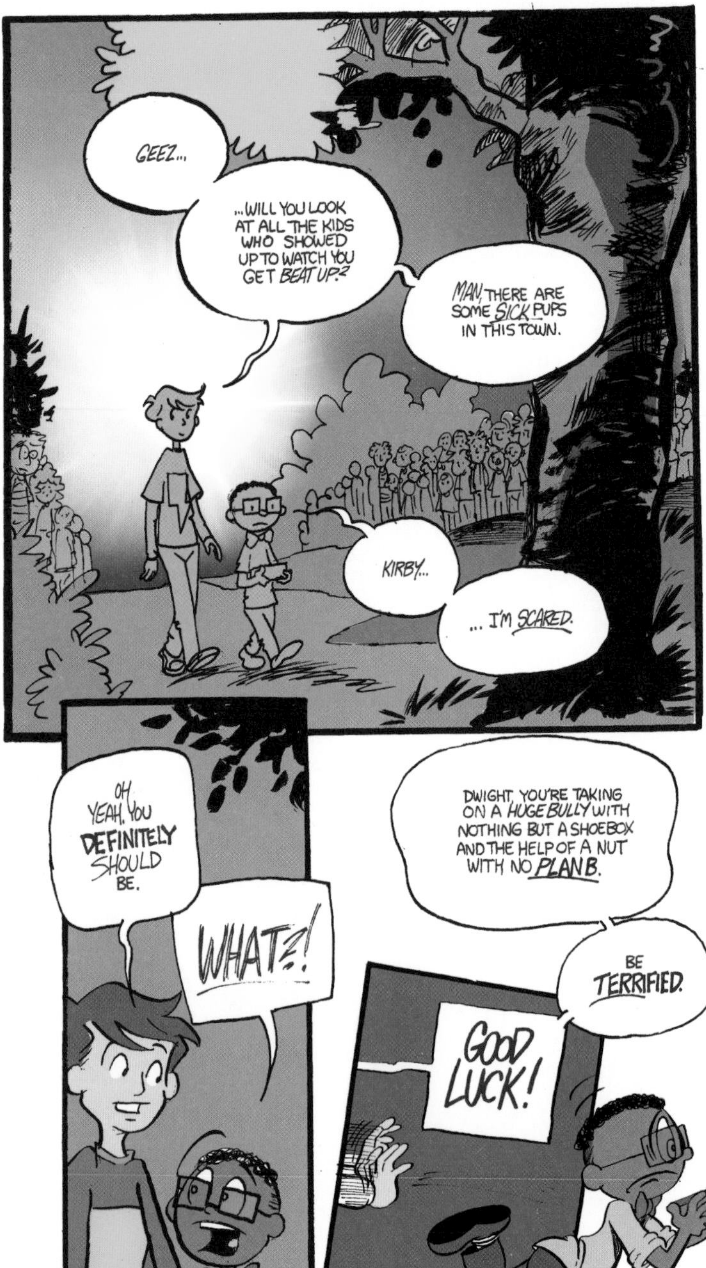
GEEZ...
...WILL YOU LOOK AT ALL THE KIDS WHO SHOWED UP TO WATCH YOU GET BEAT UP?
MAN, THERE ARE SOME SICK PUPS IN THIS TOWN.
KIRBY...
... I'M SCARED.
OH YEAH, YOU DEFINITELY SHOULD BE.
WHAT?!
DWIGHT, YOU'RE TAKING ON A HUGE BULLY WITH NOTHING BUT A SHOEBOX AND THE HELP OF A NUT WITH NO PLAN B.
BE TERRIFIED.
GOOD LUCK!

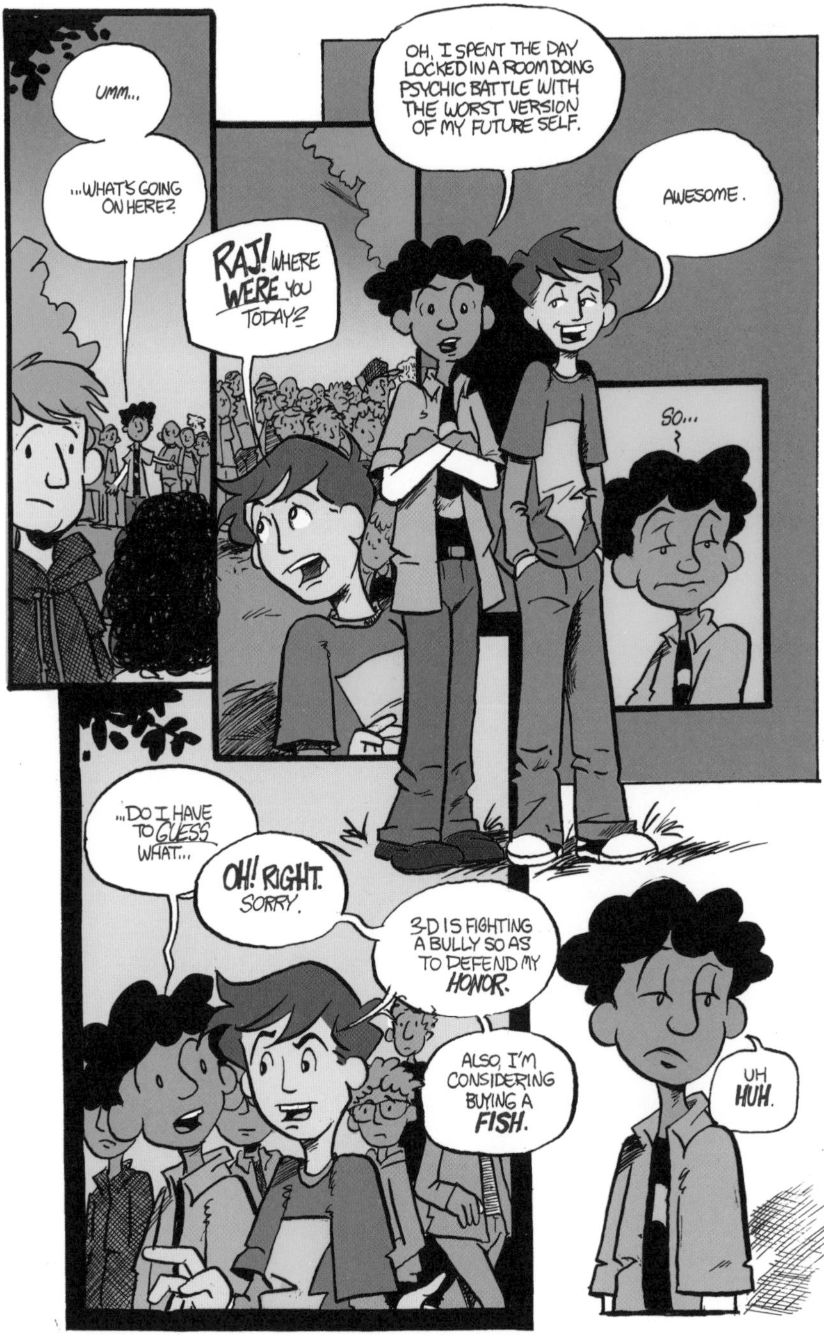
UMM...
...WHAT'S GOING ON HERE?
RAJ! WHERE WERE YOU TODAY?
OH, I SPENT THE DAY LOCKED IN A ROOM DOING PSYCHIC BATTLE WITH THE WORST VERSION OF MY FUTURE SELF.
AWESOME.
SO...
...DO I HAVE TO GUESS WHAT...
OH! RIGHT. SORRY.
3-D IS FIGHTING A BULLY SO AS TO DEFEND MY HONOR.
ALSO, I'M CONSIDERING BUYING A FISH.
UH HUH.

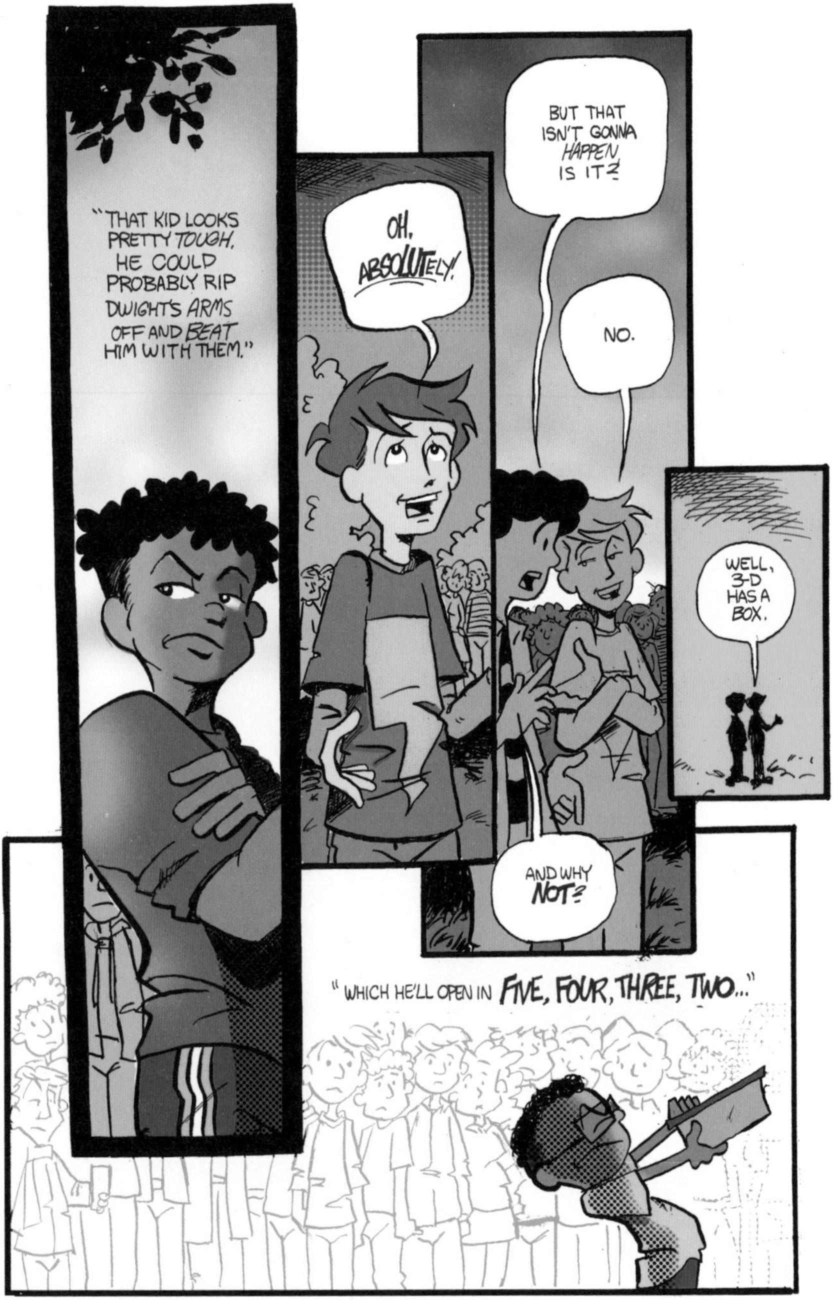
"THAT KID LOOKS PRETTY TOUGH. HE COULD PROBABLY RIP DWIGHT'S ARMS OFF AND BEAT HIM WITH THEM."
OH, ABSOLUTELY!
BUT THAT ISN'T GONNA HAPPEN, IS IT?
NO.
AND WHY NOT?
WELL, 3-D HAS A BOX.
"WHICH HE'LL OPEN IN FIVE, FOUR, THREE, TWO..."

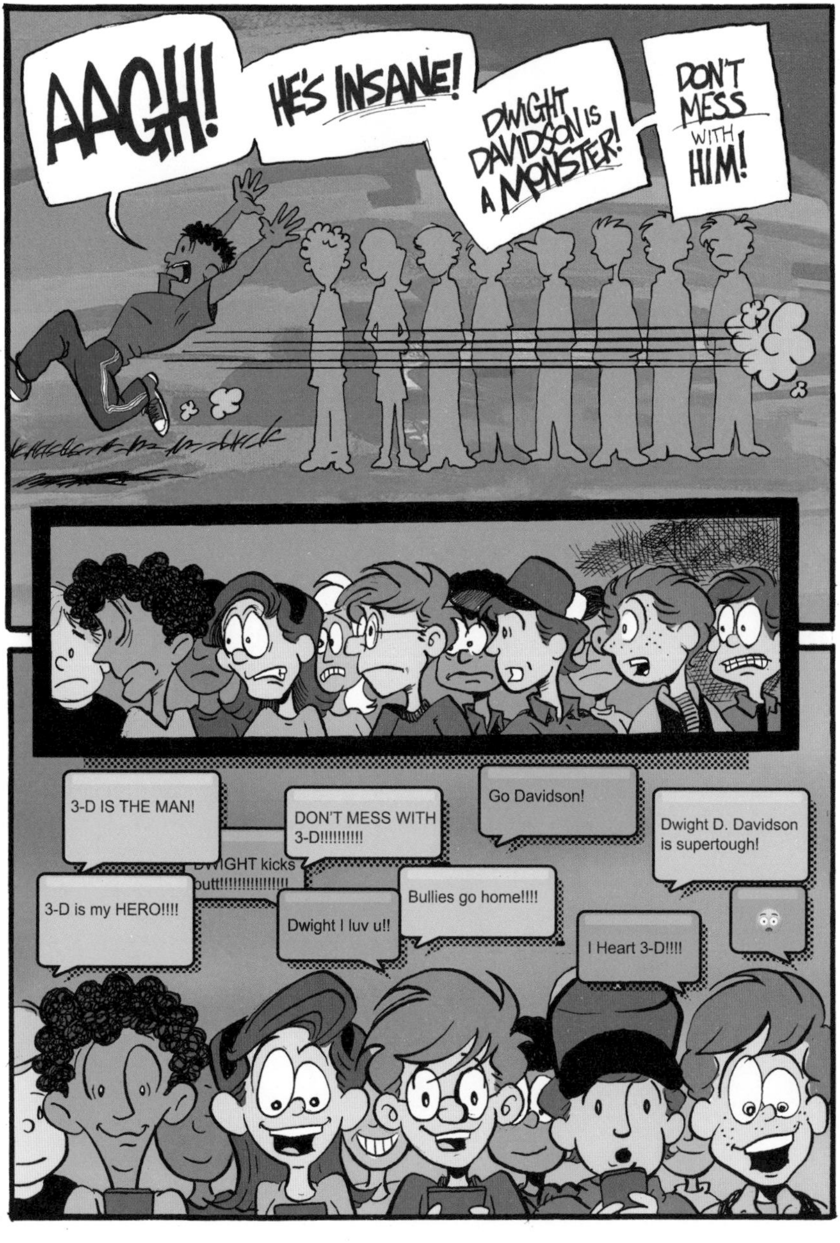
AAGH!
HE'S INSANE!
DWIGHT DAVIDSON IS A MONSTER!
DON'T MESS WITH HIM!
3-D IS THE MAN!
DON'T MESS WITH 3-D!!!!!!!!!!
IGHT kicks utt!!!!!!!!!!!!!!!!
Go Davidson!
Dwight D. Davidson is supertough!
3-D is my HERO!!!!
Dwight I luv u!!
Bullies go home!!!!
I Heart 3-D!!!!

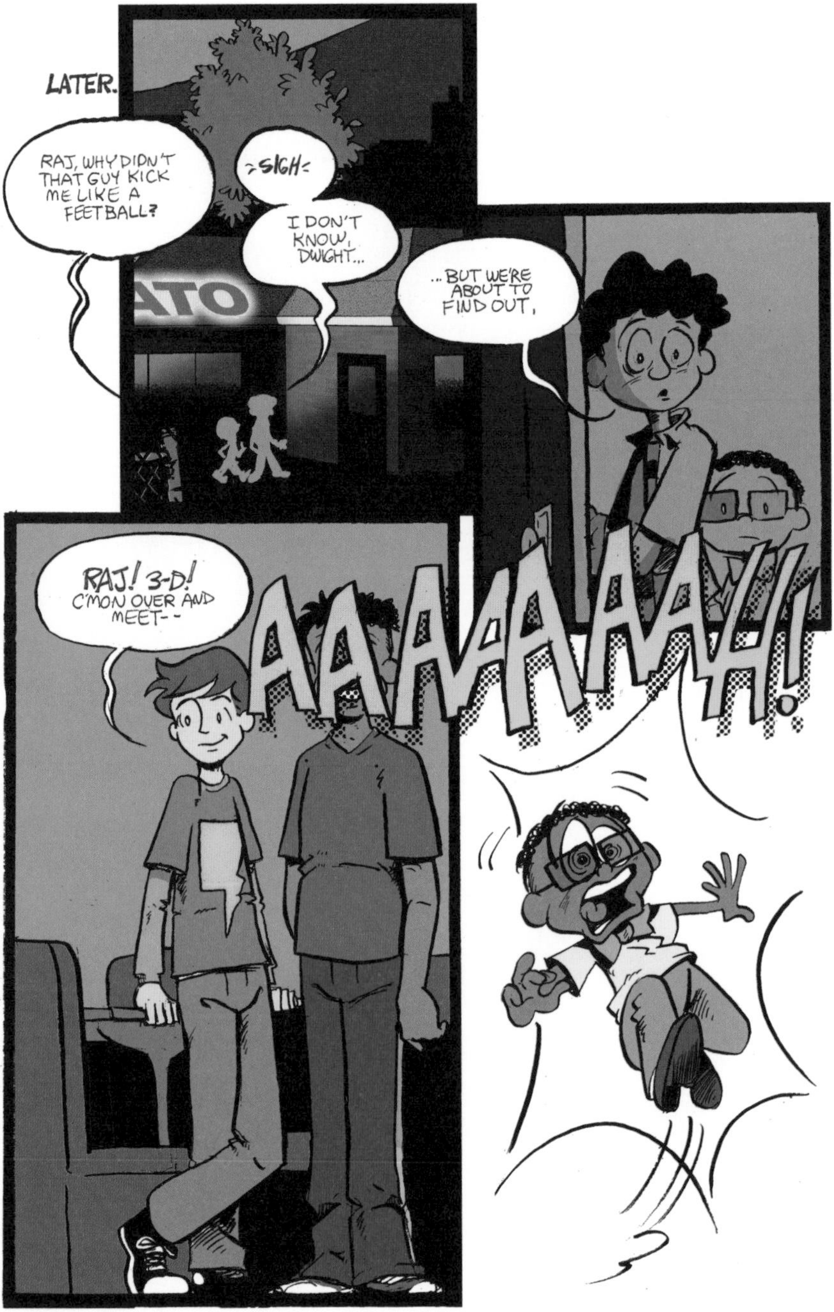
LATER.
RAJ, WHY DIDN'T THAT GUY KICK ME LIKE A FEETBALL?
SIGH
I DON'T KNOW, DWIGHT...
...BUT WE'RE ABOUT TO FIND OUT.
RAJ! 3-D! C'MON OVER AND MEET--
AAAAAAAH!!

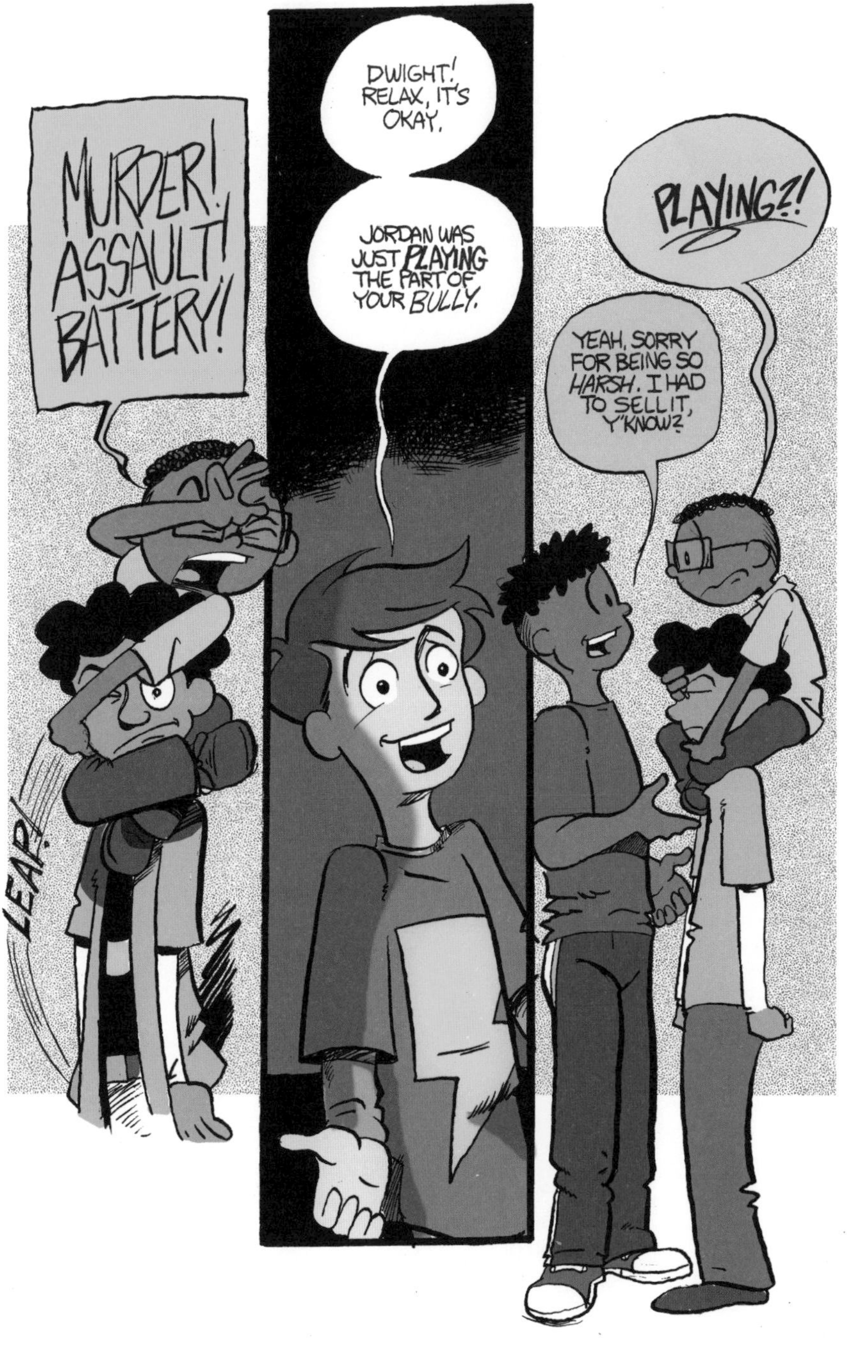
MURDER! ASSAULT! BATTERY!
LEAP!
DWIGHT! RELAX, IT'S OKAY.
JORDAN WAS JUST PLAYING THE PART OF YOUR BULLY.
PLAYING?!
YEAH, SORRY FOR BEING SO HARSH. I HAD TO SELL IT, Y'KNOW?

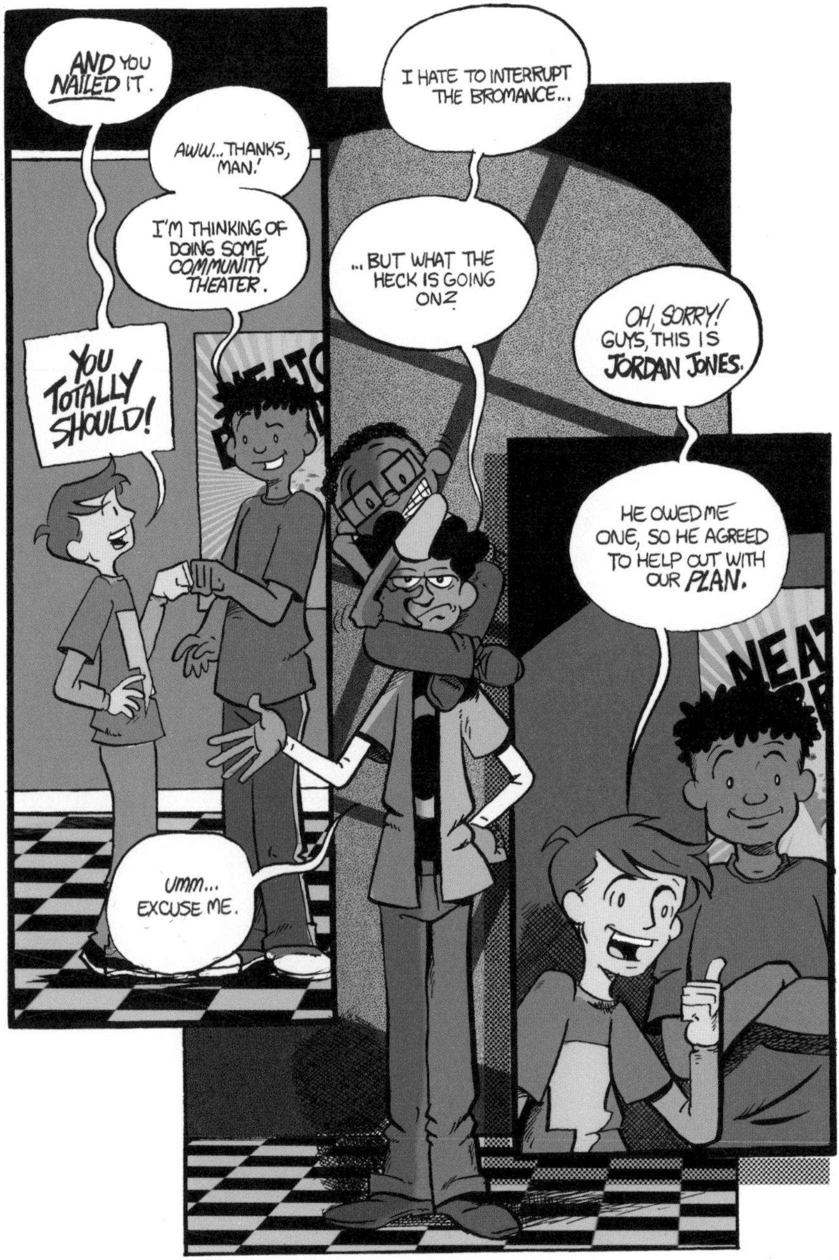
AND YOU NAILED IT.
AWW... THANKS, MAN.'
I'M THINKING OF DOING SOME COMMUNITY THEATER.
YOU TOTALLY SHOULD!
UMM... EXCUSE ME.
I HATE TO INTERRUPT THE BROMANCE...
... BUT WHAT THE HECK IS GOING ON?
OH, SORRY! GUYS, THIS IS JORDAN JONES.
HE OWED ME ONE, SO HE AGREED TO HELP OUT WITH OUR PLAN.
NEATO

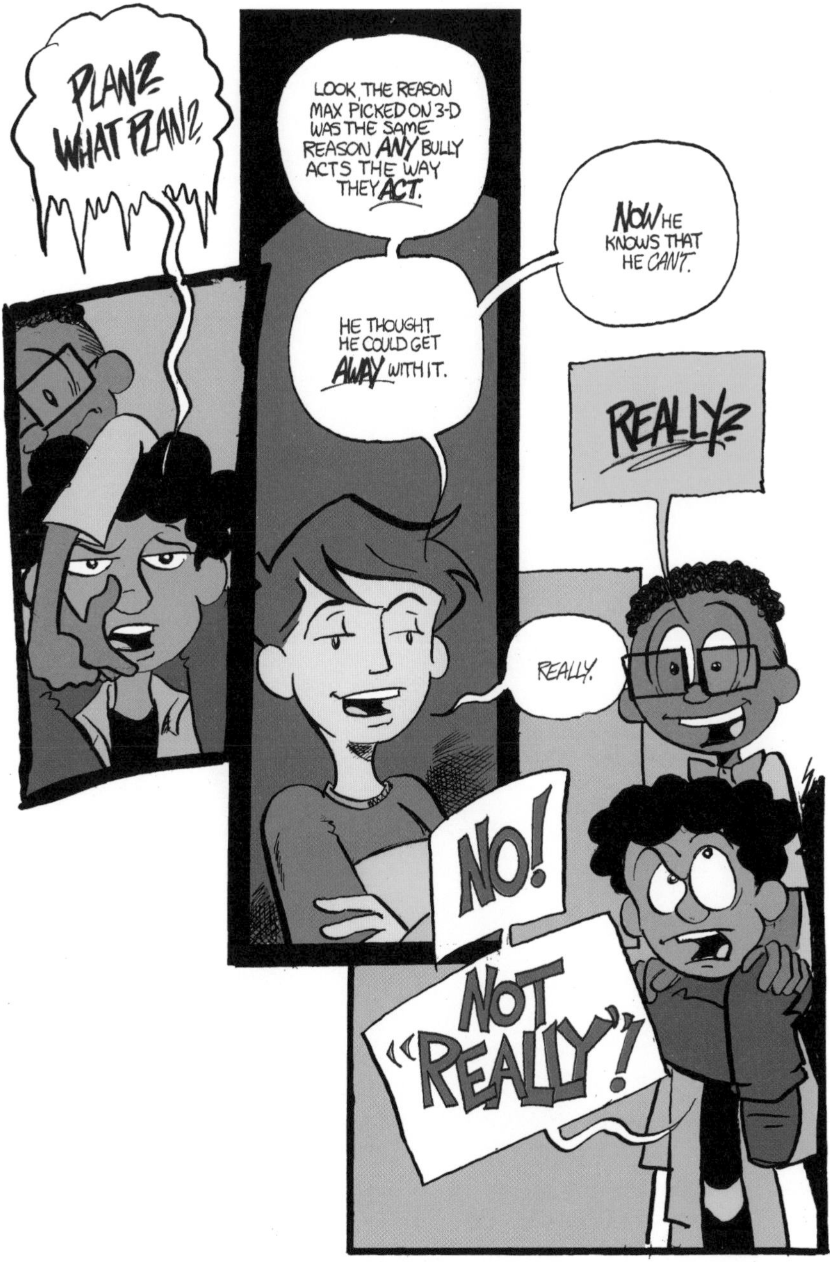
PLAN? WHAT PLAN?
LOOK, THE REASON MAX PICKED ON 3-D WAS THE SAME REASON ANY BULLY ACTS THE WAY THEY ACT.
HE THOUGHT HE COULD GET AWAY WITH IT.
NOW HE KNOWS THAT HE CAN'T.
REALLY?
REALLY.
NO!
NOT "REALLY"!

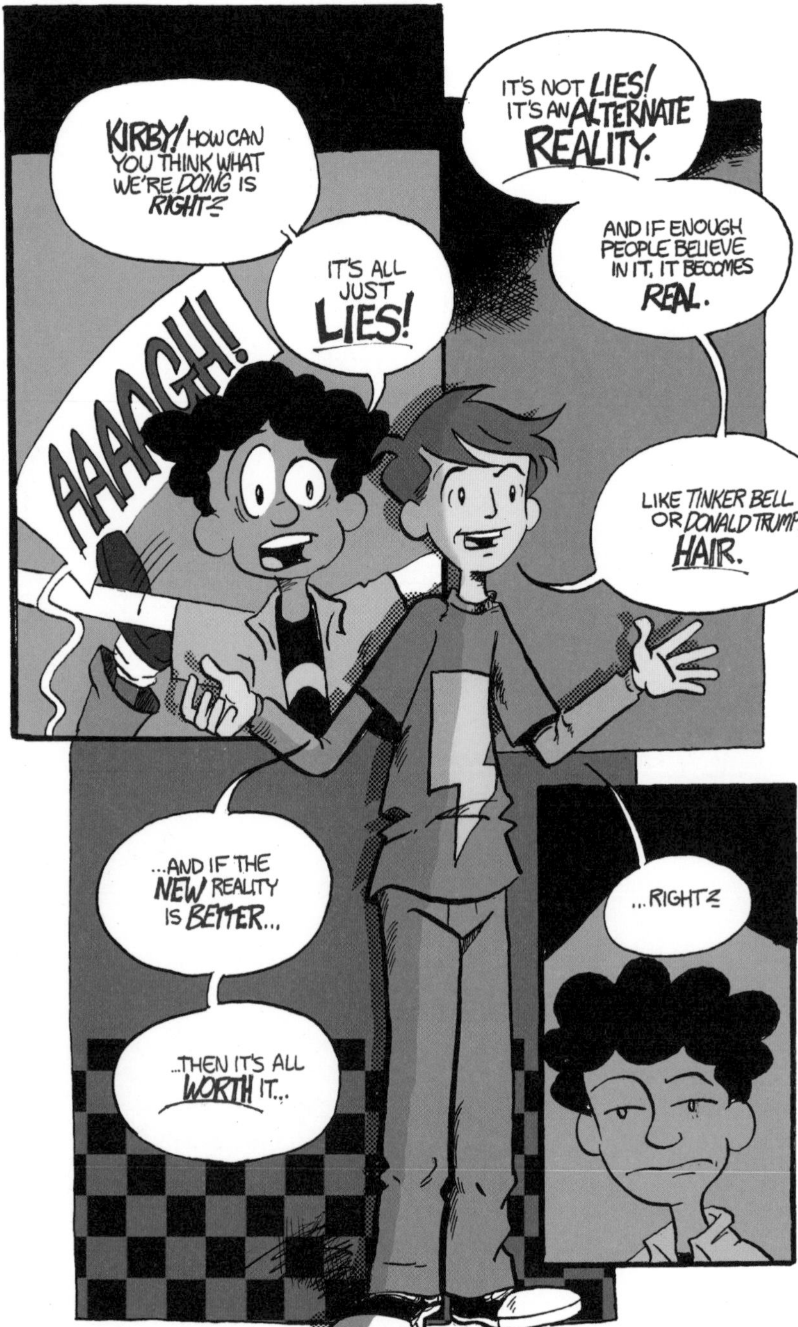
KIRBY! HOW CAN YOU THINK WHAT WE'RE DOING IS RIGHT?
IT'S ALL JUST LIES!
AAAAGH!
IT'S NOT LIES! IT'S AN ALTERNATE REALITY.
AND IF ENOUGH PEOPLE BELIEVE IN IT, IT BECOMES REAL.
LIKE TINKER BELL OR DONALD TRUMP'S HAIR.
...AND IF THE NEW REALITY IS BETTER...
...THEN IT'S ALL WORTH IT...
...RIGHT?

LOOK, I LOVED KIRBY LIKE A BROTHER.
HONESTLY.
NB
BUT... THERE WERE TWO REASONS I ALSO WANTED TO KICK HIM A LITTLE.
NEATO
THE FIRST WAS WHEN KIRBY SAID STUFF LIKE THAT.
THE SECOND...

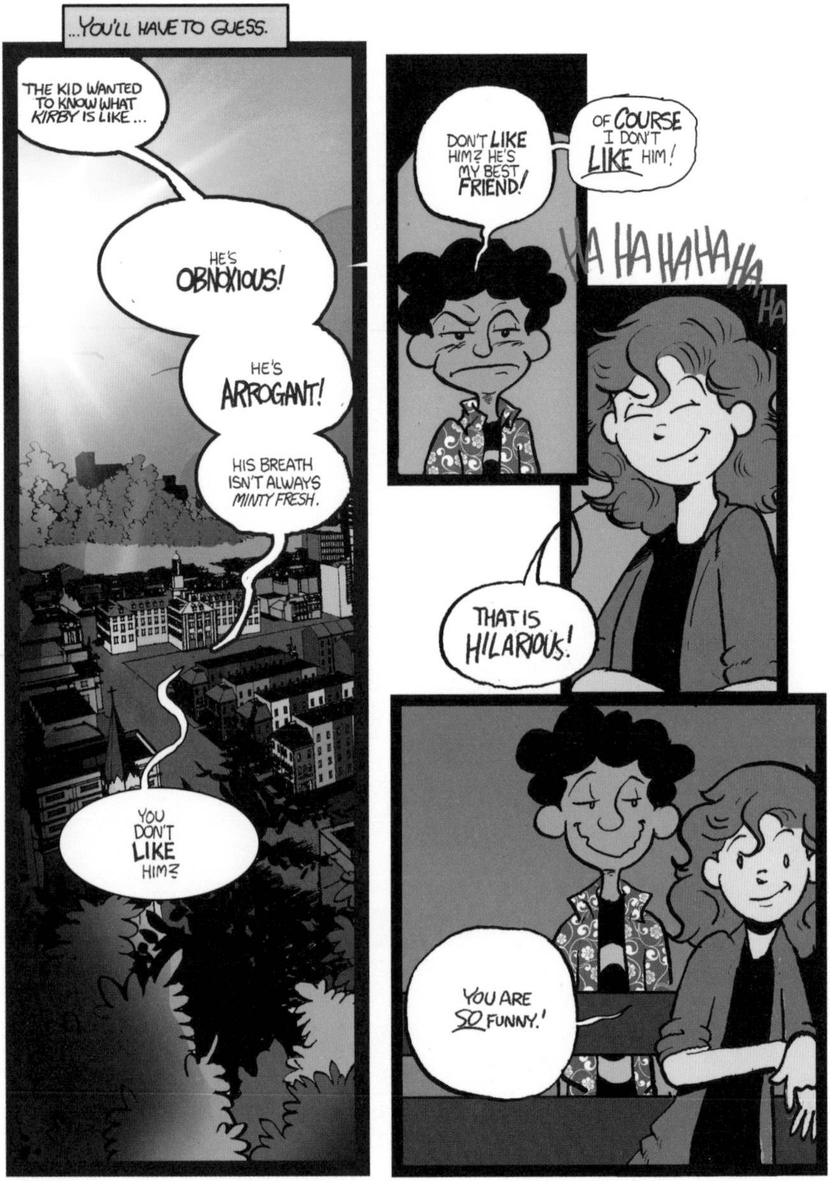
...YOU'LL HAVE TO GUESS.
THE KID WANTED TO KNOW WHAT KIRBY IS LIKE...
HE'S OBNOXIOUS!
HE'S ARROGANT!
HIS BREATH ISN'T ALWAYS MINTY FRESH.
YOU DON'T LIKE HIM?
DON'T LIKE HIM? HE'S MY BEST FRIEND!
OF COURSE I DON'T LIKE HIM!
HA HA HAHAHAHA HA HA
THAT IS HILARIOUS!
YOU ARE SO FUNNY!

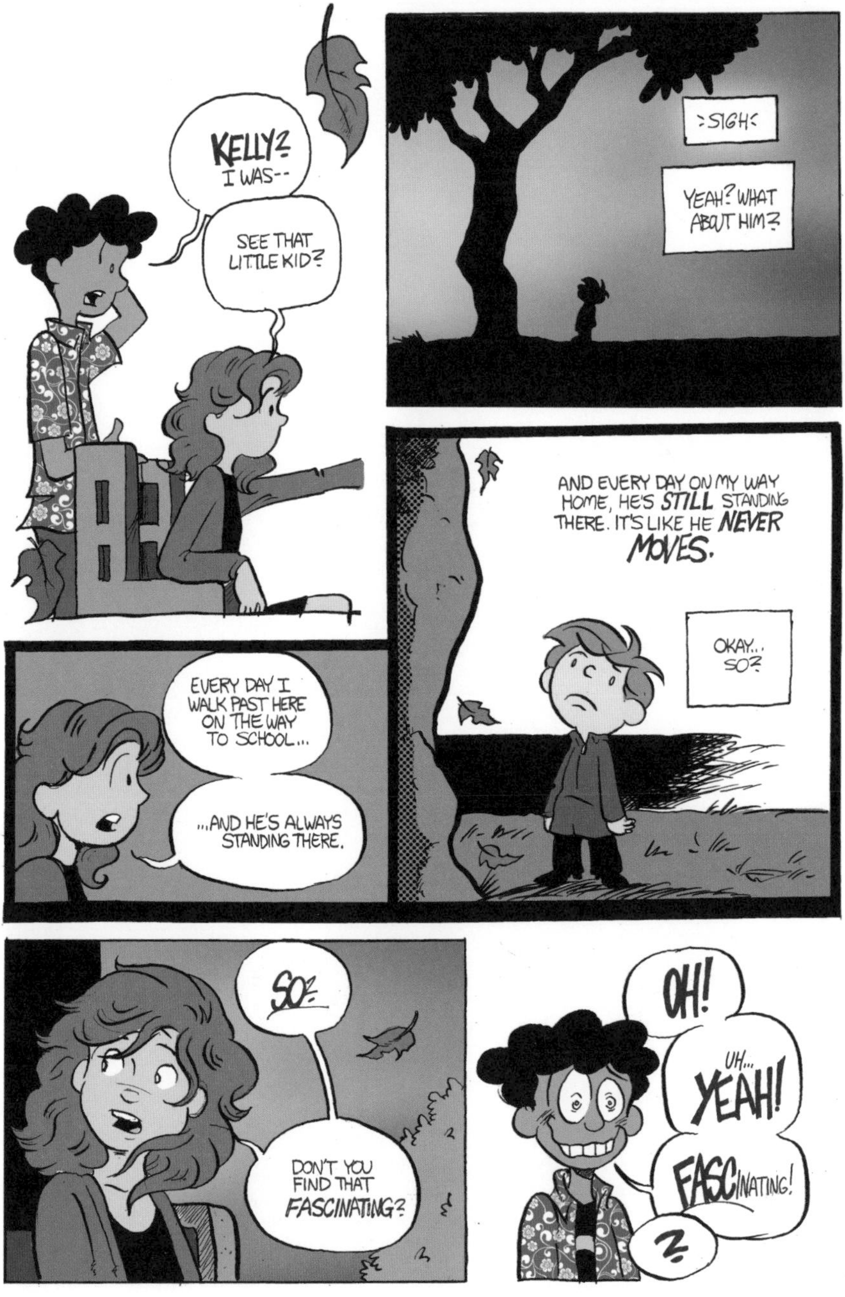

KELLY? I WAS--
SEE THAT LITTLE KID?
>SIGH<
YEAH? WHAT ABOUT HIM?
EVERY DAY I WALK PAST HERE ON THE WAY TO SCHOOL...
...AND HE'S ALWAYS STANDING THERE.
AND EVERY DAY ON MY WAY HOME, HE'S STILL STANDING THERE. IT'S LIKE HE NEVER MOVES.
OKAY... SO?
SO?
DON'T YOU FIND THAT FASCINATING?
OH!
UH... YEAH!
FASCINATING!
?

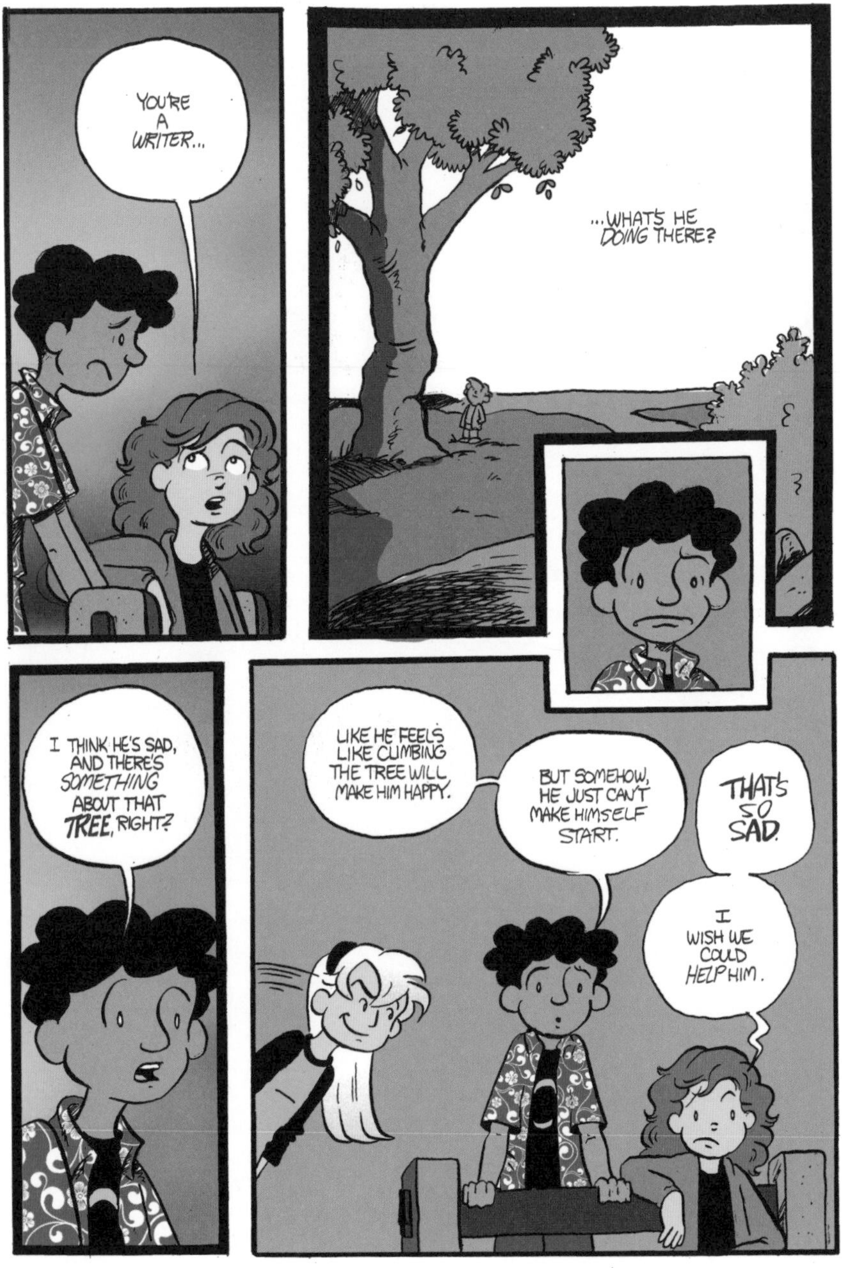

YOU'RE A WRITER...
...WHAT'S HE DOING THERE?
I THINK HE'S SAD, AND THERE'S SOMETHING ABOUT THAT TREE, RIGHT?
LIKE HE FEELS LIKE CLIMBING THE TREE WILL MAKE HIM HAPPY.
BUT SOMEHOW, HE JUST CAN'T MAKE HIMSELF START.
THAT'S SO SAD.
I WISH WE COULD HELP HIM.

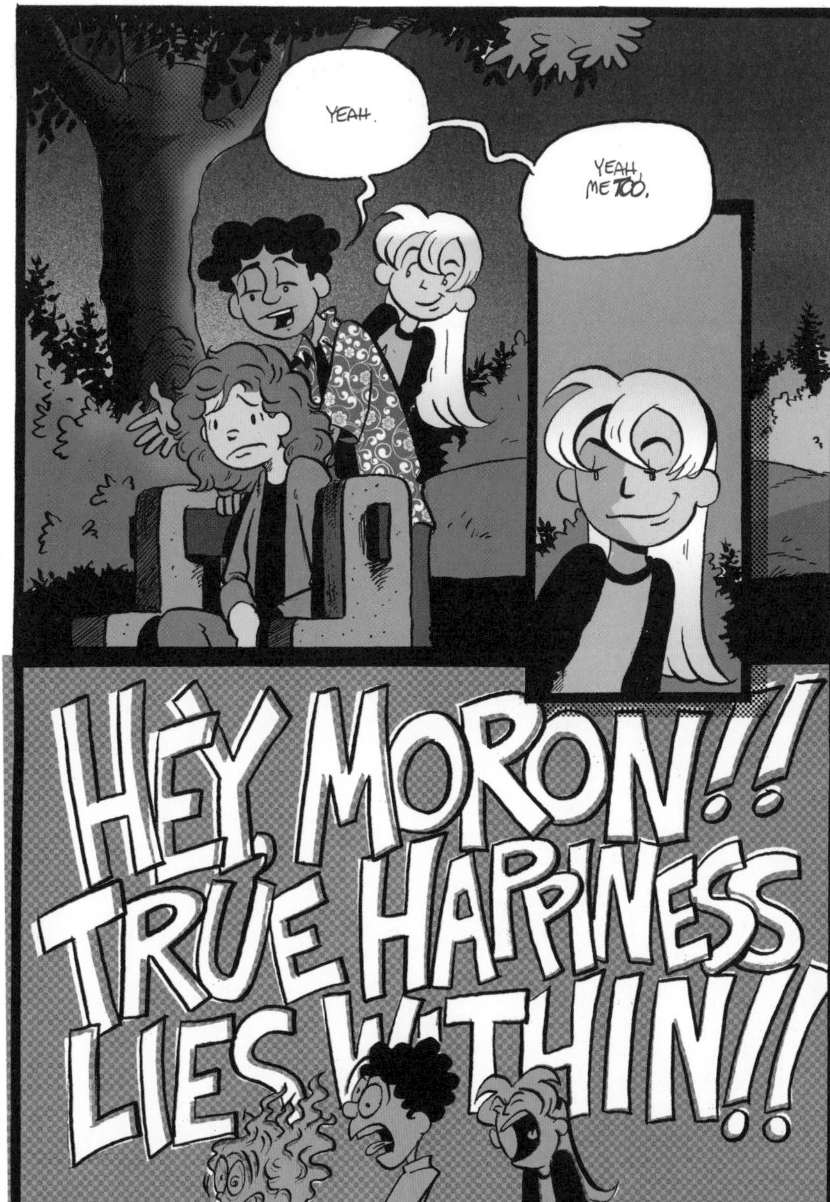
YEAH.
YEAH, ME TOO.
HEY, MORON!! TRUE HAPPINESS LIES WITHIN!!

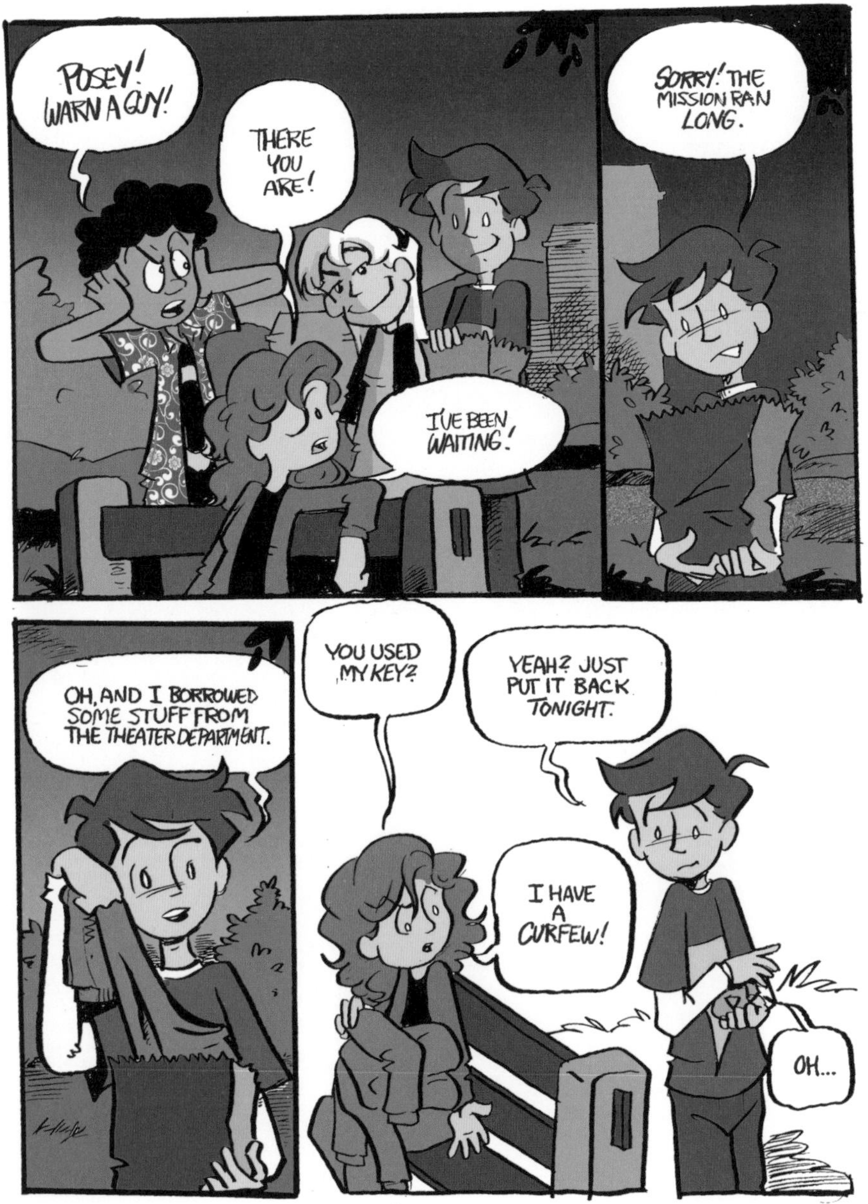
POSEY! WARN A GUY!
THERE YOU ARE!
I'VE BEEN WAITING!
SORRY! THE MISSION RAN LONG.
OH, AND I BORROWED SOME STUFF FROM THE THEATER DEPARTMENT.
YOU USED MY KEY?
YEAH? JUST PUT IT BACK TONIGHT.
I HAVE A CURFEW!
OH...

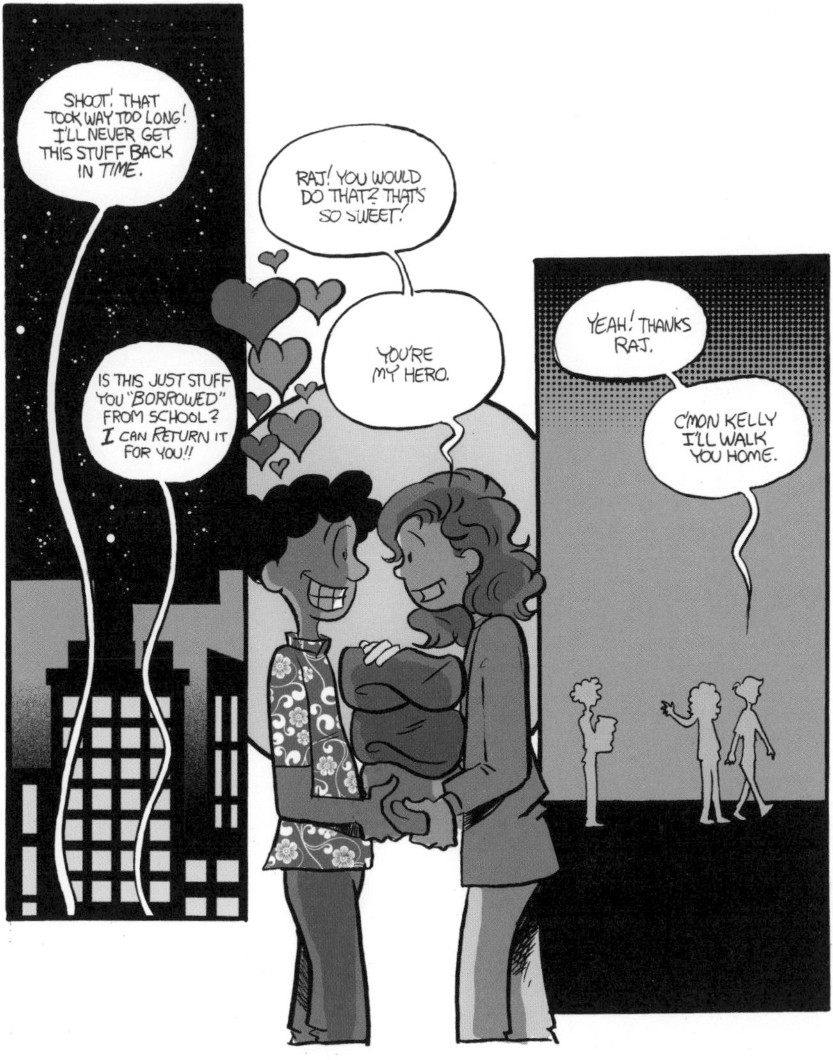
SHOOT! THAT TOOK WAY TOO LONG! I'LL NEVER GET THIS STUFF BACK IN *TIME*.
IS THIS JUST STUFF YOU "BORROWED" FROM SCHOOL? *I* CAN RETURN IT FOR YOU!!
RAJ! YOU WOULD DO THAT? THAT'S SO SWEET!
YOU'RE MY HERO.
YEAH! THANKS RAJ.
C'MON KELLY I'LL WALK YOU HOME.

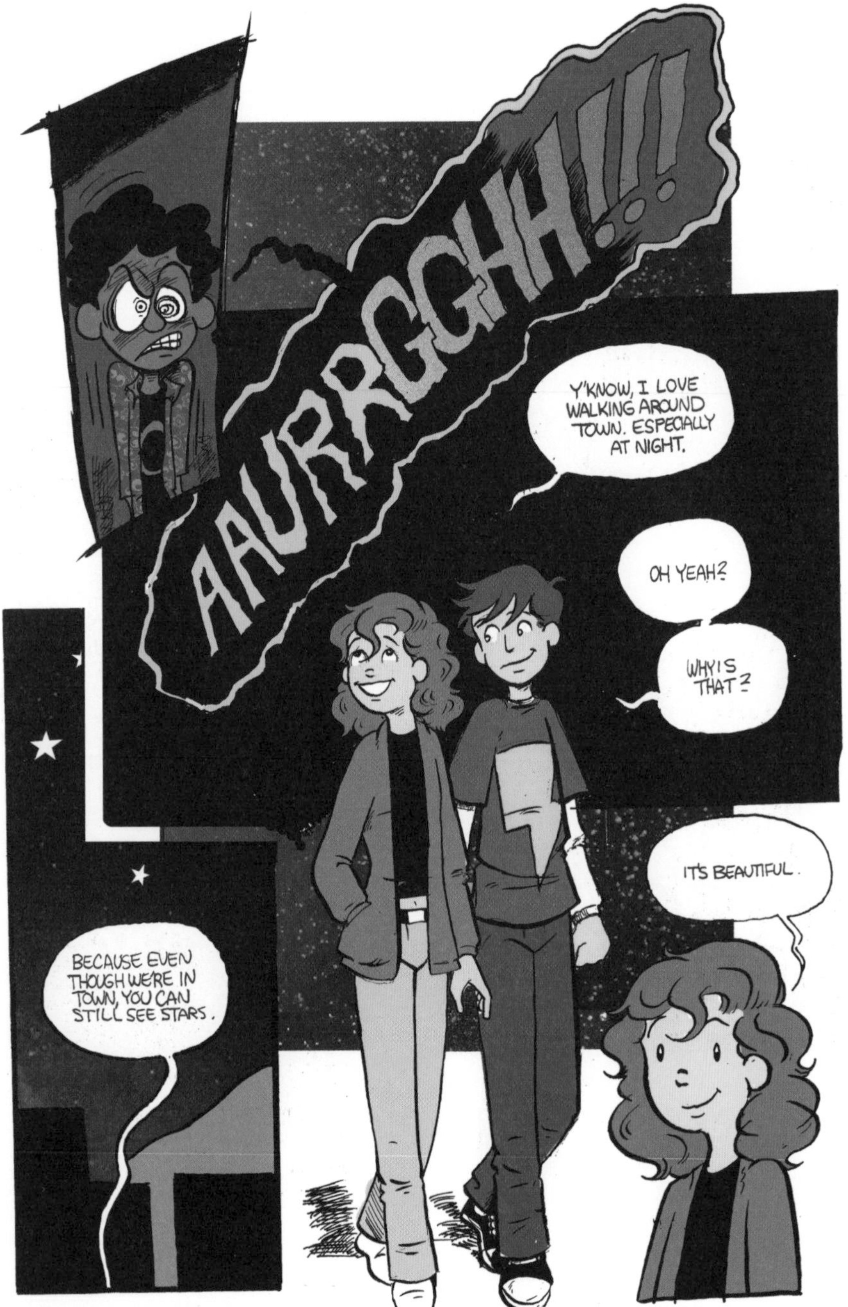
AAURRGGHH!!!!
Y'KNOW, I LOVE WALKING AROUND TOWN. ESPECIALLY AT NIGHT.
OH YEAH?
WHY IS THAT?
BECAUSE EVEN THOUGH WE'RE IN TOWN, YOU CAN STILL SEE STARS.
IT'S BEAUTIFUL.

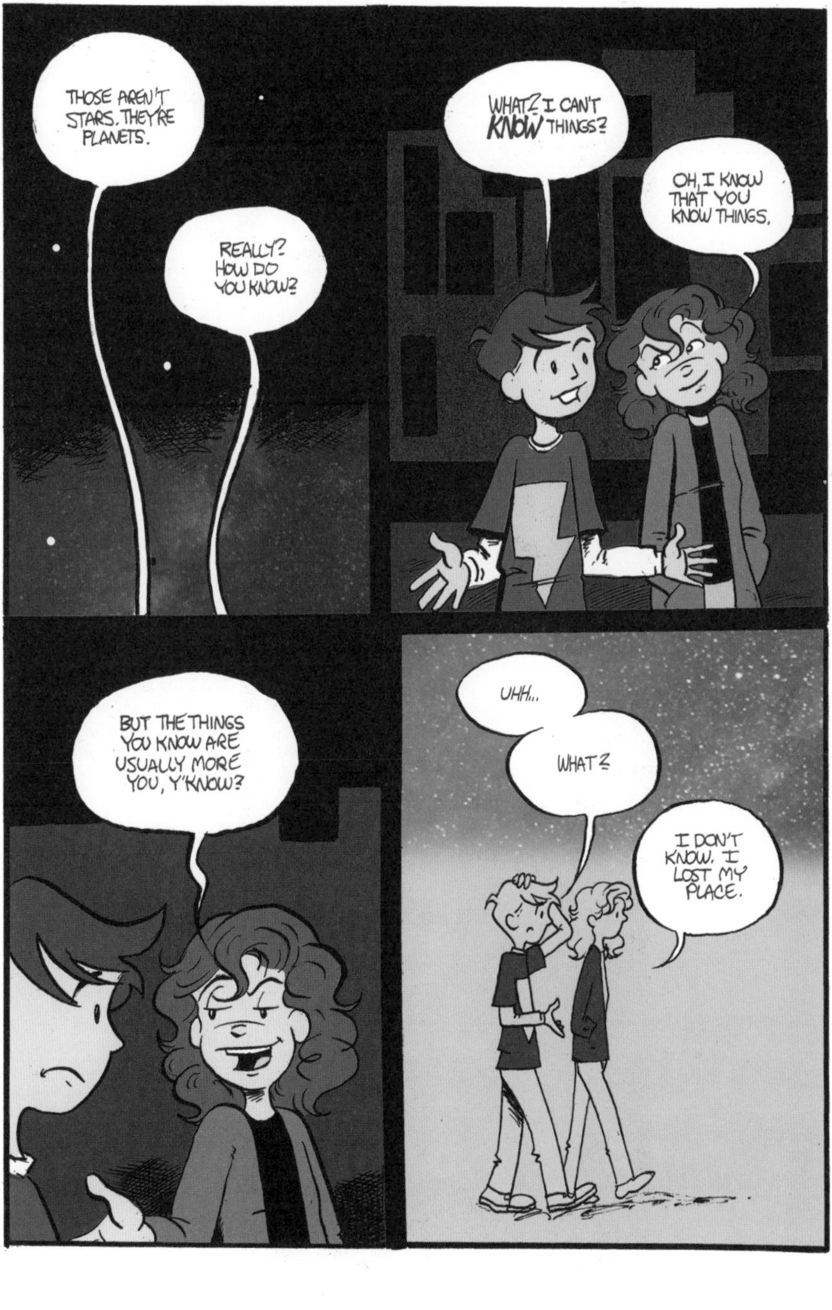
THOSE AREN'T STARS. THEY'RE PLANETS.
REALLY? HOW DO YOU KNOW?
WHAT? I CAN'T KNOW THINGS?
OH, I KNOW THAT YOU KNOW THINGS.
BUT THE THINGS YOU KNOW ARE USUALLY MORE YOU, Y'KNOW?
UHH...
WHAT?
I DON'T KNOW. I LOST MY PLACE.

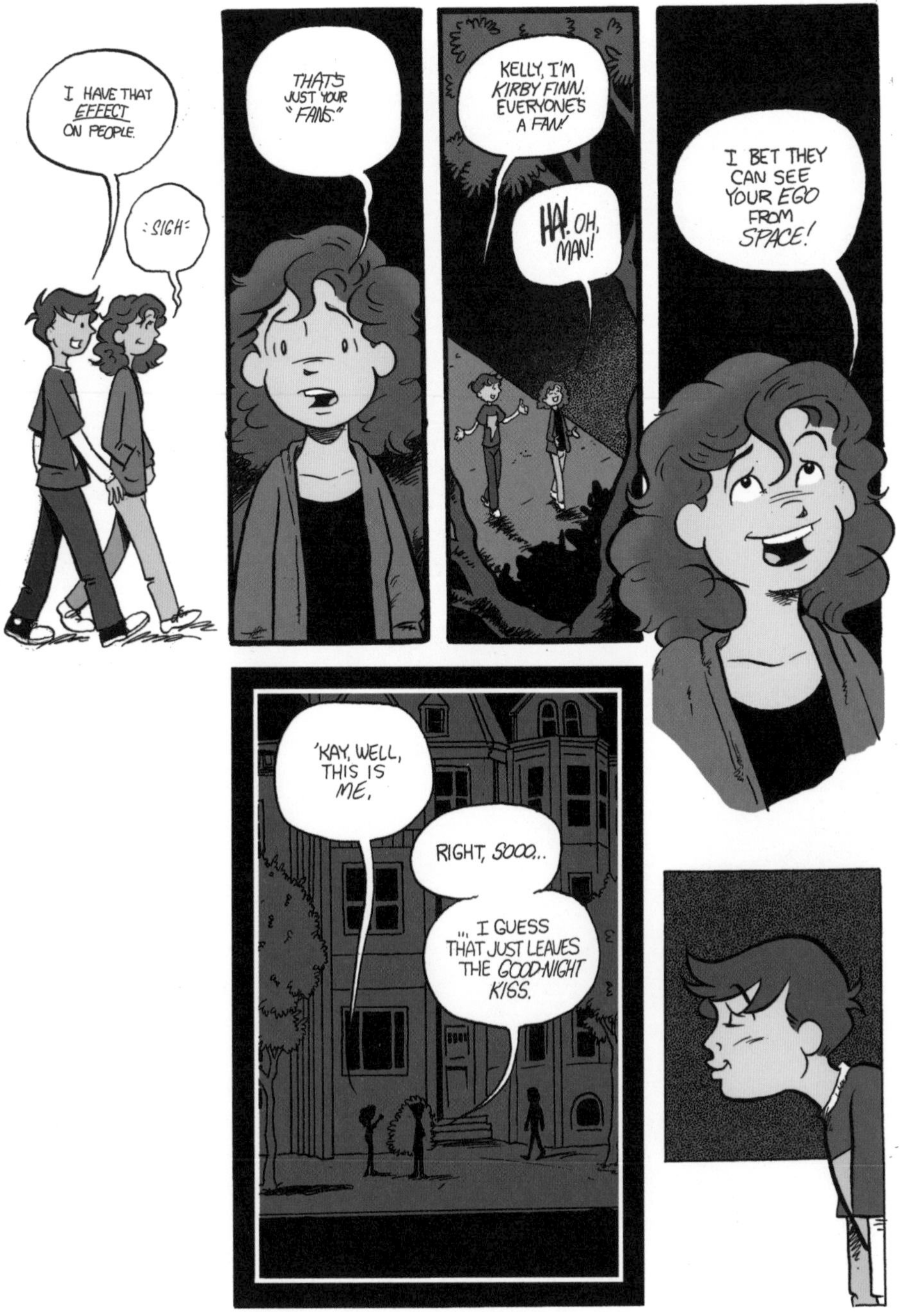
I HAVE THAT EFFECT ON PEOPLE.
:SIGH:
THAT'S JUST YOUR "FANS."
KELLY, I'M KIRBY FINN. EVERYONE'S A FAN!
HA! OH, MAN!
I BET THEY CAN SEE YOUR EGO FROM SPACE!
'KAY, WELL, THIS IS ME.
RIGHT, SOOO...
... I GUESS THAT JUST LEAVES THE GOOD-NIGHT KISS.

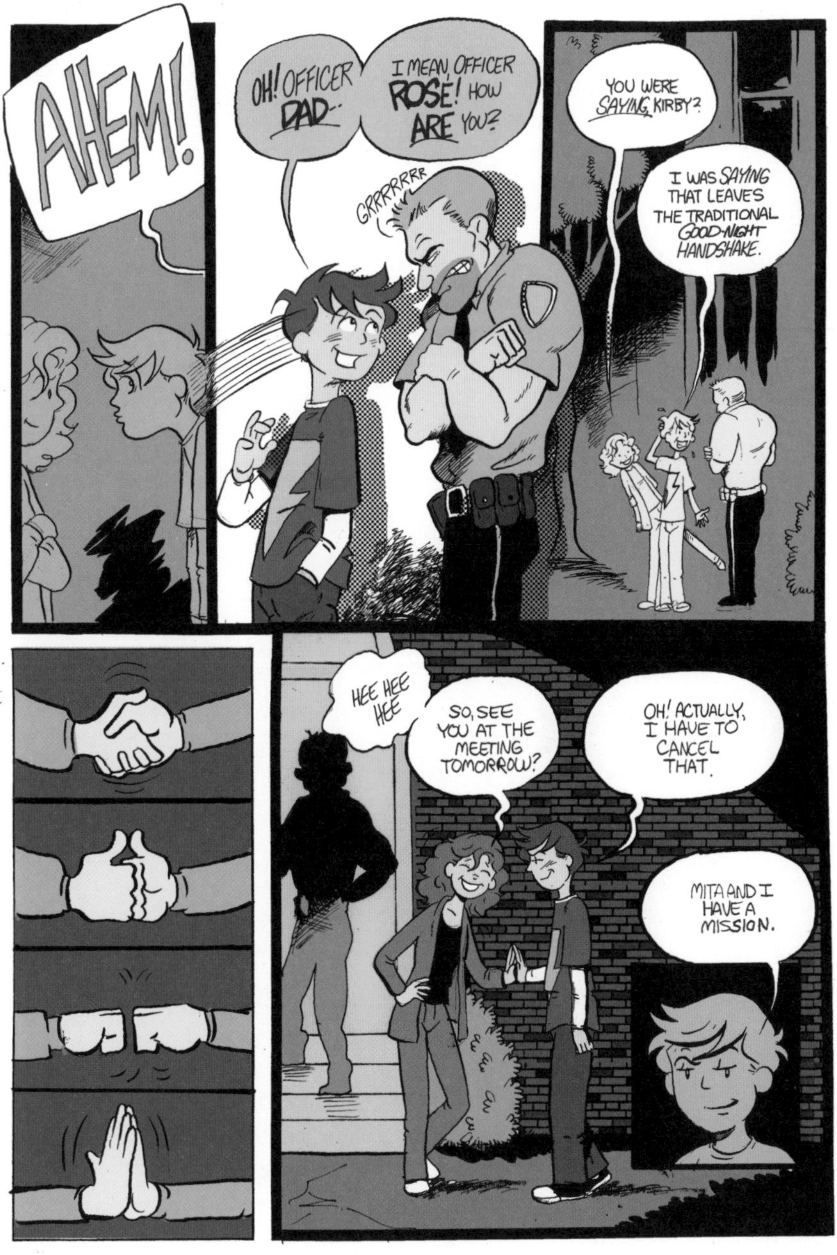
AHEM!
OH! OFFICER DAD--
I MEAN, OFFICER ROSE! HOW ARE YOU?
GRRRRRRR
YOU WERE SAYING, KIRBY?
I WAS SAYING THAT LEAVES THE TRADITIONAL GOOD-NIGHT HANDSHAKE.
HEE HEE HEE
SO, SEE YOU AT THE MEETING TOMORROW?
OH! ACTUALLY, I HAVE TO CANCEL THAT.
MITA AND I HAVE A MISSION.

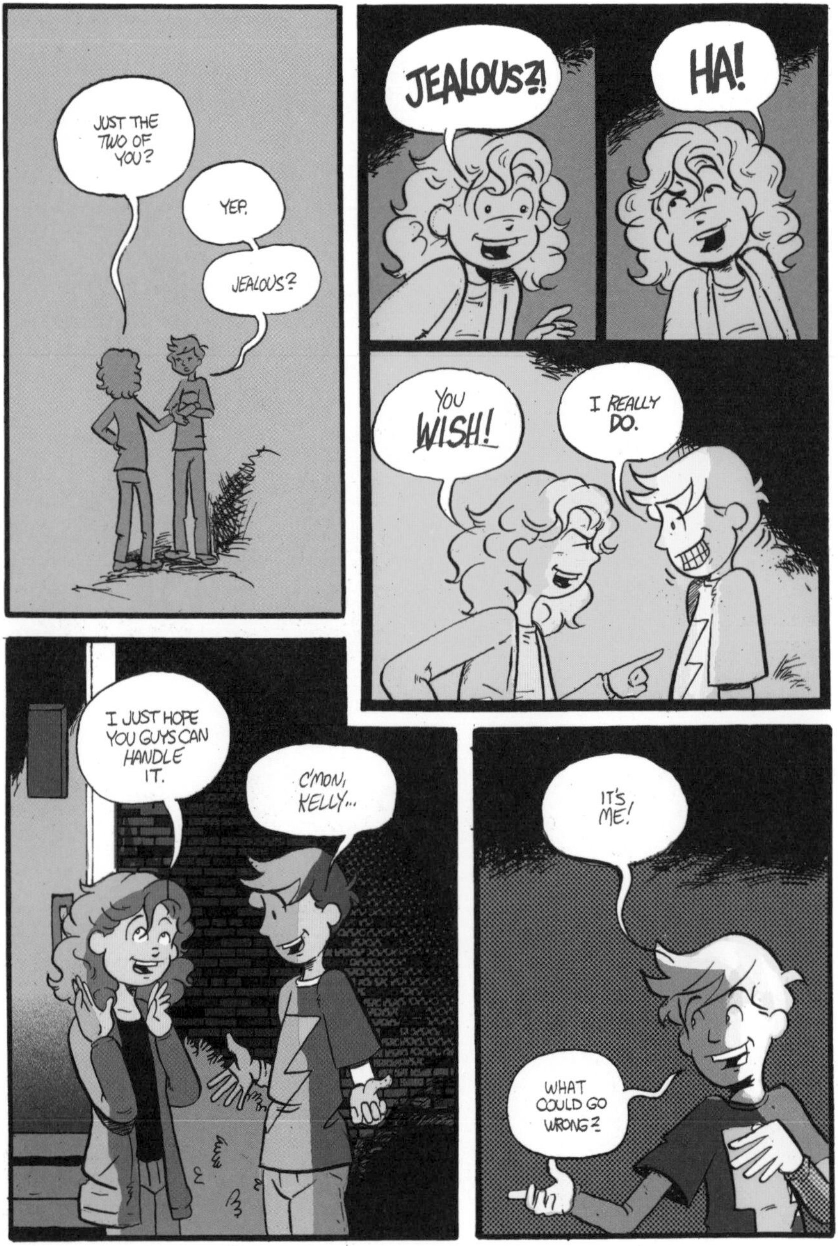
JUST THE TWO OF YOU?
YEP.
JEALOUS?
JEALOUS?!
HA!
YOU WISH!
I REALLY DO.
I JUST HOPE YOU GUYS CAN HANDLE IT.
C'MON, KELLY...
IT'S ME!
WHAT COULD GO WRONG?

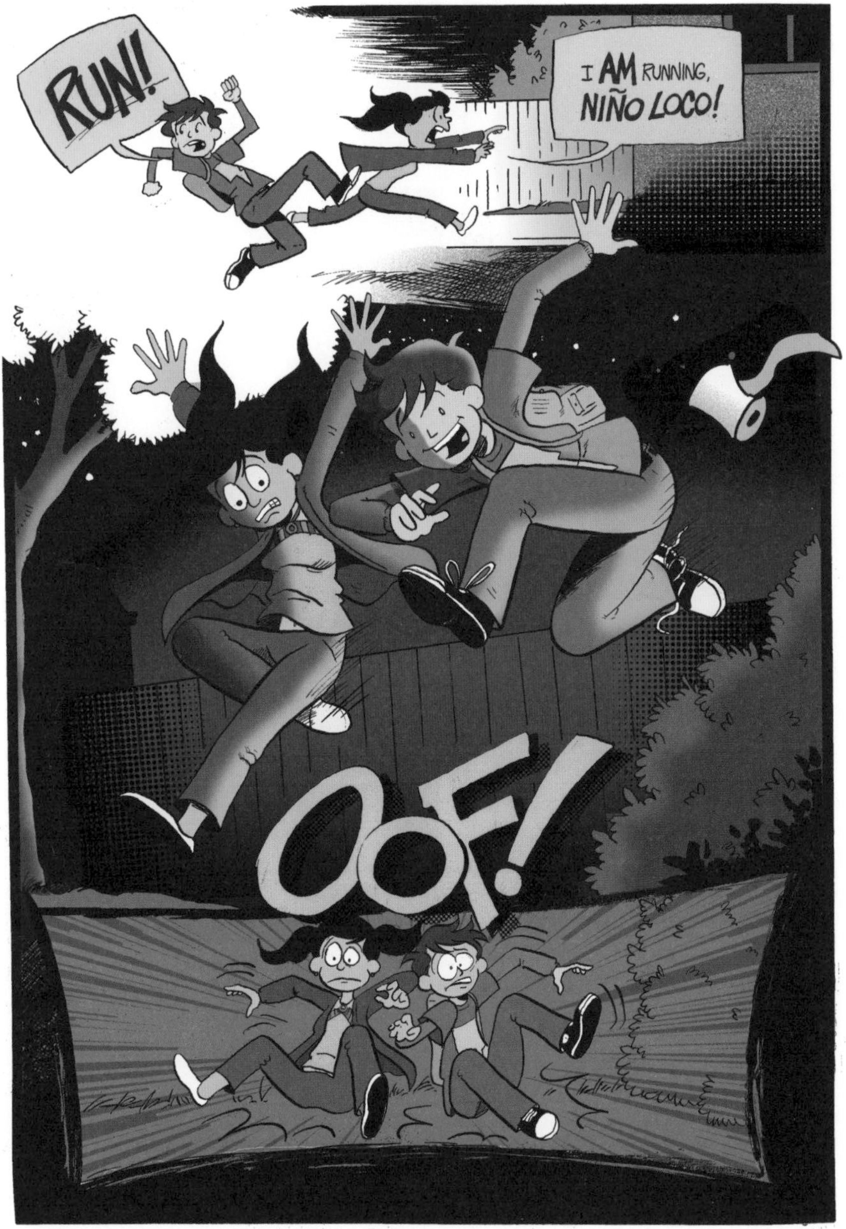
RUN!
I AM RUNNING, NIÑO LOCO!
OOF!

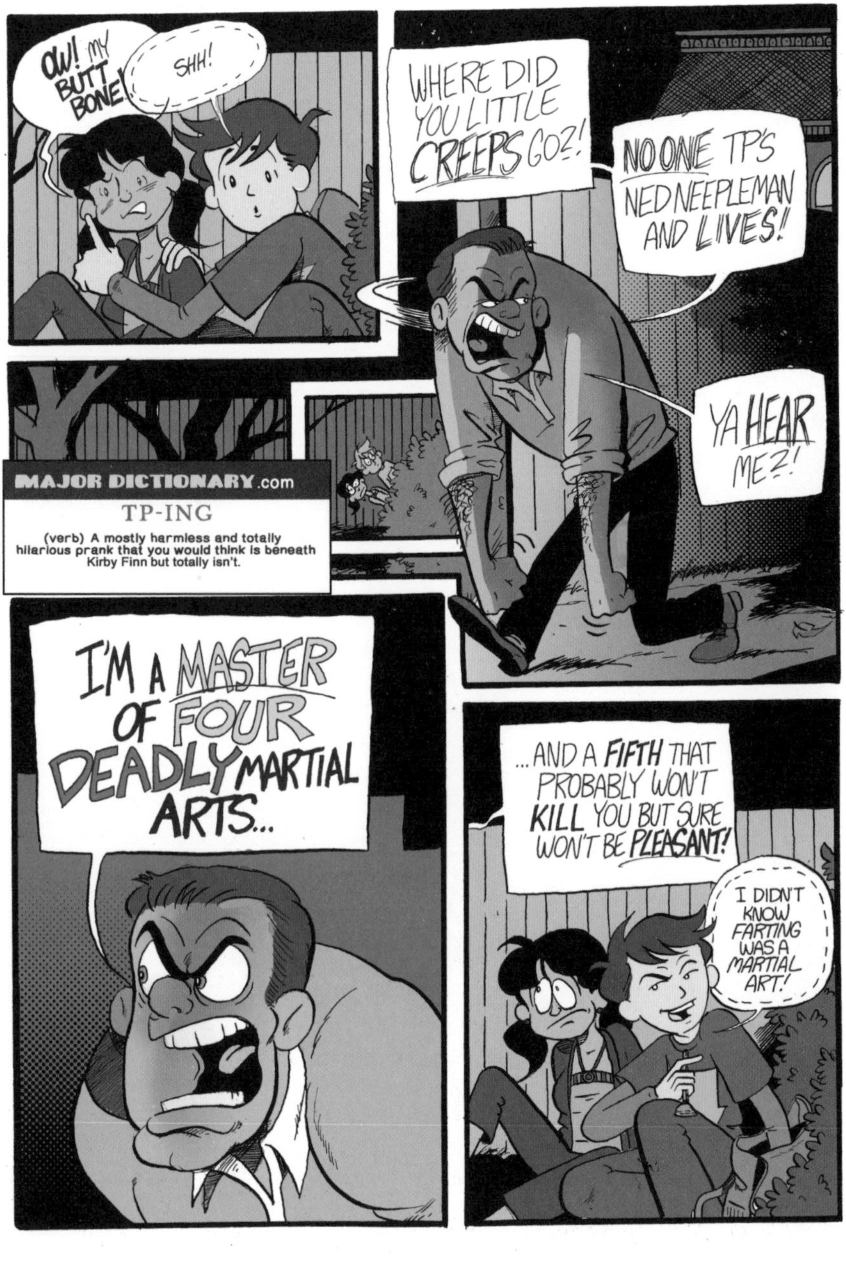
OW! MY BUTT BONE!
SHH!
WHERE DID YOU LITTLE CREEPS GO?!
NO ONE TP'S NED NEEPLEMAN AND LIVES!
YA HEAR ME?!
MAJOR DICTIONARY.com
TP-ING
(verb) A mostly harmless and totally hilarious prank that you would think is beneath Kirby Finn but totally isn't.
I'M A MASTER OF FOUR DEADLY MARTIAL ARTS...
...AND A FIFTH THAT PROBABLY WON'T KILL YOU BUT SURE WON'T BE PLEASANT!
I DIDN'T KNOW FARTING WAS A MARTIAL ART!

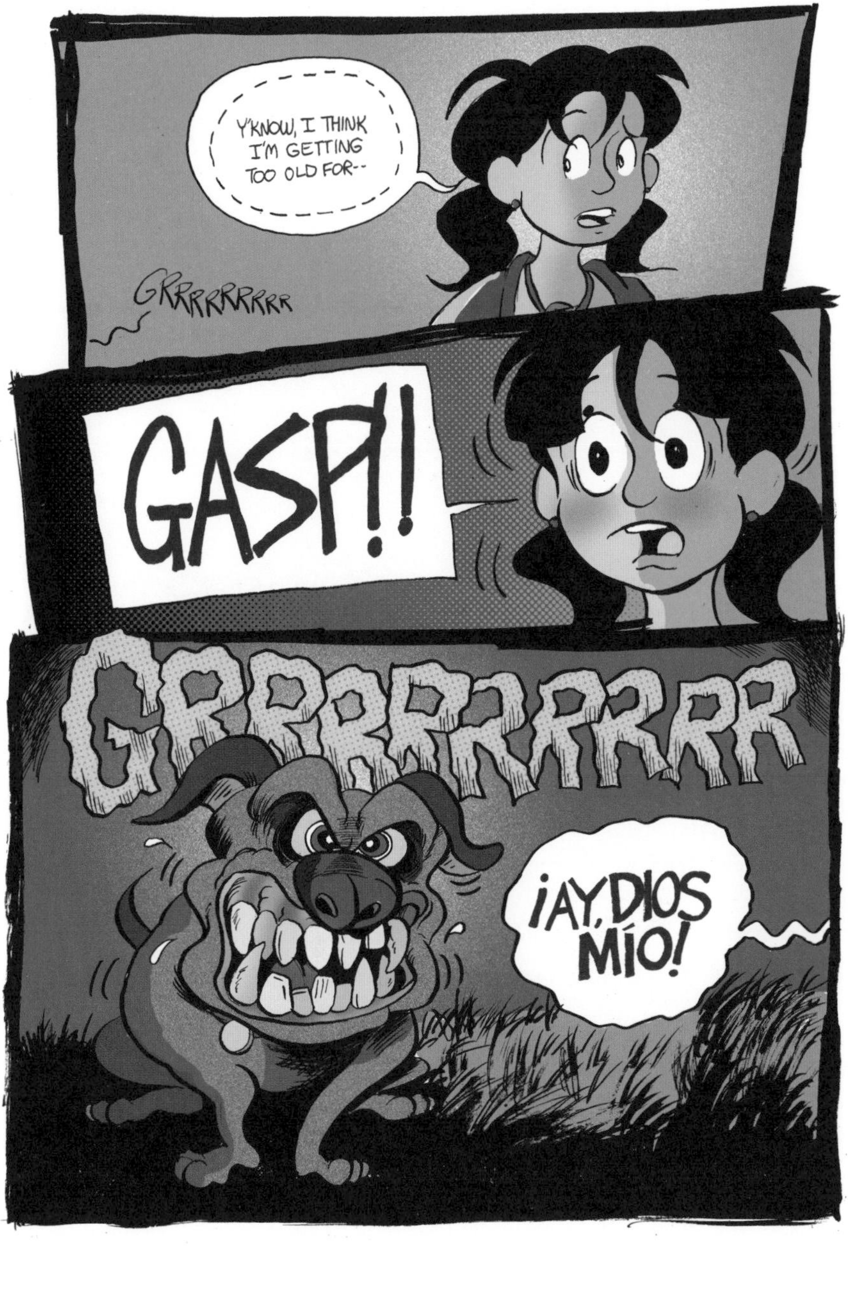
Y'KNOW, I THINK I'M GETTING TOO OLD FOR--
GRRRRRRRRR
GASP!!
GRRRRRRRRRR
¡AY, DIOS MÍO!

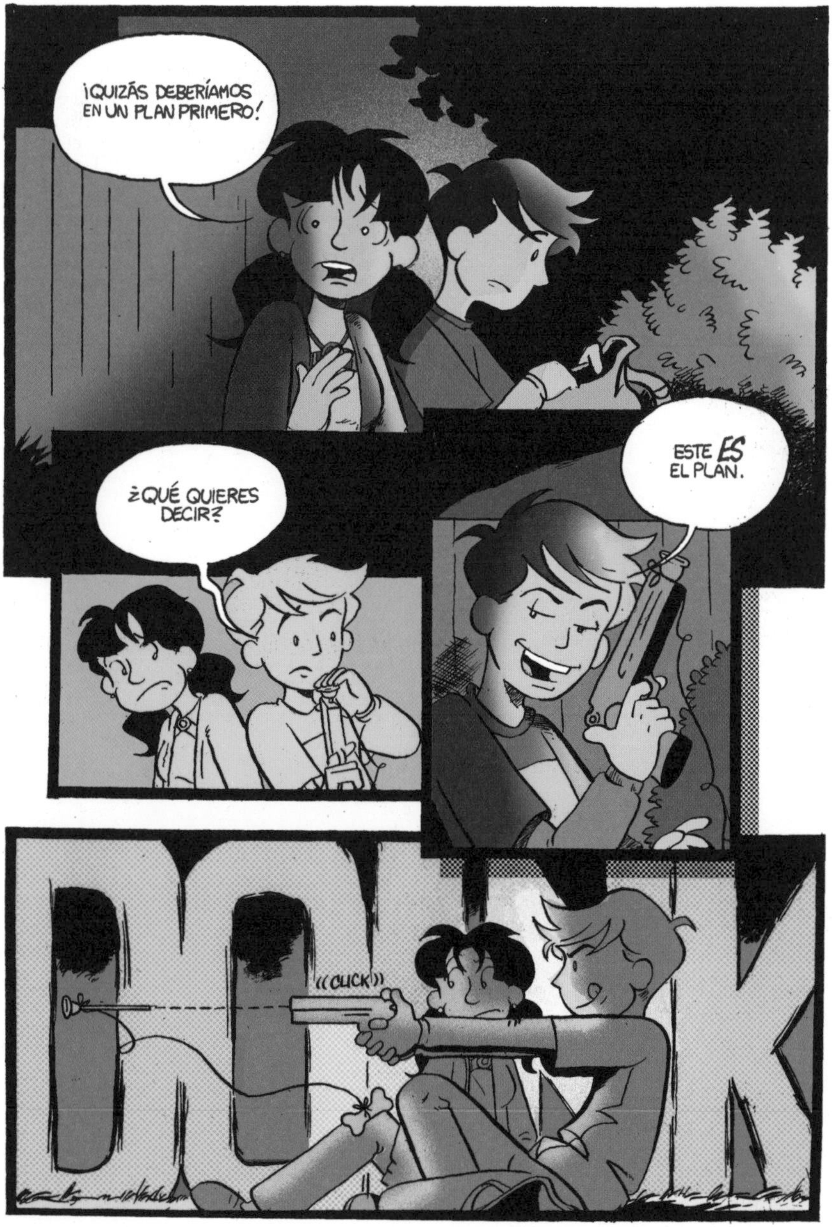
¡QUIZÁS DEBERÍAMOS EN UN PLAN PRIMERO!
¿QUÉ QUIERES DECIR?
ESTE ES EL PLAN.
DONK
((CLICK))

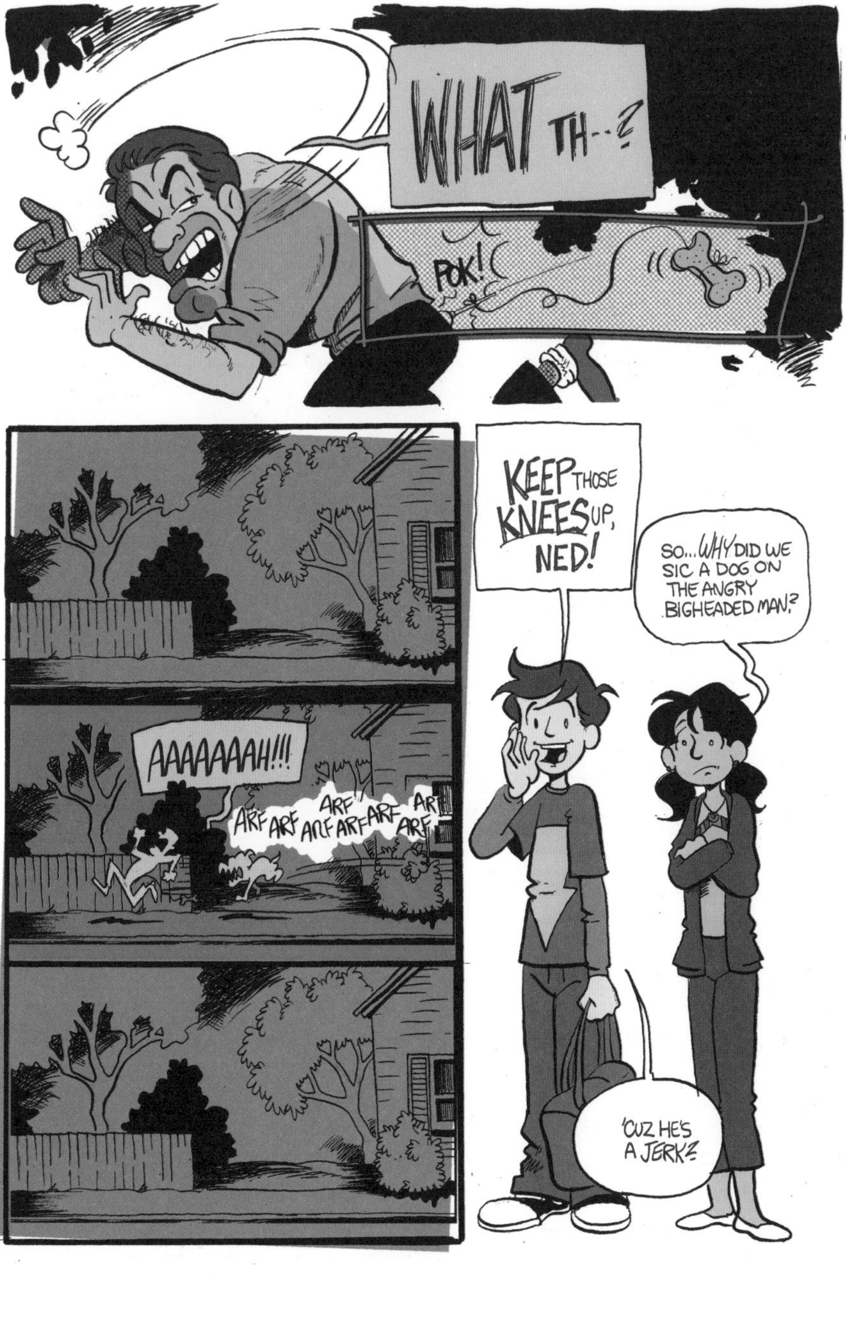
POK!
WHAT TH--?
AAAAAAAH!!!
ARF ARF ARF ARF ARF ARF ARF ARF ARF
KEEP THOSE KNEES UP, NED!
SO... WHY DID WE SIC A DOG ON THE ANGRY BIGHEADED MAN?
'CUZ HE'S A JERK.

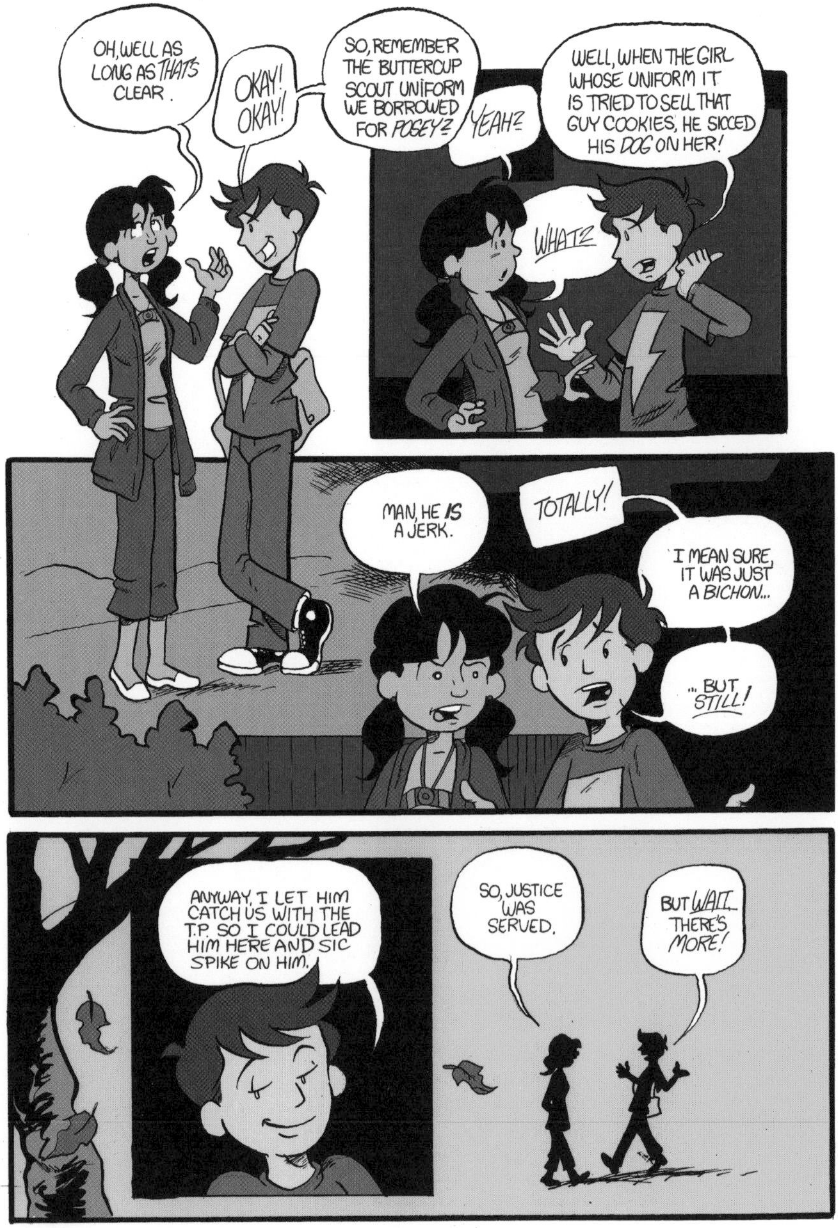
OH, WELL AS LONG AS THAT'S CLEAR.
OKAY! OKAY!
SO, REMEMBER THE BUTTERCUP SCOUT UNIFORM WE BORROWED FOR POSEY?
YEAH?
WELL, WHEN THE GIRL WHOSE UNIFORM IT IS TRIED TO SELL THAT GUY COOKIES, HE SICCED HIS DOG ON HER!
WHAT?
MAN, HE IS A JERK.
TOTALLY!
I MEAN SURE, IT WAS JUST A BICHON...
... BUT STILL!
ANYWAY, I LET HIM CATCH US WITH THE T.P. SO I COULD LEAD HIM HERE AND SIC SPIKE ON HIM.
SO, JUSTICE WAS SERVED.
BUT WAIT, THERE'S MORE!

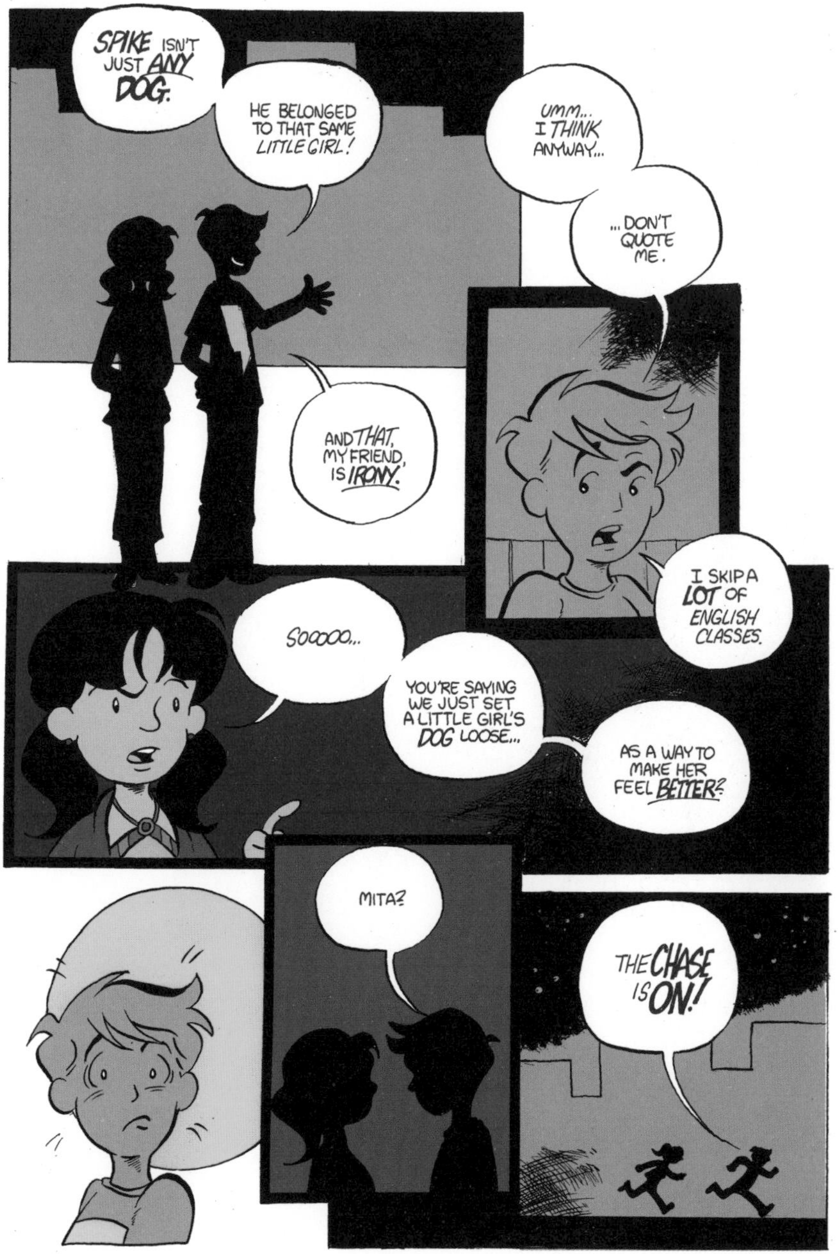
SPIKE ISN'T JUST ANY DOG.
HE BELONGED TO THAT SAME LITTLE GIRL!
AND THAT, MY FRIEND, IS IRONY.
UMM... I THINK ANYWAY...
...DON'T QUOTE ME.
I SKIP A LOT OF ENGLISH CLASSES.
SOOOOO...
YOU'RE SAYING WE JUST SET A LITTLE GIRL'S DOG LOOSE...
AS A WAY TO MAKE HER FEEL BETTER?
MITA?
THE CHASE IS ON!

HA! HA! HA! I DO NOT!
OH, YOU SOOOOOOO DO!
I DO NOT RUN LIKE A FRIGHTENED DUCK!!
OUCH!
OH NO?
'CUZ THIS IS YOU...
"...DUH! WAIT UP, KIRBY! QUACK! QUACK!"
SO?
THIS IS YOU...
"DUH! UH DUH! THE CHASE IS DUH!"
GOD, YOU'RE A WEIRDO.
WELL, AT LEAST WE GOT THE DOG BACK.
?
Y'KNOW, THE PHONE WILL DING IF KELLY TEXTS.

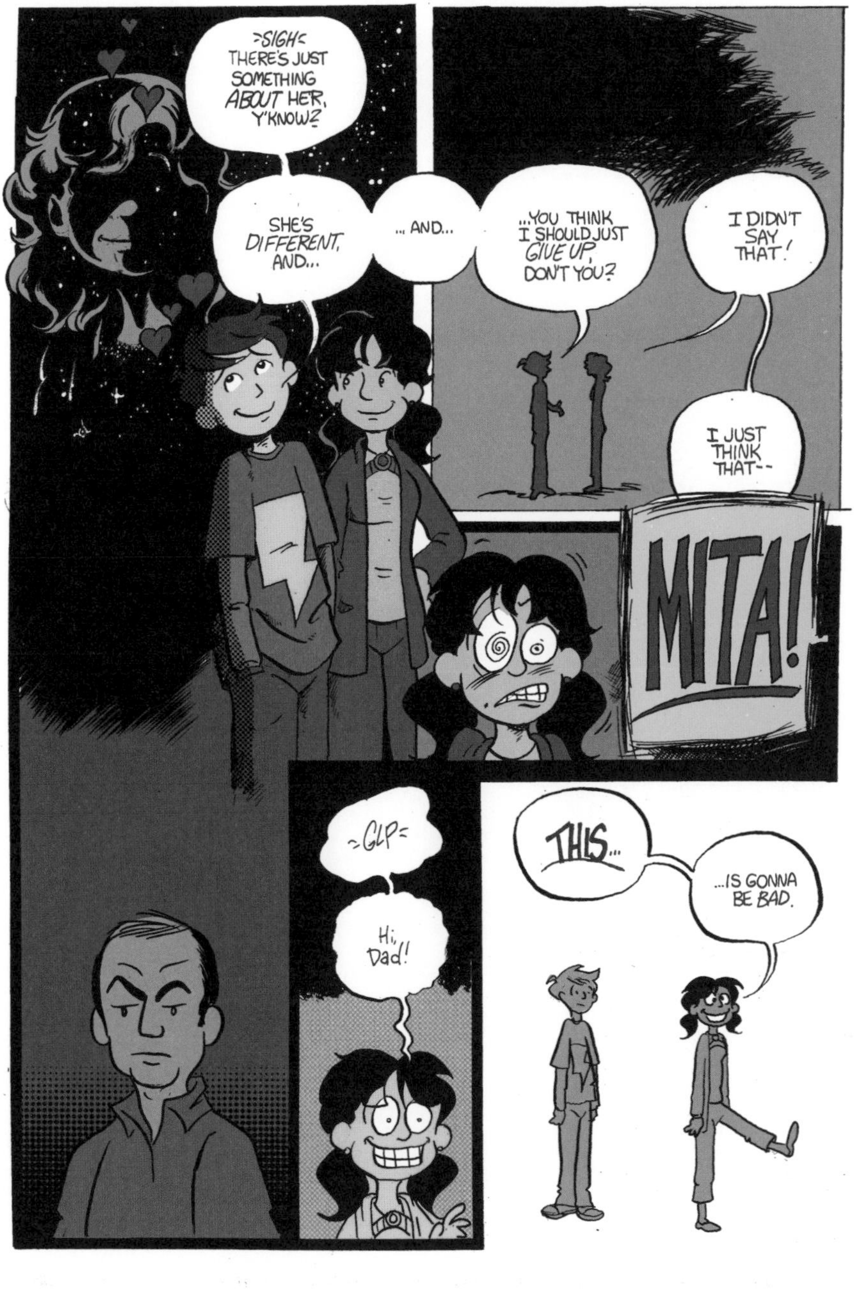
>SIGH< THERE'S JUST SOMETHING ABOUT HER, Y'KNOW?
SHE'S DIFFERENT, AND...
... AND...
...YOU THINK I SHOULD JUST GIVE UP, DON'T YOU?
I DIDN'T SAY THAT!
I JUST THINK THAT--
MITA!
=GLP=
Hi, Dad!
THIS...
...IS GONNA BE BAD.

REASON FIVE: THE BUCK STOPS

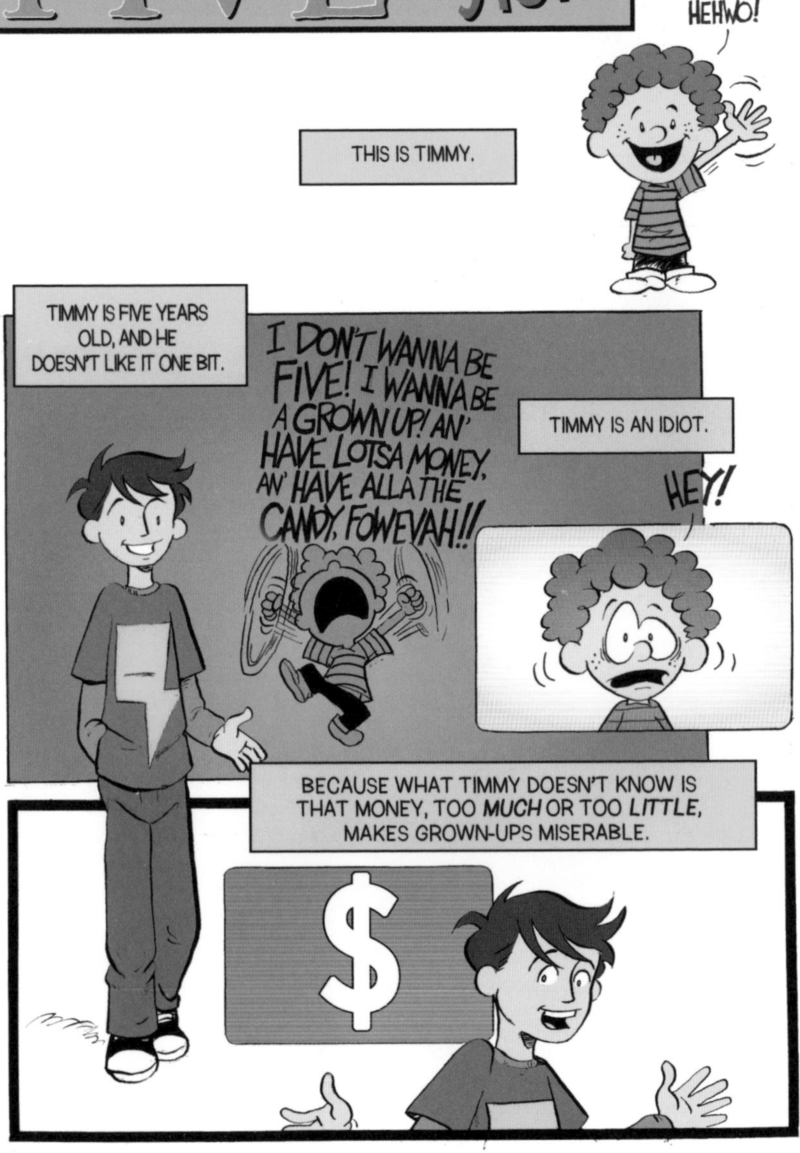
HEHWO!
THIS IS TIMMY.
TIMMY IS FIVE YEARS OLD, AND HE DOESN'T LIKE IT ONE BIT.
I DON'T WANNA BE FIVE! I WANNA BE A GROWN UP! AN' HAVE LOTSA MONEY, AN' HAVE ALLA THE CANDY, FOWEVAH!!
TIMMY IS AN IDIOT.
HEY!
BECAUSE WHAT TIMMY DOESN'T KNOW IS THAT MONEY, TOO *MUCH* OR TOO *LITTLE*, MAKES GROWN-UPS MISERABLE.
$

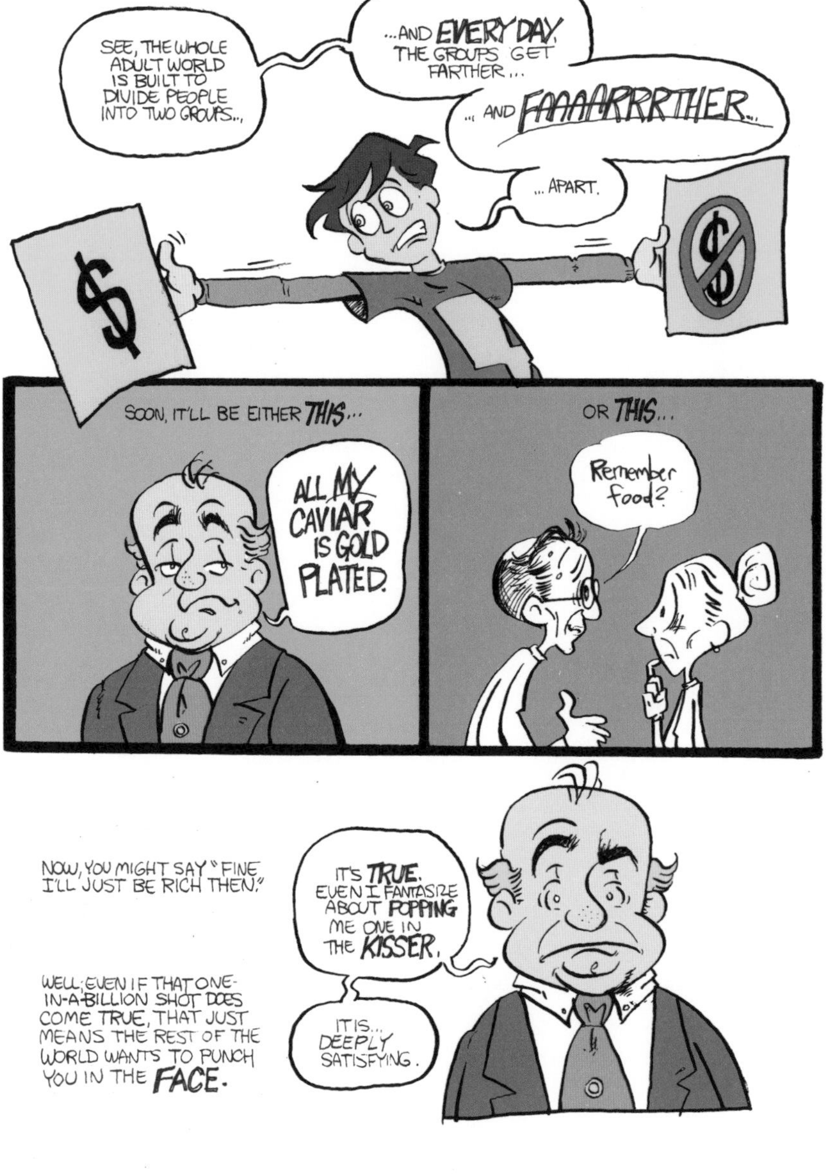
SEE, THE WHOLE ADULT WORLD IS BUILT TO DIVIDE PEOPLE INTO TWO GROUPS...
...AND EVERY DAY, THE GROUPS GET FARTHER...
... AND FAAAARRRTHER...
... APART.
SOON, IT'LL BE EITHER THIS...
ALL MY CAVIAR IS GOLD PLATED.
OR THIS...
Remember food?
NOW, YOU MIGHT SAY "FINE. I'LL JUST BE RICH THEN."
IT'S TRUE. EVEN I FANTASIZE ABOUT POPPING ME ONE IN THE KISSER.
IT IS... DEEPLY SATISFYING.
WELL, EVEN IF THAT ONE-IN-A-BILLION SHOT DOES COME TRUE, THAT JUST MEANS THE REST OF THE WORLD WANTS TO PUNCH YOU IN THE FACE.

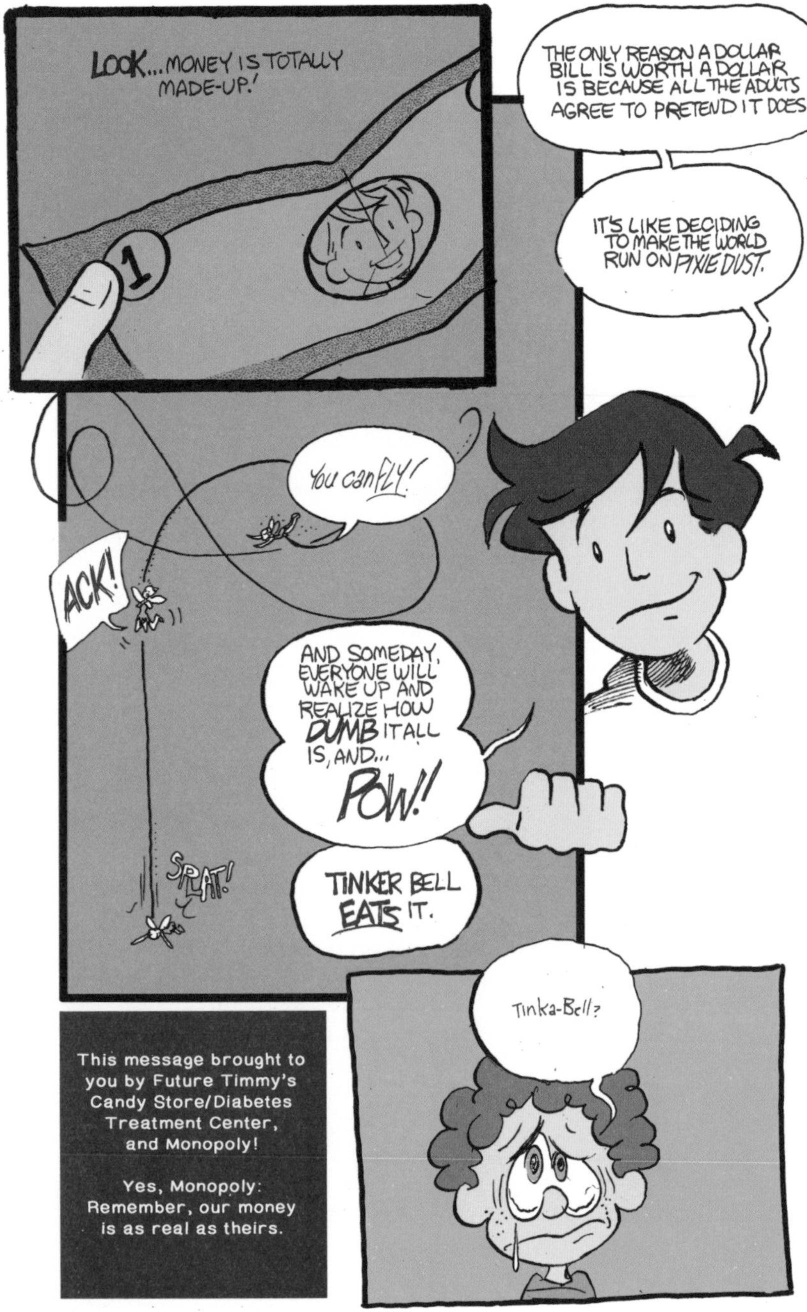
LOOK... MONEY IS TOTALLY MADE-UP!
THE ONLY REASON A DOLLAR BILL IS WORTH A DOLLAR IS BECAUSE ALL THE ADULTS AGREE TO PRETEND IT DOES.
IT'S LIKE DECIDING TO MAKE THE WORLD RUN ON PIXIE DUST.
You can FLY!
ACK!
AND SOMEDAY, EVERYONE WILL WAKE UP AND REALIZE HOW DUMB IT ALL IS, AND...
POW!!
SPLAT!
TINKER BELL EATS IT.
Tinka-Bell?
This message brought to you by Future Timmy's Candy Store/Diabetes Treatment Center, and Monopoly!
Yes, Monopoly: Remember, our money is as real as theirs.

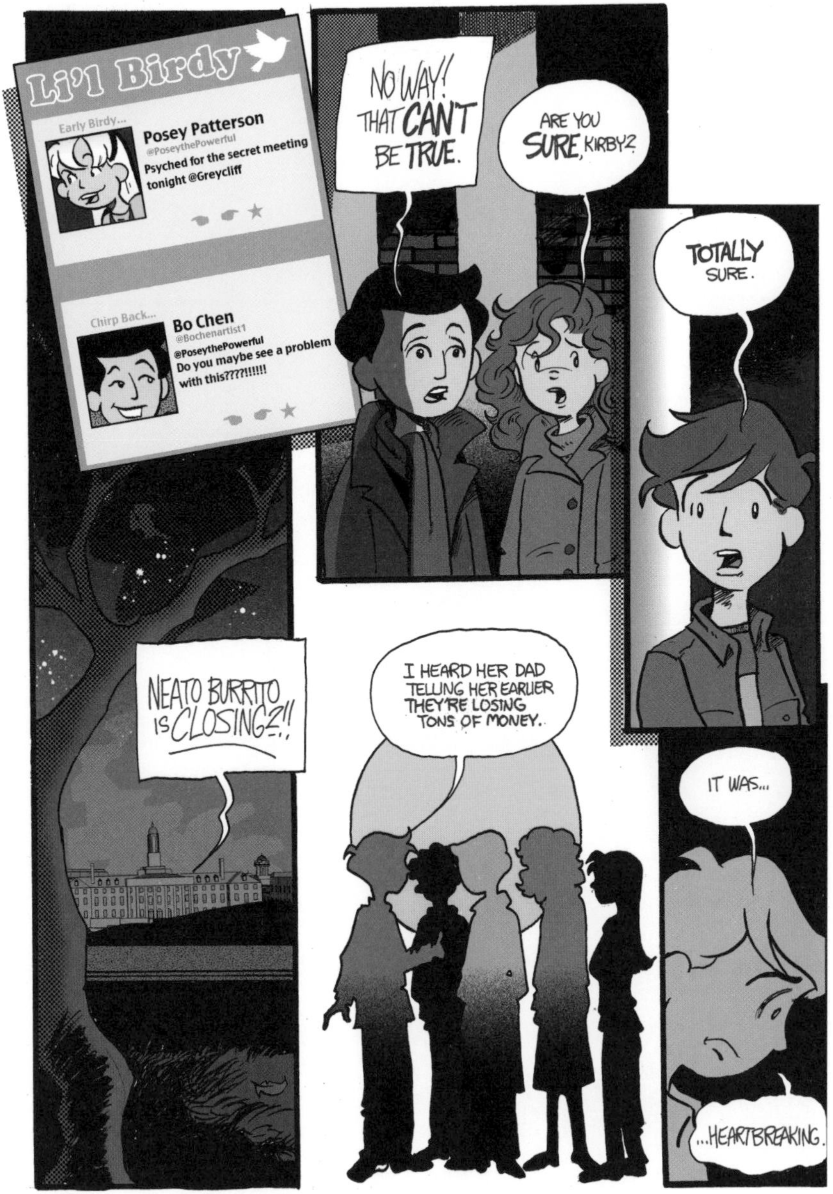
Li'l Birdy
Early Birdy...
Posey Patterson
@PoseythePowerful
Psyched for the secret meeting tonight @Greycliff
Chirp Back...
Bo Chen
@Bochenartist1
@PoseythePowerful
Do you maybe see a problem with this????!!!!!!
NO WAY! THAT CAN'T BE TRUE.
ARE YOU SURE, KIRBY?
TOTALLY SURE.
NEATO BURRITO IS CLOSING?!!
I HEARD HER DAD TELLING HER EARLIER THEY'RE LOSING TONS OF MONEY.
IT WAS...
...HEARTBREAKING.

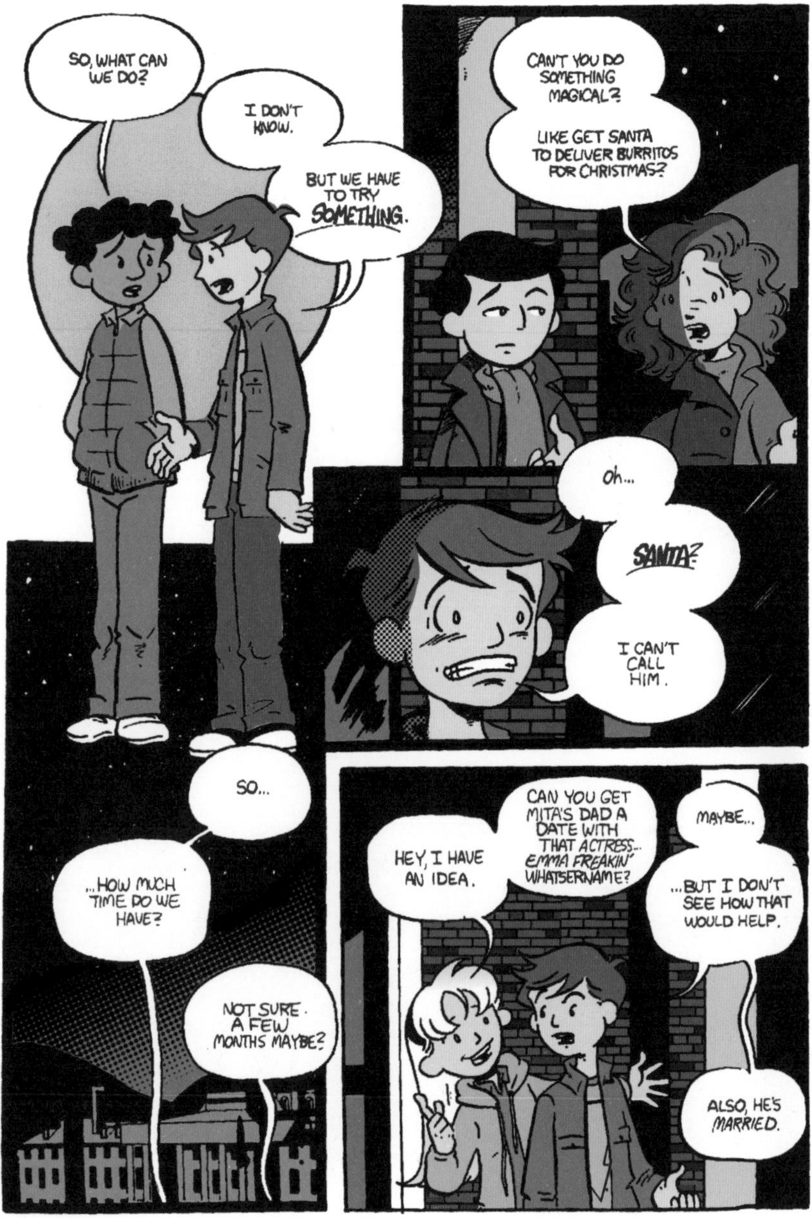
SO, WHAT CAN WE DO?
I DON'T KNOW.
BUT WE HAVE TO TRY SOMETHING.
CAN'T YOU DO SOMETHING MAGICAL?
LIKE GET SANTA TO DELIVER BURRITOS FOR CHRISTMAS?
oh...
SANTA?
I CAN'T CALL HIM.
SO...
...HOW MUCH TIME DO WE HAVE?
NOT SURE. A FEW MONTHS MAYBE?
HEY, I HAVE AN IDEA.
CAN YOU GET MITA'S DAD A DATE WITH THAT ACTRESS... EMMA FREAKIN' WHATSERNAME?
MAYBE...
...BUT I DON'T SEE HOW THAT WOULD HELP.
ALSO, HE'S MARRIED.

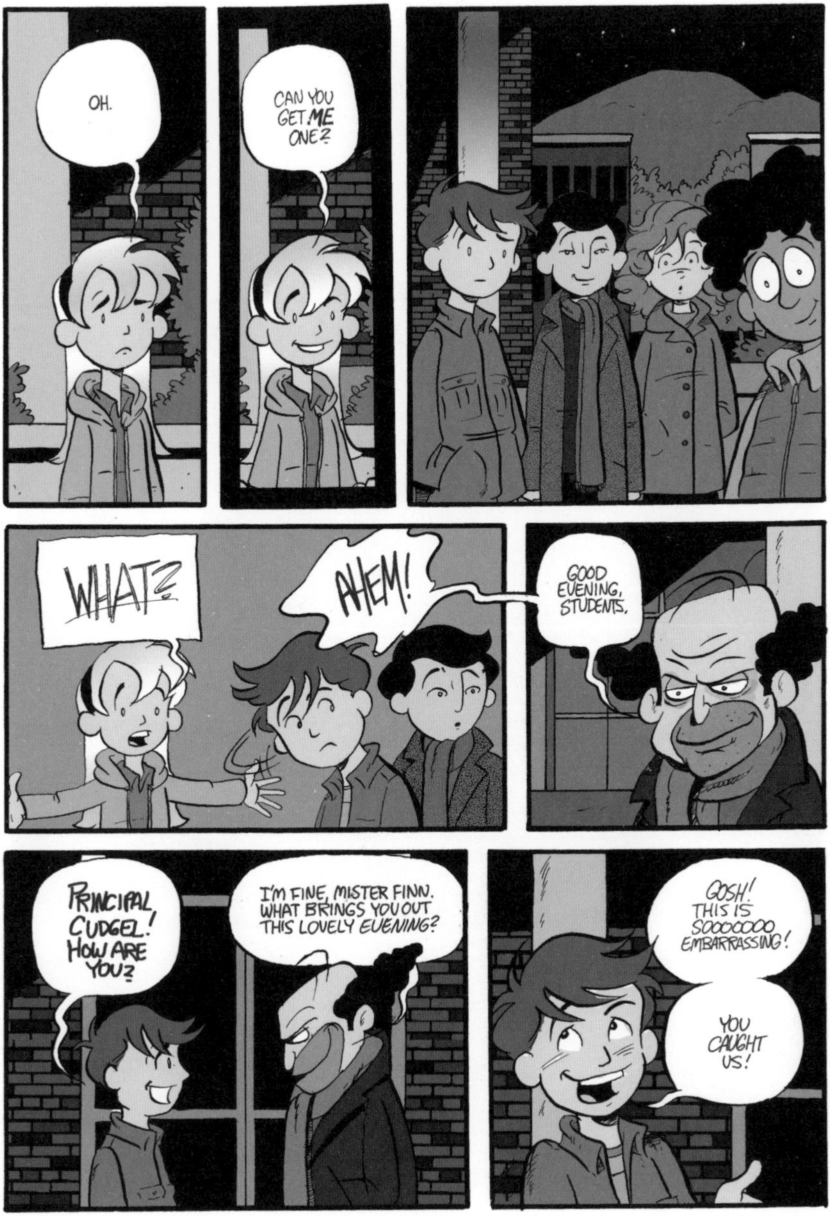
OH.
CAN YOU GET ME ONE?
WHAT?
AHEM!
GOOD EVENING, STUDENTS.
PRINCIPAL CUDGEL! HOW ARE YOU?
I'M FINE, MISTER FINN. WHAT BRINGS YOU OUT THIS LOVELY EVENING?
GOSH! THIS IS SOOOOOOO EMBARRASSING!
YOU CAUGHT US!

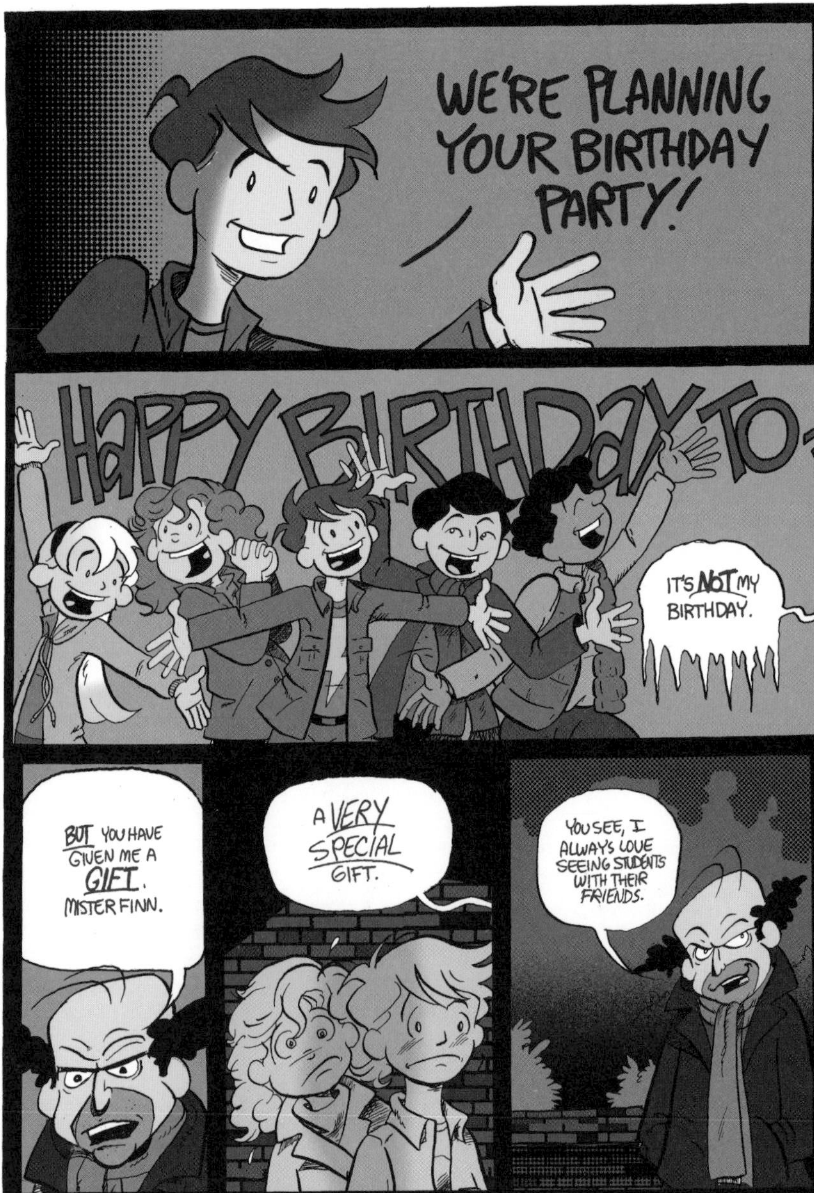
WE'RE PLANNING YOUR BIRTHDAY PARTY!
HAPPY BIRTHDAY TO-
IT'S NOT MY BIRTHDAY.
BUT YOU HAVE GIVEN ME A GIFT. MISTER FINN.
A VERY SPECIAL GIFT.
YOU SEE, I ALWAYS LOVE SEEING STUDENTS WITH THEIR FRIENDS.

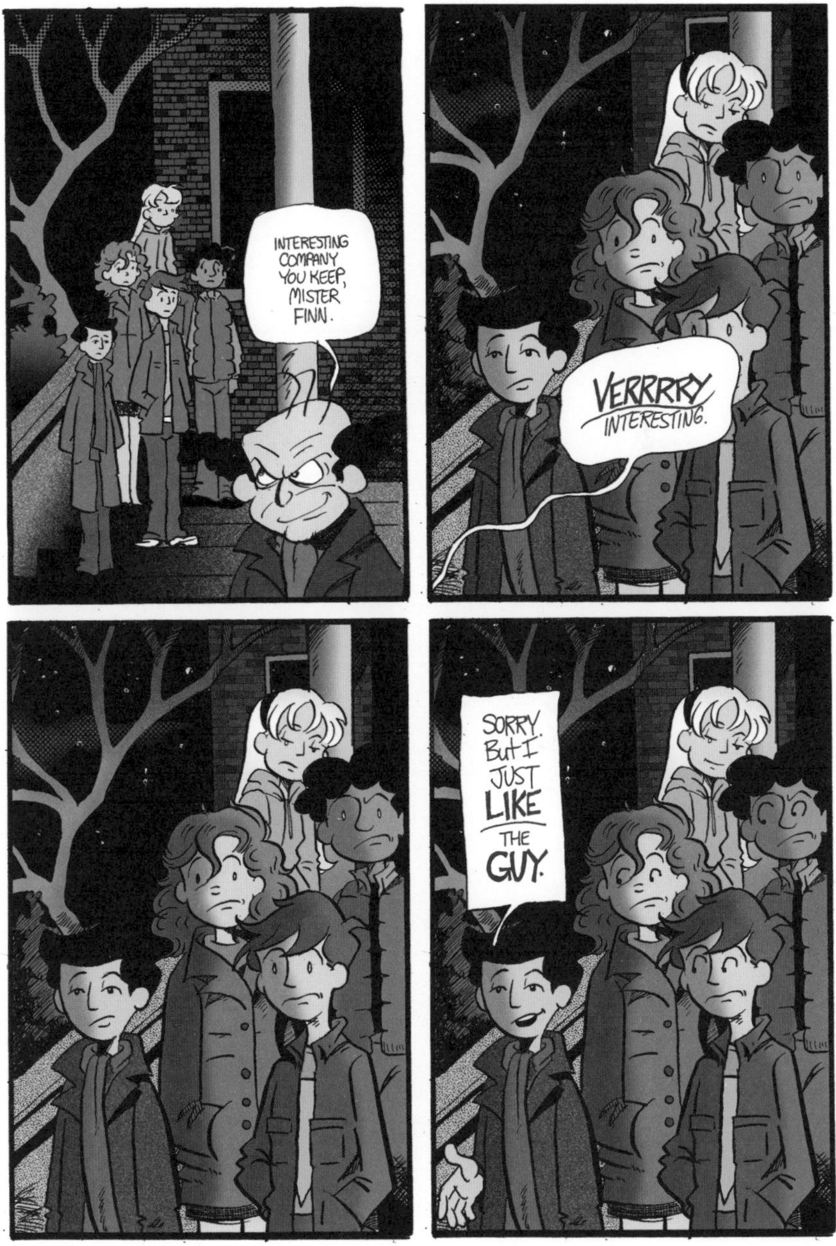
INTERESTING COMPANY YOU KEEP, MISTER FINN.
VERRRRY INTERESTING.
SORRY. But I JUST LIKE THE GUY.

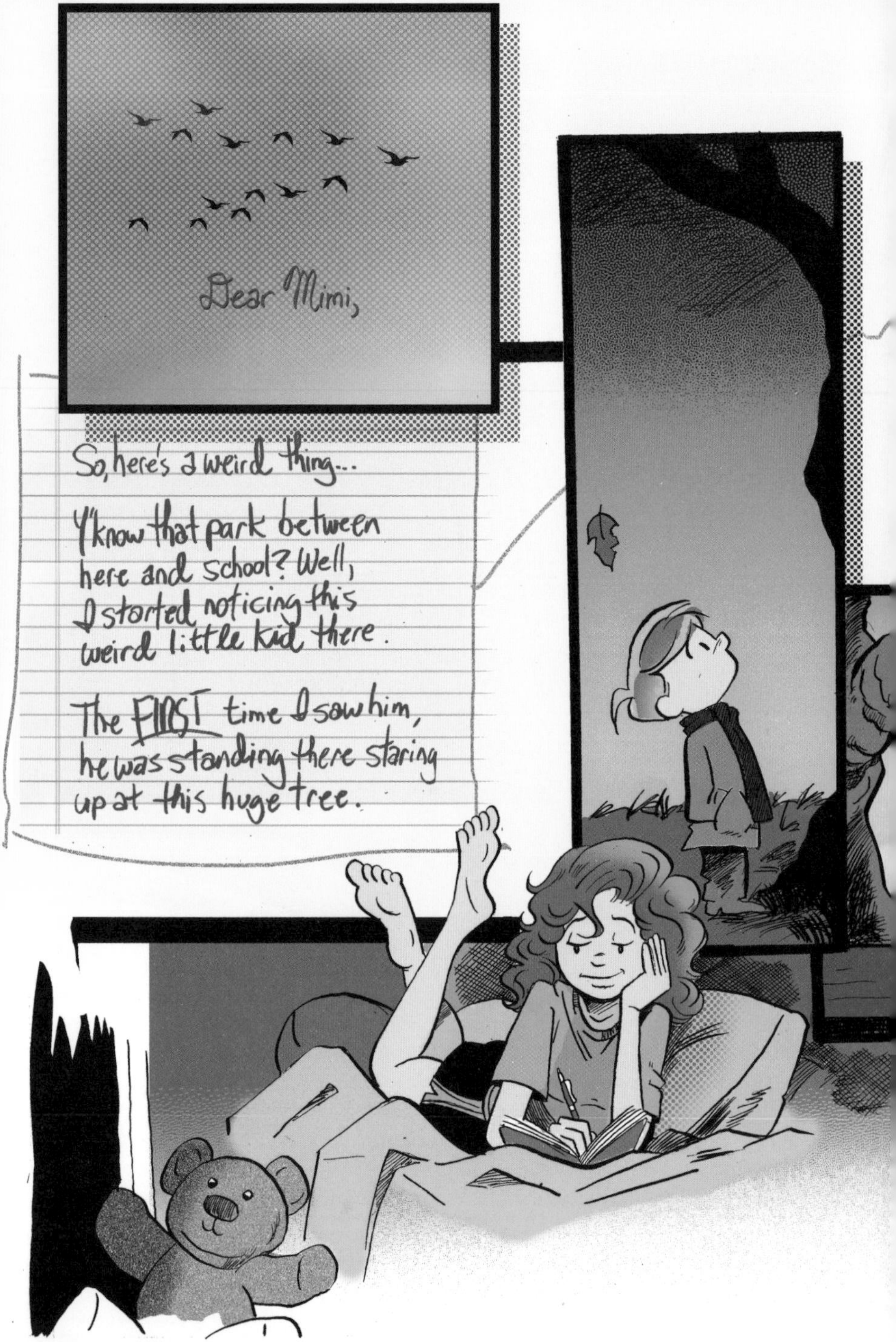
Dear Mimi,
So, here's a weird thing...
Y'know that park between here and school? Well, I started noticing this weird little kid there.
The FIRST time I saw him, he was standing there staring up at this huge tree.

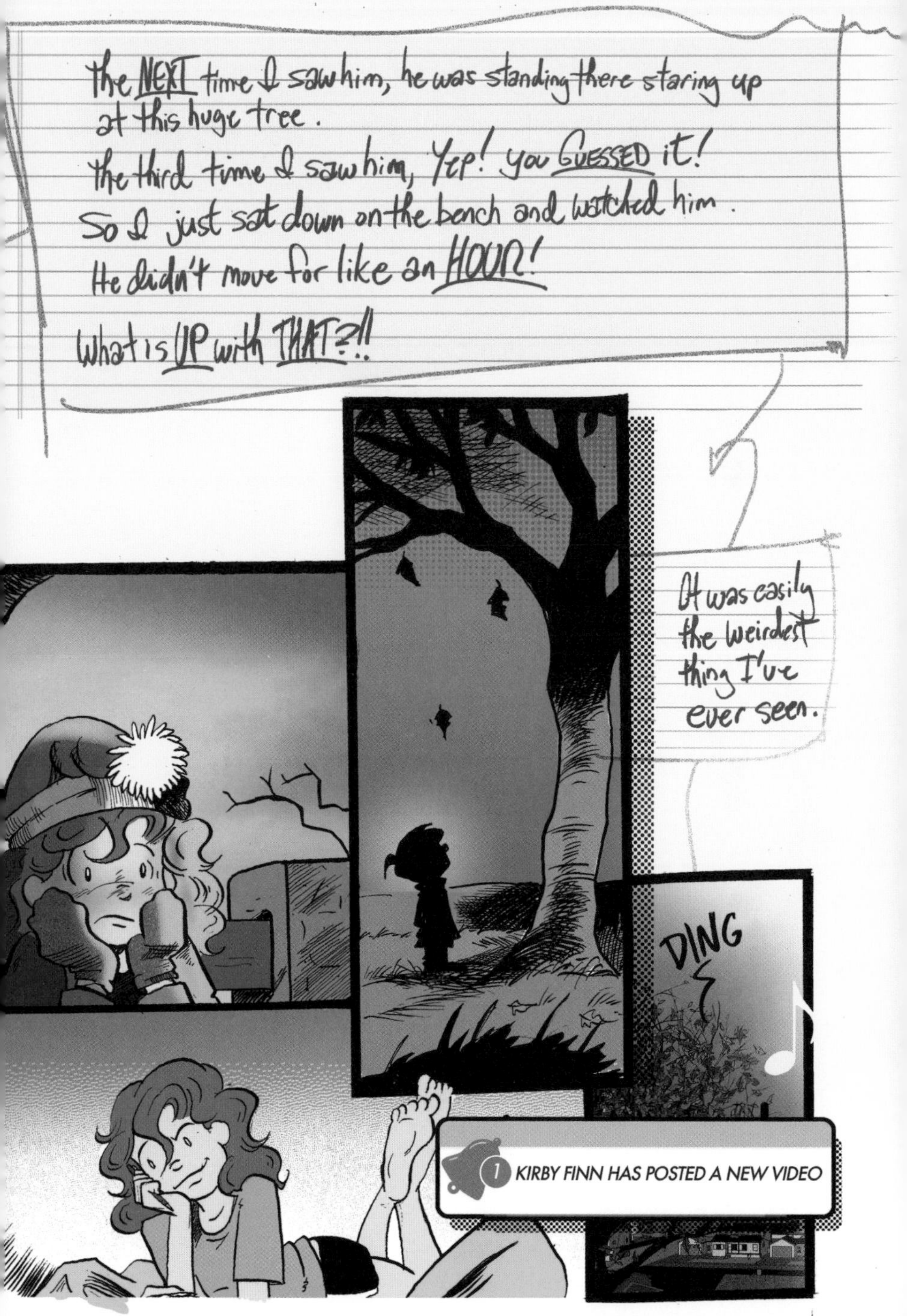
the NEXT time I saw him, he was standing there staring up at this huge tree.
the third time I saw him, Yep! you GUESSED it!
So I just sat down on the bench and watched him.
He didn't move for like an HOUR!
What is UP with THAT?!!
It was easily the weirdest thing I've ever seen.
DING
KIRBY FINN HAS POSTED A NEW VIDEO

REASON FOUR: IT ALL DEPENDS

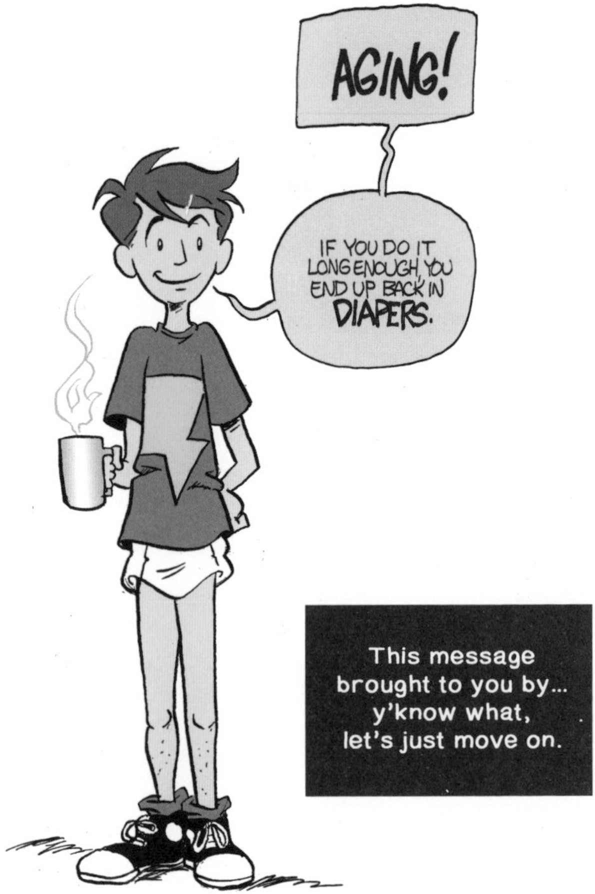
AGING!
IF YOU DO IT LONG ENOUGH, YOU END UP BACK IN DIAPERS.
This message brought to you by... y'know what, let's just move on.

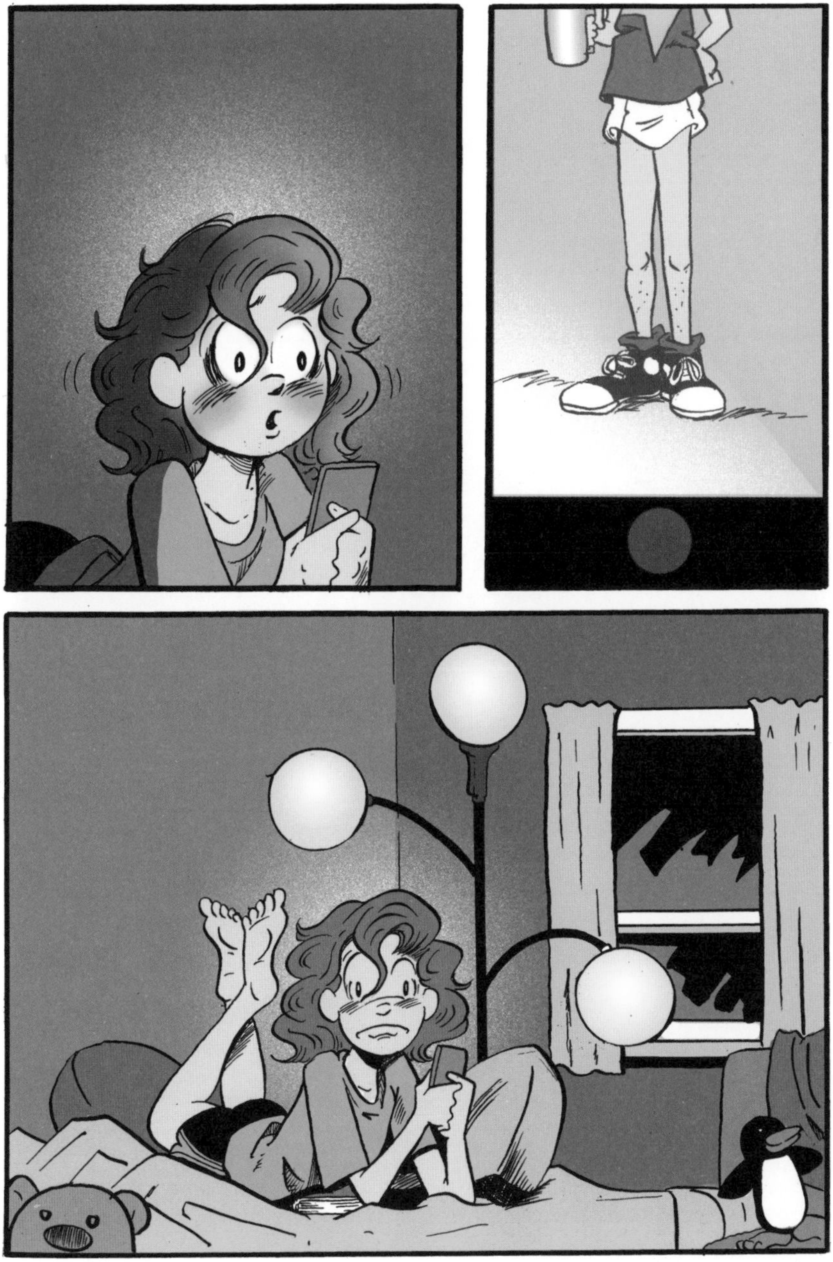

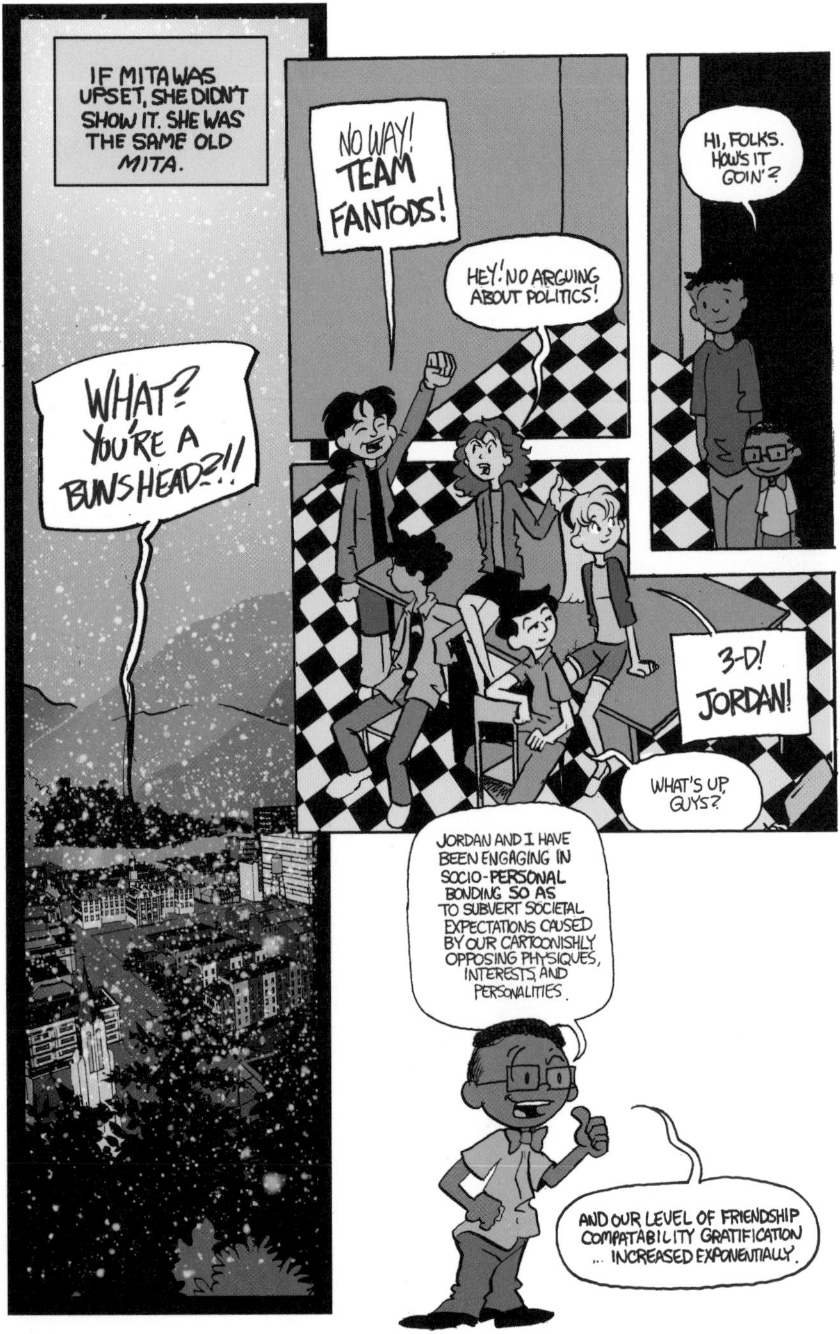
IF MITA WAS UPSET, SHE DIDN'T SHOW IT. SHE WAS THE SAME OLD MITA.
WHAT? YOU'RE A BUNSHEAD?!!
NO WAY! TEAM FANTODS!
HEY! NO ARGUING ABOUT POLITICS!
HI, FOLKS. HOW'S IT GOIN'?
3-D! JORDAN!
WHAT'S UP, GUYS?
JORDAN AND I HAVE BEEN ENGAGING IN SOCIO-PERSONAL BONDING SO AS TO SUBVERT SOCIETAL EXPECTATIONS CAUSED BY OUR CARTOONISHLY OPPOSING PHYSIQUES, INTERESTS, AND PERSONALITIES.
AND OUR LEVEL OF FRIENDSHIP COMPATABILITY GRATIFICATION ... INCREASED EXPONENTIALLY.

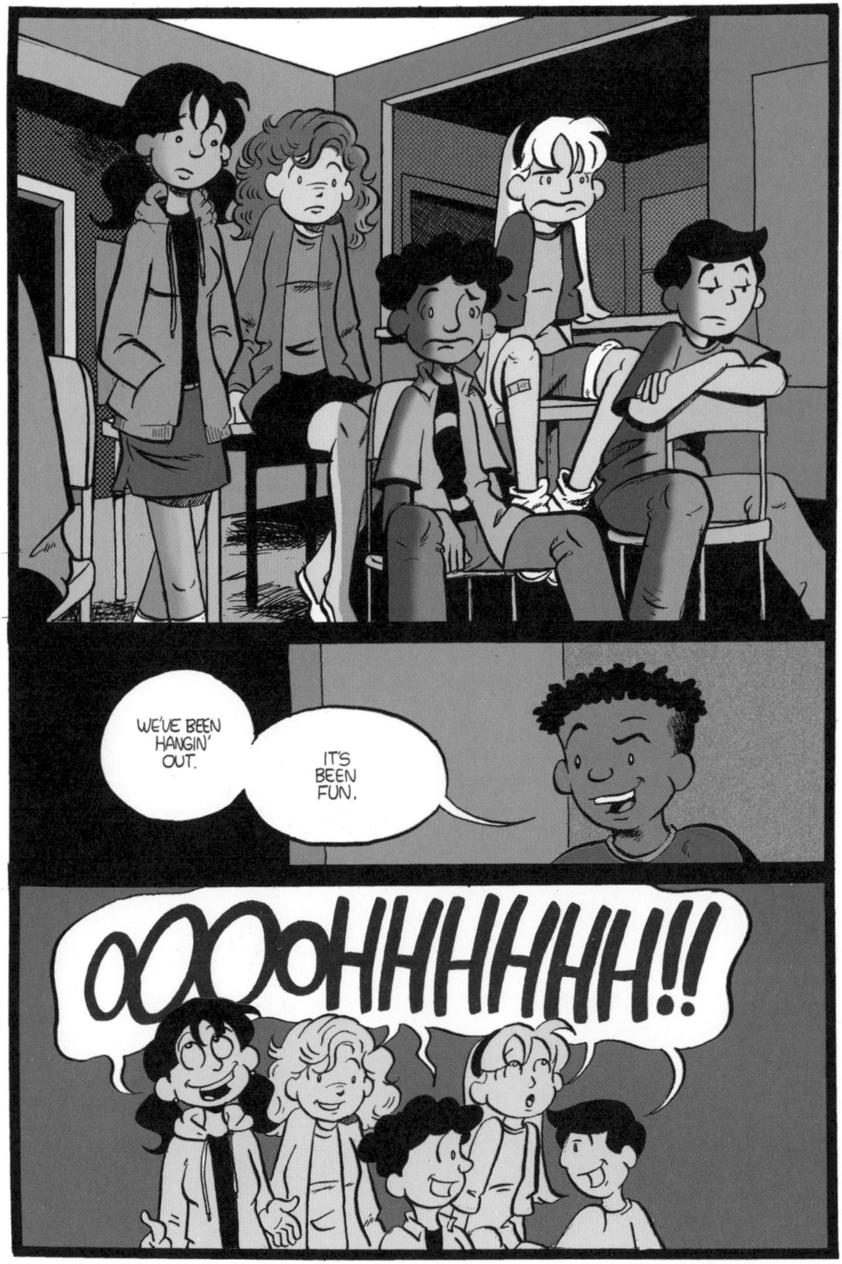
WE'VE BEEN HANGIN' OUT.
IT'S BEEN FUN.
OOOOHHHHHHH!!

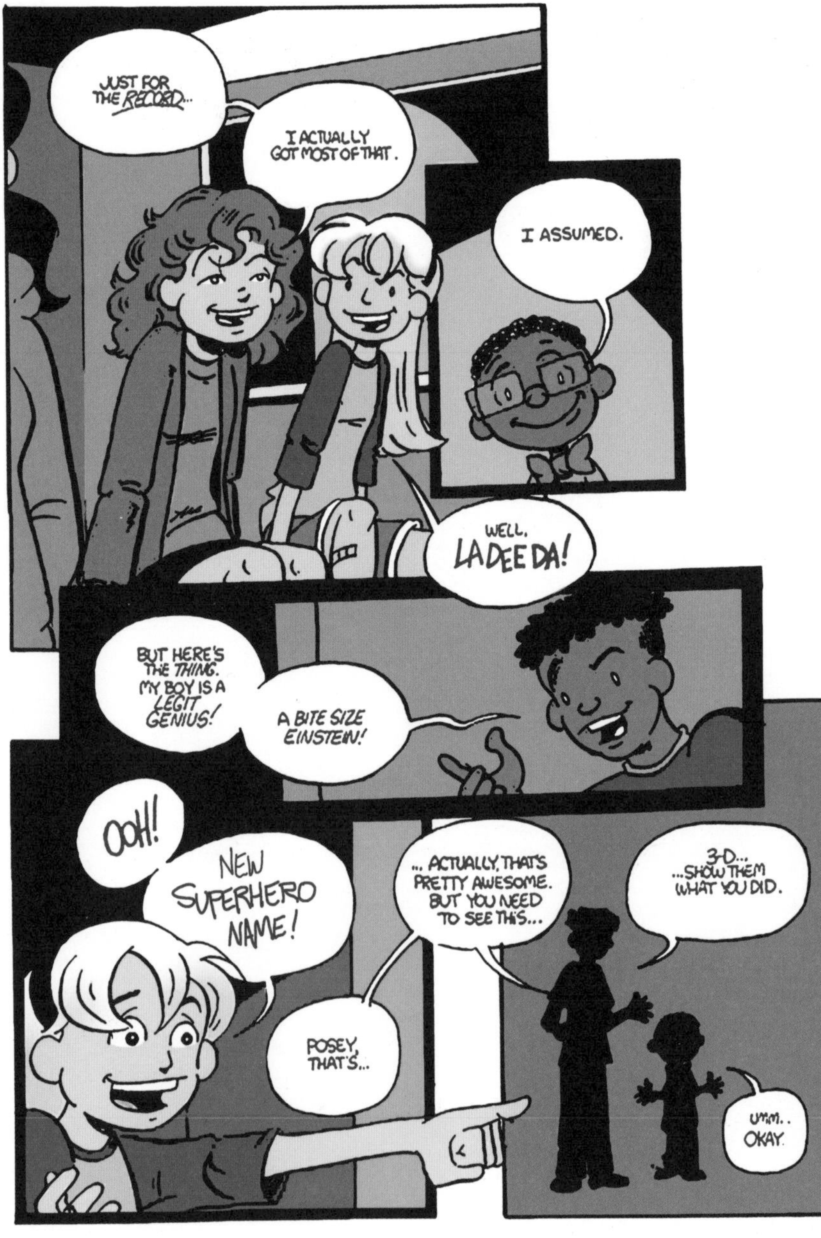
JUST FOR THE RECORD...
I ACTUALLY GOT MOST OF THAT.
I ASSUMED.
WELL, LA DEE DA!
BUT HERE'S THE THING. MY BOY IS A LEGIT GENIUS!
A BITE SIZE EINSTEIN!
OOH!
NEW SUPERHERO NAME!
POSEY, THAT'S...
... ACTUALLY, THAT'S PRETTY AWESOME. BUT YOU NEED TO SEE THIS...
3-D... ...SHOW THEM WHAT YOU DID.
UMM.. OKAY.

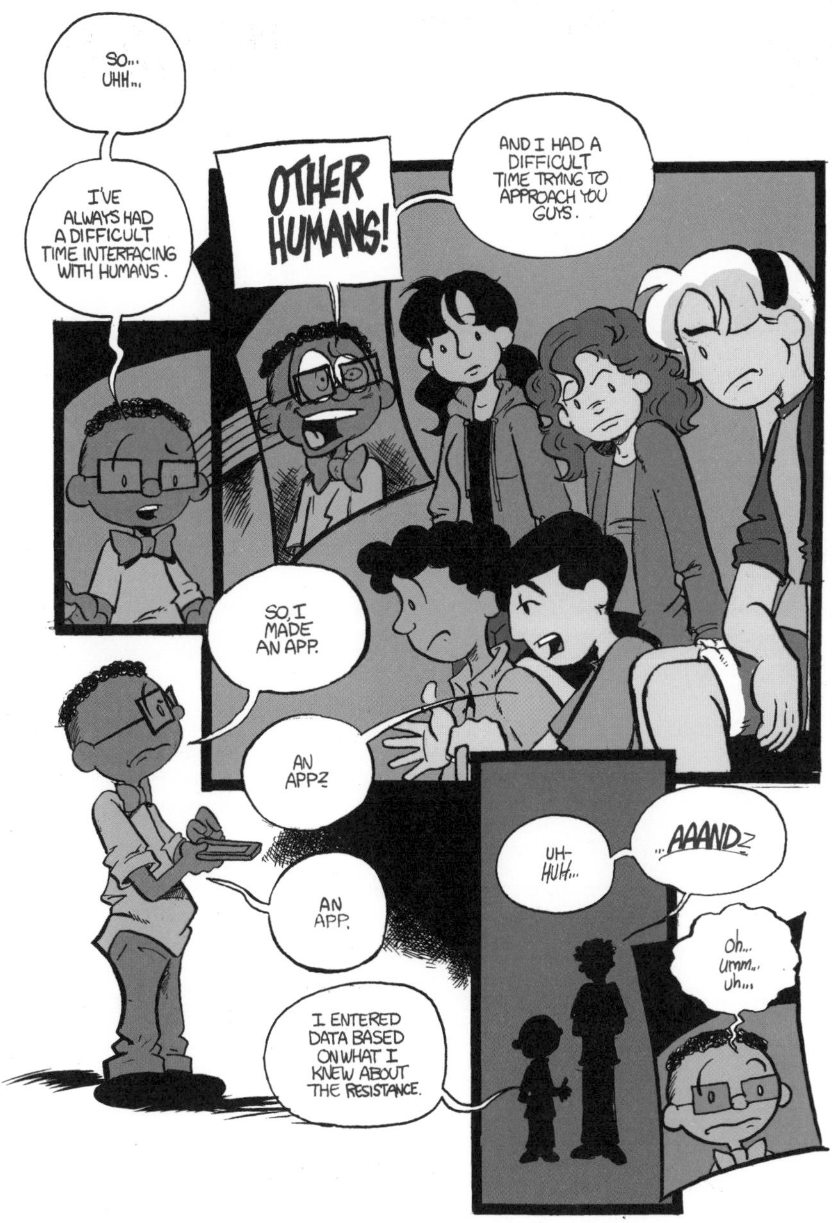
SO... UHH...
I'VE ALWAYS HAD A DIFFICULT TIME INTERFACING WITH HUMANS.
OTHER HUMANS!
AND I HAD A DIFFICULT TIME TRYING TO APPROACH YOU GUYS.
SO, I MADE AN APP.
AN APP?
AN APP.
UH-HUH...
...AAAND?
Oh... umm... uh...
I ENTERED DATA BASED ON WHAT I KNEW ABOUT THE RESISTANCE.

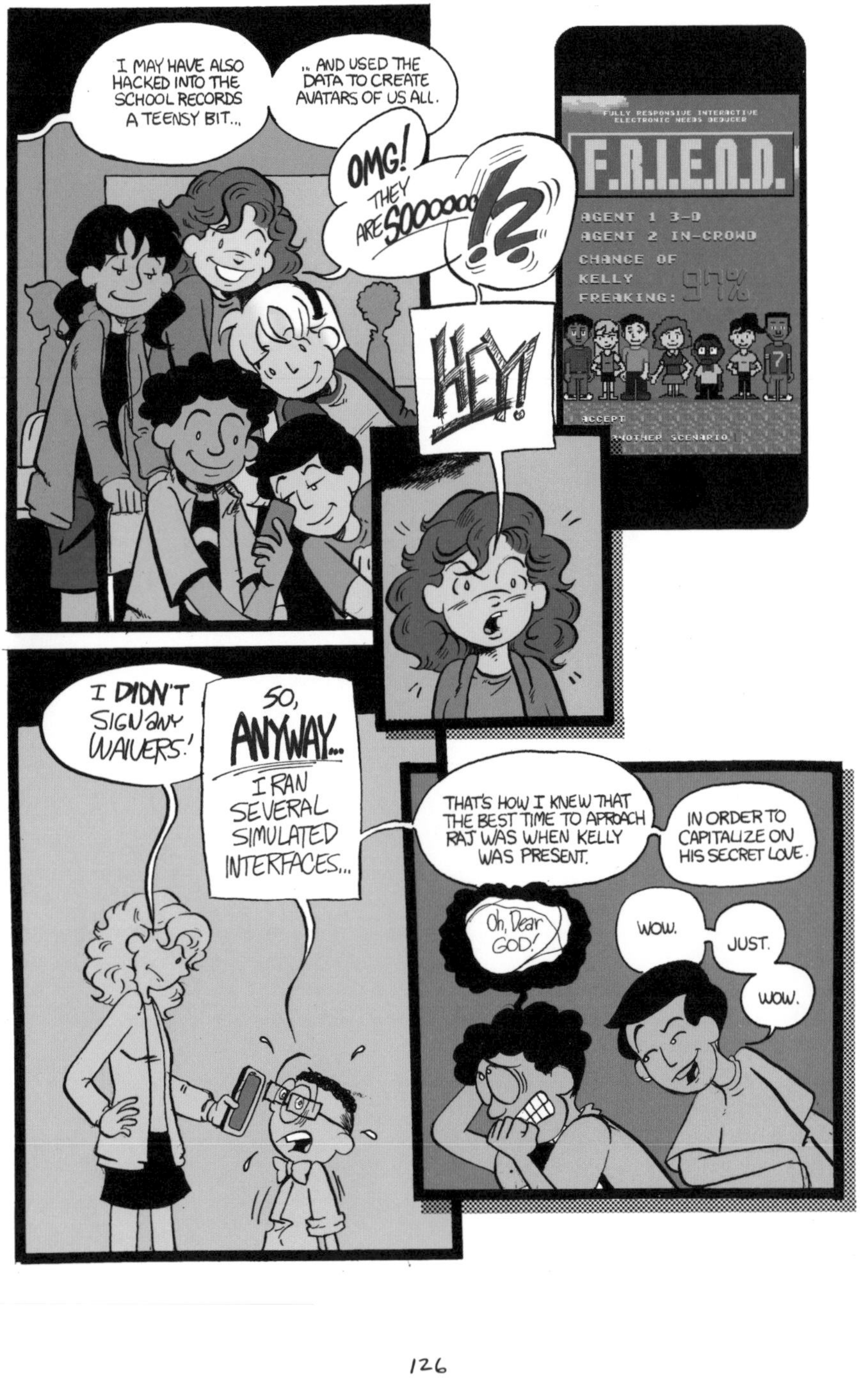
I MAY HAVE ALSO HACKED INTO THE SCHOOL RECORDS A TEENSY BIT...
.. AND USED THE DATA TO CREATE AVATARS OF US ALL.
OMG! THEY ARE SOOOOOO
!?
FULLY RESPONSIVE INTERACTIVE ELECTRONIC NEEDS DEDUCER
F.R.I.E.N.D.
AGENT 1 3-D
AGENT 2 IN-CROWD
CHANCE OF KELLY FREAKING: 97%
ACCEPT
ANOTHER SCENARIO
HEY!
I DIDN'T SIGN any WAIVERS!
SO, ANYWAY...
I RAN SEVERAL SIMULATED INTERFACES...
THAT'S HOW I KNEW THAT THE BEST TIME TO APROACH RAJ WAS WHEN KELLY WAS PRESENT.
IN ORDER TO CAPITALIZE ON HIS SECRET LOVE.
Oh, Dear GOD!
WOW.
JUST.
WOW.

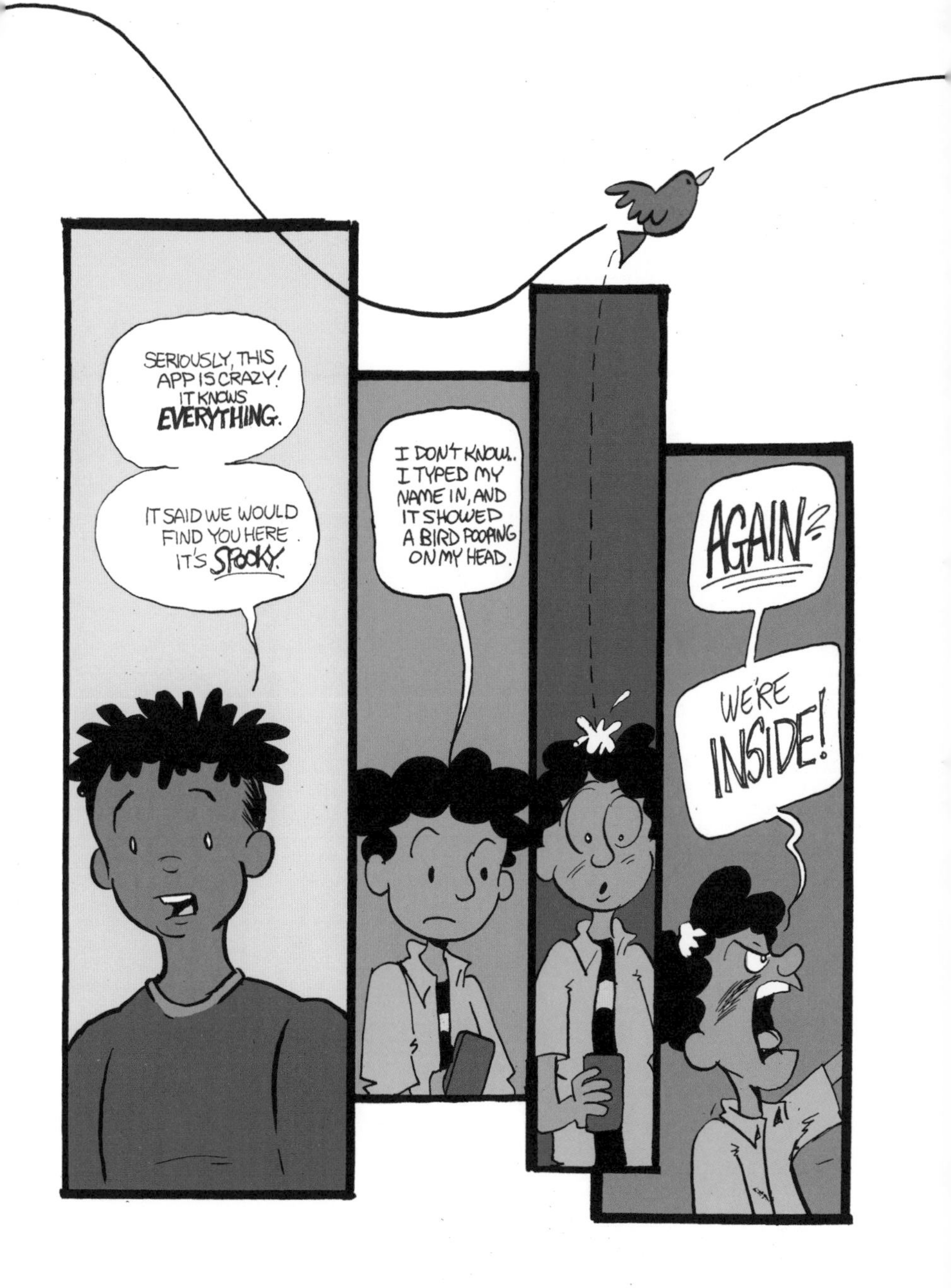
SERIOUSLY, THIS APP IS CRAZY! IT KNOWS EVERYTHING.
IT SAID WE WOULD FIND YOU HERE. IT'S SPOOKY.
I DON'T KNOW... I TYPED MY NAME IN, AND IT SHOWED A BIRD POOPING ON MY HEAD.
AGAIN?
WE'RE INSIDE!

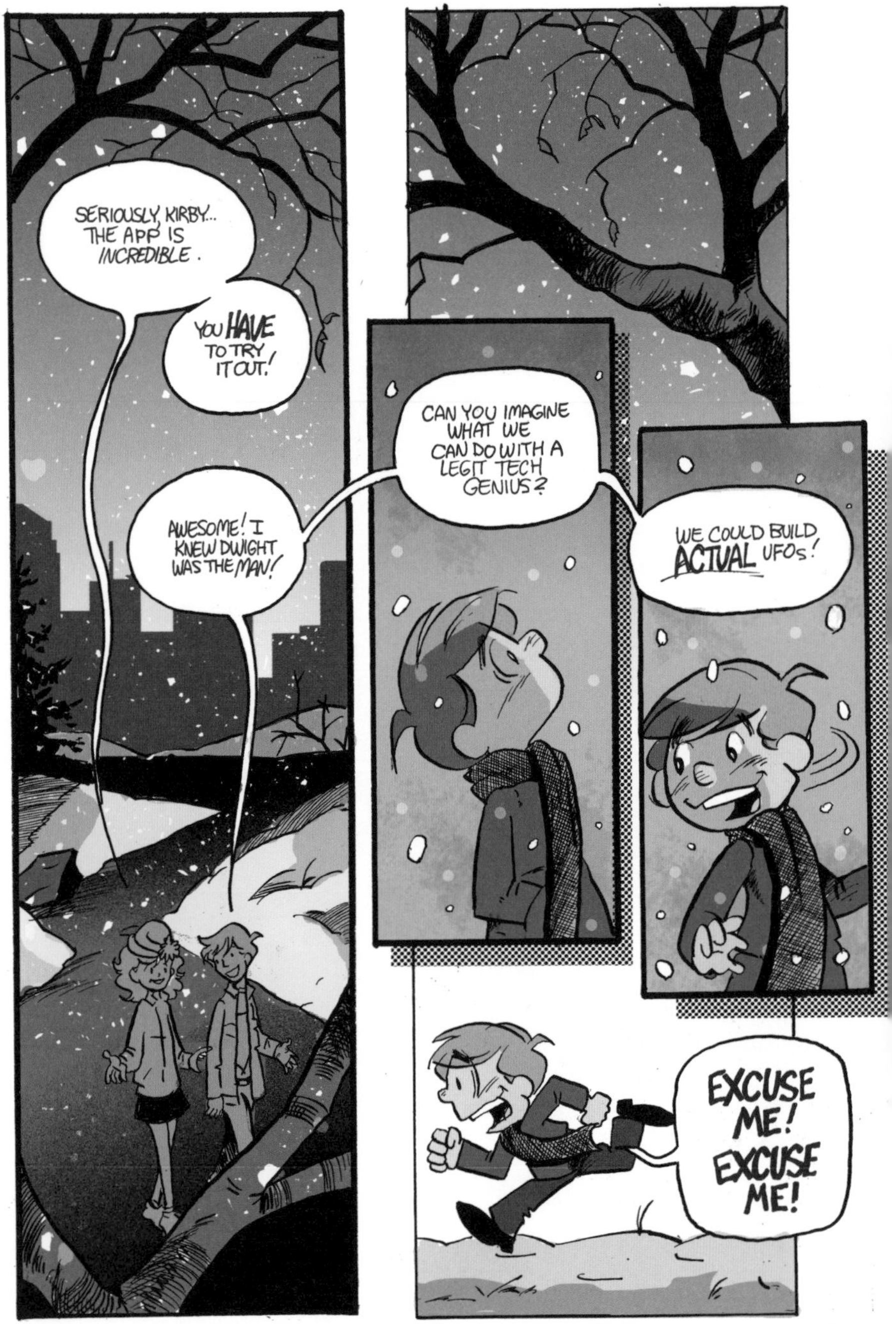
SERIOUSLY, KIRBY... THE APP IS INCREDIBLE.
YOU HAVE TO TRY IT OUT!
AWESOME! I KNEW DWIGHT WAS THE MAN!
CAN YOU IMAGINE WHAT WE CAN DO WITH A LEGIT TECH GENIUS?
WE COULD BUILD ACTUAL UFOs!
EXCUSE ME! EXCUSE ME!

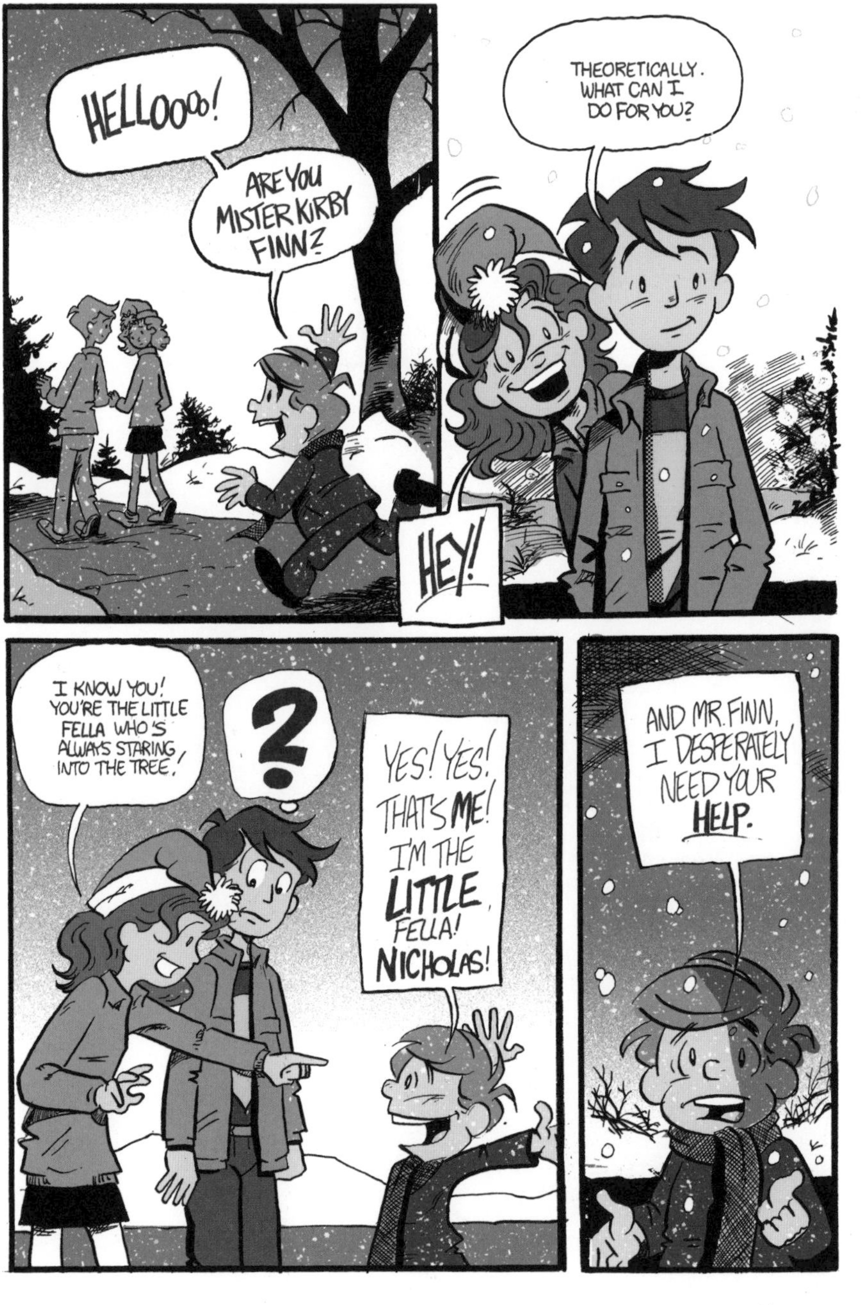
HELLOooo!
ARE YOU MISTER KIRBY FINN?
HEY!
THEORETICALLY. WHAT CAN I DO FOR YOU?
I KNOW YOU! YOU'RE THE LITTLE FELLA WHO'S ALWAYS STARING INTO THE TREE!
?
YES! YES! THAT'S ME! I'M THE LITTLE FELLA! NICHOLAS!
AND MR. FINN, I DESPERATELY NEED YOUR HELP.

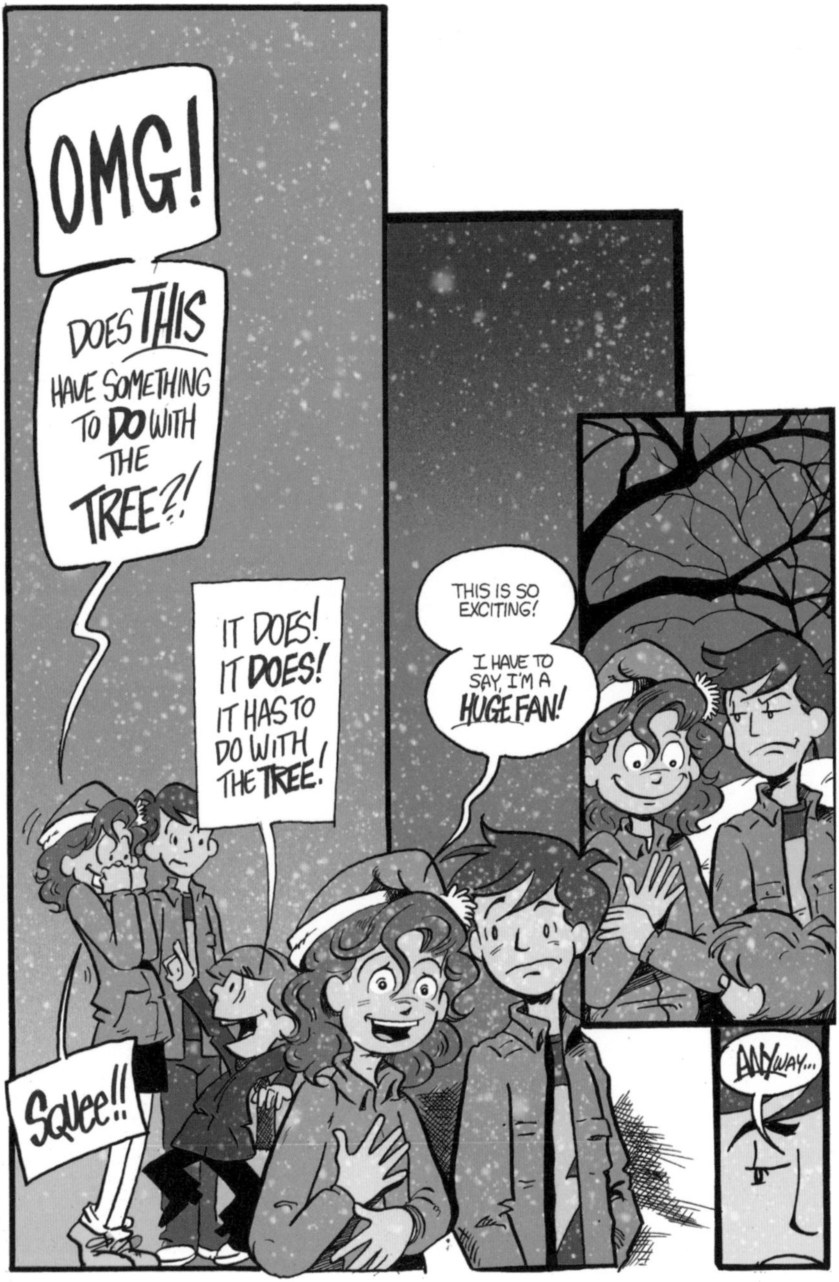
OMG!
DOES THIS HAVE SOMETHING TO DO WITH THE TREE?!
IT DOES! IT DOES! IT HAS TO DO WITH THE TREE!
Squee!!
THIS IS SO EXCITING!
I HAVE TO SAY, I'M A HUGE FAN!
ANYWAY...

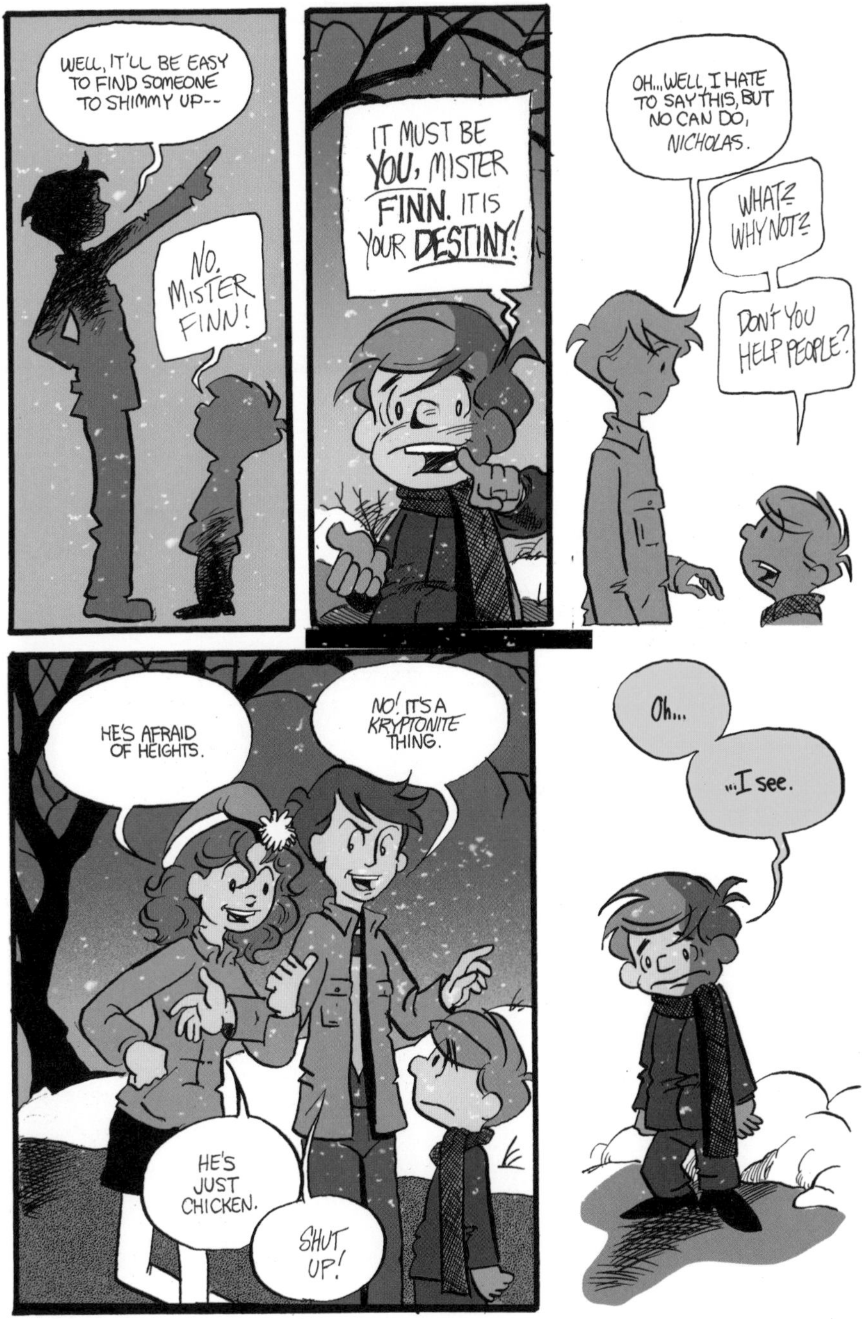

WELL, IT'LL BE EASY TO FIND SOMEONE TO SHIMMY UP--
NO. MISTER FINN!
IT MUST BE YOU, MISTER FINN. IT IS YOUR DESTINY!
OH... WELL, I HATE TO SAY THIS, BUT NO CAN DO, NICHOLAS.
WHAT? WHY NOT?
DON'T YOU HELP PEOPLE?
HE'S AFRAID OF HEIGHTS.
NO! IT'S A KRYPTONITE THING.
HE'S JUST CHICKEN.
SHUT UP!
Oh...
...I see.

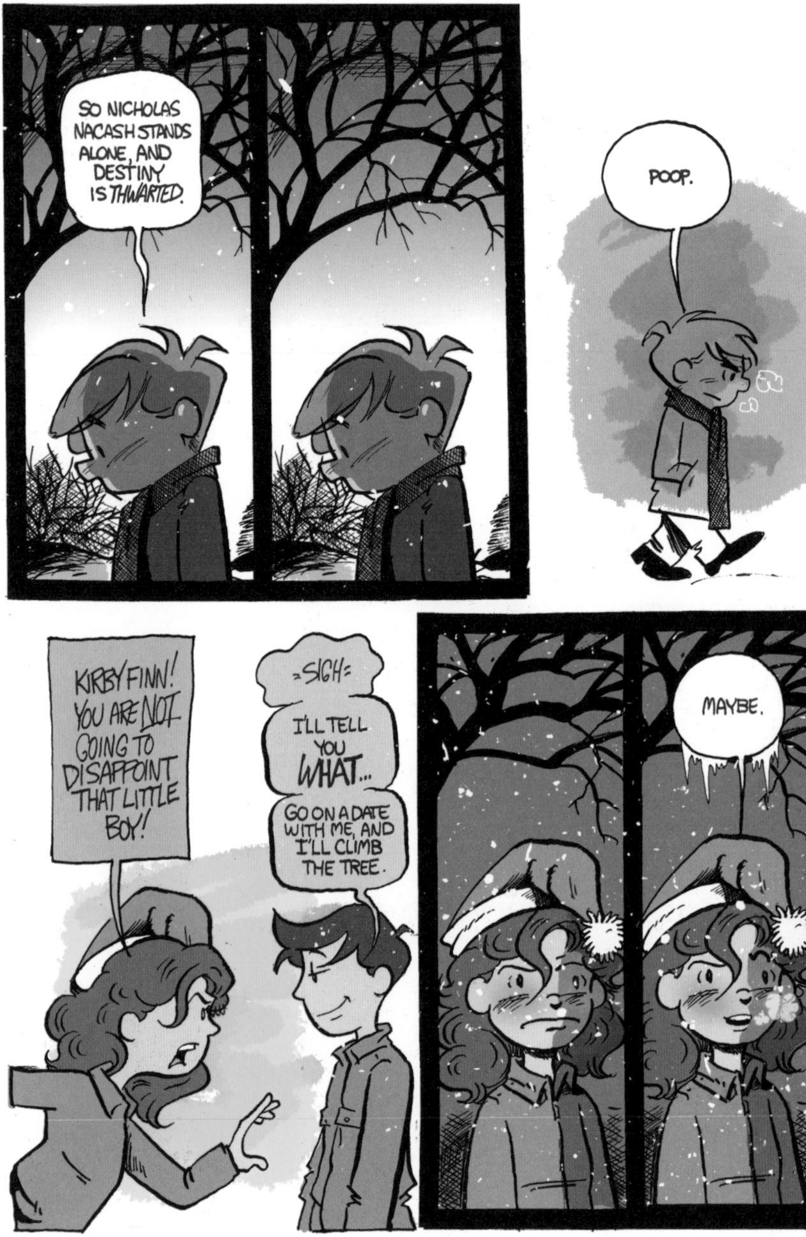
SO NICHOLAS NACASH STANDS ALONE, AND DESTINY IS THWARTED.
POOP.
KIRBY FINN! YOU ARE NOT GOING TO DISAPPOINT THAT LITTLE BOY!
=SIGH=
I'LL TELL YOU WHAT...
GO ON A DATE WITH ME, AND I'LL CLIMB THE TREE.
MAYBE.

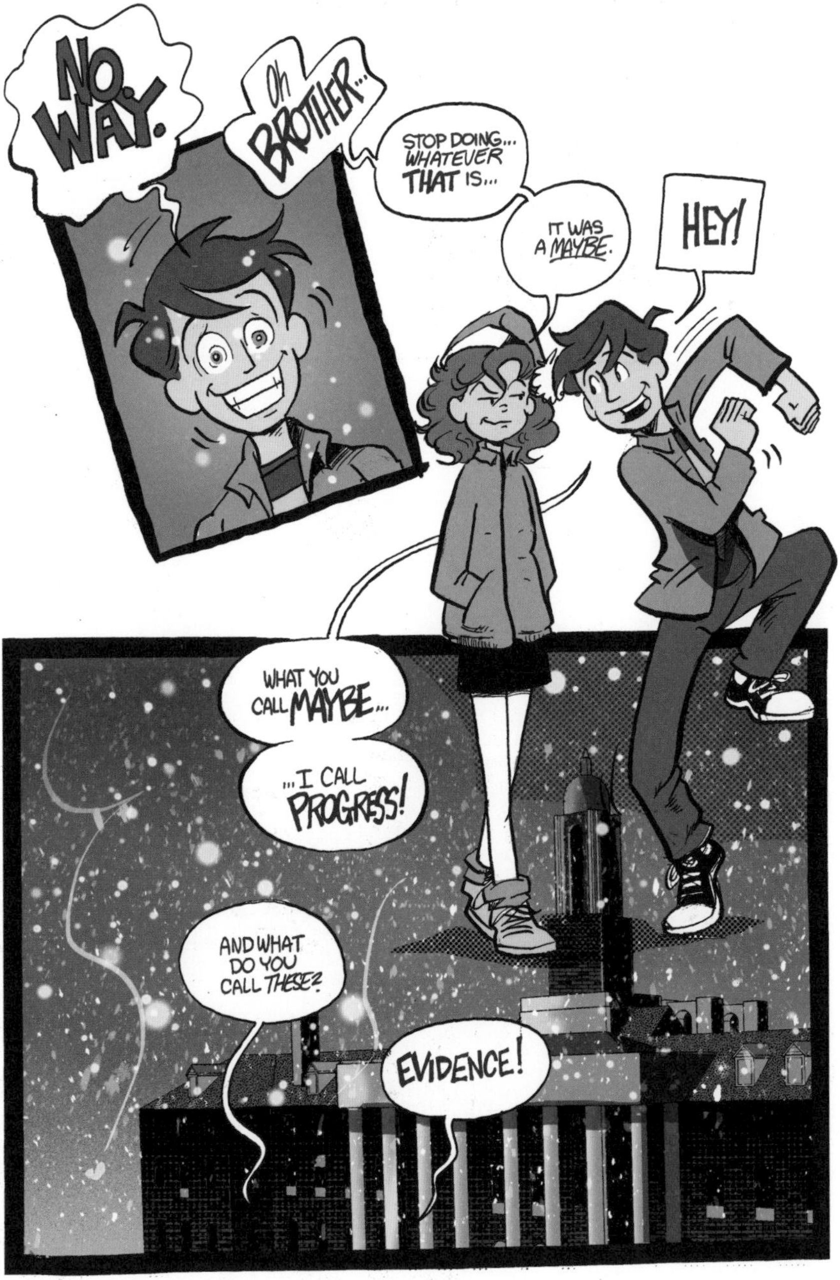
NO. WAY.
Oh BROTHER...
STOP DOING... WHATEVER THAT IS...
IT WAS A MAYBE.
HEY!
WHAT YOU CALL MAYBE...
...I CALL PROGRESS!
AND WHAT DO YOU CALL THESE?
EVIDENCE!

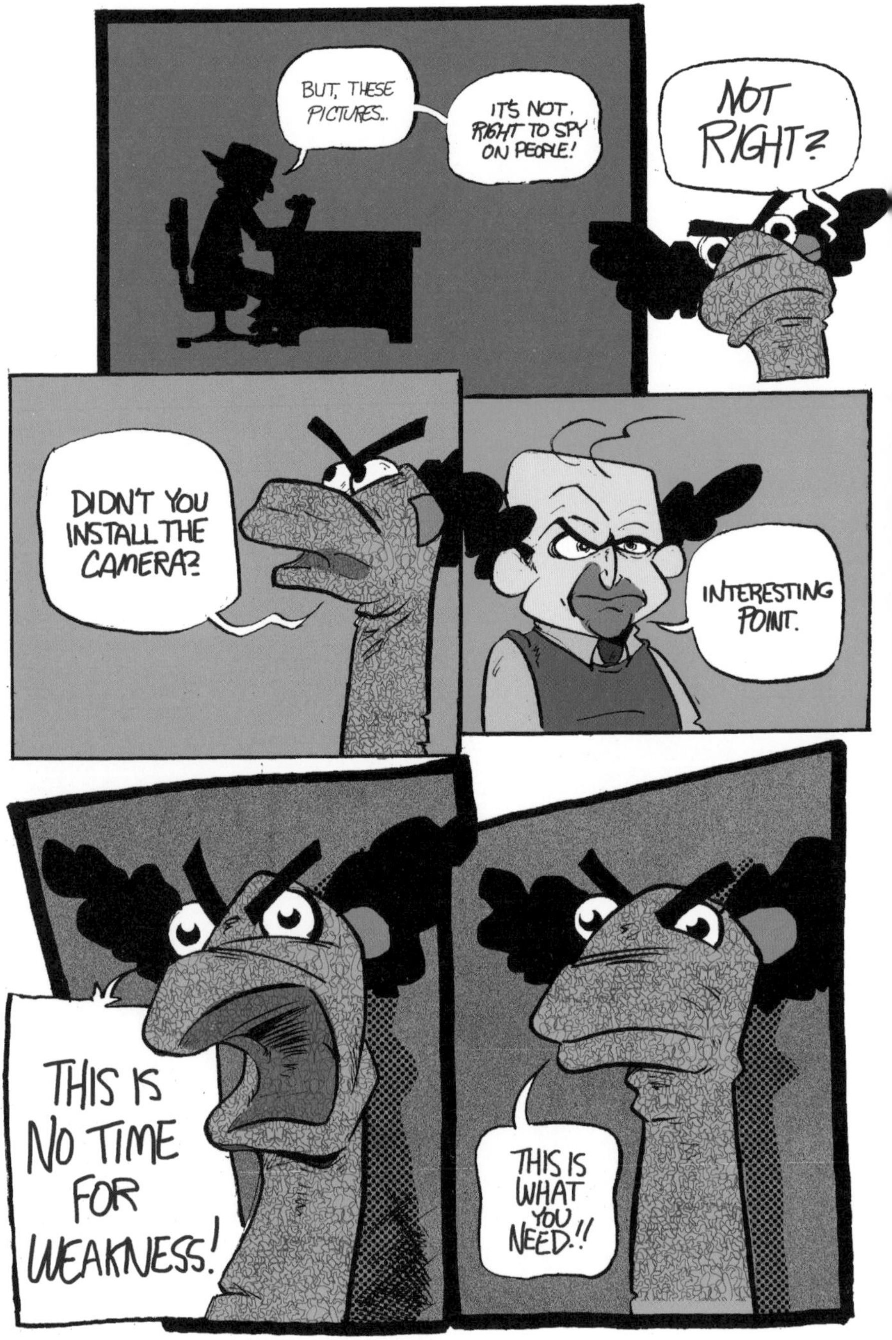
BUT, THESE PICTURES..
IT'S NOT RIGHT TO SPY ON PEOPLE!
NOT RIGHT?
DIDN'T YOU INSTALL THE CAMERA?
INTERESTING POINT.
THIS IS NO TIME FOR WEAKNESS!
THIS IS WHAT YOU NEED!!

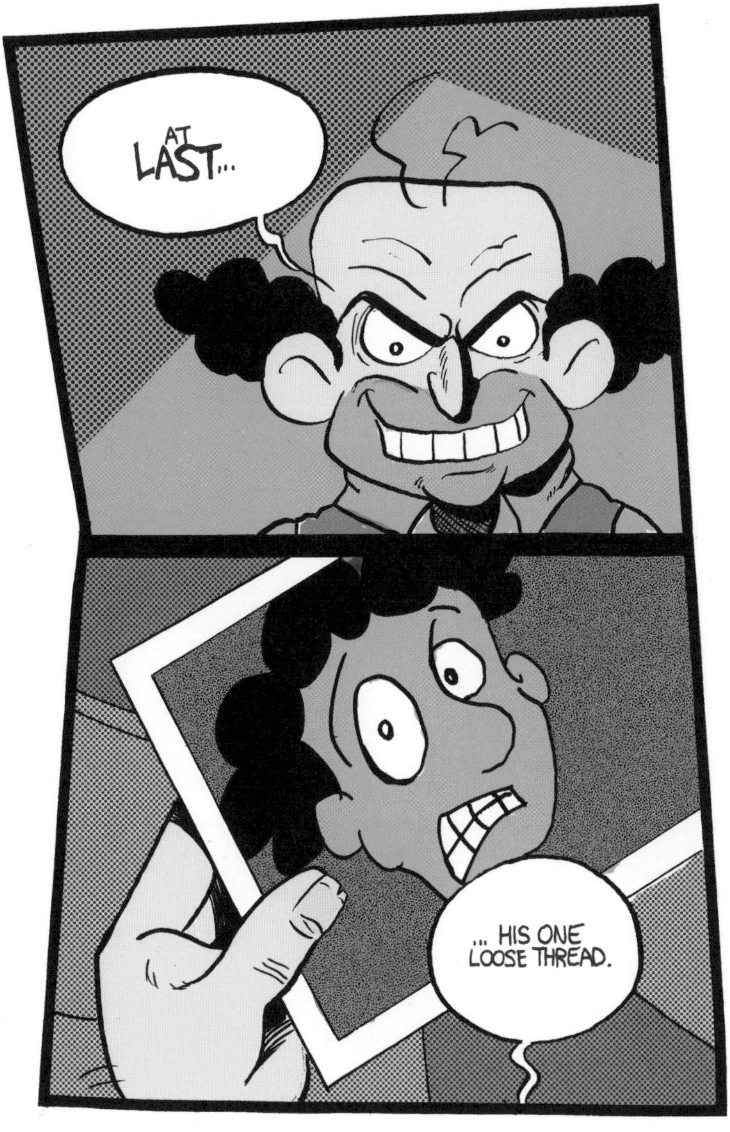
AT LAST...
... HIS ONE LOOSE THREAD.

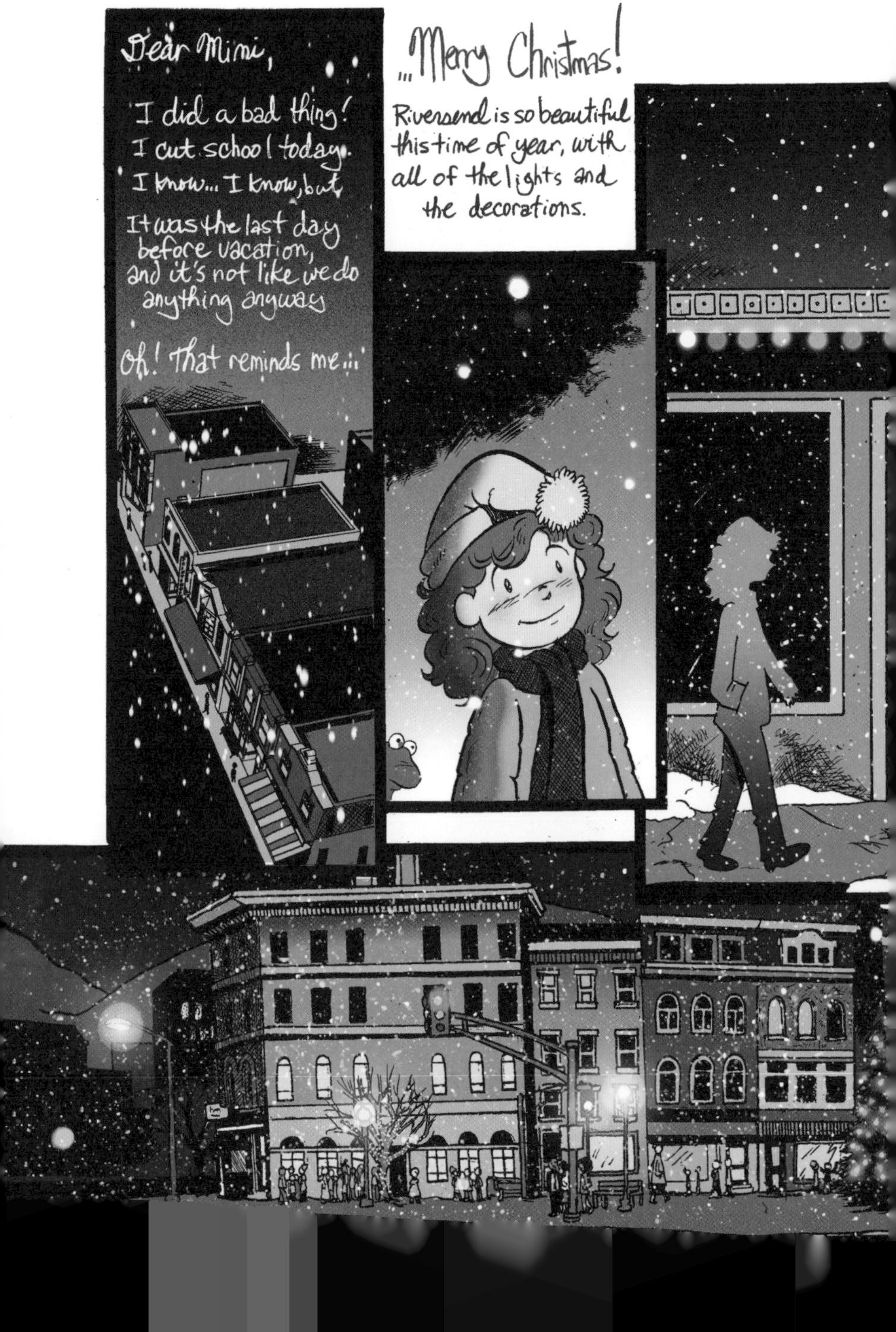
Dear Mimi,
I did a bad thing! I cut school today. I know... I know, but
It was the last day before vacation, and it's not like we do anything anyway
Oh! That reminds me...
...Merry Christmas!
Riversend is so beautiful this time of year, with all of the lights and the decorations.

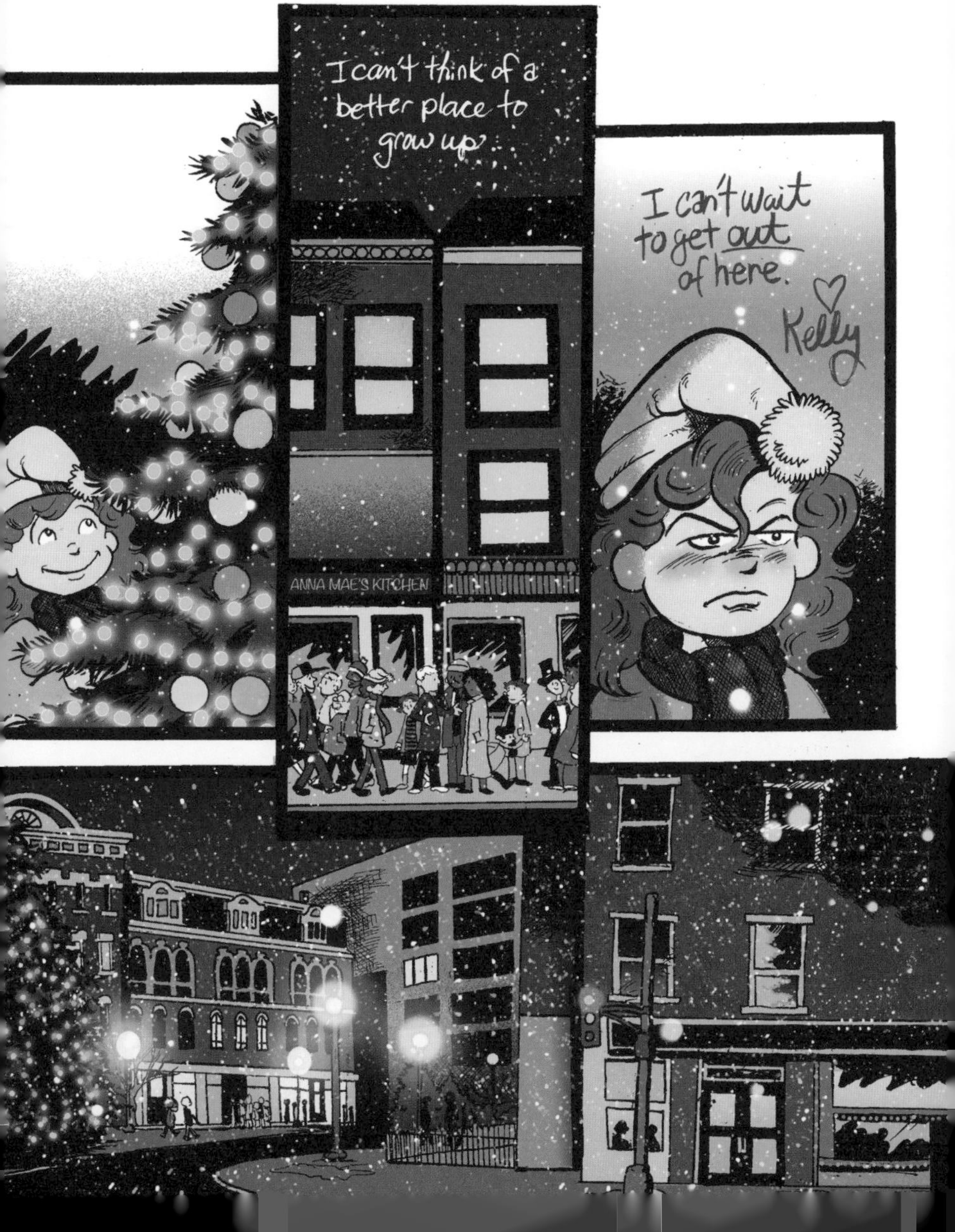
I can't think of a better place to grow up...
ANNA MAE'S KITCHEN
I can't wait to get out of here.
Kelly

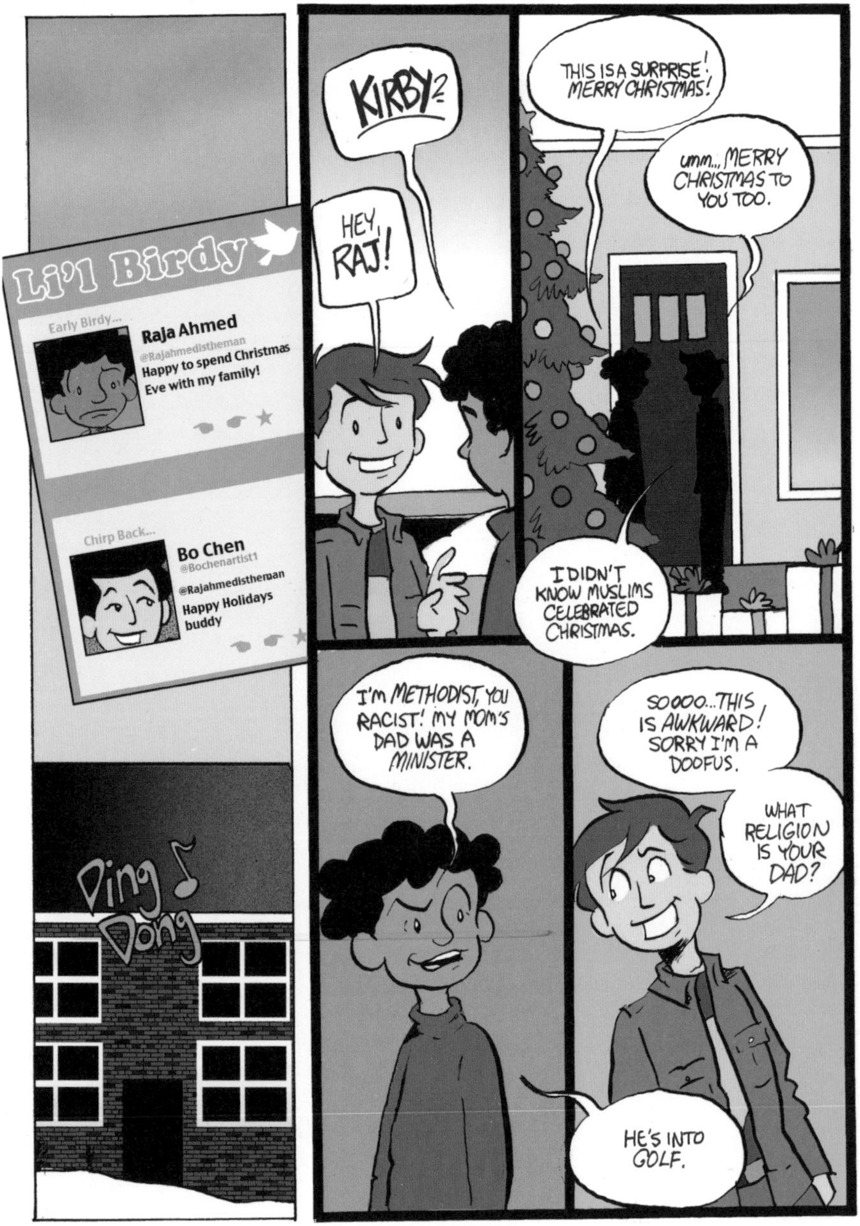

Li'l Birdy
Early Birdy...
Raja Ahmed
@Rajahmedistheman
Happy to spend Christmas Eve with my family!
Chirp Back...
Bo Chen
@Bochenartist1
@Rajahmedistheman
Happy Holidays buddy
Ding Dong
KIRBY?
HEY, RAJ!
THIS IS A SURPRISE! MERRY CHRISTMAS!
umm... MERRY CHRISTMAS TO YOU TOO.
I DIDN'T KNOW MUSLIMS CELEBRATED CHRISTMAS.
I'M METHODIST, YOU RACIST! MY MOM'S DAD WAS A MINISTER.
SOOOO...THIS IS AWKWARD! SORRY I'M A DOOFUS.
WHAT RELIGION IS YOUR DAD?
HE'S INTO GOLF.

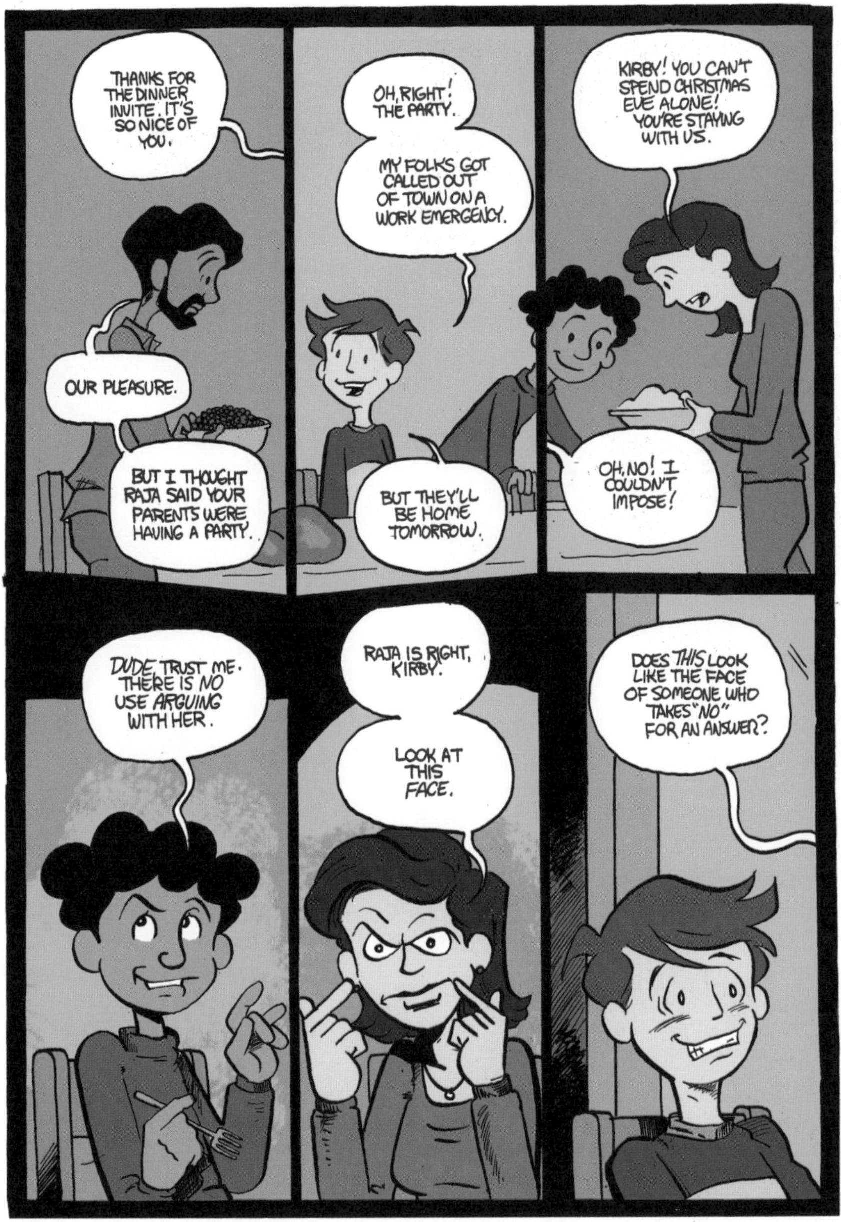
THANKS FOR THE DINNER INVITE. IT'S SO NICE OF YOU.
OUR PLEASURE.
BUT I THOUGHT RAJA SAID YOUR PARENTS WERE HAVING A PARTY.
OH, RIGHT! THE PARTY.
MY FOLKS GOT CALLED OUT OF TOWN ON A WORK EMERGENCY.
BUT THEY'LL BE HOME TOMORROW.
KIRBY! YOU CAN'T SPEND CHRISTMAS EVE ALONE! YOU'RE STAYING WITH US.
OH, NO! I COULDN'T IMPOSE!
DUDE TRUST ME. THERE IS NO USE ARGUING WITH HER.
RAJA IS RIGHT, KIRBY.
LOOK AT THIS FACE.
DOES THIS LOOK LIKE THE FACE OF SOMEONE WHO TAKES "NO" FOR AN ANSWER?

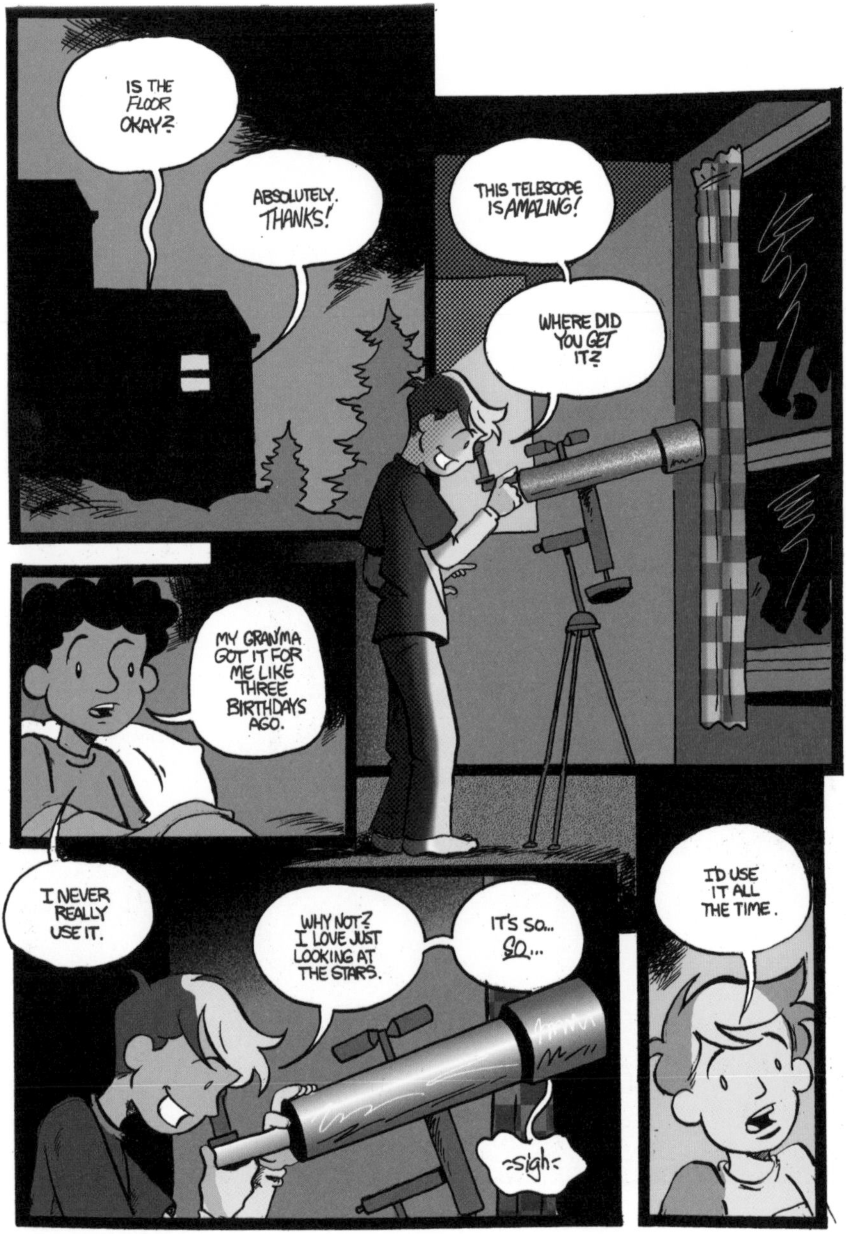
IS THE FLOOR OKAY?
ABSOLUTELY. THANKS!
THIS TELESCOPE IS AMAZING!
WHERE DID YOU GET IT?
MY GRAN'MA GOT IT FOR ME LIKE THREE BIRTHDAYS AGO.
I NEVER REALLY USE IT.
WHY NOT? I LOVE JUST LOOKING AT THE STARS.
IT'S SO... SO...
:sigh:
I'D USE IT ALL THE TIME.

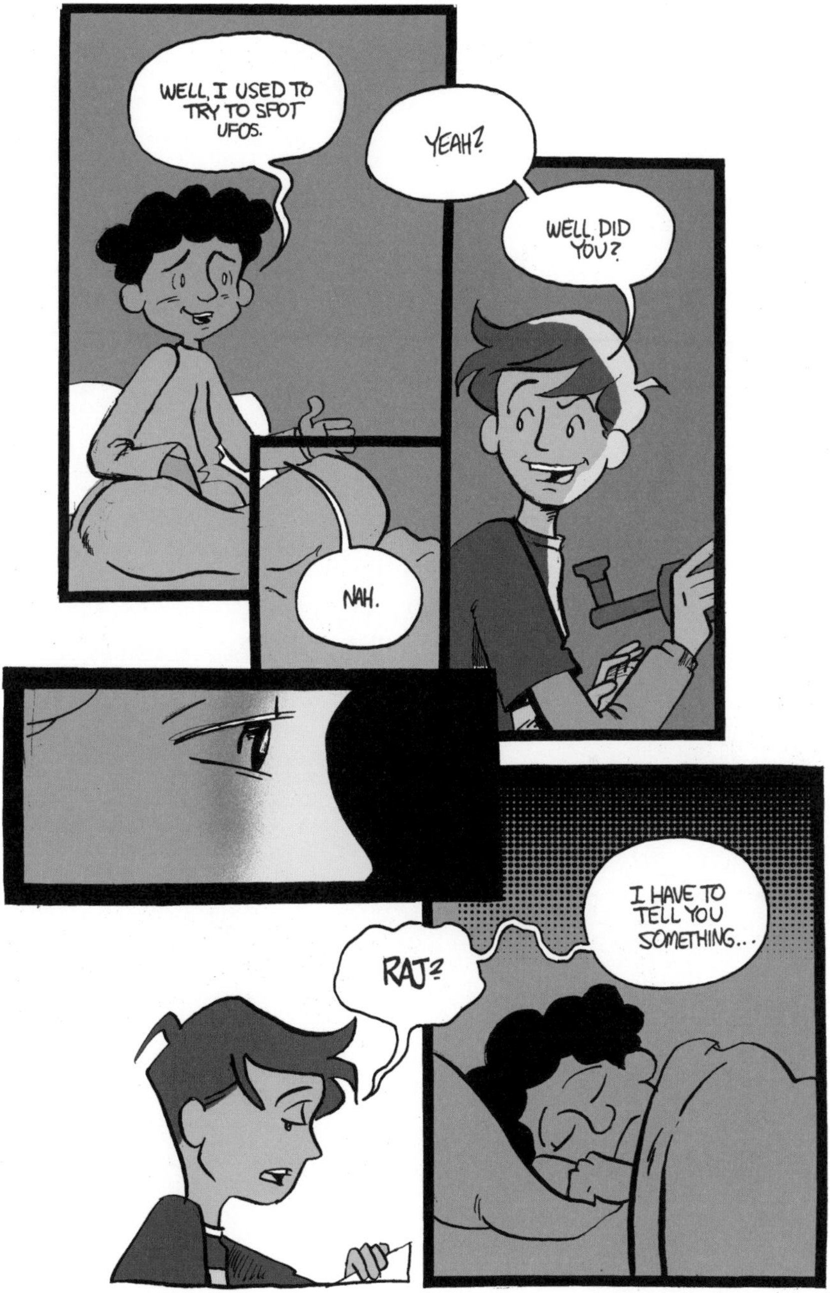
WELL, I USED TO TRY TO SPOT UFOS.
YEAH?
WELL, DID YOU?
NAH.
RAJ?
I HAVE TO TELL YOU SOMETHING...

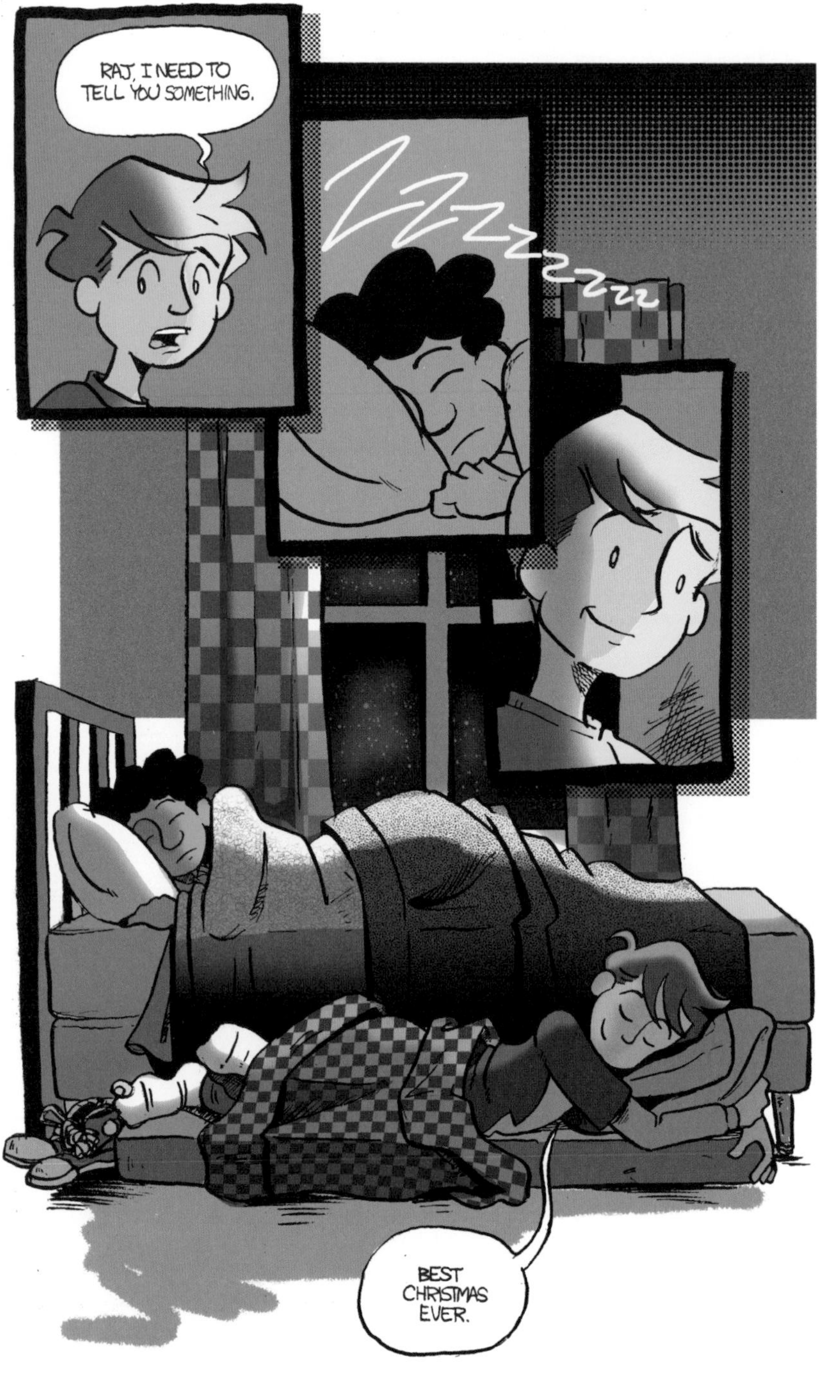
RAJ, I NEED TO TELL YOU SOMETHING.
ZZZZZZzzz
BEST CHRISTMAS EVER.

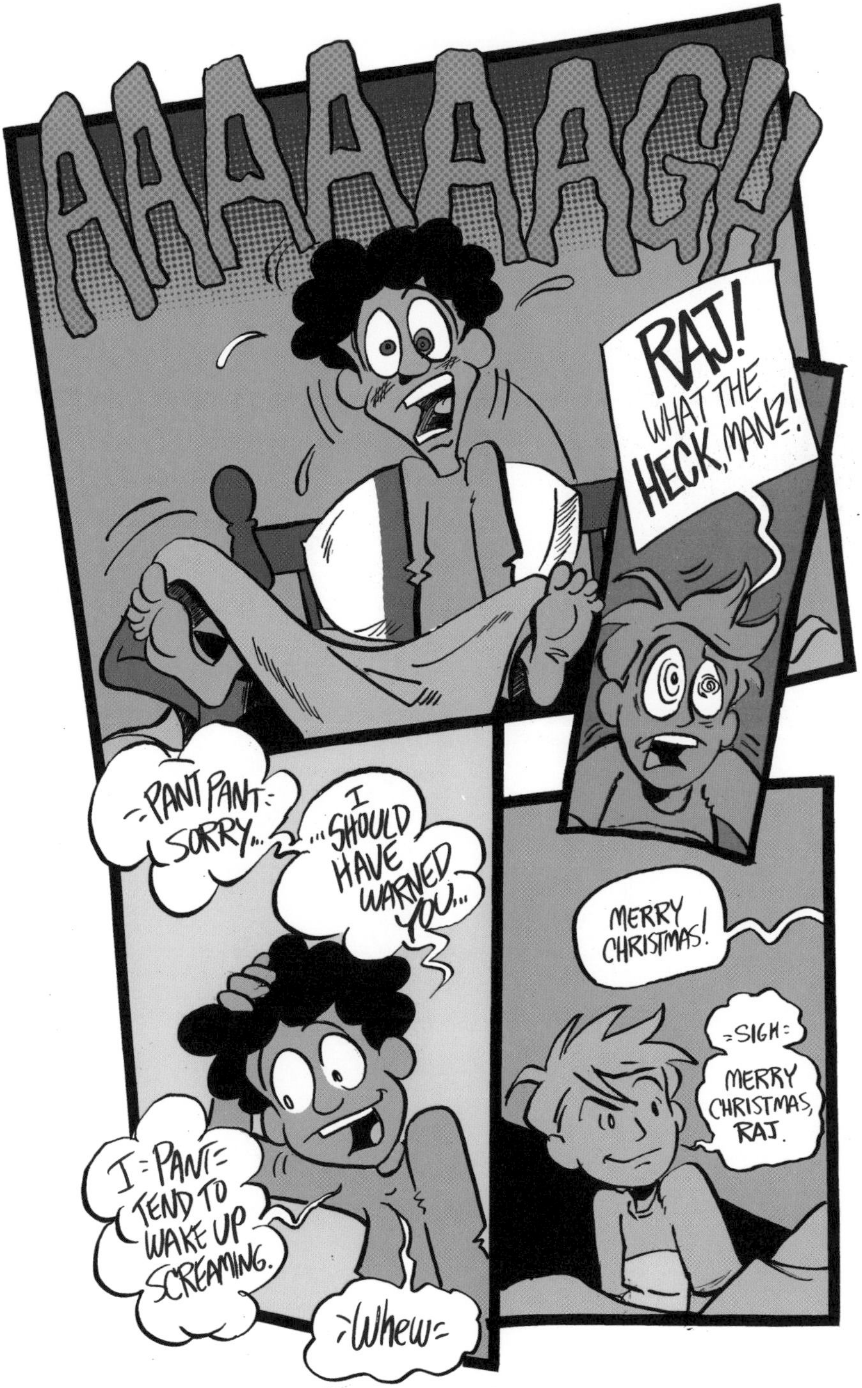
AAAAAAGH
RAJ! WHAT THE HECK, MAN?!
PANT PANT SORRY...
...I SHOULD HAVE WARNED YOU...
I PANT TEND TO WAKE UP SCREAMING.
Whew
MERRY CHRISTMAS!
SIGH
MERRY CHRISTMAS, RAJ.

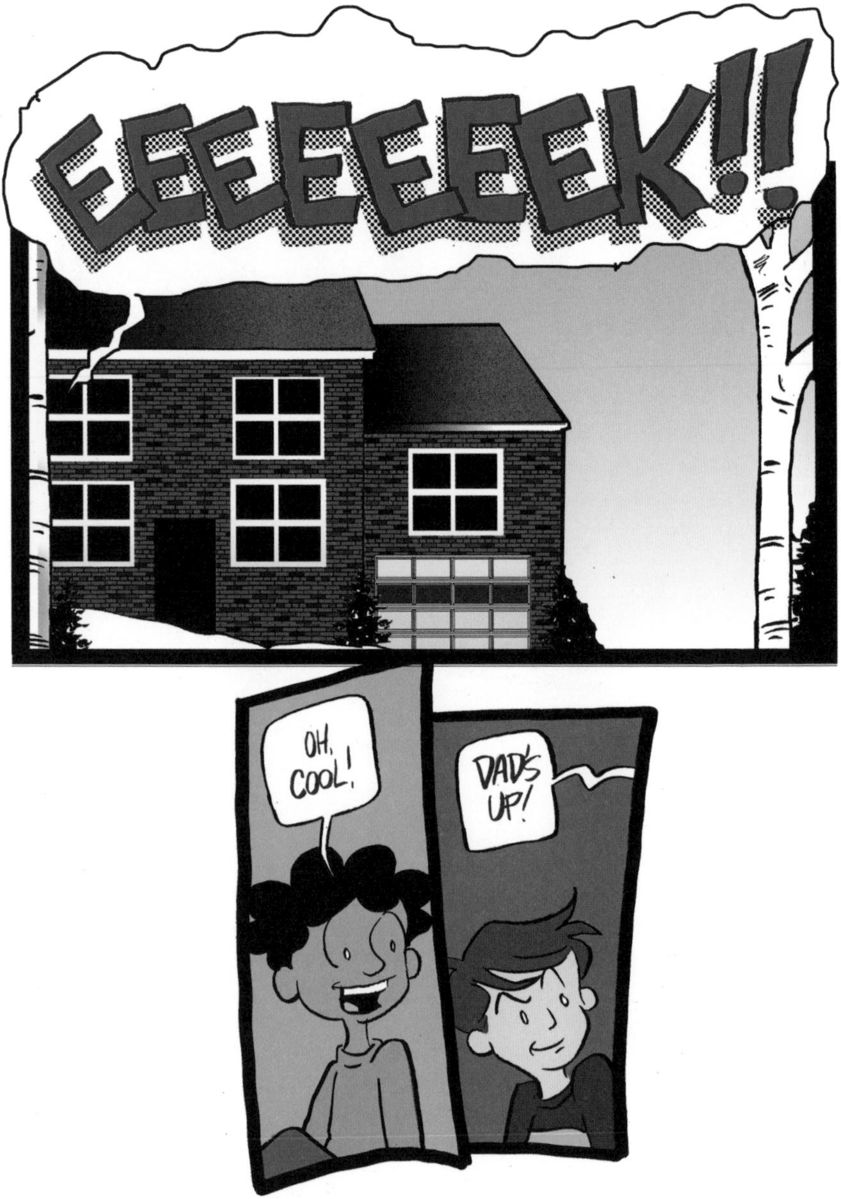
EEEEEEEK!!
OH, COOL!
DAD'S UP!

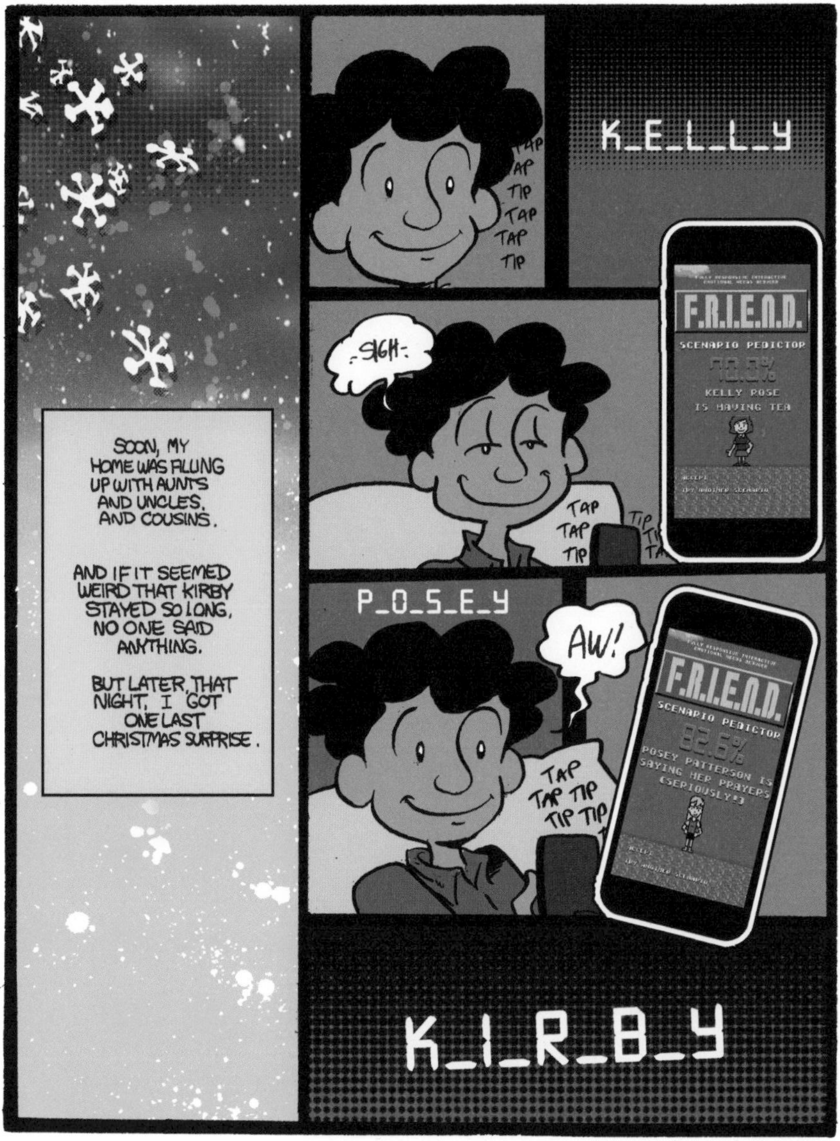
SOON, MY HOME WAS FILLING UP WITH AUNTS AND UNCLES, AND COUSINS.
AND IF IT SEEMED WEIRD THAT KIRBY STAYED SO LONG, NO ONE SAID ANYTHING.
BUT LATER, THAT NIGHT, I GOT ONE LAST CHRISTMAS SURPRISE.
TAP TAP TIP TAP TAP TIP
K_E_L_L_Y
F.R.I.E.N.D.
SCENARIO PEDICTOR
KELLY ROSE IS HAVING TEA
-SIGH-
TAP TAP TIP
P_O_S_E_Y
AW!
FULLY RESPONSIVE INTERACTIVE EMOTIONAL NEEDS DEFINER
F.R.I.E.N.D.
SCENARIO PEDICTOR
POSEY PATTERSON IS SAYING HER PRAYERS (SERIOUSLY!)
TAP TAP TIP TIP TIP
K_I_R_B_Y

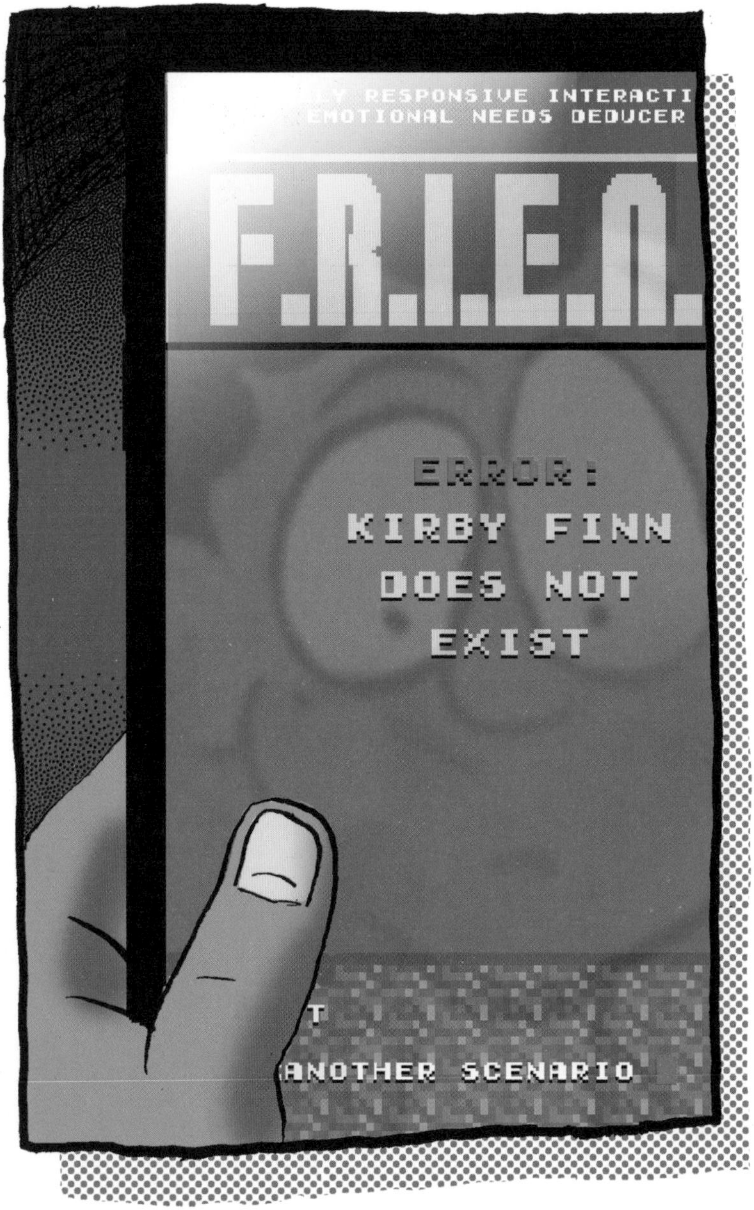
RESPONSIVE INTERACTI
EMOTIONAL NEEDS DEDUCER
F.R.I.E.N.
ERROR:
KIRBY FINN
DOES NOT
EXIST
ANOTHER SCENARIO

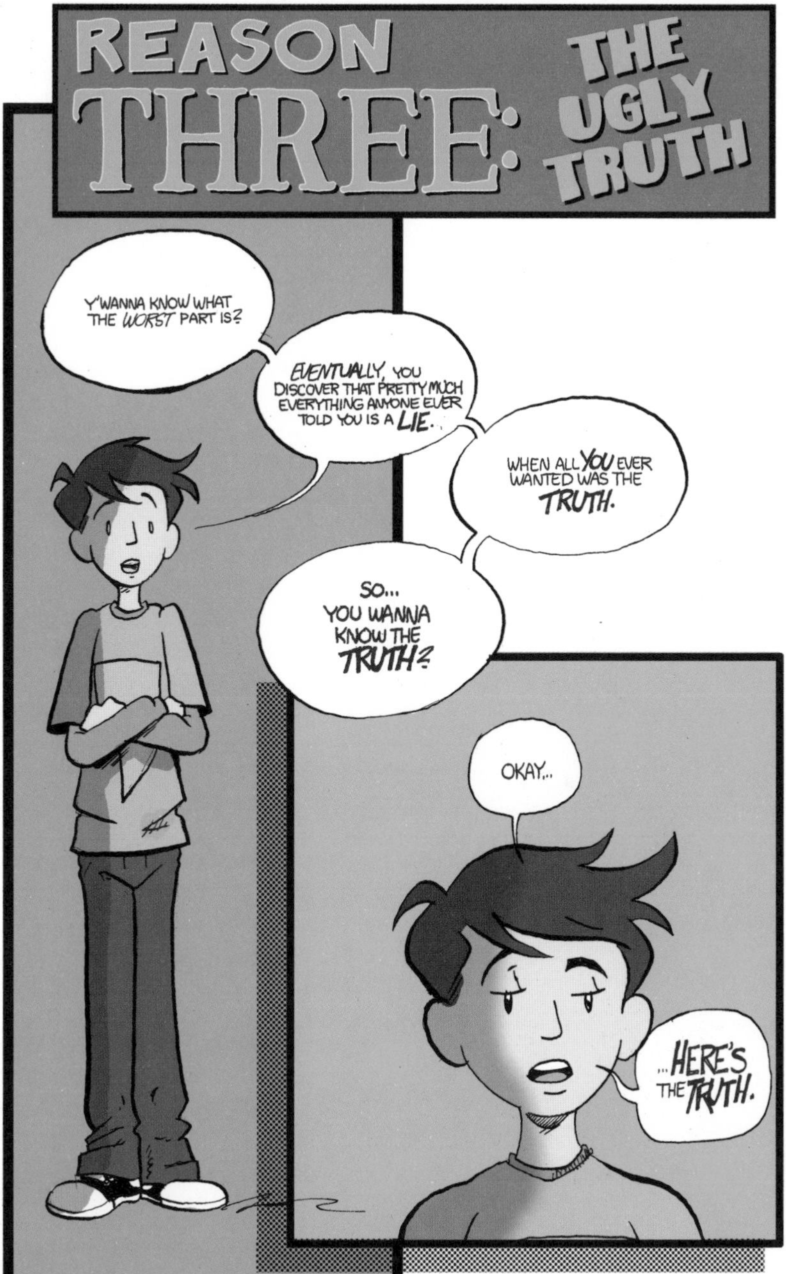
REASON THREE: THE UGLY TRUTH
Y'WANNA KNOW WHAT THE WORST PART IS?
EVENTUALLY, YOU DISCOVER THAT PRETTY MUCH EVERYTHING ANYONE EVER TOLD YOU IS A LIE.
WHEN ALL YOU EVER WANTED WAS THE TRUTH.
SO... YOU WANNA KNOW THE TRUTH?
OKAY...
...HERE'S THE TRUTH.

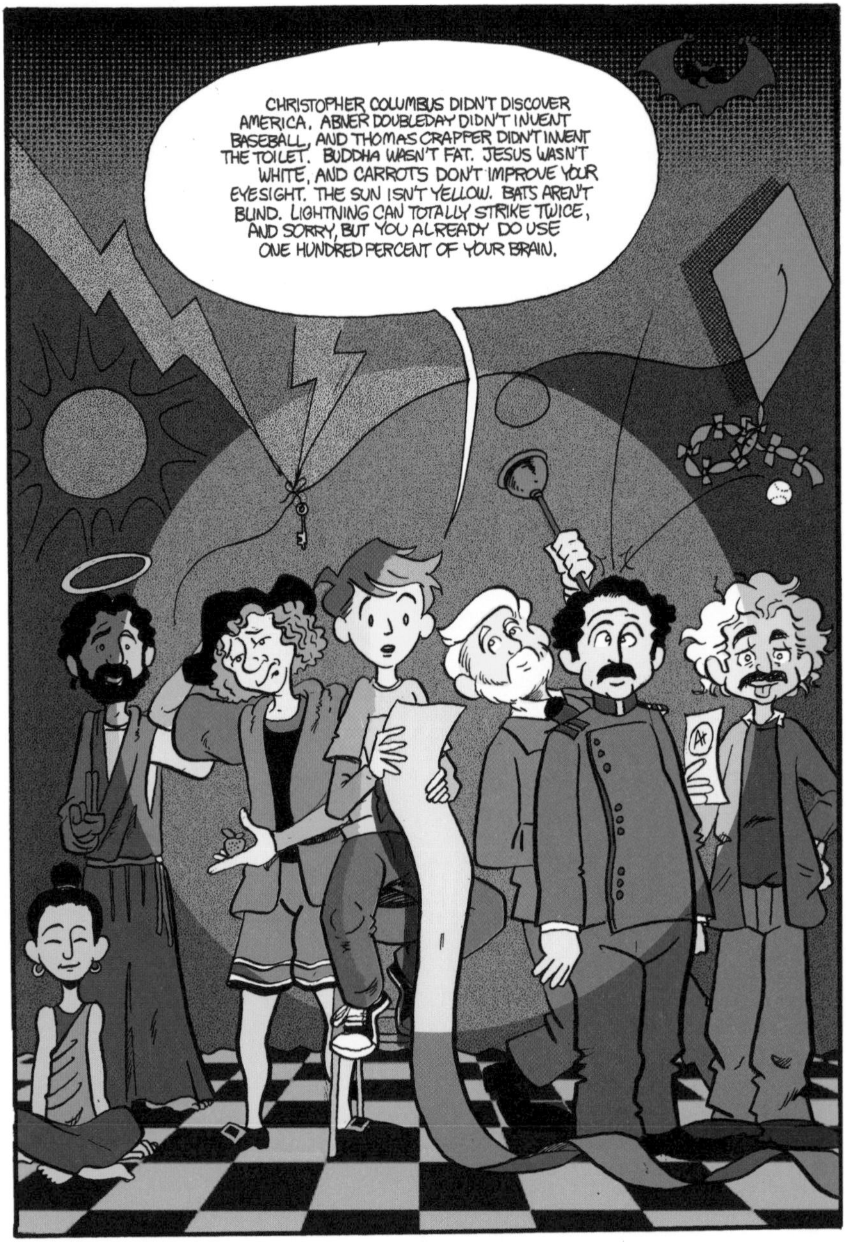
CHRISTOPHER COLUMBUS DIDN'T DISCOVER AMERICA, ABNER DOUBLEDAY DIDN'T INVENT BASEBALL, AND THOMAS CRAPPER DIDN'T INVENT THE TOILET. BUDDHA WASN'T FAT. JESUS WASN'T WHITE, AND CARROTS DON'T IMPROVE YOUR EYESIGHT. THE SUN ISN'T YELLOW. BATS AREN'T BLIND. LIGHTNING CAN TOTALLY STRIKE TWICE, AND SORRY, BUT YOU ALREADY DO USE ONE HUNDRED PERCENT OF YOUR BRAIN.
A+

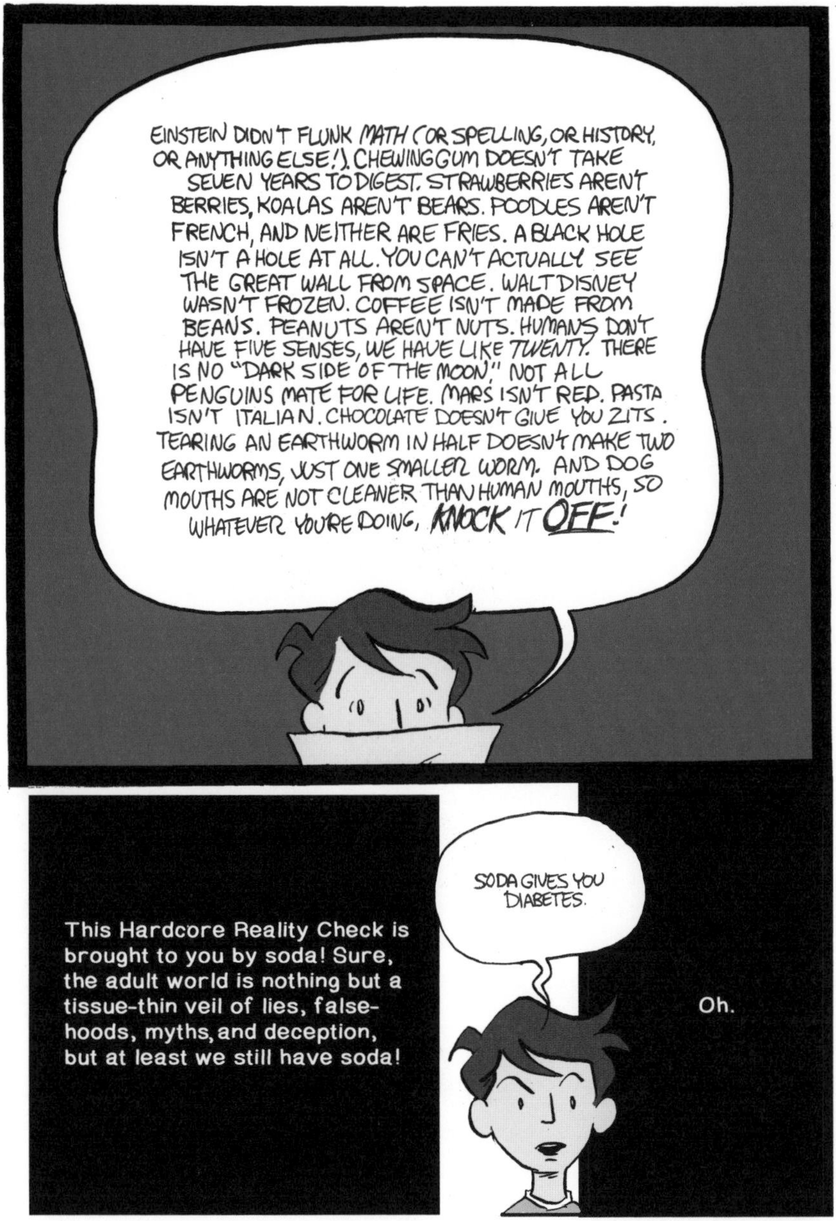
EINSTEIN DIDN'T FLUNK MATH (OR SPELLING, OR HISTORY, OR ANYTHING ELSE!). CHEWING GUM DOESN'T TAKE SEVEN YEARS TO DIGEST. STRAWBERRIES AREN'T BERRIES, KOALAS AREN'T BEARS. POODLES AREN'T FRENCH, AND NEITHER ARE FRIES. A BLACK HOLE ISN'T A HOLE AT ALL. YOU CAN'T ACTUALLY SEE THE GREAT WALL FROM SPACE. WALT DISNEY WASN'T FROZEN. COFFEE ISN'T MADE FROM BEANS. PEANUTS AREN'T NUTS. HUMANS DON'T HAVE FIVE SENSES, WE HAVE LIKE TWENTY. THERE IS NO "DARK SIDE OF THE MOON," NOT ALL PENGUINS MATE FOR LIFE. MARS ISN'T RED. PASTA ISN'T ITALIAN. CHOCOLATE DOESN'T GIVE YOU ZITS. TEARING AN EARTHWORM IN HALF DOESN'T MAKE TWO EARTHWORMS, JUST ONE SMALLER WORM. AND DOG MOUTHS ARE NOT CLEANER THAN HUMAN MOUTHS, SO WHATEVER YOU'RE DOING, KNOCK IT OFF!
This Hardcore Reality Check is brought to you by soda! Sure, the adult world is nothing but a tissue-thin veil of lies, falsehoods, myths, and deception, but at least we still have soda!
SODA GIVES YOU DIABETES.
Oh.

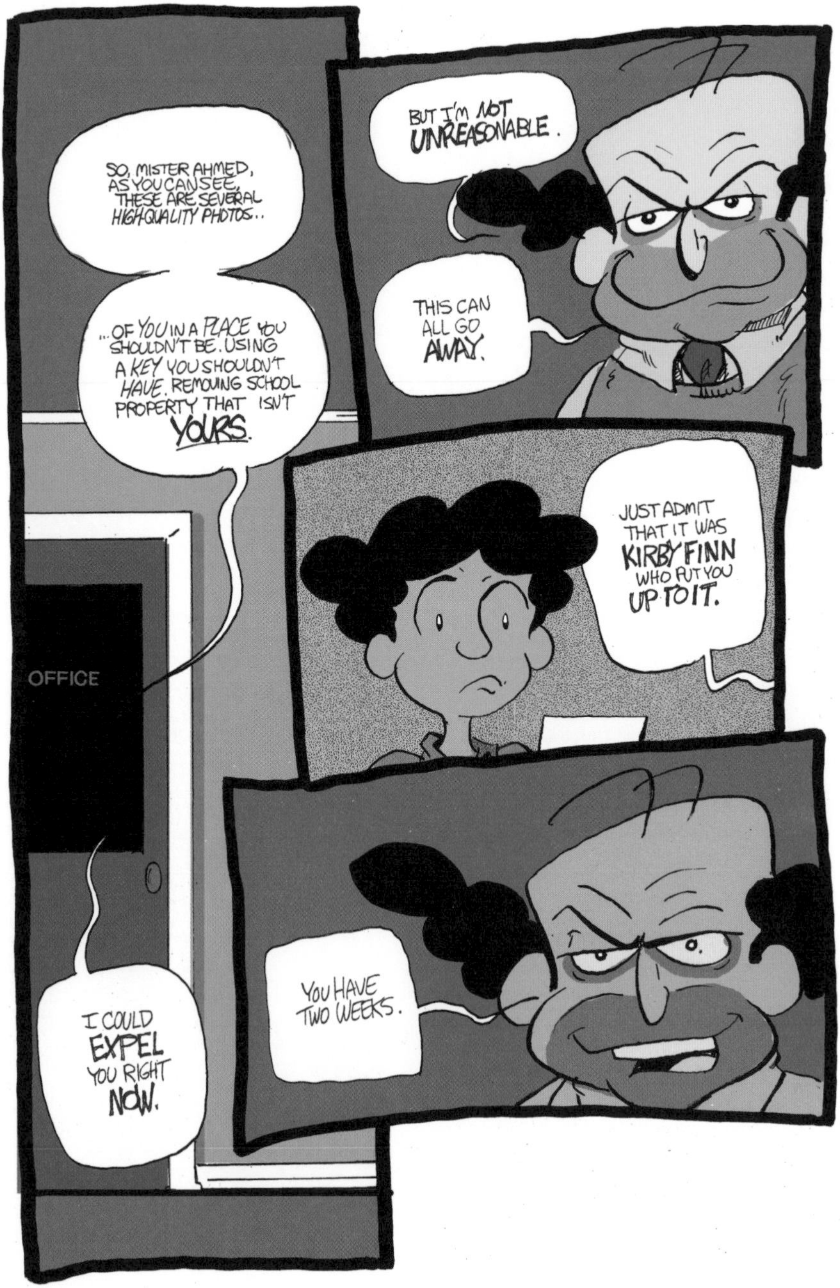
SO, MISTER AHMED, AS YOU CAN SEE, THESE ARE SEVERAL HIGH-QUALITY PHOTOS...
...OF YOU IN A PLACE YOU SHOULDN'T BE. USING A KEY YOU SHOULDN'T HAVE. REMOVING SCHOOL PROPERTY THAT ISN'T YOURS.
OFFICE
I COULD EXPEL YOU RIGHT NOW.
BUT I'M NOT UNREASONABLE.
THIS CAN ALL GO AWAY.
JUST ADMIT THAT IT WAS KIRBY FINN WHO PUT YOU UP TO IT.
YOU HAVE TWO WEEKS.

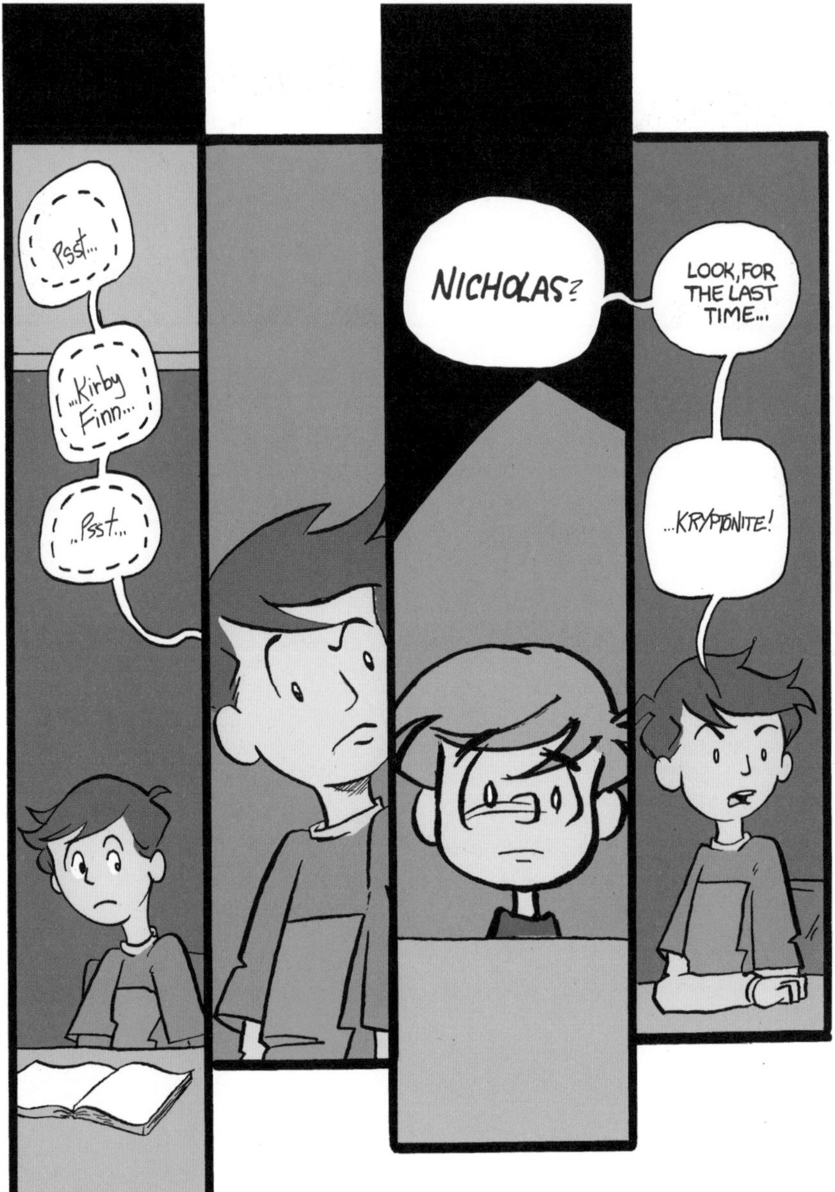
Psst...
...Kirby Finn...
...Psst...
NICHOLAS?
LOOK, FOR THE LAST TIME...
...KRYPTONITE!

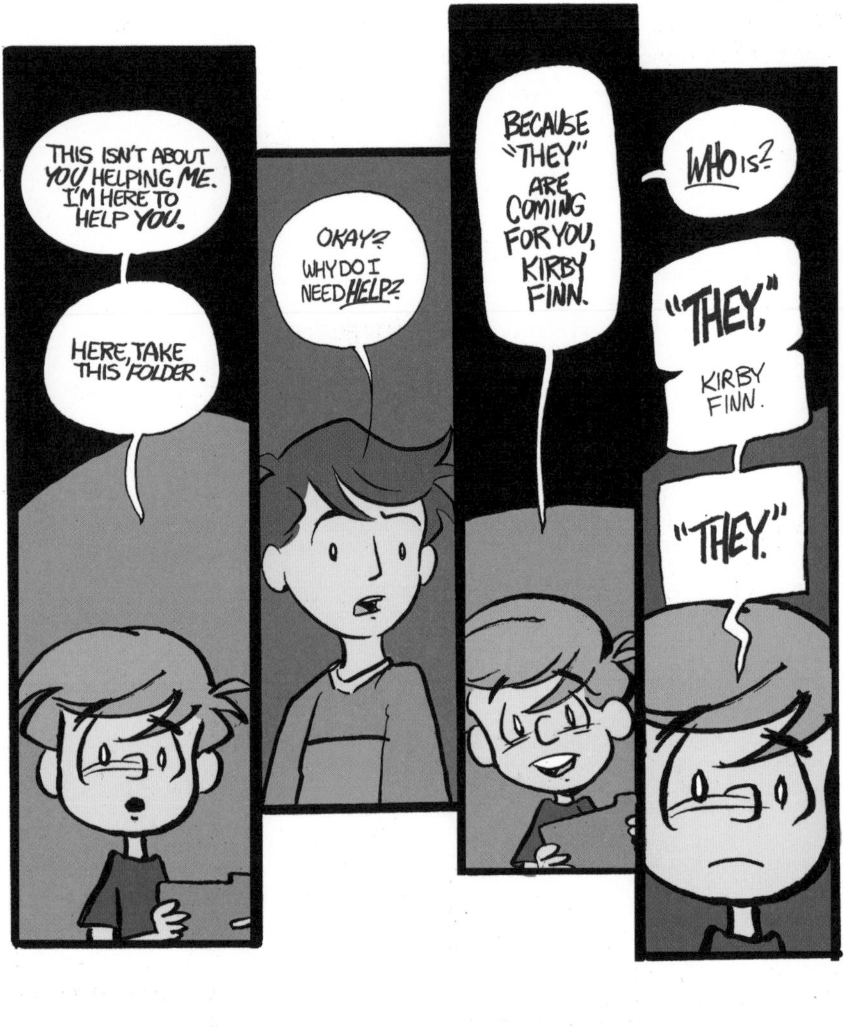
THIS ISN'T ABOUT YOU HELPING ME. I'M HERE TO HELP YOU.
HERE, TAKE THIS FOLDER.
OKAY? WHY DO I NEED HELP?
BECAUSE "THEY" ARE COMING FOR YOU, KIRBY FINN.
WHO IS?
"THEY," KIRBY FINN.
"THEY."

MAJOR DICTIONARY.com

"THE PHANTOM MOMENT"

(noun)The point where even the die-hard supporters begin to lose faith.

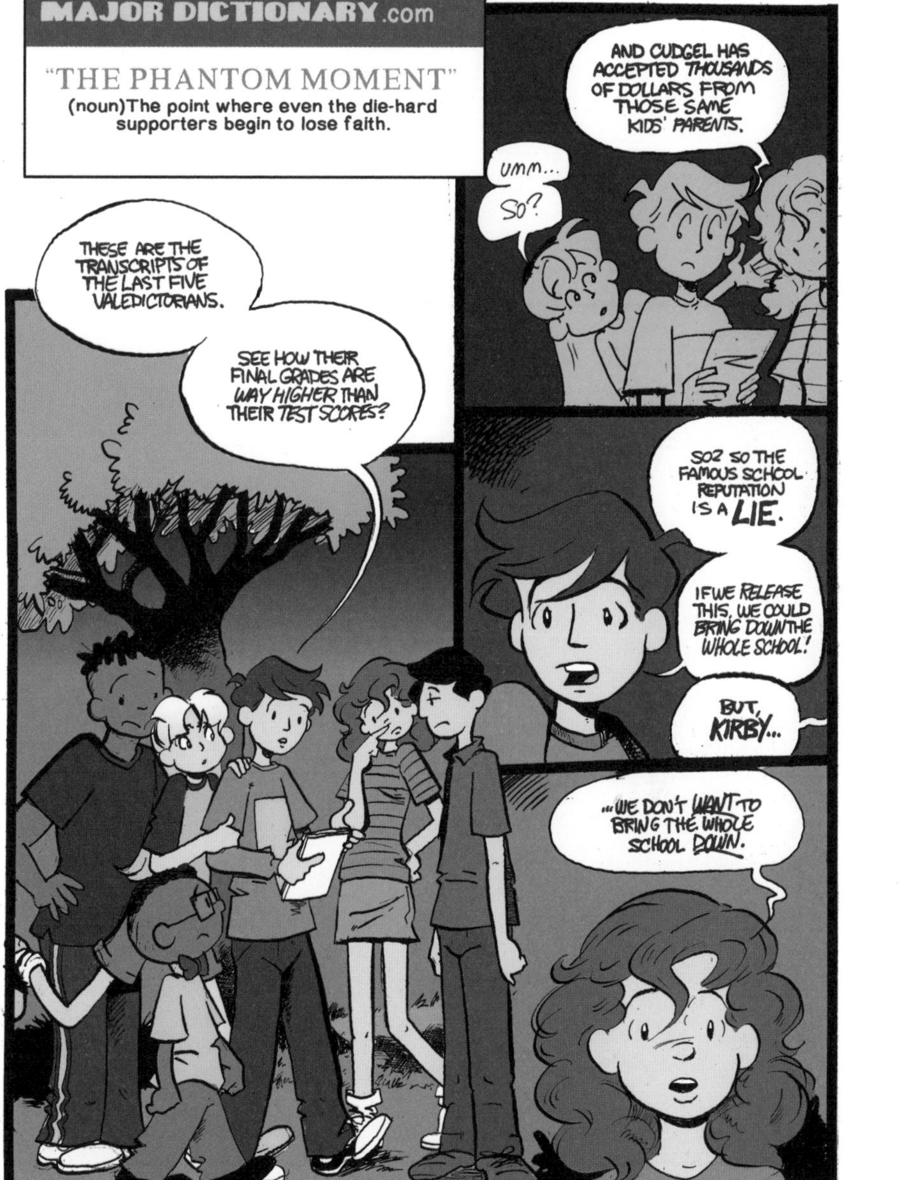

THESE ARE THE TRANSCRIPTS OF THE LAST FIVE VALEDICTORIANS.
SEE HOW THEIR FINAL GRADES ARE *WAY HIGHER* THAN THEIR *TEST SCORES*?
AND CUDGEL HAS ACCEPTED *THOUSANDS* OF DOLLARS FROM THOSE SAME KIDS' *PARENTS*.
UMM... SO?
SO? SO THE FAMOUS SCHOOL REPUTATION IS A **LIE**.
IF WE *RELEASE* THIS, WE COULD *BRING DOWN* THE *WHOLE SCHOOL*!
BUT, **KIRBY**...
...WE DON'T WANT TO BRING THE WHOLE SCHOOL DOWN.

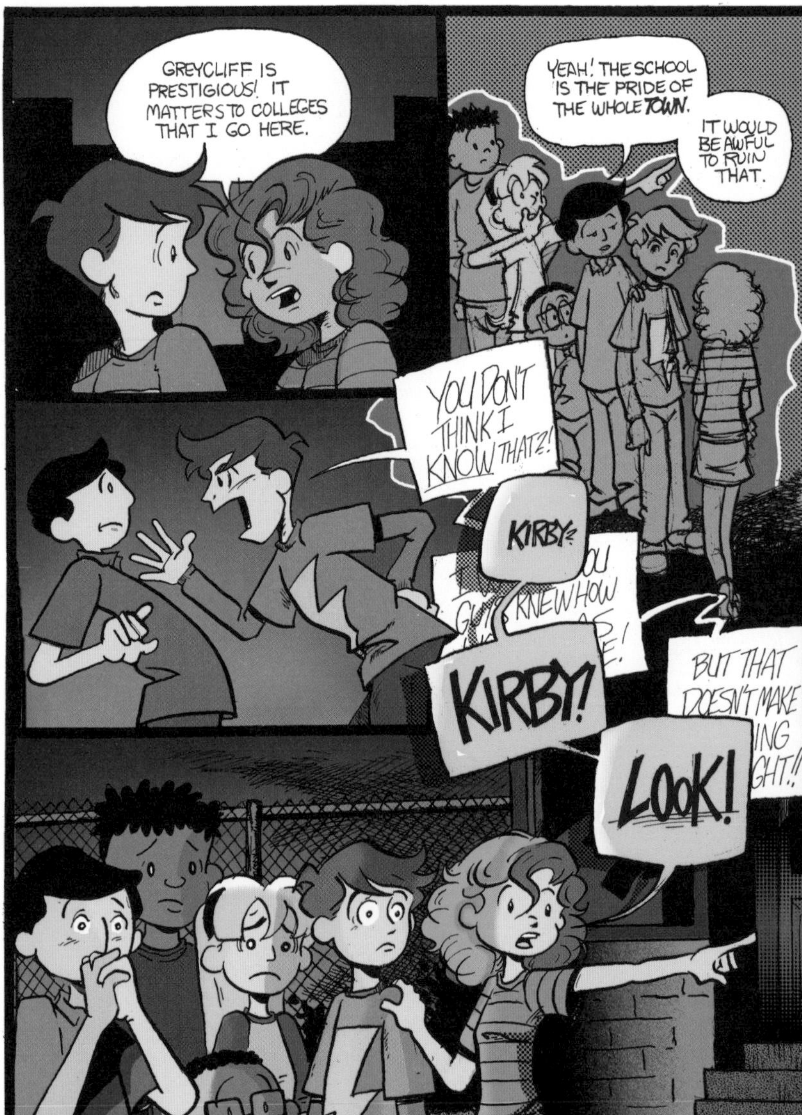
GREYCLIFF IS PRESTIGIOUS! IT MATTERS TO COLLEGES THAT I GO HERE.
YEAH! THE SCHOOL IS THE PRIDE OF THE WHOLE TOWN.
IT WOULD BE AWFUL TO RUIN THAT.
YOU DON'T THINK I KNOW THAT?!
KIRBY?!
KIRBY!
LOOK!

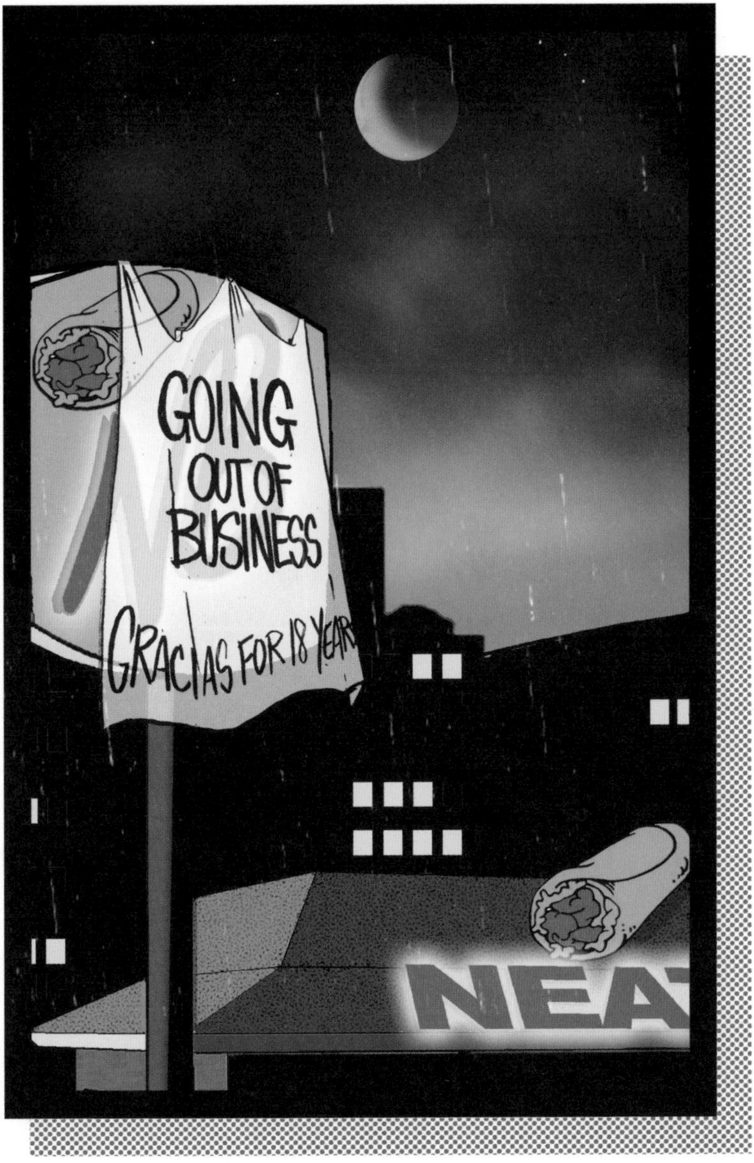
GOING
OUT OF
BUSINESS
GRACIAS FOR 18 YEARS
NEA

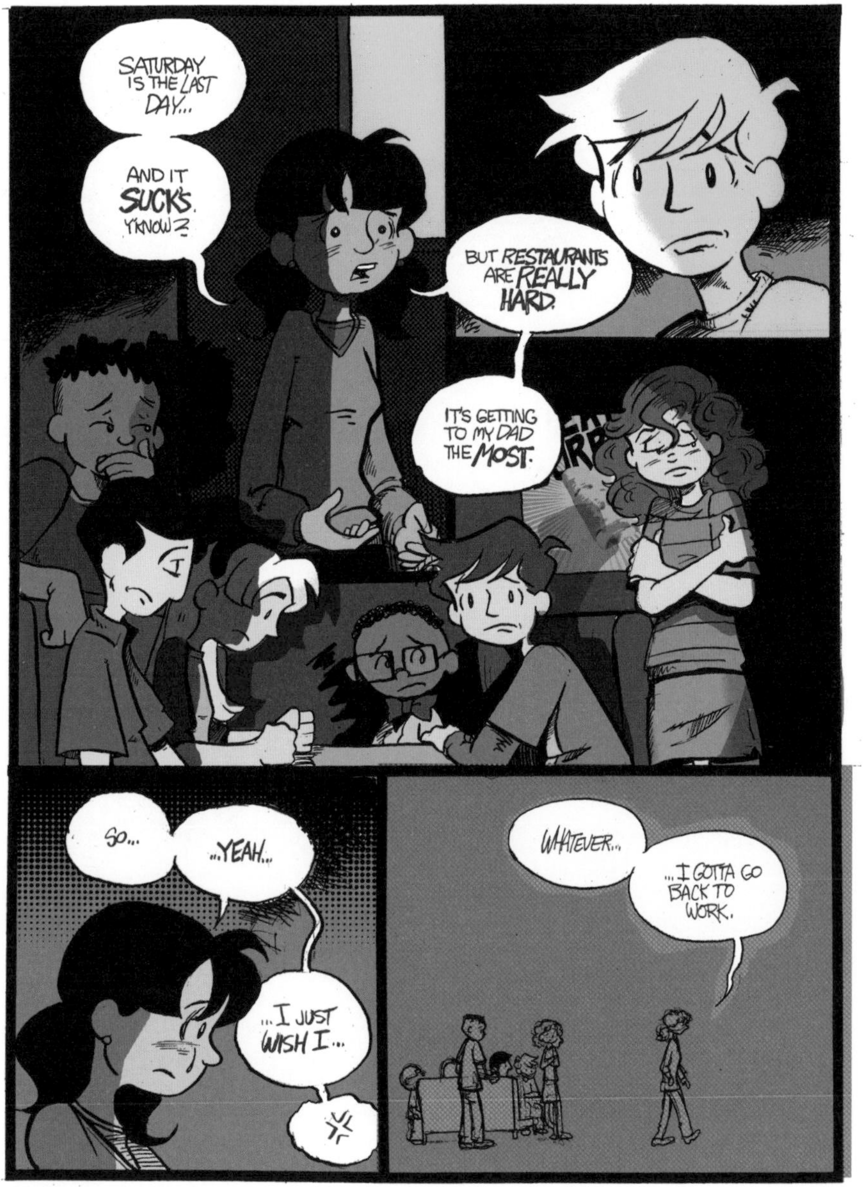
SATURDAY IS THE LAST DAY...
AND IT SUCKS. Y'KNOW?
BUT RESTAURANTS ARE REALLY HARD.
IT'S GETTING TO MY DAD THE MOST.
SO...
...YEAH...
...I JUST WISH I...
WHATEVER...
...I GOTTA GO BACK TO WORK.

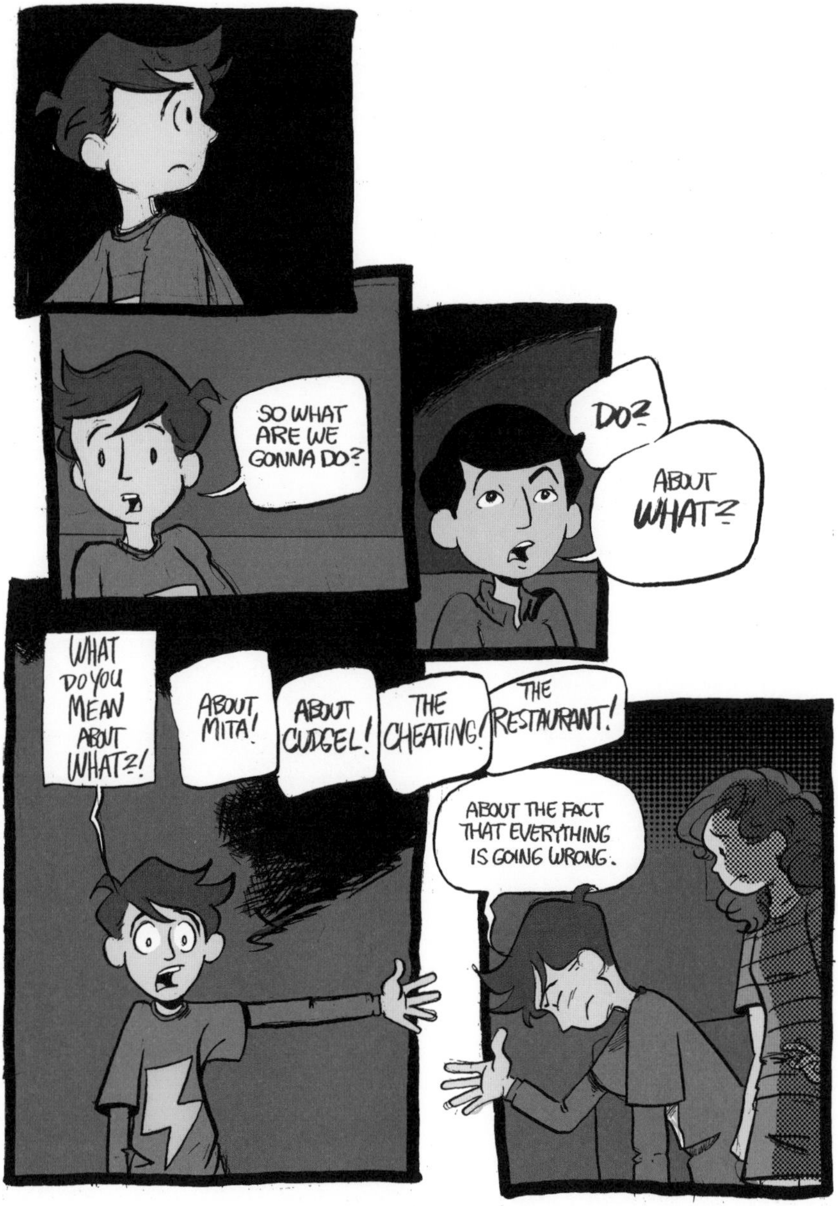
SO WHAT ARE WE GONNA DO?
DO?
ABOUT WHAT?
WHAT DO YOU MEAN ABOUT WHAT?!
ABOUT, MITA!
ABOUT CUDGEL!
THE CHEATING!
THE RESTAURANT!
ABOUT THE FACT THAT EVERYTHING IS GOING WRONG.

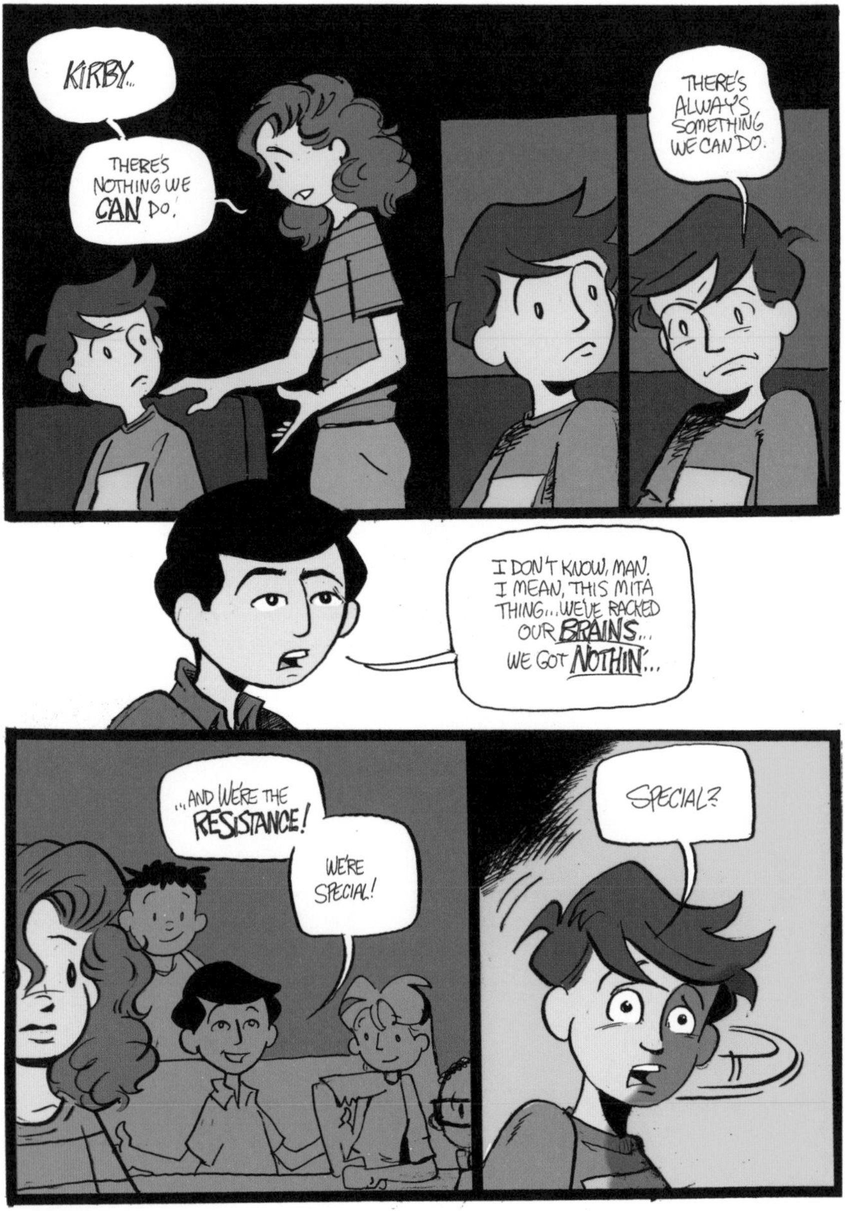
KIRBY...
THERE'S NOTHING WE CAN DO.
THERE'S ALWAYS SOMETHING WE CAN DO.
I DON'T KNOW, MAN. I MEAN, THIS MITA THING... WE'VE RACKED OUR BRAINS... WE GOT NOTHIN'...
...AND WE'RE THE RESISTANCE!
WE'RE SPECIAL!
SPECIAL?

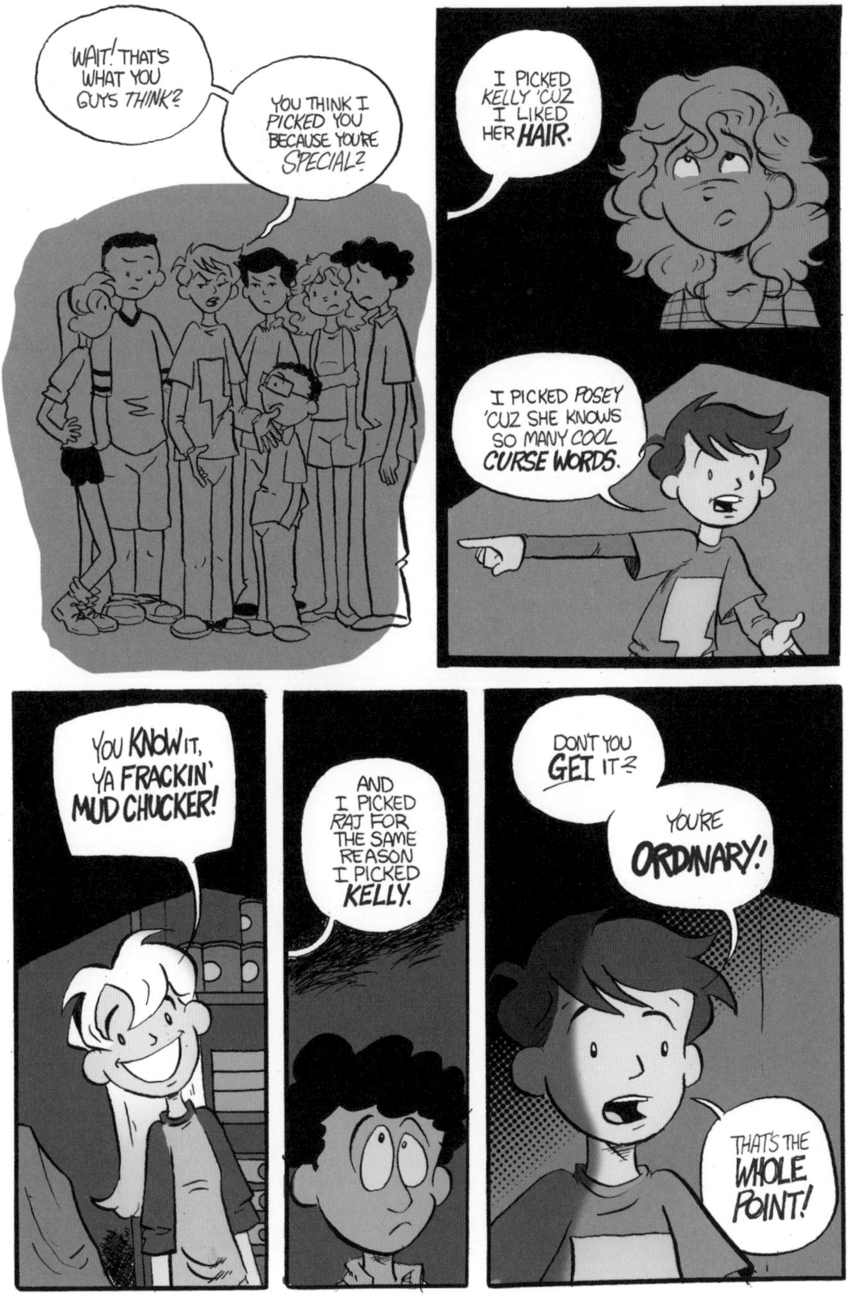
WAIT! THAT'S WHAT YOU GUYS THINK?
YOU THINK I PICKED YOU BECAUSE YOU'RE SPECIAL?
I PICKED KELLY 'CUZ I LIKED HER HAIR.
I PICKED POSEY 'CUZ SHE KNOWS SO MANY COOL CURSE WORDS.
YOU KNOW IT, YA FRACKIN' MUD CHUCKER!
AND I PICKED RAJ FOR THE SAME REASON I PICKED KELLY.
DON'T YOU GET IT?
YOU'RE ORDINARY!
THAT'S THE WHOLE POINT!

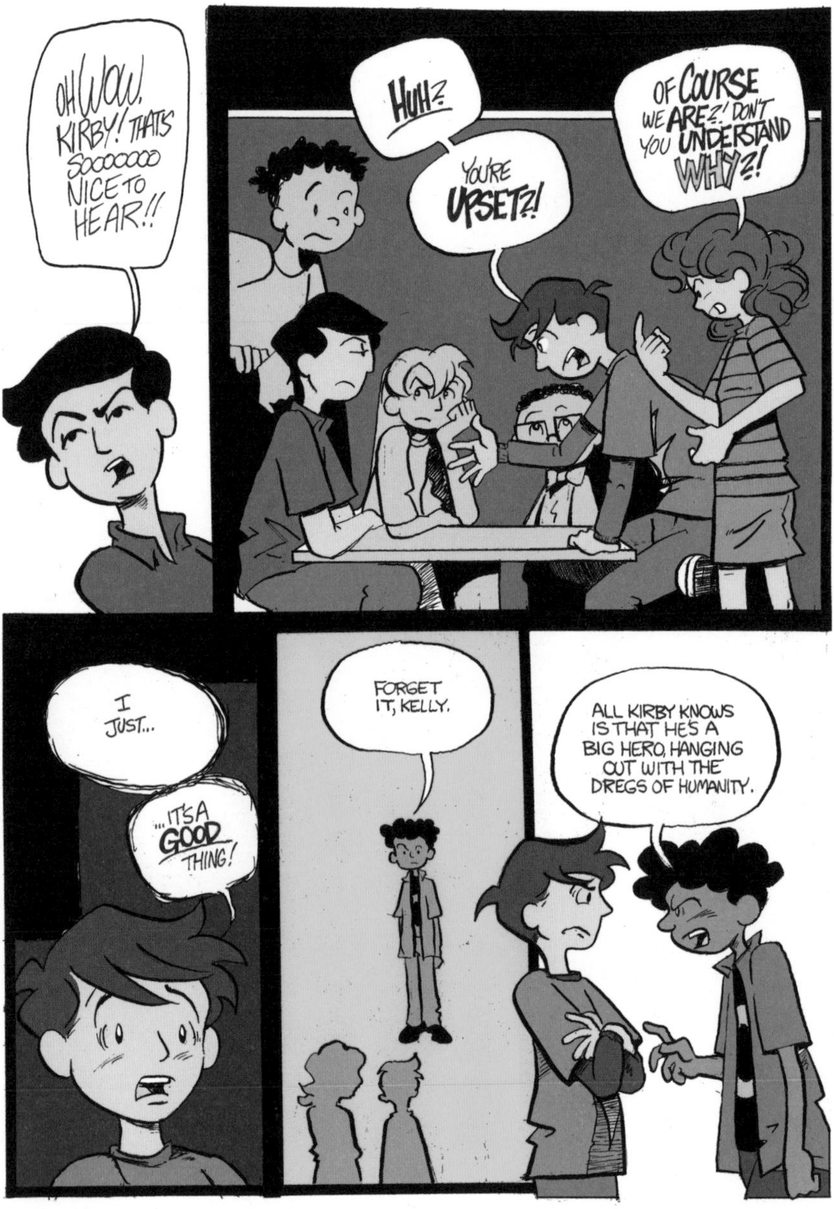
OH WOW, KIRBY! THAT'S SOOOOOOO NICE TO HEAR!!
HUH?!
YOU'RE UPSET?!
OF COURSE WE ARE?! DON'T YOU UNDERSTAND WHY?!
I JUST...
...IT'S A GOOD THING!
FORGET IT, KELLY.
ALL KIRBY KNOWS IS THAT HE'S A BIG HERO, HANGING OUT WITH THE DREGS OF HUMANITY.

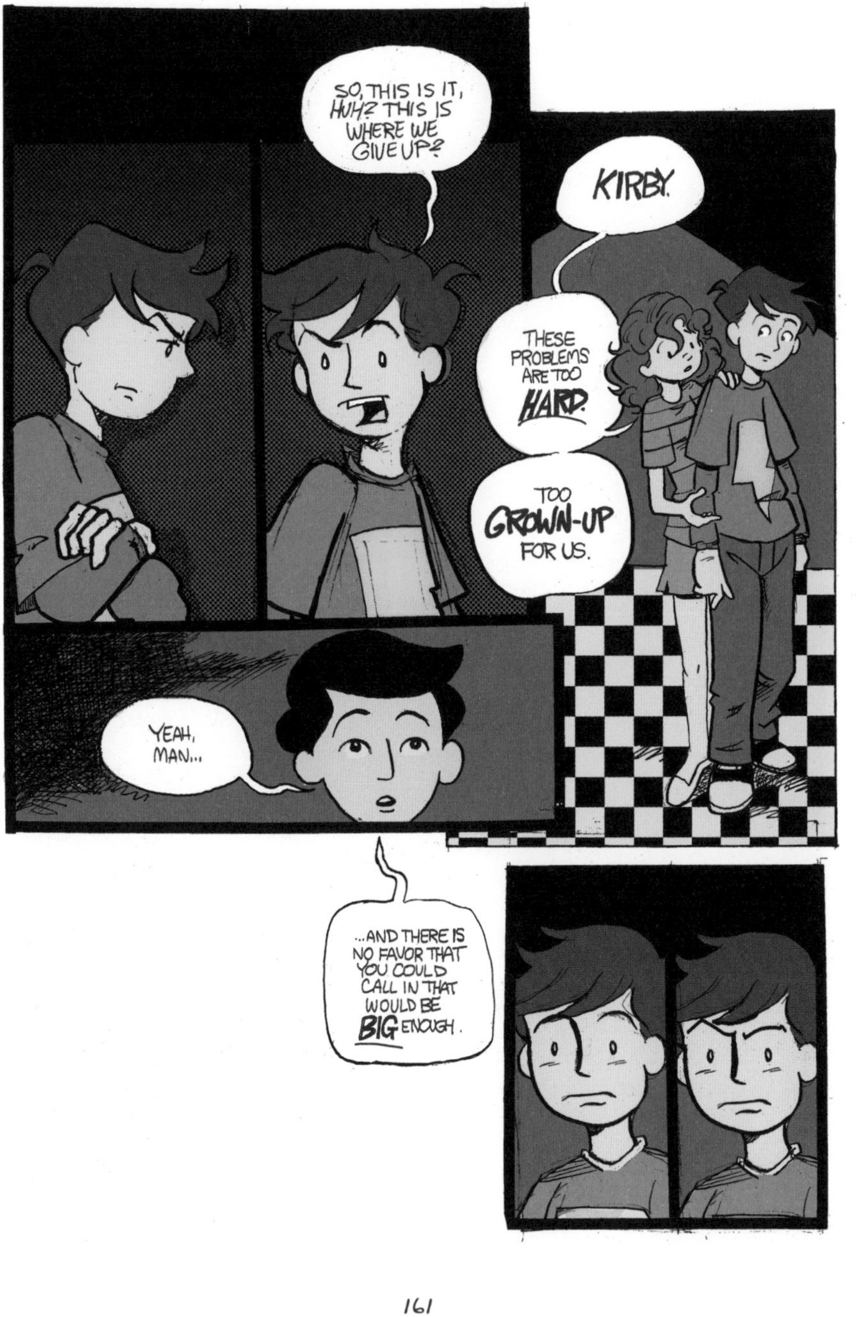
SO, THIS IS IT, HUH? THIS IS WHERE WE GIVE UP?
KIRBY.
THESE PROBLEMS ARE TOO HARD.
TOO GROWN-UP FOR US.
YEAH, MAN...
...AND THERE IS NO FAVOR THAT YOU COULD CALL IN THAT WOULD BE BIG ENOUGH.

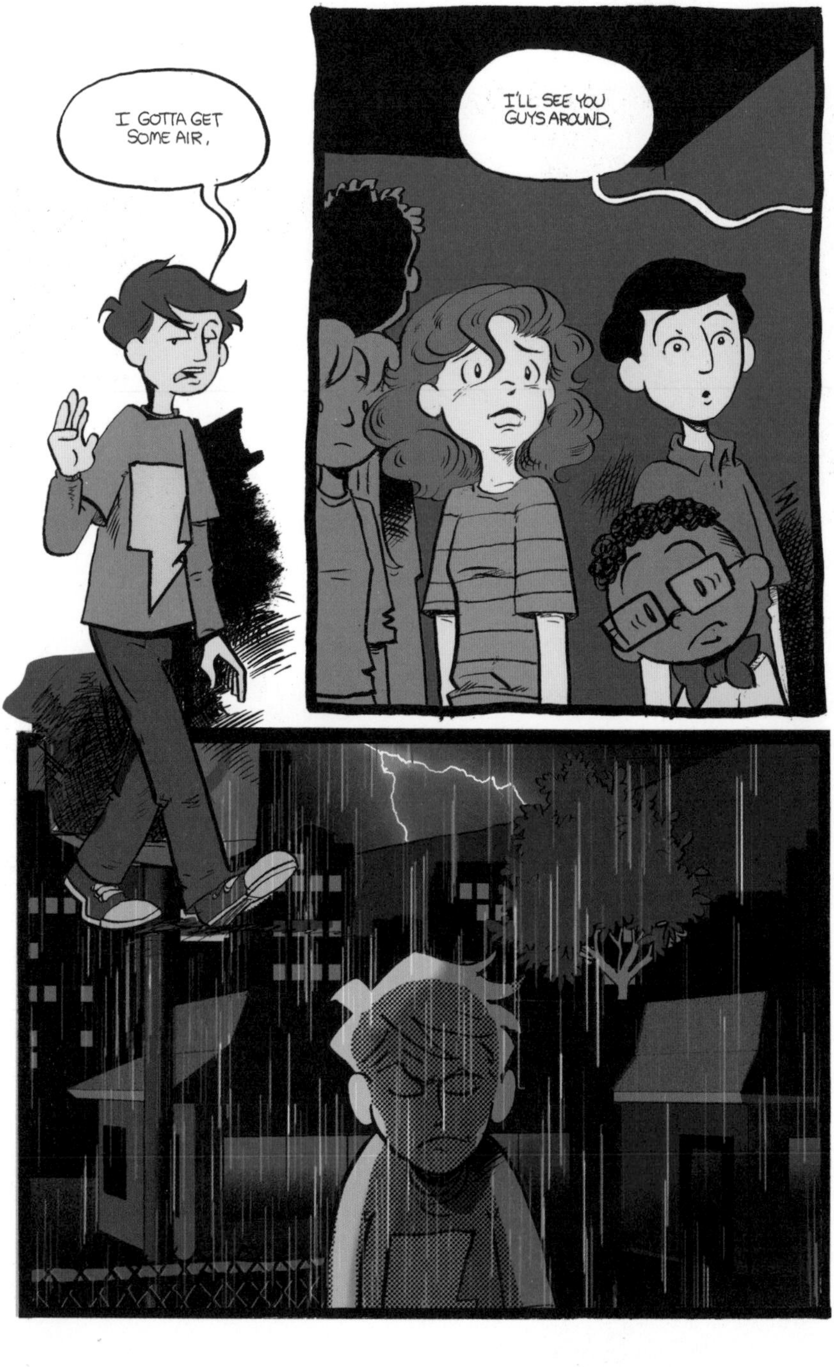
I GOTTA GET SOME AIR.
I'LL SEE YOU GUYS AROUND.

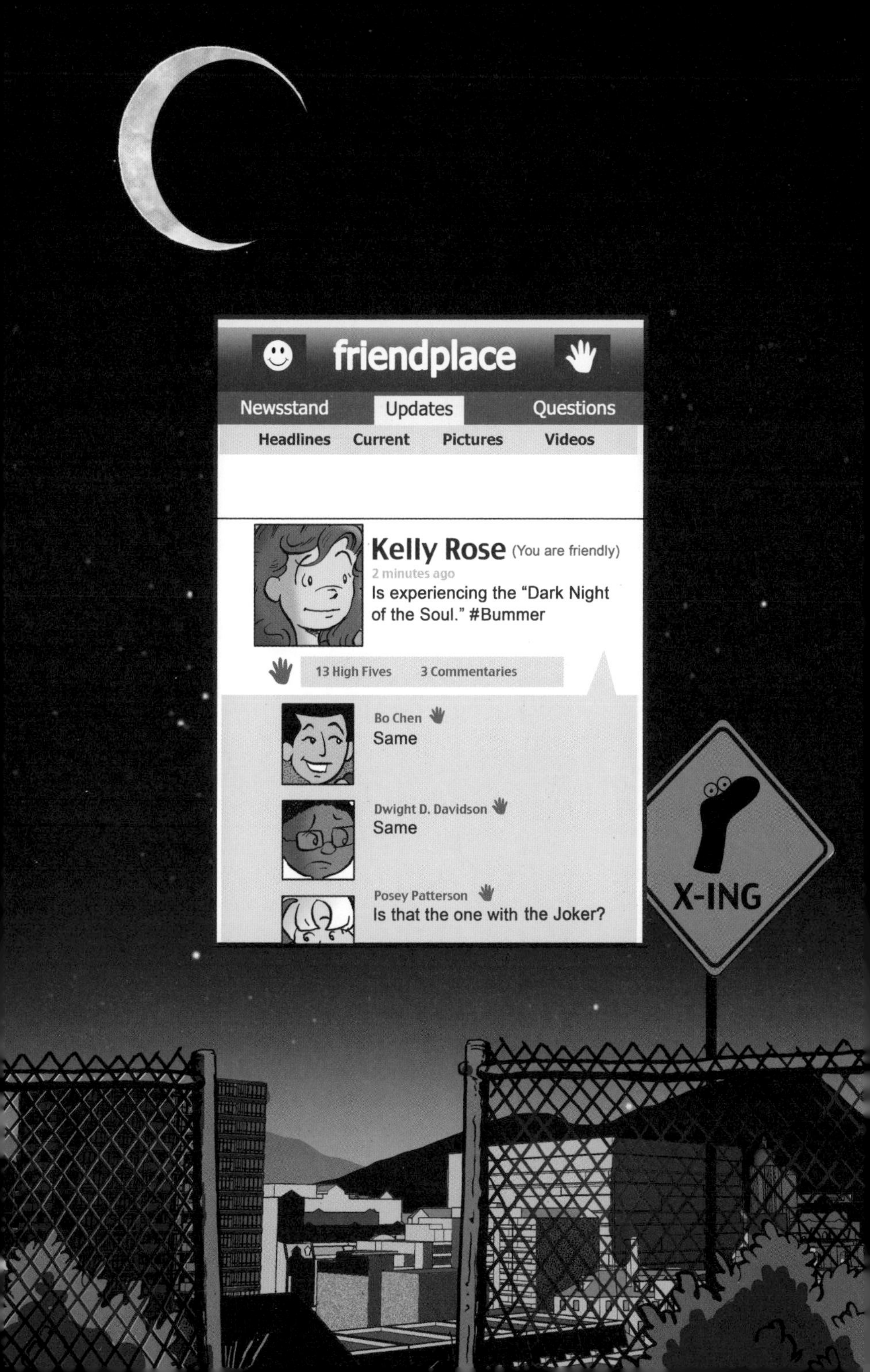
friendplace
Newsstand
Updates
Questions
Headlines
Current
Pictures
Videos
Kelly Rose (You are friendly)
2 minutes ago
Is experiencing the "Dark Night of the Soul." #Bummer
13 High Fives
3 Commentaries
Bo Chen
Same
Dwight D. Davidson
Same
Posey Patterson
Is that the one with the Joker?
X-ING

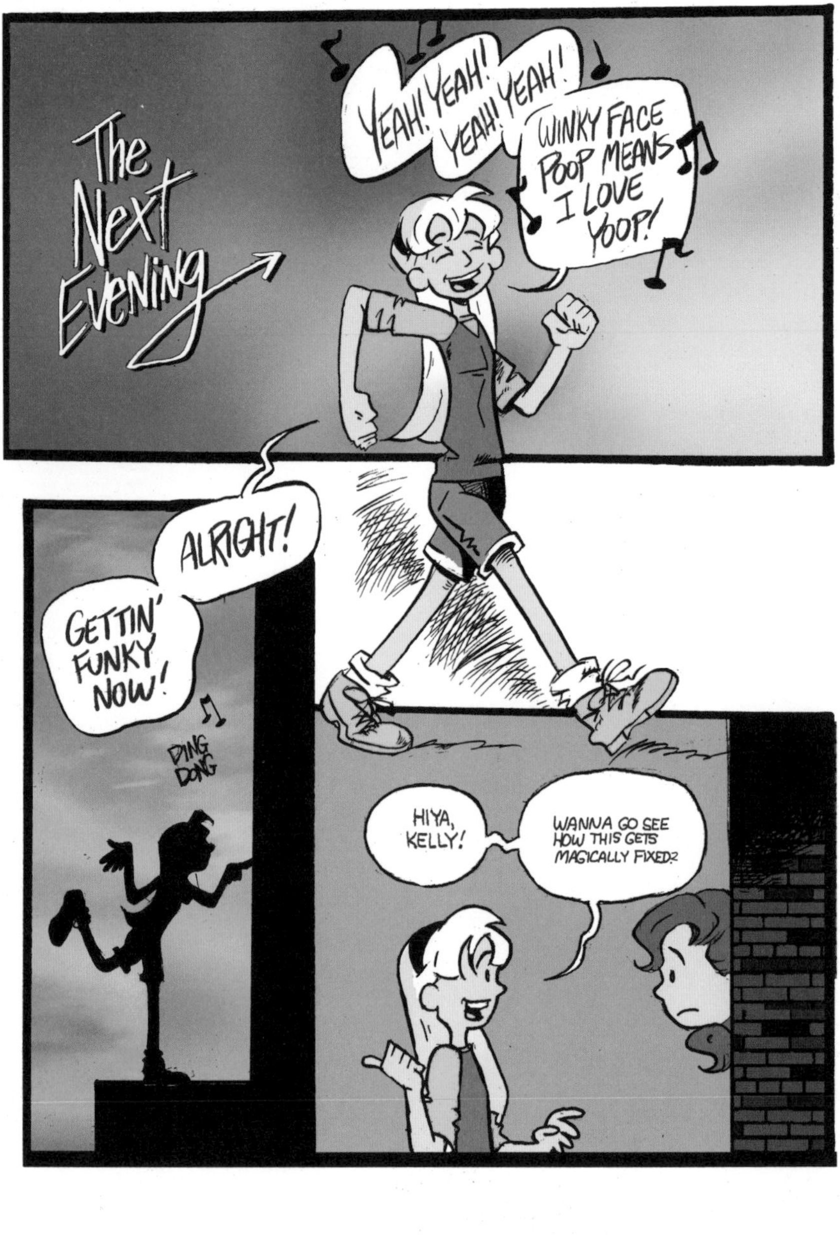
The Next Evening
YEAH! YEAH! YEAH! YEAH!
WINKY FACE POOP MEANS I LOVE YOOP!
ALRIGHT!
GETTIN' FUNKY NOW!
DING DONG
HIYA, KELLY!
WANNA GO SEE HOW THIS GETS MAGICALLY FIXED?

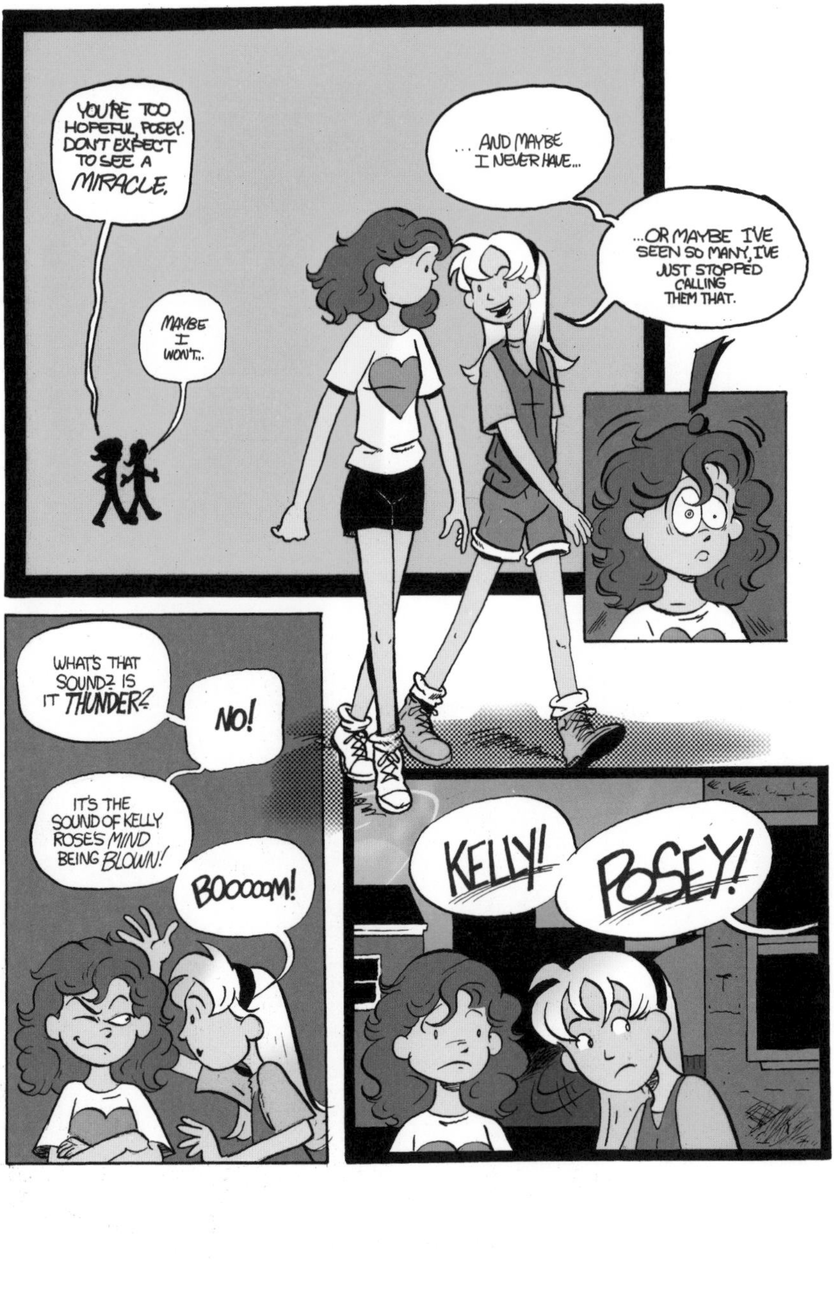
YOU'RE TOO HOPEFUL, POSEY. DON'T EXPECT TO SEE A MIRACLE.
MAYBE I WON'T...
... AND MAYBE I NEVER HAVE...
...OR MAYBE I'VE SEEN SO MANY, I'VE JUST STOPPED CALLING THEM THAT.
WHAT'S THAT SOUND? IS IT THUNDER?
NO!
IT'S THE SOUND OF KELLY ROSE'S MIND BEING BLOWN!
BOOOOOM!
KELLY!
POSEY!

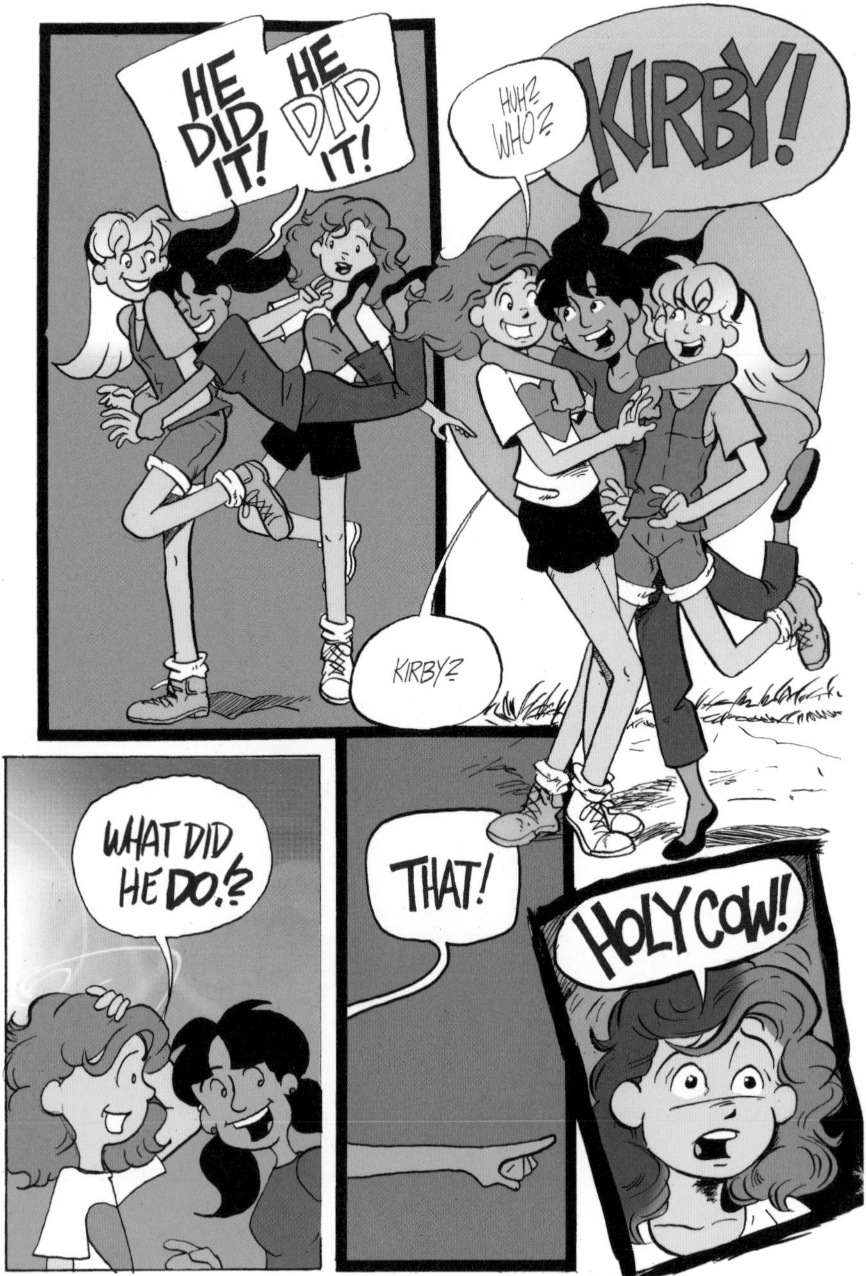
HE DID IT!
HE DID IT!
HUH? WHO?
KIRBY!
KIRBY?
WHAT DID HE DO?!?
THAT!
HOLY COW!

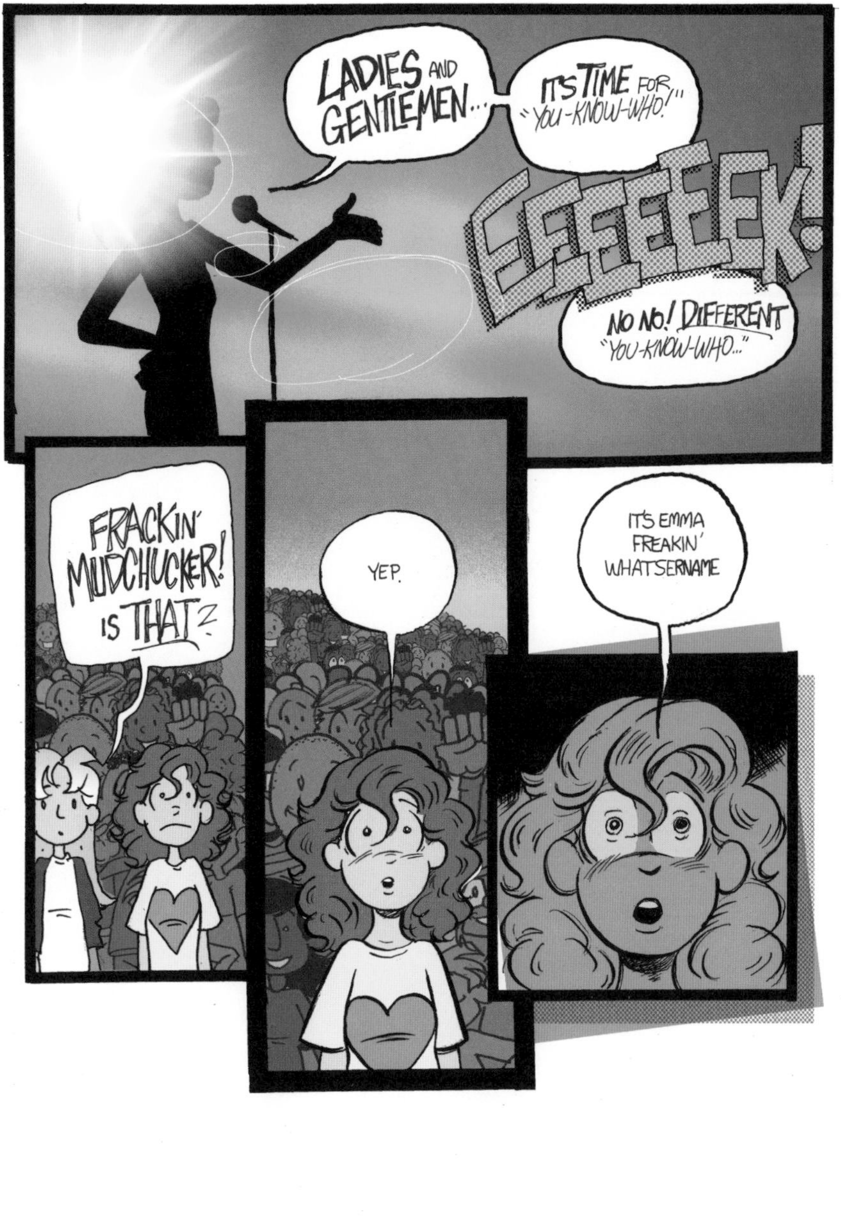
LADIES AND GENTLEMEN...
IT'S TIME FOR "YOU-KNOW-WHO!"
EEEEEEK!
NO NO! DIFFERENT "YOU-KNOW-WHO..."
FRACKIN' MUDCHUCKER! IS THAT?
YEP.
IT'S EMMA FREAKIN' WHATSERNAME

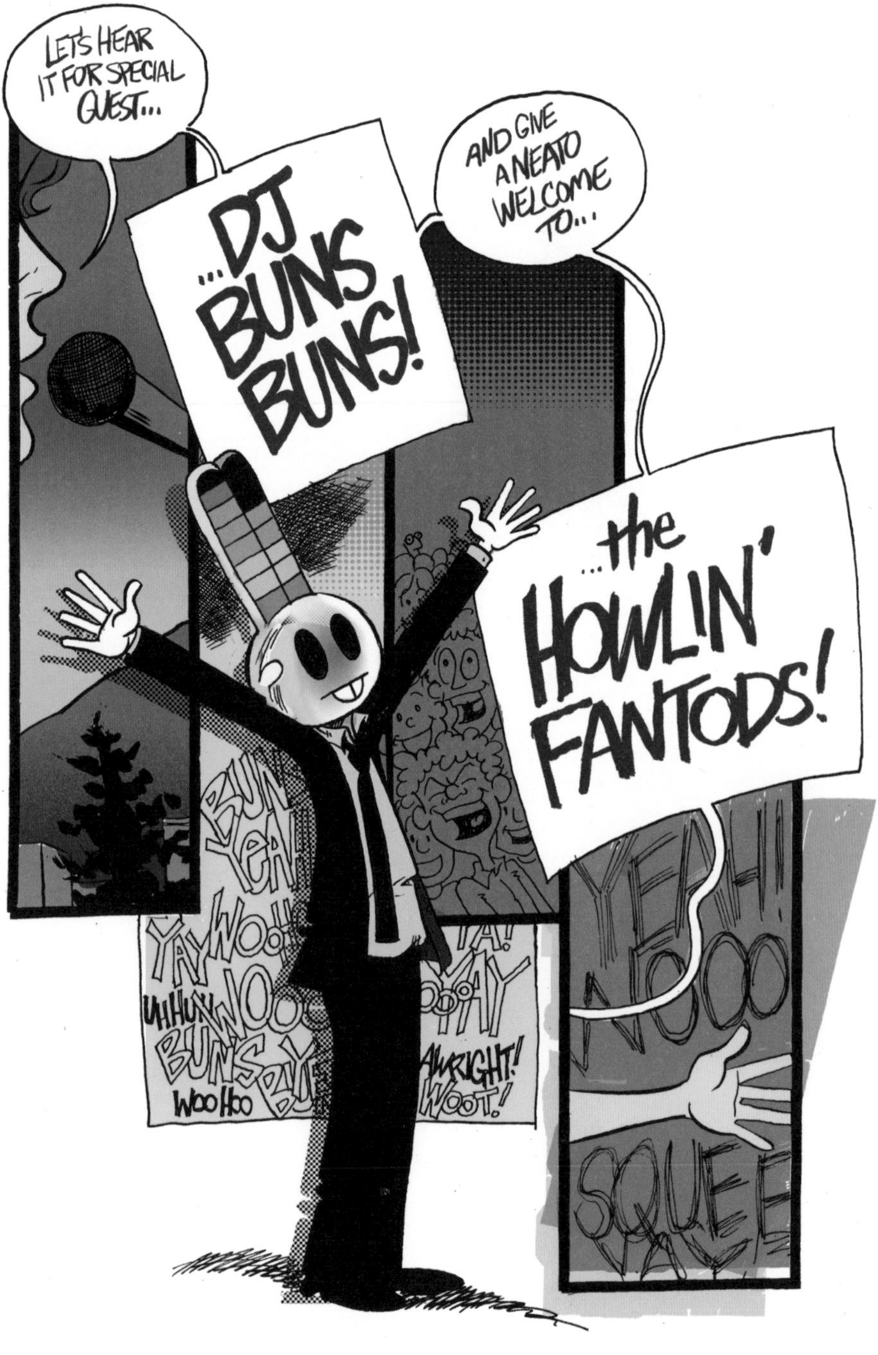
LET'S HEAR IT FOR SPECIAL GUEST...
...DJ BUNS BUNS!
AND GIVE A NEATO WELCOME TO...
...the HOWLIN' FANTODS!
YEAH! WOO YAY UHHUH BUNS WOOHOO
YAY WOOT! AWRIGHT!
YEAH! WOOOO SQUEE

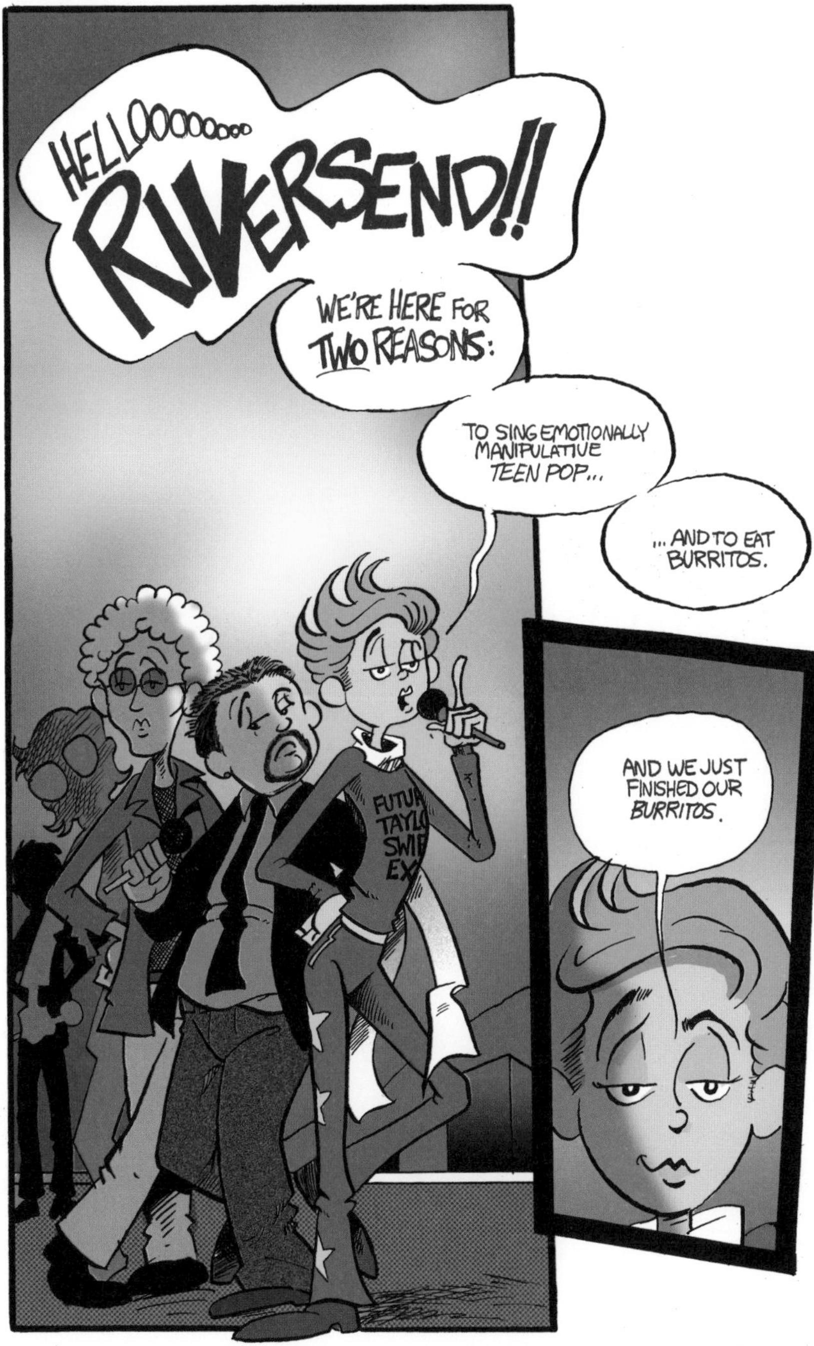
HELLOOOOOooo RIVERSEND!!
WE'RE HERE FOR TWO REASONS:
TO SING EMOTIONALLY MANIPULATIVE TEEN POP...
...AND TO EAT BURRITOS.
AND WE JUST FINISHED OUR BURRITOS.

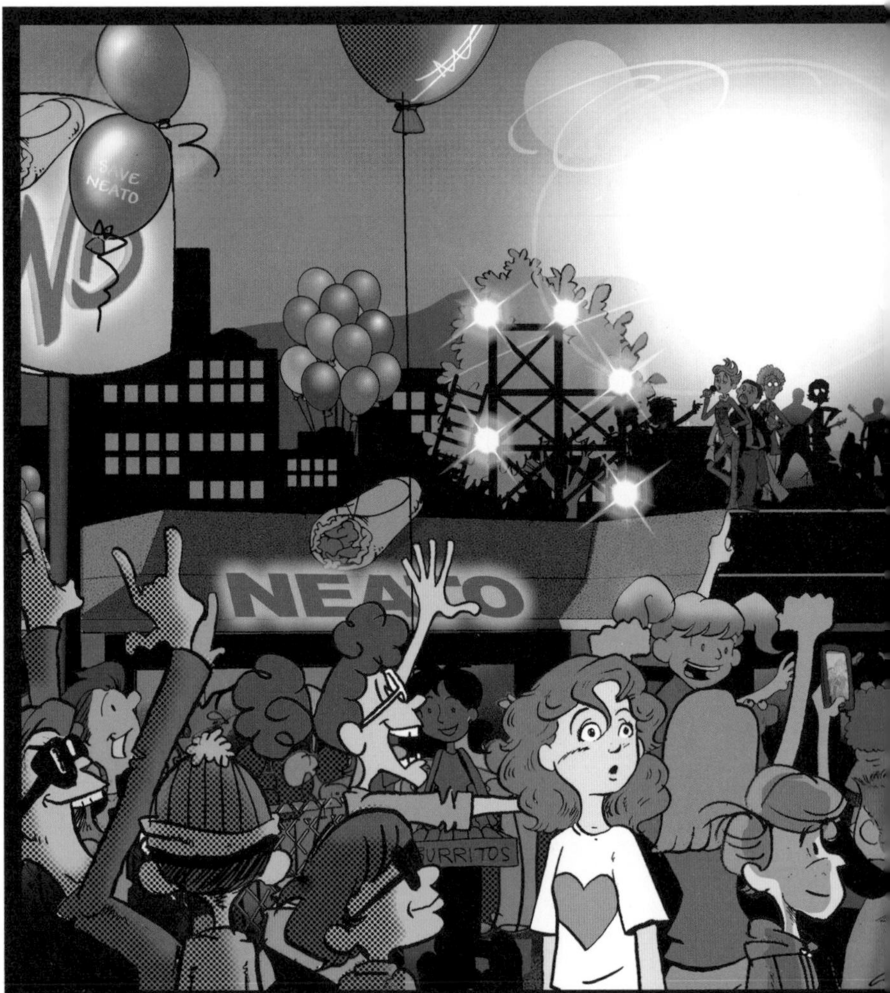
SAVE NEATO
NEATO
BURRITOS

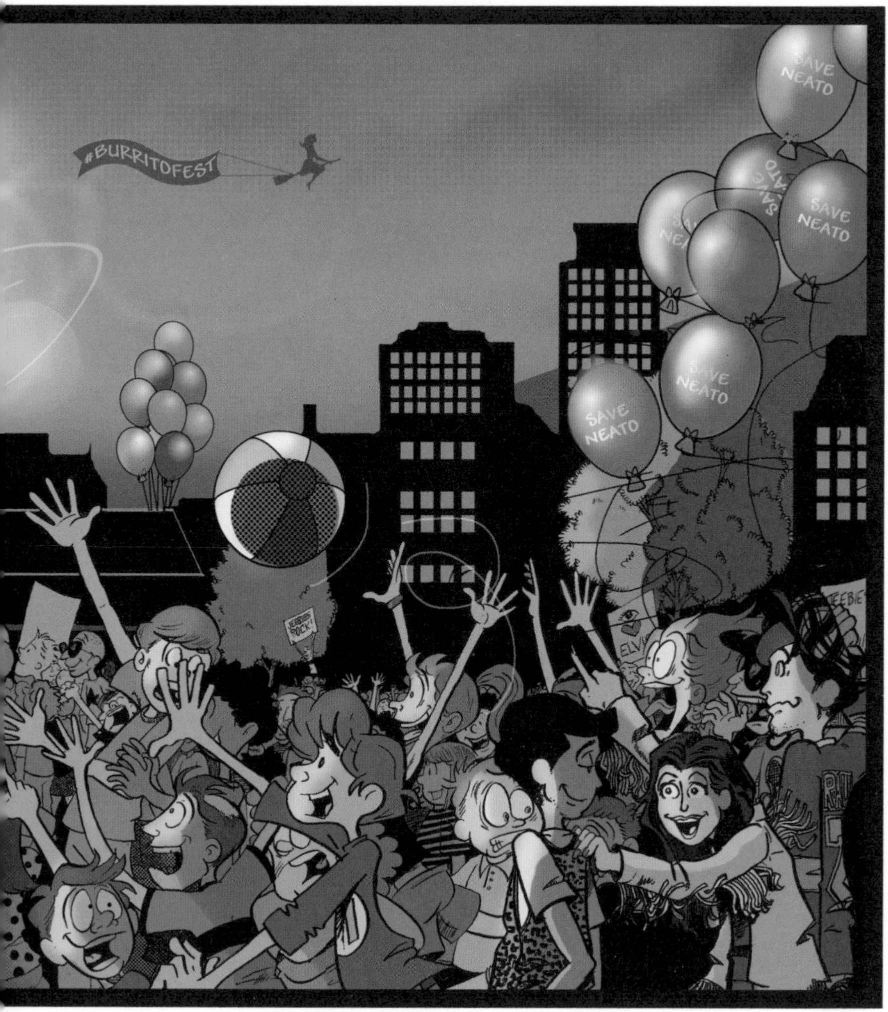
#BURRITOFEST
SAVE NEATO
SAVE NEATO
SAVE NEATO
SAVE NEATO

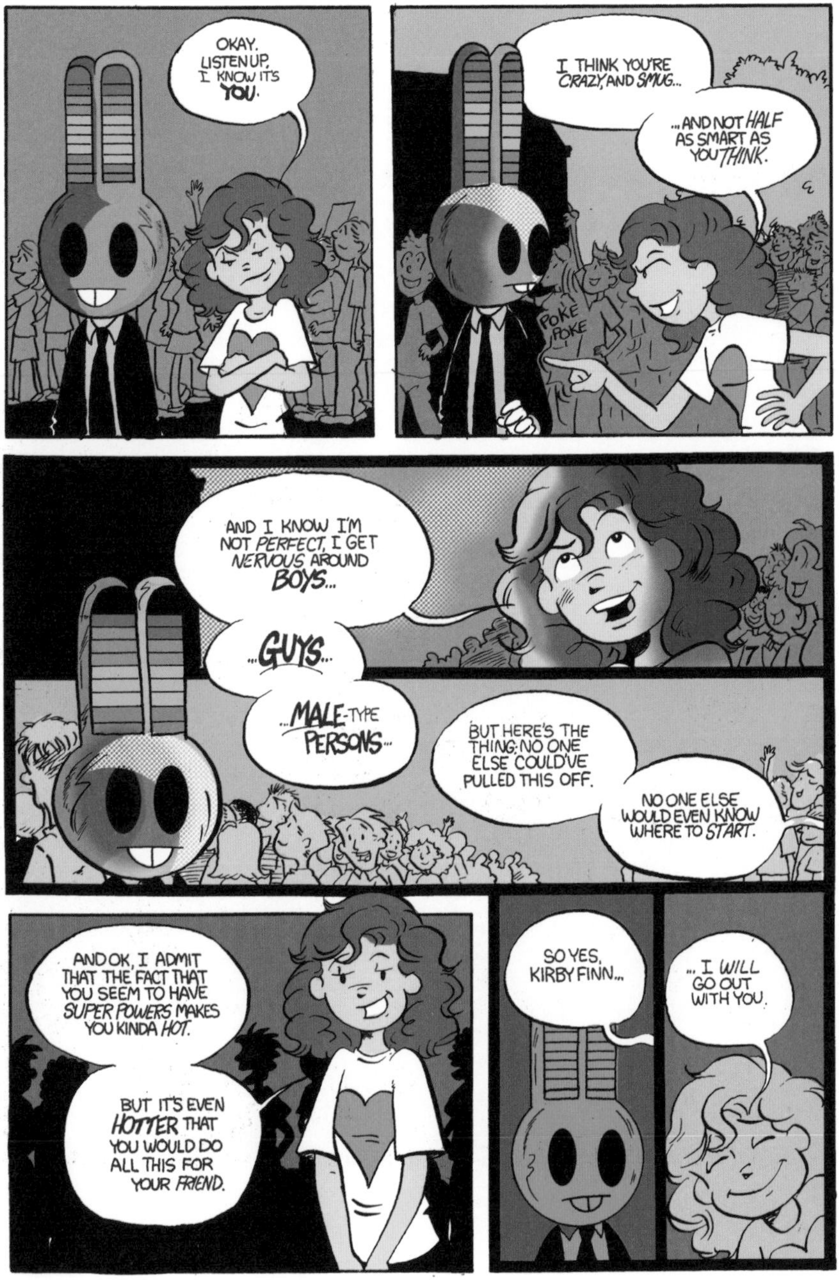
OKAY. LISTEN UP, I KNOW IT'S YOU.
I THINK YOU'RE CRAZY, AND SMUG...
...AND NOT HALF AS SMART AS YOU THINK.
POKE POKE
AND I KNOW I'M NOT PERFECT, I GET NERVOUS AROUND BOYS...
...GUYS...
...MALE-TYPE PERSONS...
BUT HERE'S THE THING: NO ONE ELSE COULD'VE PULLED THIS OFF.
NO ONE ELSE WOULD EVEN KNOW WHERE TO START.
AND OK, I ADMIT THAT THE FACT THAT YOU SEEM TO HAVE SUPER POWERS MAKES YOU KINDA HOT.
BUT IT'S EVEN HOTTER THAT YOU WOULD DO ALL THIS FOR YOUR FRIEND.
SO YES, KIRBY FINN...
...I WILL GO OUT WITH YOU.

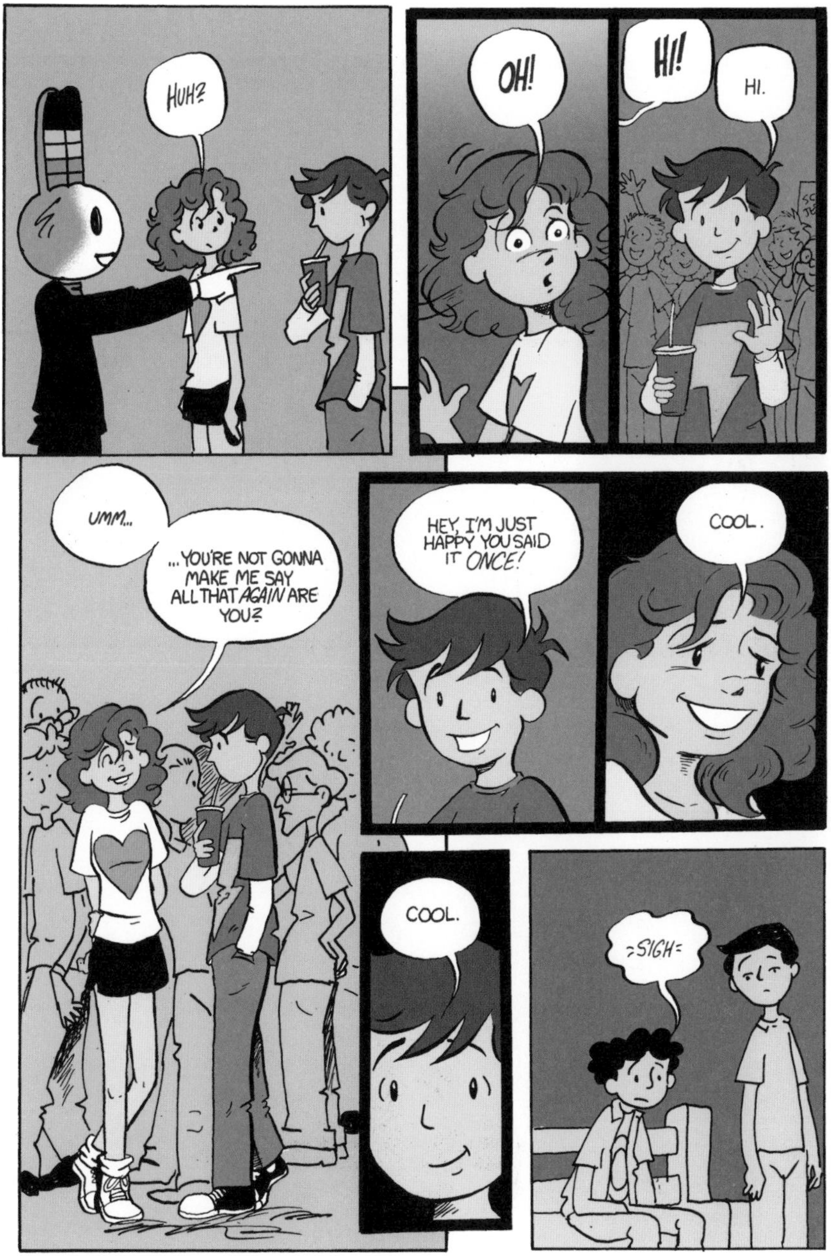
HUH?
OH!
HI!
HI.
UMM...
...YOU'RE NOT GONNA MAKE ME SAY ALL THAT AGAIN ARE YOU?
HEY, I'M JUST HAPPY YOU SAID IT ONCE!
COOL.
COOL.
SIGH

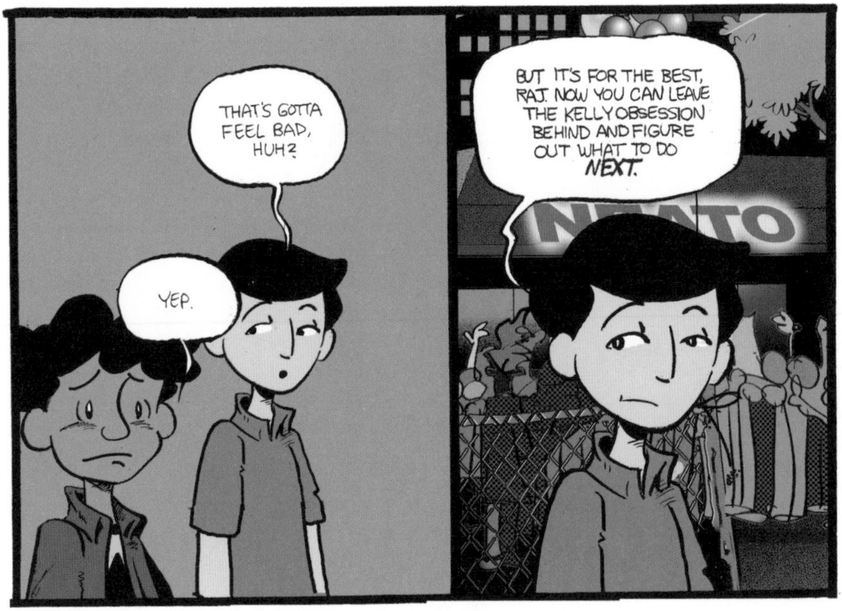
THAT'S GOTTA FEEL BAD, HUH?
YEP.
BUT IT'S FOR THE BEST, RAJ. NOW YOU CAN LEAVE THE KELLY OBSESSION BEHIND AND FIGURE OUT WHAT TO DO *NEXT.*

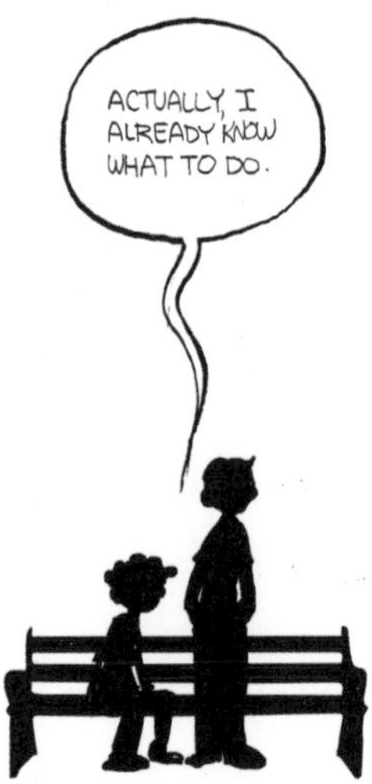
ACTUALLY, I ALREADY KNOW WHAT TO DO.

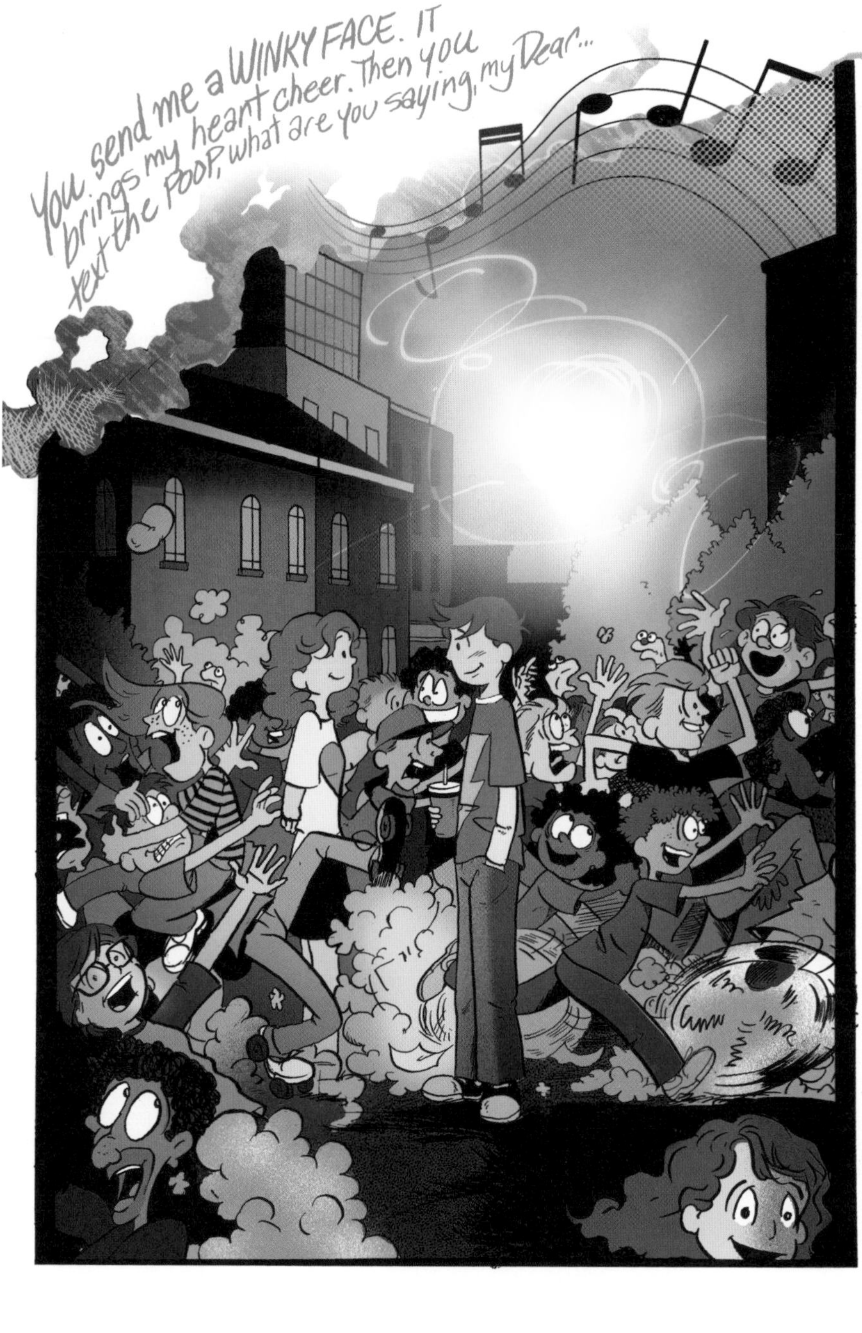
You send me a WINKY FACE. IT brings my heart cheer. Then you text the POOP, what are you saying, my Dear...

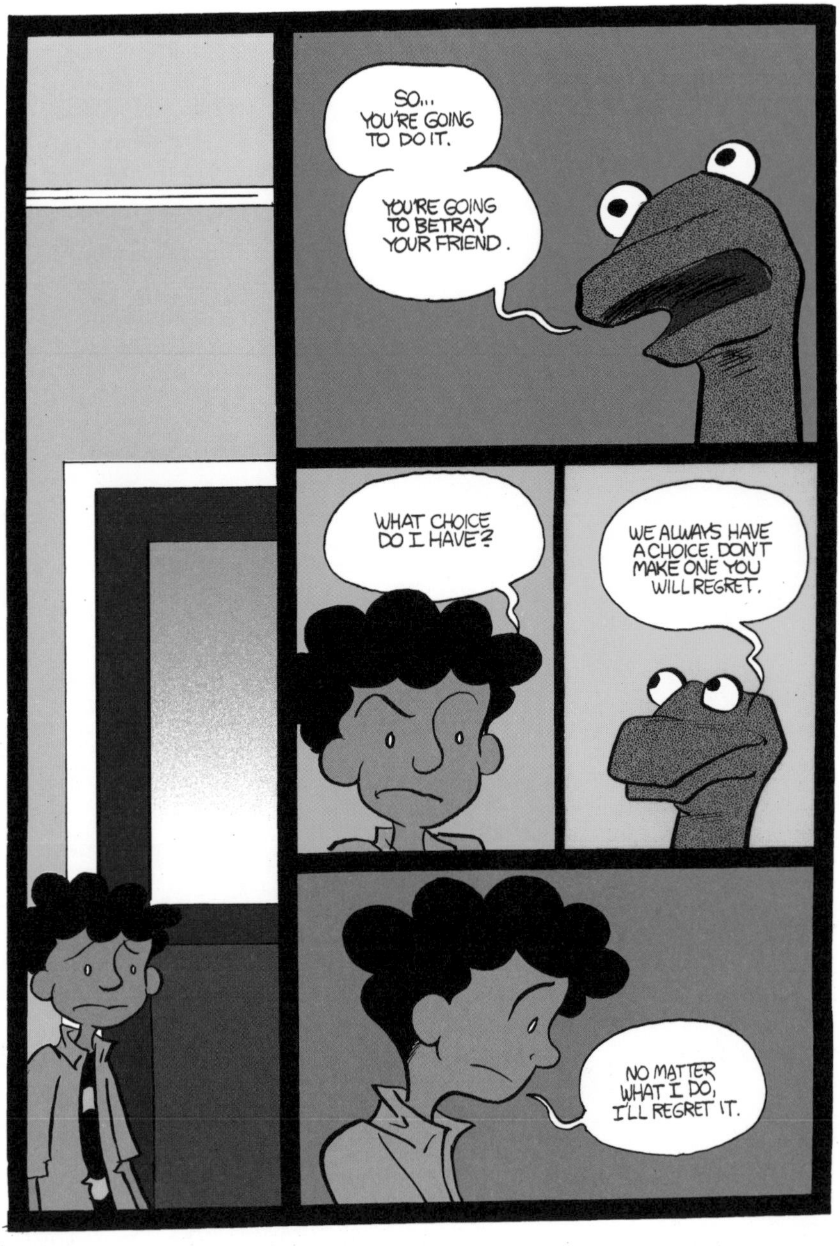
SO...
YOU'RE GOING
TO DO IT.
YOU'RE GOING
TO BETRAY
YOUR FRIEND.
WHAT CHOICE
DO I HAVE?
WE ALWAYS HAVE
A CHOICE. DON'T
MAKE ONE YOU
WILL REGRET.
NO MATTER
WHAT I DO,
I'LL REGRET IT.

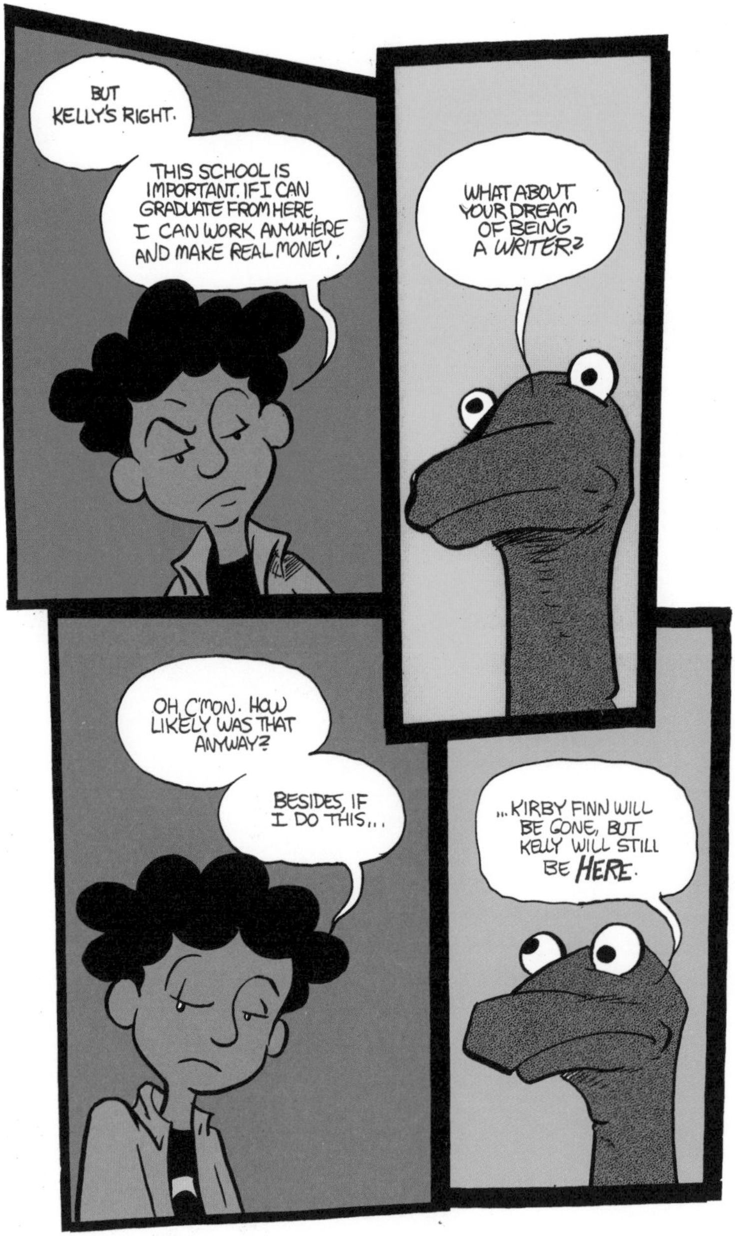
BUT KELLY'S RIGHT.
THIS SCHOOL IS IMPORTANT. IF I CAN GRADUATE FROM HERE, I CAN WORK ANYWHERE AND MAKE REAL MONEY.
WHAT ABOUT YOUR DREAM OF BEING A *WRITER*?
OH, C'MON. HOW LIKELY WAS THAT ANYWAY?
BESIDES, IF I DO THIS...
...KIRBY FINN WILL BE GONE, BUT KELLY WILL STILL BE **HERE**.

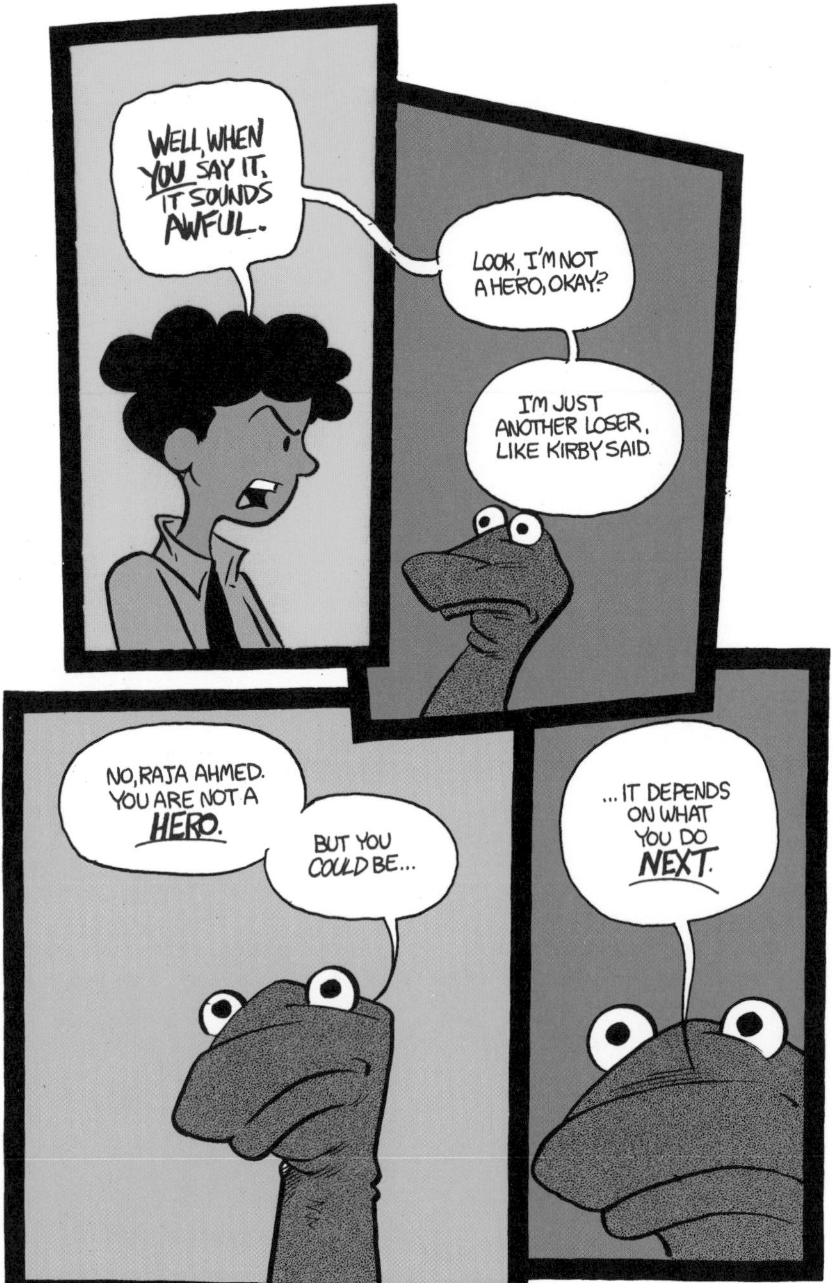

WELL, WHEN YOU SAY IT, IT SOUNDS AWFUL.
LOOK, I'M NOT A HERO, OKAY?
I'M JUST ANOTHER LOSER. LIKE KIRBY SAID.
NO, RAJA AHMED. YOU ARE NOT A HERO.
BUT YOU COULD BE...
...IT DEPENDS ON WHAT YOU DO NEXT.

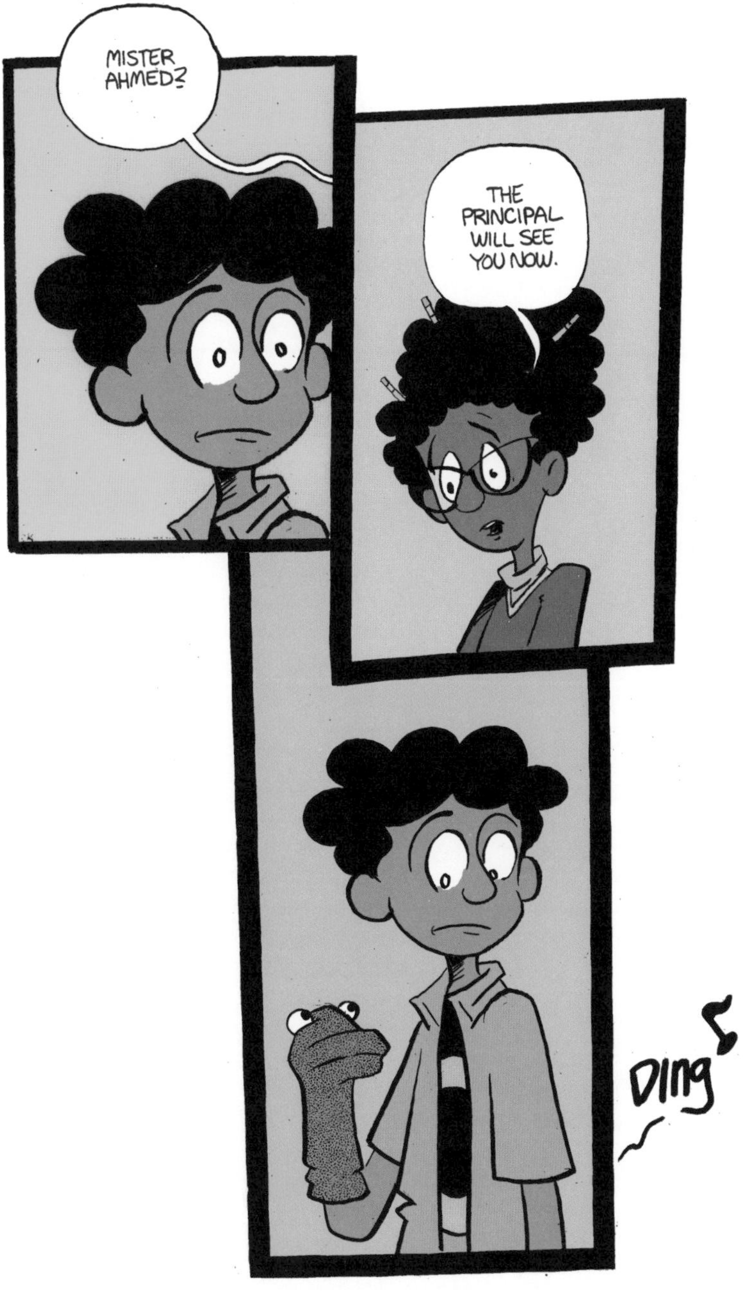
MISTER AHMED?
THE PRINCIPAL WILL SEE YOU NOW.
DING

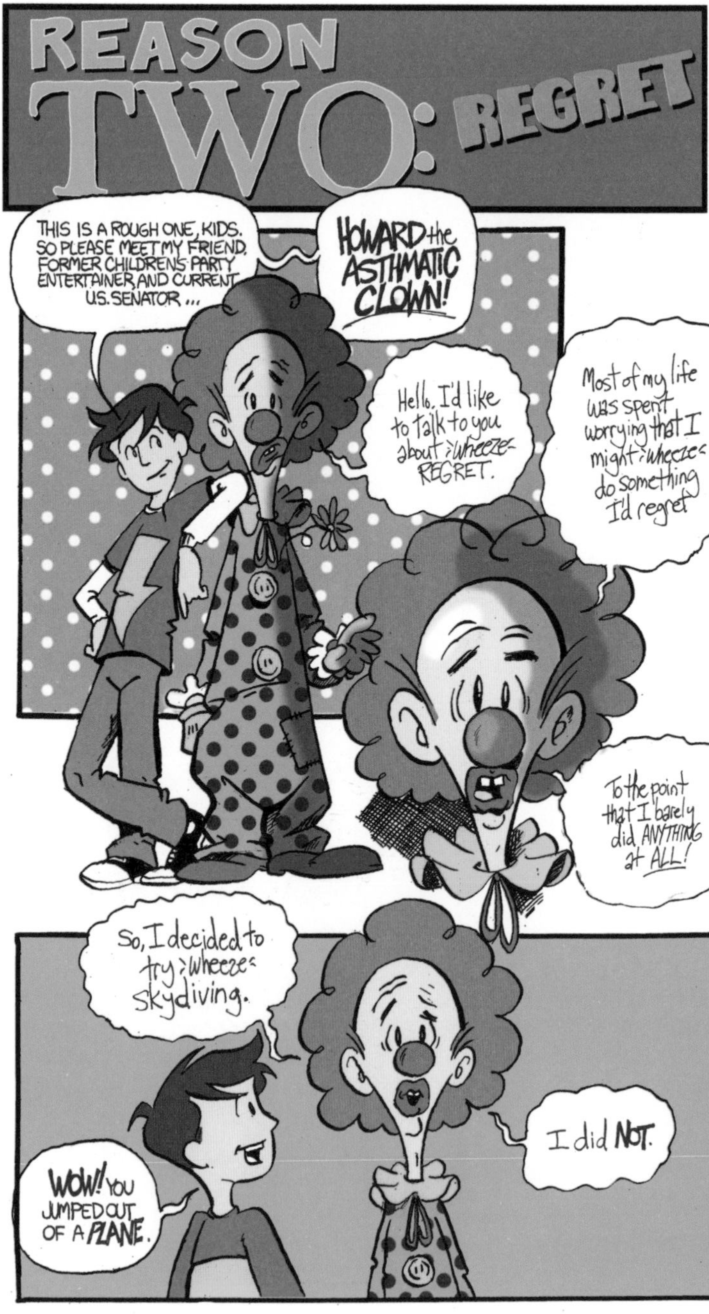
REASON TWO: REGRET
THIS IS A ROUGH ONE, KIDS. SO PLEASE MEET MY FRIEND, FORMER CHILDRENS PARTY ENTERTAINER, AND CURRENT U.S. SENATOR ...
HOWARD the ASTHMATIC CLOWN!
Hello. I'd like to talk to you about >wheeze< REGRET.
Most of my life was spent worrying that I might >wheeze< do something I'd regret
To the point that I barely did ANYTHING at ALL!
So, I decided to try >wheeze< skydiving.
WOW! YOU JUMPED OUT OF A PLANE.
I did NOT.

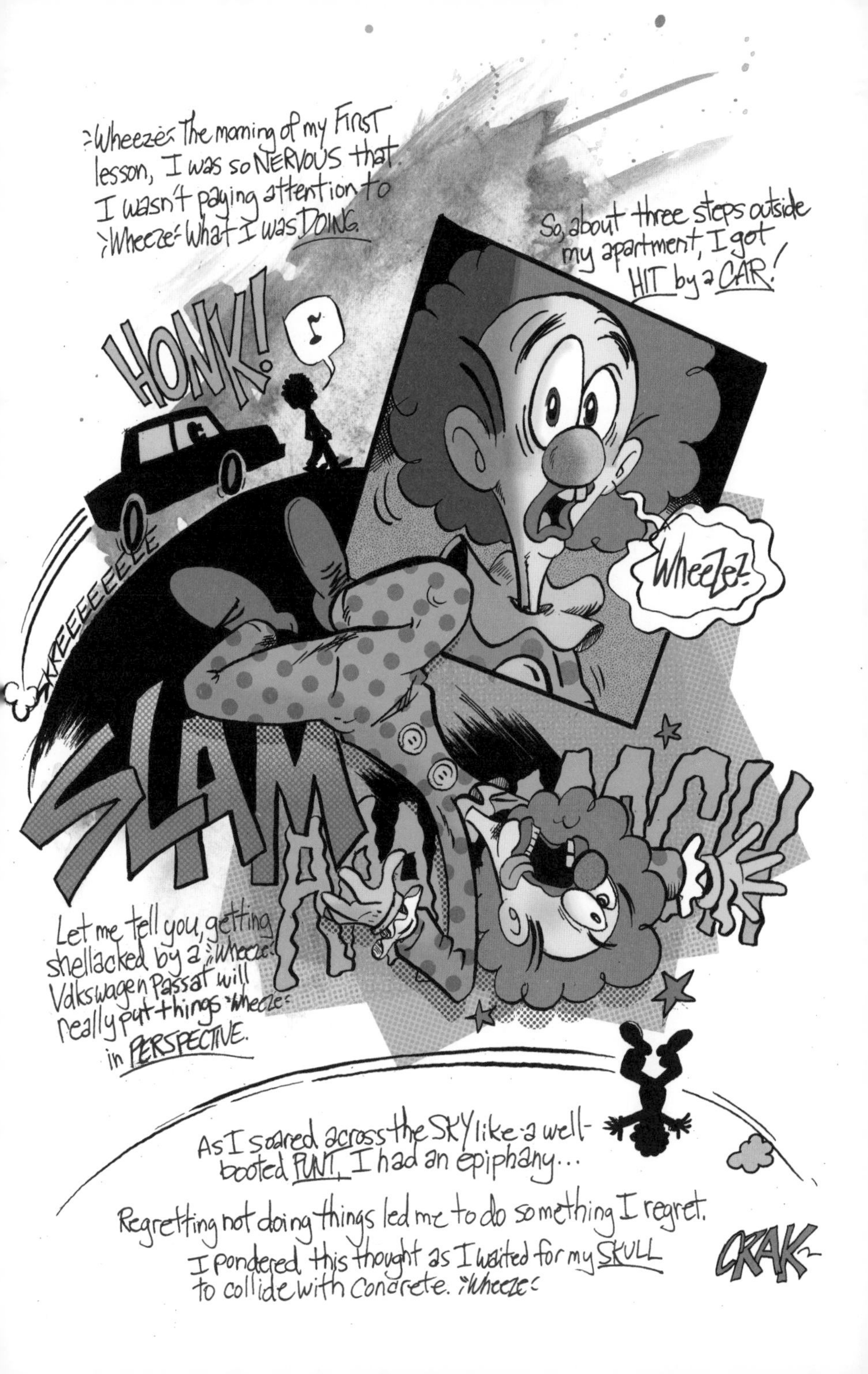
:Wheeze: The morning of my FIRST lesson, I was so NERVOUS that I wasn't paying attention to :Wheeze: what I was DOING.
So, about three steps outside my apartment, I got HIT by a CAR!
HONK!
♪
SKREEEEEEEEEE
Wheeze
SLAM
WHACK
Let me tell you, getting shellacked by a :Wheeze: Volkswagen Passat will really put things :Wheeze: in PERSPECTIVE.
As I soared across the SKY like a well-booted PUNT, I had an epiphany...
Regretting not doing things led me to do something I regret.
I pondered this thought as I waited for my SKULL to collide with concrete. :Wheeze:
CRAK

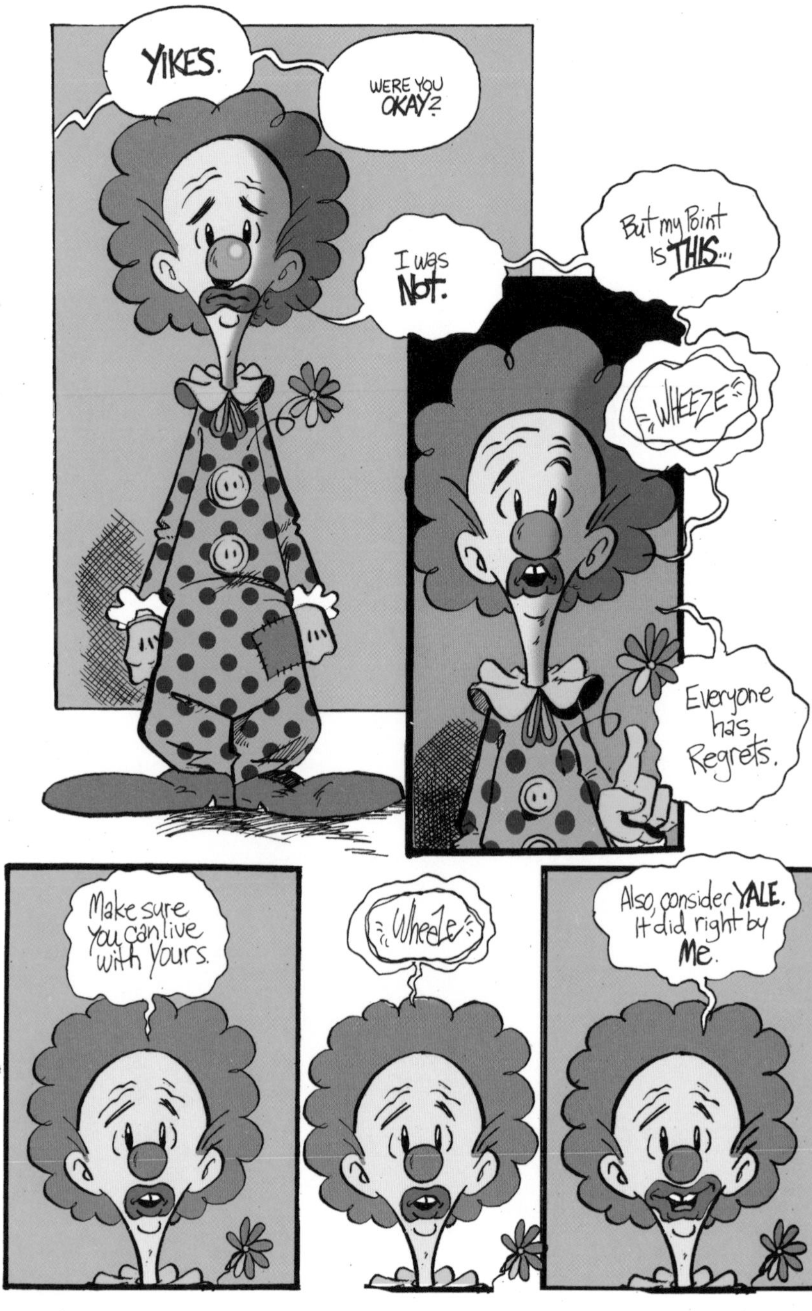
YIKES.
WERE YOU OKAY?
I was NOT.
But my Point is THIS...
WHEEZE
Everyone has Regrets.
Make sure you can live with Yours.
Wheeze
Also, consider YALE. It did right by Me.

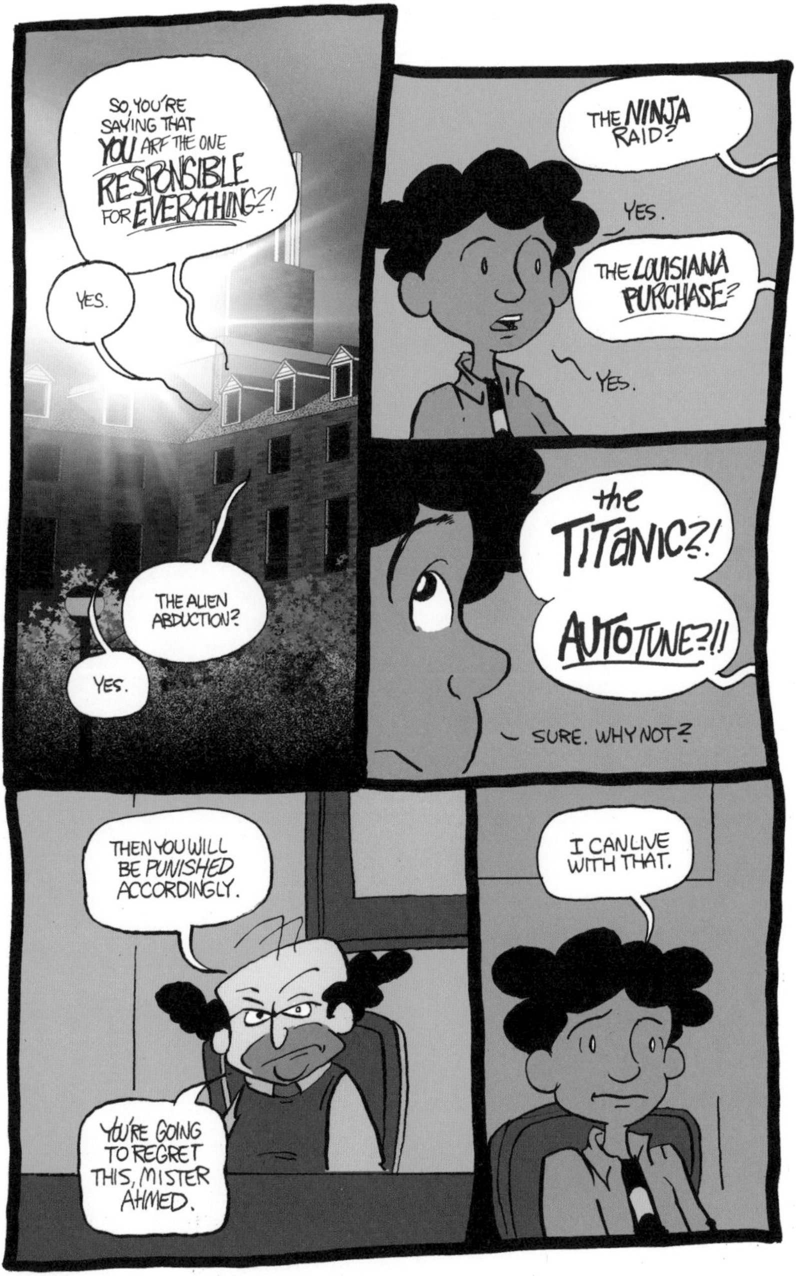
SO, YOU'RE SAYING THAT YOU ARE THE ONE RESPONSIBLE FOR EVERYTHING?!
YES.
THE ALIEN ABDUCTION?
YES.
THE NINJA RAID?
YES.
THE LOUISIANA PURCHASE?
YES.
the TITANIC?!
AUTOTUNE?!!
SURE. WHY NOT?
THEN YOU WILL BE PUNISHED ACCORDINGLY.
YOU'RE GOING TO REGRET THIS, MISTER AHMED.
I CAN LIVE WITH THAT.

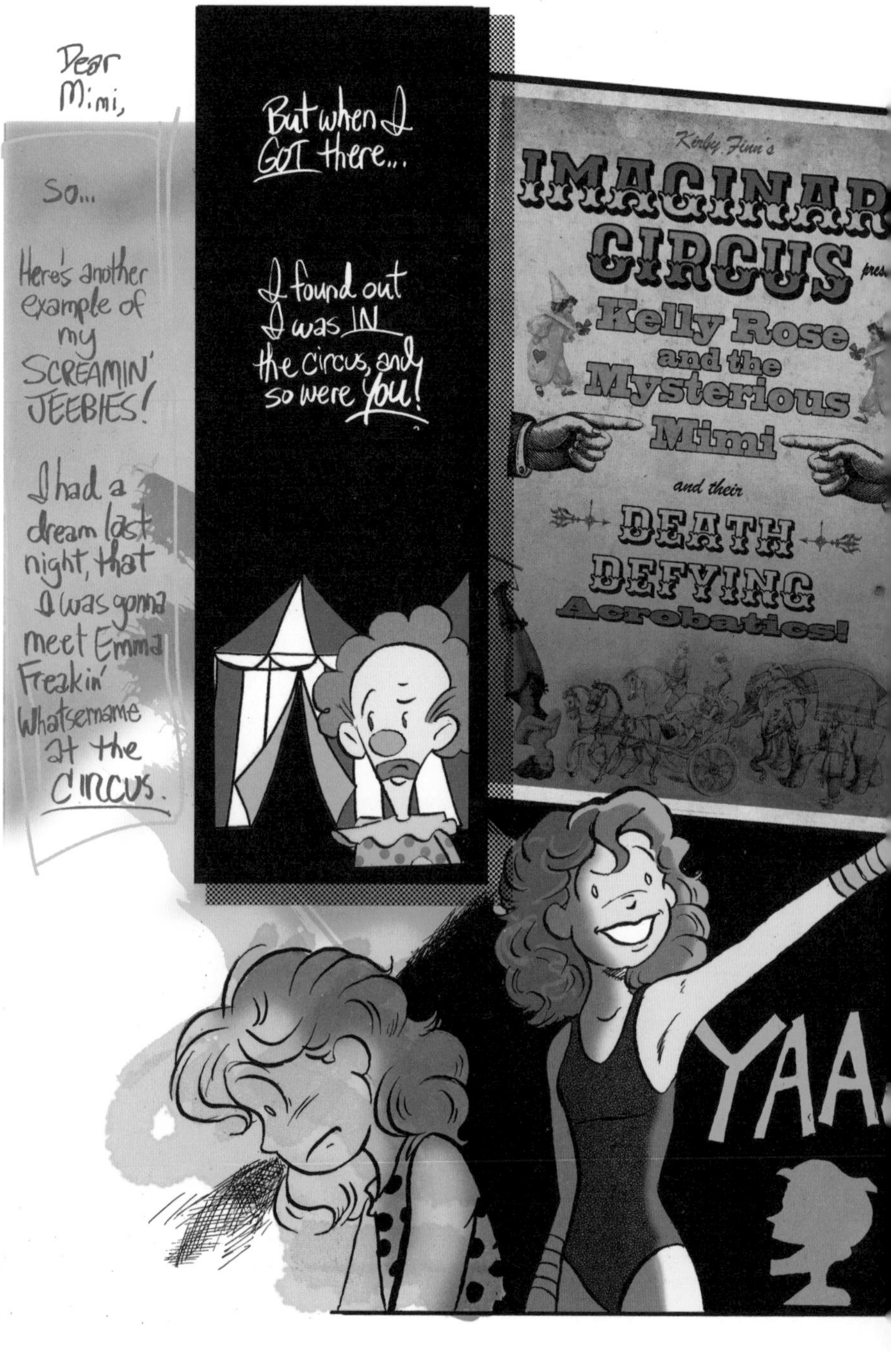

Dear Mimi,
So...
Here's another example of my SCREAMIN' JEEBIES!
I had a dream last night, that I was gonna meet Emma Freakin' Whatsername at the CIRCUS.
But when I GOT there...
I found out I was IN the circus, and so were YOU!
Kirby Finn's
IMAGINAR
CIRCUS
Kelly Rose
and the
Mysterious
Mimi
and their
DEATH
DEFYING
Acrobatics!
YAA

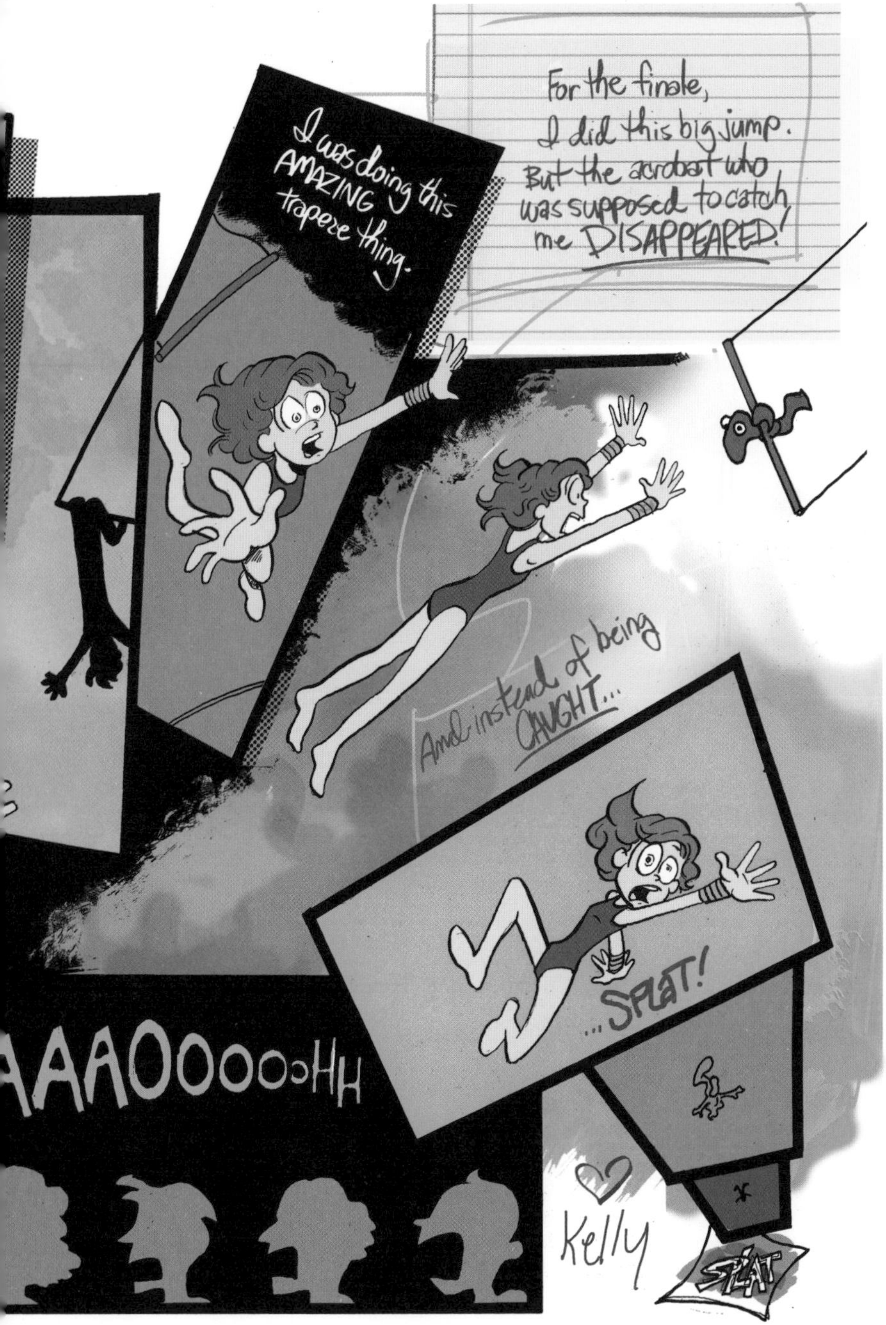
I was doing this AMAZING trapeze thing.
For the finale, I did this big jump. But the acrobat who was supposed to catch me DISAPPEARED!
And instead of being CAUGHT...
...SPLAT!
AAAOOOoHH
Kelly
SPLAT

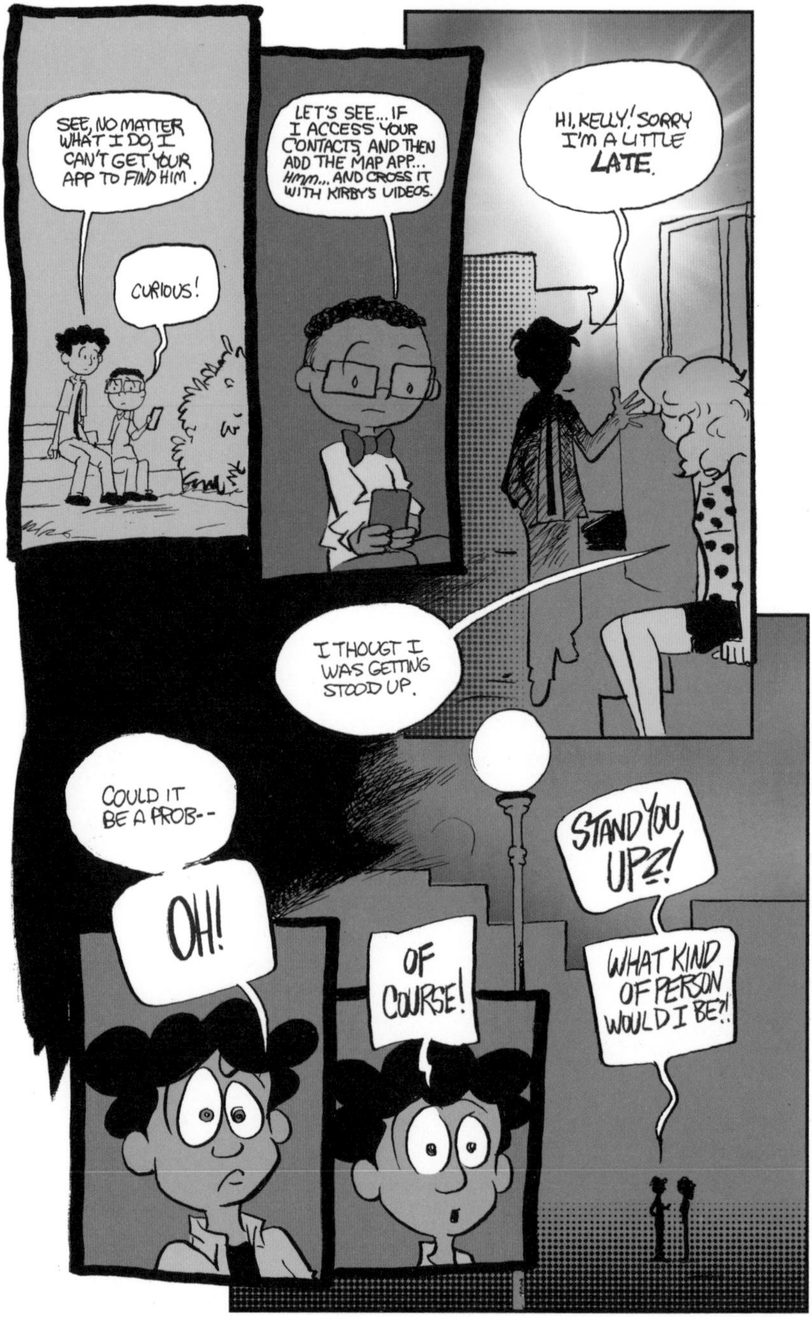
SEE, NO MATTER WHAT I DO, I CAN'T GET YOUR APP TO FIND HIM.
CURIOUS!
LET'S SEE... IF I ACCESS YOUR CONTACTS, AND THEN ADD THE MAP APP... HMM... AND CROSS IT WITH KIRBY'S VIDEOS.
HI, KELLY! SORRY I'M A LITTLE LATE.
I THOUGT I WAS GETTING STOOD UP.
COULD IT BE A PROB--
OH!
OF COURSE!
STAND YOU UP?!
WHAT KIND OF PERSON WOULD I BE?!

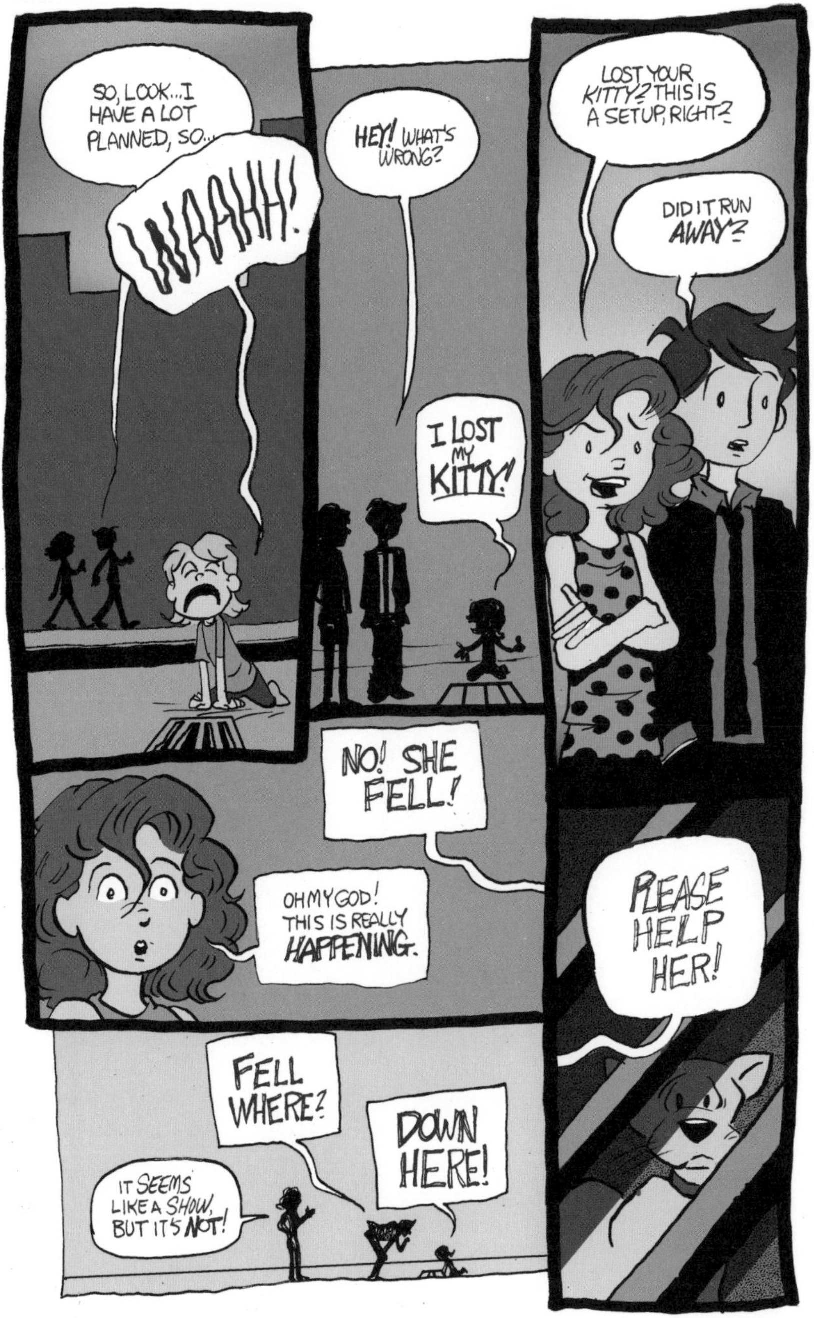
SO, LOOK...I HAVE A LOT PLANNED, SO...
WAAHH!
HEY! WHAT'S WRONG?
I LOST MY KITTY!
LOST YOUR KITTY? THIS IS A SETUP, RIGHT?
DID IT RUN AWAY?
NO! SHE FELL!
OH MY GOD! THIS IS REALLY HAPPENING.
PLEASE HELP HER!
FELL WHERE?
DOWN HERE!
IT SEEMS LIKE A SHOW, BUT IT'S NOT!

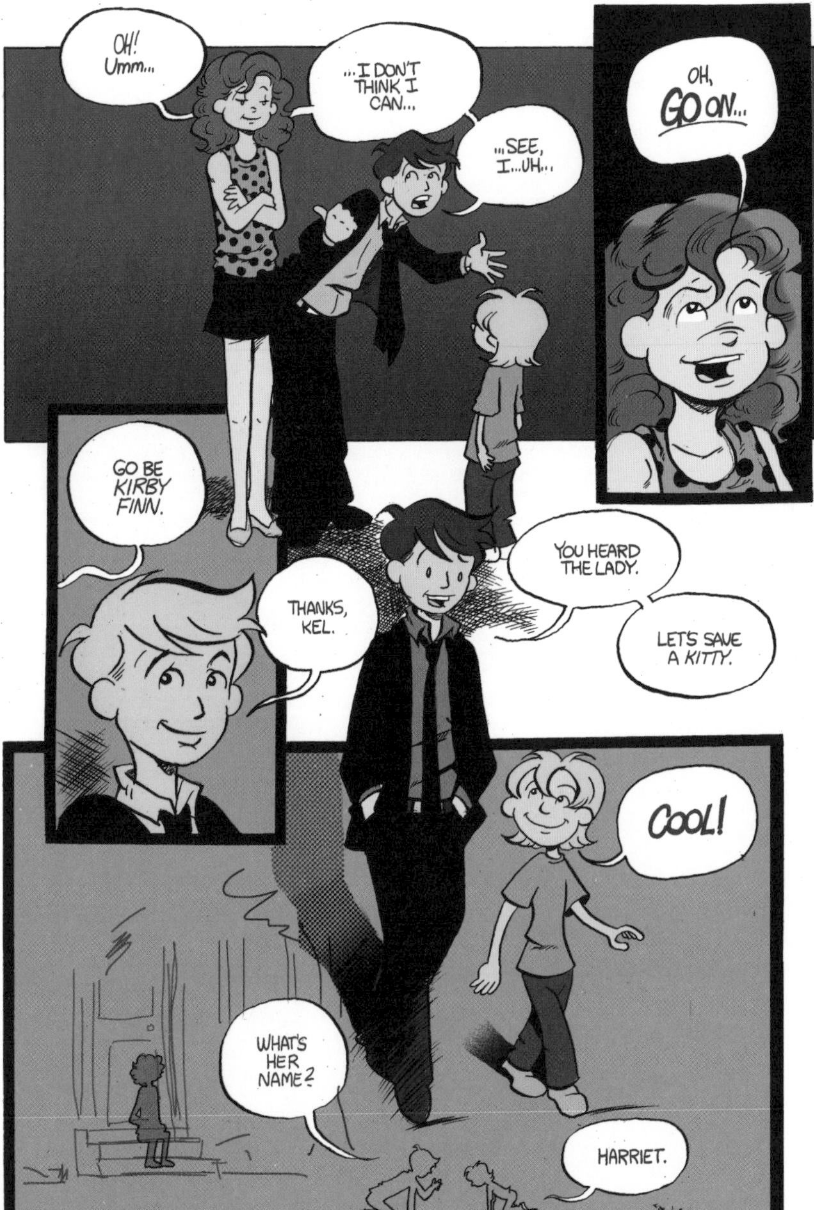
OH! Umm...
...I DON'T THINK I CAN...
...SEE, I...UH...
OH, GO ON...
GO BE KIRBY FINN.
THANKS, KEL.
YOU HEARD THE LADY.
LET'S SAVE A KITTY.
COOL!
WHAT'S HER NAME?
HARRIET.
MRRRROWWWWW.

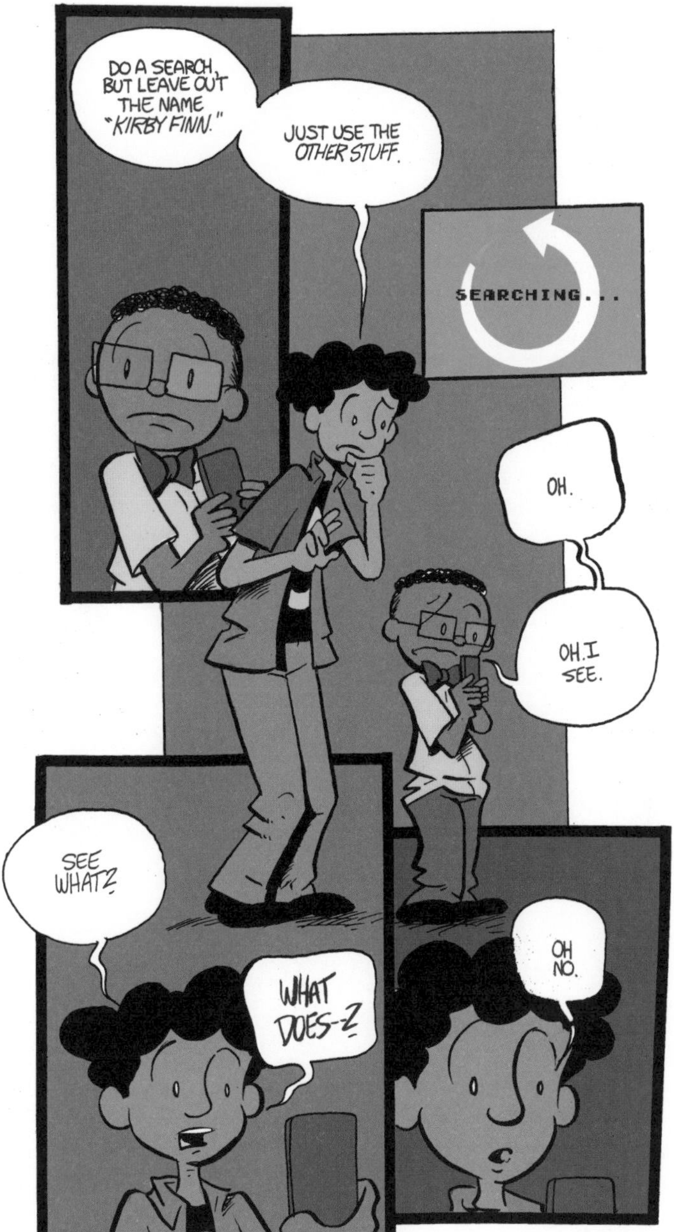
DO A SEARCH, BUT LEAVE OUT THE NAME "KIRBY FINN."
JUST USE THE OTHER STUFF.
SEARCHING...
OH.
OH. I SEE.
SEE WHAT?
WHAT DOES--?
OH NO.

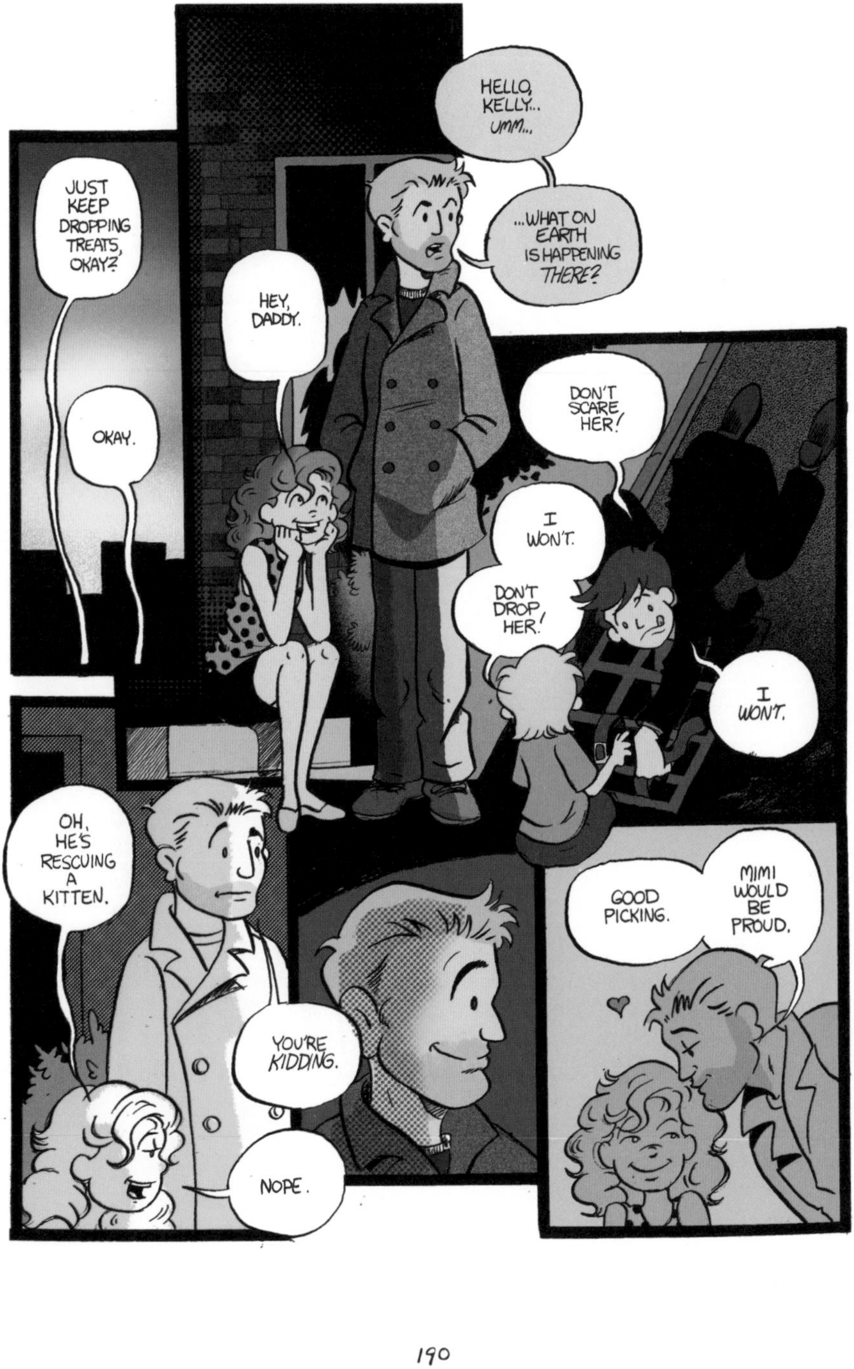
JUST KEEP DROPPING TREATS, OKAY?
OKAY.
HELLO, KELLY... UMM...
...WHAT ON EARTH IS HAPPENING THERE?
HEY, DADDY.
DON'T SCARE HER!
I WON'T.
DON'T DROP HER!
I WON'T.
OH, HE'S RESCUING A KITTEN.
YOU'RE KIDDING.
NOPE.
GOOD PICKING.
MIMI WOULD BE PROUD.

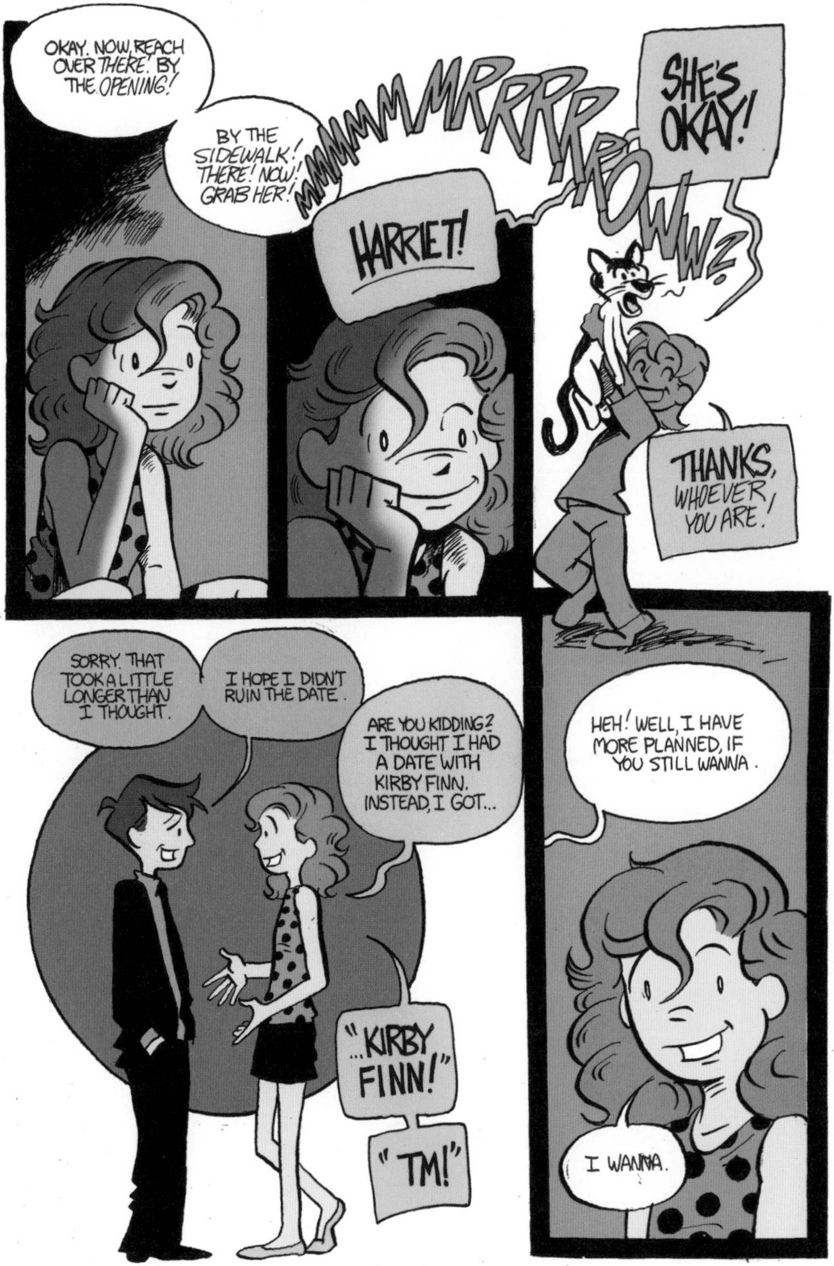
OKAY. NOW, REACH OVER THERE! BY THE OPENING!
BY THE SIDEWALK! THERE! NOW! GRAB HER!
HARRIET!
MMMMMMRRRRROWW?
SHE'S OKAY!
THANKS, WHOEVER YOU ARE!
SORRY. THAT TOOK A LITTLE LONGER THAN I THOUGHT.
I HOPE I DIDN'T RUIN THE DATE.
ARE YOU KIDDING? I THOUGHT I HAD A DATE WITH KIRBY FINN. INSTEAD, I GOT...
"...KIRBY FINN!"
"TM!"
HEH! WELL, I HAVE MORE PLANNED, IF YOU STILL WANNA.
I WANNA.

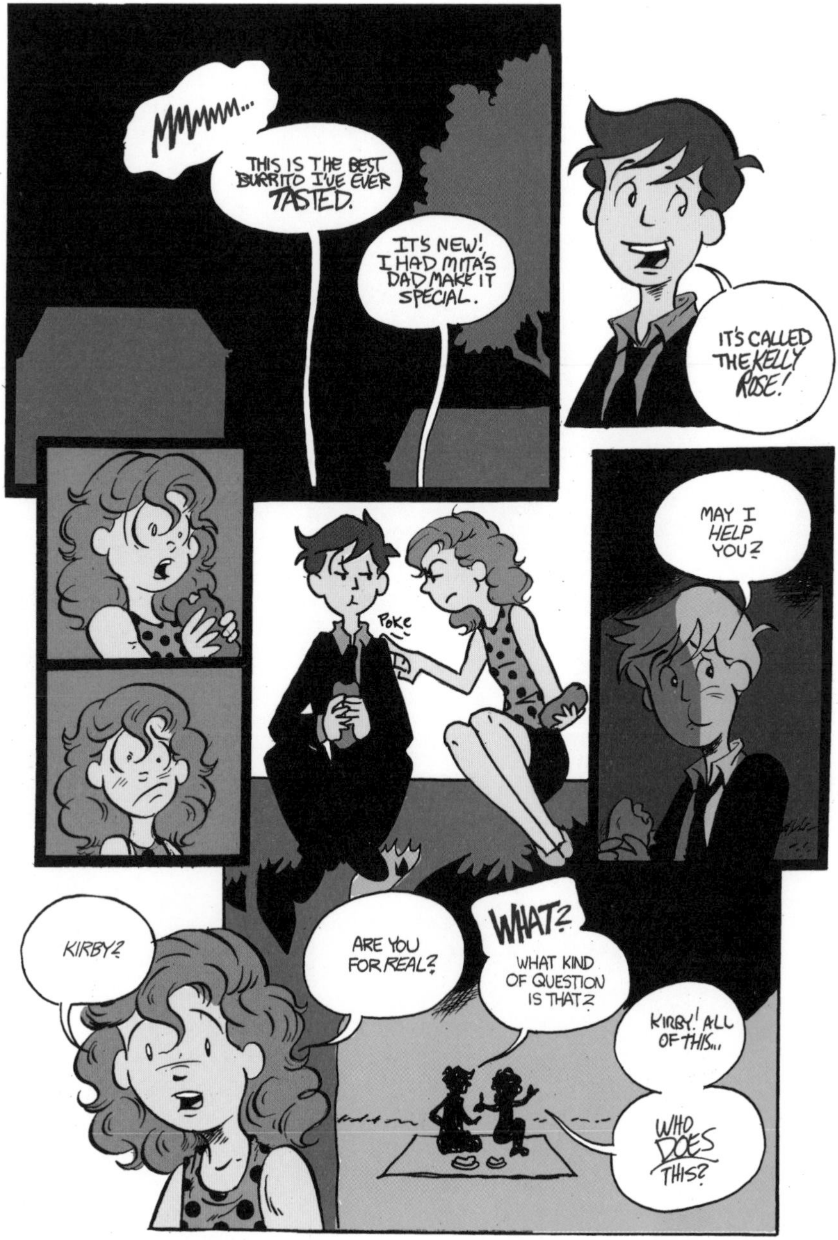
MMMMM...
THIS IS THE BEST BURRITO I'VE EVER TASTED.
IT'S NEW! I HAD MITA'S DAD MAKE IT SPECIAL.
IT'S CALLED THE KELLY ROSE!
POKE
MAY I HELP YOU?
KIRBY?
ARE YOU FOR REAL?
WHAT?
WHAT KIND OF QUESTION IS THAT?
KIRBY! ALL OF THIS...
WHO DOES THIS?

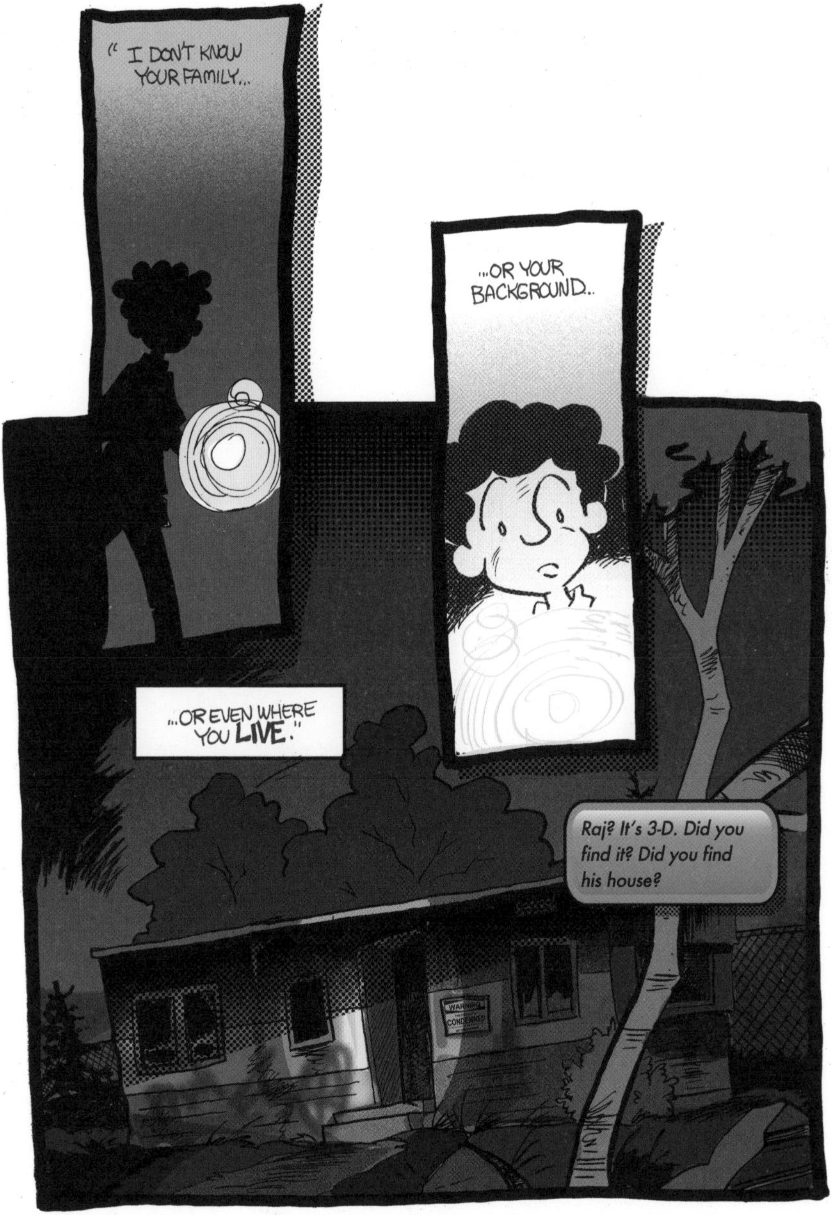
" I DON'T KNOW YOUR FAMILY...
...OR YOUR BACKGROUND..
...OR EVEN WHERE YOU LIVE."
Raj? It's 3-D. Did you find it? Did you find his house?
WARNING
CONDEMNED

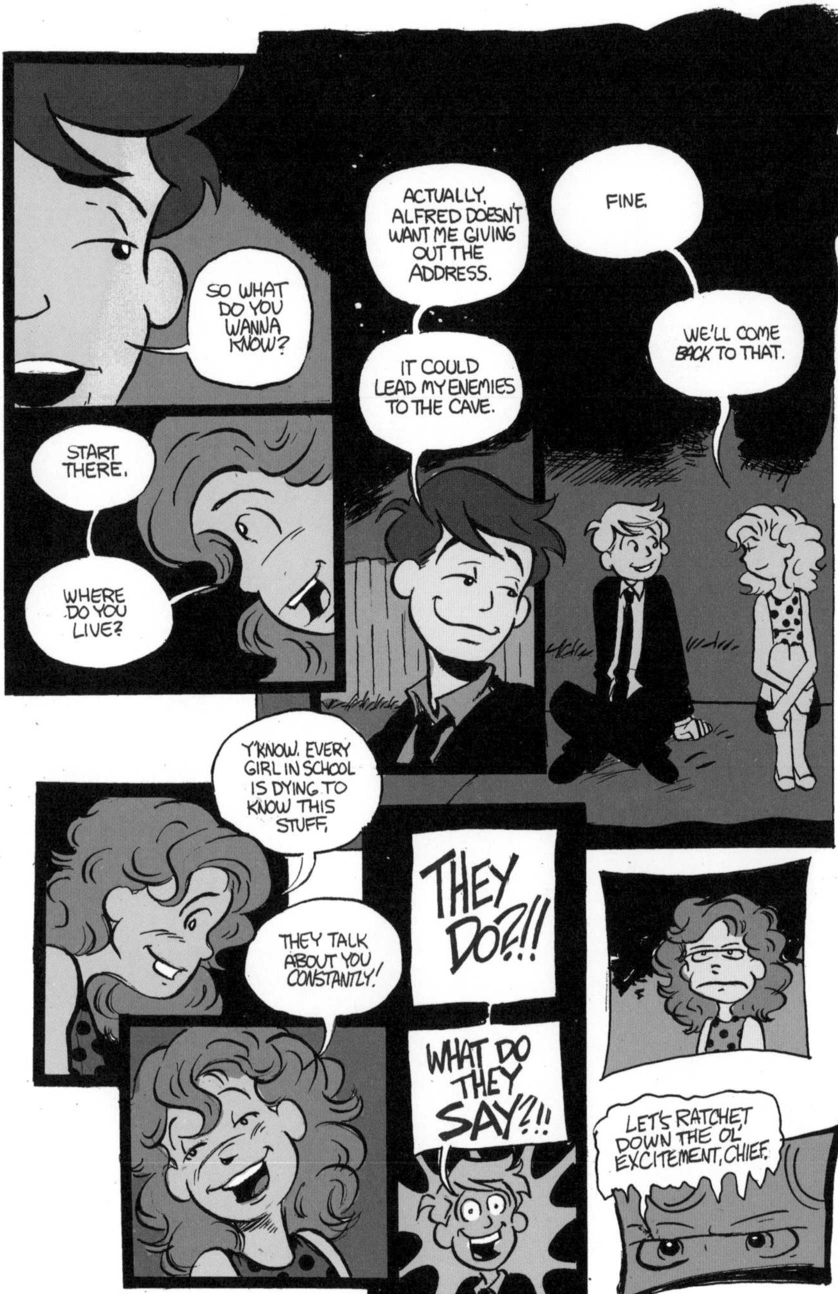
SO WHAT DO YOU WANNA KNOW?
START THERE.
WHERE DO YOU LIVE?
ACTUALLY, ALFRED DOESN'T WANT ME GIVING OUT THE ADDRESS.
IT COULD LEAD MY ENEMIES TO THE CAVE.
FINE.
WE'LL COME BACK TO THAT.
Y'KNOW, EVERY GIRL IN SCHOOL IS DYING TO KNOW THIS STUFF.
THEY TALK ABOUT YOU CONSTANTLY!
THEY DO?!!
WHAT DO THEY SAY?!!
LET'S RATCHET DOWN THE OL' EXCITEMENT, CHIEF.

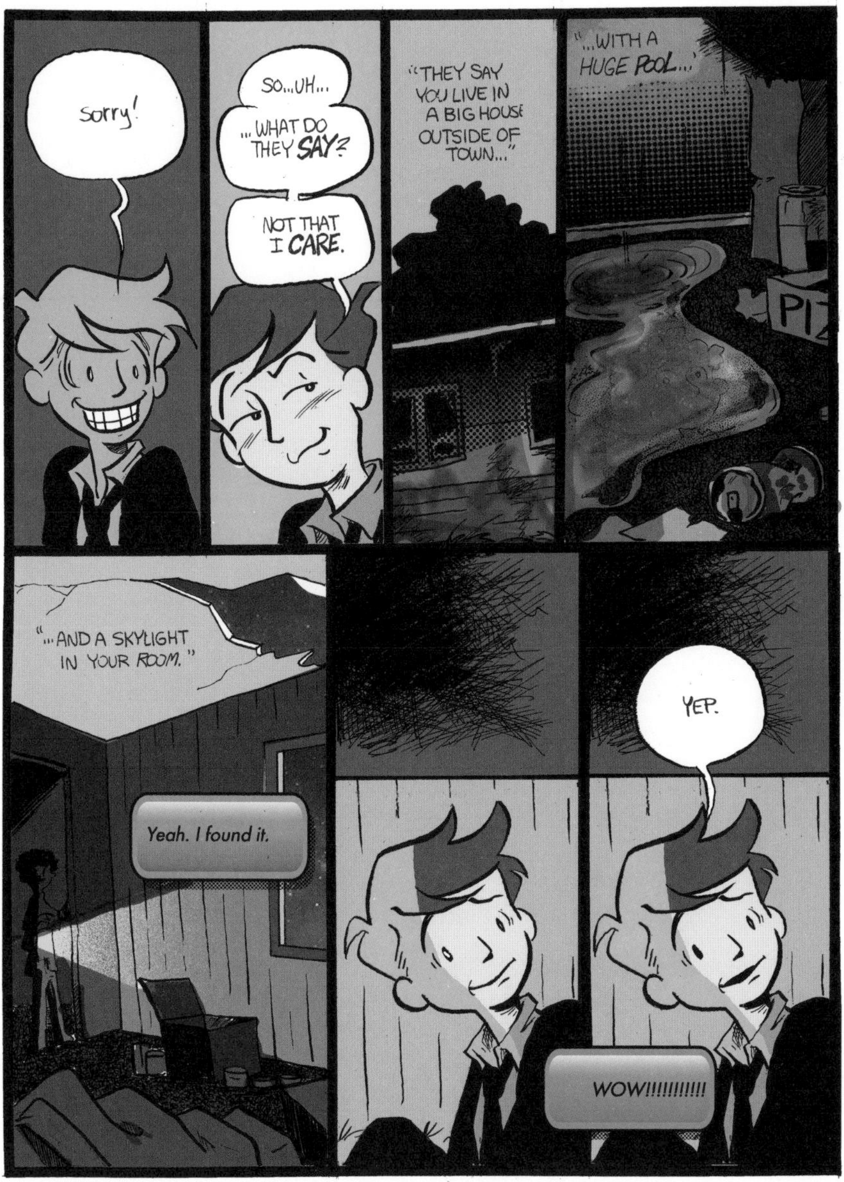

Sorry!
SO...UH...
...WHAT DO THEY SAY?
NOT THAT I CARE.
"THEY SAY YOU LIVE IN A BIG HOUSE OUTSIDE OF TOWN..."
"...WITH A HUGE POOL..."
PIZ
"...AND A SKYLIGHT IN YOUR ROOM."
Yeah. I found it.
YEP.
WOW!!!!!!!!!!

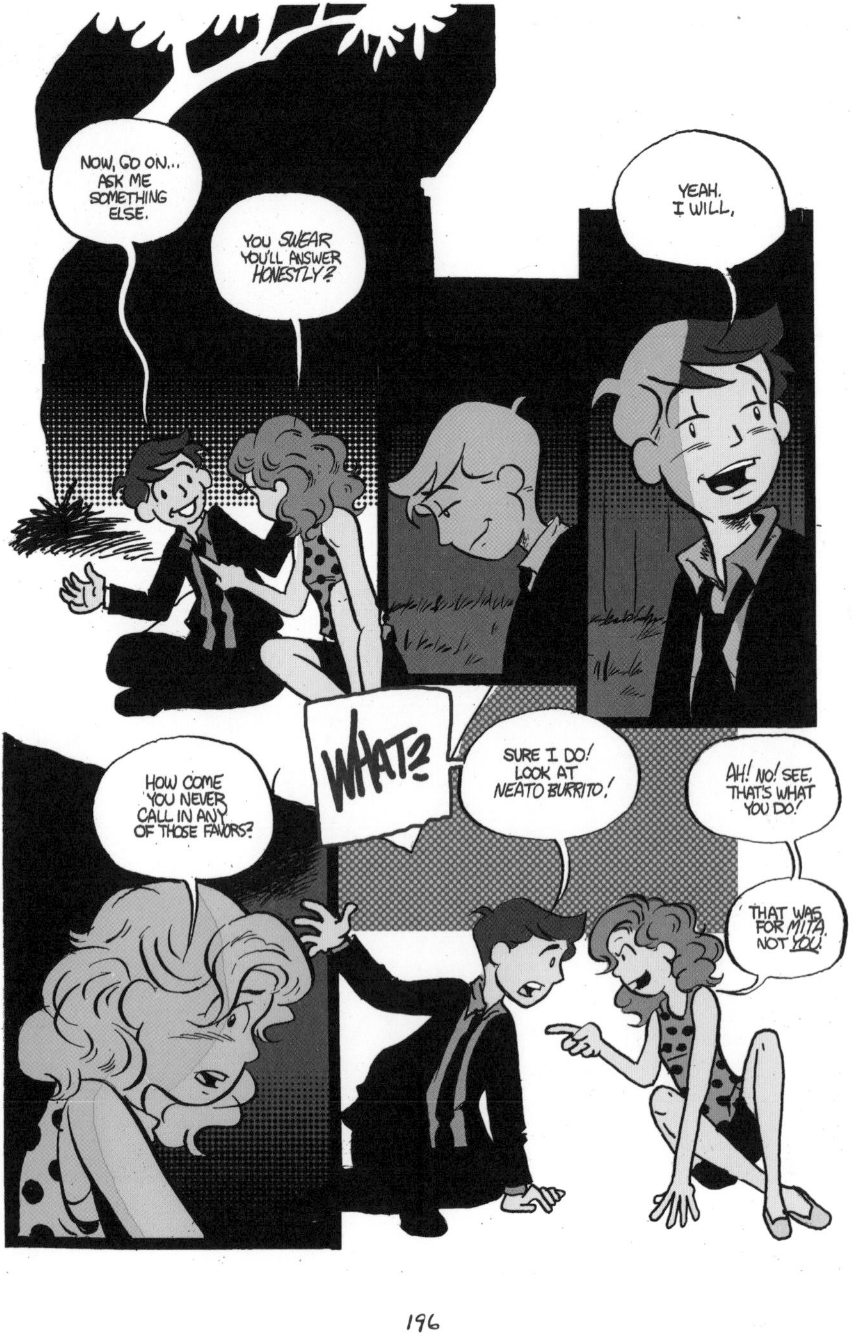
NOW, GO ON... ASK ME SOMETHING ELSE.
YOU SWEAR YOU'LL ANSWER HONESTLY?
YEAH. I WILL.
HOW COME YOU NEVER CALL IN ANY OF THOSE FAVORS?
WHAT?
SURE I DO! LOOK AT NEATO BURRITO!
AH! NO! SEE, THAT'S WHAT YOU DO!
THAT WAS FOR MITA, NOT YOU.

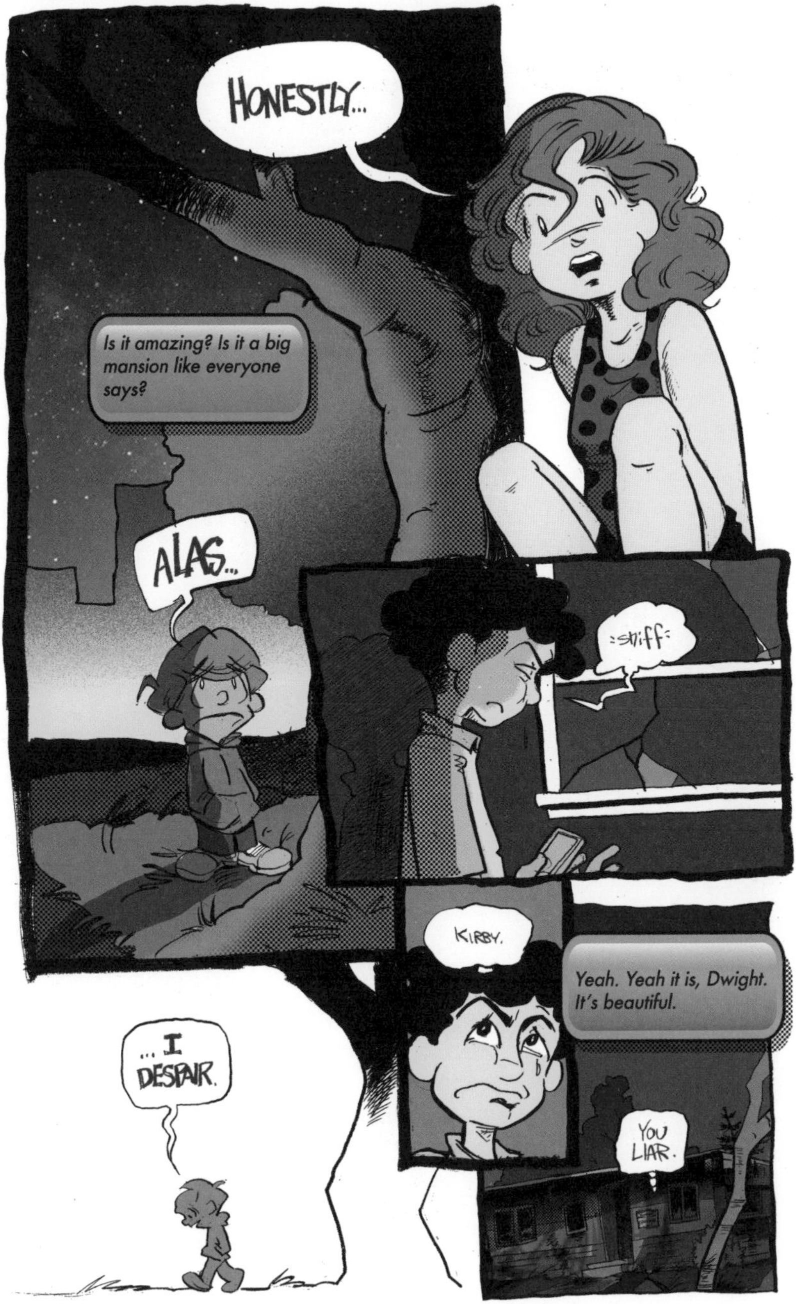
HONESTLY...
Is it amazing? Is it a big mansion like everyone says?
ALAS...
=SNIFF=
...I DESPAIR.
KIRBY.
Yeah. Yeah it is, Dwight. It's beautiful.
YOU LIAR.

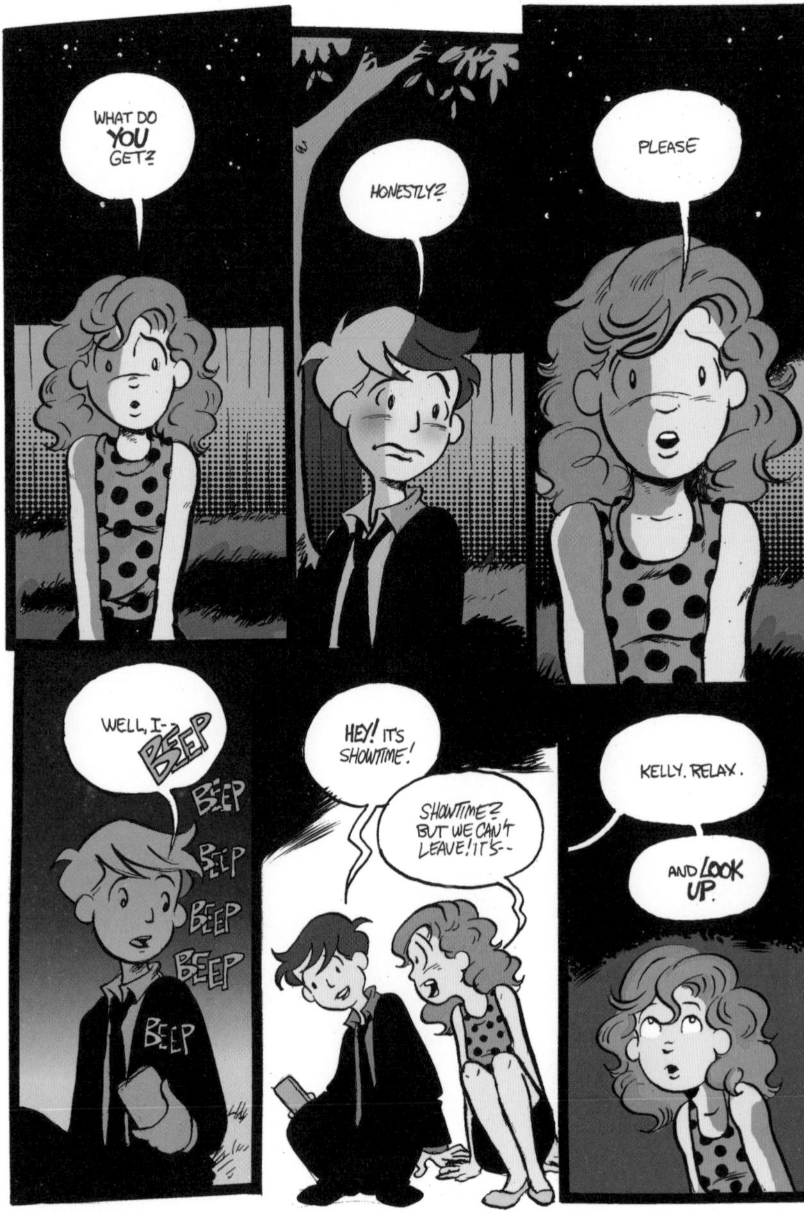
WHAT DO YOU GET?
HONESTLY?
PLEASE
WELL, I--
BEEP
BEEP
BEEP
BEEP
BEEP
BEEP
HEY! IT'S SHOWTIME!
SHOWTIME? BUT WE CAN'T LEAVE! IT'S--
KELLY. RELAX.
AND LOOK UP.

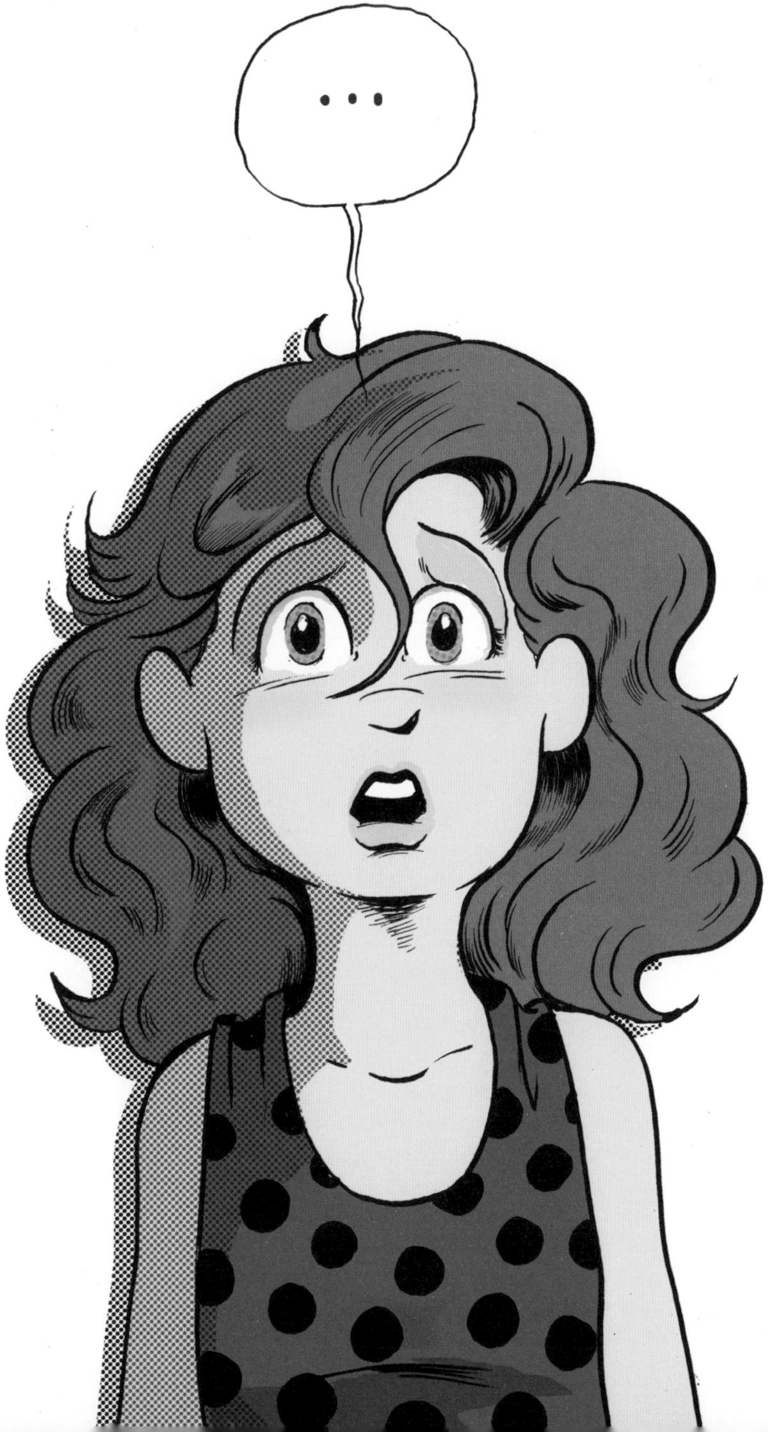
...

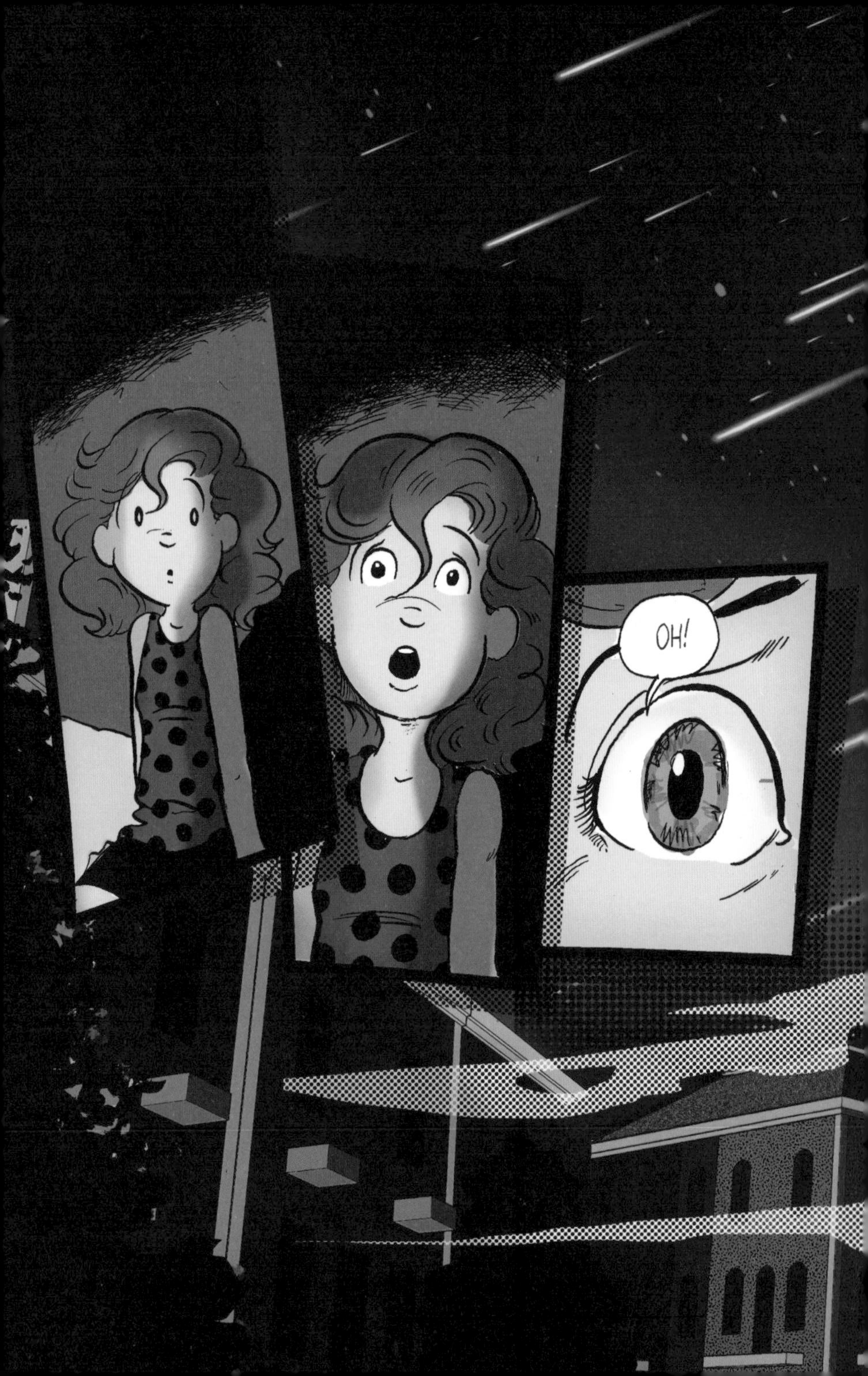
OH!

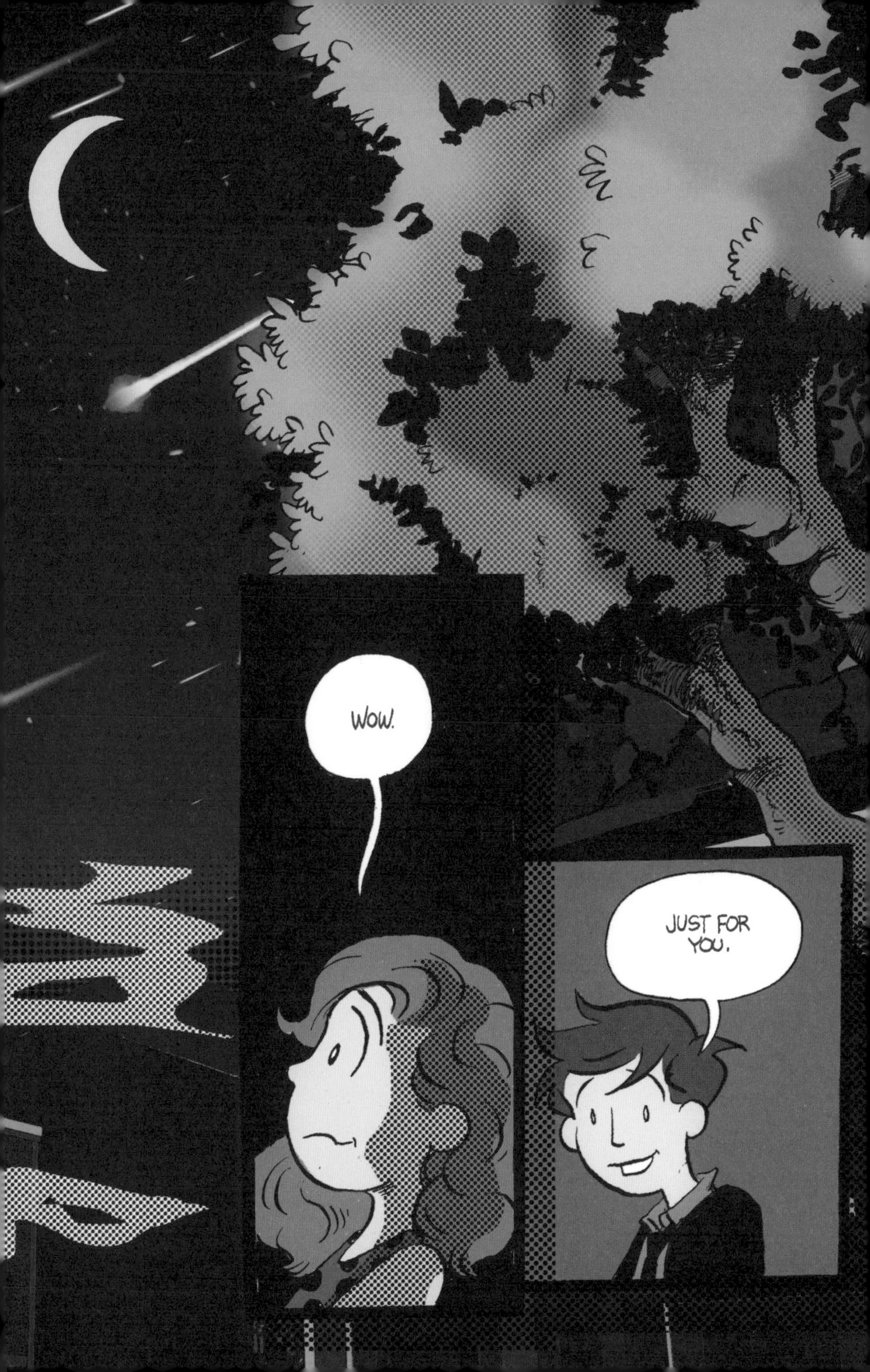
WOW.
JUST FOR YOU.

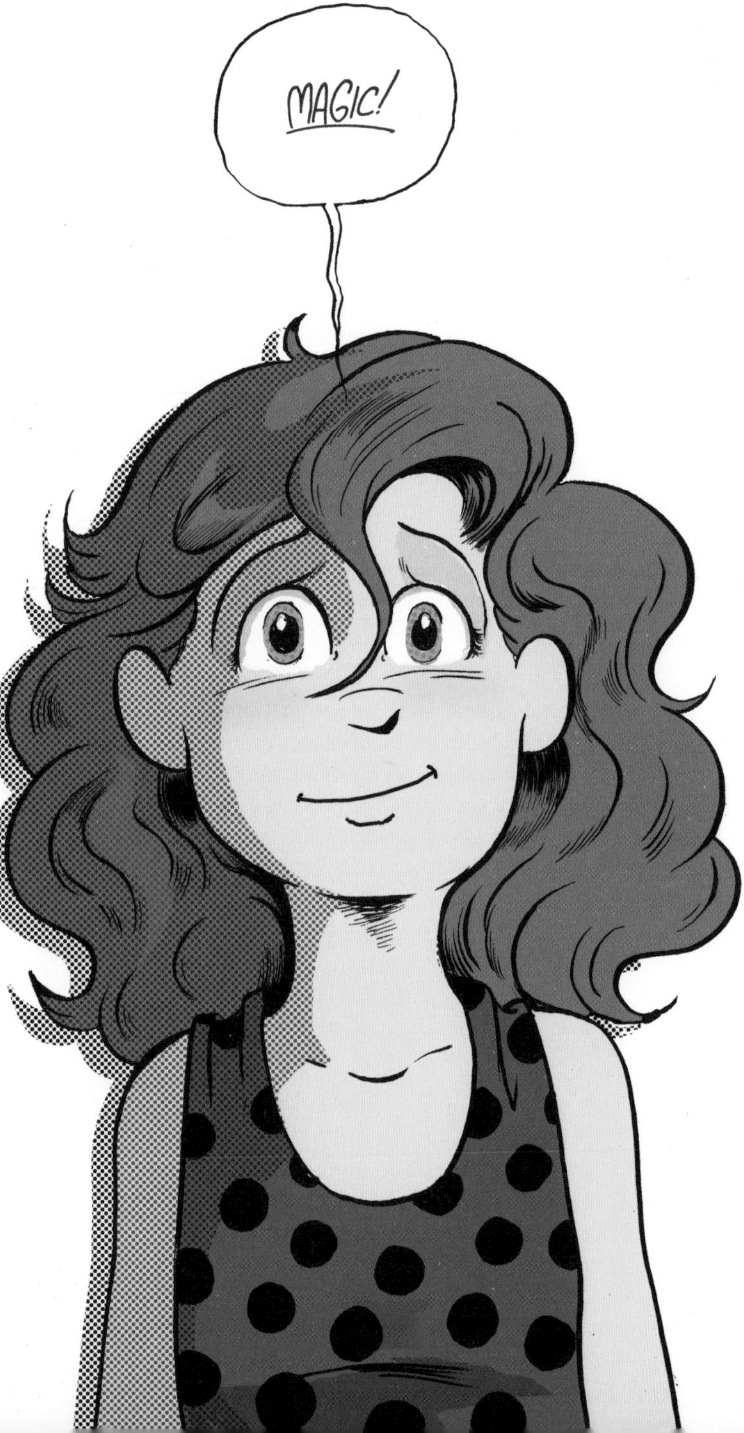
MAGIC!

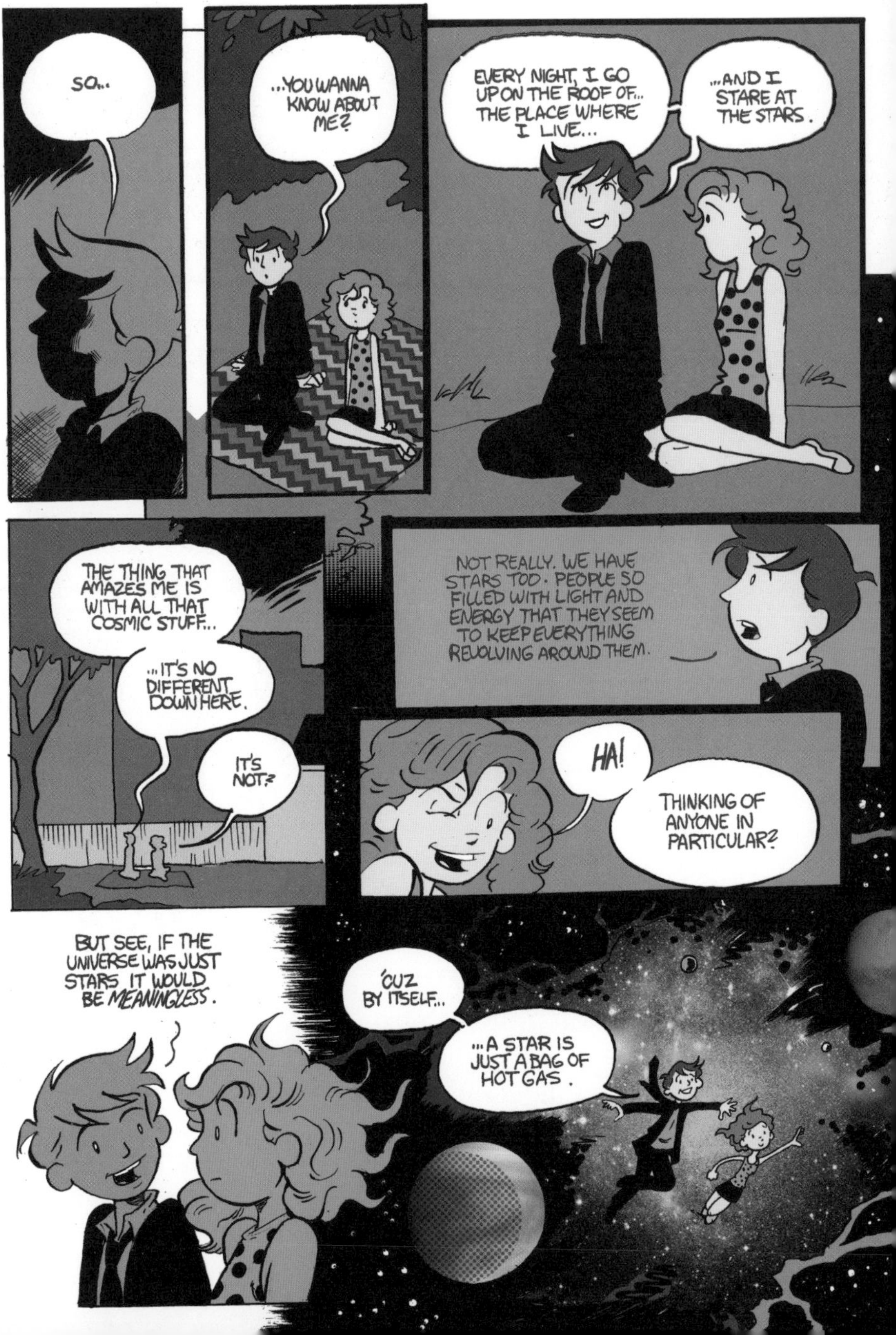
SO...
...YOU WANNA KNOW ABOUT ME?
EVERY NIGHT, I GO UP ON THE ROOF OF... THE PLACE WHERE I LIVE...
...AND I STARE AT THE STARS.
THE THING THAT AMAZES ME IS WITH ALL THAT COSMIC STUFF...
...IT'S NO DIFFERENT DOWN HERE.
IT'S NOT?
NOT REALLY. WE HAVE STARS TOO. PEOPLE SO FILLED WITH LIGHT AND ENERGY THAT THEY SEEM TO KEEP EVERYTHING REVOLVING AROUND THEM.
HA!
THINKING OF ANYONE IN PARTICULAR?
BUT SEE, IF THE UNIVERSE WAS JUST STARS IT WOULD BE *MEANINGLESS*.
'CUZ BY ITSELF...
...A STAR IS JUST A BAG OF HOT GAS.

BUT, IT'S NOT JUST THE STARS; THERE ARE COMETS.
WHOOP!
MARS, HERE I COME!
THEY GO WHIPPING BY LIKE A RUNAWAY FREIGHT TRAIN.
HA! LIKE ROSEY!
EXACTLY!
AND THERE ARE ASTEROIDS... PEOPLE WHO WERE SUPPOSED TO BE PLANETS...
(...OR MAYBE USED TO BE PLANETS...)
...AND NOW ARE JUST RUBBLE...
SO SAD.
I MEANT TO DO THIS!

AND, OF COURSE, THERE ARE THE PLANETS.
THOSE ARE MY FAVORITES.
OH, YEAH? WHY IS THAT, PROFESSOR?
BECAUSE, THERE ARE TRILLIONS, AND TRILLIONS OF THEM, AND EVERY ONE IS UNIQUE.
AND, EVERY ONCE IN A WHILE... HECK! MAYBE ONLY ONCE... THERE IS ONE FILLED WITH LIFE!

BUT WHAT I LIKE BEST IS HOW IT ALL FITS TOGETHER...
...LIKE US!
YOU AND ME?
ALL OF US!
A BUNCH OF WEIRD, CRAZY, INDIVIDUAL MESSES...
...THAT SOMEHOW ALL COME TOGETHER...
...TO MAKE SOMETHING BEAUTIFUL.

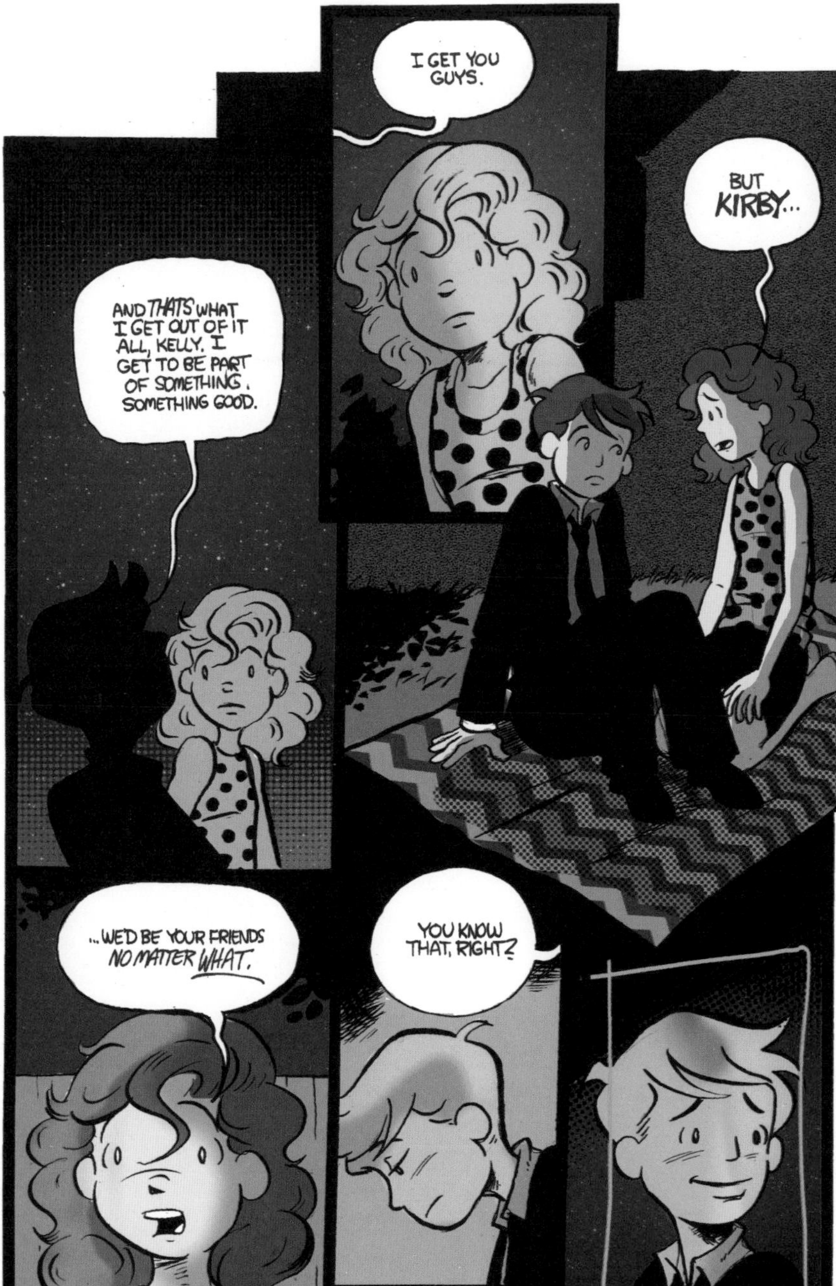
AND THAT'S WHAT I GET OUT OF IT ALL, KELLY. I GET TO BE PART OF SOMETHING. SOMETHING GOOD.
I GET YOU GUYS.
BUT KIRBY...
...WE'D BE YOUR FRIENDS NO MATTER WHAT.
YOU KNOW THAT, RIGHT?

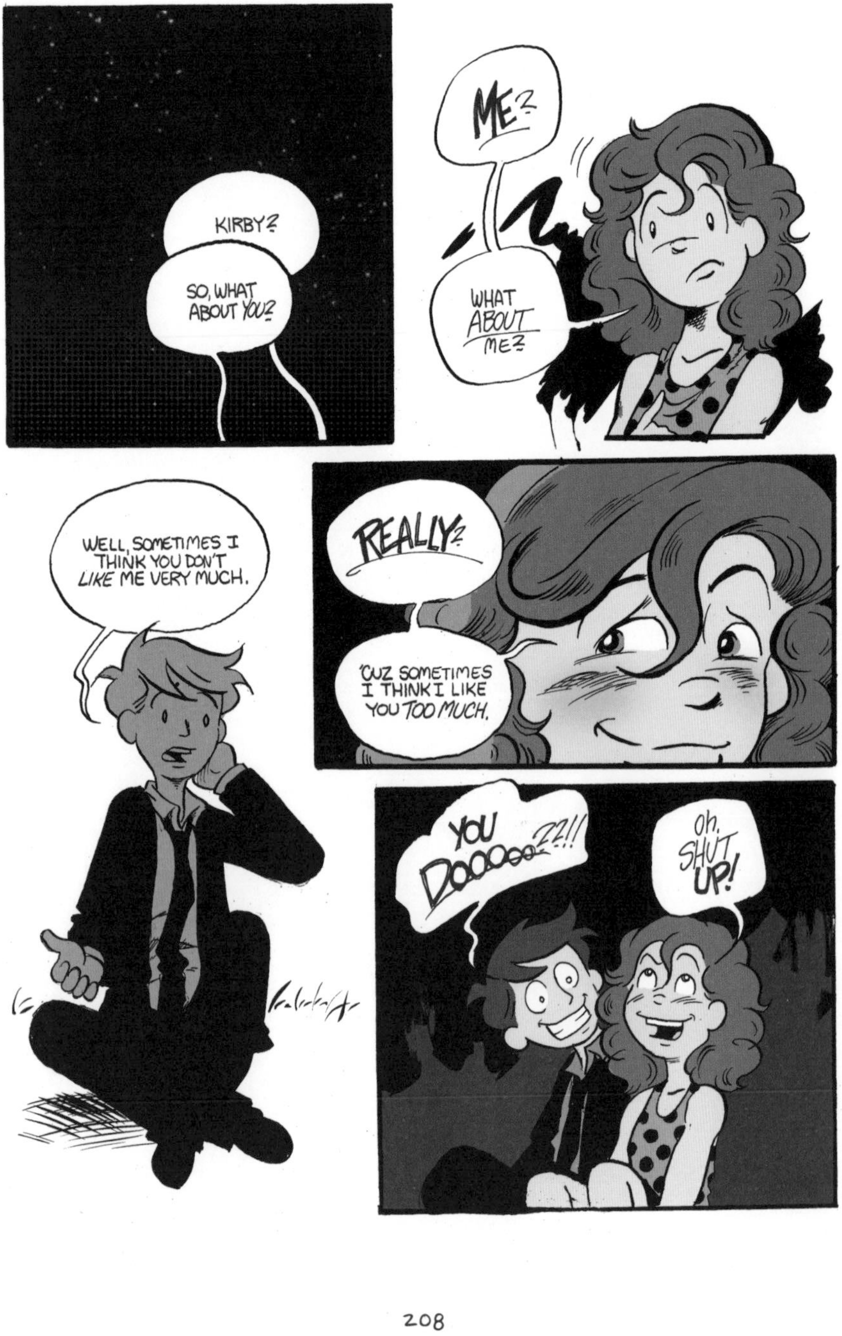
KIRBY?
SO, WHAT ABOUT YOU?
ME?
WHAT ABOUT ME?
WELL, SOMETIMES I THINK YOU DON'T LIKE ME VERY MUCH.
REALLY?
'CUZ SOMETIMES I THINK I LIKE YOU TOO MUCH.
YOU DOOOOOO??!!
Oh, SHUT UP!

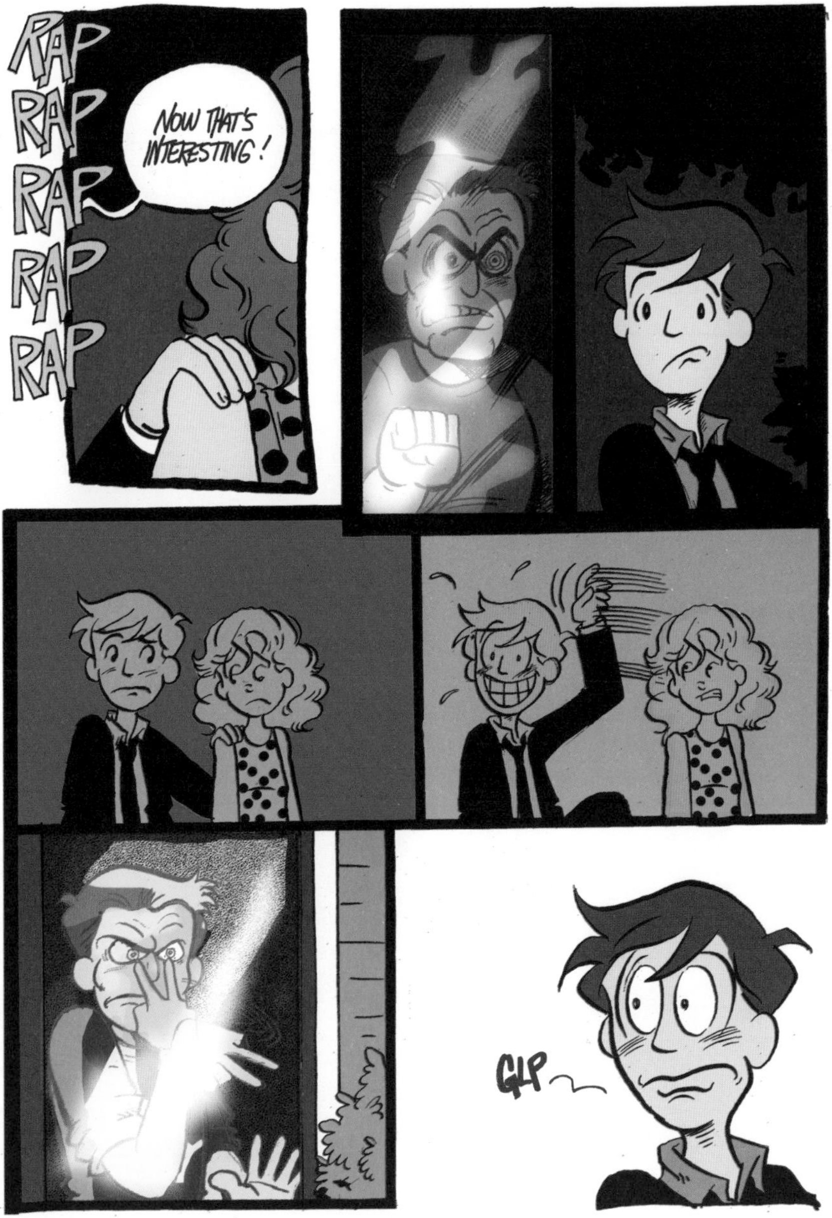
RAP RAP RAP RAP RAP
NOW THAT'S INTERESTING!
GLP

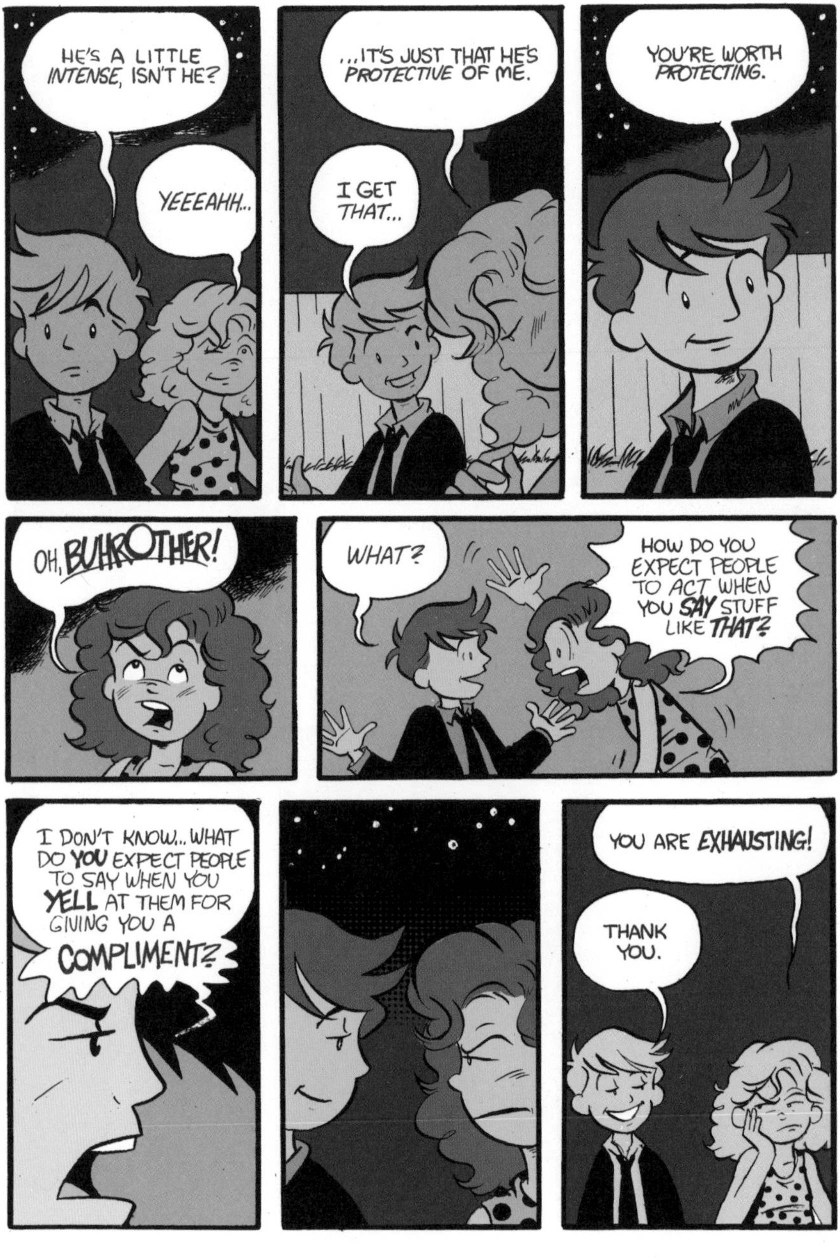
HE'S A LITTLE INTENSE, ISN'T HE?
YEEEAHH...
...IT'S JUST THAT HE'S PROTECTIVE OF ME.
I GET THAT...
YOU'RE WORTH PROTECTING.
OH, BUHROTHER!
WHAT?
HOW DO YOU EXPECT PEOPLE TO ACT WHEN YOU SAY STUFF LIKE THAT?!
I DON'T KNOW... WHAT DO YOU EXPECT PEOPLE TO SAY WHEN YOU YELL AT THEM FOR GIVING YOU A COMPLIMENT?!
YOU ARE EXHAUSTING!
THANK YOU.

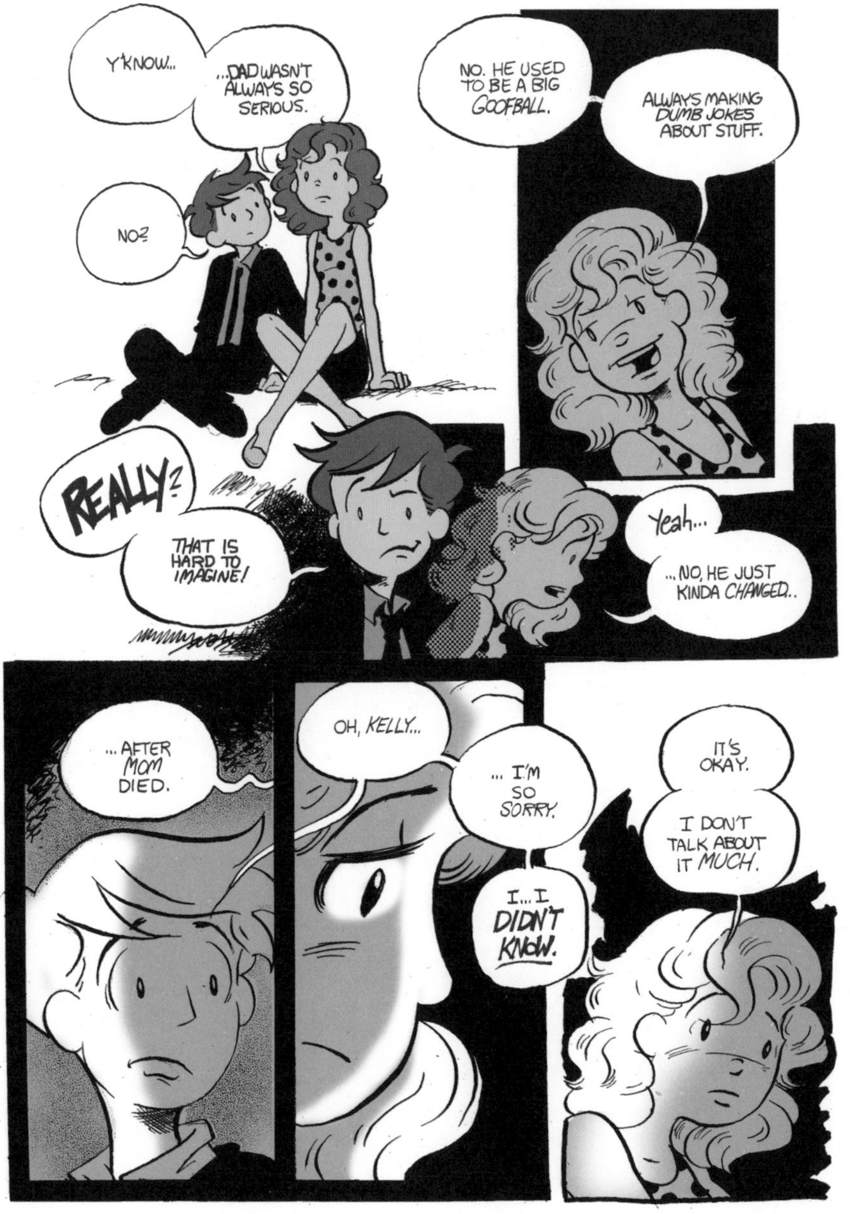
Y'KNOW...
...DAD WASN'T ALWAYS SO SERIOUS.
NO?
NO. HE USED TO BE A BIG GOOFBALL.
ALWAYS MAKING DUMB JOKES ABOUT STUFF.
REALLY?
THAT IS HARD TO IMAGINE!
Yeah...
...NO, HE JUST KINDA CHANGED...
...AFTER MOM DIED.
OH, KELLY...
...I'M SO SORRY.
I...I DIDN'T KNOW.
IT'S OKAY.
I DON'T TALK ABOUT IT MUCH.

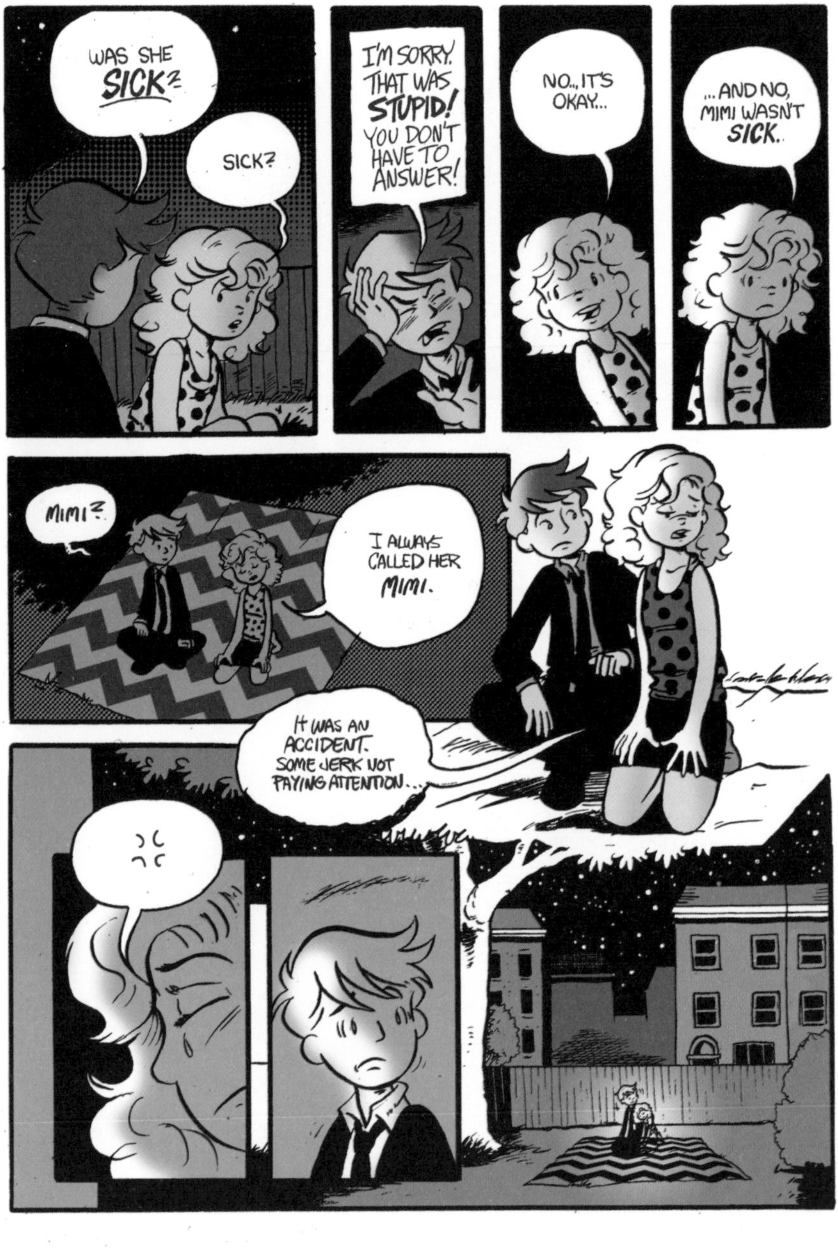
WAS SHE SICK?
SICK?
I'M SORRY. THAT WAS STUPID! YOU DON'T HAVE TO ANSWER!
NO... IT'S OKAY...
...AND NO, MIMI WASN'T SICK.
MIMI?
I ALWAYS CALLED HER MIMI.
IT WAS AN ACCIDENT. SOME JERK NOT PAYING ATTENTION...

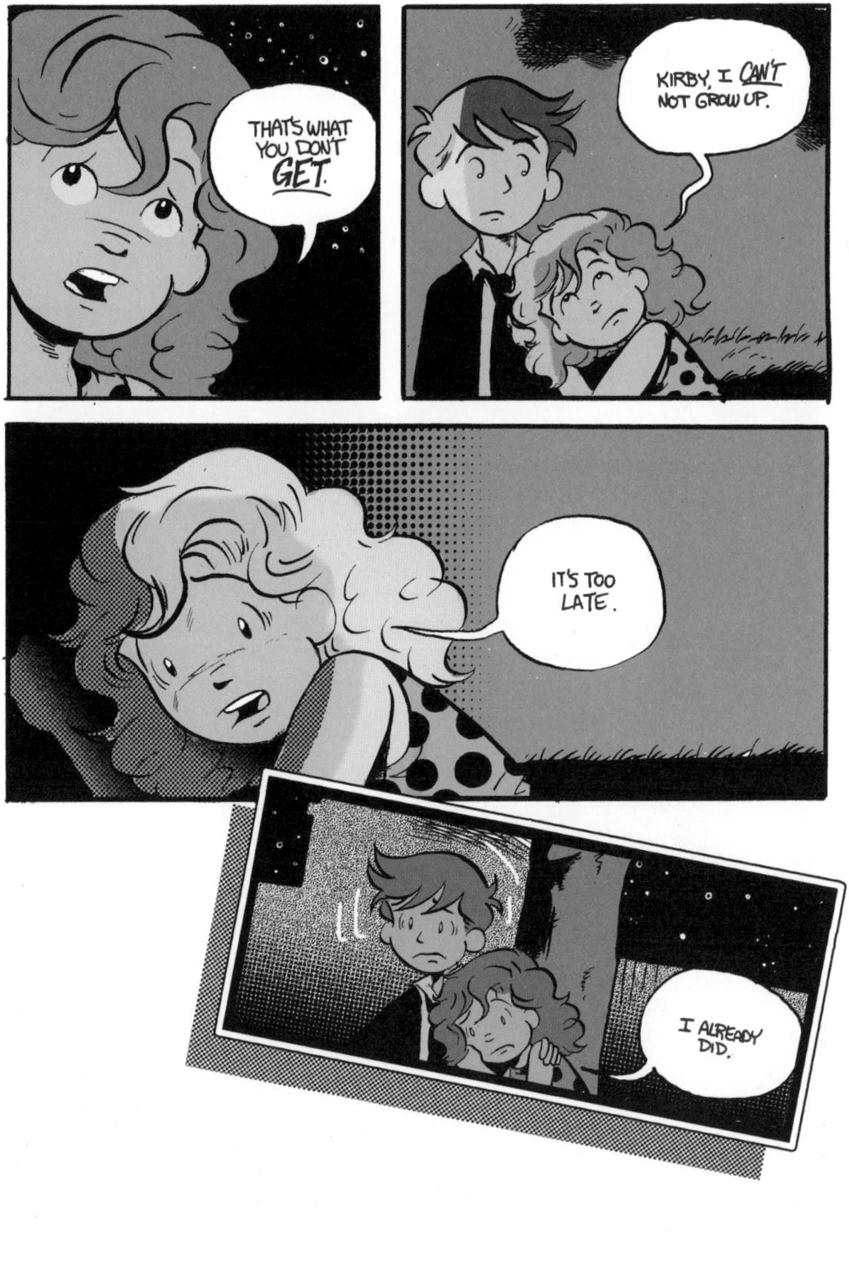
THAT'S WHAT YOU DON'T GET.
KIRBY, I CAN'T NOT GROW UP.
IT'S TOO LATE.
I ALREADY DID.

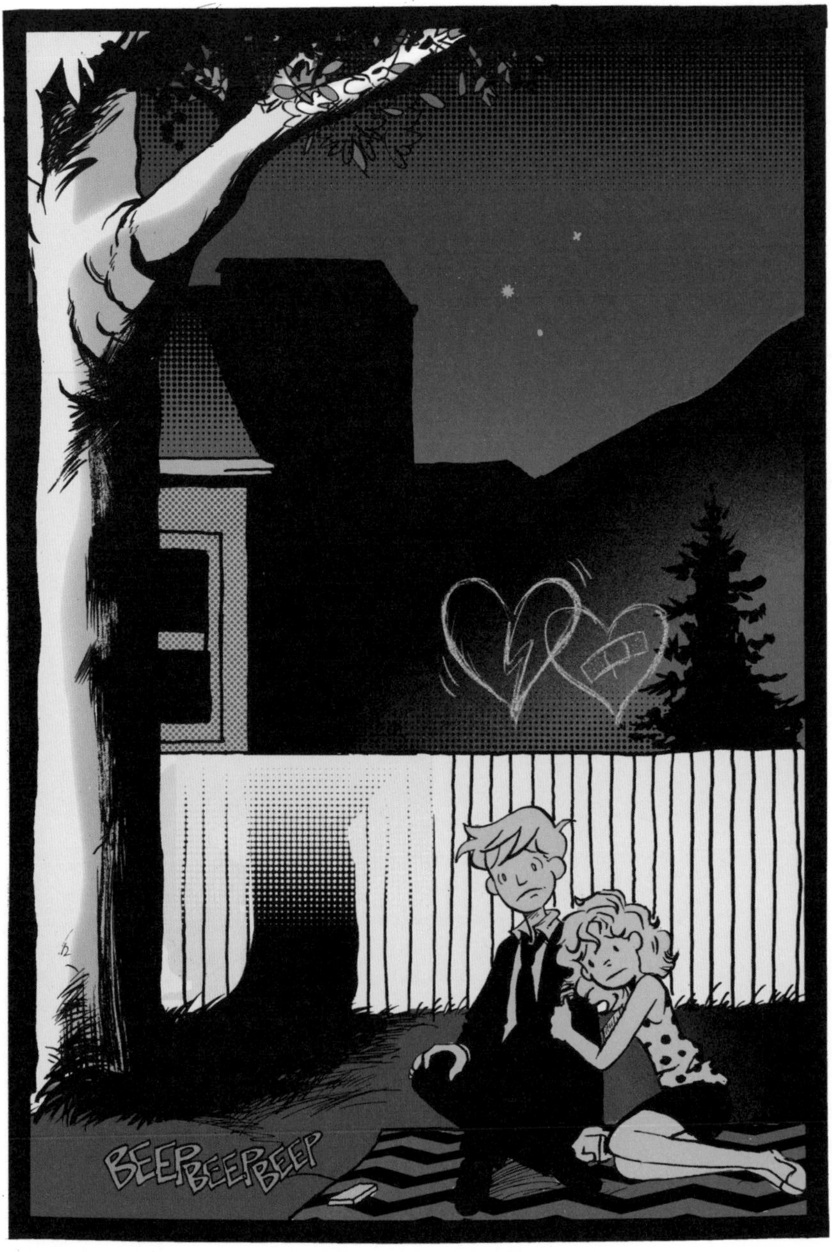
BEEP BEEP BEEP

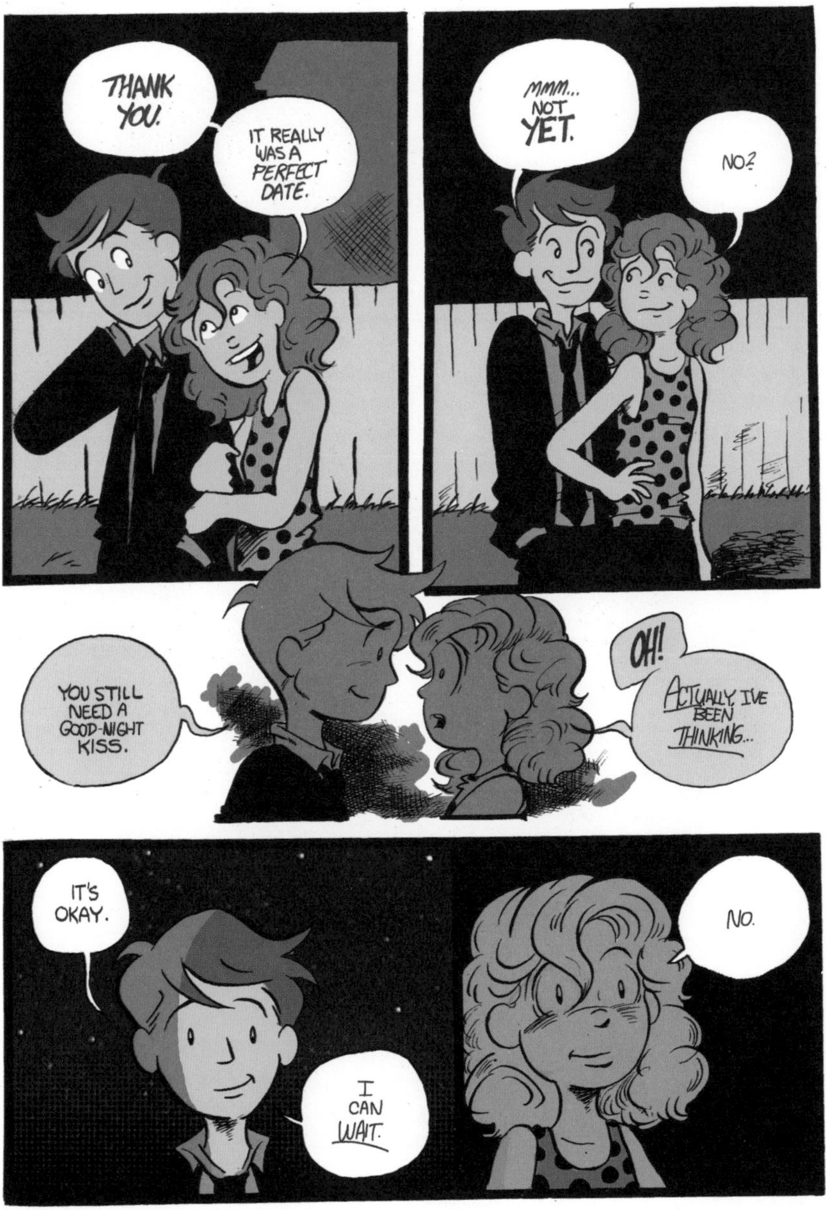
THANK YOU.
IT REALLY WAS A PERFECT DATE.
MMM... NOT YET.
NO?
YOU STILL NEED A GOOD-NIGHT KISS.
OH!
ACTUALLY, I'VE BEEN THINKING...
IT'S OKAY.
I CAN WAIT.
NO.

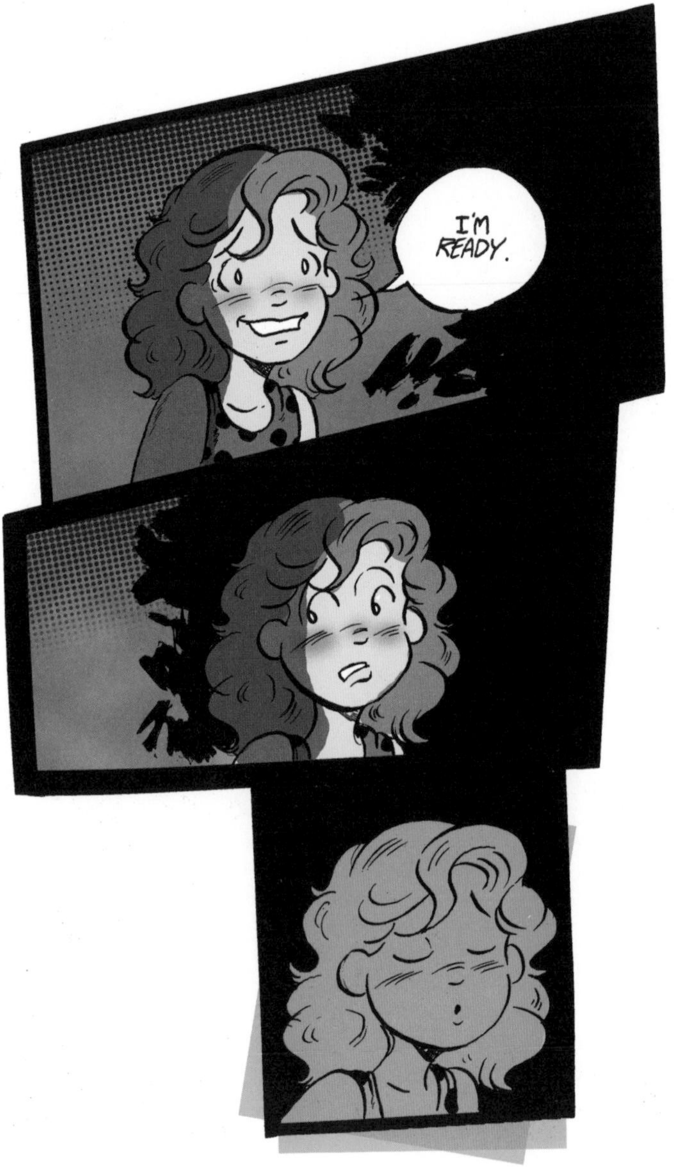
I'M READY.

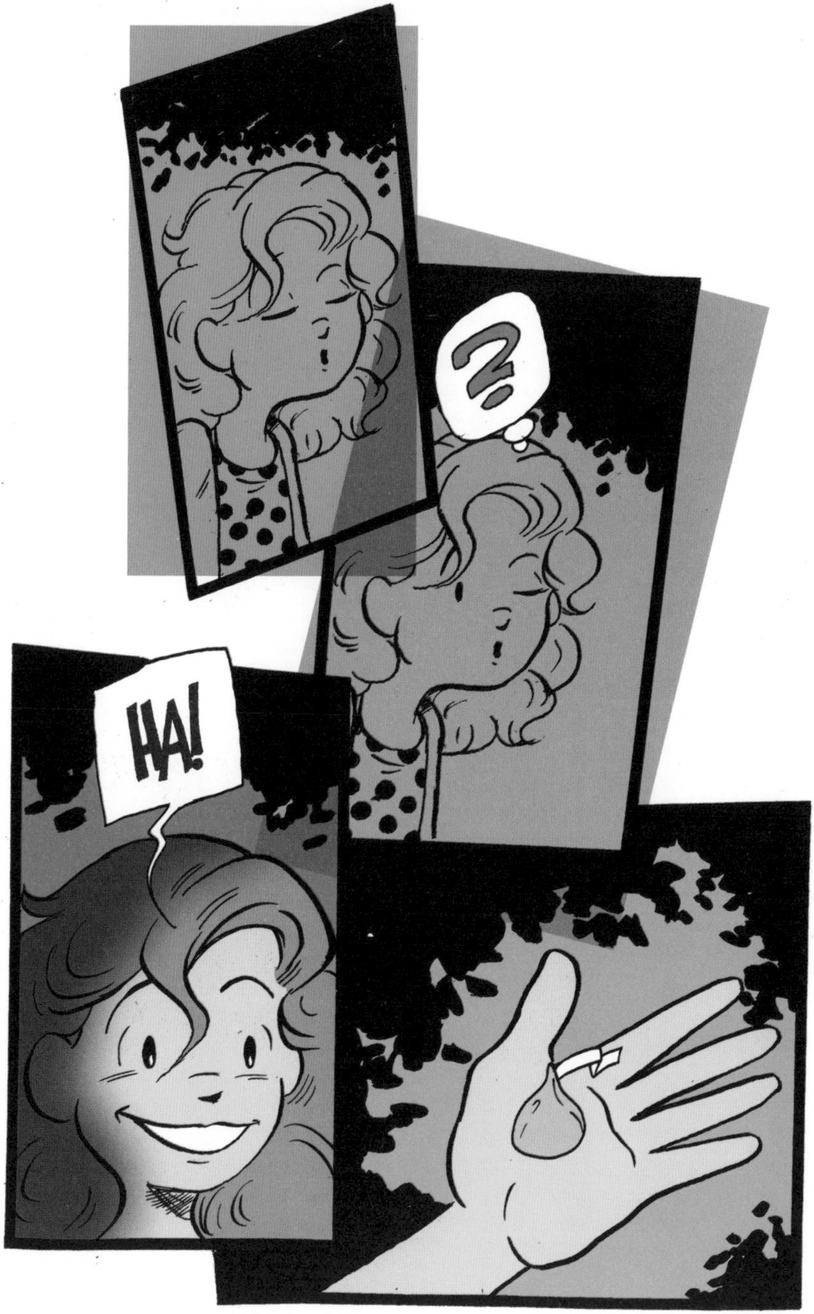
?
HA!

PSST!
good night, Perfect Girl.
>kiss<
GOOD-BYE, KIRBY FINN.

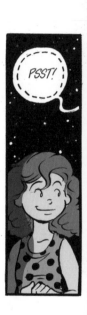

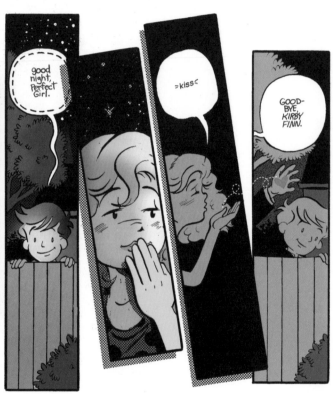

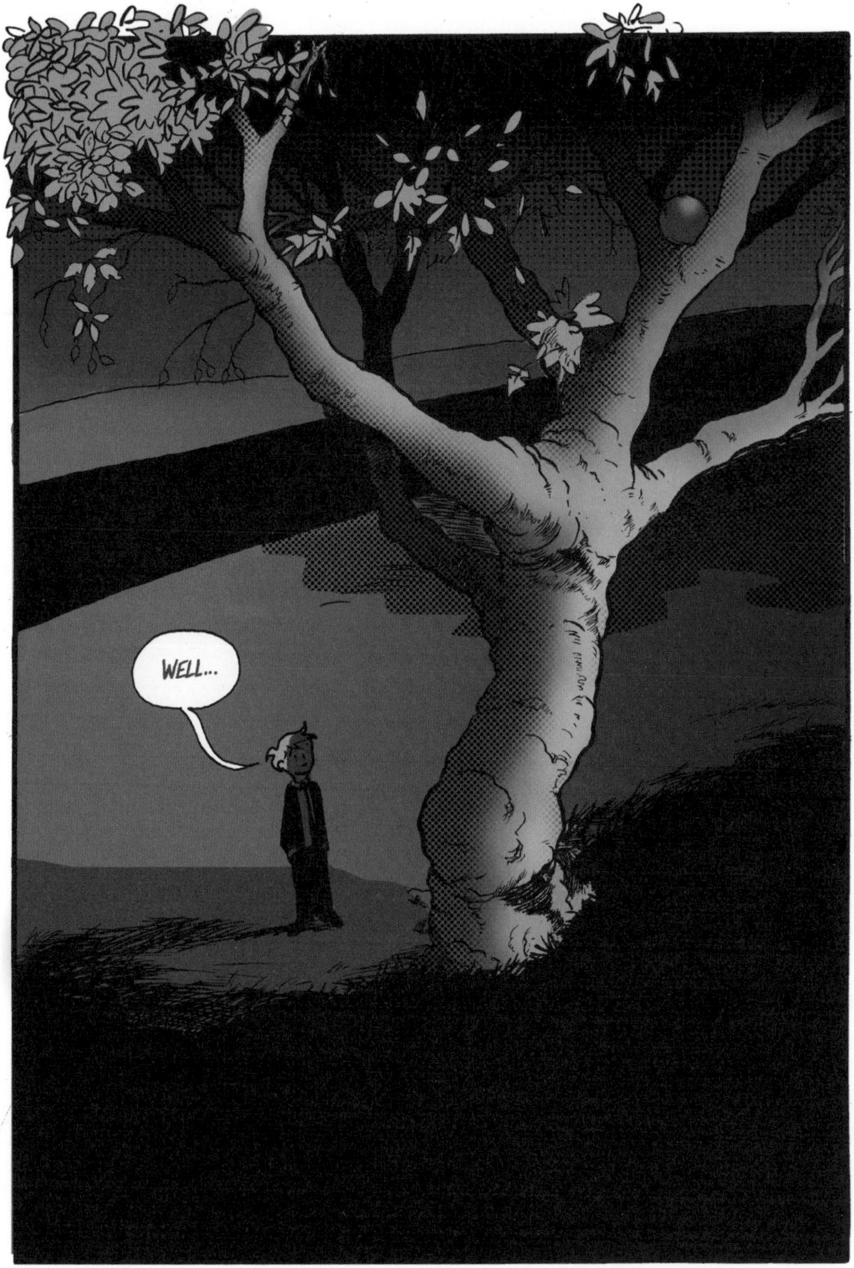
WELL...

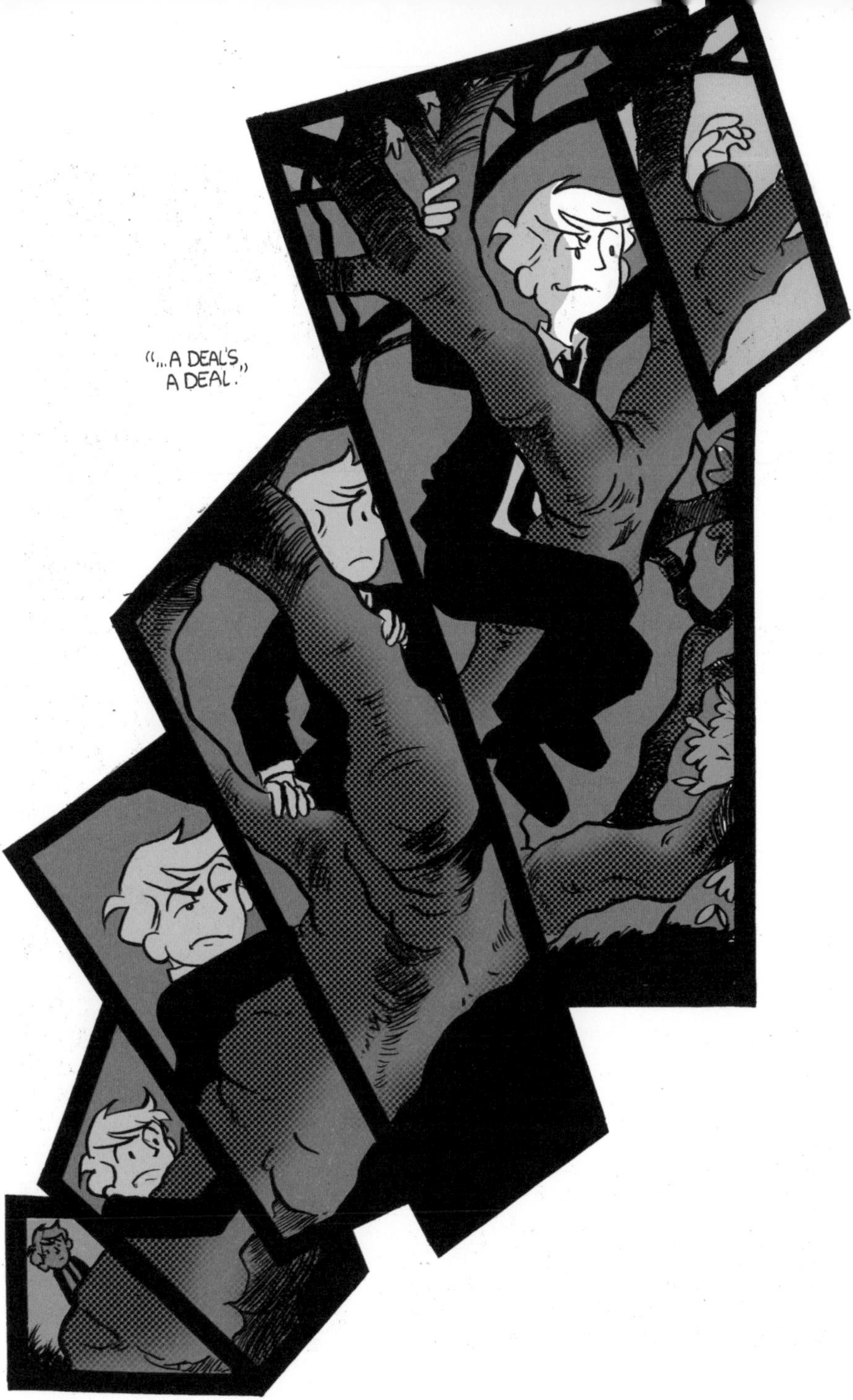
"...A DEAL'S A DEAL."

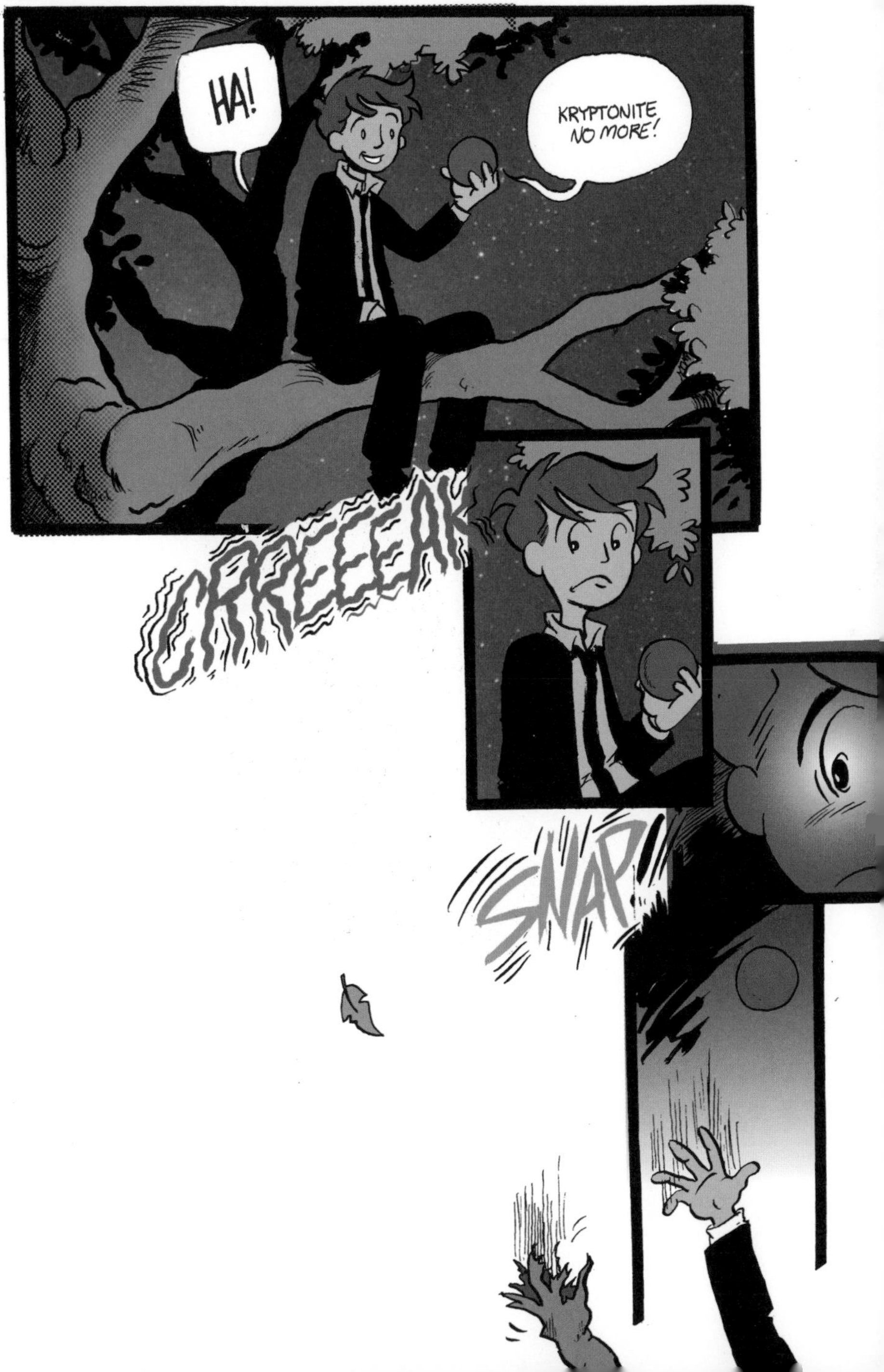
HA!
KRYPTONITE NO MORE!
CRREEEAK
SNAP

REASON ONE: DEATH

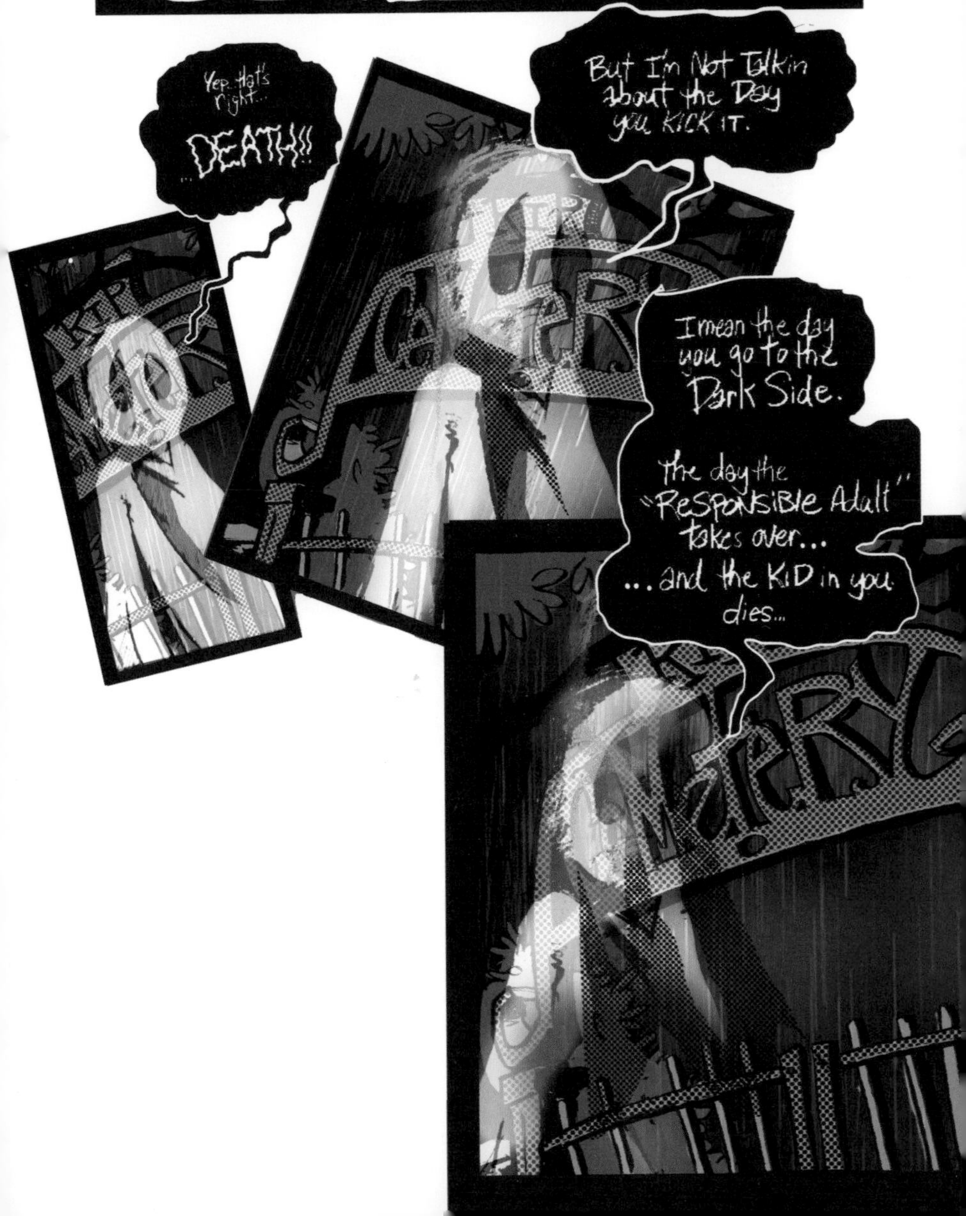
Yep..that's right...
...DEATH!!
But I'm Not Talkin about the Day you KICK IT.
I mean the day you go to the Dark Side.
The day the "RESPONSIBLE Adult" takes over...
...and the KID in you dies...

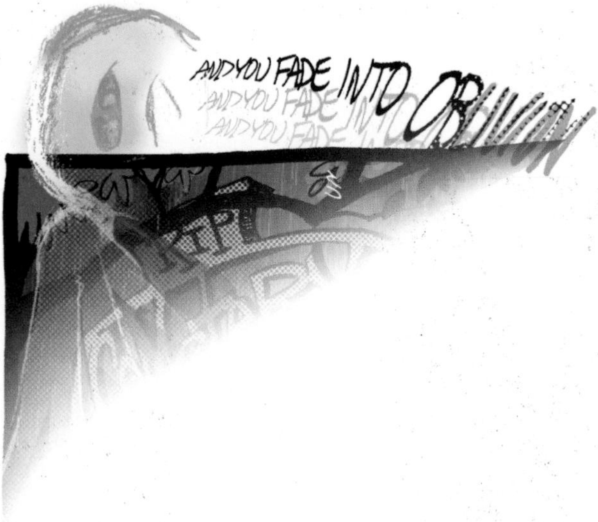
AND YOU FADE INTO OB
RIP

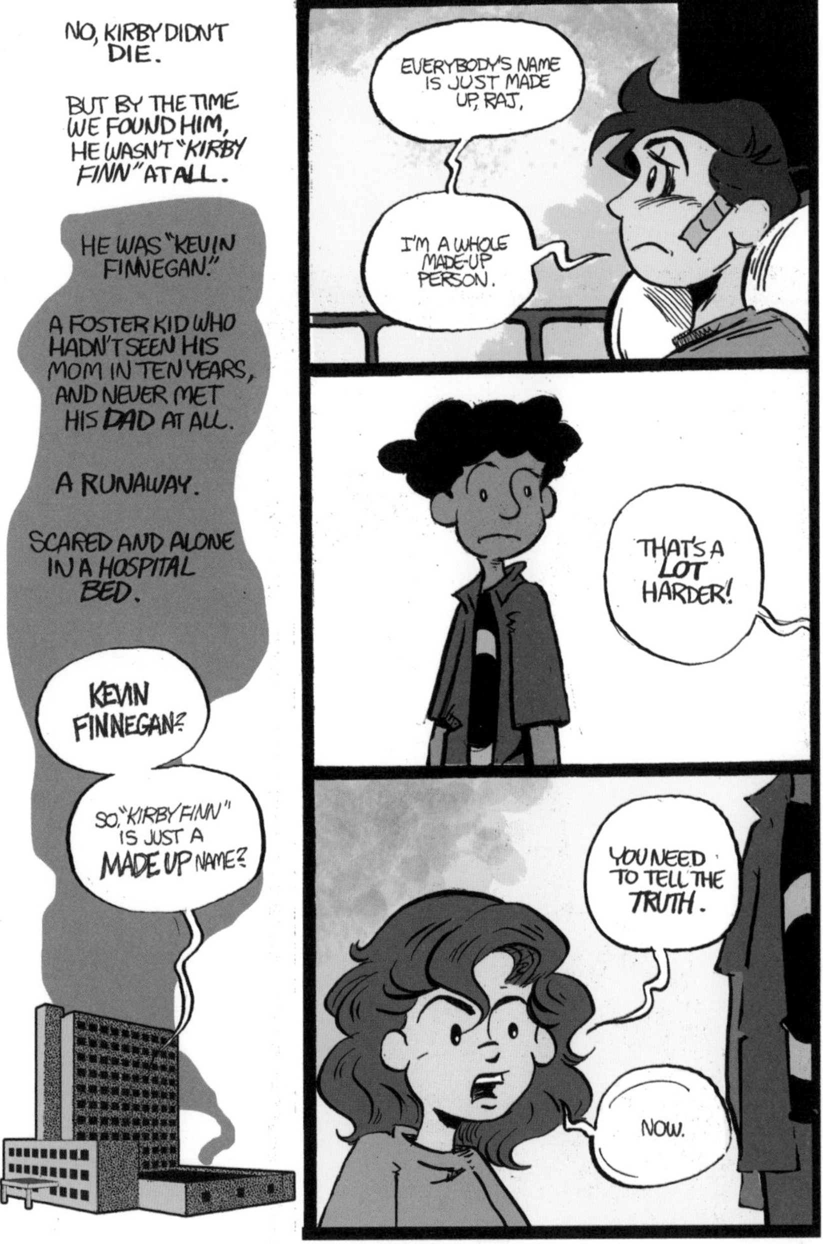
NO, KIRBY DIDN'T DIE.
BUT BY THE TIME WE FOUND HIM, HE WASN'T "KIRBY FINN" AT ALL.
HE WAS "KEVIN FINNEGAN."
A FOSTER KID WHO HADN'T SEEN HIS MOM IN TEN YEARS, AND NEVER MET HIS DAD AT ALL.
A RUNAWAY.
SCARED AND ALONE IN A HOSPITAL BED.
KEVIN FINNEGAN?
SO, "KIRBY FINN" IS JUST A MADE UP NAME?
EVERYBODY'S NAME IS JUST MADE UP, RAJ.
I'M A WHOLE MADE-UP PERSON.
THAT'S A LOT HARDER!
YOU NEED TO TELL THE TRUTH.
NOW.

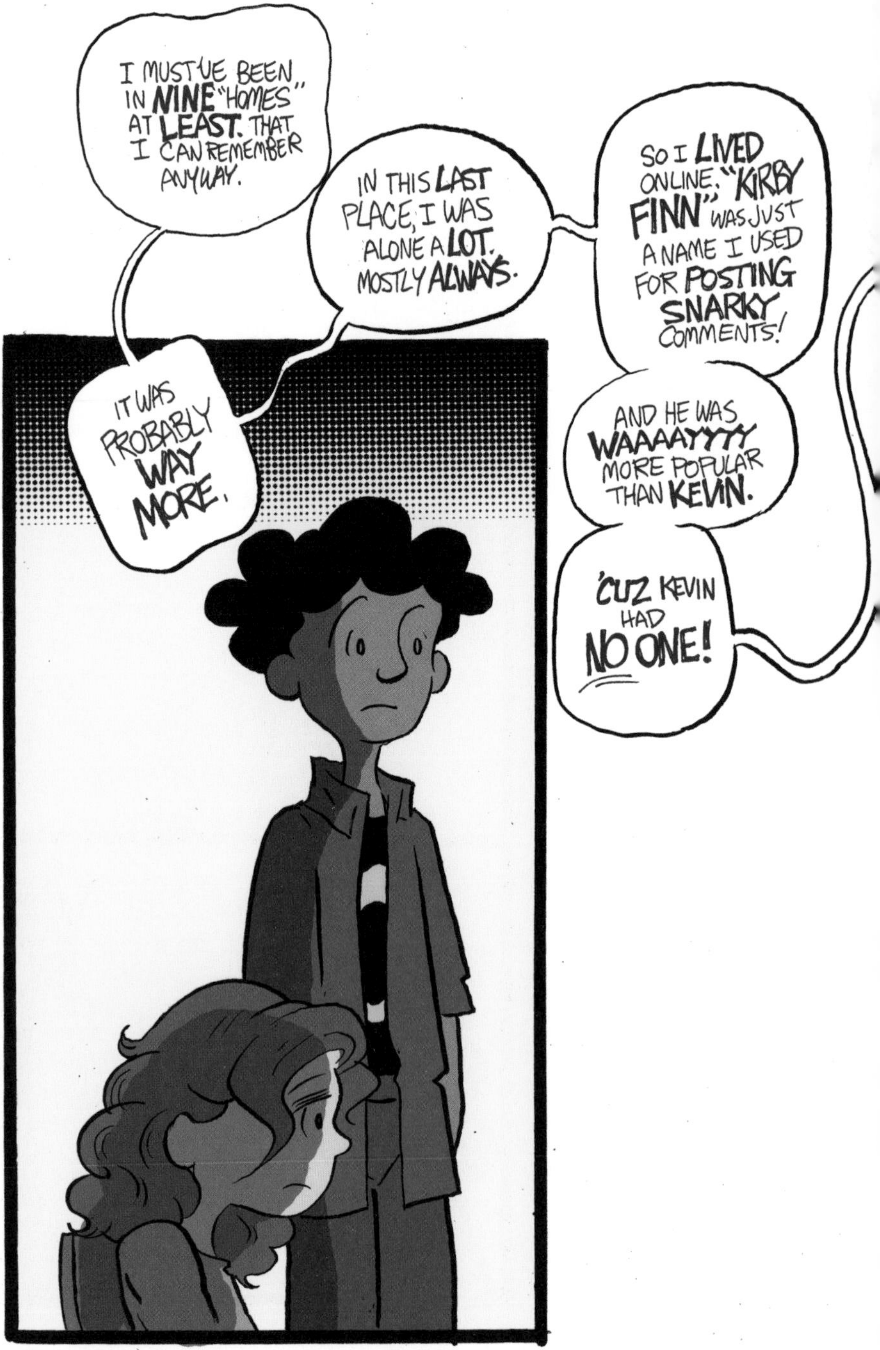
I MUST'VE BEEN IN NINE "HOMES" AT LEAST. THAT I CAN REMEMBER ANYWAY.
IT WAS PROBABLY WAY MORE.
IN THIS LAST PLACE, I WAS ALONE A LOT. MOSTLY ALWAYS.
SO I LIVED ONLINE. "KIRBY FINN" WAS JUST A NAME I USED FOR POSTING SNARKY COMMENTS!
AND HE WAS WAAAAYYYY MORE POPULAR THAN KEVIN.
'CUZ KEVIN HAD NO ONE!

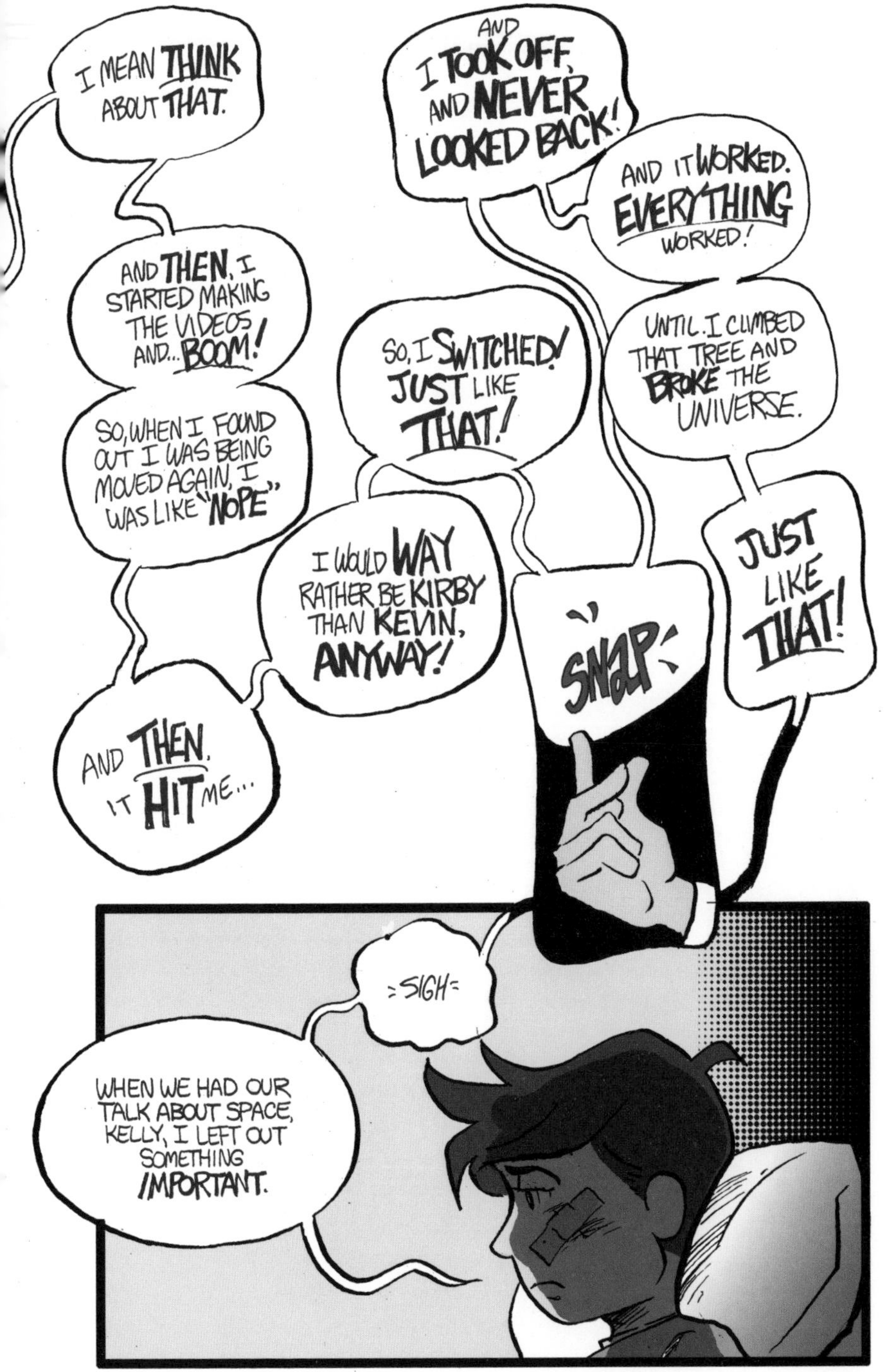
I MEAN THINK ABOUT THAT.
AND THEN, I STARTED MAKING THE VIDEOS AND... BOOM!
SO, WHEN I FOUND OUT I WAS BEING MOVED AGAIN, I WAS LIKE "NOPE"
AND THEN, IT HIT ME...
I WOULD WAY RATHER BE KIRBY THAN KEVIN, ANYWAY!
SO, I SWITCHED! JUST LIKE THAT!
AND I TOOK OFF, AND NEVER LOOKED BACK!
AND IT WORKED. EVERYTHING WORKED!
UNTIL I CLIMBED THAT TREE AND BROKE THE UNIVERSE.
JUST LIKE THAT!
SNAP
=SIGH=
WHEN WE HAD OUR TALK ABOUT SPACE, KELLY, I LEFT OUT SOMETHING IMPORTANT.

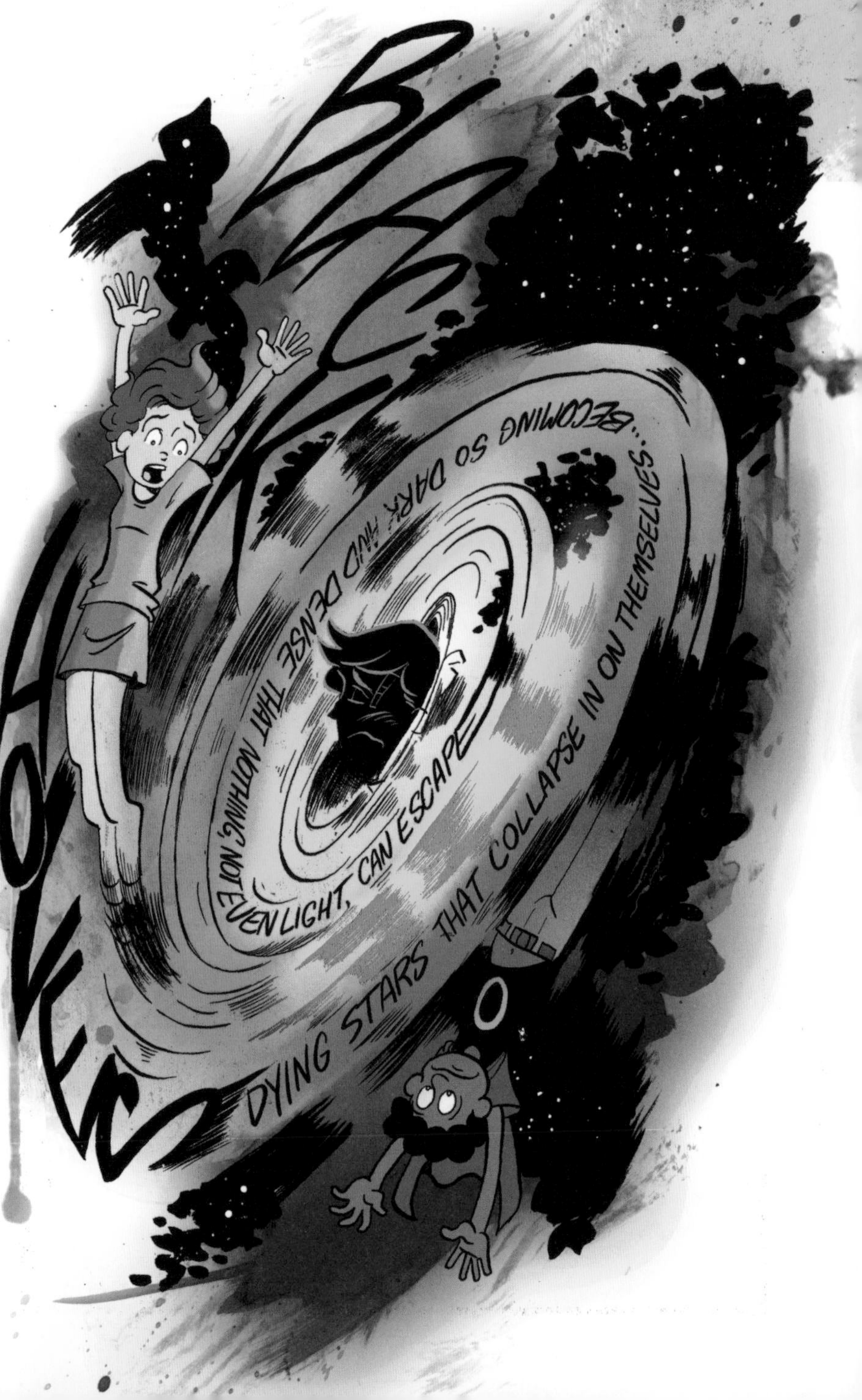
BLACK HOLES
DYING STARS THAT COLLAPSE IN ON THEMSELVES...
BECOMING SO DARK AND DENSE THAT NOTHING, NOT EVEN LIGHT, CAN ESCAPE

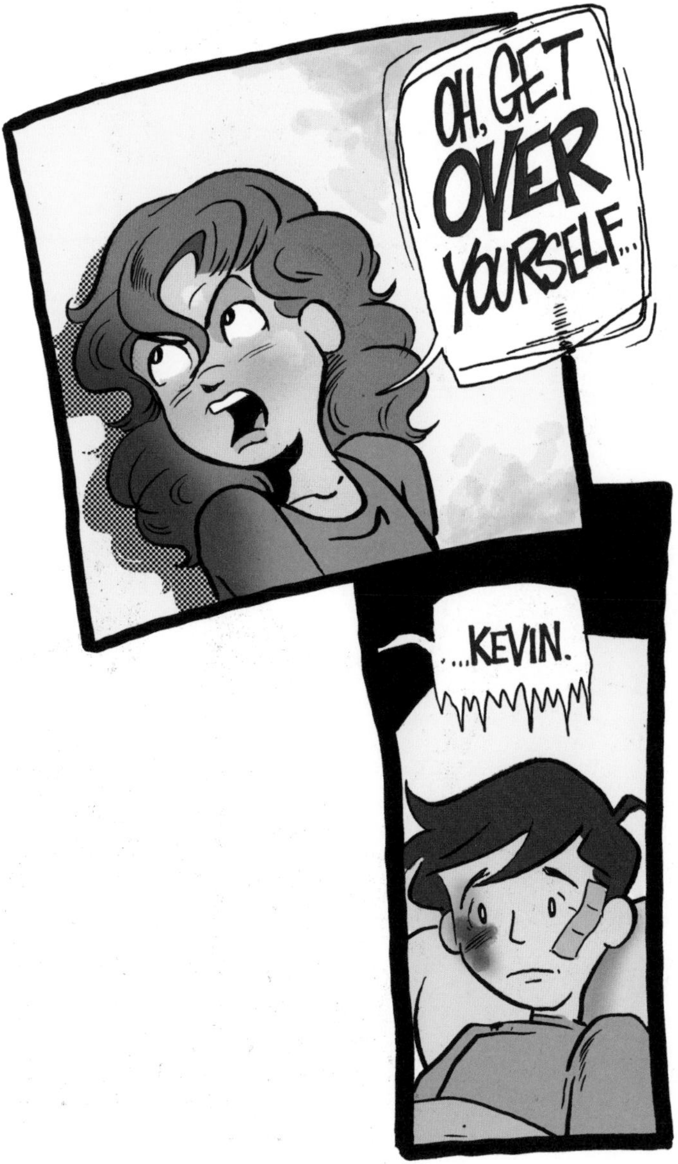
OH, GET OVER YOURSELF...
...KEVIN.

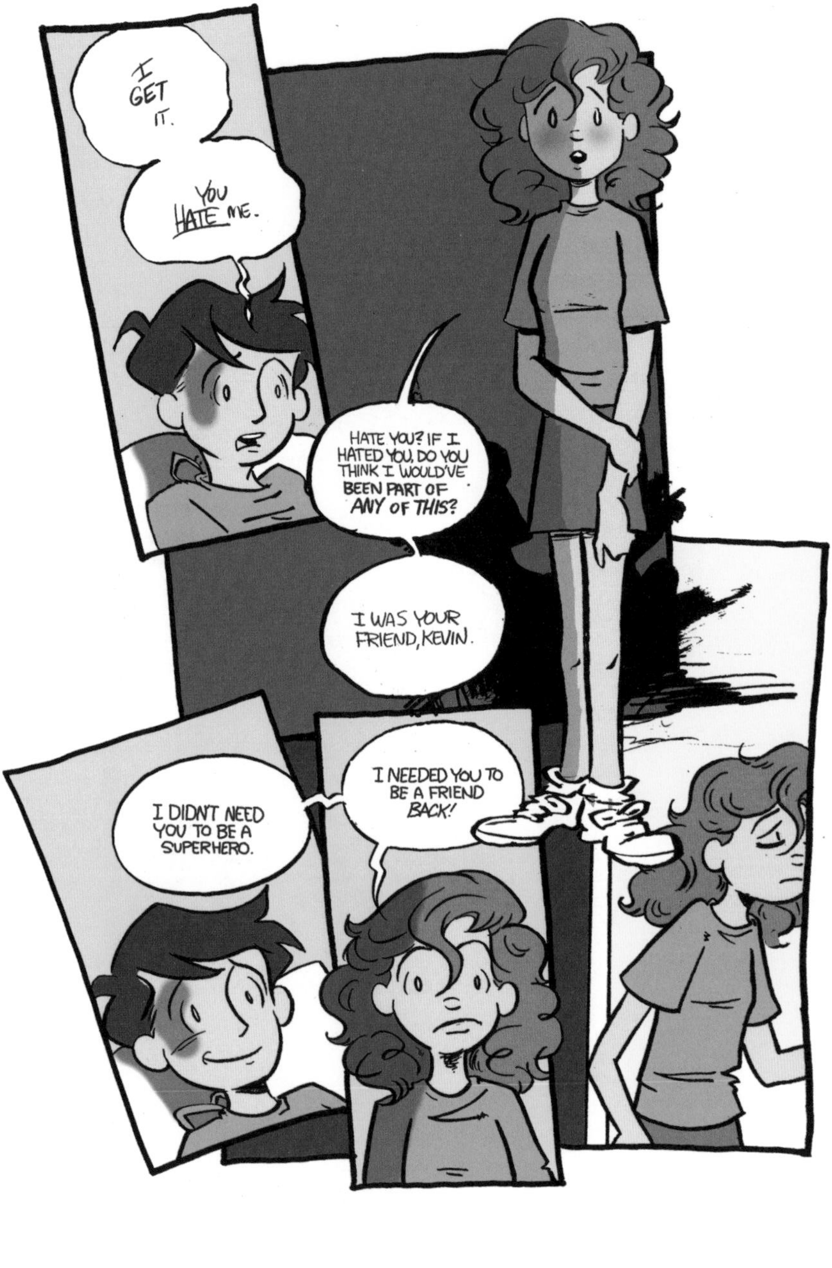
I GET IT.
YOU HATE ME.
HATE YOU? IF I HATED YOU, DO YOU THINK I WOULD'VE BEEN PART OF ANY OF THIS?
I WAS YOUR FRIEND, KEVIN.
I DIDN'T NEED YOU TO BE A SUPERHERO.
I NEEDED YOU TO BE A FRIEND BACK!

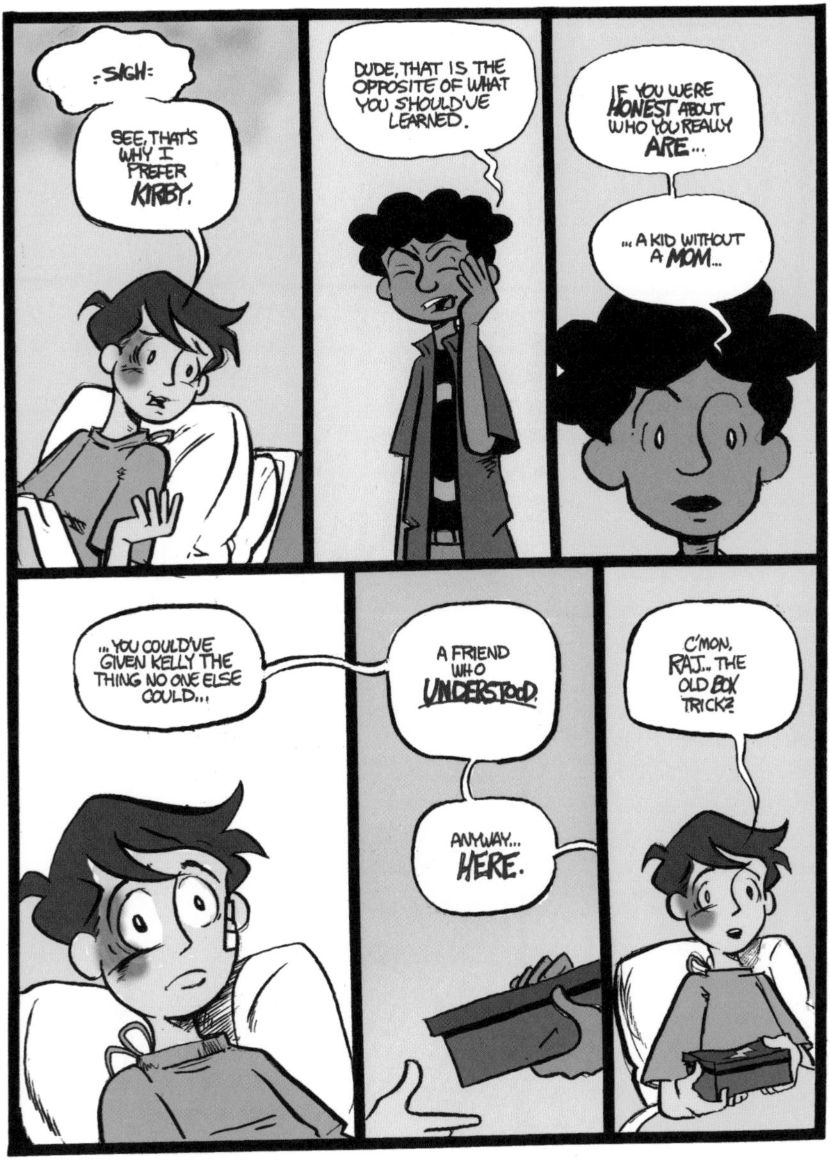
=SIGH=
SEE, THAT'S WHY I PREFER KIRBY.
DUDE, THAT IS THE OPPOSITE OF WHAT YOU SHOULD'VE LEARNED.
IF YOU WERE HONEST ABOUT WHO YOU REALLY ARE...
...A KID WITHOUT A MOM...
...YOU COULD'VE GIVEN KELLY THE THING NO ONE ELSE COULD...
A FRIEND WHO UNDERSTOOD.
ANYWAY... HERE.
C'MON, RAJ.. THE OLD BOX TRICK?

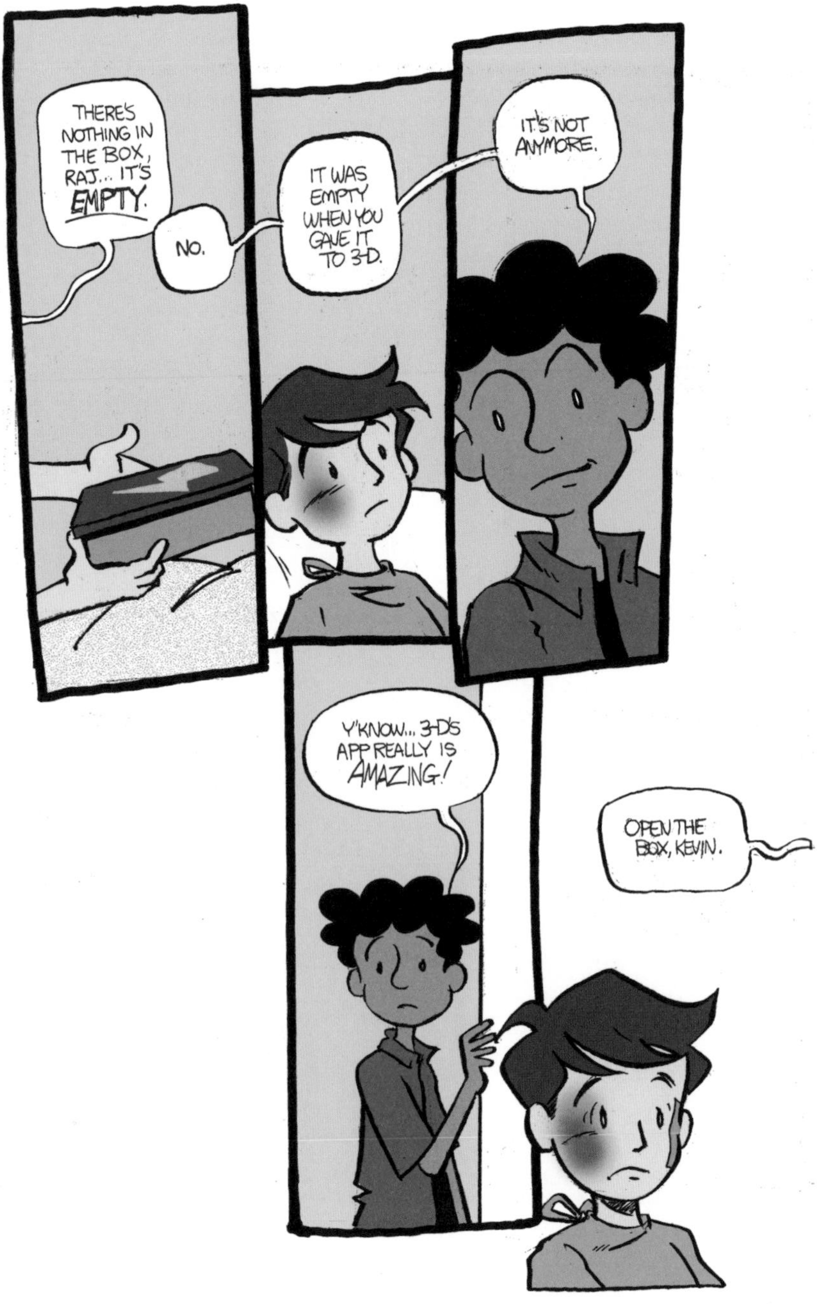
THERE'S NOTHING IN THE BOX, RAJ... IT'S EMPTY.
NO.
IT WAS EMPTY WHEN YOU GAVE IT TO 3-D.
IT'S NOT ANYMORE.
Y'KNOW... 3-D'S APP REALLY IS AMAZING!
OPEN THE BOX, KEVIN.

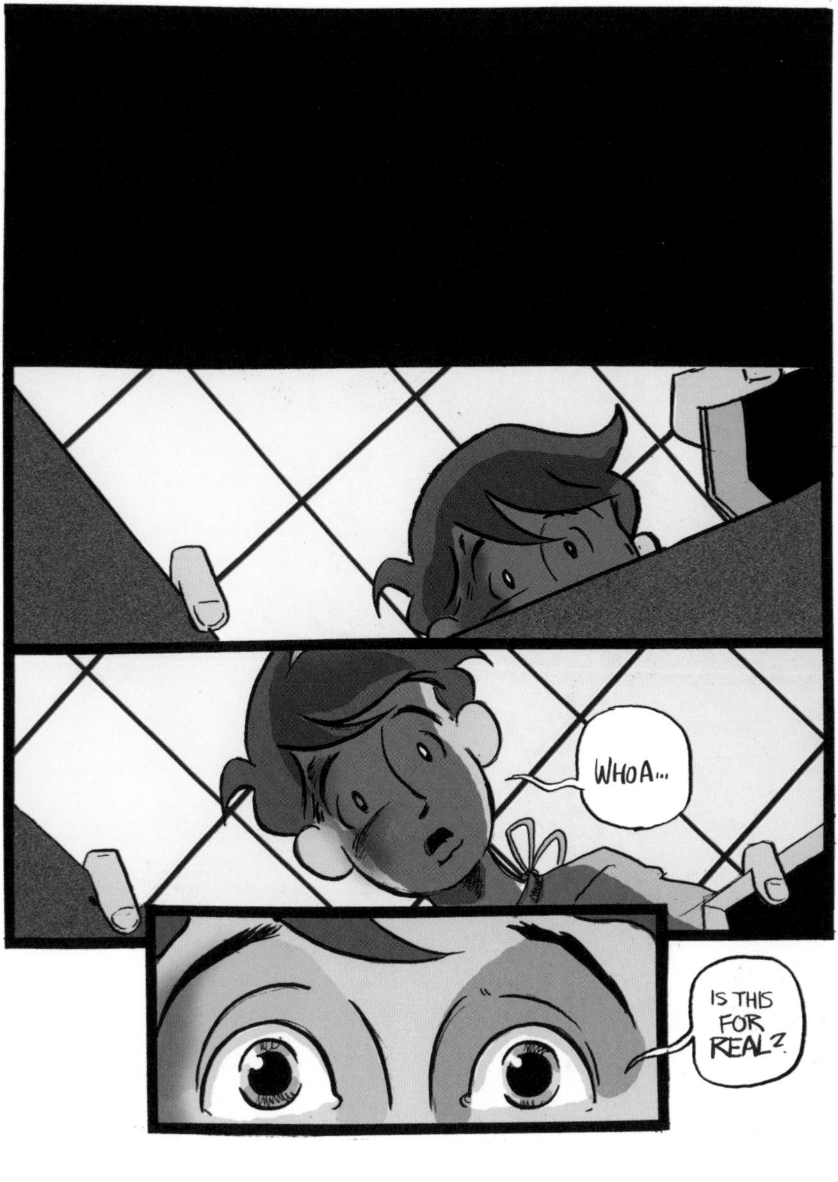
WHOA...
IS THIS FOR REAL?

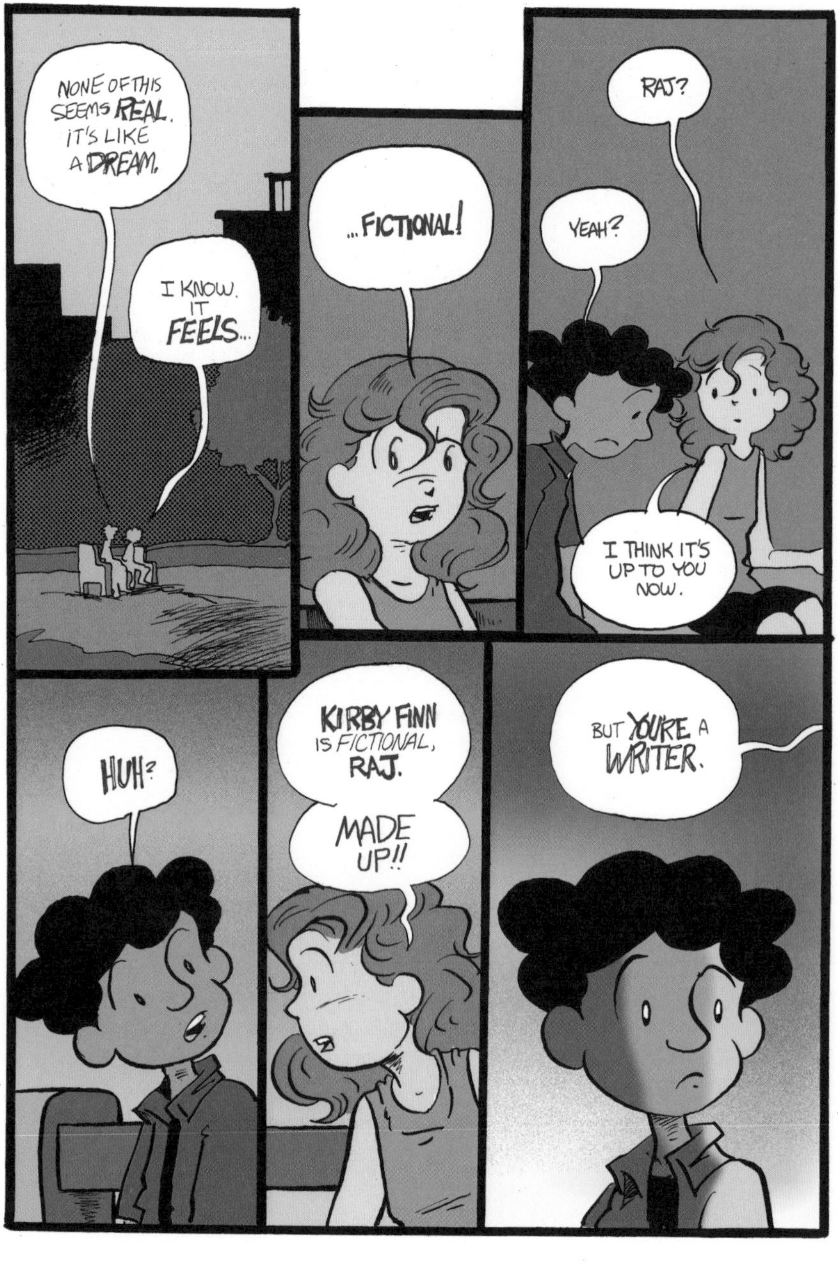
NONE OF THIS SEEMS REAL. IT'S LIKE A DREAM.
I KNOW. IT FEELS...
...FICTIONAL!
RAJ?
YEAH?
I THINK IT'S UP TO YOU NOW.
HUH?
KIRBY FINN IS FICTIONAL, RAJ.
MADE UP!!
BUT YOU'RE A WRITER.

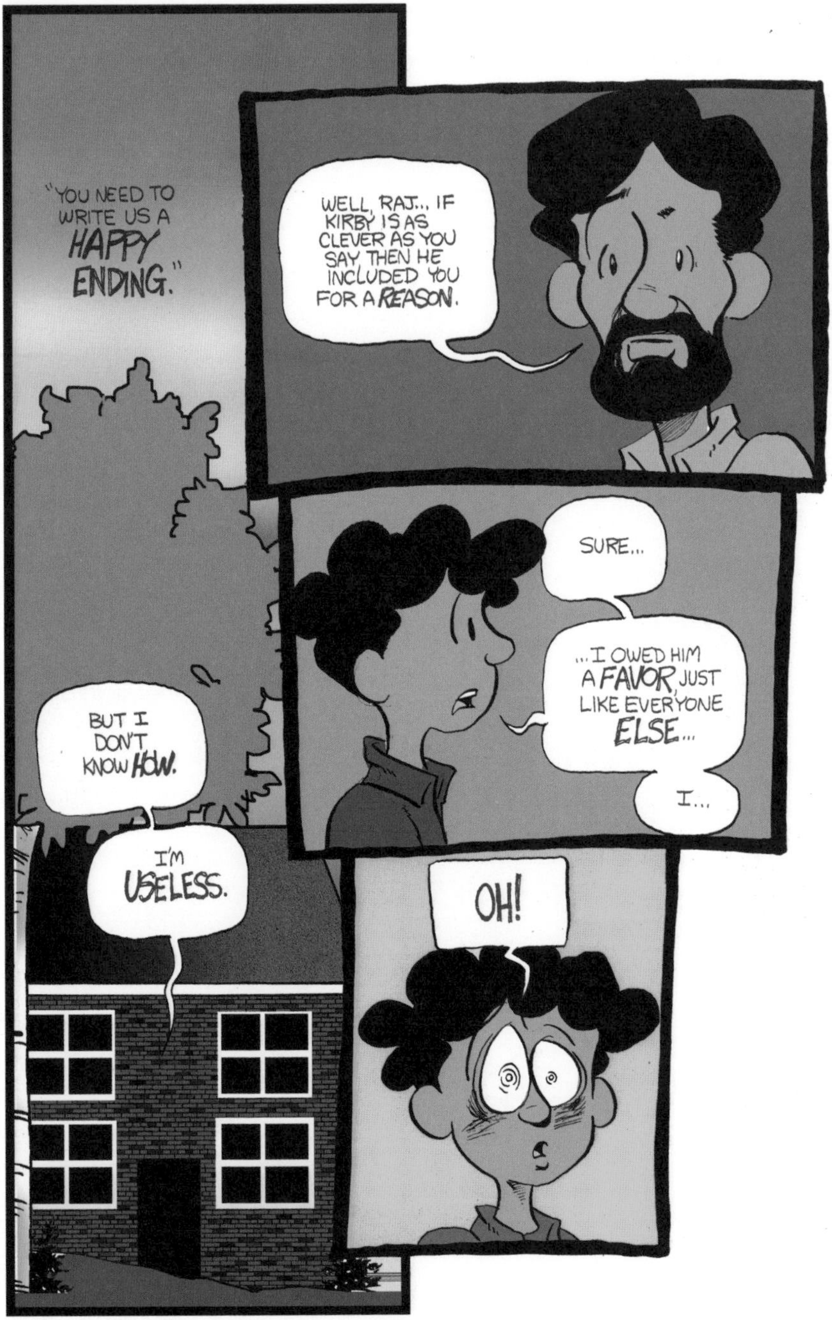
"YOU NEED TO WRITE US A HAPPY ENDING."
WELL, RAJ... IF KIRBY IS AS CLEVER AS YOU SAY THEN HE INCLUDED YOU FOR A REASON.
SURE...
...I OWED HIM A FAVOR, JUST LIKE EVERYONE ELSE...
I...
BUT I DON'T KNOW HOW.
I'M USELESS.
OH!

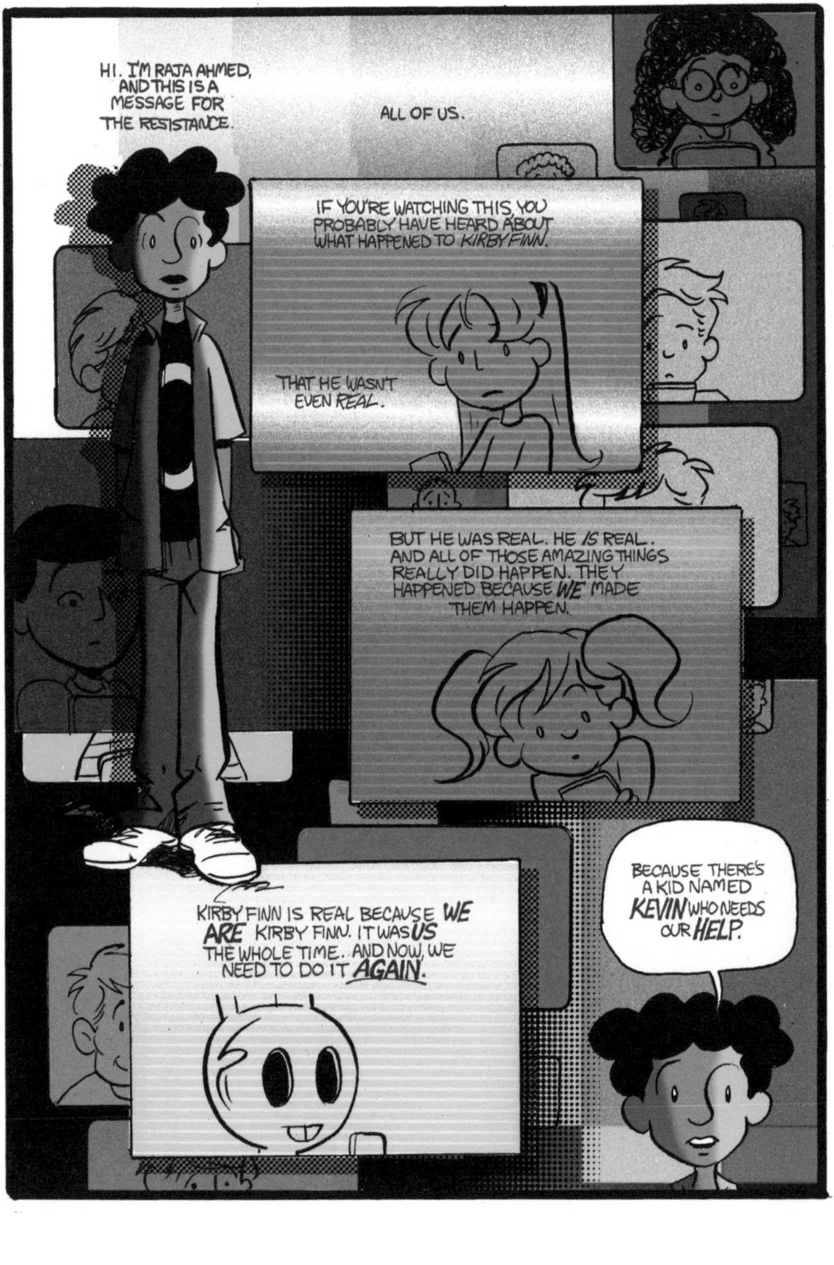
HI. I'M RAJA AHMED, AND THIS IS A MESSAGE FOR THE RESISTANCE.
ALL OF US.
IF YOU'RE WATCHING THIS, YOU PROBABLY HAVE HEARD ABOUT WHAT HAPPENED TO KIRBY FINN.
THAT HE WASN'T EVEN REAL.
BUT HE WAS REAL. HE IS REAL. AND ALL OF THOSE AMAZING THINGS REALLY DID HAPPEN. THEY HAPPENED BECAUSE WE MADE THEM HAPPEN.
KIRBY FINN IS REAL BECAUSE WE ARE KIRBY FINN. IT WAS US THE WHOLE TIME. AND NOW, WE NEED TO DO IT AGAIN.
BECAUSE THERE'S A KID NAMED KEVIN WHO NEEDS OUR HELP.

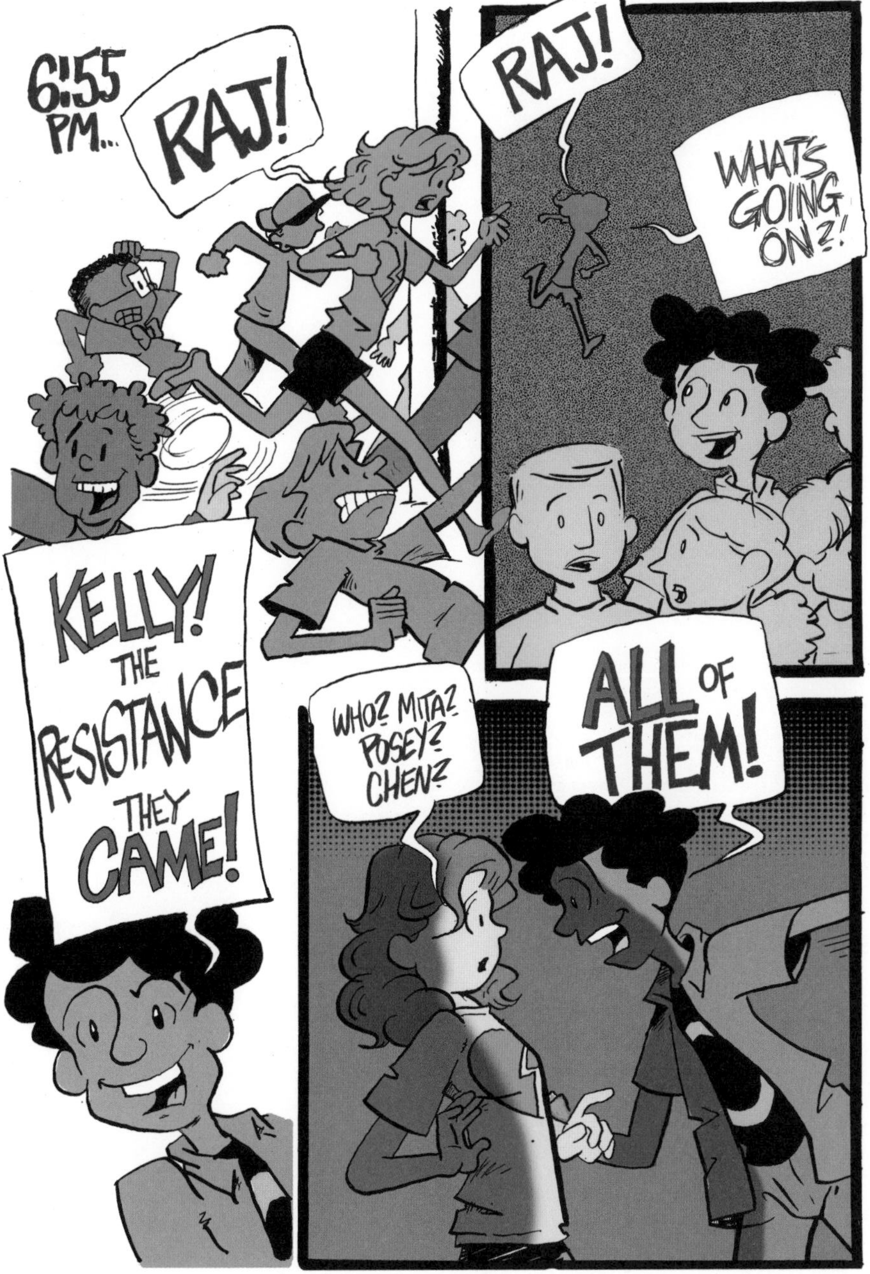
6:55 PM...
RAJ!
RAJ!
WHAT'S GOING ON?!
KELLY! THE RESISTANCE THEY CAME!
WHO? MITA? POSEY? CHEN?
ALL OF THEM!

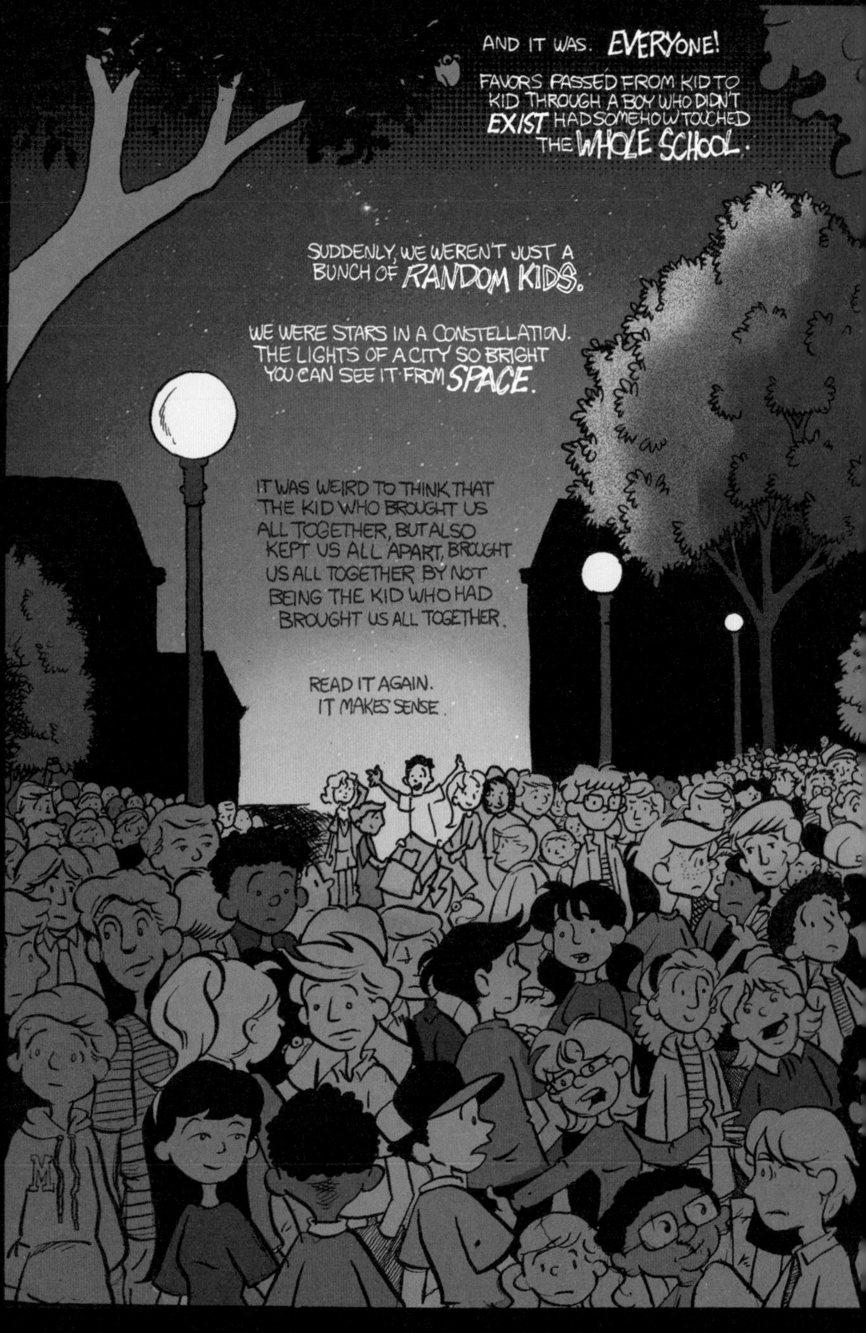
AND IT WAS. EVERYONE!
FAVORS PASSED FROM KID TO KID THROUGH A BOY WHO DIDN'T EXIST HAD SOMEHOW TOUCHED THE WHOLE SCHOOL.
SUDDENLY, WE WEREN'T JUST A BUNCH OF RANDOM KIDS.
WE WERE STARS IN A CONSTELLATION. THE LIGHTS OF A CITY SO BRIGHT YOU CAN SEE IT FROM SPACE.
IT WAS WEIRD TO THINK THAT THE KID WHO BROUGHT US ALL TOGETHER, BUT ALSO KEPT US ALL APART, BROUGHT US ALL TOGETHER BY NOT BEING THE KID WHO HAD BROUGHT US ALL TOGETHER.
READ IT AGAIN. IT MAKES SENSE.

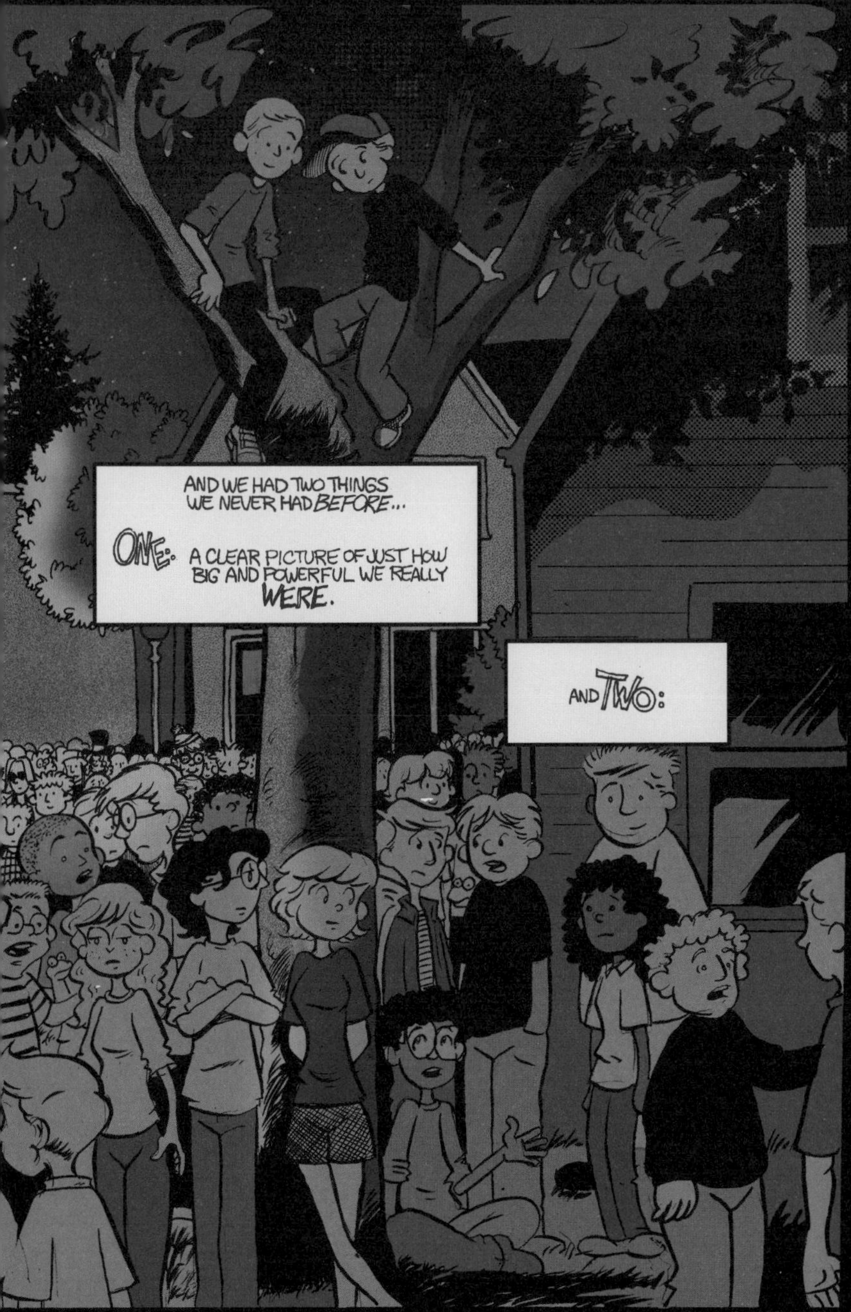
AND WE HAD TWO THINGS WE NEVER HAD BEFORE...
ONE: A CLEAR PICTURE OF JUST HOW BIG AND POWERFUL WE REALLY WERE.
AND TWO:

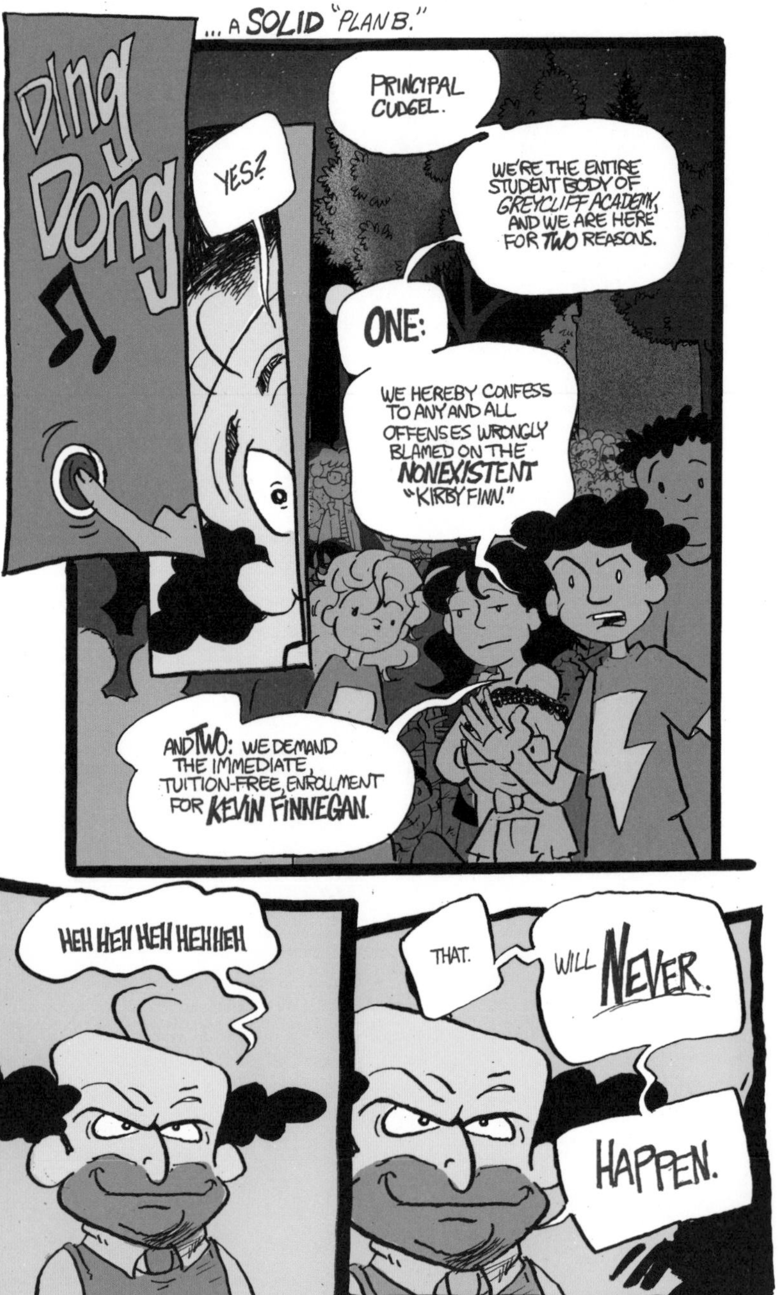
... A SOLID "PLAN B."
DING DONG
YES?
PRINCIPAL CUDGEL.
WE'RE THE ENTIRE STUDENT BODY OF GREYCLIFF ACADEMY, AND WE ARE HERE FOR TWO REASONS.
ONE:
WE HEREBY CONFESS TO ANY AND ALL OFFENSES WRONGLY BLAMED ON THE NONEXISTENT "KIRBY FINN."
AND TWO: WE DEMAND THE IMMEDIATE, TUITION-FREE, ENROLLMENT FOR KEVIN FINNEGAN.
HEH HEH HEH HEHHEH
THAT.
WILL NEVER.
HAPPEN.

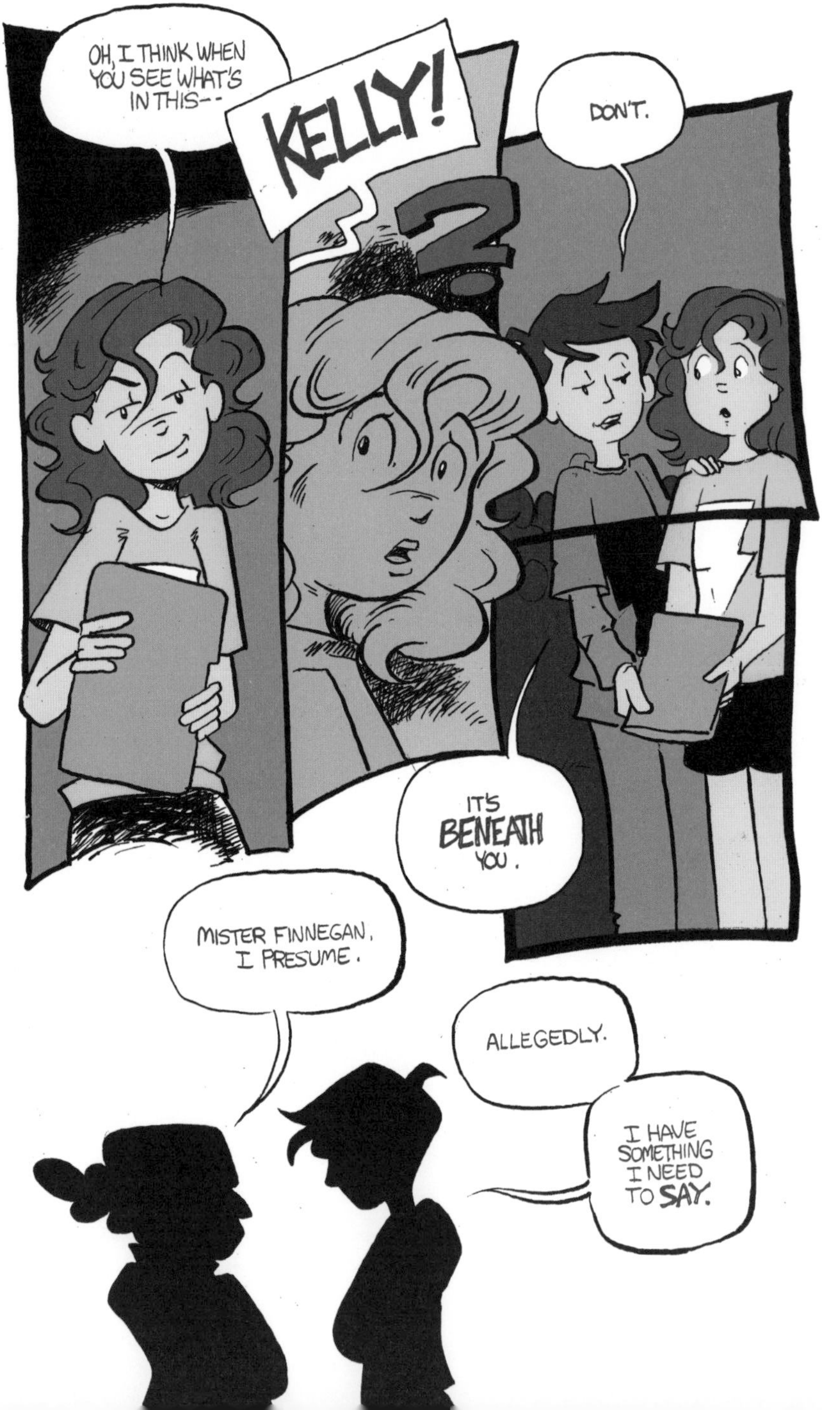
OH, I THINK WHEN YOU SEE WHAT'S IN THIS--
KELLY!
DON'T.
IT'S BENEATH YOU.
MISTER FINNEGAN, I PRESUME.
ALLEGEDLY.
I HAVE SOMETHING I NEED TO SAY.

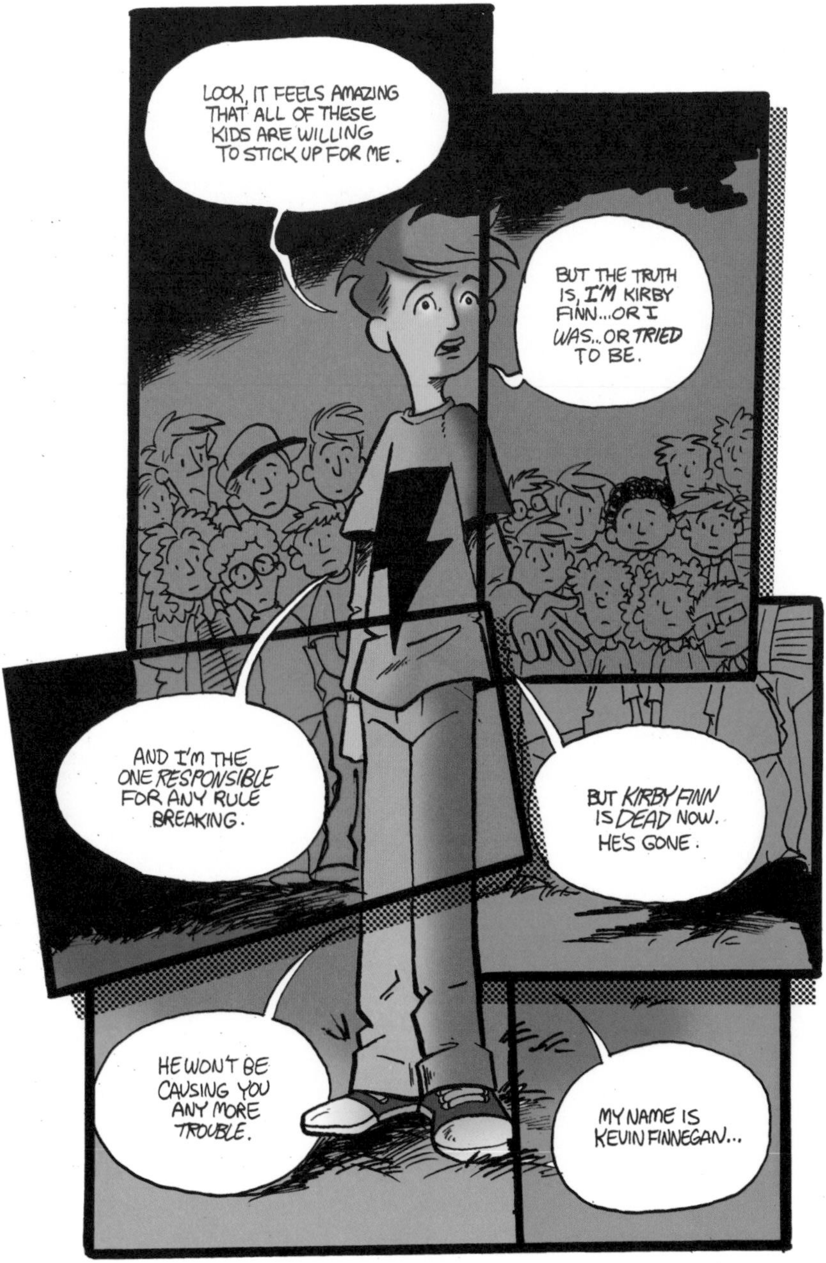
LOOK, IT FEELS AMAZING THAT ALL OF THESE KIDS ARE WILLING TO STICK UP FOR ME.
BUT THE TRUTH IS, I'M KIRBY FINN...OR I WAS...OR TRIED TO BE.
AND I'M THE ONE RESPONSIBLE FOR ANY RULE BREAKING.
BUT KIRBY FINN IS DEAD NOW. HE'S GONE.
HE WON'T BE CAUSING YOU ANY MORE TROUBLE.
MY NAME IS KEVIN FINNEGAN...

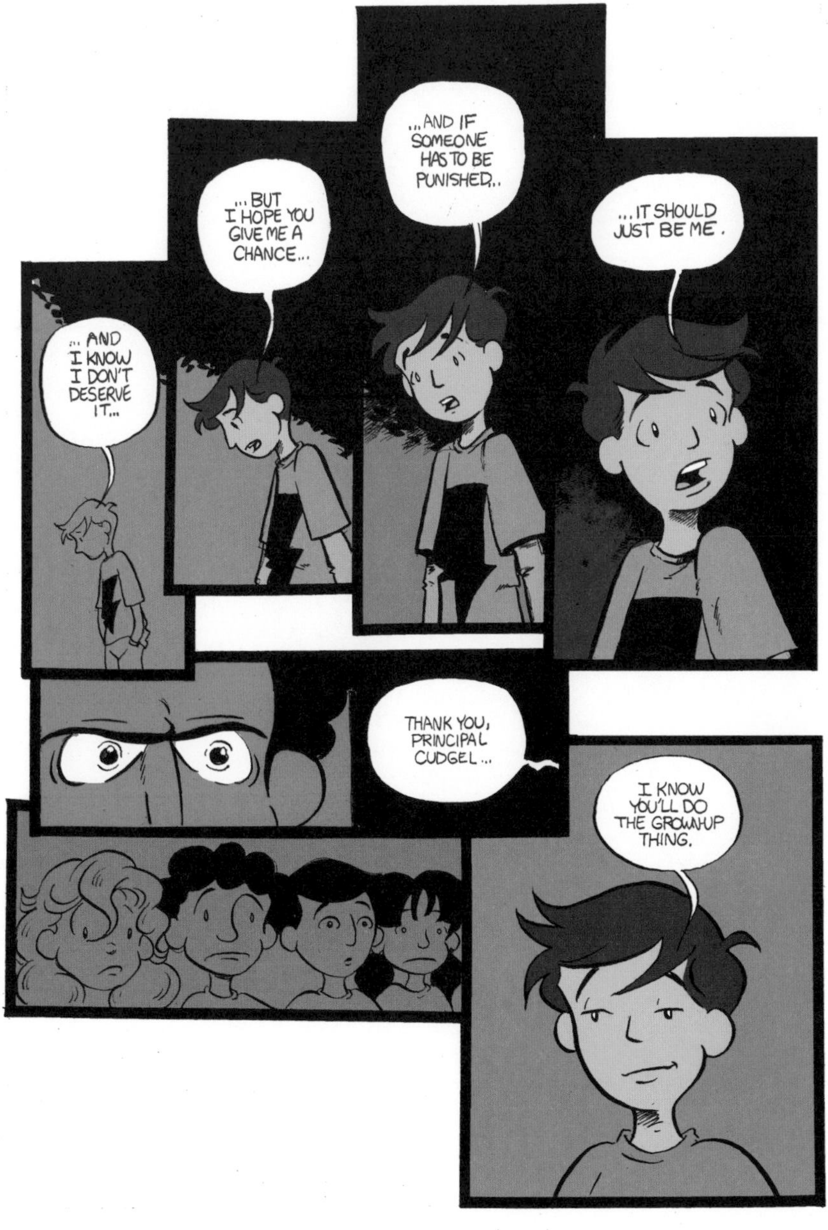

... AND I KNOW I DON'T DESERVE IT...
... BUT I HOPE YOU GIVE ME A CHANCE...
... AND IF SOMEONE HAS TO BE PUNISHED...
... IT SHOULD JUST BE ME.
THANK YOU, PRINCIPAL CUDGEL...
I KNOW YOU'LL DO THE GROWNUP THING.

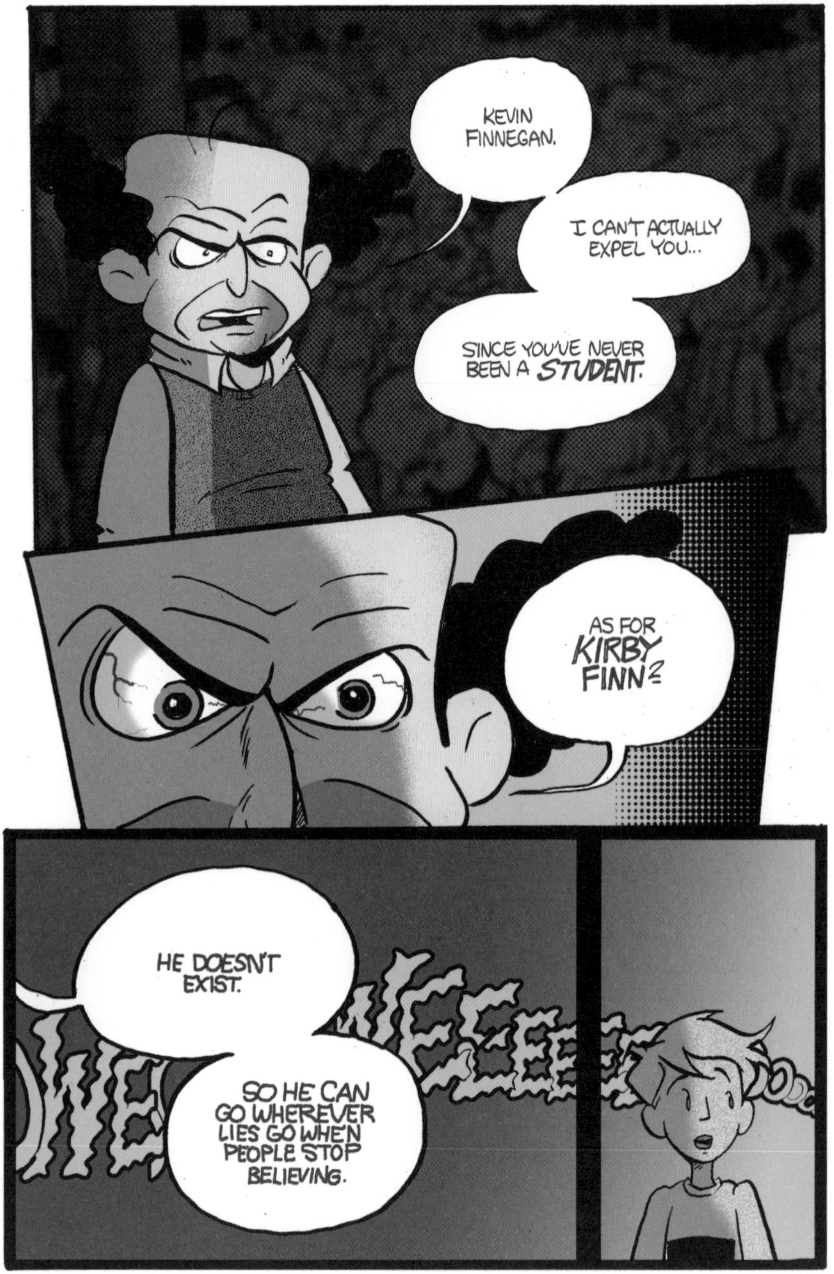
KEVIN FINNEGAN.
I CAN'T ACTUALLY EXPEL YOU...
SINCE YOU'VE NEVER BEEN A STUDENT.
AS FOR KIRBY FINN?
HE DOESN'T EXIST.
SO HE CAN GO WHEREVER LIES GO WHEN PEOPLE STOP BELIEVING.
WEEEEEE

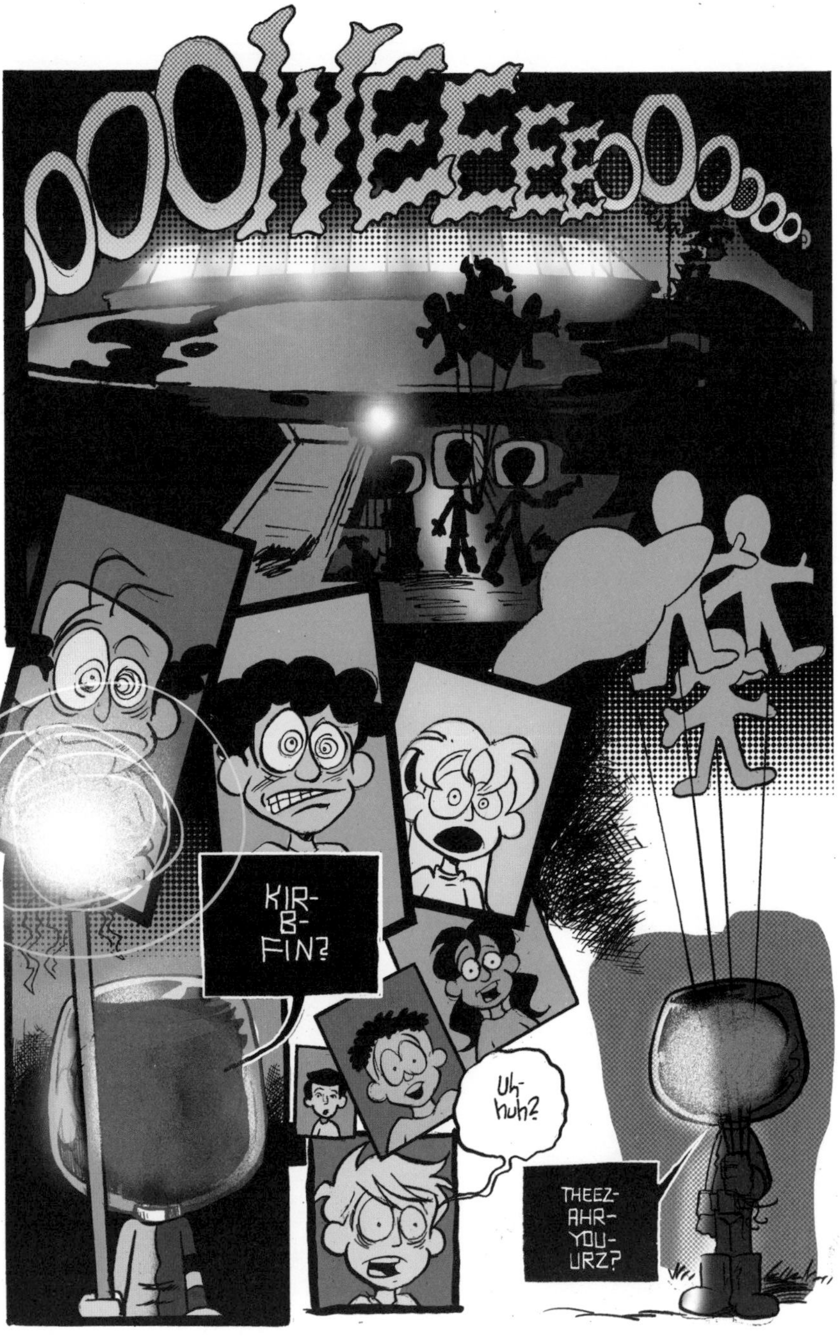
OOOOWEEEEOOOOOOO
KIR-B-FIN?
Uh-huh?
THEEZ-AHR-YOU-URZ?

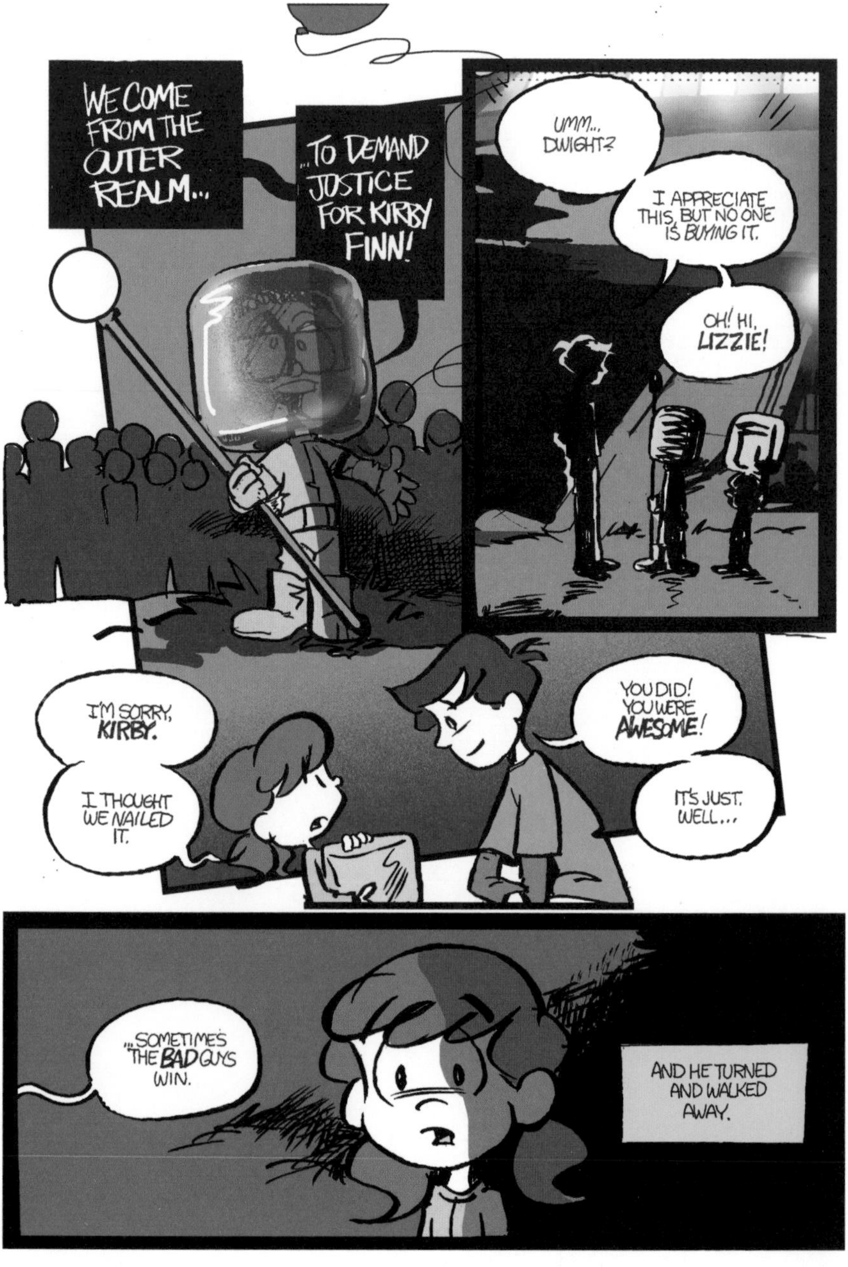

WE COME FROM THE OUTER REALM...
...TO DEMAND JUSTICE FOR KIRBY FINN!
UMM... DWIGHT?
I APPRECIATE THIS, BUT NO ONE IS *BUYING* IT.
OH! HI, **LIZZIE!**
I'M SORRY, **KIRBY.**
I THOUGHT WE *NAILED* IT.
YOU DID! YOU WERE **AWESOME!**
IT'S JUST, WELL...
...SOMETIMES THE ***BAD*** GUYS WIN.
AND HE TURNED AND WALKED AWAY.

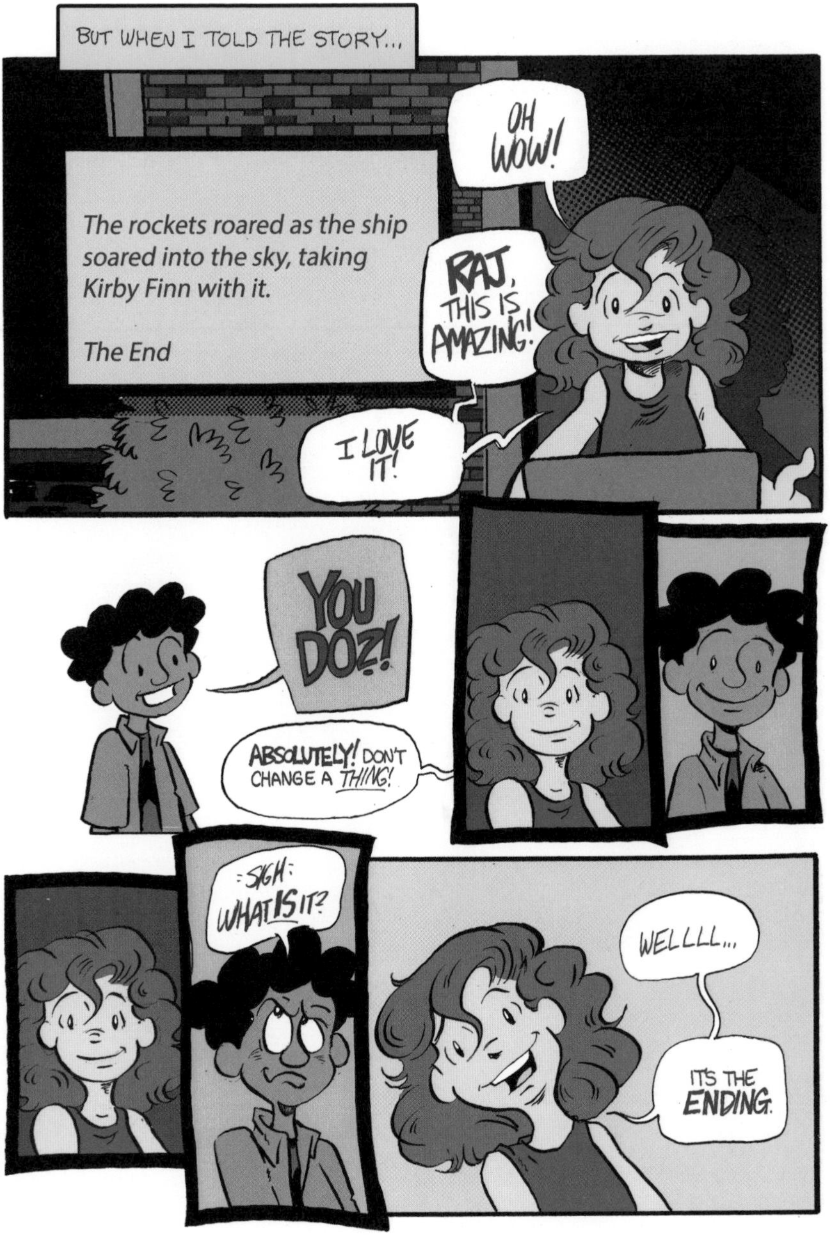

BUT WHEN I TOLD THE STORY...
The rockets roared as the ship soared into the sky, taking Kirby Finn with it.
The End
OH WOW!
RAJ, THIS IS AMAZING!
I LOVE IT!
YOU DOZ!
ABSOLUTELY! DON'T CHANGE A THING!
=SIGH= WHAT IS IT?
WELLLL...
IT'S THE ENDING.

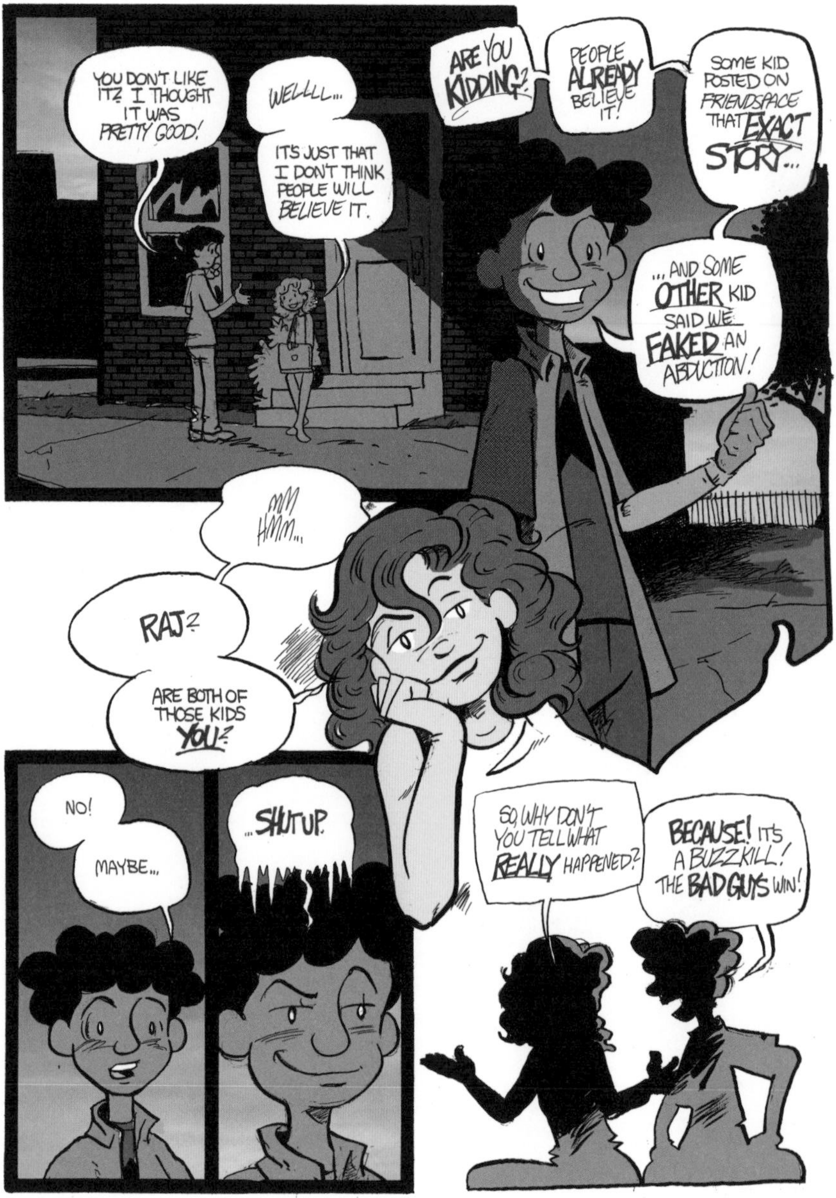
YOU DON'T LIKE IT? I THOUGHT IT WAS PRETTY GOOD!
WELLLL...
IT'S JUST THAT I DON'T THINK PEOPLE WILL BELIEVE IT.
ARE YOU KIDDING?
PEOPLE ALREADY BELIEVE IT!
SOME KID POSTED ON FRIENDSPACE THAT EXACT STORY...
...AND SOME OTHER KID SAID WE FAKED AN ABDUCTION!
MM HMM...
RAJ?
ARE BOTH OF THOSE KIDS YOU?
NO!
MAYBE...
...SHUT UP.
SO, WHY DON'T YOU TELL WHAT REALLY HAPPENED?
BECAUSE! IT'S A BUZZKILL! THE BAD GUYS WIN!

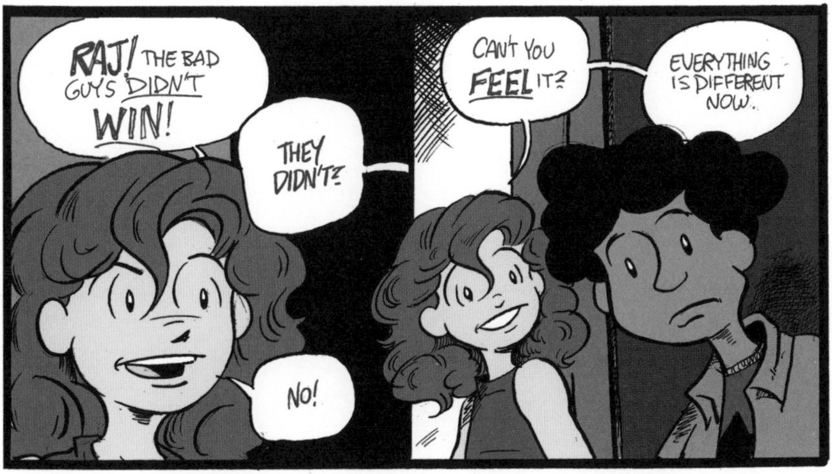
RAJ! THE BAD GUYS DIDN'T WIN!
THEY DIDN'T?
NO!
CAN'T YOU FEEL IT?
EVERYTHING IS DIFFERENT NOW.

EVER SINCE THAT NIGHT... SEEING US ALL TOGETHER... KNOWING WE WERE PART OF SOMETHING SO **BIG**... SO **REAL**...

...EVERYONE GOT A LITTLE **NICER**... A LITTLE **CLOSER**...

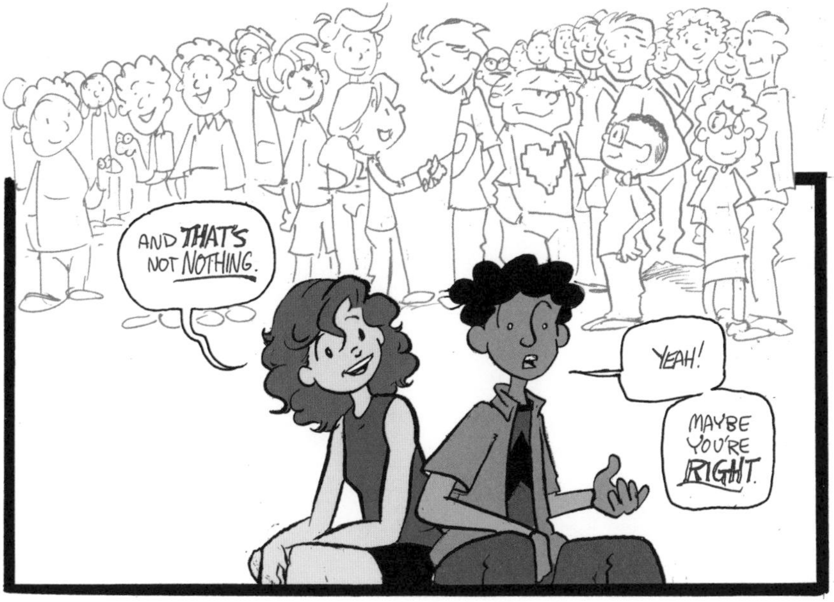
AND THAT'S NOT NOTHING.
YEAH!
MAYBE YOU'RE RIGHT.

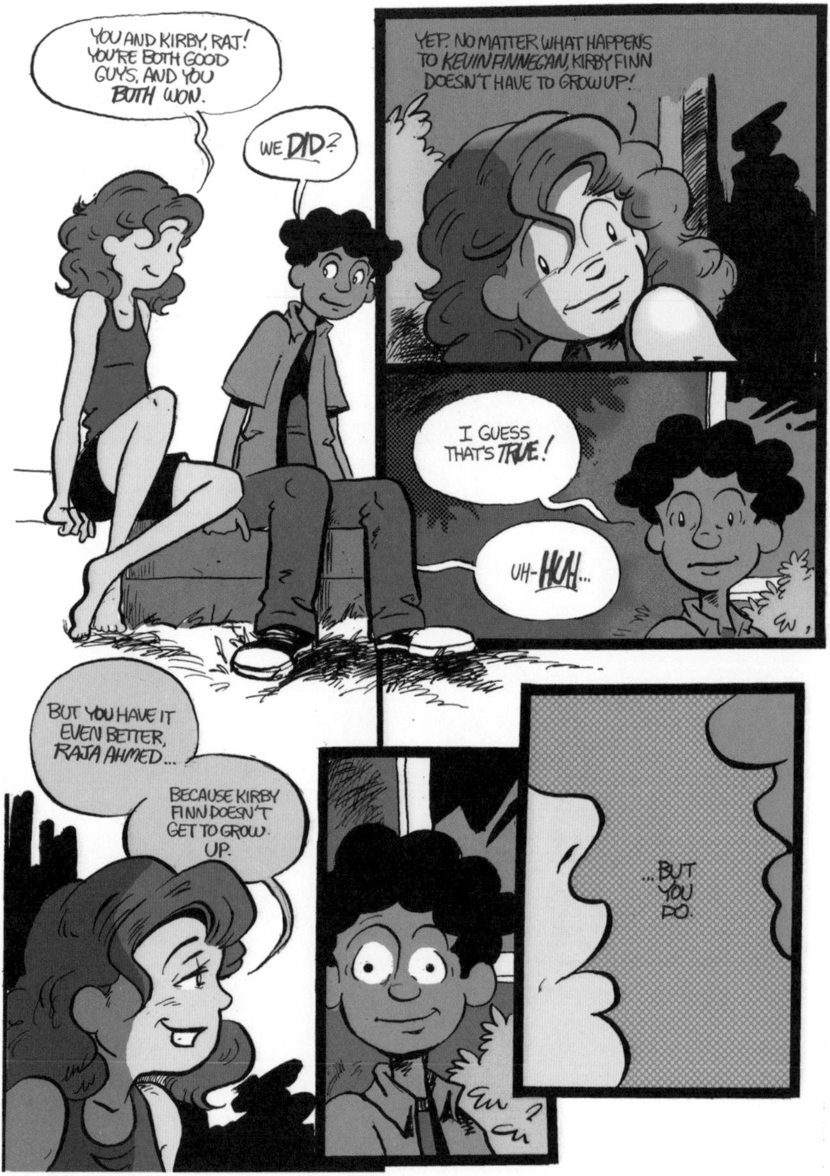
YOU AND KIRBY, RAJ! YOU'RE BOTH GOOD GUYS, AND YOU BOTH WON.
WE DID?
YEP. NO MATTER WHAT HAPPENS TO KEVIN FINNEGAN, KIRBY FINN DOESN'T HAVE TO GROW UP!
I GUESS THAT'S TRUE!
UH-HUH...
BUT YOU HAVE IT EVEN BETTER, RAJA AHMED...
BECAUSE KIRBY FINN DOESN'T GET TO GROW UP.
...BUT YOU DO.

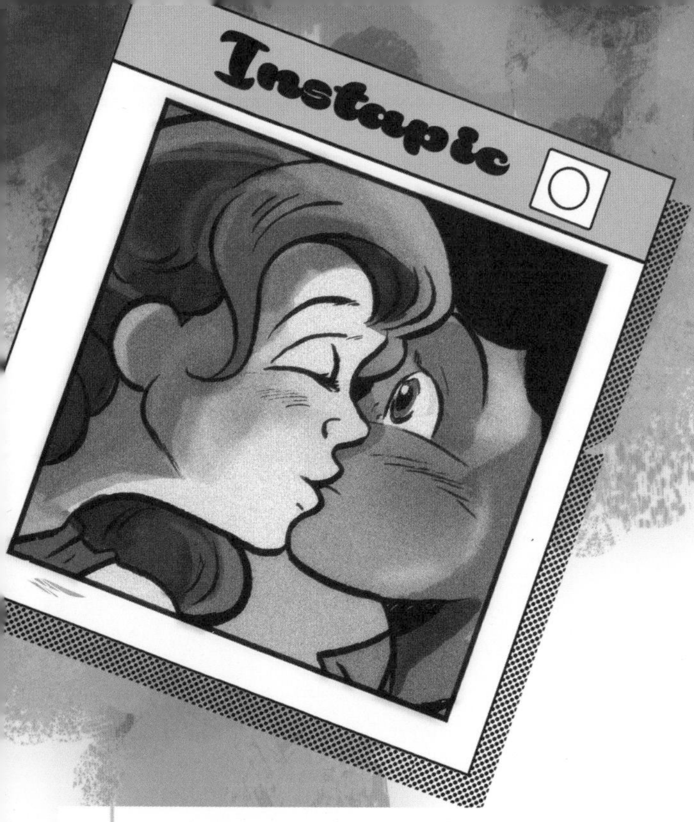
Instapic

Dear Mimi,

My bad dream came true. I took a leap, and the person who was supposed to catch me wasn't there.

So I fell.

I fell really far, and I landed really hard.

But, you know what? I survived.

And maybe that's the silver lining in having to grow up too fast.

It gave me the courage to make the leap, but it also gave me the strength to survive the fall.

I love you, mom, Yeah, I got hurt, but I'm okay.

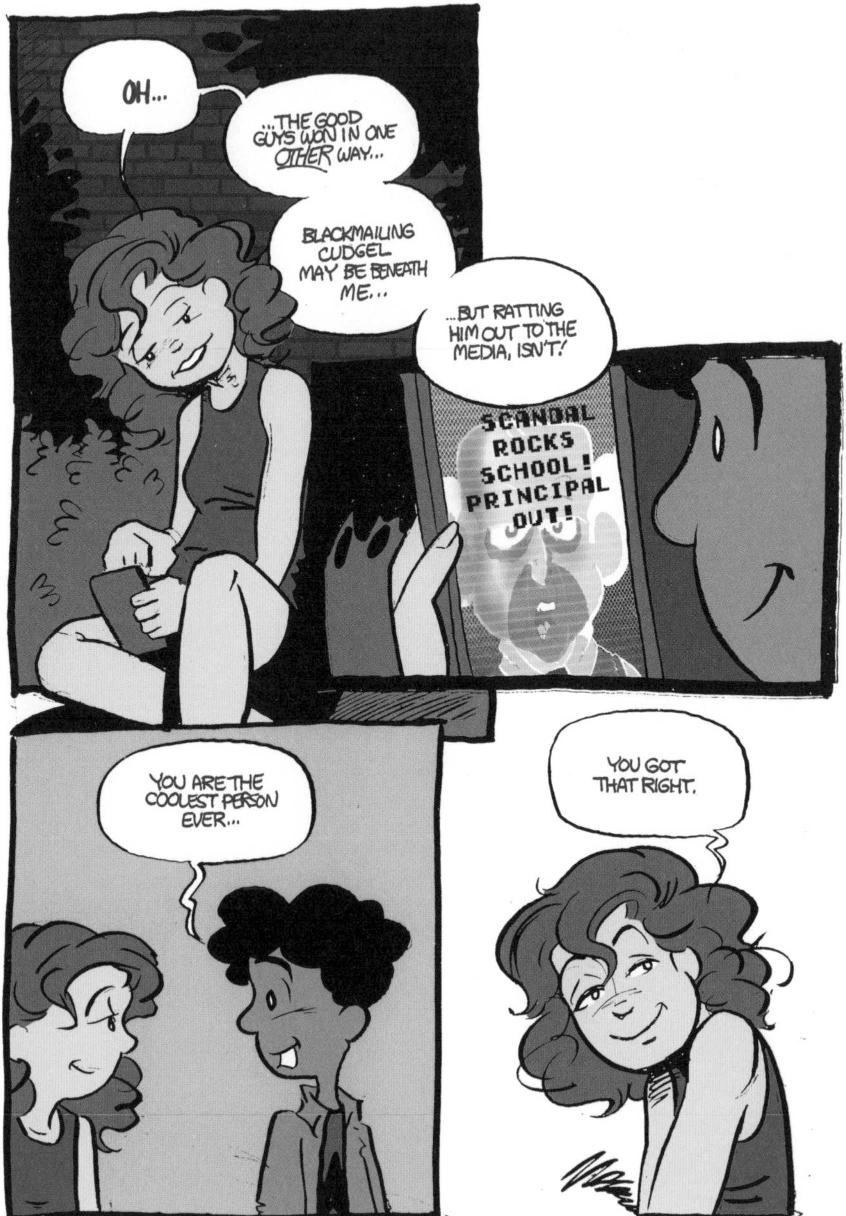
OH...
...THE GOOD GUYS WON IN ONE OTHER WAY...
BLACKMAILING CUDGEL MAY BE BENEATH ME...
...BUT RATTING HIM OUT TO THE MEDIA, ISN'T!
SCANDAL ROCKS SCHOOL! PRINCIPAL OUT!
YOU ARE THE COOLEST PERSON EVER...
YOU GOT THAT RIGHT.

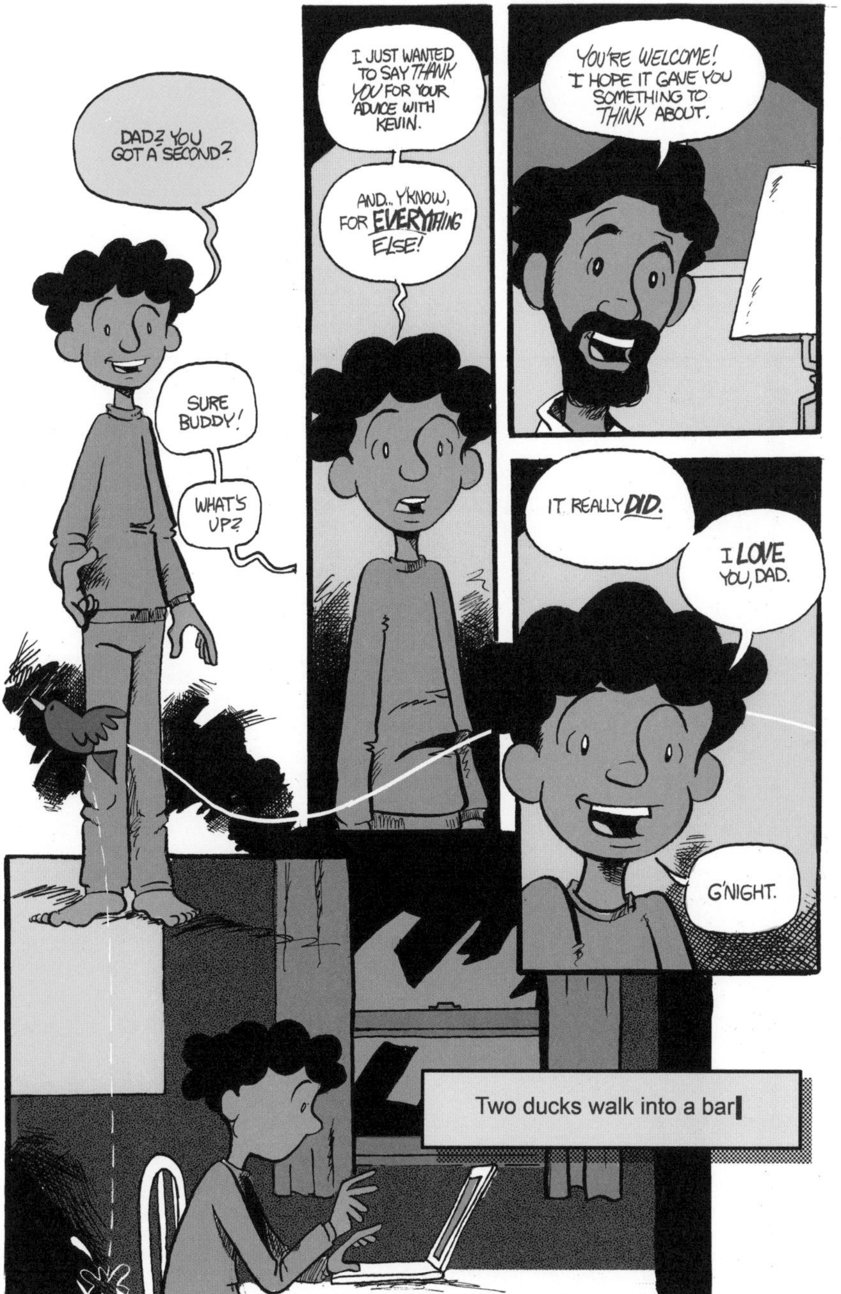
DAD? YOU GOT A SECOND?
SURE BUDDY!
WHAT'S UP?
I JUST WANTED TO SAY THANK YOU FOR YOUR ADVICE WITH KEVIN.
AND... Y'KNOW, FOR EVERYTHING ELSE!
YOU'RE WELCOME! I HOPE IT GAVE YOU SOMETHING TO THINK ABOUT.
IT REALLY DID.
I LOVE YOU, DAD.
G'NIGHT.
Two ducks walk into a bar

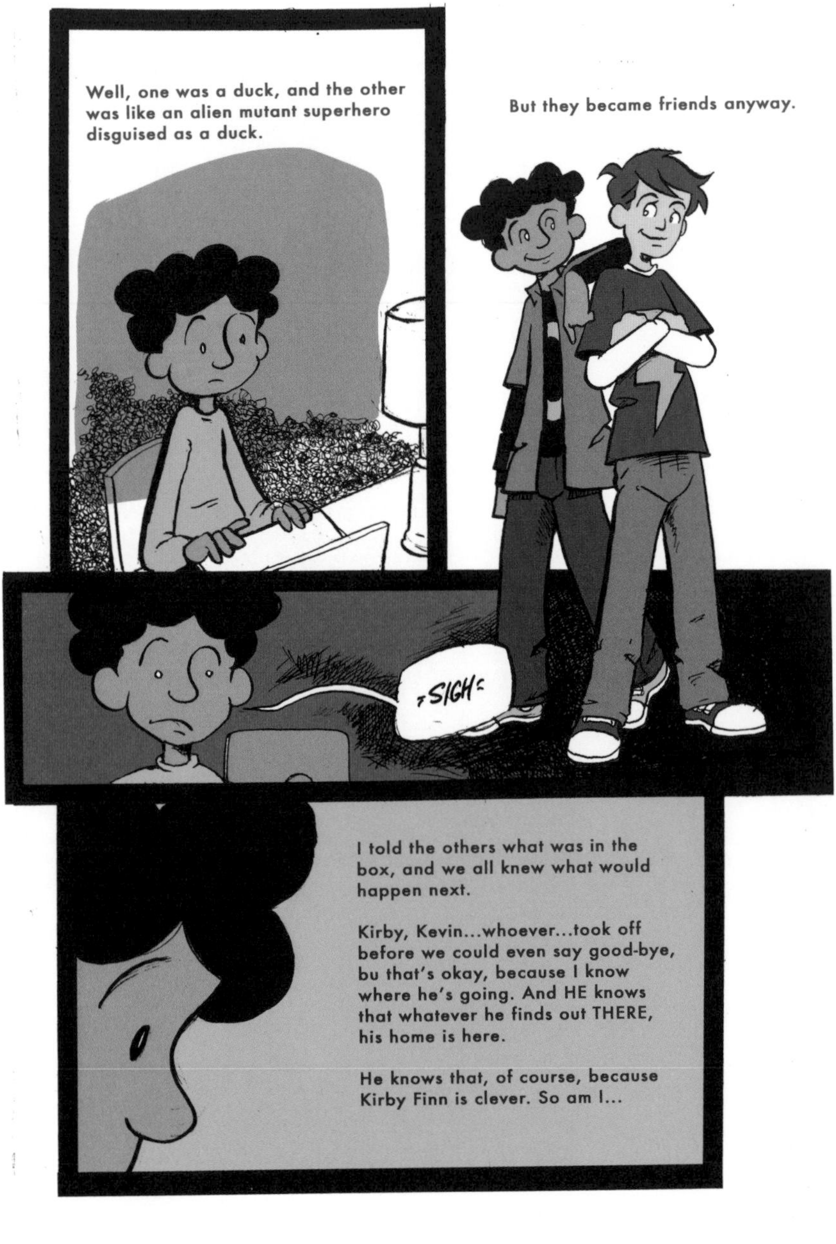
Well, one was a duck, and the other was like an alien mutant superhero disguised as a duck.
But they became friends anyway.
SIGH
I told the others what was in the box, and we all knew what would happen next.
Kirby, Kevin...whoever...took off before we could even say good-bye, bu that's okay, because I know where he's going. And HE knows that whatever he finds out THERE, his home is here.
He knows that, of course, because Kirby Finn is clever. So am I...

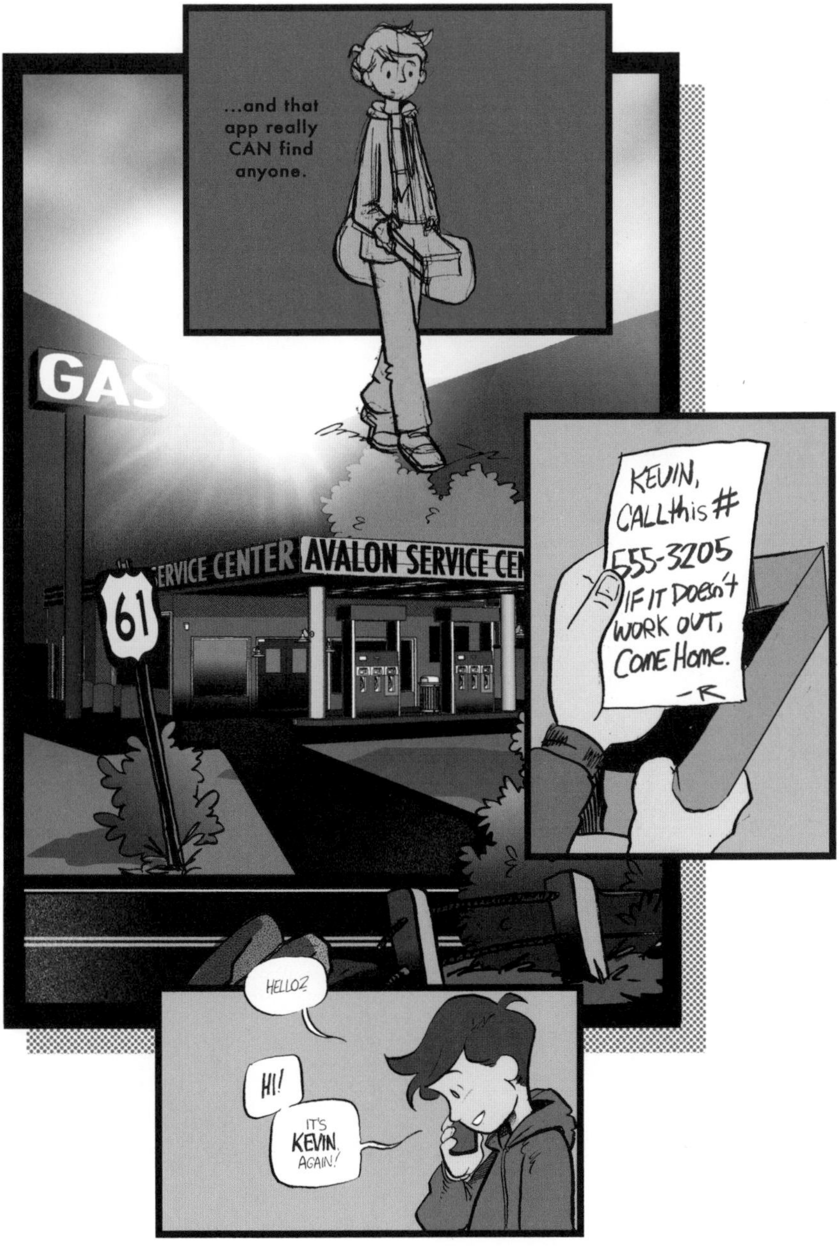
...and that app really CAN find anyone.
GAS
SERVICE CENTER
AVALON SERVICE CEN
61
KEVIN, CALL this # 555-3205 IF IT Doesn't WORK OUT, Come Home. -R
HELLO?
HI!
IT'S KEVIN. AGAIN!

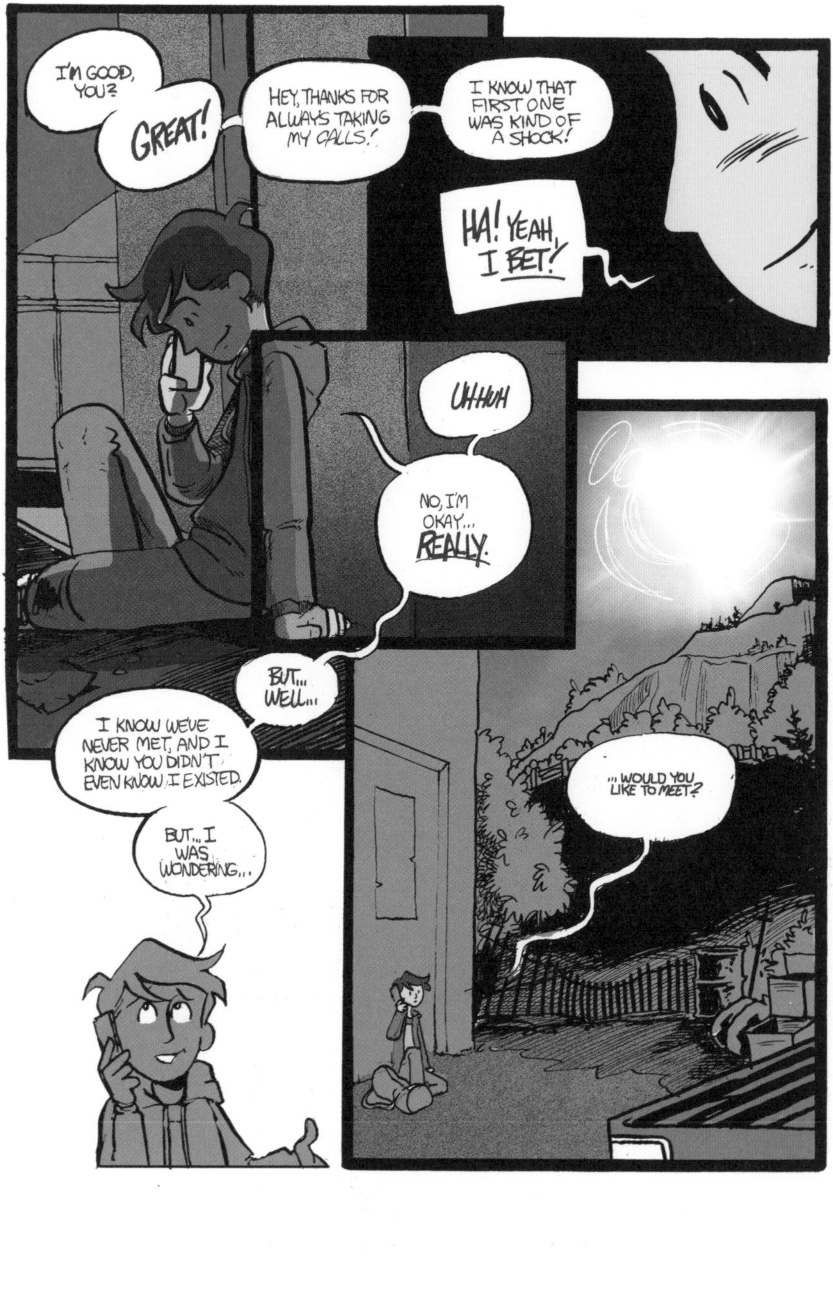
I'M GOOD, YOU?
GREAT!
HEY, THANKS FOR ALWAYS TAKING MY CALLS!
I KNOW THAT FIRST ONE WAS KIND OF A SHOCK!
HA! YEAH, I BET!
UH-HUH
NO, I'M OKAY... REALLY.
BUT... WELL...
I KNOW WE'VE NEVER MET, AND I KNOW YOU DIDN'T EVEN KNOW I EXISTED.
BUT... I WAS WONDERING...
...WOULD YOU LIKE TO MEET?

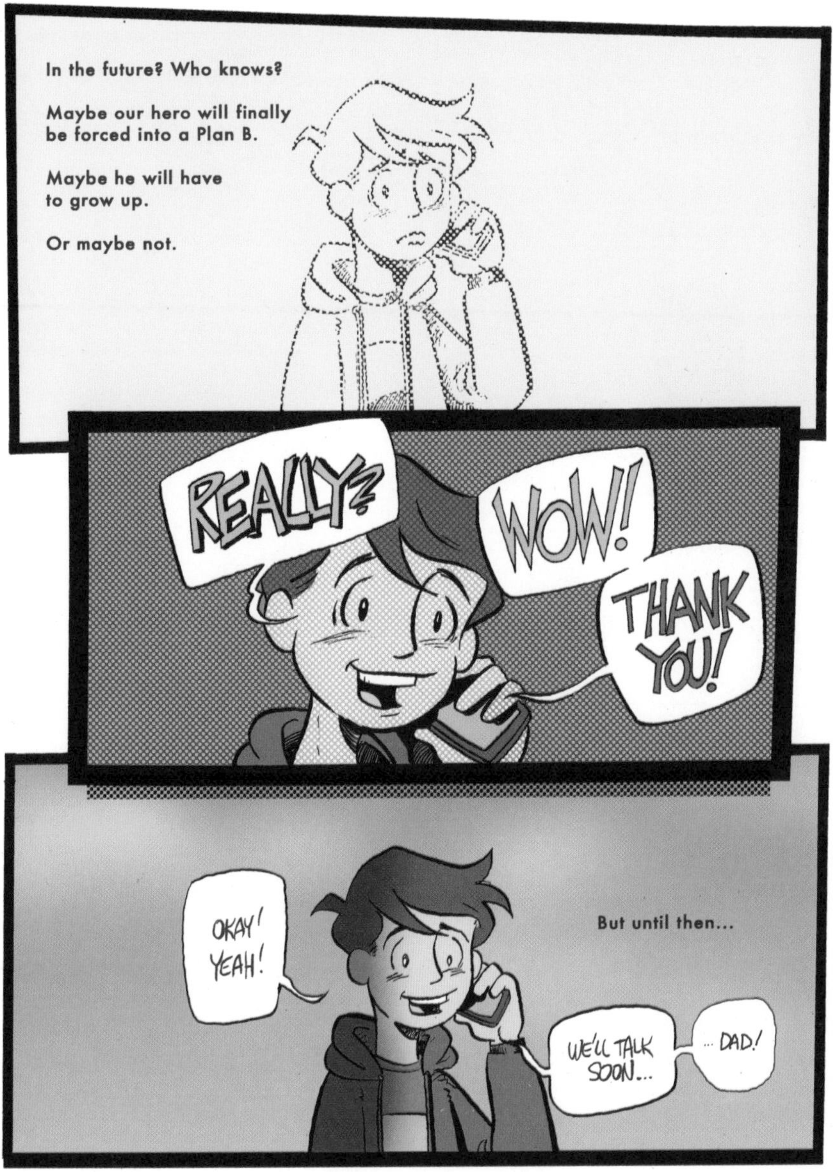
In the future? Who knows?
Maybe our hero will finally be forced into a Plan B.
Maybe he will have to grow up.
Or maybe not.
REALLY?
WOW!
THANK YOU!
OKAY! YEAH!
But until then...
WE'LL TALK SOON...
...DAD!

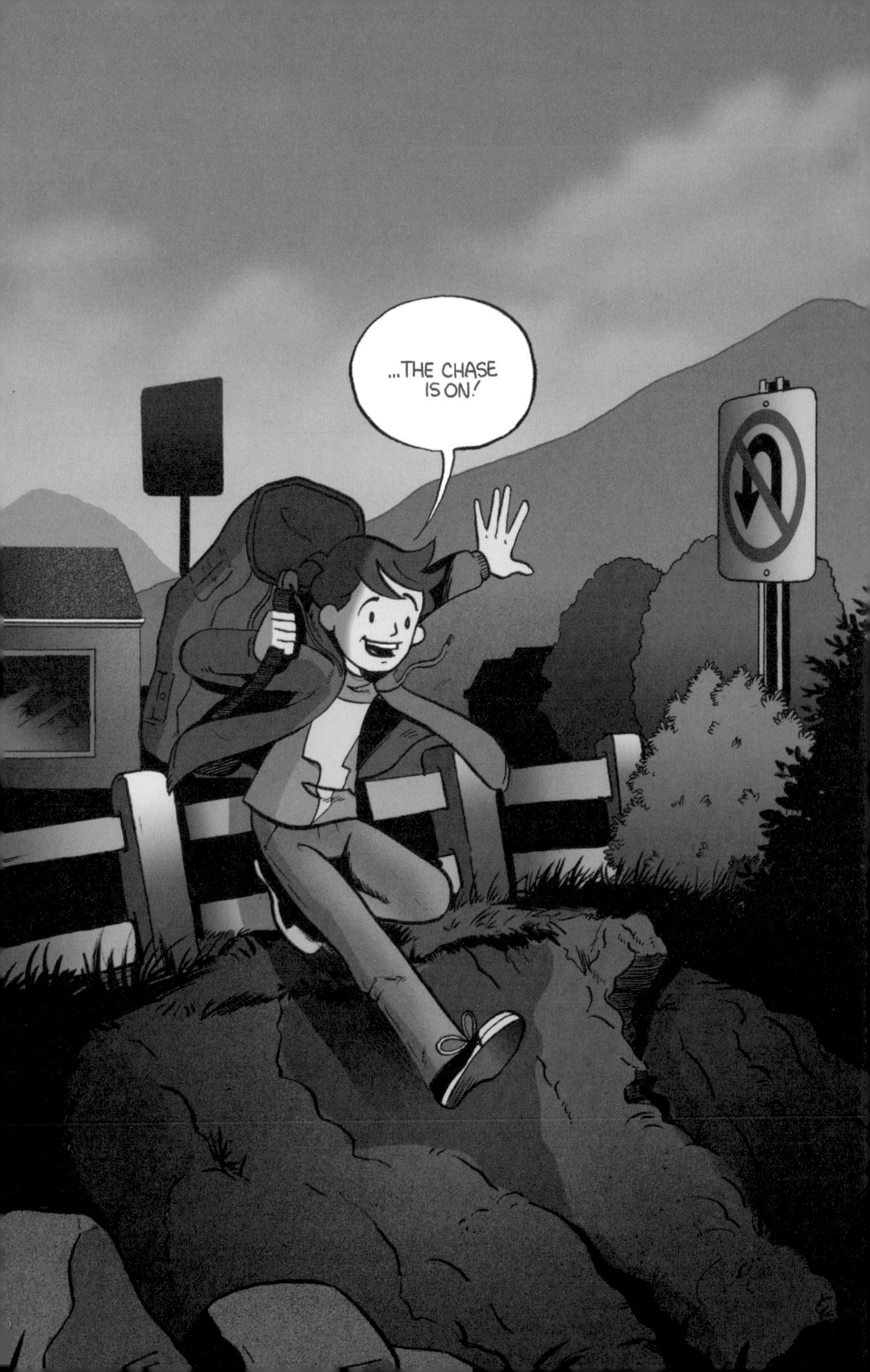
...THE CHASE IS ON!

FIN

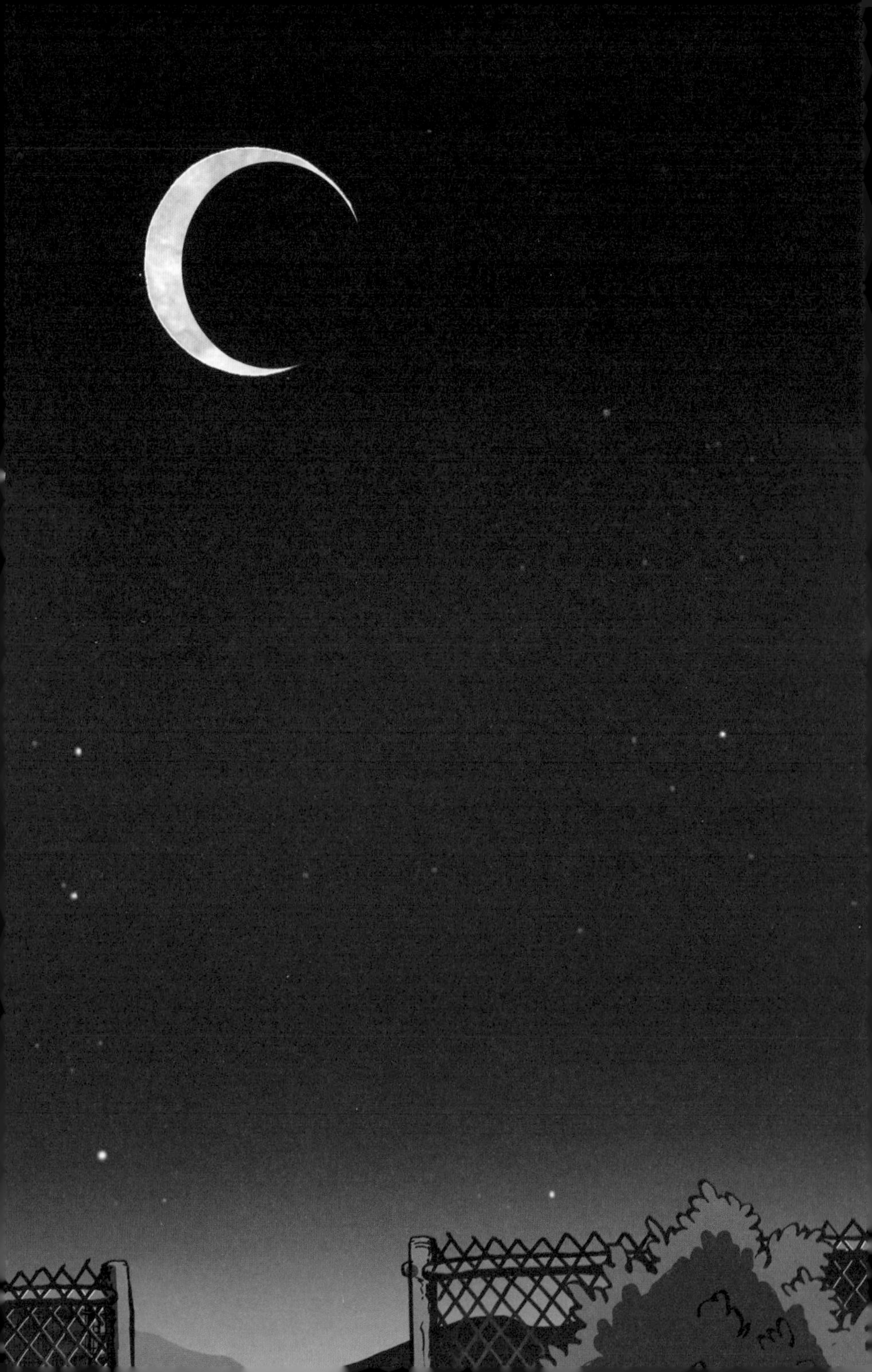

A NOTE FROM THE AUTHOR

Some books are easy. They simply pour out of one's pen, onto the page in their final form.

So I've heard anyway. That's never really happened to me.

It REALLY didn't happen on this book, which took more than three and a half years for me to complete.

I wanted to do something that was about the strange, wild, meta-moment we are all living in, and also make it funny and weird. Which is a lot easier to type than it is to do.

Characters DO tend to just pop into my head now and again, though. Kirby Finn was definitely one of those. He just appeared out of nowhere, filled with all of these wild, exciting stories about his exploits. It was a long time before I realized that there was more to this kid than he was letting on. Finding out who "Kirby Finn" really was.

This book was a challenge, but most rewarding things are. The only thing left is for me to thank my family, friends, agent, and everyone at Scholastic for all their patience and help as I worked to bring this story to completion.

It's here now, and I'm really proud of it. I hope you enjoy it too.

JIMMY GOWNLEY

BEHIND THE SCENES

Here are some sketches, drawings, and deleted scenes for you to enjoy. I hope you get a kick out of this peek behind the curtain.

AAAAAAAGH

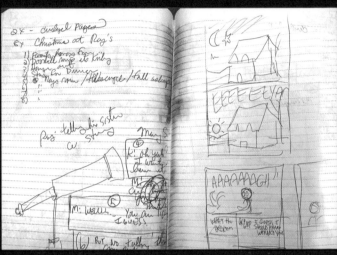

All of my stories start in simple notebooks. Just jotting down any idea that comes into my mind until things start to gel.

YOU DON'T LIKE IT? I THOUGHT IT WAS PRETTY GOOD!
WELLLL...
IT'S JUST THAT I DON'T THINK PEOPLE WILL BELIEVE IT.
ARE YOU KIDDING?
PEOPLE ALREADY BELIEVE IT!
SOME KID POSTED ON FRIENDSPACE THAT EXACT STORY...
...AND SOME OTHER KID SAID WE FAKED AN ABDUCTION!
RAJ?
ARE BOTH OF THOSE KIDS YOU!?
NO!
MAYBE...
...SHUT UP.
SO WHY DON'T YOU TELL WHAT REALLY HAPPENED?
BECAUSE! IT'S A BUZZKILL! THE BAD GUYS WIN!

Once I have the idea of a scene pretty firmly in mind, I start doodling little rough outlines. The words and pictures need to work together, so I try to develop them both at the same time.

All of my artwork is done on illustration board with old-fashioned pen and ink. I even letter the books by hand!

JIMMY GOWNLEY is an award-winning comics author who began writing and drawing comics at age fifteen. His acclaimed series, Amelia Rules!, was launched in 2001 to a flurry of rave reviews. He has been nominated for multiple Eisner awards and his book, *The Dumbest Idea Ever!*, won the Children's Choice Award. He co-founded the organization Kids Love Comics, which works to promote comic books and graphic novels as a valuable tool for literacy. Jimmy lives in Harrisburg, Pennsylvania.

ALSO BY JIMMY GOWNLEY

Jimmy Gownley shares his adventures as he grows from an eager-to-please boy into a teenage comic book artist. This is the real-life story of how the DUMBEST idea ever became the BEST thing that ever happened to him.

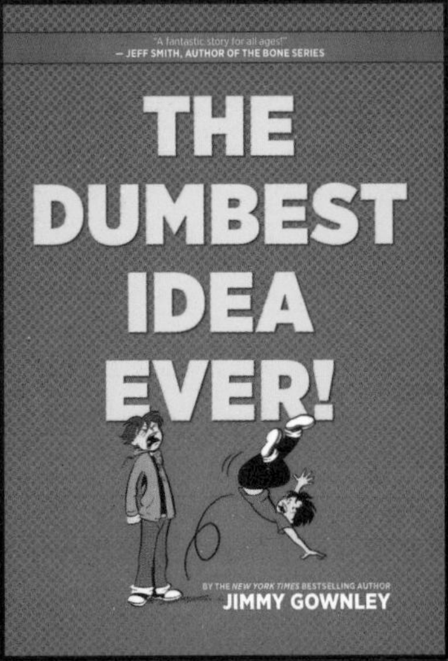
"A fantastic story for all ages!"
— JEFF SMITH, AUTHOR OF THE BONE SERIES
THE DUMBEST IDEA EVER!
BY THE *NEW YORK TIMES* BESTSELLING AUTHOR
JIMMY GOWNLEY

★ "Humble, endearing and utterly easy to relate to; don't miss this one." — *Kirkus*, starred review

"It's a deeply personal and genuine work of autobiography, and an open letter of assurance to aspiring artists everywhere." — *Publishers Weekly*

"This is an excellent example of autobiographical sequential art at its most deeply felt." — *Booklist*

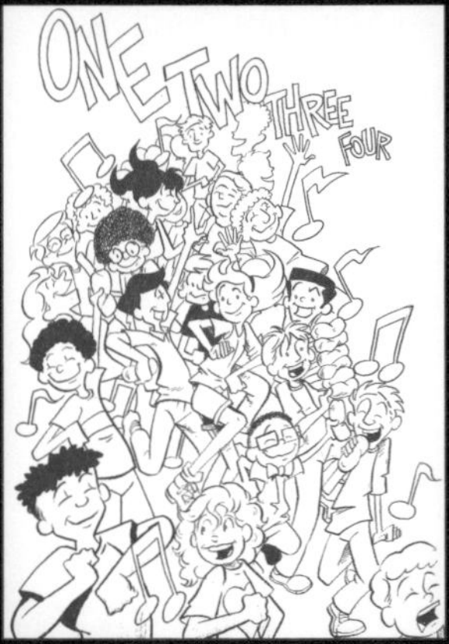
ONE TWO THREE FOUR

Not all of the scenes work, and sometimes some things have to be redone. Not too often though.

Believe it or not this image below was a scene in the book at one point! If you want to see that version of the story, write your congresspersoon!

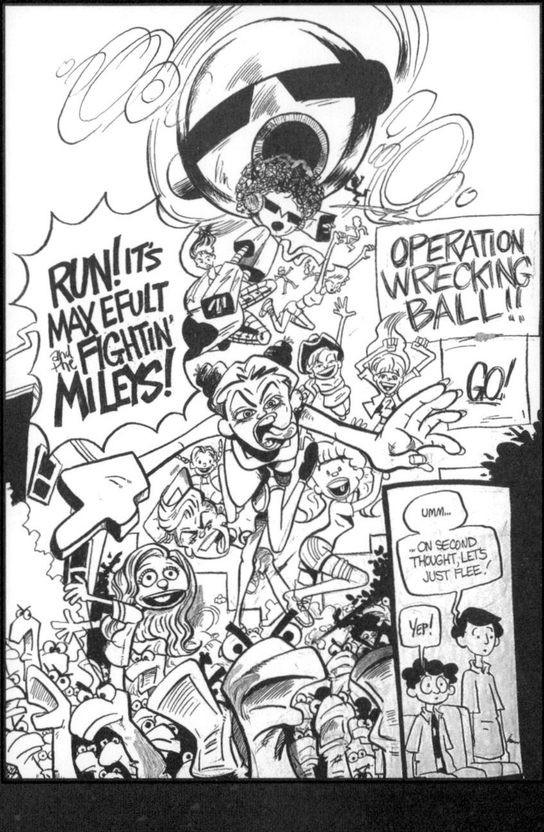
RUN! IT'S MAX EFULT and the FIGHTIN' MILEYS!
OPERATION WRECKING BALL!!
GO!
UMM...
...ON SECOND THOUGHT, LET'S JUST FLEE!
YEP!

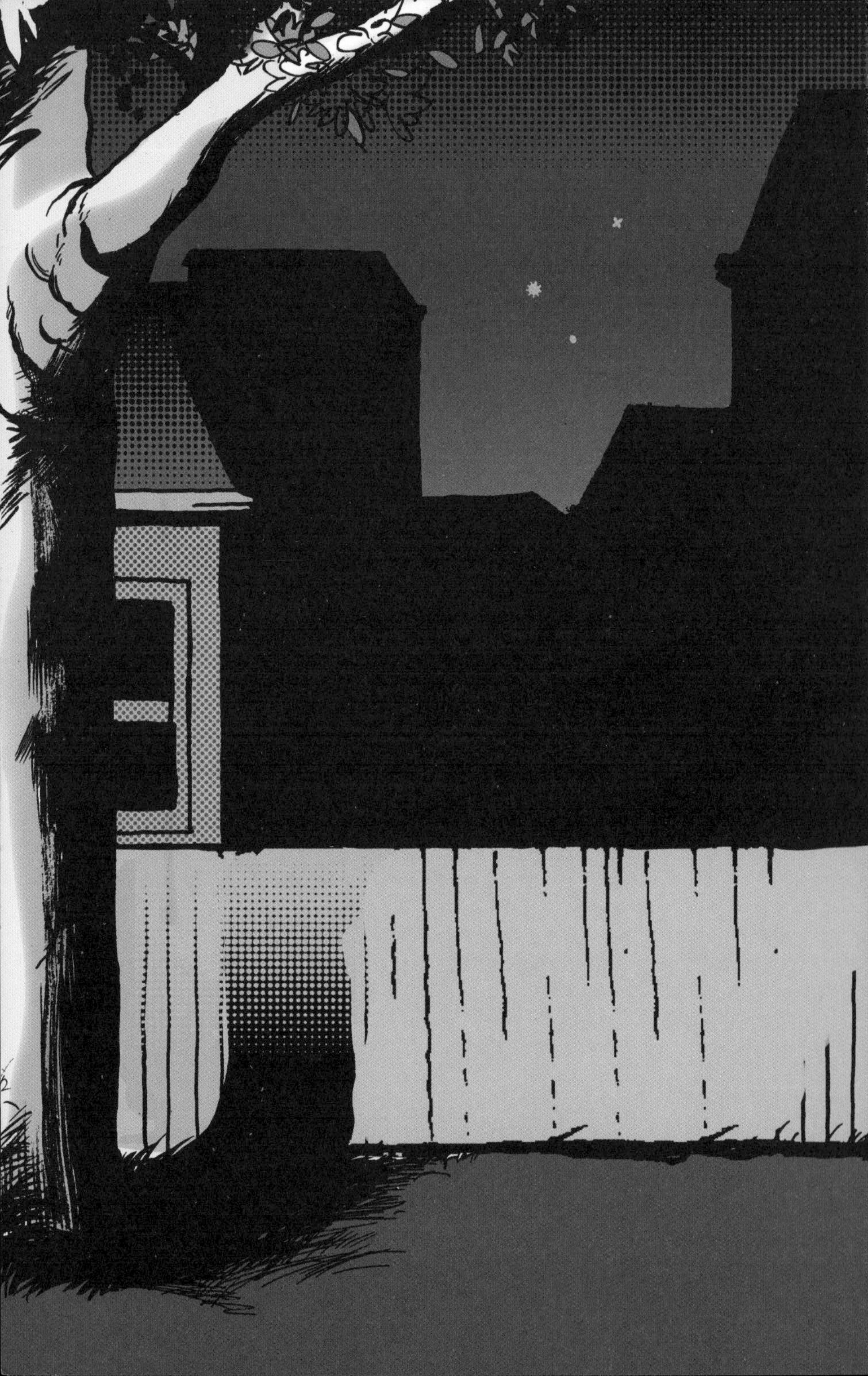